PHOTO-FINISH
LIGHT THICKENS
BLACK BEECH AND HONEYDEW

Dame Ngaio Marsh was born in New Zealand in 1895 and died in February 1982. She wrote over 30 detective novels and many of her stories have theatrical settings, for Ngaio Marsh's real passion was the theatre. Both actress and producer, she almost single-handedly revived the New Zealand public's interest in the theatre. It was for this work that she received what she called her 'damery' in 1966.

'The finest writer in the English language of the pure, classical puzzle whodunit. Among the crime queens, Ngaio Marsh stands out as an Empress.' *The Sun*

'Ngaio Marsh transforms the detective story from a mere puzzle into a novel.' *Daily Express*

'Her work is as nearly flawless as makes no odds. Character, plot, wit, good writing, and sound technique.' *Sunday Times*

'She writes better than Christie!' *New York Times*

'Brilliantly readable . . . first class detection.' *Observer*

'Still, quite simply, the greatest exponent of the classical English detective story.' *Daily Telegraph*

'Read just one of Ngaio Marsh's novels and you've go to read them all . . . ' *Daily M*

BY THE SAME AUTHOR

A Man Lay Dead

Enter a Murderer

The Nursing Home Murder

Death in Ecstasy

Vintage Murder

Artists in Crime

Death in a White Tie

Overture to Death

Death at the Bar

Surfeit of Lampreys

Death and the Dancing Footman

Colour Scheme

Died in the Wool

Final Curtain

Swing, Brother, Swing

Opening Night

Spinsters in Jeopardy

Scales of Justice

Off With His Head

Singing in the Shrouds

False Scent

Hand in Glove

Dead Water

Death at the Dolphin

Clutch of Constables

When in Rome

Tied up in Tinsel

Black As He's Painted

Last Ditch

Grave Mistake

Photo-Finish

Light Thickens

Black Beech and Honeydew (autobiography)

NGAIO MARSH

Photo-Finish

Light Thickens

Black Beech and Honeydew

AND

Morepork

HARPER

HARPER

an imprint of HarperCollins*Publishers*
77-85 Fulham Palace Road
Hammersmith, London W6 8JB
www.harpercollins.co.uk

This omnibus edition 2009
1

Photo-Finish first published in Great Britain by Collins 1980
Light Thickens first published in Great Britain by Collins 1982
Black Beech and Honeydew first published in Great Britain
by Collins 1966; revised and enlarged edition published 1981
Morepork first published in Great Britain in
Death on the Air and Other Stories by HarperCollins*Publishers* 1995

Ngaio Marsh asserts the moral right to
be identified as the author of these works

ISBN 978 0 00 732879 6
Printed and bound in Great Britain by
Clays Ltd, St Ives plc

Mixed Sources
Product group from well-managed
forests and other controlled sources
www.fsc.org Cert no. SW-COC-1806
© 1996 Forest Stewardship Council

FSC is a non-profit international organisation established to promote the
responsible management of the world's forests. Products carrying the FSC
label are independently certified to assure consumers that they come
from forests that are managed to meet the social, economic and
ecological needs of present and future generations.

Find out more about HarperCollins and the environment at
www.harpercollins.co.uk/green

CONTENTS

Photo-Finish
1

Light Thickens
223

Black Beech and Honeydew
431

BONUS STORY:
Morepork
723

Photo-Finish

For Fredaneve
with love

Contents

1 The Sommita 5

2 The Lodge 23

3 Rehearsal 45

4 Performance 66

5 Nocturne 99

6 Storm Continued 128

7 Strix 157

8 The Police 187

9 Departure 211

Cast of Characters

Isabella Sommita (née Pepitone)	
Ben Ruby	*Her manager*
Montague V. Reece	*Her friend*
Rupert Bartholomew	*Her protégé*
Maria	*Her maid*
Chief Superintendent Roderick Alleyn CID	
Troy Alleyn RA	*His wife*
His Assistant Commissioner, Scotland Yard	
Bert	*A chauffeur*
Les	*A launchman*
Marco	*A manservant*
Ned Hanley	*Mr Reece's secretary*
Signor Beppo Lattienzo	*The Sommita's Master of Singing*
Hilda Dancy	*A contralto*
Eru Johnstone	*A bass*
Sylvia Parry	*A mezzo-soprano*
Rodolfo Romano	*A tenor*
Sir David Baumgartner	*A critic*
Mrs Bacon	*Housekeeper*
Dr John Carmichael, MD	*A guest*
Inspector Hazelmere	*Rivermouth Constabulary*
Detective-Sergeant Franks	*Rivermouth Constabulary*
Detective-Sergeant Barker	*Rivermouth Constabulary*
Dr Winslow	

CHAPTER 1

The Sommita

One of the many marvels of Isabella Sommita's technique was her breathing: it was totally unobservable. Even in the most exacting passages, even in the most staggering flights of coloratura, there was never the slightest disturbance of the corsage.

'You could drop an ice cube down her cleavage,' boasted her manager, Ben Ruby, 'and not a heave would you get for your trouble.'

He had made this observation when sitting in a box immediately above the diva at the Royal Festival Hall and had spoken no more than the truth. Offstage, when moved by one of her not infrequent rages, La Sommita's bosom would heave with the best of them.

It did so now, in her private suite at the Château Australasia in Sydney. She was *en negligé* and it was sumptuously evident that she was displeased and that the cause of her displeasure lay on the table at her elbow: a newspaper folded to expose a half-page photograph with a banner headline, CROSS-PATCH? and underneath, LA SOMMITA IS NOT AMUSED!

It had been taken yesterday in Double Bay, Sydney. The photographer, wearing a floppy white hat, a white scarf over his mouth and dark spectacles had stepped out from an alleyway and gone snap. She had not been quick enough to turn her back but her jaw had dropped and her left eye had slewed; its habit when rage overtook her. The general effect was that of a gargoyle at the dentist's: an elderly and infuriated gargoyle. The photograph was signed Strix.

She beat on the paper with her largish white fist and her ring into it. She panted lavishly.

'Wants horsewhipping,' Montague Reece mumbled. He was generally accepted as the Sommita's established lover and he filled this role in the manner commonly held to be appropriate, being large, rich, muted, pale, dyspeptic and negative. He was said to wield a great deal of power in his own world.

'Of course he needs horsewhipping,' shouted his dear one. 'But where's the friend who will go out and do it?' She laughed and executed a wide contemptuous gesture that included all present. The newspaper fluttered to the carpet.

'Personally,' Ben Ruby offered, 'I wouldn't know one end of a horsewhip from the other.' She dealt him a glacial stare. 'I didn't mean to be funny,' he said.

'Nor were you.'

'No.'

A young man of romantic appearance in a distant chair behind the diva clasped a portfolio of music to his midriff and said in a slightly Australian voice: 'Can't something be done? Can't they be sued?'

'What for?' asked Mr Ruby.

'Well – libel. Look at it, for God's sake!' the young man brought out. 'Well, I mean to say, *look*!'

The other two men glanced at him, but the Sommita without turning her head said: 'Thank you, darling,' and extended her arm. The intention was unmistakable: an invitation, nay, a command. The young man's beautiful face crimsoned, he rose and, maintaining a precarious hold on his portfolio, advanced crouchingly to imprint a kiss upon the fingers. He lost control of his portfolio. Its contents shot out of their confine and littered the carpet: sheet upon sheet of music in manuscript.

He fell on his knees and scrabbled about the floor. 'I'm so sorry,' he gabbled. 'Oh hell, I'm so bloody sorry.'

The Sommita had launched a full-scale attack upon the Australian press. Rupert, she said, indicating the young man, was absolutely right. The press should be sued. The police should be called in. The photographer should be kicked out of the country. Was he to be suffered to wreck her life, her career, her sanity, to make her the laughing stock of both hemispheres? (She was in the habit of instancing graphical data.) Had she not, she demanded, consented to the Australian appearances solely as a means of escape from his infamy?

'You are sure, I suppose,' said Mr Reece in his pallid manner, 'that it's the same man? Strix?'

This produced a tirade. 'Sure! Sure!' Had not the detested Strix bounced out of cover in all the capitals of Europe as well as in New York and San Francisco? Had he not shot her at close quarters and in atrocious disarray? *Sure!* She drew a tempestuous breath. Well, she shouted, what were they going to do about it? Was she to be protected or was she to have a breakdown, lose her voice and spend the rest of her days in a straitjacket? She only asked to be informed.

The two men exchanged deadpan glances.

'We can arrange for another bodyguard,' Montague Reece offered without enthusiasm.

'She didn't much fancy the one in New York,' Mr Ruby pointed out.

'Assuredly I did not,' she agreed, noisily distending her nostrils. 'It is not amusing to be closely followed by an imbecile in unspeakable attire who did nothing, but nothing, to prevent the outrage on Fifth Avenue. He merely goggled. As, by the way, did you all.'

'Sweetheart, what else could we do? The fellow was a passenger in an open car. It was off like a bullet as soon as he'd taken his picture.'

'Thank you, Benny. I remember the circumstances.'

'But *why*?' asked the young man called Rupert, still on his knees assembling his music. 'What's got into him? I mean to say, it doesn't make sense and it must cost a lot of money to follow you all over the globe. He must be bonkers.'

He recognized his mistake as soon as it escaped his lips and began to gabble. Perhaps because he was on his knees and literally at her feet the Sommita who had looked explosive leant forward and tousled his blond hair. 'My poorest!' she said. 'You are quite, *quite* ridiculous and I adore you. I haven't introduced you,' she added as an afterthought. 'I've forgotten your surname.'

'Bartholomew.'

'Really? Very well, Rupert Bartholomew,' she proclaimed, with an introductory wave of her hand.

'. . . d'you do,' he muttered. The others nodded.

'Why does he do it? He does it,' Montague Reece said impatiently, reverting to the photographer, 'for money. No doubt the idea arose from the Jacqueline Kennedy affair. He's carried it much further and he's been successful. Enormously so.'

'That's right,' Ruby agreed. 'And the more he does it the more – ' he hesitated – 'outrageous the results become.'

'He re-touches,' the Sommita intervened. 'He distorts. I know it.'

They all hurriedly agreed with her.

'I'm going,' she said unexpectedly, 'to dress. Now. And when I return I wish to be given an intelligent solution. I throw out, for what they are worth, my suggestions. The police. Prosecution. The Press. Who owns this – ' she kicked the offending newspaper and had some difficulty in disengaging her foot – 'this garbage? Who is the proprietor? Attack him.' She strode to the bedroom door. 'And I warn you, Monty. I warn you, Benny. This is my final word. Unless I am satisfied that there is an end to my persecution I shall not sing in Sydney. They can,' said the Sommita, reverting to her supposed origins, 'stuff their Sydney Opera House.'

She made her exit and did not neglect to slam the door.

'Oh dear,' said Benjamin Ruby quietly.

'Quite,' said Montague Reece.

The young man called Rupert Bartholomew, having reinstated his portfolio, got to his feet.

'I reckon I'd better – ?'

'Yes?' said Mr Reece.

'Take myself off. I mean to say, it's a bit awkward.'

'What's awkward?'

'Well, you see, Madame – Madame Sommita asked me – I mean to say, she said I was to bring this – ' he indicated, precariously, his portfolio.

'Look out,' said Ben Ruby. 'You'll scatter it again.' He did not try to suppress a note of resignation. 'Is it something you've written?' he said. It was more a statement than an enquiry.

'This is right. She said I could bring it.'

'When,' Reece asked, 'did she say it?'

'Last night. Well – this morning. About one o'clock. You were leaving that party at the Italian Embassy. You had gone back to fetch something: her gloves, I think, and she was in the car. She saw me.'

'It was raining.'

'Heavily,' said the young man proudly. 'I was the only one.'

'You spoke to her?'

'She beckoned me. She put the window down. She asked me how long I'd been there. I said three hours. She asked my name and what I did. I told her. I play the piano in a small orchestra and give lessons. And I type. And then I told her I had all her recordings and – well, she was so wonderful. I mean to me, there in the rain. I just found myself telling her I've written an opera – short – a one-acter – sort of dedicated to her, *for* her. Not, you know, not because I dreamt she would ever hear of it. Good God no!'

'And so,' Benjamin Ruby suggested, 'she said you could show it to her.'

'This is right. This morning. I think she was sorry I was so wet.'

'And have you shown it to her?' asked Mr Reece. 'Apart from throwing it all over the carpet?'

'No. I was just going to when the waiter came up with this morning's papers and – she saw that thing. And then you came. I suppose I'd better go.'

'It's hardly the moment perhaps – ' Mr Reece began when the bedroom door opened and an elderly woman with ferociously black hair came into the room. She held up a finger at Rupert, rather in the manner of summoning a waiter.

'She wanta you,' said the woman. 'Also the music.'

'All right, Maria,' said Mr Ruby, and to the young man, 'Maria is Madame's dresser. You'd better go.'

So Rupert, whose surname was Bartholomew, clutching his opera, walked into La Sommita's bedroom as a fly, if he'd only known it, into a one-way web.

'She'll eat that kid,' Mr Ruby said dispassionately, 'in one meal.'

'Half way down her throat already,' her protector agreed.

II

'I've wanted to paint that woman,' said Troy Alleyn, 'for five years. And now look!'

She pushed the letter across the breakfast table. Her husband rea it and raised an eyebrow. 'Remarkable,' he said.

'I know. Especially the bit about you. What does it say, exactly? I was too excited to take it all in. Who's the letter *from*, actually? Not from *her*, you'll notice?'

'It's from Montague Reece, no less.'

'Why, "no less". Who's Montague Reece?'

'I wish,' said Alleyn, 'he could hear you ask.'

'Why?' Troy repeated. 'Oh, I know! Isn't he very well off?'

'You may say so. In the stinking-of-it department. Mr Onassis Colossus, in fact.'

'I remember now. Isn't he her lover?'

'That's it.'

'All is made clear to me. I think. Do read it, darling. Aloud.'

'All of it?'

'Please.'

'Here goes,' said Alleyn and read:

'Dear Mrs Alleyn,
   'I hope that is the correct way to address you. Should I perhaps have used your most celebrated soubriquet?
   'I write to ask if from November 1st you and your husband will be my guests at Waihoe Lodge, an island retreat I have built on a lake in New Zealand. It is recently completed and I dare to hope it will appeal to you. The situation is striking and I think I may say that my guests will be comfortable. You would have, as your studio, a commodious room, well-lit, overlooking the lake, with a view of distant mountains and, of course, complete freedom as to time and privacy.'

'He sounds like a land-and-estate agent – all mod cons and the usual offices. Pray continue,' said Troy.

'I must confess that this invitation is the prelude to another and that is for you to paint a portrait of Madame Isabella Sommita who will be staying with us at the time proposed. I have long hoped for this. In my opinion, and I am permitted to say in hers also, none of her portraits hitherto has given us the true "Sommita".
   'We are sure that a "Troy" would do so quite marvellously!

'Please say you approve the proposal. We will arrange transport, as my guest, of course, by air, and will settle details as soon as we hear, as I so greatly hope, that you will come. I shall be glad if you will be kind enough to inform me of your terms.

'I shall write, under separate cover, to your husband whom we shall be delighted to welcome with you to the Lodge.

'I am, believe me, dear Mrs Alleyn,

'Yours most sincerely,

'*Montague Reece*.'

After a longish pause Troy said: 'Would it be going too far to paint her singing? You know, mouth wide open for a top note.'

'Mightn't she look as if she were yawning?'

'I don't *think* so,' Troy brooded, and then with a sidelong grin at her husband, 'I could always put a balloon coming out of her mouth with "A in alt" written in it.'

'That would settle any doubts, of course. Except that I fancy it refers to male singers.'

'You haven't looked at your letter. Do look.'

Alleyn looked. 'Here it is,' he said. 'Over-posh and posted in Sydney.' He opened it.

'What's he say?'

'The preamble's much the same as yours and so's the follow-up: the bit about him having to confess to an ulterior motive.'

'Does he want *you* to paint *his* portrait, my poor Rory?'

'He wants me to give them "my valued opinion" as to the possibility of obtaining police protection "in the matter of the persecution of Madame Sommita by a photographer of which I am no doubt aware." Well, of all the damn cheek!' said Alleyn. 'Travel thirteen thousand miles to sit on an island in the middle of a lake and tell him whether or not to include a copper in his house party.'

'Oh! Yes. The penny's dropped. All that stuff in the papers. I didn't really read it.'

'You must be the only English-speaking human being who didn't.'

'Well, I did, really. Sort of. But the photographs were so hideous they put me off. Fill me, as I expect they say in Mr Reece' circles, in.'

'You remember how Mrs Jacqueline Kennedy, as she was then, was pestered by a photographer?'

'Yes.'

'It's the same situation but much exaggerated. The Kennedy rumpus may have put the idea into this chap's head. He signs himself "Strix". He's actually followed the Sommita all over the world. Wherever she has appeared in opera or on the concert stage: Milan, Paris, Covent Garden, New York, Sydney. At first the photographs were the usual kind of thing with the diva flashing gracious smiles at the camera, but gradually differences crept in. They became more and more unflattering and he became more and more intrusive. He hid behind bushes. He trespassed on private ground and cropped up when and where he was least expected. On one occasion he joined the crowd round the stage door with the rest of the press, and contrived to get right up to the front.

'As she came into the doorway and did her usual thing of being delighted and astonished at the size of the crowd he aimed his camera and at the same time blew a piercingly loud whistle. Her jaw dropped and her eyes popped and in the resulting photograph she looked as if someone had thumped her between the shoulder blades.

'From then on the thing ripened into a sort of war of attrition. It caught the fancy of her enormous public, the photos became syndicated and the man is said to be making enormous sums of money. Floods of angry letters from her fans to the papers concerned. Threats. Unkind jokes in the worst possible taste. Bets laid. Preposterous stories suggesting he's a cast-off lover taking his revenge or a tenor who fell out with her. Rumours of a nervous breakdown. Bodyguards. The lot.'

'Isn't it rather feeble of them not to spot him and manhandle him off?'

'You'd have thought so, but he's too smart for them. He disguises himself – sometimes bearded and sometimes not. Sometimes in the nylon stocking mask. At one time turned out like a City gent, at another like a Skid Row drop-out. He's said to have a very, *very* sophisticated camera.'

'Yes, but when he's done it, why hasn't somebody grabbed him ▪nd jumped on the camera? And what about her celebrated tem-
▪rament? You'd think she'd set about him herself.'

'You would, but so far she hasn't done any better than yelling pen-and-ink.'

'Well,' Troy said, 'I don't see what you could be expected to do about it.'

'Accept with pleasure and tell my AC that I'm off to the antipodes with my witch-wife? Because,' Alleyn said, putting his hand on her head, 'you are going, aren't you?'

'I do madly want to have a go at her: a great big flamboyant rather vulgar splotch of a thing. Her arms,' Troy said reminiscently, 'are indecent. White and flowing. You can see the brush strokes. She's so shockingly sumptuous. Oh yes, Rory love, I'm afraid I must go.'

'We could try suggesting that she waits till she's having a bash at Covent Garden. No,' said Alleyn, watching her, 'I can see that's no go, you don't want to wait. You must fly to your commodious studio and in between sittings you must paint pretty peeps of snowy mountains reflected in the lucid waters of the lake. You might knock up a one-man show while you're about it.'

'You shut up,' said Troy, taking his arm.

'I think you'd better write a rather formal answer giving your terms, as he so delicately suggests. I suppose I decline under separate cover.'

'It might have been fun if we'd dived together into the flesh pots.'

'The occasions when your art and my job have coincided haven't been all that plain sailing, have they, my love?'

'Not,' she agreed, 'so's you'd notice. Rory, do you mind? My going?'

'I always mind but I try not to let on. I must say I don't go much for the company you'll be keeping.'

'Don't you? High operatic with tantrums between sittings? Will that be the form, do you suppose?'

'Something like that, I dare say.'

'I shan't let her look at the thing until it's finished and if she cuts up rough, her dear one needn't buy it. One thing I will *not* do,' said Troy calmly. 'I will not oblige with asinine alterations. If she's that sort.'

'I should think she well might be. So might he.'

'Taking the view that if he's paying he's entitled to a return for his cash? What is he? English? New Zealand? American? Australian?'

'I've no idea. But I don't much fancy you being his guest, darling, and that's a fact.'

'I can hardly offer to pay my own way. Perhaps,' Troy suggested, 'I should lower my price in consideration of board and lodging.'

'All right, smarty-pants.'

'If it turns out to be a pot-smoking party or worse, I can always beat a retreat to my pretty peepery and lock the door on all comers.'

'What put pot into your fairly pretty little head?'

'I don't know. Here!' said Troy. 'You're not by any chance suggesting the diva is into the drug scene?'

'There have been vague rumours. Probably false.'

'He'd hardly invite *you* to stay if she was.'

'Oh,' Alleyn said lightly, 'their effrontery knows no bounds. I'll write my polite regrets before I go down to the Factory.'

The telephone rang and he answered it with the noncommittal voice Troy knew meant the Yard.

'I'll be down in a quarter of an hour, sir,' he said and hung up. 'The AC,' he explained. 'Up to something. I always know when he goes all casual on me.'

'Up to what, do you suppose?'

'Lord knows. Undelicious by the sound of it. He said it was of no particular moment but would I drop in: an ominous opening. I'd better be off.' He made for the door, looked at her, returned and rounded her face between his hands. 'Fairly pretty little head,' he repeated and kissed it.

Fifteen minutes later his Assistant Commissioner received him in the manner to which he had become accustomed: rather as if he was some sort of specimen produced in a bad light to be peered at, doubtfully. The AC was as well furnished with mannerisms as he was with brains and that would be underestimating them.

'Hullo, Rory,' he said. 'Morning to you. Morning. Troy well? Good.' (Alleyn had not had time to answer.) 'Sit down. Sit down. Yes.'

Alleyn sat down. 'You wanted to see me, sir?' he suggested.

'It's nothing much, really. Read the morning papers?'

'*The Times*.'

'Seen last Friday's *Mercury*?'

'No.'

'I just wondered. That silly stuff with the press photographer and the Italian singing woman. What's-her-name?'

After a moment's pause Alleyn said woodenly: 'Isabella Sommita.'

'That's the one,' agreed the AC, one of whose foibles it was to pretend not to remember names. 'Silly of me. Chap's been at it again.'

'Very persistent.'

'Australia. Sydney or somewhere. Opera House, isn't it?'

'There is one: yes.'

'On the steps at some sort of function. Here you are.'

He pushed over the newspaper folded to expose the photograph. It had indeed been taken a week ago on the steps of the magnificent Sydney Opera House on a summer's evening. La Sommita, gloved in what seemed to be cloth of gold topped by a tiara, stood among VIPs of the highest calibre. Clearly she was not yet poised for the shot. The cameraman had jumped the gun. Again, her mouth was wide open but on this occasion she appeared to be screaming at the Governor General of Australia. Or perhaps shrieking with derisive laughter. There is a belief held by people of the theatre that nobody over the age of twenty-five should allow themselves to be photographed from below. Here, the camera had evidently been half a flight beneath the diva who therefore appeared to be richly endowed with chins and more than slight *embonpoint*. The Governor General, by some momentary accident, seemed to regard her with incredulity and loathing.

A banner headline read: WHO DO YOU THINK YOU ARE!

The photograph, as usual, was signed 'Strix' and was reproduced, by arrangement, from a Sydney newspaper.

'That, I imagine,' said Alleyn, 'will have torn it!'

'So it seems. Look at this.'

It was a letter addressed to 'The Head of Scotland Yard, London' and written a week before the invitations to the Alleyns on heavy paper endorsed with an elaborate monogram: I.S. lavishly entwined with herbage. The envelope was bigger than the ones received by the Alleyns but of the same make and paper. The letter itself occupied two and a half pages, with a gigantic signature. It had been typed, Alleyn noticed, on a different machine. The address was Château Australasia, Sydney.

'The Commissioner sent it down,' said the AC. 'You'd better read it.'

Alleyn did so. The typed section merely informed the recipient that the writer hoped to meet one of his staff, Mr Alleyn, at Waihoe Lodge, New Zealand, where Mr Alleyn's wife was commissioned to paint the writer's portrait. The writer gave the dates proposed. The recipient was of course aware of the outrageous persecution – 'and so on along the already familiar lines. Her object in writing to him, she concluded, was because she hoped Mr Alleyn would be accorded full authority by the Yard to investigate this outrageous affair and she remained – '

'Good God,' said Alleyn quietly.

'You've still got a postscript,' the AC observed.

It was handwritten and all that might be expected. Points of exclamation proliferated. Underscorings doubled and trebled to an extent that would have made Queen Victoria's correspondence appear by contrast a model of stony reticence. The subject matter lurched into incoherence but the general idea was to the effect that if the 'Head of Scotland Yard' didn't do something pretty smartly he would have only himself to blame when the writer's career came to a catastrophic halt. On her knees she remained distractedly and again in enormous calligraphy, sincerely, Isabella Sommita.

'Expound,' the AC invited with his head on one side. He was being whimsical. 'Comment. Explain in your own words.'

'I can only guess that the letter was typed by a secretary who advised moderation. The postscript seems to be all her own and written in a frenzy.'

'*Is* Troy going to paint the lady? And do you propose to be absent without leave in the antipodes?'

Alleyn said: 'We got our invitations this morning. I was about to decline, sir, when you rang up. Troy's accepting.'

'*Is* she?' said the AC thoughtfully. '*Is* she, now? A good subject, um? To paint? What?'

'Very,' Alleyn said warily. What *is* he on about? he wondered.

'Yes. Ah well,' said the AC, freshening his voice with a suggestion of dismissal. Alleyn started to get up. 'Hold on,' said the AC. 'Know anything about this man she lives with? Reece, isn't it?'

'No more than everyone knows.'

'Strange coincidence, really,' mused the AC.

'Coincidence?'

'Yes. The invitations. Troy going out there and all this.' He flipped his finger at the papers on his desk. 'All coming together as it were.'

'Hardly a coincidence, sir, would you say? I mean, these dotty letters were all written with the same motive.'

'Oh, I don't mean *them*,' said the AC contemptuously. 'Or only in so far as they turn up at the same time as the other business.'

'What other business?' said Alleyn, and managed to keep the weary note out of his voice.

'Didn't I tell you? Stupid of me. Yes. There's a bit of a flap going on in the international Drug Scene: the USA in particular. Interpol picked up a lead somewhere and passed it on to the French who talked to the FBI who've been talking to our lot. It seems there's been some suggestion that the diva might be a big, big girl in the remotest background. Very nebulous it sounded to me but our Great White Chief is slightly excited.' This was the AC's habitual manner of alluding to the Commissioner. 'He's been talking to the Special Squad. And, by the way, to MI6.'

'How do they come into it?'

'Somewhere along the line. Cagey, as usual, I gather,' said the AC. 'But they did divulge that there was a leak from an anonymous source to the effect that the Sommita is thought to have operated in the past.'

'What about Reece?'

'Clean as a whistle, as far as is known.'

'Montague Reece,' Alleyn mused. 'Almost too good to be true. Like something out of *Trilby*. Astrakhan coat-collar and glistening beard. Anything about his origin, sir?'

'Thought to be American-Sicilian.'

During the pause that followed the AC hummed, uncertainly, the habañera from *Carmen*. 'Ever heard her in that?' he said. 'Startling. Got the range – soprano, mezzo, you name it, got the looks, got the sex. Stick you like a pig for tuppence and make you like it.' He shot one of his disconcerting glances at Alleyn. 'Troy'll have her hands full,' he said. 'What?'

'Yes,' Alleyn agreed, and with a strong foreboding of what was in store, added: 'I don't much fancy her going.'

'Quite. Going to put your foot down, are you, Rory?'

Alleyn said: 'As far as Troy's concerned I haven't got feet.'

'Tell that to the Fraud Squad,' said the AC and gave a slight whinny.

'Not where her work's concerned. It's a must. For both of us.'

'Ah,' said the AC. 'Mustn't keep you,' he said, and shifted without further notice into the tone that meant business. 'It just occurs to me that in the circumstances you might, after all, take this trip. And by the way you know New Zealand, don't you? Yes?' And when Alleyn didn't answer: 'What I meant when I said "coincidence". The invitation and all that. Drops like a plum into our lap. We're asked to keep a spot of very inconspicuous observation on this article and here's the article's boyfriend asking you to be his guest and Bob, so to speak, is your uncle. Incidentally, you'll be keeping an eye on Troy and her termagant subject, won't you? Well?'

Alleyn said: 'Am I to take it, sir, that this is an order?'

'I must say,' dodged the AC, 'I thought you would be delighted.'

'I expect I ought to be.'

'Very well, then,' said the AC testily. 'Why the hell aren't you?'

'Well, sir, you talked about coincidences. It so happens that by a preposterous series of them Troy has been mixed up to a greater and lesser degree in four of my cases. And – '

'And by all accounts behaved quite splendidly. Hul-*lo*!' said the AC. 'That's it, is it? You don't like her getting involved?'

'On general principles, no, I don't.'

'But, my dear man, you're not going out to the antipodes to involve yourself in an investigation. You're on observation. There won't,' said the AC, 'as likely as not, be anything to observe. Except, of course, your most attractive wife. You're not going to catch a murderer. You're not going to catch anyone. What?'

'I didn't say anything.'

'All right. It's an order. You'd better ring your wife and tell her. Morning to you.'

III

In Melbourne all was well. The Sydney season had been a fantastic success artistically, financially and, as far as Isabella Sommita was concerned, personally. 'Nothing to equal it had been experienced,' as the press raved, 'within living memory.' One reporter laboriously joked that if cars were motivated by real instead of statistical horse-power the quadrupeds would undoubtedly have been unhitched and the diva drawn in triumph and by human propulsion through the seething multitudes.

There had been no further offensive photography.

Young Rupert Bartholomew had found himself pitchforked into a milieu that he neither understood nor criticized but in which he floundered in a state of complicated bliss and bewilderment. Isabella Sommita had caused him to play his one-act opera. She had listened with an approval that ripened quickly with the realization that the soprano role was, to put it coarsely, so large that the rest of the cast existed only as trimmings. The opera was about Ruth and the title was *The Alien Corn*. ('Corn,' muttered Ben Ruby to Monty Reece, but not in the Sommita's hearing, 'is dead right.') There were moments when the pink clouds amid which Rupert floated thinned and a small, ice-cold pellet ran down his spine and he wondered if his opera was any good. He told himself that to doubt it was to doubt the greatest soprano of the age and the pink clouds quickly re-formed. But the shadow of unease did not absolutely leave him.

Mr Reece was not musical. Mr Ruby, in his own untutored way, was. Both accepted the advisability of consulting an expert and such was the pitch of the Sommita's mounting determination to stage this piece that they treated the matter as one of top urgency. Mr Ruby, under pretence of wanting to study the work, borrowed it from the Sommita. He approached the doyen of Australian music critics, and begged him, for old times' sake, to give his strictly private opinion on the opera. He did so and said that it stank.

'Menotti-and-water,' he said. 'Don't let her touch it.'

'Will you tell her so?' Mr Ruby pleaded.

'Not on your Nelly,' said the great man, and as an afterthought, 'What's the matter with her? Has she fallen in love with the composer?'

'Boy,' said Mr Ruby deeply, 'you said it.'

It was true. After her somewhat tigerish fashion the Sommita was in love. Rupert's Byronic appearance, his melting glance, and his undiluted adoration had combined to do the trick. At this point she had a flaring row with her Australian secretary who stood up to her and when she sacked him said she had taken the words out of his mouth. She then asked Rupert if he could type and when he said yes promptly offered him the job. He accepted, cancelled all pending appointments, and found himself booked in at the same astronomically expensive hotel as his employer. He not only dealt with her correspondence. He was one of her escorts to the theatre and was permitted to accompany her at her practices. He supped with her after the show and stayed longer than any of the other guests. He was in Heaven.

On a night when this routine had been observed and Mr Reece had retired early, in digestive discomfort, the Sommita asked Rupert to stay while she changed into something comfortable. This turned out to be a ruby silken negligée which may indeed have been comfortable for the wearer but which caused the beholder to shudder in an agony of excitement.

He hadn't a hope. She had scarcely embarked upon the preliminary phases of her formidable techniques when she was in his arms, or more strictly, he in hers.

An hour later he floated down the long passage to his room, insanely inclined to sing at the top of his voice.

'My first!' he exulted. 'My very first. And, incredibly – Isabella Sommita.'

He was, poor boy, as pleased as Punch with himself.

IV

As far as his nearest associates could discover Mr Reece was not profoundly disturbed by his mistress's goings-on. Indeed he appeared to ignore them but, really, it was impossible to tell, he was so remarkably uncommunicative. Much of his time, most of it, in fact, was spent with a secretary, manipulating, it was widely conjectured, the Stock Markets and receiving long-distance telephone calls. His manner towards Rupert Bartholomew was precisely the same as his manner towards the rest of the Sommita's following: so neutral that it could scarcely be called a manner at all. Occasionally when Rupert thought of Mr Reece he was troubled by stabs of uncomfortable speculation, but he was too far gone in incredulous rapture to be greatly concerned.

It was at this juncture that Mr Reece flew to New Zealand to inspect his island lodge, now completed.

On his return, three days later, to Melbourne, he found the Alleyns' letters of acceptance and the Sommita in a high state of excitement.

'Dar-leeng,' she said, 'you will show me everything. You have photographs, of course? Am I going to be pleased? Because I must tell you I have great plans. But such plans!' cried the Sommita and made mysterious gestures. 'You will never guess.'

'What are they?' he asked in his flat-voiced way.

'Ah-ah!' she teased. 'You must be patient. First the pictures which Rupert, too, must see. Quick, quick, the pictures.'

She opened the bedroom door into the sitting room and in two glorious notes sang, 'Rupert!'

Rupert had been coping with her fan mail. When he came in he found that Mr Reece had laid out a number of glossy coloured photographs on the bed. They were all of the island lodge.

The Sommita was enchanted. She exclaimed, purred, exulted. Several times she burst into laughter. Ben Ruby arrived and the photographs were re-exhibited. She embraced all three men severally and more or less together.

And then with a sudden drop into the practical she said, 'The music room. Let me see it again. Yes. How big is it?'

'From memory,' said Mr Reece, 'sixty feet long and forty wide.' Mr Ruby whistled. 'That's quite a size,' he remarked. 'That's more like a bijou theatre than a room. You settling to give concerts, honey?'

'Better than that!' she cried. 'Didn't I tell you, Monty my darleeng, that we have made plans. Ah, we have cooked up *such* plans, Rupert and I. Haven't we, *caro*? Yes?'

'Yes,' Rupert said with an uncertain glance at Mr Reece. 'I mean – Marvellous.'

Mr Reece had an extremely passive face but Rupert thought he detected a shade of resignation pass over it. Mr Ruby, however, wore an expression of the deepest apprehension.

The Sommita flung her right arm magnificently across Rupert's shoulders. 'This dear child,' she said and if she had made it: 'this adorable lover' she could have scarcely been more explicit, 'has

genius. I tell you – I who know. *Genius*.' They said nothing and she
continued. 'I have lived with his opera. I have studied his opera. I
have studied the leading role. The "Ruth". The arias, the solos, the
duets – there are two – and the *ensembles*. All, but all, have the unmistakable stigmata of genius. I do not,' she amended, 'use the word
"stigmata" in the sense of martyrdom. Better, perhaps, to say "they
bear the banner of genius". *Genius!*' she shouted.

To look at Rupert at this moment one might have thought that
'martyrdom' was, after all, the more appropriate word. His face was
dark red and he shifted in her embrace. She shook him, none too
gently. 'Clever, *clever* one,' she said and kissed him noisily.

'Are we to hear your plan?' Mr Reece asked.

The hour being seven o'clock she hustled them into the sitting
room and told Rupert to produce cocktails. He was glad to secrete
himself in the chilly cabinet provided for drinks, ice and glasses. A
few desultory and inaudible remarks came from the other three. Mr
Ruby cleared his throat once or twice. Then, so unexpectedly that
Rupert spilt Mr Reece's whisky and soda over his hands, the piano
in the sitting room sketched the opening statement of what he had
hoped would be the big aria from his opera: and the superb voice, in
heart-rending pianissimo, sang: 'Alone, alone amidst the alien corn.'

It was at that moment with no warning at all that Rupert was visited by a catastrophic certainty. He had been mistaken in his opera.
Not even the most glorious voice in all the world could ever make it
anything but what it was – third rate.

It's no good, he thought. It is ridiculously commonplace. And
then: She has no judgement. She is not a musical woman.

He was shattered.

CHAPTER 2

The Lodge

Early on a fine morning in the antipodean spring the Alleyns were met at their New Zealand airport by a predictably rich car and were driven along roads that might have been ruled across the plains to vanishing points on the horizon. The Pacific was out of sight somewhere to their left and before them rose foothills. These were the outer ramparts of the Southern Alps.

'We're in luck,' Alleyn said. 'On a grey day when there are no hills to be seen, the plains can be deadly. Would you want to paint?'

'I don't think so,' Troy said after considering it. 'It's all a bit inhuman, isn't it? One would have to find an idiom. I get the feeling that the people only move across the surface. They haven't evolved with it. They're not included,' said Troy, 'in the anatomy. What cheek!' she exclaimed, 'to generalize when I've scarcely arrived in the country.'

The driver, who was called Bert, was friendly and anxious for his passengers to be impressed. He pointed out mountains that had been sheep-farmed by the first landholders.

'Where we're going,' Troy asked, 'to Waihoe Lodge – is that sheep country?'

'No way. We're going into Westland, Mrs Alleyn. The West Coast. It's all timber and mining over there. Waihoe's quite a lake. And the Lodge! You know what they reckon it's cost him? Half a million. And more. That's what they reckon. Nothing like it anywhere else in N'yerzillun. You'll be surprised.'

'We've heard about it,' Alleyn said.

'Yeah? You'll still be surprised.' He slewed his head towards Troy. 'You'll be the painting lady,' he said. 'Mr Reece reckoned you might get the fancy to take a picture up at the head of the Pass. Where we have lunch.'

'I don't think that's likely,' Troy said.

'You're going to paint the famous lady: is that right?' His manner was sardonic. Troy said yes, she was.

'Rather you than me,' said the driver.

'Do you paint, then?'

'Me? Not likely. I wouldn't have the patience.'

'It takes a bit more than patience,' Alleyn said mildly.

'Yeah? That might be right, too,' the driver conceded. There was a longish pause. 'Would she have to keep still, then?' he asked.

'More or less.'

'I reckon it'll be more "less" than "more",' said the driver. 'They tell me she's quite a celebrity,' he added.

'Worldwide,' said Alleyn.

'What they reckon. Yeah,' said the driver with a reflective chuckle, 'they can keep it for mine. Temperamental! You can call it that if you like.' He whistled. 'If it's not one thing it's another. Take the dog. She had one of these fancy hound things, white with droopy hair. The boss give it to her. Well, it goes crook and they get a vet and he reckons it's hopeless and it ought to be put out of its misery. So *she* goes crook. Screechin' and moanin', something remarkable. In the finish the boss says get it over with, so me and the vet take it into the hangar and he chloroforms it and then gives it an injection and we bury it out of sight. Cripes!' said the driver. 'When they told her you'd of thought they'd committed a murder.' He sucked his teeth reminiscently.

'Maria,' he said presently, 'that's her personal help or maid or whatever it's called – she was saying there's been some sort of a schemozzle over in Aussie with the papers. But you'll know about that, Mr Alleyn. Maria reckons you've taken on this situation. Is that right?'

'I'm afraid not,' said Alleyn. Troy gave him a good nudge.

'What she reckons. You being a detective. 'Course Maria's a foreigner. Italian,' said the driver. 'You can't depend on it with that mob. They get excited.'

'You're quartered there, are you? At the Lodge?'

'This is right. For the duration. When they pack it in there'll only be a caretaker and his family on the island. Monty Reece has built a garage and boathouse on the lake shore and his launch takes you over to the Lodge. He's got his own chopper, mind. No trouble. Ring through when required.'

The conversation died. Troy wondered if the driver called his employer 'Monty Reece' to his face and decided that quite possibly he did.

The road across the plains mounted imperceptibly for forty miles and a look backward established their height. Presently they stared down into a wide riverbed laced with milky-turquoise streaks.

At noon they reached the top where they lunched from a hamper with wine in a chiller-kit. Their escort had strong tea from a Thermos flask. 'Seeing I'm the driver,' he said, 'and seeing there's the Zig-Zag yet to come.' He was moved to entertain them with stories about fatal accidents in the gorge.

The air up here was wonderfully fresh and smelt aromatically of manuka scrub patching warm tussocky earth. They were closer now to perpetual snow.

'We better be moving,' said the driver. 'You'll notice a big difference when we go over the head of the Pass. Kind of sudden.'

There was a weathered notice at the top: CORNISHMAN'S PASS. 1000 METRES.

The road ran flat for a short distance and then dived into a new world. As the driver had said: it was sudden. So sudden, so new and so dramatic that for long afterwards Troy would feel there had been a consonance between this moment and the events that were to follow, as if, on crossing over the Pass, they entered a region that was prepared and waiting.

It was a world of very dark rain forest that followed, like velvet, the convolutions of the body it enfolded. Here and there waterfalls glinted. Presiding over the forests, snow-tops caught the sun, but down below the sun never reached and there, thread-like in its gorge, a river thundered. 'You can just hear 'er,' said the driver who had stopped the car.

But all they heard at first was birdsong – cool statements, incomparably wild. After a moment Troy said she thought she could hear the river. The driver suggested they go to the edge and look down.

Troy suffered horridly from height-vertigo but went, clinging to
Alleyn's arm. She looked down once as if from a gallery in a theatre
on an audience of treetops, and saw the river.

The driver, ever-informative, said that you could make out the
roof of a car that six years ago went over from where they stood.
Alleyn said, 'So you can,' put his arm round his wife and returned
her to the car.

They embarked upon the Zig-Zag.

The turns in this monstrous descent were so acute that vehicles
travelling in the same direction would seem to approach each other
and indeed did pass on different levels. They had caught up with
such a one and crawled behind it. They met a car coming up from
the gorge. Their own driver pulled up on the lip of the road and the
other sidled past on the inner running with half an inch to spare.
The drivers wagged their heads at each other.

Alleyn's arm was across Troy's shoulders. He pulled her ear. 'First
prize for intrepidity, Mrs A.,' he said. 'You're being splendid.'

'What did you expect me to do? Howl like a banshee?'

Presently the route flattened out and the driver changed into top
gear. They reached the floor of the gorge and drove beside the river,
roaring in its courses, so that they could scarcely hear each other
speak. It was cold down there.

'Now you're in Westland,' shouted the driver.

Evening was well advanced when, after a two-hour passage
through the wet loam-scented forest that New Zealanders call 'bush'
they came out into more open country and stopped at a tiny railway
station called Kai-kai. Here they collected the private mailbag for the
Lodge and then drove parallel with the railway for twenty miles,
rounded the nose of a hill and there lay a great floor of water: Lake
Waihoe.

'There you are,' said the driver, 'That's the Lake for you. *And* the
Island.'

'Stay me with flagons!' said Alleyn and rubbed his head.

The prospect was astonishing. At this hour the Lake was perfectly unruffled and held the blazing image of an outrageous sunset.
Fingers of land reached out bearing elegant trees that reversed themselves in the water. Framed by these and far beyond them was the
Island and on the Island Mr Reece's Lodge.

It was a house designed by a celebrated architect in the modern idiom but so ordered that one might have said it grew organically out of its primordial setting. Giants that carried their swathy foliage in clusters stood magnificently about a grassy frontage. There was a jetty in the foreground with a launch alongside. Grossly incongruous against the uproarious sunset, like some intrusive bug, a helicopter hovered. As they looked it disappeared behind the house.

'I don't believe in all this,' said Troy. 'It's out of somebody's dream. It can't be true.'

'You reckon?' asked the driver.

'I reckon,' said Troy.

They turned into a lane that ran between tree ferns and underbrush down to the lake edge where there was a garage, a landing stage, a boathouse and a bell in a miniature belfry. They left the car and walked out into evening smells of wet earth, fern and moss and the cold waters of the lake.

The driver rang the bell, sending a single echoing note across the lake. He then remarked that they'd been seen from the Island. Sure enough the launch put out. So still was the evening they could hear the putt-putt of the engine. 'Sound travels a long way over the water,' said the driver.

The sunset came to its preposterous climax. Everything that could be seen, near and far, was sharpened and gilded. Their faces reddened. The far-off windows of the Lodge turned to fire. In ten minutes it had all faded and the landscape was cold. Troy and Alleyn walked a little way along the water's edge and Troy looked at the house and wondered about the people inside it. Would Isabella Sommita feel that it was a proper showplace for her brilliance and what would she look like posing in the 'commodious studio' against those high windows, herself flamboyant against another such sunset as the one that had gone by?

Troy said: 'This really *is* an adventure.'

Alleyn said: 'Do you know, in a cockeyed sort of way it reminds me of one of those Victorian romances by George Macdonald where the characters find a looking glass and walk out of this world into another one inhabited by strange beings and unaccountable on-goings.'

'Perhaps,' said Troy, 'the entrance to that great house will turn out to be our own front door and we'll be back in London.'

They talked about the house and the way in which it rose out of its setting in balanced towers. Presently the launch, leaving an arrowhead of rippled silk in its wake, drew in to the landing stage. It was a large, opulent craft. The helmsman came out of his wheelhouse and threw a mooring rope to the car driver.

'Meet Les Smith,' said the driver.

'Gidday,' said Les Smith. 'How's tricks, then, Bert? Good trip?'

'No trouble, Les.'

'Good as gold,' said the helmsman.

Alleyn helped them stow the luggage. Troy was handed on board and they puttered out on the lake.

The driver went into the wheelhouse with Les Smith. Troy and Alleyn sat in the stern.

'Here we go,' he said. 'Liking it?'

'It's a lovely beginning,' said Troy. 'It's so lovely it hurts.'

'Keep your fingers crossed,' he said lightly.

II

Perhaps because their day had been so long and had followed so hard on their flight from England, the first night at the Lodge went by rather like a dream for Troy.

They had been met by Mr Reece's secretary and a dark man dressed like a tarted-up ship's steward who carried their baggage. They were taken to their room to 'freshen up'. The secretary, a straw-coloured youngish man with a gushing manner, explained that Mr Reece was on the telephone but would be there to meet them when they came down and that everyone was 'changing' but they were not to bother as everybody would 'quite understand'. Dinner was in a quarter of an hour. There was a drinks tray in the room and he suggested that they should make use of it and said he knew they would be angelic and excuse him as Mr Reece had need of his services. He then, as an apparent afterthought, was lavish in welcome, flashed smiles and withdrew. Troy thought vaguely that he was insufferable.

'I don't know about you,' she said, 'but I refuse to be quite understood and I'm going to shift my clothes. I require a nice wash and a change. And a drink, by the way.'

She opened her suitcase, scuffled in it and lugged out a jump suit which was luckily made of uncrushable material. She then went into the bathroom which was equipped like a plumber-king's palace. Alleyn effected a lightning change at which exercise he was a past master and mixed two drinks. They sat side by side on an enormous bed and contemplated their room.

'It's all been done by some super American interior decorator, wouldn't you say?' said Troy, gulping down her brandy-and-dry.

'You reckon?' said Alleyn, imitating the driver.

'I reckon,' said Troy. 'You have to wade through the carpet, don't you? Not walk on it.'

'It's not a carpet: it's about two hundred sheepskins sewn together. The local touch.'

'All jolly fine for us to snigger. It's pretty smashing, really, let's face it. Not human, though. If only there was something shabby and out of character somewhere.'

'Us,' Alleyn said. 'We're all of that. Drink up. We'd better not be late.'

On their way downstairs they took in the full effect of the hall with its colossal blazing fireplace, display on the walls of various lethal weapons and hangings woven in the Maori fashion, and a large semi-abstract wood sculpture of a pregnant nude with a complacent smirk. From behind one of the doors there came sounds of conversation. An insistent male voice rose above the rest. There followed a burst of multiple laughter.

'Good Lord,' said Alleyn, 'it's a house party.'

The dark man who had taken their baggage up was in the hall.

'In the drawing room, sir,' he said unnecessarily and opened the door.

About a dozen or so people, predominantly male, were grouped at the far end of a long room. The focal point seemed to be a personage with a grey imperial beard and hair *en brosse*, wearing a velvet jacket and flowing tie, an eyeglass and a flower in his lapel. His manner was that of a practised *raconteur* who, after delivering a *mot*, is careful to preserve an expressionless face. His audience

was barely recovered from its fits of merriment. The straw-
coloured secretary, indeed, with glass in hand, gently tapped his
fingers against his left wrist by way of applause. In doing this he
turned, saw the Alleyns and bent over someone in a sofa with its
back to the door.

A voice said: 'Ah yes,' and Mr Reece rose and came to greet them.

He was shortish and dark and had run a little to what is sometimes called expense-account fat. His eyes were large, and his face
closed: a face that it would be easy to forget since it seemed to say
nothing.

He shook hands and said how glad he was to receive them: to
Troy he added that it was an honour and a privilege to welcome her.
There were, perhaps, American overtones in his speech but on the
whole his voice, like the rest of him, seemed neutral. He introduced
the Alleyns formally to everybody. To the *raconteur* who was Signor
Beppo Lattienzo and who kissed Troy's hand. To a rotund gentleman
who looked like an operatic tenor and turned out to be one: the celebrated Rodolfo Romano. To Mr Ben Ruby who was jocular and said
they all knew Troy would do better than *that*: indicating a vast academic portrait of La Sommita's gown topped up by her mask. Then
came a young man of startling physical beauty who looked apprehensive – Rupert Bartholomew; a pretty girl whose name Troy,
easily baffled by mass introductions, didn't catch, and a largish lady
on a sofa who was called Miss Hilda Dancy and had a deep voice,
and finally there loomed up a gentleman with an even deeper voice
and a jolly brown face who proclaimed himself a New Zealander and
was called Mr Eru Johnstone.

Having discharged his introductory duties Mr Reece retained his
hold on Alleyn, supervised his drink, led him a little apart and, as
Troy could see by the sort of attentive shutter that came over her
husband's face, engaged him in serious conversation.

'You have had a very long day, Mrs Alleyn,' said Signor Lattienzo
who spoke with a marked Italian accent. 'Do you feel as if all your
time signals had become – ' he rotated plump hands rapidly round
each other – 'jumbled together?'

'Exactly like that,' said Troy. 'Jet hangover, I think.'

'It will be nice to retire?'

'Gosh, yes!' she breathed, surprised into ardent agreement.

'Come and sit down,' he said, and led her to a sofa removed from that occupied by Miss Dancy.

'You must not begin to paint before you are ready,' he said. 'Do not permit them to bully you.'

'Oh, I'll be ready, I hope, tomorrow.'

'I doubt it and I doubt even more if your subject will be available.'

'Why?' asked Troy quickly. 'Is anything the matter? I mean – '

'The *matter*? That depends on one's attitude.' He looked fixedly at her. He had very bright eyes. 'You have not heard evidently of the great event,' he said. 'No? Ah. Then I must tell you that the night after next we are to be audience at the first performance on any stage of a brand-new one-act opera. A world première, in fact,' said Signor Lattienzo and his tone was exceedingly dry. 'What do you think about that?'

'I'm flabbergasted,' said Troy.

'You will be even more so when you have heard it. You do not know who I am, of course.'

'I'm afraid I only know that your name is Lattienzo.'

'Ah-ha.'

'I expect I ought to have exclaimed, "No! Not *the* Lattienzo?"'

'Not at all. I am that obscure creature a vocal pedagogue. I take the voice and teach it to know itself.'

'And did you – ?'

'Yes. I took to pieces the most remarkable vocal instrument of these times and put it together again and gave it back to its owner. I worked her like a horse for three years and I am probably the only living person to whom she pays the slightest professional attention. I am commanded here because she wishes me to fall into a rapture over this opera.'

'Have you seen it? Or should one say "read it"?'

He cast up his eyes and made a gesture of despair.

'Oh dear,' said Troy.

'Alas, alas,' agreed Signor Lattienzo. Troy wondered if he was habitually so unguarded with complete strangers.

'You have, of course,' he said, 'noticed the fair young man with the appearance of a quattrocento angel and the expression of a soul in torment?'

'I have indeed. It's a remarkable head.'

'What devil, one asks oneself, inserted into it the notion that it could concoct an opera. And yet,' said Signor Lattienzo, looking thoughtfully at Rupert Bartholomew, 'I fancy the first-night horrors the poor child undoubtedly suffers are not of the usual kind.'

'No?'

'No. I fancy he has discovered his mistake and feels deadly sick.'

'But this is dreadful,' Troy said. 'It's the worst that can happen.'

'Can it happen to painters, then?'

'I think painters know while they are still at it, if the thing they are doing is no good. I know I do,' said Troy. 'There isn't perhaps the time-lag that authors and, from what you tell me, musicians can go through before they come to the awful moment of truth. Is the opera really so bad?'

'Yes. It is bad. Nevertheless, here and there, perhaps three times, one hears little signs that make one regret he is being spoilt. Nothing is to be spared him. He is to conduct.'

'Have you spoken to him? About it being wrong?'

'Not yet. First I shall let him hear it.'

'Oh,' Troy protested, 'but why! Why let him go through with it. Why not tell him and advise him to cancel the performance.'

'First of all, because she would pay no attention.'

'But if he refused?'

'She has devoured him, poor dear. He would not refuse. She has made him her secretary-accompanist-composer, but beyond all that and most destructively, she has taken him for her lover and gobbled him up. It is very sad,' said Signor Lattienzo and his eyes were bright as coal nuggets. 'But you see,' he added, 'what I mean when I say that La Sommita will be too much *engagée* to pose for you until all is over. And then she may be too furious to sit still for thirty seconds. The first dress rehearsal was yesterday. Tomorrow will be occupied in alternately resting and making scenes and attending a second dress rehearsal. And the next night – the performance! Shall I tell you of their first meeting and how it has all come about?'

'Please.'

'But first I must fortify you with a drink.'

He did tell her, making a good story of it. 'Imagine! Their first encounter. All the ingredients of the soap opera. A strange young man, pale as death, beautiful as Adonis, with burning eyes and water pouring off the end of his nose, gazes hungrily at his goddess at one a.m. during a deluge. She summons him to the window of her car. She is kind and before long she is even kinder. And again, kinder. He shows her his opera – it is called *The Alien Corn*, it is dedicated to her and since the role of Ruth is virtually the entire score and has scarcely finished ravishing the audience with one coloratura embellishment before another sets in, she is favourably impressed. You know, of course, of her celebrated A above high C.'

'I'm afraid not!'

'No? It's second only to the achievement recorded in the *Guinness Book of Records*. This besotted young man has been careful to provide for it in her aria. I must tell you by the way that while she sings like the Queen of Heaven, musically speaking this splendid creature is as stupid as an owl.'

'Oh, come!'

'Believe me. It is the truth. You see before you the assembled company engaged at vast cost for this charade. The basso: a New Zealander and a worthy successor to Inia te Wiata. He is the Boaz and, believe me, finds himself knee deep in corn for which "alien" is all too inadequate a description. The dear Hilda Dancy on the sofa is the Naomi who escapes with a duet, a handful of recitatives and the contralto part in an enfeebled pastiche of "*Bella figlia del amore*". There she is joined by a mezzo-soprano – (the little Sylvia Parry now talking to the composer) She is, so to speak, Signora Boaz. Next comes the romantic element in the person of Rodolfo Romano who is the head gleaner and adores the Ruth at first sight. She, I need not tell you, dominates the quartet. You find me unsympathetic, perhaps?' said Signor Lattienzo.

'I find you very funny,' said Troy.

'But spiteful? Yes?'

'Well – ruthless, perhaps.'

'Would we were all.'

'What?'

'"Ruth"-less, my dear.'

'Oh, *really*!' said Troy and burst out laughing.

'I am very hungry. She is twenty minutes late as usual and our good Monty consults his watch. Ah! we are to be given the full performance – the Delayed Entrance. Listen.'

A musical whooping could at that moment be heard rapidly increasing in volume.

'The celestial fire engine,' said Signor Lattienzo, 'approaches.' He said this loudly to Alleyn who had joined them.

The door into the hall was flung wide, Isabella Sommita stood on the threshold and Troy thought: This is it. O, praise the Lord all ye lands, this is it.

The first thing to be noticed about the Sommita was her eyes. They were enormous, black and baleful, and set slantwise in her magnolia face. They were topped by two jetty arcs, thin as a camel-hair brush but one knew that if left to themselves they would bristle and meet angrily above her nose. Her underlip was full, her teeth slightly protuberant with the little gap at the front which is said to denote an amorous disposition.

She wore green velvet and diamonds and her celebrated bosom, sumptuously displayed, shone like marble.

Everyone who had been sitting rose. Alleyn thought: A bit more of this and the ladies would fall to the ground in curtseys. He looked at Troy and recognized the quickened attention, the impersonal scrutiny that meant his wife was hooked.

'Dar-leengs!' sang La Sommita. 'So late! Forgive, forgive.' She directed her remarkably searching gaze upon them all, and let it travel slowly, rather, Alleyn thought, in the manner of a lighthouse, until it rested upon him, and then upon Troy. An expression of astonishment and rapture dawned. She advanced upon them both with outstretched arms and cries of excitement, seized their hands, giving them firm little shakes as if she was congratulating them on their union and found her joy in doing so too great for words.

'But you have COME!' she cried at last and appealed to everyone else. 'Isn't it wonderful!' she demanded. 'They have COME!' She displayed them, like trophies, to her politely responsive audience.

Alleyn said 'Hell' inaudibly and as a way of releasing himself kissed the receptive hand.

There followed cascades of welcome. Troy was gripped by the shoulders and gazed at searchingly and asked if she (the Sommita) would 'do' and told that already she knew they were *en rapport* and that she (the Sommita) always '*knew*'. Didn't Troy always *know*? Alleyn was appealed to: 'Didn't she?'

'Oh,' Alleyn said, 'she's as cunning as a bagload of monkeys, Madame. You've no idea.'

Further melodious hoots, this time of laughter, greeted the far from brilliant sally. Alleyn was playfully chided.

They were checked by the entry at the far end of the room of another steward-like personage who announced dinner. He carried a salver with what was no doubt the mail that had come with the Alleyns and took it to the straw-coloured secretary who said: 'On my desk.' The man made some inaudible reply and seemed to indicate a newspaper on his salver. The secretary looked extremely perturbed and repeated, loudly enough for Alleyn to hear. 'No, no. I'll attend to it. In the drawer of my desk. Take it away.'

The man bowed slightly and returned to the doors.

The guests were already in motion and the scene now resembled the close of the first act of an Edwardian comedy, voices pitched rather high, movements studied, the sense, even, of some approach to a climax which would develop in the next act.

It developed, however, there and then. The bass, Mr Eru Johnstone, said in his enormous voice: 'Do I see the evening paper? It will have the results of the Spring Cup, won't it?'

'I should imagine so,' said Mr Reece. 'Why?'

'We had a sweep on Top Note. It seemed a clear indication,' and he boomed up the room. 'Everybody! The Cup!'

The procession halted. They all chattered in great excitement but were, as actors say, 'topped' by the Sommita demanding to see the paper there and then. Alleyn saw the secretary, who looked agitated, trying to reach the servant but the Sommita had already seized the newspaper and flapped it open.

The scene that followed bore for three or four seconds a far-fetched resemblance to an abortive ruck in rugby football. The guests, still talking eagerly, surged round the prima donna. And then, suddenly, fell silent, backed away and left her isolated, speechless and cross-eyed, holding out the open newspaper as if she intended to drop-kick it to eternity. Alleyn said afterwards that he could have sworn she foamed at the mouth.

Across the front page of the paper a banner headline was splashed.

SOMMITA SAYS NO FALSIES

And underneath:

SIGNED STATEMENT: BY FAMOUS PRIMA DONNA.
HER CURVES ARE ALL HER OWN. BUT ARE THEY????

Boxed in a heavy outline, at the centre of the page, were about nine lines of typescript and beneath them the enormous signature –

Isabella Sommita

III

Dinner had been catastrophic, a one-man show by the Sommita. To say she had run through the gamut of the passions would be a rank understatement: she began where the gamut left off and bursts of hysteria were as passages-of-rest in the performance. Occasionally she would come to an abrupt halt and wolf up great mouthfuls of the food that had been set before her, for she was a greedy lady. Her discomforted guests would seize the opportunity to join her, in a more conservative manner, in taking refreshment. The dinner was superb.

Her professional associates were less discomforted, the Alleyns afterwards agreed, than a lay audience would have been and indeed seemed more or less to take her passion in their stride, occasionally contributing inflammatory remarks while Signor Romano who was on her left made wide ineffable gestures and when he managed to get hold of it, kissed her hand. Alleyn was on her right. He was frequently appealed to and came in for one or two excruciating prods in the ribs as she drove home her points. He was conscious that Troy had her eyes on him and when he got the chance, made a lightning grimace of terror at her. He saw she was on the threshold of giggles.

Troy was on Mr Reece's right. He seemed to think that in the midst of this din he was under an obligation to make conversation and remarked upon the lack of journalistic probity in Australia. The offending newspaper, it seemed, was an Australian weekly with a wide circulation in New Zealand.

When the port had been put before him and his dear one had passed for the time being into a baleful silence, he suggested tonelessly that the ladies perhaps wished to withdraw.

The Sommita made no immediate response and a tricky hiatus occurred during which she glowered at the table. Troy thought: Oh, to hell with all this, and stood up. Hilda Dancy followed with alacrity and so after a moment's hesitation did wide-eyed Sylvia Parry. The men got to their feet.

The Sommita rose, assumed the posture of a Cassandra about to give tongue, appeared to change her mind and said she was going to bed.

About twenty minutes later Alleyn found himself closeted in a room that looked like the setting for a science-fiction film but was Mr Reece's study. With him were Mr Reece himself, Mr Ben Ruby, Rupert Bartholomew and the straw-coloured secretary whose name turned out to be Hanley.

The infamous sheet of newsprint was laid out on a table round which the men had gathered. They read the typewritten letter reproduced in the central box.

To The Editor
The Watchman
Sir: I wish, through your column, to repudiate utterly an outrageous calumny which is circulating in this country. I wish to state, categorically, that I have no need of, and therefore have never resorted to, cosmetic surgery or to artificial embellishment of any kind whatsoever. I am, and I present myself to my public, as God made me. Thank you.

Isabella Sommita.

(*Picture on page 30*)

'And you tell me,' Alleyn said, 'that the whole thing is a forgery?'

'You bet it's a forgery,' said Ben Ruby. 'Would she ever help herself to a plateful of poisonous publicity! My God, this is going to make her the big laugh of a lifetime over in Aussie. *And* it'll spread overseas, you better believe it.'

'*Have* there in fact been any rumours, any gossip of this sort?'

'Not that we have knowledge of,' said Mr Reece. 'And if it had been at all widespread, we certainly would have heard. Wouldn't we, Ben?'

'Well, face it, old boy, anyone that's seen her would know it was silly. I meantersay, look at her cleavage! Speaks for itself.' Mr Ruby turned to Alleyn. 'You've seen. You couldn't miss it. She's got the best twinset you're likely to meet in a lifetime. Beautiful! Here! Take a look at this picture.'

He turned to page 30 and flattened it out. The 'picture' was a photograph of the Sommita in profile with her head thrown back, her hands behind her resting on a table and taking the weight. She was in character as Carmen and an artificial rose was clenched between her teeth. She was powerfully décolletée and although at first glance there seemed to be no doubt of the authenticity of the poitrine, on closer examination there were certain curious little marks in that region suggestive of surgical scars. The legend beneath read 'Seeing's believing!'

'She never liked that picture,' Mr Ruby said moodily. 'Never. But the press did, so we kept it in the handouts. Here!' he exclaimed jamming a forefinger at it. 'Here, take a look at this, will you? This has been interfered with. This has been touched up. This has been tinkered with. Those scars are phoney.'

Alleyn examined it. 'I think you're right,' he said and turned back to the front page.

'Mr Hanley,' he said, 'do you think that typewriter could have been one belonging to anybody in Madame Sommita's immediate circle? Can you tell that?'

'Oh? Oh!' said the secretary and stooped over the paper. 'Well,' he said after a moment, 'it wasn't typed on my machine.' He laughed uncomfortably. 'I can promise you that much,' he said. 'I wouldn't know about hers. How about it, Rupert?'

'Bartholomew,' explained Mr Reece in his flattened way, 'is Madame's secretary.' He stood back and motioned Rupert to examine the page.

Rupert who had a tendency to change colour whenever Mr Reece paid him any attention, did so now. He stooped over the paper.

'No,' he said, 'it's not our – I mean my – machine. The letter p is out of alignment in ours. And anyway it's not the same type.'

'And the signature? That looks convincing enough, doesn't it?' Alleyn asked his host.

'Oh yes,' he said. 'It's Bella's signature.'

'Can any of you think of any cause Madame Sommita may have had to put her signature at the foot of a blank sheet of letter paper?'

Nobody spoke.

'Can she type?'

'No,' they all said and Ben Ruby added irritably, 'Ah, for Chrissake, what's the point of labouring at it? There've been no rumours about her bosom, pardon my candour, and, hell, she never wrote that bloody letter. It's got to be a forgery and, by God, in my book it's got to be that sodding photographer at the bottom of it.'

The two young men made sounds of profound agreement.

Mr Reece raised his hand and they were silenced. 'We are fortunate enough,' he announced, 'to have Mr Alleyn, or rather Chief Superintendent Alleyn, with us. I suggest that we accord him our full attention, gentlemen.'

He might have been addressing a board meeting. He turned to Alleyn and made a slight inclination. 'Will you – ?' he invited.

Alleyn said: 'Of course, if you think I can be of use. But I expect I ought just to mention that if there's any idea of calling in the police it will have to be the New Zealand police. I'm sure you will understand that.'

'Oh, quite so, quite so,' said Mr Reece. 'Let us say we will value, immensely, your unofficial expertise.'

'Very well. But it won't be at all startling.'

The men took chairs round the table, as if, Alleyn thought, they were resigning themselves to some damned lecture. The whole scene, he thought, was out of joint. They might have arranged between themselves how it should be played but were not quite sure of their lines.

He remembered his instructions from the AC. He was to observe, act with extreme discretion, fall in with the terms of his invitation and treat the riddle of the naughty photographer as he would any case to which he had been consigned in the ordinary course of his duties.

He said: 'Here goes then. First of all: if this was a police job one of the first things to be done would be to make an exhaustive examination of the letter which seems to be a reproduction in print of an original document. We would get it blown up on a screen, search the result for any signs of fingerprints or indications of what sort of paper the original might be. Same treatment for the photograph with particular attention to the rather clumsy faking of surgical scars.

'At the same time someone would be sent to the offices of *The Watchman* to find out everything available about when the original letter was received and whether by post or pushed into the correspondence box at the entrance or wherever of *The Watchman*'s office. And also who dealt with it. *The Watchman*, almost certainly, would be extremely cagey about this and would, when asked to produce the original, say it had not been kept, which might or might not be true. Obviously,' Alleyn said, 'they didn't ask for any authorization of the letter or take any steps to assure themselves that it was genuine.'

'It's not that sort of paper,' said Ben Ruby. 'Well, look at it. If we sued for libel it'd be nothing new to *The Watchman*. The scoop would be worth it.'

'Didn't I hear,' Alleyn asked, 'that on one occasion the photographer – "Strix" isn't it? – dressed as a woman, asked for her autograph and then fired his camera at point-blank range and ducked out?'

Mr Ruby slammed the table. 'By God, you're right,' he shouted, 'and he got it. She signed. He got her signature.'

'It's too much, I suppose, to ask if she remembers any particular book or whether she ever signed at the bottom of a blank page or how big the page was.'

'She remembers! Too right she remembers!' Mr Ruby shouted. 'That one *was* an outsize book. Looked like something special for famous names. She remembers it on account it was not the usual job. As for the signature she's most likely to have made it extra big to fill out the whole space. She does that.'

'Were any of you with her? She was leaving the theatre, wasn't she? At the time?'

'I was with her,' Mr Reece offered. 'So were you, Ben. We always escort her from the stage door to her car. I didn't actually see the book. I was looking to make sure the car was in the usual place. There was a big crowd.'

'I was behind her,' said Mr Ruby. '*I* couldn't see anything. The first thing *I* knew was the flash and the rumpus. She was yelling out for somebody to stop the photographer. Somebody else was scream-ing "Stop that woman!" and fighting to get through. And it turned out afterwards, the screamer was the woman herself who was the photographer Strix if you can follow me.'

'Just,' said Alleyn.

'He's made monkeys out of the lot of us; all along the line he's made us look like monkeys,' Mr Ruby complained.

'What does *he* look like? Surely someone must have noticed something about him?'

But, no, it appeared. Nobody had come forward with a reliable description. He operated always in a crowd where everyone's atten-tion was focused on his victim and cameramen abounded. Or unex-pectedly he would pop round a corner with his camera held in both hands before his face, or from a car that shot off before any action could be taken. There had been one or two uncertain impressions – he was bearded, he had a scarf pulled over his mouth, he was dark. Mr Ruby had a theory that he never wore the same clothes twice and always went in for elaborate make-ups but there was nothing to support this idea.

'What action,' Mr Reece asked Alleyn, 'would you advise?'

'To begin with: *not* an action for libel. Can she be persuaded against it, do you think?'

'She may be all against it in the morning. You never know,' said Hanley, and then with an uneasy appeal to his employer: 'I *beg* your pardon, sir, but I mean to say you *don't*, do you? Actually?'

Mr Reece, with no change of expression in his face, merely looked at his secretary who subsided nervously.

Alleyn had returned to *The Watchman*. He tilted the paper this way and that under the table lamp. 'I think,' he said, 'I'm not *sure* but I *think* the original paper was probably glossy.'

'I'll arrange for someone to deal with *The Watchman* end,' said Mr Reece, and to Hanley: 'Get through to Sir Simon Marks in Sydney,' he ordered. 'Or wherever he is. Get him.'

Hanley retreated to a distant telephone and huddled over it in soundless communication.

Alleyn said: 'If I were doing this as a conscientious copper I would now ask you all if you have any further ideas about the per-petrator of these ugly tricks – assuming for the moment that the

photographer and the concoctor of the letter are one and the same
person. Is there anybody you can think of who bears a grudge deep
enough to inspire such persistent and malicious attacks? Has she an
enemy, in fact?'

'Has she a hundred bloody enemies?' Mr Ruby heatedly returned.
'Of course she has. Like the homegrown baritone she insulted in
Perth or the top hostess in Los Angeles who threw a high-quality
party for her and asked visiting royalty to meet her.'

'What went wrong?'

'She didn't go.'

'Oh dear!'

'Took against it at the last moment because she'd heard the host's
money came from South Africa. We talked about a sudden attack of
migraine, which might have answered if she hadn't gone to supper
at Angelo's and the press hadn't reported it with pictures the next
morning.'

'Wasn't "Strix" already in action by then, though?'

'That's true,' agreed Mr Ruby gloomily. 'You've got something
there. But enemies! My oath!'

'In my view,' said Mr Reece, 'the matter of enmity doesn't arise.
This has been from first to last a profitable enterprise. I've ascer-
tained that "Strix" can ask what he likes for his photographs. It's
only a matter of time, one imagines, before they reappear in book-
form. He's hit on a money-spinner and unless we can catch him in
the act he'll go on spinning as long as the public interest lasts. Simple
as that.'

'If he concocted the letter,' Alleyn said, 'it's hard to see how he'd
make money out of that. He could hardly admit to forgery.'

Rupert Bartholomew said: 'I think the letter was written out of
pure spite. She thinks so, too: you heard her. A sort of black practical joke.'

He made this announcement with an air of defiance, almost of
proprietorship. Alleyn saw Mr Reece look at him for several
seconds with concentration as if his attention had been unexpectedly aroused. He thought: That boy's getting himself into
deep water.

Hanley had been speaking into the telephone. He stood up and
said, 'Sir Simon Marks, sir.'

Mr Reece took the call inaudibly. The others fell into an unrestful silence, not wishing to seem as if they listened but unable to find anything to say to each other. Alleyn was conscious of Rupert Bartholomew's regard which as often as he caught it was hurriedly turned away. He's making some sort of appeal, Alleyn thought and went over to him. They were now removed from the others.

'Do tell me about your opera,' he said. 'I've only gathered the scantiest picture from our host of what is going to happen but it all sounds most exciting.'

Rupert muttered something about not being too sure of that.

'But,' said Alleyn, 'it must be an enormous thing for you, isn't it? For the greatest soprano of our time to bring it all about? A wonderful piece of good fortune, I'd have thought.'

'Don't,' Rupert muttered. 'Don't say that.'

'Hullo! What's all this? First night nerves?'

Rupert shook his head. Good Lord, Alleyn thought, a bit more of this and he'll be in tears. Rupert stared at him and seemed to be on the edge of speech when Mr Reece put back the receiver and rejoined the others. 'Marks will attend to *The Watchman*,' he said. 'If the original is there he'll see that we get it.'

'Can you be sure of that?' Ruby asked.

'Certainly. He owns the group and controls the policy.'

They began to talk in a desultory way and for Alleyn their voices sounded a long way off and disembodied. The spectacular room became unsteady and its contents swelled, diminished and faded. I'm going to sleep on my feet, he thought and pulled himself together.

He said to his host, 'As I can't be of use, I wonder if I may be excused? It's been a long day and one didn't get much sleep on the plane.'

Mr Reece was all consideration. 'How very thoughtless of us,' he said. 'Of course. Of course.' He made appropriate hospitable remarks about hoping the Alleyns had everything they required, suggested that they breakfasted late in their room and ring when they were ready for it. He sounded as if he was playing some sort of internal cassette of his own recording. He glanced at Hanley who advanced, all eager to please.

'We're in unbelievable bliss,' Alleyn assured them, scarcely know-ing what he said. And to Hanley: 'No, please don't bother. I promise not to doze off on my way up. Good night, everyone.'

He crossed the hall which was now dimly lit. The pregnant woman loomed up and stared at him through slitted eyes. Behind her the fire, dwindled to a glow, pulsated quietly.

As he passed the drawing-room door he heard a scatter of desul-tory conversation: three voices at the most, he thought, and none of them belonging to Troy.

And, sure enough, when he reached their room he found her in bed and fast asleep. Before joining her he went to the heavy window curtains, parted them and saw the lake in moonlight close beneath him, stretching away like a silver plain into the mountains. Incongruous, he thought, and impertinent, for this little knot of noisy, self-important people with their self-imposed luxury and serio-comic concerns to be set down at the heart of such an immense serenity.

He let the curtain fall and went to bed.

He and Troy were coming back to earth in Mr Reece's aeroplane. An endless road rushed towards them. Appallingly far below, the river thundered and water lapped at the side of their boat. He fell quietly into it and was immediately fathoms deep.

CHAPTER 3

Rehearsal

Troy slept heavily and woke at ten o'clock to find Alleyn up and dressed and the room full of sunshine.

'I've never known you so unwakeable,' he said. 'Deep as the lake itself. I've asked for our breakfast.'

'Have you been up long?'

'About two hours. The bathroom's tarted up to its eyebrows. Jets of water smack you up where you least expect it. I went downstairs. Not a soul about apart from the odd slave who looked at me as if I was dotty. So I went outside and had a bit of an explore. Troy, it really is quite extraordinarily beautiful, this place; so still; the lake clear, the trees motionless, everything new and fresh and yet, or so one feels, empty and belonging to primordial time. Dear me,' said Alleyn, rubbing his nose, 'I'd better not try. Let's tell each other about what went on after that atrocious dinner party.'

'I've nothing to tell. When we left you the diva merely said in a volcanic voice: 'Excuse me, ladies,' and swept upstairs. I gave her time to disappear and then followed suit. I can scarcely remember getting myself to bed. What about you?'

Alleyn told her.

'If you ask me,' Troy said, 'it needs only another outrage like this and she'll break down completely. She was literally shaking all over as if she had a rigor. She can't go on like that. Don't you agree?'

'Not really. Not necessarily. Have you ever watched two Italians having a discussion in the street? Furious gestures, shrieks, glaring eyes, faces close together. Any moment, you think, it'll be a free-for-all

and then without warning they burst out laughing and hit each other's
shoulders in comradely accord. I'd say she was of the purest Italian –
perhaps Sicilian – peasant stock and utterly uninhibited. Add to that
the propensity of all public performers to cut up rough and throw tem-
peraments right and left when they think they've been slighted and
you've got La Sommita. You'll see.'

But beyond staring bemusedly out of the windows, Troy was not
given much chance of seeing for herself. Instead, she and Alleyn
were to be taken on a tour of the house by Mr Reece, beginning with
the 'studio' which turned out to be on the same level as their bedroom. Grand pianos being as chicken feed to Mr Reece, there was
one in here and Troy was given to understand that the Sommita
practised at it and that the multiple-gifted Rupert Bartholomew
acted as her accompanist, having replaced an Australian lady in that
capacity. She found, with astonishment, that an enormous easel of
sophisticated design and a painter's table and stool had been introduced into the room for her use. Mr Reece was anxious, he said, to
know if they suited. Troy, tempted to ask if they were on sale or
return, said they did and was daunted by their newness. There was
also a studio throne with a fine lacquer screen on it. Mr Reece
expressed a kind of drab displeasure that it was not large enough to
accommodate the grand piano as well. Troy, who had already made
up her mind what she wanted to do with her subject, said it was of
no consequence. When, she asked, would she be able to start? Mr
Reece, she thought, was slightly evasive. He had not spoken this
morning to Madame, he said, but he understood there would be
rehearsals for the greater part of the day. The orchestra was to arrive.
They had been rehearsing, with frequent visits from Bartholomew,
and would arrive by bus. The remaining guests were expected
tomorrow.

The studio window was of the enormous plate-glass kind.
Through it they had a new view of lake and mountains. Immediately
beneath them, adjoining the house, was a patio and close by an
artificially enclosed swimming pool, round which and in which
members of the house party were displayed. On the extreme right,
separated from the pool and surrounded by native bush, was an
open space and a hangar which, Mr Reece said, accommodated the
helicopter.

Mr Reece was moved to talk about the view which he did in a grey, factual manner, stating that the lake was so deep in many parts that it had never been sounded and that the region was famous for a storm, known locally as The Rosser, which rose unheralded in the mountains and whipped the lake into fury and had been responsible for many fatal accidents.

He also made one or two remarks on the potential for 'development' and Alleyn saw the look of horrified incredulity on his wife's face. Fortunately, it appeared, pettifogging legislation about land-tenure and restrictions on imported labour would prohibit what Mr Reece called 'worthwhile touristic planning' so that the prospect of marinas, high-rise hotels, speedboats, loud music and floodlit bathing pools did not threaten those primordial shores. Sandflies by day and mosquitoes by night, Mr Reece thought, could be dealt with and Troy envisaged low-flying aircraft delivering millions of gallons of kerosene upon the immaculate face of the lake.

Without warning she was overcome by a return of fatigue and felt quite unable to face an extended pilgrimage of this unending mansion. Seeing her dilemma, Alleyn asked Mr Reece if he might fetch her gear and unpack it. There was immediate talk of summoning a 'man' but they managed to avoid this. And then a 'man' in fact did appear, the dark, Italianate-looking person who had brought their breakfast. He had a message for Mr Reece. Madame Sommita wished to see him urgently.

'I think I had better attend to this,' he said. 'We all meet on the patio at eleven for drinks. I hope you will both join us there.'

So they were left in peace. Alleyn fetched Troy's painting gear and unpacked it. He opened up her old warrior of a paintbox, unstrapped her canvases and set out her sketchbook, and the collection of materials that were like signatures written across any place where Troy worked. She sat in a chair by the window and watched him and felt better.

Alleyn said: 'This room will be de-sterilized when it smells of turpentine and there are splotches of flake white on the ledge of that easel and paint rags on the table.'

'At the moment it can *not* be said to beckon one to work. They might as well have hung Please Don't Touch notices on everything.'

'You won't mind once you get going.'

'You think? P'raps you're right,' she said, cheering up. She looked down at the house party round the pool. 'That's quite something,' she said. 'Very frisky colour and do notice Signor Lattienzo's stomach. Isn't it superb!'

Signor Lattienzo was extended on an orange-coloured chaise longue. He wore a green bathrobe which had slid away from his generous torso upon which a book with a scarlet cover was perched. He glistened.

Prompted, perhaps by that curious telepathy which informs people that they are being stared at, he threw back his head, saw Troy and Alleyn and waved energetically. They responded. He made eloquent Italianate gestures which he wound up by kissing both his hands at once to Troy.

'You've got off, darling,' said Alleyn.

'I like him, I think. But I'm afraid he's rather malicious. I didn't tell you. He thinks that poor beautiful young man's opera is awful. Isn't that sad?'

'Is *that* what's the matter with the boy!' Alleyn exclaimed. 'Does *he* know it's no good?'

'Signor Lattienzo thinks he might.'

'And yet they're going on with all this wildly extravagant business.'

'She insists, I imagine.'

'Ah.'

'Signor Lattienzo says she's as stupid as an owl.'

'Musically?'

'Yes. But I rather gathered generally, as well.'

'The finer points of attitudes towards a hostess don't seem to worry Signor Lattienzo.'

'Well, if we're going to be accurate, I suppose she's not his hostess. She's his ex-pupil.'

'True.'

Troy said: 'That boy's out of his depth altogether. She's made a nonsense of him. She's a monster and I can't wait to get it on canvas. A monster,' Troy repeated with relish.

'He's not down there with the rest of them,' Alleyn pointed out. 'I suppose he's concerned with the arrival of his orchestra.'

'I can't bear to think of it. Imagine! All these musical VIPs converging on him and he knowing, if he *does* know, that it's going to be a fiasco. He's going to conduct. Imagine!'

'Awful. Rubbing his nose in it.'

'We'll have to be there.'

'I'm afraid so, darling.'

Troy had turned away from the window and now faced the door of the room. She was just in time to see it gently closing.

'What's wrong?' Alleyn asked quickly.

Troy whispered: 'The door. Someone's just shut it.'

'Really?'

'Yes. Truly.'

He went to the door and opened it. Troy saw him look to his right.

'Hullo, Bartholomew,' he said. 'Good morning to you. Looking for Troy, by any chance?'

There was a pause and then Rupert's Australian voice, unevenly pitched, not fully audible: 'Oh, good morning. I – yes – matter of fact – message – '

'She's here. Come in.'

He came in, white-faced and hesitant. Troy welcomed him with what she felt might be overdone cordiality and asked if his message was for her.

'Yes,' he said, 'yes, it is. She – I mean Madame Sommita – asked me to say she's very sorry but in case you might be expecting her she can't – she's afraid she won't be able – to sit for you today because – because – '

'Because of rehearsals and everything? Of course. I wasn't expecting it and in fact I'd rather *not* start today.'

'Oh,' he said, 'yes. I see. Good-oh, then. I'll tell her.'

He made as if to go but seemed inclined to stay.

'Do sit down,' said Alleyn, 'unless you're in a hurry, of course. We're hoping someone – you, if you've time – will tell us a little more about tomorrow night.'

He made a movement with both hands almost as if he wanted to cover his ears but checked it and asked if they minded if he smoked. He produced a cigarette case; gold with a jewelled motif.

'Will you?' he said to Troy and when she declined, turned to Alleyn. The open case slipped out of his uncertain grasp. He said;

'Oh. Sorry,' and looked as if he'd been caught shoplifting. Alleyn picked it up. The inside of the lid was inscribed. There in all its flamboyance was the now familiar signature: Isabella Sommita.

Rupert was making a dreadfully clumsy business of shutting the case and lighting his cigarette. Alleyn, as if continuing a conversation, asked Troy where she would like him to put the easel. They improvised an argument about light and the possibility of the bathing pool as a subject. This enabled them both to look out of the window.

'Very tricky subject,' Troy said. 'I don't think I'm up to it!'

'Better maintain a masterly inactivity, you think?' Alleyn cheerfully rejoined. 'You may be right.'

They turned back into the room and there was Rupert Bartholomew, sitting on the edge of the model's throne and crying.

He possessed male physical beauty to such a remarkable degree that there was something unreal about his tears. They trickled over the perfect contours of his face and might have been drops of water on a Greek mask. They were distressing but they were also incongruous.

Alleyn said: 'My dear chap, what's the matter?' and Troy: 'Would you like to talk about it? We're very discreet.'

He talked. Disjointedly at first and with deprecating interruptions – they didn't want to hear all this – he didn't want them to think he was imposing – it could be of no interest to them. He wiped his eyes, blew his nose, drew hard on his cigarette and became articulate.

At first it was simply a statement that *The Alien Corn* was no good, that the realization had come upon him out of the blue and with absolute conviction. 'It was ghastly,' he said. 'I was pouring out drinks and suddenly, without warning, I knew. Nothing could alter it: the thing's punk.'

'Was this performance already under consideration?' Alleyn asked him.

'She had it all planned. It was meant to be a – well – a huge surprise. And the ghastly thing is,' said Rupert, his startlingly blue eyes opened in horror, 'I'd thought it all fantastic. Like one of those schmaltzy young-genius-makes-it films. I'd been in – well – in ecstasy.'

'Did you tell her, there and then?' asked Troy.

'Not then. Mr Reece and Ben Ruby were there. I – well, I was so – you know – shattered. Sort of. I waited,' said Rupert, and blushed, 'until that evening.'

'How did she take it?'

'She didn't take it. I mean she simply wouldn't listen. I mean she simply swept it aside. She said – my God, she said genius always had moments like these, moments of what she called divine despair. She said *she* did. Over her singing. And then, when I sort of tried to stick it out, she – was – well, very angry. And you see – I mean she had cause. All her plans and arrangements. She'd written to Beppo Lattienzo and Sir David Baumgartner and she'd fixed up with Rodolfo and Hilda and Sylvia and the others. And the press. The big names. All that. I did hang out for a bit but – '

He broke off, looked quickly at Alleyn and then at the floor. 'There were other things. It's more complicated than I've made it sound,' he muttered.

'Human relationships can be hellishly awkward, can't they?' Alleyn said.

'You're telling me,' Rupert fervently agreed. Then he burst out: 'I think I must have been mad! Or ill, even. Like running a temperature and now it's gone and – and – I'm cleaned out and left with tomorrow.'

'And you *are* sure?' Troy asked. 'What about the company and the orchestra? Do you know what they think? And Signor Lattienzo?'

'She made me promise not to show it to him. I don't know if *she's* shown it. I think she has. He'll have seen at once that it's awful, of course. And the company: they know all right. Rodolfo Romano very tactfully suggests alterations. I've seen them looking at each other. They stop talking when I turn up. Do you know what they call it? They think I haven't heard but I've heard all right. They call it *Corn*. Very funny. Oh,' Rupert cried out, 'she shouldn't have done it! It hasn't been a fair go: I hadn't got a hope. Not a hope in hell. My God, she's making me *conduct*. There I'll stand, before those VIPs, waving my arms like a bloody puppet and they won't know which way to look for embarrassment.'

There was a long silence, broken at last by Troy.

'Well,' she said vigorously, 'refuse. Never mind about the celebrities and the fuss and the phoney publicity. It'll be very unpleasant and it'll take a lot of guts but at least it'll be honest. To the devil with the lot of them. Refuse.'

He got to his feet. He had been bathing and his short yellow robe had fallen open. He's apricot-coloured, Troy noted, not blackish tan and coarsened by exposure like most sun addicts. He's really too much of a treat. No wonder she grabbed him. He's a collector's piece, poor chap.

'I don't think,' Rupert said, 'I'm any more chicken than the next guy. It's not that. It's her – Isabella. You saw last night what she can be like. And coming on top of this letter business – look, she'd either break down and make herself ill or – or go berserk and murder somebody. Me, for preference.'

'Oh, come *on*!' said Troy.

'No,' he said, 'it's not nonsense. Really. She's a Sicilian.'

'Not *all* Sicilians are tigers,' Alleyn remarked.

'Her kind are.'

Troy said, 'I'm going to leave you to Rory. I think this calls for male-chauvinist gossip.'

When she had gone, Rupert began apologizing again. What, he asked, would Mrs Alleyn think of him?

'Don't start worrying about that,' Alleyn said. 'She's sorry, she's not shocked and she's certainly not bored. And I think she may be right. However unpleasant it may be, I think perhaps you should refuse. But I'm afraid it's got to be your decision and nobody else's.'

'Yes, but you see you don't know the worst of it. I couldn't bring it out with Mrs Alleyn here. I – Isabella – we – '

'Good Lord, my dear chap – ' Alleyn began and then pulled himself up. 'You're lovers, aren't you?' he said.

'If you can call it that,' he muttered.

'And you think if you take this stand against her you'll lose her? That it?'

'Not exactly – I mean, yes, of course, I suppose she'd kick me out.'

'Would that be such a very bad thing?'

'It'd be a bloody good thing,' he burst out.

'Well, then – '

'I can't expect you to understand. I don't understand myself. At first it was marvellous: magical. I felt equal to anything. Way up. Out of this world. To hear her sing, to stand at the back of the theatre and see two thousand people go mad about her and to know that for *me* it didn't end with the curtain calls and flowers and ovations but that for *me* the best was still to come. Talk about the crest of the wave – gosh, it was super.'

'I can imagine.'

'And then, after that – you know – that moment of truth about the opera, the whole picture changed. You could say that the same thing happened about her. I saw all at once what she really is like and that she only approved of that bloody fiasco because she saw herself making a success in it and that she ought never, *never* to have given me the encouragement she did. And I knew she had no real musical judgement and that I was lost.'

'All the more reason – ' Alleyn began and was shouted down.

'You can't tell me anything I don't know. But I was *in* it. Up to my eyes. Presents – like this thing, this cigarette case. Clothes, even. A fantastic salary. At first I was so far gone in – I suppose you could call it – rapture, that it didn't seem degrading. And now, in spite of seeing it all as it really is, I can't get out. I can't.'

Alleyn waited. Rupert got to his feet. He squared his shoulders, pocketed his awful cigarette case and actually produced a laugh of sorts.

'Silly, isn't it?' he said, with an unhappy attempt at lightness. 'Sorry to have bored you.'

Alleyn said: 'Are you familiar with Shakespeare's sonnets?'

'No. Why?'

'There's a celebrated one that starts off by saying the expense of spirit in a waste of shame is lust in action. I suppose it's the most devastating statement you can find of the sense of degradation that accompanies passion without love. *La Belle Dame Sans Merci* is schmaltz alongside it. That's your trouble, isn't it? The gilt's gone off the gingerbread but the gingerbread is still compulsive eating. And that's why you can't make the break.'

Rupert twisted his hands together and bit his knuckles.

'You could put it like that,' he said.

The silence that followed was interrupted by an outbreak of voices on the patio down below: exclamations, sounds of arrival and unmistakably the musical hoots that were the Sommita's form of greeting.

'Those are the players,' said Rupert. 'I must go down. We have to rehearse.'

II

By midday Troy's jet-lag had begun to fade and with it the feeling of unreality in her surroundings. A familiar restlessness replaced it and this, as always, condensed into an itch to work. She and Alleyn walked round the island and found that, apart from the landing ground for the helicopter and the lawnlike frontage with its sentinel trees, it was practically covered by house. The clever architect had allowed small areas of original bush to occur where they most could please. On the frontal approach from the lake to the Lodge, this as well as the house itself served to conceal a pole from which power lines ran across the lake to a spit of land with a dado of trees that reached out from the far side of the island.

'For the moment,' said Troy, 'don't let's think about what it all cost.'

They arrived at the bathing pool at eleven o'clock; drinks were being served. Two or three guests had arrived at the same time as the quartet of players who turned out to be members of a South Island Regional Orchestra. The musicians, three men and a lady, sticking tight to each other and clearly overawed, were painstakingly introduced by Rupert. The Sommita, in white sharkskin with a tactful tunic, conversed with them very much *de haut en bas* and then engulfed the Alleyns, particularly Troy whose arm and hand she secured, propelling her to a canopied double seat and retaining her hold after they had occupied it. Troy found all this intensely embarrassing but at least it gave her a good opportunity to notice the markedly asymmetric structure of the face, the distance between the corner of the heavy mouth and that of the burning eye being greater on the left side. And there was a faint darkness, the slightest change of colour on the upper lip. You couldn't have a better face for Carmen, Troy thought.

The Sommita talked of the horrible letter and the touched-up photograph and what they had done to her and how shattering it was that the activities of the infamous photographer – for of course he was at the bottom of it – should have extended to New Zealand and even to the Island when she had felt safe at last from persecution.

'It *is* only the paper, though,' Troy pointed out. 'It's not as though the man himself was here. Don't you think it's quite likely that now the tour of Australia is over he may very well have gone back to his country of origin, wherever that may be? Mightn't the letter have just been his final effort? You had gone and he couldn't take any more photographs so he cooked up the letter?'

The Sommita stared at her for a long time and in a most uncomfortable manner, gave her hand a meaningful squeeze and released it. Troy did not know what to make of this.

'But,' the Sommita was saying, 'we must speak of your art, must we not? And of the portrait. We begin the day after tomorrow, yes? And I wear my crimson décolleté which you have not yet seen. It is by Saint-Laurent and is dramatic. And for the pose – this.'

She sprang to her feet, curved her sumptuous right arm above her head, rested her left palm upon her thigh, threw back her head and ogled Troy frowningly in the baleful, sexy manner of Spanish dancers. The posture provided generous exposure to her frontage and gave the lie to any suggestions of plastic surgery.

'I think,' Troy said, 'the pose might be a bit exacting to maintain. And if it's possible I'd like to make some drawings as a sort of limbering-up. Not posed drawings. Only slight notes. If I could just be inconspicuously on the premises and make scribbles with a stick of charcoal.'

'Yes? Ah! Good. This afternoon there will be rehearsal. It will be only a preparation for the dress rehearsal tonight. You may attend it. You must be very inconspicious, you understand.'

'That will be ideal,' said Troy. 'Nothing could suit me better.'

'My poor Rupert,' the Sommita suddenly proclaimed, again fixing Troy with that disquieting regard, 'is nervous. He has the sensitivity of the true artist, the creative temperament. He is strung like a violin.'

She suspects something, Troy thought. She's pumping. Damn.

She said: 'I can well imagine.'

'I'm sure you can,' said the Sommita with what seemed to be all too meaningful an emphasis.

'Darling Rupert,' she called to him: 'if your friends are ready perhaps you should show them – ?'

The players gulped down the rest of their drinks and professed themselves ready.

'Come!' invited the Sommita, suddenly all sparkle and gaiety. 'I show you now our music room. Who knows? There may be inspiration for you, as for us. We bring also our great diviner who is going to rescue me from my persecutors.'

She towed Troy up to Alleyn and unfolded this proposition. Her manner suggested the pleasurable likelihood of his offering to seduce her at the first opportunity. 'So you come to the salon too,' she said, 'to hear music?' And in her velvet tones the word 'music' was fraught with much the same meaning as 'china' in *The Country Wife*.

Troy hurried away to get her sketching block, charcoal and conté pencil. Alleyn waited for her and together they went to the 'music room'.

It was entered by double doors from the rear of the main hall. It was, as Mr Ruby had once indicated, more like a concert chamber than a room. It were tedious to insist upon the grandiloquences of Waihoe Lodge: enough to say that the stage occupied one end of this enormous room, was approached from the auditorium by three wide steps up to a projecting apron and thence to the main acting area. Beautifully proportioned pillars were ranged across the back flanking curtained doorways. The musicians were in a little huddle by a grand piano on the floor of the auditorium and in the angle of the apron. They were tuning their instruments and Rupert, looking ill, was with them. The singers came in and sat together in the auditorium.

There was a change now in the Sommita; an air of being in her own professional climate and with no nonsense about it. She was deep in conversation with Romano when the Alleyns came in. She saw them and pointed to chairs halfway down the auditorium. Then she folded her arms and stood facing the stage. Every now and then she shouted angry instructions. As if on some stage director's instruction, a shaft of sunlight from an open window found her. The effect was startling. Troy settled herself to make a drawing.

Now the little orchestra began to play: tentatively at first with stoppages when they consulted with Rupert. Then with one and another of the soloists, repeating passages, making adjustments. Finally the Sommita said, 'We take the aria, darling,' and swept up to stage centre.

Rupert's back was turned to the audience and facing the musicians. He gave them the beat conservatively. They played and were stopped by the Sommita. 'More authority,' she said. 'We should come in like a lion. Again.'

Rupert waited for a moment. Troy saw that his left hand was clenched so hard that the knuckles shone white. He flung back his head, raised his right hand and gave a strong beat. The short introduction was repeated with much more conviction, it reached a climax of sorts and then the whole world was filled with one long sound: '*Ah!*' sang the Sommita. '*A-a-a-h!*' and then: '*What joy is here, what peace, what plentitude!*'

At first it was impossible to question the glory, so astonishing was the sound, so absolute the command. Alleyn thought: Perhaps it hardly matters what she sings. Perhaps she could sing 'A bee-eye-ee-eye-ee sat on a wall-eye-all-eye-all' and distil magic from it. But before the aria had come to its end he thought that even if he hadn't been warned he would have known that musically it was no great shakes. He thought he could detect clichés and banalities. And the words! He supposed in opera they didn't matter all that much but the thought occurred that she might more appropriately have sung: 'What joy is here, what peace, what platitude.'

Troy was sitting two seats in front of Alleyn, holding her breath and drawing in charcoal. He could see the lines that ran out like whiplashes under her hand, the thrown-back head and the wide mouth. Not a bit, he thought, remembering their joke, as if the Sommita was yawning: the drawing itself sang. Troy ripped the sketch off her pad and began again. Now her subject talked to the orchestra who listened with a kind of avid respect, and Troy drew them in the graphic shorthand that was all her own.

Alleyn thought that if Rupert was correct in believing the players had rumbled the inadequacies of the music, the Sommita had ravished them into acceptance, and he wondered if, after all, she could work this magic throughout the performance and save poor Rupert's face for him.

A hand was laid on Alleyn's shoulder. He turned his head and found Mr Reece's impassive countenance close to his own. 'Can you come out?' he said very quietly. 'Something has happened.'

As they went out the Sommita and Rodolfo Romano had begun to sing their duet.

The servant who had brought the Alleyns their breakfast was in the study looking uneasy and deprecating.

'This is Marco,' said Mr Reece. 'He has reported an incident that I think you should know about. Tell Chief Superintendent Alleyn exactly what you told me.'

Marco shied a little on hearing Alleyn's rank, but he told his story quite coherently and seemed to gather assurance as he did so. He had the Italian habit of gesture but only a slight accent.

He said that he had been sent out to the helicopter hangar to fetch a case of wine that had been brought in the previous day. He went in by a side door and as he opened it heard a scuffle inside the hangar. The door dragged a little on the floor. There was, unmistakably, the sound of someone running. 'I think I said something, sir, "Hullo" or something, as I pushed the door open. I was just in time to catch sight of a man in bathing costume, running out at the open end of the hangar. There's not much room when the chopper's there. I had to run back and round the tail and by the time I got out he was gone.'

Alleyn said: 'The hangar, of course, opens on to the cleared space for take-off.'

'Yes, sir. And it's surrounded by a kind of shrubbery. The proper approach follows round the house to the front. I ran along it about sixty feet but there wasn't a sign of him so I returned and had a look at the bush as they call it. It was very overgrown and I saw at once he couldn't have got through it without making a noise. But there wasn't a sound. I peered about in case he was lying low and then I remembered that on the far side of the clearing there's another path through the bush going down to the lakeside. So I took this path. With the same result: nothing. Well, sir,' Marco amended, and an air of complacency if not of smugness crept over his face, 'I say "nothing". But that's not quite right. There was something. Lying by the path. There was this.'

With an admirable sense of timing he thrust forward his open palm. On it lay a small round metal or plastic cap.

'It's what they use to protect the lens, sir. It's off a camera.'

III

'I don't think,' Alleyn said, 'we should jump to alarming conclusions about this but certainly it should be followed up. I imagine,' he said drily, 'that anything to do with photography is a tricky subject at the Lodge.'

'With some cause,' said Mr Reece.

'Indeed. Now then, Marco. You've given us a very clear account of what happened and you'll think I'm being unduly fussy if we go over it all again.'

Marco spread his hands as if offering him the earth.

'First of all, then: this man. Are you sure it wasn't one of the guests or one of the staff?'

'No, no, no, no, no,' said Marco rapidly, shaking his finger sideways as if a wasp had stung it. 'Not possible. No!'

'Not, for instance, the launchman?'

'No, sir. No! Not anyone of the household. I am certain. I would swear it.'

'Dark or fair?'

'Fair. Bareheaded. Fair. Certainly a blond.'

'And bare to the waist?'

'Of course. Certainly.'

'Not even a camera slung over his shoulder?'

Marco closed his eyes, bunched his fingers and laid the tips to his forehead. He remained like that for some seconds.

'Well? What about it?' Mr Reece asked a trifle impatiently.

Marco opened his eyes and unbunched his fingers. 'It could have been in his hands,' he said.

'This path,' Alleyn said. 'The regular approach from the front of the house round to the hangar. As I recollect, it passes by the windows of the concert chamber?'

'Certainly,' Mr Reece said and nodded very slightly at Alleyn. 'And this afternoon they were not curtained.'

'And open?'

'And open.'

'Marco,' Alleyn said, 'did you at any point hear anything going on in the concert chamber?'

'But yes!' Marco cried, staring at him. 'Madame, sir. It was Madame. She sang. With the voice of an angel.'

'Ah.'

'She was singing still, sir, when I returned to the clearing.'

'After you found this cap, did you go on to the lakeside?'

'Not quite to the lakeside, sir, but far enough out of the bush to see that he was not there. And then I thought I should not continue but that I should report at once to Signor Reece. And that is what I did.'

'Very properly.'

'Thank you, sir.'

'And I,' said Mr Reece, 'have sent the house staff to search the grounds, and most of the guests.'

'If I remember correctly,' Alleyn said, 'at the point where Marco emerged from the bush it is only a comparatively short distance across from the Island to that narrow tree-clad spit that reaches out from the mainland towards the Island and is linked to it by your power lines?'

'You suggest he might have swum it?' Mr Reece asked.

'No, sir,' Marco intervened. 'Not possible. I would have seen him.' He stopped and then asked with a change of voice. 'Or would I?'

'If he's on the Island he will be found,' said Mr Reece coldly. And then to Alleyn: 'You were right to say we should not make too much of this incident. It will probably turn out to be some young hoodlum or another with a camera. But it is a nuisance. Bella has been very much upset by this Strix and his activities. If she hears of it she might well begin to imagine all sorts of things. I suggest we say nothing of it to the guests and performers. You hear that, Marco?'

Marco was all acquiescence.

Alleyn thought that if what was no doubt a completely unco-ordinated search was thundering about the premises the chances of keeping the affair secret were extremely slender. But, he reminded himself, for the present the rehearsal should be engaging everybody's attention.

When he had gone, Mr Reece, with a nearer approach to cosiness than Alleyn would have thought within his command, said: 'What do you make of all that? Simply a loutish trespasser or – something else?'

'Impossible to say. Is it pretty widely known in New Zealand that Madame Sommita is your guest?'

'Oh yes. One tries to circumvent the press but one never totally succeeds. It has come out. There have been articles about the Lodge itself and there are pressmen who try to bribe the launchman to bring them over. He is paid a grotesquely high wage and has the sense to refuse. I must say,' Mr Reece confided, 'it would be very much in character for one of these persons to skulk about the place, having, by whatever means, swimming perhaps, got himself on the Island. The hangar would be a likely spot, one might think, for him to hide.'

'He would hear the rehearsal from there.'

'Precisely. And await his chance to come out and take a photograph through an open window. It's possible. As long,' Mr Reece said, and actually struck his right fist into his left palm, 'as long as it isn't that filthy Strix at it again. Anything rather than that.'

'Will you tell me something about your staff? You've asked me to do my constabulary stuff and this would be a routine question.'

'Ned Hanley is better qualified than I to answer it. He came over here from Australia and saw to it. An over-ambitious hotel had gone into liquidation. He engaged eight of the staff and a housekeeper for the time we shall be using the Lodge. Marco was not one of these but we had excellent references, I understand. Ned would tell you.'

'An Italian, of course?'

'Oh yes. But a naturalized Australian. He made a great thing, just now, of his story but I would think it was substantially correct. I'm hoping the guests and performers will not, if they do get hold of the story, start jumping to hysterical conclusions. Perhaps we should let it be known quite casually that a boy had swum across and has been sent packing. What do you think?'

Before Alleyn could answer, the door opened and Signor Beppo Lattienzo entered. His immaculate white shorts and silken *matelot* were in disarray and he sweated copiously.

'My dears!' he said. 'Drama! The hunt is up. The Hound of Heaven itself – or should I say Himself? – could not be more diligent.'

He dropped into a chair and fanned himself with an open palm. '"Over hill, over dale, thorough bush, thorough brier," as the industrious fairy remarks and so do I. What fun to be known as "The Industrious Fairy", ' panted Signor Lattienzo coyly.

'Any luck?' Alleyn asked.

'Not a morsel. The faithful Maria, my dear Monty, is indomitable. Into the underbrush with the best of us. She has left her hairnet as a votive offering on a thorny entanglement known, I am informed, as a Bush Lawyer.'

Signor Lattienzo smiled blandly at Mr Reece and tipped Alleyn a lewdish wink. 'This,' he remarked, 'will not please our diva, no? And if we are to speak of hounds and of persistence, how about the intrepid Strix? What zeal! What devotion! Though she flee to the remotest antipodes, though she, as it were, to go to earth (in, one must add, the greatest possible comfort) upon an enchanted island, there shall he nose her out. One can only applaud. Admit it, my dear Monty.'

Mr Reece said: 'Beppo, there is no reason to suppose that the man Strix has had any part in this incident. The idea is ridiculous and I am most anxious that Bella should not entertain it. It is a trivial matter involving some local lout and must not be blown up into a ridiculous drama. You know very well, none better, how she can overreact and after last night's shock – I really must ask you to use the greatest discretion.'

Signor Lattienzo wiped the sweat away from the area round his left eye. He breathed upon his glass, polished it and with its aid contemplated his host. 'But, of course, my dear Monty,' he said quietly, 'I understand. Perfectly. I dismiss the photographer. Poof! He is gone. And now – '

The door burst open and Ben Ruby strode in. He also showed signs of wear and tear.

'Here! Monty!' he shouted. 'What the hell's the idea? These servants of yours are all saying bloody Strix is back and you ought to call in the police. What about it?'

IV

Mr Reece, white with annoyance, summoned his entire staff, including the driver and the launchman, into the study. Alleyn, who was asked to remain, admired the manner in which the scene was handled and the absolute authority which Mr Reece seemed to command. He repeated the explanation that had been agreed upon. The theory of the intrusive lout was laid before them and the idea of Strix's recrudescence soundly rubbished. 'You will forget this idiotic notion, if you please,' said Mr Reece and his voice was frigid. He looked pointedly at Maria. 'You understand,' he said, 'you are not to speak of it to Madame.' He added something in Italian – not one of Alleyn's strongest languages but he thought it was a threat of the instant sack if Maria disobeyed orders.

Maria, who had shut her mouth like a trap, glared back at Mr Reece and muttered incomprehensibly. The household was then dismissed.

'I don't like your chances,' said Ben Ruby. 'They'll talk.'

'They will behave themselves. With the possible exception of the woman.'

'She certainly didn't sound cooperative.'

'Jealous.'

'Ah!' said Signor Lattienzo. 'The classic situation: Mistress and Abigail. No doubt Bella confides extensively.'

'No doubt.'

'Well, she can't do so for the moment. The *ripetizione* is still in full swing.'

Ben Ruby opened the door. From beyond the back of the hall and the wall of the concert chamber but seeming to come from nowhere in particular there was singing: disembodied as if heard through the wrong end of some auditory telescope. Above three unremarkable voices there soared an incomparable fourth.

'Yes,' said Signor Lattienzo. 'It is the *ripetizione* and they are only at the quartet: a third of the way through. They will break for luncheon at one-thirty and it is now twenty minutes past noon. For the time being we are safe.'

'I wouldn't bet on that one, either,' said Ben Ruby. 'She likes to have Maria on tap at rehearsals.'

'If you don't mind,' Alleyn said, 'I think I'll just take a look at the terrain.'

The three men stared at him and for a moment said nothing. And then Mr Reece stood up. 'You surely cannot for a moment believe – ' he said.

'Oh no, no. But it strikes me that one might find something that would confirm the theory of the naughty boy.'

'Ah.'

'What, for instance?' asked Ben Ruby.

'This or that,' Alleyn said airily. 'You never know. The unexpected has a way of turning up. Sometimes. Like you, I wouldn't bet on it.'

And before any of them had thought of anything else to say he let himself out and gently closed the door.

He went out of the house by the main entrance, turned left and walked along the gravelled front until he came to a path that skirted the western façade. He followed it and as he did so the sound of music and of singing, broken by discussion and the repetition of short passages, grew louder. Presently he came to the windows of the concert chamber and saw that one of them, the first, was still open. It was at the end farthest removed from the stage, which was screened from it by a curtain that operated on a hinged bracket.

He drew nearer. There, quite close, was the spot in the auditorium where the Sommita had stood with her arms folded, directing the singers.

And there, still in her same chair, still crouched over her sketching block with her short hair tousled and her shoulders hunched, was his wife. She was still hard at work. Her subject was out of sight haranguing the orchestra but her image leapt up under Troy's grubby hand. She was using a conté pencil and the lines she made, sometimes broadly emphatic, sometimes floating into extreme delicacy, made one think of the bowing of an accomplished fiddler.

She put the drawing on the floor, pushed it away with her foot, and stared at it, sucking her knuckles and scowling. Then she looked up and saw her husband. He pulled a face at her, laid a finger across his lips and ducked out of sight.

He had been careful not to tread on the narrow strip of earth that separated the path from the wall and now, squatting, was able to examine it. It had been recently trampled by a number of persons. To hell with the search party, thought Alleyn.

He moved further along the path, passing a garden seat and keeping as far away as was possible from the windows. The thicket of fern and underbrush on his right was broken here and there by forays, he supposed, of the hunt, successfully ruining any signs there might have been of an intruder taking cover. Presently the path branched away from the house into the bush to emerge, finally, at the hangar.

Inside the hangar there was ample evidence of Marco's proceedings. The earthy short cut he had taken had evidently been damp and Alleyn could trace his progress on the asphalt floor exactly as he had described it.

Alleyn crossed the landing ground, scorching under the noonday sun. Sounds from the concert chamber had faded. There was no birdsong. He found the path through the bush to the lakeside and followed it: dark green closed about him and the now familiar conservatory smell of wet earth and moss.

It was only a short distance to the lake and soon the bush began to thin out, admitting shafts of sunlight. It must have been about here that Marco said he had spotted the protective cap from the camera. Alleyn came out into the open and there, as he remembered them from his morning walk, were the shore and the lake and overhead power lines reaching away to the far shore.

Alleyn stood for a time out there by the lakeside. The sun that beat down on his head spread a kind of blankness over the landscape, draining it of colour. He absent-mindedly reached into his pocket for his pipe and touched a small hard object. It was the lens cap, wrapped in his handkerchief. He took it out and uncovered it, being careful not to touch the surface: a futile precaution, he thought, after Marco's handling of the thing.

It was from a well-known make of Japanese camera that produced self-developing instant results. The trade name 'Koto' was stamped on the top.

He folded it up and returned it to his pocket. In a general way he did not go much for 'inspiration' in detective work, but if ever he had been visited by such a bonus, it was at that moment down by the lake.

CHAPTER 4

Performance

Early in the morning of the following day there was a change in the weather. A wind came up from the north-west, not a strong wind and not steady but rather it was a matter of occasional brushes of cooler air on the face and a vague stirring among the trees around the house. The sky was invaded by oncoming masses of cloud, turrets and castles that mounted and changed and multiplied. The lake was no longer glassy but wrinkled. Wavelets slapped gently at the shore.

At intervals throughout the morning new guests would arrive: some by chartered plane to the nearest airport and thence by helicopter to the Island, others by train and car, and a contingent of indigenous musical intelligentsia by bus. The launch would be very active.

A piano-tuner arrived and could be heard dabbing away at single notes and, to the unmusical ear, effecting no change in their pitch.

Sir David Baumgartner, the distinguished musicologist and critic, was to stay overnight at the Lodge, together with a Dr Carmichael, a celebrated consultant who was also President of the New Zealand Philharmonic Society. The remainder faced many dark hours in launch, bus and cars and in mid-morning would be returned wan and bemused to their homes in Canterbury.

The general idea, as far as the Sommita had concerned herself with their reaction to these formidable exertions, was that the guests would be so enraptured by their entertainment as to be perfectly oblivious of all physical discomfort. In the meantime she issued a command that the entire house party was to assemble outside the house for Mr Ben Ruby to take a mass photograph. They did so in chilly discomfort under a lowering sky.

'Eyes and teeth to the camera, everybody,' begged Mr Ruby.

The Sommita did not reappear at luncheon and was said to be resting. It was, on the whole, a quiet meal. Even Signor Lattienzo did little to enliven it. Rupert Bartholomew, looking anguished, ate nothing, muttered something to the effect that he was needed in the concert chamber and excused himself. Mr Reece made ponderous small talk with Troy, while Alleyn, finding himself next to Miss Hilda Dancy, did his best. He asked her if she found opening nights trying and she replied in vibrant contralto: 'When they are important,' clearly indicating that this one was not. After Rupert had left them she said, 'It's a crying shame.'

'A crying shame?' he ventured. 'How?'

'You'll see,' she prophesied. 'Cannibal!' she added, and apart from giving him a dark look which he was unable to interpret, though he thought he could make a fairly good guess, she was disinclined for any further conversation.

After luncheon the Alleyns went up to the studio where he related the story of the interloper and the camera cap. When he had finished and Troy had taken time to think it over, she said: 'Rory, do you think he's still on the Island? The photographer?'

'The photographer? Yes,' he said and something in his voice made her stare at him. 'I think the photographer's here. I'll tell you why.' And he did.

For the rest of the afternoon Troy brooded over her drawings and made some more. Sounds of arrival were heard from time to time. Beyond the great window the prospect steadily darkened and the forest on the far shore moved as if brushed by an invisible hand. 'The arrivals by launch will have a rough trip,' said Alleyn. The helicopter flapped down to its landing place and discharged an imposing personage in a black overcoat and hat. 'Sir David Baumgartner, no less,' said Alleyn, and then, 'Troy, you saw me outside that window, didn't you? Do you think you would have been bound to notice a photographer if one had operated through that same window?'

'Oh no,' she said, 'not bound to at all. I was working.'

'So you were,' he agreed. 'I think I'll take a look.'

And he went downstairs to the concert chamber. When he arrived, there was no one to be seen but Hanley, who was evidently stage manager for the production, superintending three imported electricians in the management of the lights and seeming to be in a state of controlled dementia. Whatever the climate outside might be, inside it was electric.

Alleyn heard Hanley demand at large: 'Well, where the hell is he? He ought to be *here*. I've never seen anything like it.'

The curtain that separated the apron from the stage proper was open and the acting areas were prepared for the performance. A realistic set had not been attempted. A blue cloth had been hung behind the pillars and the central entrance was flanked by two stylized sheaves of corn. Three sumptuously draped seats completed the decor.

Alleyn sat where Troy had sat to make her drawings. The window in question was still uncurtained and open. Such had been her concentration that he thought she would not have noticed him if he had not leant over the sill.

Hanley said to the electricians, 'It's easy, really. You've marked the areas where Madame Sommita stands and you've got them covered. Fade up when she's there and fade down when she moves away. Otherwise there are no lights cues: they stay as set throughout. Cover the windows and we'll run it through once more.'

He turned to Alleyn. 'Have *you* seen Rupert?' he asked. 'He was to be here half an hour ago to give the music cues. They went all to blazes at the dress rehearsal. Honestly, it's too much.'

'I'll see if I can find him,' he volunteered.

'Super of you,' gushed Hanley with a desperate return to his secretarial manner. 'Thank you *so* much.'

Alleyn thought that a hunt for the unhappy Rupert might well turn out to be as fruitless as the one for a problematical photographer but he struck it lucky, if that was the appropriate word, at the first cast, which was Mr Reece's spectacular study.

He wondered if a visitor was expected to knock or even to make appointment before venturing upon this sanctum but decided to ct an entrance in the normal manner. He opened the door and ed in.

The actual entrance was shut off from the room by a large leather screen, the work of a decorator much in vogue. Alleyn came in to the sound of Mr Reece's voice.

' – remind you of the favours you have taken at her hands. And this is how you would choose to repay them. By making her a laughing stock. You allow us to engage celebrated artistes, to issue invitations, to bring people of the utmost distinction halfway across the world to hear this thing and now propose to tell them that after all there will be no performance and they can turn round and go back again.'

'I know. Do you think I haven't thought of all this! Do you think – Please, *please* believe me – Bella, I beg you – '

'*Stop!*'

Alleyn, behind the screen and about to beat a retreat, fetched up short as if the command had been directed at him. It was the Sommita.

'The performance,' she announced, 'will take place. The violin is competent. He will lead. And you, you who have determined to break my heart, will sulk in your room. And when it is over you will come to me and weep your repentance. And it will be too late. Too late. You will have murdered my love for you. Ingrate!' shouted the Sommita. 'Poltroon! So!'

Alleyn heard her masterful tread. As he had no time to get away, he stepped boldly out of cover and encountered her face to face.

Her own face might have been a mask for one of the Furies. She made a complicated gesture and for a moment he thought that actually she might haul off and hit him, blameless as he was, but she ended up by grasping him by his coat collar, giving him a ferocious précis of their predicament and ordering him to bring Rupert to his senses. When he hesitated she shook him like a cocktail, burst into tears and departed.

Mr Reece, standing with authority on his own hearthrug, had not attempted to stem the tide of his dear one's wrath nor was it possible to guess at his reaction to it. Rupert sat with his head in his hands, raising it momentarily to present a stricken face.

'I'm so sorry,' Alleyn said, 'I've blundered in with what is clearly an inappropriate message.'

'Don't go,' said Mr Reece. 'A message? For me?'

'For Bartholomew. From your secretary.'

'Yes? He had better hear it.'

Alleyn delivered it. Rupert was wanted to set the lights.

Mr Reece asked coldly, 'Will you do this? Or is it going too far to expect it?'

Rupert got to his feet. 'Well,' he asked Alleyn, 'what do you think now? Do you say I should refuse?'

Allen said: 'I'm not sure. It's a case of divided loyalties, isn't it?'

'I would have thought,' said Mr Reece, 'that any question of loyalty was entirely on one side. To whom is he loyal if he betrays his patrons?'

'Oh,' Alleyn said. 'To his art.'

'According to him, he has no "art".'

'I'm not sure,' Alleyn said slowly, 'whether, in making his decision, it really matters. It's a question of aesthetic integrity.'

Rupert was on his feet and walking towards the door.

'Where are you going?' Mr Reece said sharply.

'To set the lights. I've decided,' said Rupert loudly. 'I can't stick this out any longer. I'm sorry I've given so much trouble. I'll see it through.'

II

When Alleyn went up to their room in search of Troy he found her fast asleep on their enormous bed. At a loose end, and worried about Rupert Bartholomew's sudden capitulation, Alleyn returned downstairs. He could hear voices in the drawing room and concert chamber. Outside the house, a stronger wind had got up.

Midway down the hall, opposite the dining room, there was a door which Mr Reece had indicated as opening into the library. Alleyn thought he would find himself something to read and went in.

It might have been created by a meticulous scene-painter for an Edwardian drama. Uniform editions rose in irremovable tiers from floor to ceiling, the result, Alleyn supposed, of some mass-ordering process; classics, biographies and travel. There was a section devoted to contemporary novels each a virgin in its unmolested jacket. There was an assembly of 'quality' productions that would have broken the backs of elephantine coffee tables and there were orderly stacks of the most popular weeklies.

He wandered along the ranks at a loss for a good read and high up in an ill-lit corner came upon a book that actually bore signs of usage. It was unjacketed and the spine was rubbed. He drew it out and opened it at the title page.

Il Mistero di Bianca Rossi by Pietro Lamparelli. Alleyn didn't read Italian with the complete fluency that alone gives easy pleasure but the title was an intriguing surprise. He allowed the verso to flip over and there on the flyleaf in sharp irregular characters was the owner's name M. V. Rossi.

He settled down to read it.

An hour later he went upstairs and found Troy awake and refreshed.

The opera, a one-acter which lasted only an hour, was to begin at eight o'clock. It would be prefaced by light snacks with drinks and followed by a grand dinner party.

'Do you suppose,' Troy wondered, as they dressed, 'that a reconciliation has taken place?'

'I've no idea. She may go for a magnificent acceptance of his surrender or she may not be able to do herself out of the passionate rapture bit. My bet would be that she's too professional to allow herself to be upset before a performance.'

'I wish he hadn't given in.'

'He's made the harder choice, darling.'

'I suppose so. But if she does take him back – it's not a pretty thought.'

'I don't think he'll go. I think he'll pack his bags and go back to teaching the piano and playing with his small Sydney group and doing a little typing on the side.'

'Signor Lattienzo did say there were two or three signs of promise in the opera.'

'Did he? If he's right, the more shame on that termagant for what she's done to the boy.'

They were silent for a little while after this and then Troy said: 'Is there a window open? It's turned chilly, hasn't it?'

'I'll look.'

The curtains had been closed for the night. Alleyn parted them, and discovered an open window. It was still light outside. The wind had got up strongly now, there was a great pother of hurrying clouds in the sky and a wide vague sound abroad in the evening.

'It's brewing up out there,' Alleyn said. 'The lake's quite rough.' He shut the window.

'Not much fun for the guests going home,' said Troy, and then: 'I'll be glad, won't you, when this party's over?'

'Devoutly glad.'

'Watching that wretched boy's ordeal, it'll be like sitting out an *auto-da-fé*,' she said.

'Would you like to have a migraine? I'd make it sound convincing.'

'No. He'd guess. So, oh Lord, would she.'

'I'm afraid you're right. Should we go down now, darling, to our champagne and snacks?'

'I expect so. Rory, your peculiar mission seems to have got mislaid, doesn't it? I'd almost forgotten about it. Do you by any chance suppose Mr Reece to be a "Godfather" with an infamous Sicilian "Family" background?'

'He's a cold enough fish to be anything, but – ' Alleyn hesitated for a moment. 'No,' he said. 'So far there's been nothing to report. I shall continue to accept his hospitality and will no doubt return empty-handed to my blasted boss. I've little stomach for the job, and that's a fact. If it wasn't for you, my particular dish, and your work in hand, I'd have even less. Come on.'

Notwithstanding the absence of Rupert and all the performers, the drawing room was crowded. About thirty guests had arrived by devious means and were being introduced to each other by Mr Reece and his secretary. There were top people from the Arts Council, various conductors and a selection of indigenous critics, notably a prestigious authority from the *New Zealand Listener*. Conspicuous among the distinguished guests from abroad was a large rubicund man with drooping eyelids and a dictatorial nose: Sir David Baumgartner, the celebrated critic and musicologist. He was in close conversation with Signor Lattienzo who, seeing the Alleyns, gave them one of his exuberant bows, obviously told Sir David who they were and propelled him towards them.

Sir David told Troy that it really was a great honour and a delightful surprise to meet her and asked if it could be true that she was
going to paint the Great Lady. He chaffed Alleyn along predictable
lines, saying that they would all have to keep their noses clean,
wouldn't they? He spoke gravely of the discomforts of his journey. It
had come upon him, to put it bluntly, at a most inconvenient time
and if it had been anybody else – here he gave them a roguish
glance – he wouldn't have dreamt of – he need say no more. The
implication clearly was that *The Alien Corn* had better be good.

Lobster sandwiches, pâté, and miniature concoctions of the kind
known to Mr Justice Shallow as 'pretty little tiny kickshaws' were
handed round and champagne galore. Sir David sipped, raised his
eyebrows and was quickly ready for a refill. So were all the new
arrivals. Conversation grew noisy.

'Softening-up process,' Alleyn muttered.

And indeed by ten minutes to eight all signs of travel fatigue had
evaporated and when Marco, who had been much in evidence,
tinkled up and down on a little xylophone, he was obliged to do so
for some time like a ship's steward walking down corridors with a
summons to dinner.

Ben Ruby and Mr Reece began a tactful herding towards the concert chamber.

The doors were open. The audience assembled itself.

The chairs in the front rows were ticketed with the names of the
house guests and some of the new arrivals who evidently qualified
as VIPs. Troy and Alleyn were placed on the left of Mr Reece's empty
chair, Sir David and Signor Lattienzo on its right with Ben Ruby
beyond them. The rest of the élite comprised the conductor of the
New Zealand Philharmonic Orchestra and his wife, three professors
of music from as many universities, an Australian newspaper mag-
nate and four representatives of the press – which press exactly had
not been defined. The remainder of an audience of about fifty chose
their own seats while at the back the household staff was feudally
accommodated.

The collective voice was loud and animated and the atmosphere
of expectancy fully established. 'If only they keep it up,' Troy whispered to Alleyn. She glanced along the row to Signor Lattienzo. His
arms were folded and his head inclined towards Sir David who was

full of animation and bonhomie. Lattienzo looked up from under his brows, saw Troy and crossed the fingers of his right hand.

The players came in and tuned their instruments, a sound that always caught Troy under the diaphragm. The lights in the auditorium went out. The stage curtain glowed. Mr Reece slipped into his seat beside Troy. Rupert Bartholomew came in from behind the stage so inconspicuously that he had raised his baton before he had been noticed. The overture began.

Troy always wished she knew more about music and could understand why one sound moved her and another left her disengaged. Tonight she was too apprehensive to listen properly. She tried to catch the response of the audience, watched Rupert's back and wondered if he was able to distil any magic from his players, wondered, even, how long the ephemeral good nature induced by champagne could be expected to last with listeners who knew what music was about. She was so distracted by these speculations that the opening of the curtain caught her by surprise.

She had dreamt up all sorts of awful possibilities: Rupert breaking down and walking out, leaving the show to crawl to disaster; Rupert stopping the proceedings and addressing the audience; or the audience itself growing more and more restless or apathetic and the performance ending on the scantiest show of applause and the audience being harangued by an infuriated Sommita.

None of these things took place. True, as the opera developed the boisterous good humour of the audience seemed to grow tepid but the shock of that Golden Voice, the astonishment it engendered note by note, was so extraordinary that no room was left for criticism. And there was, or so it seemed to Troy, a passage in the duet with Hilda Dancy – 'Whither thou goest' – when suddenly the music came true. She thought: That's one of the bits Signor Lattienzo meant. She looked along the row and he caught her glance and nodded.

Sir David Baumgartner, whose chin was sunk in his shirt frill in what passed for profound absorption, raised his head. Mr Reece, sitting bolt upright in his chair, inconspicuously consulted his watch.

The duet came to its end and Troy's attention wandered. The show was well-dressed, the supporting artists being clad in low-profile biblical gear hired from a New Zealand company who had recently revived the York Cycle. The Sommita's costume, created for the occasion, was white and virginal and if it was designed to make Ruth look like a startling social misfit amidst the alien corn, succeeded wonderfully in achieving this end.

The quartet came and went and left no mark. Sir David looked irritated. The Sommita, alone on stage, sailed into a recitative and thence to her big aria. Troy now saw her purely in terms of paint, fixing her in the memory, translating her into a new idiom. The diva had arrived at the concluding *fioritura*, she moved towards her audience, she lifted her head, she spread her arms and rewarded them with her trump card – A above high C.

No doubt she would have been very cross if they had observed the rule about not applauding until the final curtain. They did not observe it. They broke into a little storm of clapping. She raised a monitory hand. The performance entered into its penultimate phase: a lachrymose parting between Ruth and Signor Romano, plump in kilted smock and leg strappings and looking like a late photograph of Caruso. Enter Boaz, discovering them and ordering the gleaner to be beaten. Ruth and Naomi pleading with Boaz to relent, which he did, and the opera ended with a rather cursory reconciliation of all hands in chorus.

The sense of relief when the curtains closed was so overwhelming that Troy found herself clapping wildly. After all, it had not been so bad. None of the horrors she had imagined had come to pass, it was over and they were in the clear.

Afterwards, she wondered if the obligatory response from the audience could have been evoked by the same emotion.

Three rapid curtain calls were taken. The first by the company, the second by the Sommita who was thinly cheered by backbenchers, and the third again by the Sommita who went through her customary routine of extended arms, kissed hands and deep curtsies.

And then she turned to the orchestra, advanced upon it with outstretched hand and beckoning smile only to find that her quarry had vanished. Rupert Bartholomew was gone. The violinist stood up and said something inaudible but seemed to suggest that Rupert was backstage. The Sommita's smile had become fixed. She swept to an upstage entrance and vanished through it. The audience, nonplussed, kept up a desultory clapping which had all but died out when she re-entered, bringing, almost dragging, Rupert after her.

He was sheet-white and dishevelled. When she exhibited him, retaining her grasp of his hand, he made no acknowledgement of the applause she exacted. It petered out into a dead silence. She whispered something and the sound was caught up in a giant enlargement: the north-west wind sighing round the island.

The discomfiture of the audience was extreme. Someone, a woman, behind Troy said: 'He's not well. He's going to faint,' and there was a murmur of agreement. But Rupert did not faint. He stood bolt upright, looked at nothing, and suddenly freed his hand.

'Ladies and Gentlemen,' he said loudly.

Mr Reece began to clap and was followed by the audience. Rupert shouted: 'Don't do that,' and they stopped. He then made his curtain speech.

'I expect I ought to thank you. Your applause is for a Voice. It's a wonderful Voice, insulted by the stuff it has been given to sing tonight. For that I am responsible. I should have withdrawn it at the beginning when I realized – when I first realized – when I knew – '

He swayed a little and raised his hand to his forehead.

'When I knew,' he said. And then he did faint. The curtains closed.

III

Mr Reece handled the catastrophe with expertise. He stood up, faced his guests and said that Rupert Bartholomew had been unwell for some days and no doubt the strain of the production had been a little too much for him. He (Mr Reece) knew that they would all appreciate this and he asked them to reassemble in the drawing room. Dinner would be served as soon as the performers were ready to join them.

So out they all trooped and Mr Reece, followed by Signor Lattienzo, went backstage.

As they passed through the hall the guests became more aware of what was going on outside: irregular onslaughts of wind, rain and, behind these immediate sounds, a vague groundswell of turbulence. Those guests who were to travel through the night by way of launch, bus and car began to exchange glances. One of them, a woman, who was near the windows parted the heavy curtains and looked out releasing the drumming sound of rain against glass and a momentary glimpse of the blinded pane. She let the curtain fall and pulled an anxious grimace. A hearty male voice said loudly: 'Not to worry. She'll be right.'

More champagne in the drawing room and harder drinks for the asking. The performers began to come in and Hanley with them. He circulated busily. 'Doing his stuff,' said Alleyn.

'Not an easy assignment,' said Troy and then: 'I'd like to know how that boy is.'

'So would I.'

'Might we be able to do anything, do you suppose?'

'Shall we ask?'

Hanley saw them, flashed his winsome smile and joined them. 'We're going in now,' he said. 'The Lady asks us not to wait.'

'How's Rupert?'

'Poor dear! *Wasn't* it a pity? Everything had gone *so* well. He's in his room. Lying down, you know, but quite all right. Not to be disturbed. He'll be *quite* all right,' Hanley repeated brightly. 'Straight-out case of nervous fatigue. Ah, there's the gong. Will you give a lead? Thank you *so* much.'

On this return passage through the hall, standing inconspicuously just inside the entrance and partly screened by the vast pregnant woman whose elfin leer suggested a clandestine rendezvous, was a figure in dripping oilskins: Les, the launchman. Hanley went to speak to him.

The dining room had been transformed, two subsidiary tables being introduced to form an E with the middle stroke missing. The three central places at the 'top' table were destined for the Sommita, her host and Rupert Bartholomew, none of whom appeared to occupy them. All the places were named and the Alleyns were again among the VIPs. This time Troy found herself with Mr Reece's chair on her left and Signor Lattienzo on her right. Alleyn was next to the Sommita's empty chair with the wife of the New Zealand conductor on his left.

'This is delightful,' said Signor Lattienzo.

'Yes, indeed,' said Troy who was not in the mood for badinage.

'I arranged it.'

'You, what?' she exclaimed.

'I transposed the cards. You had been given the New Zealand *maestro* and I his wife. She will be enraptured with your husband's company and will pay no attention to her own husband. He will be less enraptured but that cannot be helped.'

'Well,' said Troy, 'for sheer effrontery, I must say – !'

'I take, as you say, the buttery bun? Apropos, I am much in need of refreshment. That was a most painful débâcle, was it not?'

'Is he all right? Is someone doing something? I'm sure I don't know what anybody *can* do,' Troy said, 'but is there someone?'

'I have seen him.'

'You have?'

'I have told him that he took a courageous and honest course. I was also able to say that there was a shining moment – the duet when you and I exchanged signals. He has rewritten it since I saw the score. It is delightful.'

'That will have helped.'

'A little, I think.'

'Yesterday he confided rather alarmingly in us, particularly in Rory. Do you think he might like to see Rory?'

'At the moment I hope he is asleep. A Dr Carmichael has seen him and I have administered a pill. I suffer,' said Signor Lattienzo, 'from insomnia.'

'Is she coming down, do you know?'

'I understand from our good Monty – yes. After the débâcle she appeared to have been in two minds about what sort of temperament it would be appropriate to throw. Obviously an attack upon the still unconscious Rupert was out of the question. There remained the flood of remorse which I fancy she would not care to entertain since it would indicate a flaw in her own behaviour. Finally there could be a demonstration as from a distracted lover. Puzzled by this choice, she burst into a storm of ambiguous tears and Retired, as they say in your Shakespeare, Above. Escorted by Monty. To the ministrations of the baleful Maria and with the intention of making another delayed entrance. We may expect her at any moment, no doubt. In the meantime the grilled trout was delicious and here comes the coq-au-vin.'

But the Sommita did not appear. Instead, Mr Reece arrived to say that she had been greatly upset by poor Rupert Bartholomew's collapse which had no doubt been due to nervous exhaustion, but would rejoin them a little later. He then said that he was sorry indeed to have to tell them that he had been advised by the launchman that the local storm, known as The Rosser, had blown up and would increase in force, probably reaching its peak in about an hour when it would then become inadvisable to make the crossing to the mainland. Loath as he was to break up the party, he felt perhaps . . . He spread his hands.

The response was immediate. The guests, having finished their marrons glacés, professed themselves, with many regrets, ready to leave. There was a general exodus for them to prepare themselves for the journey, Sir David Baumgartner, who had been expected to stay, among them. He had an important appointment looming up, he explained, and dare not risk missing it.

There would be room enough for all the guests and the performers in the bus and cars that waited across the lake. Anyone so inclined could spend the tag end of the night at the Cornishman's Pass pub on the east side of the Pass and journey down-country by train the next day. The rest would continue through the night, descending to the plains and across them to their ultimate destinations.

The Alleyns agreed that the scene in the hall bore a resemblance to rush hour on the Underground. There was a sense of urgency and scarcely concealed impatience. The travellers were to leave in two batches of twenty which was the maximum accommodation in the launch. The house-staff fussed about with raincoats and umbrellas. Mr Reece stood near the door repeating valedictory remarks of scant originality and shaking hands. Some of the guests, as their anxiety mounted, became perfunctory in their acknowledgements, a few actually neglected him altogether being intent upon manoeuvring themselves into the top twenty. Sir David Baumgartner, in awful isolation and a caped mackintosh, sat in a porter's chair looking very cross indeed.

The entrance doors opened admitting wind, rain and cold all together. The first twenty guests were gone: swallowed up and shut out as if, Troy thought – and disliked herself for so thinking – they were condemned.

Mr Reece explained to the remainder that it would be at least half an hour before the launch returned and advised them to wait in the drawing room. The servants would keep watch and would report as soon as they sighted the lights of the returning launch.

A few followed this suggestion but most remained in the hall, sitting round the enormous fireplace or in scattered chairs, wandering about, getting themselves behind the window curtains and coming out, scared by their inability to see anything beyond streaming panes.

Eru Johnstone was speaking to the tenor, Rodolfo Romano, and the little band of musicians who listened to him in a huddle of apprehension. Alleyn and Troy joined them. Eru Johnstone was saying: 'It's something one doesn't try to explain. I come from the far north of the North Island and have only heard about the Island indirectly from some of our people down here on the Coast. I had forgotten. When we were engaged for this performance, I didn't connect the two things.'

'But it's tapu?' asked the pianist. 'Is that it?'

'In very early times an important person was buried here,' he said, as it seemed unwillingly. 'Ages afterwards, when the pakehas came, a man named Ross, a prospector, rowed out to the island. The story is that the local storm blew up and he was drowned. I had forgotten,' Eru Johnstone repeated in his deep voice. 'I suggest you do, too. There have been many visitors since those times and many storms – '

'Hence "Rosser"?' Alleyn asked.

'So it seems.'

'How long does it usually last?'

'About twenty-four hours, I'm told. No doubt it varies.'

Alleyn said: 'On my first visit to New Zealand I met one of your people who told me about Maoritanga. We became friends and I learnt a lot from him – Dr Te Pokiha!'

'Rangi Te Pokiha?' Johnstone exclaimed. 'You know him? He is one of our most prominent elders.'

And he settled down to talk at great length of his people. Alleyn led the conversation back to the Island. 'After what you have told me,' he said, 'do you mind my asking if you believe it to be tapu?'

After a long pause Eru Johnstone said: 'Yes.'

'Would you have come,' Troy asked, 'if you had known?'

'No,' said Eru Johnstone.

'Are you staying here?' asked Signor Lattienzo, appearing at Troy's elbow, 'or shall we fall back upon our creature comforts in the drawing room? One can't go on saying goodbye to people who scarcely listen.'

'I've got a letter I want to get off,' said Alleyn. 'I think I'll just scribble it and ask one of these people if they'd mind putting it in the post. What about you, Troy?'

'I rather thought – the studio. I ought to "fix" those drawings.'

'I'll join you there,' he said.

'Yes, darling, do.'

Troy watched him run upstairs.

'Surely you are not going to start painting after all this!' Signor Lattienzo exclaimed.

'Not I!' Troy said. 'It's just that I'm restless and can't settle. It's been a bit of a day, hasn't it? Who's in the drawing room?'

'Hilda Dancy and the little Parry who are staying on. Also the Dr Carmichael who suffers excruciatingly from seasickness. It is not very gay in the drawing room although the lissom Hanley weaves in and out. Is it true that you have made drawings this afternoon?'

'One or two preliminary canters.'

'Of Bella?'

'Mostly of her, yes.'

Signor Lattienzo put his head on one side and contrived to look wistful. In spite of herself Troy laughed. 'Would you like to see them?' she said.

'Naturally I would like to see them. *May* I see them?'

'Come on, then,' said Troy.

They went upstairs to the studio. Troy propped her drawings, one by one, on the easel, blew fixative through a diffuser over each and laid them side by side on the throne to dry: Signor Lattienzo screwed in his eyeglass, folded his plump hands over his ample stomach and contemplated them.

After a long pause during which vague sounds of activity down in the hall drifted up and somewhere a door slammed, Signor Lattienzo said: 'If you had not made that last one, the one on the right, I would have said you were a merciless lady, Madame Troy.'

It was the slightest of the drawings. The orchestra was merely indicated playing like mad in the background. In the foreground La Sommita, having turned away from them, stared at vacancy and in everything that Troy had set down with such economy there was desolation.

'Look what you've done with her,' Signor Lattienzo said. 'Did she remain for long like that? Did she, for once, face reality? I have never seen her look so and now I feel I have never seen her at all.'

'It only lasted for seconds.'

'Yes? Shall you paint her like that?'

Troy said slowly: 'No, I don't think so.' She pointed to the drawing of La Sommita in full cry, mouth wide open, triumphant. 'I rather thought this – '

'This is the portrait of a Voice.'

'I would have liked to call it "A in alt" because that sounds so nice. I don't know what it means but I understand it would be unsuitable.'

'Highly so. *Mot juste*, by the way.'

'"A in sop" wouldn't have the same charm.'

'No.'

'Perhaps, simply "Top Note". Though why I should fuss about a title when I haven't as yet clapped paint to canvas, I can't imagine.'

'Has she seen the drawings?'

'No.'

'And won't if you can help it?'

'That's right,' said Troy.

They settled down. Signor Lattienzo discoursed cosily, telling Troy of droll occurrences in the world of opera and of a celebrated company half-Italian and half-French of which the Sommita had been the star and in which internal feuding ran so high that when people asked at the Box Office what opera was on tonight the manager would intervene and say, 'Wait till the curtain goes up, Madame,' or (Dear Boy!) 'Just wait till the curtain goes up.' With this and further discourse he entertained Troy exceedingly. After some time Alleyn came in and said the launch had been sighted on its return trip and the last batch of travellers were getting ready to leave.

'The wind is almost gale force,' he said. 'The telephone's out of order – probably a branch across the line. Radio and television are cut off.'

'Will they be all right?' Troy asked. 'The passengers?'

'Reece says that Les knows his job and that he wouldn't undertake the passage if he thought there was any risk. Hanley's swanning about telling everyone that the launch is seaworthy, cost the earth and crossed the English Channel in a blizzard.'

'*How* glad I am,' Signor Lattienzo remarked, 'that I am not on board her.'

Alleyn opened the window-curtains. 'She could be just visible from here,' he said, and after a pause, 'Yes, there she is. Down at the jetty.'

Troy joined him. Beyond the half-blinded window lights, having no background, moved across the void, distorted by the runnels of water streaming down the pane. They rose, tilted, sank, rose again, vanished, reappeared and were gone.

'They are going aboard,' said Alleyn. 'I wonder if Eru Johnstone is glad to have left the Island?'

'One would have thought – ' Signor Lattienzo began and was cut short by a scream.

It came from within the house and mounted like a siren. It broke into a gabble, resumed and increased in volume.

'Oh *no*!' said Signor Lattienzo irritably. 'What now, for pity's sake!' A piercing scream answered him.

And then he was on his feet. 'That is not Bella's voice,' he said loudly.

It was close. On their landing. Outside their door. Alleyn made for the door but before he could reach it, it opened and there was Maria, her mouth wide open, yelling at the top of her voice.

'*Soccorso! Soccorso!*'

Alleyn took her by the upper arms. '*Che succede?*' he demanded. 'Control yourself, Maria. What are you saying?'

She stared at him, broke free, and ran to Signor Lattienzo, beat him with her clenched fists and poured out a stream of Italian.

He held her by the wrists and shook her. '*Taci!*' he shouted, and to Alleyn: 'She is saying that Bella has been murdered.

IV

The Sommita lay on her back across a red counterpane. The bosom of her biblical dress had been torn down to the waist and under her left breast, irrelevantly, unbelievably, the haft of a knife stuck out. The wound was not visible, being masked by a piece of glossy coloured paper or card that had been pierced by the knife and trans-fixed to the body. From beneath this a thin trace of blood had slid down towards naked ribs like a thread of red cotton. The Sommita's face, as seen from the room, was upside down. Its eyes bulged and its mouth was wide open. The tongue protruded as if at the moment of death she had pulled a gargoyle's grimace at her killer. The right arm, rigid as a branch, was raised in the fascist salute. She might have been posed for the jacket on an all-too-predictable shocker.

Alleyn turned to Montague Reece who stood halfway between the door and the bed with Beppo Lattienzo holding his arm. The secretary, Hanley, had stopped short just inside the room, his hand over his mouth and looking as if he was going to be sick. Beyond the door Maria could be heard to break out afresh in bursts of hysteria. Alleyn said: 'That doctor – Carmichael, isn't it? – he stayed behind, didn't he?'

'Yes,' said Mr Reece. 'Of course,' and to Hanley: 'Get him.'

'And shut the door after you,' said Alleyn. 'Whoever's out there on the landing, tell them to go downstairs and wait in the drawing room.'

'And get rid of that cursed woman,' Mr Reece ordered savagely. 'No! Stop! Tell the housekeeper to take charge of her. I – ' he appealed to Alleyn. 'What should we do? You know about these things. I – need a few moments.'

'Monty, my dear! Monty,' Lattienzo begged him, 'don't look. Come away. Leave it to other people. To Alleyn. Come with me.' He turned on Hanley. 'Well. Why do you wait? Do as you're told, imbe-cile. The doctor!'

'There's no call to be insulting,' Hanley quavered. He looked dis-tractedly about him and his gaze fell upon the Sommita's face. 'God Almighty!' he said and bolted.

When he had gone, Alleyn said to Mr Reece: 'Is your room on this floor? Why not let Signor Lattienzo take you there? Dr Carmichael will come and see you.'

'I would like to see Ben Ruby. I do not require a doctor.'

'We'll find Ben for you,' soothed Lattienzo. 'Come along.'

'I am perfectly all right, Beppo,' Mr Reece stated. He freed himself and actually regained a sort of imitation of his customary manner. He said to Alleyn: 'I will be glad to leave this to you. You will take charge, if you please. I will be available and wish to be kept informed.' And then: 'The police. The police must be notified.'

Alleyn said: 'Of course they must. When it's possible. At the moment it's not. We are shut off.'

Mr Reece stared at him dully. 'I had forgotten,' he conceded. And then astonishingly: 'That is extremely awkward,' he said, and walked out of the room.

'He is in trauma,' said Lattienzo uncertainly. 'He is in shock. Shall I stay with him?'

'If you would. Perhaps when Mr Ruby arrives – '

'*Si, si, sicuro,*' said Signor Lattienzo. 'Then I make myself scarce.'

'Only if so desired,' Alleyn rejoined in his respectable Italian.

When he was alone he returned to the bed. Back on the job, he thought, and with no authority.

He thought of Troy: of six scintillating drawings, of a great empty canvas waiting on the brand-new easel and he wished to God he could put them all thirteen thousand miles away in a London studio.

There was a tap on the door. He heard Lattienzo say: 'Yes. In there,' and Dr Carmichael came in.

He was a middle-aged to elderly man with an air of authority. He looked sharply at Alleyn and went straight to the bed. Alleyn watched him make the expected examination and then straighten up.

'I don't need to tell you that nothing can be done,' he said. 'This is a most shocking thing. Who found her?'

'It seems, her maid. Maria. She raised the alarm and was largely incoherent. No doubt you all heard her.'

'Yes.'

'She spoke Italian,' Alleyn explained. 'I understood a certain amount and Lattienzo, of course, much more. But even to him she was sometimes incomprehensible. Apparently after the performance Madame Sommita was escorted to her room by Mr Reece.'

'That's right,' said the doctor. 'I was there. They'd asked me to have a look at the boy. When I arrived they were persuading her to go.'

'Ah yes. Well. Maria was here expecting she would be needed. Her mistress, still upset by young Bartholomew's collapse, ordered them to leave her alone. Maria put out one of her tablets, whatever they are. She also put out her dressing gown – there it is, that fluffy object still neatly folded over the chair – and she and Reece did leave. As far as I could make out she was anxious about Madame Sommita and after a time returned to the room with a hot drink – there it is untouched – and found her as you see her now. Can you put a time to the death?'

'Not precisely, of course, but I would think not more than an hour ago. Perhaps much less. The body is still warm.'

'What about the raised arm? Rigor mortis? Or cadaveric spasm?'

'The latter, I should think. There doesn't appear to have been a struggle. And that card or paper or whatever it is?' said Dr Carmichael.

'I'll tell you what that is,' said Alleyn, 'it's a photograph.'

V

Dr Carmichael, after an incredulous stare at Alleyn, stooped over the body.

'It'd be as well not to touch the paper,' said Alleyn, 'but look at it.'

He took a ballpoint pen from his pocket and used it to open out the creases. 'You can see for yourself,' he said.

Dr Carmichael looked. 'Good God!' he exclaimed. 'You're right. It's a photograph of her. With her mouth open. Singing.'

'And the knife has been pushed through the photograph at the appropriate place – the heart.'

'It's – grotesque. When – where could it have been taken?'

'This afternoon, in the concert chamber,' said Alleyn. 'Those are the clothes she wore. She stood in a shaft of sunlight. My wife made a drawing of her standing as she is here. The photograph must have been taken from outside a window. One of those instant self-developing jobs.'

Dr Carmichael said: 'What should we do? I feel helpless.'

'So, believe me, do I! Reece tells me I am to "take charge", which is all very well but I have no real authority.'

'Oh – surely!'

'I can only assume it until the local police take over. And when that will be depends on this blasted "Rosser" and the telephone breakdown.'

'I heard the young man who seems to be more or less in charge – I don't know his name – '

'Hanley.'

' – say that if the lake got rougher the launchman would stay on the mainland and sleep on board or in the boatshed. He was going to flash a lamp when they got there from the second trip to show they were all right. I think Hanley said something about him ringing a bell, though how they could expect anyone to hear it through the storm I can't imagine.

'Eru Johnstone said the "Rosser" usually lasts about twenty-four hours.'

'In the meantime – ?' Dr Carmichael motioned with his head, indicating the bed and its occupant. 'What should be the drill? Usually?'

'An exhaustive examination of the scene. Nothing moved until the crime squad have gone over the ground: photographer, dabs – fingerprints – pathologist's first report. See any self-respecting whodunit,' said Alleyn.

'So we cover her up and maintain a masterly inactivity?'

Alleyn waited for a moment or two. 'As it happens,' he said, 'I have got my working camera with me. My wife has a wide camel-hair watercolour brush. Talc powder would work all right. It's a hell of a time since I did this sort of field work but I think I can manage. When it's done the body can be covered.'

'Can I be of help?'

Alleyn hesitated for a very brief moment and then said: 'I'd be very glad of your company and of your help. You will of course be asked to give evidence at the inquest and I'd like to have a witness to my possibly irregular activities.'

'Right.'

'So if you don't mind I'll leave you here while I collect what I need and see my wife. And I suppose I'd better have a word with Hanley and the hangovers in the drawing room. I won't be long.'

'Good.'

An onslaught of wind shook the window frames.

'Not much letting-up out there,' Alleyn said. He parted the heavy curtains. 'By George!' he exclaimed. 'He's signalling! Have a look.'

Dr Carmichael joined him. Out in the blackness a pinpoint of light appeared, held for a good second and went out. It did this three times. A pause followed. The light reappeared for a full second, was followed by a momentary flash and then a long one. A pause and the performance was repeated.

'Is that Morse?' asked the doctor.

'Yes, it reads "OK",' said Alleyn. 'Somewhat ironically, under the circumstances. It was to let us know they'd made it in the launch.'

The signals were repeated.

'Here!' Alleyn said. 'Before he goes. Quick. Open up.'

They opened the curtains wide. Alleyn ran to the group of light switches on the wall and threw them all on.

The Sommita, gaping on her bed, was as she had always demanded she should be, fully lit.

Alleyn blacked out. 'Don't say anything,' he begged the doctor, 'or I'll muck it up. Do you know Morse?'

'No.'

'Oh, for a tiny boy scout. Here goes, then.'

Using both hands on the switches, he began to signal. The Sommita flashed up and out, up and out. The storm lashed the windows, the switches clicked: *Dot-dot-dot. Dash-dash-dash* and *Dot-dot-dot.*'

He waited. 'If he's still watching,' he said. 'He'll reply.'

And after a daunting interval, he did. The point of light reappeared and vanished.

Alleyn began again: slowly, laboriously. *'SOS. Urgent. Contact. Police. Murder.'* And again: *'SOS. Urgent. Contact. Police. Murder.'*

He did it three times and waited an eternity.

And at last the acknowledgement: *'Roger.'*

Alleyn said: 'Let's hope it works. I'll be off. If you'd rather leave the room, get her key from the housekeeper. Lock it from the outside and wait for me on the landing. There's a chair behind a screen. Half a minute. I'd better just look round here before I go.'

There was another door in the Sommita's enormous bedroom: it opened into her bathroom, an extraordinarily exotic apartment carpeted in crimson with a built-in dressing table and a glass surrounded by lights and flanked by shelves thronged with flasks, atomizers, jars, boxes and an arrangement of crystal flowers in a Venetian vase.

Alleyn looked at the hand basin. It was spotless but damp, and the soap wet. Of the array of scarlet towels on heated rails, one was wet but unstained.

He returned to the bedroom and had a quick look round. On the bedside table was a full cup of some milky concoction. It was still faintly warm and a skin had formed on top. Beside this was a glass of water and a bottle of sleeping tablets of a well-known proprietary brand. One had been laid out beside the water. Dr Carmichael waited with his back to the bed.

They left the room together. At Dr Carmichael's suggestion Alleyn took charge of the key.

'If it's all right,' said the doctor, 'I thought I'd have a look at the young chap. He was rather under the weather after that faint.'

'Yes,' said Alleyn. 'So I gathered. Did you look after him?'

'Reece asked me to. The secretary came round to the front in a great taking-on. I went backstage with him.'

'Good. What did you find?'

'I found Bartholomew coming to, Madame Sommita shaking him like a rabbit and that Italian singing master of hers – Lattienzo – ordering her to stop. She burst out crying and left. Reece followed her. I suppose it was then that she came upstairs. The ingénue – little Miss Parry – had the good sense to bring a glass of water for the boy. We got him to a seat and from there, when he was ready for it, to his room. Lattienzo offered to give him one of his own sleeping pills and put him to bed, but he wanted to be left to himself. I returned to the drawing room. If it's OK by you I think I'll take a look-see at him.'

'Certainly. I'd like to come with you.'

'Would you?' said Dr Carmichael, surprised. And then: 'I see. Or do I? You're checking up. Right?'

'Well – sort of. Hold on a jiffy, will you?'

Below in the hall a door had shut and he caught the sound of a bolt being pushed home. He went to the head of the stairs and looked down. There was the unmistakable, greatly foreshortened figure of their driver: short ginger hair and heavy shoulders. He was coming away from the front door and had evidently been locking up. What was his name? Ah yes. Bert.

Alleyn gave a not too loud whistle between his teeth. 'Hi! Bert!' he said. The head tilted back and the dependable face was presented. Alleyn beckoned and Bert came upstairs.

'G'day,' he said. 'This is no good. Murder, eh?'

Alleyn said: 'Look, do you feel like lending a hand? Dr Carmichael and I have got a call to make but I don't want to leave this landing unguarded. Would you be a good chap and stay here? We won't be too long. I hope.'

'She'll be right,' said Bert. And then, with a motion of his head towards the bedroom door: 'Would that be where it is?'

'Yes. The door's locked.'

'But you reckon somebody might get nosey?'

'Something like that. How about it?'

'I don't mind,' said Bert. 'Got it all on your own, eh?'

'With Dr Carmichael. I *would* be grateful. Nobody, no matter who, is to go in.'

'Good as gold,' said Bert.

So they left him there, lounging in the chair behind the screen.

'Come on,' Alleyn said to Dr Carmichael. 'Where's his room?'

'This way.'

They were passing the studio door. Alleyn said: 'Half a second, will you?' and went in. Troy was sitting on the edge of the throne looking desolate. She jumped to her feet.

He said: 'You know about it?'

'Signor Lattienzo came and told me. Rory, how terrible!'

'I know. Wait here. All right? Or would you rather go to bed?'

'I'm all right. I don't think I really believe it has happened.'

'I won't be long, I promise.'

'Don't give it another thought. I'm OK. Rory, Signor Lattienzo seems to think it was Strix – the photographer. Is that possible?'

'Remotely, I suppose.'

'I don't quite believe in the photographer.'

'If you want to talk about it, we will. In the meantime could you look me out my camera, a big sable brush and a squirt-thing of talc powder?'

'Certainly. There are at least three of the latter in our bathroom. Why,' asked Troy, rallying, 'do people perpetually give each other talc powder and never use it themselves?'

'We must work it out when we've the leisure,' said Alleyn. 'I'll come back for the things.'

He kissed her and rejoined the doctor.

Rupert Bartholomew's room was two doors along the passage. Dr Carmichael stopped. 'He doesn't know,' he said. 'Unless, of course, someone has come up and told him.'

'If he's taken Lattienzo's pill he'll be asleep.'

'Should be. But it's one of the mildest sort.'

Dr Carmichael opened the door and Alleyn followed him.

Rupert was not asleep. Nor had he undressed. He was sitting upright on his bed with his arms clasped round his knees. He looked very young.

'Hello!' said Dr Carmichael, 'what's all this? You ought to be sound asleep.' He looked at the bedside table with its switched-on lamp, glass of water and the tablet lying beside it. 'So you haven't taken your Lattienzo pill,' he said. 'Why's that?'

'I didn't want it. I want to know what's happening. All that screaming and rushing about.' He looked at Alleyn. 'Was it her? Bella? Was it because of me? I want to know. What have I done?'

Dr Carmichael slid his fingers over Rupert's wrist. 'You haven't done anything,' he said. 'Calm down.'

'Then what – ?'

'The rumpus,' Alleyn said, 'was nothing to do with you. As far as we know. Nothing. It was Maria who screamed.'

An expression that in less dramatic circumstances might almost have been described as 'huffy' appeared and faded: Rupert looked at them out of the corners of his eyes. 'Then why *did* Maria scream?' he asked.

Alleyn exchanged a glance with the doctor who slightly nodded his head.

'Well?' Rupert demanded.

'Because,' Alleyn said, 'there has been a disaster. A tragedy. A death. It will be a shock to you but, as far as we can see, which admittedly is not very far, there is no reason to link it with what happened after the performance. You will have to know of it and there would be no point in holding it back.'

'A *death*? Do you mean – ? You can't mean – ? Bella?'

'I'm afraid – yes.'

'Bella?' Rupert said and sounded incredulous. 'Bella? *Dead?*'

'It's hard to believe, isn't it?'

There was a long silence, broken by Rupert.

'But – why? What was it? Was it heart failure?'

'You could say,' Dr Carmichael observed with a macabre touch of the professional whimsy sometimes employed by doctors, 'that all deaths are due to heart failure.'

'Do you know if she had any heart trouble at all?' Alleyn asked Rupert.

'She had high blood pressure. She saw a specialist in Sydney.'

'Do you know who?'

'I've forgotten. Monty will know. So will Ned Hanley.'

'Was it a serious condition, did you gather?'

'She was told to – to slow down. Not get over-excited. That sort of thing.' He looked at them with what seemed to be apprehension. 'Should I see her?' he mumbled.

'No,' they both said quickly. He breathed out a sigh.

'I can't get hold of this,' he said, and shook his head slowly. 'I can't get hold of it at all. I can't sort of seem to believe it.'

'The best thing you can do,' said Dr Carmichael, 'is to take this tablet and settle down. There's absolutely nothing else you *can* do.'

'Oh. Oh, I see. Well; all right, then,' he replied with a strange air of speaking at random. 'But I'll put myself to bed if you don't mind.'

He took the tablet, drank the water and leant back, staring in front of him. 'Extraordinary!' he said and closed his eyes.

Alleyn and Carmichael waited for a minute or two. Rupert opened his eyes and turned off the bedside lamp. Disconcerted, they moved to the door.

'Thank you,' said Rupert in the dark. 'Good night.'

When they were in the passage Carmichael said: 'That was a very odd little conversation.'

'It was, rather.'

'You'd have almost said – well, I mean – '

'What?'

'That he was relieved. Don't get me wrong. He's had a shock – I mean, that extraordinary apology for his opera which I must say I didn't find very impressive and his faint. His pulse is still a bit erratic. But the reaction,' Carmichael repeated, '*was* odd, didn't you think?'

'People do tend to behave oddly when they hear of death. I'm sure you've found that, haven't you? In this case I rather think there *has* actually been a sense of release.'

'A *release*? From what?'

'Oh,' said Alleyn, 'from a tricky situation. From extreme anxiety. High tension. Didn't somebody say – was it Shaw? – that after the death of even one's closest and dearest, there is always a sensation of release. And relief.'

Carmichael made the noise that is written 'Humph.' He gave Alleyn a speculative look. 'You didn't,' he said, 'tell him it was murder.'

'No. Time enough in the morning. He may as well enjoy the benefit of the Lattienzo pill.'

Dr Carmichael said 'Humph,' again.

Alleyn returned to Troy who had the camera, brush and talc powder ready for him.

'How is that boy?' she asked. 'How has he taken it?'

'On the whole, very well. Remarkably well.'

'Perhaps he's run out of emotional reactions,' said Troy. 'He's been fully extended in that department.'

'Perhaps he has. You're the wisest of downy owls and had better go to roost. I'm off, and it looks like being one of those nights.'

'Oh, for Br'er Fox and Thompson and Bailey?'

'You can say that again. And oh, for you to be in your London nest thirteen thousand miles away, which sounds like the burden of a ballad,' said Alleyn. 'But as you're here you'd better turn the key in your lock when you go to bed.'

'*Me!*' said Troy incredulously. 'Why?'

'So that I'll be obliged to wake you up,' said Alleyn and left her.

He asked Bert to continue his vigil, while he himself and Dr Carmichael went down to the drawing room.

Dr Carmichael said: 'But I don't quite see – I mean you've got the key.'

'There may be other keys and other people may have them. Maria, for instance. If Bert sits behind that screen he can see anyone who tries to effect an entry.'

'I can't imagine anyone wanting to go back. Not even her murderer.'

'Can't you?' said Alleyn. 'I can.'

He and Dr Carmichael went downstairs to the drawing room.

A wan little trio of leftovers was there: Hilda Dancy, Sylvia Parry, Lattienzo. Mr Reece, Alleyn gathered, was closeted with Ben Ruby and Hanley in the study. The drawingroom had only been half-tidied of its preprandial litter when the news broke. It was tarnished with used champagne glasses, full ashtrays and buckets of melted ice. The fire had burnt down to embers and when Alleyn came in Signor Lattienzo was gingerly dropping a small log on them.

Miss Dancy at once tackled Alleyn. Was it, she boomed, true that he was in charge? If so, would he tell them exactly what had happened? Had the Sommita really been done away with? Did this mean there was a murderer at large in the house? *How* had she been done away with?

Signor Lattienzo had by this time stationed himself behind Miss Dancy in order to make deprecating faces at Alleyn.

'We have a right to be told,' said the masterful Miss Dancy.

'And told you shall be,' Alleyn replied. 'Between one and two hours ago Madame Sommita was murdered in her bedroom. That is all that any of us knows. I have been asked by Mr Reece to take charge until such time as the local police can be informed. I'm going to organize a search of the premises. There are routine questions that should be asked of everybody who was in the house after the last launch trip. If you would prefer to go to your rooms, please do so but with the knowledge that I may be obliged to knock you up when the search is completed. I'm sure Signor Lattienzo will be pleased to escort you to your rooms.'

Signor Lattienzo gave slightly incoherent assurances that he was theirs, dear ladies, to command.

'I'm staying where I am,' Miss Dancy decided. 'What about you, dear?'

'Yes. Yes, so am I,' Sylvia Parry decided: and to Alleyn: 'Does Rupert know? About Madame Sommita?'

'Dr Carmichael and I told him.'

Dr Carmichael made diffident noises.

'It will have been a terrible shock for Rupert,' said Sylvia. 'For everybody, of course, but specially for Rupert. After – what happened.' And with an air of defiance she added: 'I think Rupert did a very brave thing. It took an awful lot of guts.'

'We all know that, dear,' said Miss Dancy with a kind of gloomy cosiness.

Alleyn said, 'Before I go I wonder if you'd tell me exactly what happened after Bartholomew fainted.'

Their account was put together like a sort of unrehearsed duet with occasional stoppages when they disagreed about details and called upon Signor Lattienzo. It seemed that as soon as Rupert fell, Hanley, who was standing by, said 'Curtains' and closed them himself. Sylvia Parry knelt down by Rupert and loosened his collar and tie. Rodolfo Romano said something about fresh air and fanned Rupert with his biblical skirt. The Sommita, it appeared, after letting out an abortive shriek, stifled herself with her own hand, looked frantically round the assembly and then flung herself upon the still unconscious Rupert with such abandon that it was impossible to decide whether she was moved by remorse or fury. It was at this point that Signor Lattienzo arrived, followed in turn by Mr Reece and Ben Ruby.

As far as Alleyn could make out these three men lost no time in tackling the diva in a very businesslike manner, detaching her from Rupert and suggesting strongly that she go to her room. From here the narrative followed, more or less, the accounts already given by Signor Lattienzo and the doctor. Mr Reece accompanied the Sommita out of the concert hall, which was by this time emptied of its audience and was understood to conduct her to her room. Hanley fetched Dr Carmichael and Sylvia Parry fetched water. Rupert when sufficiently recovered was removed to his room by the doctor and Signor Lattienzo, who fetched the sleeping tablet and placed it on the bedside table. Rupert refused all offers to help him undress and get into bed so they left him and went down to dinner. The ladies and the rest of the cast were already at table.

'After Hanley had fetched Dr Carmichael, what did he do?' Alleyn asked.

Nobody had noticed. Miss Dancy said that he 'seemed to be all over the shop' and Sylvia thought it had been he who urged them into the dining room.

On this vague note Alleyn left them.

In the hall he ran into the ubiquitous Hanley, who said that the entire staff was assembled in their sitting room awaiting instructions. Alleyn gathered that Maria had, so to put it, 'stolen the show'. The New Zealand members of the staff – they of the recently bankrupt luxury hotel, including the chef and housekeeper – had grown restive under recurrent onsets of Maria's hysteria, modelled, Alleyn guessed, upon those of her late employer.

The staff sitting room, which in less democratic days would have been called the servants' hall, was large, modern in design, gaily furnished and equipped with colour television, a ping-pong table and any number of functional armchairs. The housekeeper, who turned out to be called, with Congrevian explicitness, Mrs Bacon, sat apart from her staff but adjacent to Mr Reece. She was a well-dressed, personable lady of capable appearance. Behind her was a subdued bevy of two men and three girls, the ex-hotel staff, Alleyn assumed, that she had brought with her to the Lodge.

Hanley continued in his role of restless dogsbody and hovered, apparently in readiness for something unexpected to turn up, near the door.

Alleyn spoke briefly. He said he knew how shocked and horrified they all must be and assured them that he would make as few demands upon them as possible.

'I'm sure,' he said, 'that you all wonder if there is a connection between this appalling crime and the recent activities of the elusive cameraman.' (And he wondered if Maria had noticed the photograph pinned to the body.) 'You will, I dare say, be asking yourselves if yesterday's intruder whom we failed to hunt down could be the criminal. I'm sure your search,' Alleyn said and managed to avoid a sardonic tone, 'was extremely thorough. But in a case like this every possibility, however remote, should be explored. For that reason I am going to ask the men of the household to sort themselves into pairs and to search the whole of the indoor premises. I want the pairs to remain strictly together throughout the exercise. You will not go into Madame Sommita's bedroom which is now locked. Mr Bartholomew has already gone to bed and you need not disturb him. Just look in quietly and make sure he is there. I must ask you simply to assure yourselves that there is no intruder in the house. Open any doors behind which someone might be hiding, look under beds and behind curtains, but don't handle anything else. I am going to ask Mrs Bacon and Mr Hanley to supervise this operation.'

He turned to Mrs Bacon. 'Perhaps we might just have a word?' he suggested.

'Certainly,' she said. 'In my office.'

'Good.' He looked round the assembled staff.

'I want you all to remain here,' he said. 'We won't keep you long. I'll leave Dr Carmichael in charge.'

Mrs Bacon conducted Alleyn and Hanley to her office, which turned out to be a sitting room with a large desk in it.

She said: 'I don't know whether you gentlemen would care for a drink but I do know I would,' and went to a cupboard from which she produced a bottle of whisky and three glasses. Alleyn didn't want a drink but thought it politic to accept. Hanley said: 'Oh yes. Oh *yes. Please!*'

Alleyn said: 'I see no point in pretending that I think the perpetrator of this crime has contrived to leave the island and nor do I think he is somewhere out there in the storm or skulking in the hangar. Mrs Bacon, is the entire staff collected in there? Nobody missing?'

'No. I made sure of that.'

'Good. I think it will be best to pair the members of the household with the guests and for you two, if you will, to apportion the various areas so that all are covered without overlapping. I'm not familiar enough with the topography of the Lodge to do this. I'll cruise.'

Mrs Bacon had watched him very steadily. He thought that this had probably been her manner in her hotel days when listening to complaints.

She said: 'Am I wrong in understanding that you don't believe the murderer was on the Island yesterday? That the trespasser was not the murderer, in fact?'

Alleyn hesitated and then said: 'I don't think the murderer was a trespasser, no.'

Hanley said loudly: 'Oh *no*! But you can't – I mean – that would mean – I mean – oh *no*!'

'It would mean,' said Mrs Bacon, still looking at Alleyn, 'that Mr Alleyn thinks Madame Sommita was murdered either by a guest or by a member of the household. That's correct, Mr Alleyn, isn't it? By, if I can put it that way – one of us?'

'That is perfectly correct, Mrs Bacon,' said Alleyn.

CHAPTER 5

Nocturne

The hunt turned out as Alleyn had expected it would, to be a perfectly useless exercise. The couples were carefully assorted. Marco was paired with Mrs Bacon, Ben Ruby with Dr Carmichael and Hanley with the chef for whom he seemed to have an affinity. Alleyn dodged from one pair to another, turning up where he was least expected, sometimes checking a room that had already been searched, sometimes watching the reluctant activities of the investigators, always registering in detail their reactions to the exercise.

These did not vary much. Hanley was all eyes and teeth and inclined to get up little intimate arguments with the chef. Ben Ruby, smoking a cigar, instructed his partner, Dr Carmichael, where to search, but did nothing in particular himself. Alleyn thought he seemed to be preoccupied as if confronted by a difficult crossword puzzle. Signor Lattienzo looked as if he thought the exercise was futile.

When the search was over they all returned to the staff sitting room where, on Alleyn's request, Hilda Dancy and Sylvia Parry joined them. Nobody had anything to report. The New Zealanders, Alleyn noticed, collected in a huddle. Mrs Bacon and the ex-hotel staff showed a joint tendency to eye the Italians. Marco attached himself to Signor Lattienzo. Maria entered weeping but in a subdued manner, having been chastened, Alleyn fancied, by Mrs Bacon. Hanley detached himself from his chef and joined Ben Ruby.

When they were all assembled, the door opened and Mr Reece walked in. He might have arrived to take the chair at a shareholders'

meeting. Hanley was assiduous with offers of a seat and was disregarded.

Mr Reece said to Alleyn: 'Please don't let me interrupt. Do carry
on.'

'Thank you,' Alleyn said. He told Mr Reece of the search and its
non-result and was listened to with stony attention. He then
addressed the company. He said he was grateful to them for having
carried out a disagreeable job and asked that if any of them, on afterthought, should remember something that could be of significance,
however remotely, he would at once speak of it. There was no
response. He then asked how many of them possessed cameras.

The question was received with concern. Glances were
exchanged. There was a general shuffling of feet.

'Come on,' Alleyn said. 'There's no need to show the whites of
your eyes over a harmless enquiry. I'll give you a lead.' He raised his
hand. 'I've got a camera and I don't mind betting most of you have.
Hands up.' Mr Reece, in the manner of seconding the motion, raised
his. Seven more followed suit, one after another, until only six had
not responded: Three New Zealand housemen with Maria, Marco
and Hilda Dancy.

'Good,' Alleyn said. 'Now. I'm going to ask those of you who *do*
possess a camera to tell me what the make is and if you've used it at
any time during the last week and if so what you took. Mrs Bacon?'

'Old-fashioned Simplex. I used it yesterday. I snapped the people
round the bathing pool from my sitting-room window.'

'Miss Parry?'

'It's a Pixie. I used it yesterday.' She turned pink. 'I took Rupert.
By the landing stage.'

'Signor Lattienzo?'

'Oh, my dear Mr Alleyn!' he said, spreading his hands. 'Yes, I
have a camera. It was presented to me by – forgive my conscious
looks and mantling cheeks – a grateful pupil. Isabella, in fact. I cannot remember its name and have been unable to master its ridiculously complicated mechanism. I carry it about with me, in order to
show keen.'

'And you haven't used it?'

'Well,' said Signor Lattienzo, 'in a sense I *have* used it. Yesterday.
It upsets me to remember. Isabella proposed that I take photographs

of her at the bathing pool. Rather than confess my incompetence I aimed it at her and pressed a little button. It gave a persuasive click. I repeated the performance several times. As to the results, one has grave misgivings. If there are any they rest in a prenatal state in the womb of the camera. You shall play the midwife,' offered Signor Lattienzo.

'Thank you. What about you, Mr Ruby? There's that magnificent German job, isn't there?'

Mr Ruby's camera was a very sophisticated and expensive version of instantaneous self-development. He had used it that very morning when he had lined up the entire house party with the Lodge for a background. He actually had the 'picture', as he consistently called the photograph, on him and showed it to Alleyn. There was Troy between Mr Reece, who as usual conveyed nothing, and Signor Lattienzo who playfully ogled her. And there, at the centre, of course, the Sommita with her arm laid in tigerish possession across the shoulders of a haunted Rupert while Sylvia Parry, on his other side, looked straight ahead. A closer examination showed that she had taken his hand.

Alleyn himself, head and shoulders taller than his neighbours, was, he now saw with stoic distaste, being winsomely contemplated by the ubiquitous Hanley, three places removed in the back row.

The round of camera owners was completed, the net result being that Mr Reece, Ben Ruby, Hanley and Signor Lattienzo (if he had known how to use it) all possessed cameras that could have achieved the photograph now pinned under the breast of the murdered Sommita.

To these proceedings Maria had listened with a sort of smouldering resentment. At one point she flared up and reminded Marco in vituperative Italian that he had a camera and had not declared it. He responded with equal animosity that his camera had disappeared during the Australian tour and hinted darkly that Maria herself knew more than she was prepared to let on in that connection. As neither of them could remember the make of the camera their dialogue was unfruitful.

Alleyn asked if Rupert Bartholomew possessed a camera. Hanley said he did and had taken photographs of the Island from the lake shore and of the lake shore from the Island. Nobody knew anything at all about his camera.

Alleyn wound up the proceedings, which had taken less time in performance than in description. He said that if this had been a police enquiry they would all have been asked to show their hands and roll up their sleeves and if they didn't object he would be obliged if – ?

Only Maria objected but on being called to order in no uncertain terms by Mr Reece, offered her clawlike extremities as if she expected to be stripped to the buff.

This daunting but fruitless formality completed, Alleyn told them they could all go to bed and it might be as well to lock their doors. He then returned to the landing where Bert sustained his vigil behind a large screen across whose surface ultra-modern nudes frisked busily. He had been able to keep a watch on the Sommita's bedroom door through hinged gaps between panels. The searchers in this part of the house had been Ben Ruby and Dr Carmichael. They had not tried the bedroom door but stood outside it for a moment or two, whispering, for all the world as if they were afraid the Sommita might overhear them.

Alleyn told Bert to remain unseen and inactive for the time being. He then unlocked the door and he and Dr Carmichael returned to the room.

In cases of homicide when the body has been left undisturbed, and particularly when there is an element of the grotesque or of extreme violence in its posture, there can be a strange reaction before returning to it. Might it have moved? There is something shocking about finding it just as it was, like the Sommita, still agape, still with her gargoyle tongue, still staring, still rigidly pointing. He photographed it from just inside the door.

Soon the room smelt horridly of synthetic violets as Alleyn made use of the talc powder. He then photographed the haft of the knife, a slender, vertically grooved affair with an ornate silver knob. Dr Carmichael held the bedside lamp close to it.

'I suppose you don't know where it came from?' he asked.

'I think so. One of a pair on the wall behind the pregnant woman.'

'What pregnant woman?' exclaimed the startled doctor.

'In the hall.'

'Oh. That.'

'There were two, crossed and held by brackets. Only one now.'
And after a pause during which Alleyn took three more shots, 'You
wouldn't know when it was removed?' Dr Carmichael said.

'Only that it was there before the general exodus this evening.'

'You're trained to notice details, of course.'

Using Troy's camel-hair brush, he spread the violet powder round
the mouth, turning the silent scream into the grimace of a painted
clown.

'By God, you're a cool hand,' the doctor remarked.

Alleyn looked up at him and something in the look caused Dr
Carmichael to say in a hurry: 'Sorry, I didn't mean – '

'I'm sure you didn't,' Alleyn said. 'Do you see this? Above the
corners of the mouth? Under the cheekbones?'

Carmichael stooped. 'Bruising,' he said.

'Not hypostasis?'

'I wouldn't think so. I'm not a pathologist, Alleyn.'

'No. But there are well-defined differences, aren't there?'

'Precisely.'

'She used very heavy make-up. Heavier than usual, of course, for
the performance and she hadn't removed it. Some sort of basic stuff
topped up with a finishing cream. The colouring. And then a final
powdering. Don't those bruises, if bruises they are, look as if the
make-up under the cheekbones has been disturbed? Pushed up, as
it were.'

After a considerable pause, Dr Carmichael said: 'Could be. Certainly
could be.'

'And look at the area below the lower lip. It's not very marked but
don't you think it may become more so? What does that suggest to
you?'

'Again bruising.'

'Pressure against the lower teeth?'

'Yes. That. It's possible.'

Alleyn went to the Sommita's dressing table where there was an
inevitable gold-mounted manicure box. He selected a slender nail
file, returned to the bed, slid it between the tongue and the lower
lip, exposing the inner surface.

'Bitten,' he said. He extended his left hand to within half an inch
of the terrible face with his thumb below one cheekbone, his fingers

below the other and the heel of his hand over the chin and mouth. He did not touch the face.

'Somebody with a larger hand than mine, I fancy,' he said. 'But not much. I could almost cover it.'

'You're talking about asphyxia, aren't you?'

'I'm wondering about it. Yes. There are those pinpoint spots.'

'Asphyxial haemorrhages. On the eyeballs.'

'Yes,' said Alleyn and closed his own eyes momentarily. 'Can you come any nearer to a positive answer?'

'An autopsy would settle it.'

'Of course,' Alleyn agreed.

He had again stooped over his subject and was about to take another photograph when he checked, stooped lower, sniffed, and then straightened up.

'Will you?' he said. 'It's very faint.'

Dr Carmichael stooped. 'Chloroform,' he said. 'Faint, as you say, but unmistakable. And look here, Alleyn. There's a bruise on the throat to the right of the voice-box.'

'And have you noticed the wrists?'

Dr Carmichael looked at them – at the left wrist on the end of the rigid upraised arm and at the right one on the counterpane. 'Bruising,' he said.

'Caused by – would you say?'

'Hands. So now what?' asked Dr Carmichael.

'Does a tentative pattern emerge?' Alleyn suggested. 'Chloroform. Asphyxia. Death. Ripping the dress. Two persons – one holding the wrists. The other using the chloroform. The stabbing coming later. If it's right it would account for there being so little blood, wouldn't it?'

'Certainly would,' Dr Carmichael said. 'And there's very, very little. I'd say that tells us there was a considerable gap between death and the stabbing. The blood had had time to sink.'

'How long?'

'Don't make too much of my guesswork, will you? Perhaps as much as twenty minutes – longer even. But what a picture!' said Dr Carmichael. 'You know? Cutting the dress, ripping it open, placing the photograph over the heart and then using the knife. I mean – it's so – so far-fetched. *Why?*'

'As far-fetched as a vengeful killing in a Jacobean play,' Alleyn said, and then: 'Yes. A vengeful killing.'

'Are you – are we,' Carmichael asked, 'not going to withdraw the weapon?'

'I'm afraid not. I've blown my top often enough when some well-meaning fool has interfered with the body. In this case I'd be the well-meaning fool.'

'Oh, come. But I see your point,' Carmichael said. 'I suppose I'm in the same boat myself. I should go no further than making sure she's dead. And, by God, it doesn't need a professional man to do that.'

'The law, in respect of bodies, is a bit odd. They belong to nobody. They are not the legal property of anyone. This can lead to muddles.'

'I can imagine.'

'It's all jolly fine for the lordly Reece to order me to take charge. I've no right to do so and the local police would have *every* right to cut up rough if I did.'

'So would the pathologist if I butted in.'

'I imagine,' Alleyn said, 'they won't boggle at the photographs. After all there will be – changes.'

'There will indeed. This house is central-heated.'

'There may be a local switch in this room. Yes. Over there where it could be reached from the bed. Off with it.'

'I will,' said Carmichael and switched it off.

'I wonder if we can open the windows a crack without wreaking havoc,' Alleyn said. He pulled back the heavy curtains and there was the black and streaming glass. They were sash windows. He opened one and then others half an inch at the top, admitting blades of cold air and the voice of the storm.

'At least, if we can find something appropriate, we can cover her,' he said and looked about the room. There was a sandalwood chest against the wall. He opened it and lifted out a folded bulk of black material. 'This will do,' he said. He and Carmichael opened it out, and spread it over the body. It was scented and heavy and it shone dully. The rigid arm jutted up underneath it.

'What on earth is it *for*?' Carmichael wondered.

'It's one of her black satin sheets. There are pillowcases to match in the box.'

'Good God!'

'I know.'

Alleyn locked the door into the bathroom, wrapped the key in his handkerchief and pocketed it.

He and the doctor stood in the middle of the room. Already it was colder. Slivers of wind from outside stirred the marabou trimming on the Sommita's dressing gown and even fiddled with her black satin pall so that she might have been thought to move stealthily underneath it.

'No sign of the wind dropping,' said Carmichael. 'Or is there?'

'It's not raining quite so hard, I fancy. I wonder if the launchman's got through. Where would the nearest police station be?'

'Rivermouth, I should think. Down on the coast. About sixty miles, at a guess.'

'And as, presumably, the cars are all miles away returning guests to their homes east of the ranges, and the telephone at the boathouse will be out of order, we can only hope that the unfortunate Les has set out on foot for the nearest sign of habitation. I remember that on coming here we stopped to collect the mailbag at a railway station some two miles back along the line. A very small station called Kai-kai, I think.'

'That's right. With about three *whares** and a pub. He may wait till first light,' said Dr Carmichael, 'before he goes anywhere.'

'He *did* signal "Roger", which of course may only have meant "Message received and understood." Let's leave this bloody room, shall we?'

They turned, and took two steps. Alleyn put his hand on Carmichael's arm. Something had clicked.

The door handle was turning, this way and that. Alleyn unlocked and opened it and Maria strode into the room.

II

This time Maria did not launch into histrionics. When she saw the two men she stopped, drew herself up, looked beyond them to the shrouded figure on the bed and said in English that she had come to be of service to her mistress.

*Whare – small dwelling

'I perform the last rites,' said Maria. 'This is my duty. Nobody else. It is for me.'

Alleyn said: 'Maria, certainly it would be for you if circumstances had been different, but this is murder and she must not be touched until permission has been given by the authorities. Neither Dr Carmichael nor I have touched her. We have examined but we have not touched. We have covered her for dignity's sake but that is all and so it must remain until permission is given. We can understand your wish and are sorry to prevent you. Do you understand?'

She neither replied nor looked at him. She went to a window and reached for the cord that operated it.

'No,' Alleyn said. 'Nothing must be touched.' She made for the heavier, ornate cord belonging to the curtains. 'Not that either,' Alleyn said. 'Nothing must be touched. And I'm afraid I must ask you to come away from the room, Maria.'

'I wait. I keep *veglia*.'

'It is not permitted. I am sorry.'

She said in Italian, 'It is necessary for me to pray for her soul.'

'You can do so. But not here.'

Now she did look at him, directly and for an uncomfortably long time. Dr Carmichael cleared his throat.

She walked towards the door. Alleyn reached it first. He opened it, removed the key and stood aside.

'*Sozzume*,' Maria said and spat inaccurately at him. She looked and sounded like a snake. He motioned with his head to Dr Carmichael who followed Maria quickly to the landing. Alleyn turned off the lights in the room, left it, and locked the door. He put Maria's key in his pocket. He now had two keys to the room.

'I remain,' Maria said. 'All night. Here.'

'That is as you wish,' Alleyn said.

Beside the frisky nude-embellished screen behind which Bert still kept his vigil there were chairs and a clever occasional table with a lamp carved in wood – an abstract with unmistakable phallic implications, the creation, Alleyn guessed, of the master whose pregnant lady dominated the hall.

'Sit down, Maria,' Alleyn said. 'I have something to say to you.' He moved a chair towards her. 'Please,' he said.

At first he thought she would refuse but after two seconds or so of stony immobility she did sit, poker-backed, on the edge of the offered chair.

'You have seen Madame Sommita and you know she has been murdered,' he said. 'You wish that her murderer will be found, don't you?'

Her mouth set in a tight line and her eyes flashed. She did not speak but if she had delivered herself of a tirade it could not have been more eloquent.

'Very well,' Alleyn said. 'Now then: when the storm is over and the lake is calmer the New Zealand police will come and they will ask many questions. Until they come Mr Reece has put me in charge and anything you tell me, I will tell them. Anything I ask you, I will ask for one reason only: because I hope your answer may help us to find the criminal. If your reply is of no help it will be forgotten – it will be as if you had not made it. Do you understand?'

He thought: I shall pretend she has answered. And he said: 'Good. Well, now. First question. Do you know what time it was when Madame Sommita came upstairs with Mr Reece and found you waiting for her? No? It doesn't matter. The opera began at eight and they will know how long it runs.'

He had a pocket diary on him and produced it. He made quite a business of opening it and flattening it on the table. He wrote in it, almost under her nose.

'Maria. Time of S's arrival in bedroom. No answer.'

When he looked up he found that Maria was glaring at his note-book. He pushed it nearer and turned it towards her. 'Can you see?' he asked politely.

She unclamped her mouth.

'Twenty past nine. By her clock,' she said.

'Splendid. And now, Maria – by the way I haven't got your sur-name, have I? Your *cognome*.'

'Bennini.'

'Thank you.' He added it to his note. 'I see you wear a wedding ring,' he said. 'What was your maiden name, please?'

'Why do you ask me such questions? You are impertinent.'

'You prefer not to answer?' Alleyn enquired politely.

Silence.

'Ah well,' he said. 'When you are more composed and I hope a little recovered from the terrible shock you have sustained, will you tell me exactly what happened after she arrived with Signor Reece?'

And astonishingly, with no further ado, this creature of surprises who a few seconds ago had called him 'filth' and spat at him, embarked upon a coherent and lucid account. Maria had gone straight upstairs as soon as the curtain fell on the opera. She had performed her usual duties, putting out the glass of water and the sleeping pill that the Sommita always took after an opening night, folding her negligée and nightdress over the back of a chair and turning down the crimson counterpane. The Sommita arrived with Signor Reece. She was much displeased, Maria said, which Alleyn thought was probably the understatement of the year, and ordered Maria to leave the room. This, he gathered, was a not unusual occurrence. She also ordered Mr Reece to leave, which *was*. He tried to soothe her but she became enraged.

'About what?' Alleyn asked.

About something that happened after the opera. Maria had already left the audience. The Signor Bartholomew, she gathered, had insulted the diva. Signor Reece tried to calm her, Maria herself offered to massage her shoulders but was flung off. In the upshot he and Maria left and went downstairs together, Mr Reece suggesting that Maria give the diva time to calm down and go to bed and then take her a hot drink, which had been known on similar occasions to produce a favourable reaction.

Maria had followed this advice.

How long between the time when they had left the room and Maria returned to it?

About twenty minutes, she thought.

Where was she during that time?

In the servants' quarters where she made the hot drink. Mrs Bacon and Bert the chauffeur were there most of the time and others of the staff came to and fro from their duties in the dining room where the guests were now at table. Mr Reece had joined them. Maria made the hot drink, returned to the bedroom, found her mistress murdered and raised the alarm.

'When Madame Sommita dismissed you, did she lock the door after you?'

Yes, it appeared. Maria heard the lock click. She had her own key and used it on her return.

Had anybody else a key to the room?

For the first time she boggled. Her mouth worked but she did not speak.

'Signor Reece, for instance?' Alleyn prompted.

She made the Italian negative sign with her finger.

'Who, then?'

A sly look appeared. Her eyes slid round in the direction of the passage to the right of the landing. Her hand moved to her breast.

'Do you mean Signor Bartholomew?' Alleyn asked.

'Perhaps,' she said, and he saw that, very furtively, she crossed herself.

He made a note about keys in his book.

She watched him avidly.

'Maria,' he said when he had finished writing, 'how long have you been with Madame Sommita?'

Five years, it appeared. She had come to Australia as wardrobe mistress with an Italian opera company, and had stayed on as sewing-maid at the Italian Embassy. The Signora's personal maid had displeased her and been dismissed and Signor Reece had enquired of an aide-de-camp who was a friend of his if they could tell him of anyone suitable. The Ambassador had come to the end of his term and the household staff was to be reorganized. Maria had been engaged as personal dresser and lady's maid to Isabella Sommita.

'Who do you think committed this crime?' Alleyn asked suddenly.

'The young man,' she answered venomously and at once, as if that was a foolish question. And then with another of her abrupt changes of key she urged, begged, demanded that she go back into the room and perform the last services for her mistress – lay her out with decency and close her eyes and pray it would not be held in wrath against her that she had died in a state of sin. 'I must go. I insist,' said Maria.

'That is still impossible,' said Alleyn. 'I'm sorry.'

He saw that she was on the edge of another outburst and hoped that if she was again moved to spit at him her aim would not have improved.

'You must pull yourself together,' he said. 'Otherwise I shall be obliged to ask Mr Reece to have you locked up in your own room. Be a good girl, Maria. Grieve for her. Pray for her soul but do not make scenes. They won't get you anywhere, you know.'

Dr Carmichael who had contemplated Maria dubiously throughout now said with professional authority: 'Come along like a sensible woman. You'll make yourself unwell if you go on like this. I'll take you down and we'll see if we can find the housekeeper. Mrs Bacon, isn't it? You'd much better go to bed, you know. Take an aspirin.'

'And a hot drink?' Alleyn mildly suggested.

She looked furies at him but with the abruptness that was no longer unexpected stood up, crossed the landing and walked quickly downstairs.

'Shall I see if I can find Mrs Bacon and hand her over?' Dr Carmichael offered.

'Do, like a good chap,' said Alleyn. 'And if Mrs B. has vanished, take her to bed yourself.'

'Choose your words,' said Dr Carmichael and set off in pursuit.

Alleyn caught him up at the head of the stairs. 'I'm going back in there,' he said. 'I may be a little time. Join me if you will when you've brought home the Bacon. Actually I hope they're all tucked up for the night but I'd like to know.'

Dr Carmichael ran nimbly downstairs and Alleyn returned once more to the bedroom.

III

He began a search. The bedroom was much more ornate than the rest of the house. No doubt, Alleyn thought, this reflected the Sommita's taste more than that of the clever young architect. The wardrobe doors, for instance, were carved with elegant festoons and swags of flowers in deep relief each depending from the central motif of a conventionalized sunflower with a sunken black centre: the whole concoction being rather loudly painted and reminiscent of art nouveau.

Alleyn made a thorough search of the surfaces under the bed, of the top of her dressing table, of an escritoire, in which he found the

Sommita's jewel box. This was unlocked and the contents were startling in their magnificence. The bedside table. The crimson coverlet. Nothing. Could it be under the body? Possible, he supposed, but he must not move the body.

The bathroom: all along the glass shelves, the floor, everywhere.

And yet Maria, if she was to be believed, had heard the key turned in the lock after she and Mr Reece were kicked out. And when she returned she had used her own key. He tried to picture the Sommita, at the height, it seemed, of one of her rages, turning the key in the lock, withdrawing it and then putting it – where? Hiding it? But why? There was no accommodation for it in the bosom of her Hebraic gown which was now slashed down in ribbons. He uncovered the horror that was the Sommita, and with infinite caution, scarcely touching it, examined the surface of the counterpane round the body. He even slid his hand under the body. Nothing. He recovered the body.

'When all likely places have been fruitlessly explored, begin on the unlikely and carry on into the preposterous.' This was the standard practice. He attacked the drawers of the dressingtable. They were kept, by Maria, no doubt, in perfect order. He patted, lifted and replaced lacy undergarments, stockings, gloves. Finally, in the bottom drawer on the left he arrived at the Sommita's collection of handbags. On the top was a gold mesh, bejewelled affair that he remembered her carrying on the evening of their arrival.

Using his handkerchief he gingerly opened it and found her key to the room lying on top of an unused handkerchief.

The bag would have to be fingerprinted but for the moment it would be best to leave it undisturbed.

So what was to be concluded? If she had taken her bag downstairs and left it in her dressing room, then she must have taken it back to the bedroom. Mr Reece was with her. There would have been no call for the key for Maria was already in the room, waiting for her. She was, it must never be forgotten, in a passion, and the Sommita's passions he would have thought, did not admit of methodical tidying away of handbags into drawers. She would have been more likely to chuck the bag at Mr Reece's or Maria's head, but Maria had made no mention of any such gesture. She had merely repeated that when they beat their retreat they heard the key turn in the lock and that when she came back with the hot drink she used her own key.

Was it then to be supposed that, having locked herself in, the Sommita stopped raging and methodically replaced her key in the bag and the bag in the drawer? Unlikely, because she must have used the key to admit her killer and was not likely to replace it. Being, presumably, dead.

Unless, of course, Maria was her killer. This conjured up a strange picture. The fanatically devoted Maria, hot drink in hand, re-enters the bedroom, places the brimming cup in its saucer on the bedside table and chloroforms her tigerish mistress who offers no resistance; she then produces the dagger and photograph and having completed the job, sets up her own brand of hullabaloo and rushes downstairs proclaiming the murder? No.

Back to the Sommita, then. What had she done after she had locked herself in? She had not undressed. She had not taken her pill. How had she spent her last minutes before she was murdered?

And what, oh what, about Rupert Bartholomew?

At this point there was a tap on the door and Dr Carmichael returned.

'"Safely stowed",' he said. 'At least, I hope so. Mrs Bacon was still up and ready to cope. We escorted that tiresome woman to her room, she offering no resistance. I waited outside. Mrs B. saw her undressed, be-nightied and in bed. She gave her a couple of aspirins, made sure she took them and came out. We didn't lock her up, by the way.'

'We've really no authority to do that,' said Alleyn. 'I was making an idle threat.'

'It seemed to work.'

'I really am very grateful indeed for your help, Carmichael. I don't know how I'd manage without you.'

'To tell you the truth, in a macabre sort of way, I'm enjoying myself. It's a change from general practice. What now?' asked Dr Carmichael.

'Look here. This is important. When you went backstage to succour the wretched Bartholomew the Sommita was still on deck, wasn't she?'

'She was indeed. Trying to manhandle the boy.'

'Still in her Old Testament gear, of course?'

'Of course.'

'When they persuaded her to go upstairs – Reece and Lattienzo, wasn't it? – did she take a gold handbag with her? Or did Reece take it?'

'I can't remember. I don't think so.'

'It would have looked pretty silly,' Alleyn said. 'It wouldn't exactly team up with the white samite number. I'd have thought you'd have noticed it.' He opened the drawer and showed Dr Carmichael the bag.

'She was threshing about with her arms quite a bit,' the doctor said. 'No, I'm sure she hadn't got that thing in her hand. Why?'

Alleyn explained.

Dr Carmichael closed his eyes for some seconds. 'No,' he said at last, 'I can't reconcile the available data with any plausible theory. Unless – '

'Well?'

'Well, it's a most unpleasant thought, but – unless the young man – '

'There is that, of course.'

'Maria is already making strong suggestions along those lines.'

'Is she, by George,' said Alleyn, and after a pause: 'But it's the Sommita's behaviour and her bloody key that won't fit in. Did you see anything of our host downstairs?'

'There's a light under what I believe is his study door and voices beyond.'

'Come on, then. It's high time I reported. He may be able to clear things up a bit.'

'I suppose so.'

'Either confirm or refute la bella Maria, at least,' said Alleyn. 'Would you rather go to bed?'

Dr Carmichael looked at his watch. 'Good Lord,' he exclaimed, 'it's a quarter to twelve.'

'As Iago said, "Pleasure and action make the hours seem short."'

'Who? Oh. Oh yes. No, I don't want to go to bed.'

'Come on, then.'

Again they turned off the lights and left the room. Alleyn locked the door with Maria's key.

Bert was on the landing.

'Was you still wanting a watch kept up?' he said. 'I'll take it on if you like. Only a suggestion.'

'You *are* a good chap,' Alleyn said. 'But – '

'I appreciate you got to be careful. The way things are. But seeing you suggested it yourself before and seeing I never set eyes on one of this mob until I took the job on, I don't look much like a suspect. Please yourself.'

'I accept with very many thanks. But – '

'If you was thinking I might drop off, I'd thought of that. I might, too. I could put a couple of them chairs in front of the door and doss down for the night. Just an idea,' said Bert.

'It's the answer,' Alleyn said warmly. 'Thank you, Bert.'

And he and Dr Carmichael went downstairs to the study.

Here they found, not only Mr Reece but Signor Lattienzo, Ben Ruby and Hanley, the secretary.

Mr Reece, perhaps a trifle paler than usual but he was always rather wan, sat at his trendy desk – his swivel chair turned towards the room as if he had interrupted his work to give an interview. Hanley drooped by the window curtains and had probably been looking out at the night. The other two men sat by the fire and seemed to be relieved at Alleyn's appearance. Signor Lattienzo did, in fact, exclaim: '*Ecco!* At last!' Hanley, reverting to his customary solicitude, pushed chairs forward.

'I am very glad to see you, Mr Alleyn,' said Mr Reece in his pallid way. 'Doctor,' he added with an inclination of his head towards Carmichael.

'I'm afraid we've little to report,' Alleyn said. 'Dr Carmichael is very kindly helping me but so far we haven't got beyond the preliminary stages. I'm hoping that you, sir, will be able to put us right on some points, particularly in respect of the order of events from the time Rupert Bartholomew fainted until Maria raised the alarm.'

He had hoped for some differences: something that could give him a hint of a pattern or explain the seeming discrepancies in Maria's narrative. Particularly, something about keys. But no, on all points the account corresponded with Maria's.

Alleyn asked if the Sommita made much use of her bedroom key.

'Yes; I think she did, I recommended it. She has – had – there was always – a considerable amount of jewellery in her bedroom. You may say very valuable pieces. I tried to persuade her to keep it in my safe in this room but she wouldn't do that. It was the same thing in hotels. After all, we have got a considerable staff here and it would be a temptation.'

'Her jewel case is in the escritoire – unlocked.'

Mr Reece clicked his tongue. 'She's – she was incorrigible. The artistic temperament, I am told, though I never, I'm afraid, have known precisely what that means.'

'One is never quite sure of its manifestations,' said Alleyn, surprised by this unexpected turn in the conversation. Mr Reece seemed actually to have offered something remotely suggesting a rueful twinkle.

'Well,' he said, 'you, no doubt have had first-hand experience.' And with a return to his elaborately cumbersome social manner, 'Delightful, in your case, may I hasten to say.'

'Thank you. While I think of it,' Alleyn said, 'do you, by any chance, remember if Madame Sommita carried a gold mesh handbag when you took her up to her room?'

'No,' said Mr Reece, after considering it. 'No, I'm sure she didn't.'

'Right. About these jewels. No doubt the police will ask you later to check the contents of the box.'

'Certainly. But I am not familiar with all her jewels.'

Only, Alleyn thought, with the ones he gave her, I dare say.

'They are insured,' Mr Reece offered. 'And Maria would be able to check them.'

'Is Maria completely to be trusted?'

'Oh, certainly. Completely. Like many of her class and origin she has an uncertain temper and she can be rather a nuisance, but she was devoted to her mistress, you might say fanatically so. She has been upset,' Mr Reece added with one of his own essays in understatement.

'Oh, my dear Monty,' Signor Lattienzo murmured. 'Upset! So have we all been upset. Shattered would be a more appropriate word.' He made an uncertain gesture and took out his cigarette case.

And indeed he looked quite unlike himself, being white and, as Alleyn noticed, tremulous. Monty, my dear,' he said. 'I should like a little more of your superb cognac. Is it permitted?'

'Of course, Beppo. Mr Alleyn? Doctor? Ben?'

The secretary with a sort of ghostly reminder of his customary readiness, hurried into action. Dr Carmichael had a large whisky and soda and Alleyn nothing.

Ben Ruby, whose face was puffed and blotched and his eyes bloodshot, hurriedly knocked back his cognac and pushed his glass forward. 'What say it's one of that mob?' he demanded insecurely. 'Eh? What say one of those buggers stayed behind?'

'Nonsense,' said Mr Reece.

'S'all very fine, say "nonsense".'

'They were carefully chosen guests of known distinction.'

'All ver' well. But what say,' repeated Mr Ruby, building to an unsteady climax, 'one of your sodding guestserknownstinction was not what he bloody seemed. Eh? *What say* he was Six.'

'Six?' Signor Lattienzo asked mildly. 'Did you say six?'

'I said nothing of sort. I said,' shouted Mr Ruby, '*Strix*.'

'Oh *no*!' Hanley cried out, and to Mr Reece: 'I'm sorry, but honestly! There *was* the guest list. I gave one to the launch person and he was to tick off all the names as they came aboard in case anybody had been left behind. In the loo or something. I thought you couldn't be too careful in case of accidents. Well, you know, it was – I mean *is – such* a night.'

'Yes, yes,' Mr Reece said wearily. 'Give it a rest. You acted very properly.' He turned to Alleyn. 'I really can't see why it should be supposed that Strix, if he is on the premises, could have any motive for committing this crime. On the contrary, he had every reason for wishing Bella to remain alive. She was a fortune to him.'

'All ver' well,' Mr Ruby sulked. 'If it wasn't, then who was it? Thass the point. D'you think you know who it was? Beppo? Monty? Ned? Come on. No, you don't. See what I mean?'

'Ben,' said Mr Reece quite gently, 'don't you think you'd better go to bed?'

'You may be right. I mean to say,' said Mr Ruby, appealing to Alleyn, 'I've got a hell of a lot to do. Cables. Letters. There's the US concert tour. She's booked out twelve months ahead: booked solid. All those managements.'

'They'll know about it soon enough,' said Mr Reece bitterly. 'Once this storm dies down and the police arrive it'll be world news.

Go to bed, boy. If you can use him, Ned will give you some time tomorrow.' He glanced at Hanley. 'See to that,' he said.

'Yes, of *course*,' Hanley effused, smiling palely upon Mr Ruby who acknowledged the offer without enthusiasm. 'Well, ta,' he said. 'Won't be necessary, I dare say. I can type.'

He seemed to pull himself together. He finished his brandy, rose, advanced successfully upon Mr Reece and took his hand. 'Monty,' he said. 'Dear old boy. You know me. Anything I can do? Say the word.'

'Yes, Benny,' Mr Reece said, shaking his hand. 'I know. Thank you.'

'There've been good times, haven't there?' Mr Ruby said wistfully. 'It wasn't all fireworks, was it? And now . . .'

For the first time Mr Reece seemed to be on the edge of losing his composure. 'And now,' he surprised Alleyn by saying, 'she no longer casts a shadow.' He clapped Mr Ruby on the shoulder and turned away. Mr Ruby gazed mournfully at his back for a moment or two and then moved to the door.

'Good night, all,' he said. He blew his nose like a trumpet and left them.

He was heard to fall rather heavily on his way upstairs.

'He is fortunate,' said Signor Lattienzo who was swinging his untouched cognac around in the glass. 'Now, for my part, the only occasions on which I take no consolation from alcohol are those of disaster. This is my third libation. The cognac is superb. Yet I know it will leave me stone-cold sober. It is very provoking.'

Mr Reece, without turning to face Alleyn, said: 'Have you anything further to tell me, Mr Alleyn?' and his voice was elderly and tired.

Alleyn told him about the Morse signals and he said dully that it was good news. 'But I meant,' he said, 'about the crime itself. You will appreciate, I'm sure, how – confused and shocked – to find her – like that. It was – ' He made a singular and uncharacteristic gesture as if warding off some menace. 'It was so dreadful,' he said.

'Of course it was. One can't imagine anything worse. Forgive me,' Alleyn said, 'but I don't know exactly how you learned about it. Were you prepared in any way? Did Maria – ?'

'You must have heard her. I was in the drawing room and came out and she was there on the stairs, screaming. I went straight up with her. I think I made out before we went into the room and without really taking it in, that Bella was dead. Was murdered. But not – how. Beppo, here, and Ned – arrived almost at the same moment. It may sound strange but the whole thing, at the time, seemed unreal: a nightmare, you might say. It still does.'

Alleyn said: 'You've asked me to take over until the police come. I'm very sorry indeed to trouble you – '

'No. Please,' Mr Reece interrupted with a shaky return to his customary formality. 'Please, do as you would under any other circumstances.'

'You make it easy for me. First of all, you are sure, sir, are you, that after Madame Sommita ordered you and Maria to leave the bedroom you heard her turn the key in the lock?'

'Absolutely certain. May I ask why?'

'And Maria used her own key when she returned?'

'She must have done so, I presume. The door was not locked when Maria and I returned after she raised the alarm.'

'And there are – how many keys to the room?'

If atmosphere can be said to tighten without a word being uttered it did so then in Mr Reece's study. The silence was absolute, nobody spoke, nobody moved.

'Four?' Alleyn at last suggested.

'If you know, why do you ask?' Hanley threw out.

Mr Reece said: 'That will do, Ned.'

'I'm sorry,' he said, cringing a little yet with a disreputable suggestion of blandishment. 'Truly.'

'Who has the fourth key?' Alleyn asked.

'If there is one I don't imagine it is used,' said Mr Reece.

'I think the police will want to know.'

'In that case we must find out. Maria will probably know.'

'Yes,' Alleyn agreed. 'I expect she will.' He hesitated for a moment and then said, 'Forgive me. The circumstances I know are almost unbelievably grotesque, but did you look closely? At what had been done? And how it had been done?'

'Oh, really, Alleyn – ' Signor Lattienzo protested but Mr Reece held up his hand.

'No, Beppo,' he said and cracked a dismal joke. 'As you yourself would say: I asked for it, and now I'm getting it.' And to Alleyn:

'There's something under the knife. I didn't go – near. I couldn't. What is it?'

'It is a photograph. Of Madame Sommita.'

Mr Reece's lips formed the word 'photograph' but no sound came from them.

'This is a madman,' Signor Lattienzo broke out. 'A homicidal maniac. It cannot be otherwise.'

Hanley said: 'Oh yes, *yes*!' as if there was some sort of comfort in the thought. 'A madman. Of course. A lunatic.'

Mr Reece cried out so loudly that they were all startled. 'No! What you tell me alters the whole picture. I have been wrong. From the beginning I have been wrong. The photograph proves it. If he had left a signed acknowledgement it couldn't be clearer.'

There was a long silence before Lattienzo said flatly: 'I think you may be right.'

'Right! Of course I am right.'

'And if you are, Monty, my dear, this Strix was on the Island yesterday and unless he managed to escape by the launch is still on this Island tonight. And in spite of all our zealous searching may actually be in the house. In which case we shall indeed do wisely to lock our doors.' He turned to Alleyn. 'And what does the professional say to all this?' he asked.

'I think you are probably correct in every respect, Signor Lattienzo,' said Alleyn. 'Or rather, in every respect but one.'

'And what may that be?' Lattienzo asked sharply.

'You are proposing, aren't you, that Strix is the murderer. I'm inclined to think you may be mistaken there.'

'And I would be interested to hear why?'

'Oh,' said Alleyn, 'just one of those things, you know. I would find it hard to say why. Call it a hunch.'

'But my dear sir – the photograph.'

'Ah yes,' said Alleyn. 'Quite so. There is always the photograph, isn't there?'

'You choose to be mysterious.'

'Do I? Not really. What I really came in for was to ask you all if you happened to notice that the Italian stiletto, if that is what it is, was missing from its bracket on the wall behind the nude sculpture. And if you did notice, when.'

They stared at him. After a long pause Mr Reece said: 'You will find this extraordinary but nevertheless it is a fact. I had not realized that was the weapon.'

'Had you not?'

'I am, I think I may say, an observant man but I did not notice that the stiletto was missing and I did not recognize it – ' he covered his eyes with his hands – 'when I – saw it.'

Hanley said: 'Oh God! Oh, how terrible.'

And Lattienzo: 'They were hers. You knew that, of course, Monty, didn't you? Family possessions, I always understood. I remember her showing them to me and saying she would like to use one of them in *Tosca*. I said it would be much too dangerous, however cleverly she faked it. And I may add that the Scarpia wouldn't entertain the suggestion for a second. Remembering her temperament, poor darling, it was not surprising.'

Mr Reece looked up at Alleyn. His face was deadly tired and he seemed an old man.

'If you don't mind,' he said, 'I think I must go to my room. Unless of course there is anything else.'

'Of course not.' Alleyn glanced at Dr Carmichael, who went to Mr Reece.

'You've had about as much as you can take,' he said. 'Will you let me see you to your room?'

'You are very kind. No, thank you, doctor. I am perfectly all right. Only tired.'

He stood up, straightened himself and walked composedly out of the room.

When he had gone Alleyn turned to the secretary.

'Mr Hanley,' he said. 'Did you notice one of the stilettos was missing?'

'I'd have said so, wouldn't I, if I had?' Hanley pointed out in an aggrieved voice. 'As a matter of fact, I simply loathe the things. I'm like that over knives. They make me feel sick. I expect Freud would have had something to say about it.'

'No doubt,' said Signor Lattienzo.

'It was her idea,' Hanley went on. 'She had them hung on the wall. She thought they teamed up with that marvellous pregnant female. In a way, one could see why.'

'Could one?' said Signor Lattienzo and cast up his eyes.

'I would like again to ask you all,' said Alleyn, 'if on consideration you can think of anyone – but *anyone*, however unlikely – who might have had some cause, however outrageous, to wish for Madame Sommita's death. Yes, Signor Lattienzo?'

'I feel impelled to say that while my answer is no, I can *not* think of anyone, I believe that this is a crime of passion and impulse and not a coldly calculated affair. The outrageous *grotes-querie*, the use of the photograph and of her own weapon – everything points to some – I feel inclined to say Strindbergian love-hatred of lunatic force. Strix or not, I believe you are looking for a madman, Mr Alleyn.'

IV

After that the interview began to languish and Alleyn sensed the unlikelihood of anything to the point emerging from it. He suggested that they went to bed.

'I am going to the studio,' he said. 'I shall be there for the next half-hour or so and if anything crops up, however slight, that seems to be of interest, I would be glad if you would report to me there. I do remind you all,' he said, 'that what I am trying to do is a sort of caretaker's job for the police: to see, if possible, that nothing is done inadvertently or with intention, to muddle the case for them before they arrive. Even if it were proper for me to attempt a routine police investigation, it wouldn't be possible to do so single-handed. Is that clear?'

They muttered weary assents and got to their feet.

'Good night,' said Dr Carmichael. It was the second and last time he had spoken.

He followed Alleyn into the hall and up the stairs.

When they reached the first landing they found that Bert had put two chairs together face to face, hard against the door to the Sommita's room and was lying very comfortably on this improvised couch, gently snoring.

'I'm along there,' said Dr Carmichael, pointing to the left-hand passage.

'Unless you're asleep on your feet,' said Alleyn, 'will you come into the studio for a moment or two? No need, if you can't bear the thought.'

'I'm well-trained to eccentric hours.'

'Good.'

They crossed the landing and went into the studio. The great empty canvas still stood on its easel but Troy had put away her drawings. Alleyn's dispatch case had been removed from their bedroom and placed conspicuously on the model's throne with an electric torch on top of it. Good for Troy, he thought.

Yesterday, sometime after Troy had been settled in the studio, a supply of drinks had been brought in and stored in a wall-side unit. Alleyn wondered if this was common practice at the Lodge wherever a room was inhabited.

He said: 'I didn't have a drink down there: could you do with another?'

'I believe I could. A small one, though.'

They had their drinks and lit their pipes. 'I haven't dared do this before,' said the doctor.

'Nor I,' said Alleyn. He performed what had now become a routine exercise and drew back the curtains. The voice of the wind, which he was always to remember as a kind of *leitmotif* to the action, invaded their room. The window-pane was no longer masked with water but was a black nothing with vague suggestions of violence beyond. When he leant forward his ghost-face, cadaverous with shadows, moved towards him. He closed the curtains.

'It's not raining,' he said, 'but blowing great guns.'

'What's called "blowing itself out" perhaps?'

'Hope so. But that doesn't mean the lake will automatically go calmer.'

'Unfortunately no. Everything else apart, it's bloody inconvenient,' said the doctor. 'I've got a medical conference opening in Auckland tomorrow. Eru Johnstone said he'd ring them up. I hope he remembers.'

'Why did you stay?'

'Not from choice. I'm a travel sickness subject. Ten minutes in that launch topped up by mile after mile in a closed bus would have been absolute hell for me and everyone else. Reecc was insistent that

I should stay. He wanted me to take on the Great Lady as a patient. Some notion that she was heading for a nervous crisis, it seemed.'

'One would have thought it was a chronic condition,' said Alleyn. 'All the same, I got the impression that even when she peaked, temperamentally speaking, she never went completely over the top. I'd risk a guess that she always knew jolly well what she was up to. Perhaps with one exception.'

'That wretched boy?'

'Exactly.'

'You'd say she'd gone overboard for him?' asked the doctor.

'I certainly got that impression,' Alleyn said.

'So did I, I must say. In Sydney – '

'You'd met them before?' Alleyn exclaimed. 'In Sydney?'

'Oh yes. I went over there for her season. Marvellous it was, too. I was asked to meet her at a dinner party and then to a supper Reece gave after the performance. He – they – were hospitable and kind to me for the rest of the season. Young Bartholomew was very much in evidence and she made no bones about it. I got the impression that she was – I feel inclined to say "savagely" devoted.'

'And he?'

'Oh, besotted and completely out of his depth.'

'And Reece?'

'If he objected he didn't show it. I think his might be a case of collector's satisfaction. You know? He'd acquired the biggest star in the firmament.'

'And was satisfied with the *fait accompli*? So that was that?'

'Quite. He may even have been a bit sick of her tantrums, though I must say he gave no sign of it.'

'No.'

'By the way, Alleyn, I suppose it's occurred to you that I'm a candidate for your list of suspects.'

'In common with everyone else in the house. Oh yes. But you don't come very high on the list. Of course, I didn't know you'd had a previous acquaintance with her,' Alleyn said coolly.

'Well, I must say!' Dr Carmichael exclaimed.

'I felt I really needed somebody I could call upon. You and Bert seemed my safest bets. Having had, as I then supposed, no previous connection with her and no conceivable motive.'

Dr Carmichael looked fixedly at him. Alleyn pulled a long face.

'I am a lowland Scot,' said the doctor, 'and consequently a bit heavy-handed when it comes to jokes.'

'I'll tell you when I mean to be funny.'

'Thank you.'

'Although, God knows, there's not much jokey material going in this business.'

'No, indeed.

'I suppose,' said Dr Carmichael after a companionable silence, 'that you've noticed my tact? Another lowland Scottish characteristic is commonly thought to be curiosity.'

'So I've always understood. Yes. I noticed. You didn't ask me if I know who dunnit.'

'Do you?'

'No.'

'Do you hae you suspeesions?'

'Yes. You're allowed one more.'

'Am I? What shall I choose? Do you think the photographer – Strix – is on the Island?'

'Yes.'

'And took – that photograph?'

'You've exceeded your allowance. But, yes. Of course. Who else?' said Alleyn.

'And murdered Isabella Sommita?'

'No.'

And after that they wished each other goodnight. It was now thirteen minutes past one in the morning.

When Dr Carmichael had gone Alleyn opened a note that lay on top of his dispatch case – took out an all-too-familiar file and settled down to read it for the seventh time.

Isabella Pepitone known as Isabella Sommita. Born 1940, reputedly in Palermo, Sicily. Family subsequently settled in USA.

Father Alfredo Pepitone, successful businessman USA, suspected of Mafia activities but never arrested. Suspect in Rossi homicide case 1965. Victim: Bianca Rossi, female. Pepitone subsequently killed in car accident. Homicide suspected. No arrest.

Alleyn had brought his library book upstairs. There it lay near to hand – *Il Mistero di Bianca Rossi*.

Subject trained as singer. First in New York and later for three years under Beppo Lattienzo in Milan. Subject's debut 1968 La Scala. Became celebrated. 1970–79: Associated socially with Hoffman-Beilstein group.

1977 May 10th: Self-styled 'Baron' Hoffman-Beilstein, since believed to be Mr Big behind large-scale heroin chain, cruised his yacht *Black Star* round the Bermudas. Subject was one of his guests. Visited Miami via Fort Lauderdale. First meeting with Montague V. Reece, fellow passenger.

1977 May 11th: Subject and Hoffman-Beilstein lunched at Palm Beach with Earl J. Ogden now known to be background figure in heroin trade. He dined aboard yacht same night. Subsequently a marked increase in street sales and socially high-class markets Florida and, later, New York. FBI suspects heroin brought ashore from *Black Star* at Fort Lauderdale. Interpol interested.

1977: Relations with Hoffman-Beilstein became less frequent.

1978: Relations H-B apparently terminated. Close relationship developed with Reece. Subject's circle now consists of top impeccable socialites and musical celebrities.

Written underneath these notes in the spiky, irritable hand of Alleyn's Assistant Commissioner:

For Ch. Sup. Alleyn's attn. Not much joy. Any items however insignificant will be appreciated.

Alleyn locked the file back in the case. He began to walk about the room as if he kept an obligatory watch. It would be so easy, he thought, to concoct a theory based on the meagre document. How would it go?

The Sommita, born Bella Pepitone which he thought he'd heard or read somewhere, was a common Sicilian name, but was reared in the United States. He remembered the unresolved Rossi case quite well. It was of the sort that turns up in books about actual crimes.

The feud was said to be generations deep: a hangover from some initial murder in Sicily. It offered good material for 'true crimes' collections being particularly bloody and having a peculiar twist: in the long succession of murders the victims had always been women and the style of their putting-off grisly.

The original crime which took place in 1910 in Sicily and triggered off the feud, was said to have been the killing of a Pepitone woman in circumstances of extreme cruelty. Ever since, hideous idiocies had been perpetrated on both sides at irregular intervals in the name of this vendetta.

The macabre nature of the Sommita's demise and her family connections would certainly qualify her as a likely candidate and it must be supposed would notch up several points on the Rossi score.

Accepting, for the moment, this outrageous proposition, what, he speculated, about the MO? How was it all laid on? Could Strix be slotted into the pattern? Very readily, if you let your imagination off the chain. Suppose Strix was in the Rossi interest and had been hired, no doubt at an exorbitant price, to torment the victim, but not necessarily to dispatch her? Perhaps Strix was himself a member of the Rossi Family? In this mixed stew of concoctions there was one outstanding ingredient: the identity of Strix. For Alleyn it was hardly in doubt but if he was right it followed that Strix was not the assassin. (And how readily that melodramatic word surfaced in this preposterous case.) From the conclusion of the opera until Alleyn went upstairs to write his letter this 'Strix' had been much in evidence downstairs. He had played the ubiquitous busybody. He had been present all through dinner and in the hall when the guests were milling about waiting to embark.

He had made repeated trips from house to jetty full of consoling chat, sheltering departing guests under a gigantic umbrella. He had been here, there and everywhere but he certainly had not had time to push his way through the crowd, go upstairs, knock on the Sommita's door, be admitted, administer chloroform, asphyxiate her, wait twenty minutes and then implant the stiletto and the photograph. And return to his duties, unruffled, in his natty evening get-up.

For, in Alleyn's mind, at this juncture there were no two ways about the identity of Strix.

CHAPTER 6

Storm Continued

Alleyn wrote up his notes. He sat at the brand-new paint-table Troy would never use and worked for an hour, taking great pains to be comprehensive, detailed, succinct and lucid, bearing in mind that the notes were destined for the New Zealand police. And the sooner he handed them over and he and Troy packed their bags, the better he would like it.

The small hours came and went and with them that drained sensation accompanied by the wakefulness that replaces an unsatisfied desire for sleep. The room, the passage outside, the landing and the silent house beyond seemed to change their character and lead a stealthy night life of their own.

It was raining again. Giant handfuls of rice seemed to be thrown across the windowpanes. The Lodge, new as it was, jolted under the onslaught. Alleyn thought of the bathing pool below the studio windows, and almost fancied he could hear its risen waters slapping at the house.

At a few minutes short of two o'clock he was visited by an experience Troy, ever since the early days of their marriage when he had first confided in her, called his 'Familiar', though truly a more accurate name might be 'Unfamiliar' or perhaps 'Alter Ego'. He understood that people interested in such matters were well acquainted with this state of being and that it was not at all unusual. Perhaps the ESP buffs had it taped. He had never cared to ask.

The nearest he could get to it was to say that without warning he would feel as if he had moved away from his own identity and looked at himself as if at a complete stranger. He felt that if he held on outside himself something new and very remarkable would come out of it. But he never did hang on and as suddenly as normality had gone it would return. The slightest disturbance clicked it back and he was within himself again.

As now, when he caught a faint movement that had not been there before – the sense rather than the sound – of someone in the passage outside the room.

He went to the door and opened it and was face to face with the ubiquitous and serviceable Hanley.

'Oh,' said Hanley, '*so* sorry. I was just going to knock. One saw the light under your door and wondered if – you know – one might be of use.'

'You're up late. Come in.'

He came in, embellishing his entrance with thanks and apologies. He wore a dressing gown of Noël Coward vintage and Moroccan slippers. His hair was fluffed up into a little crest like a baby's. In the uncompromising lights of the studio it could be seen that he was not very young.

'I think,' he said, 'it's absolutely fantastic of you to take on all this beastliness. Honestly!'

'Oh,' Alleyn said, 'I'm only treading water, you know, until the proper authorities arrive.'

'A prospect that doesn't exactly fill one with rapture.'

'Why are you abroad so late, Mr Hanley?'

'Couldn't you settle for "Ned"? Mr Hanley makes one feel like an undergraduate getting gated. I'm abroad in the night because I can't sleep. I can't help seeing – everything – her. Whenever I close my eyes – there it is. If I do doze – it's there. Like those crumby old horror films. An awful face suddenly rushing at one. It might as well be one of Dracula's ladies after the full treatment.' He gave a miserable giggle and then looked appalled. 'I shouldn't be like this,' he said. 'Even though, as a matter of fact, it's no more than the truth. But I mustn't bore you with my woes.'

'Where is your room?'

'One flight up. Why? Oh, I see. You're wondering what brought me down here, aren't you? You'll think it very peculiar and it's not easy to explain but actually it was that thing about being drawn towards something that gives one the horrors like edges of precipices and spiders. You know? After trying to sleep and getting nightmares I began to think I had to make myself come down to this floor and cross the landing outside – that room. When I went to bed I actually used the staff stairs to avoid doing that very thing and here I was under this beastly compulsion. So I did it. I hated it and I did it. And in the event there was our rather good-looking chauffeur, Bert, snoring on chairs. He must have very acute hearing, because when I crossed the landing he opened his eyes and stared at me. It was disconcerting because he didn't utter. I lost my head and said: "Oh, hullo, Bert, it's perfectly all right. Don't get up," and made a bolt of it into this passage and saw the light under your door. I seem to be cold. Would you think it too bold if I asked you if I might have a brandy? I didn't downstairs because I make it a rule never to unless the Boss-Man offers and anyway I don't really like the stuff. But I think – tonight – '

'Yes, of course. Help yourself.'

'Terrific,' Hanley said. Alleyn saw him half fill a small tumbler, take a pull at it, shudder violently and close his eyes.

'Would you mind awfully if I turned on that radiator?' he asked. 'Our central heating goes off between twelve and seven.'

Alleyn turned it on. Hanley sat close to it on the edge of the throne and nursed his brandy. 'That's better,' he said. 'I feel much better. Sweet of you to understand.'

Alleyn, as far as he knew, had given no sign of having understood anything. He had been thinking that Hanley was the second distraught visitor to the studio over the past forty-eight hours and that in a way he was a sort of unconvincing parody of Rupert Bartholomew. It struck him that Hanley was making the most of his distress, almost relishing it.

'As you're feeling better,' he suggested, 'perhaps you won't mind putting me straight on one or two domestic matters – especially concerning the servants.'

'If I can,' Hanley said readily enough.

'I hope you can. You've been with Mr Reece for some years, haven't you?'

'Since January 1977. I was a senior secretary with the Hoffman-Beilstein Group in New York. Transferred from their Sydney offices.

The Boss-Man was chums with them in those days and I saw quite a lot of him. And he of me. His secretary had died and in the upshot,' said Hanley, a little too casually, 'I got the job.' He finished his brandy. 'It was all quite amicable and took place during a cruise on the Caribbean in the Hoffman yacht. I was on duty. The Boss-Man was a guest. I think it was then that he found out about the Hoffman-Beilstein organization being naughty. He's absolutely Caesar's Wife himself. Well, you know what I mean. Pure as the driven snow. Incidentally, that was when he first encountered The Lady,' said Hanley and his mouth tightened. 'But without any noticeable reaction. He wasn't really a lady's man.'

'No?'

'Oh no. She made all the running. And, face it, she *was* a collector's piece. It was like pulling off a big deal. As a matter of fact, in my opinion, it was – well – far from being a *grande passion*. Oh dear, there I go again. But it was, as you might say, a very aseptic relationship.'

This chimed, Alleyn thought, with Dr Carmichael's speculation.

'Yes, I see,' he said lightly. 'Has Mr Reece any business relationships with Hoffman-Beilstein?'

'He pulled out. Like I said, he didn't fancy the way things shaped up. There were very funny rumours. He broke everything off after the cruise. Actually he rescued Madame – and me – at the same time. That's how it all started.'

'I see. And now – about the servants.'

'I suppose you mean Marco and Maria, don't you? Straight out of grand opera the two of them. Without the voice for it, of course.'

'Did they come into the household before your time?'

'Maria came with Madame, of course, at the same time as I made my paltry entrance. I understand the Boss-Man produced her. From the Italian Embassy or somewhere rather smooth. But Marco arrived after me.'

'When was that?'

'Three years ago. The Boss-Man wanted a personal servant. I advertised and Marco was easily the best bet. He had marvellous references. We thought that being Italian he might understand Maria and The Lady.'

'Would that be about the time when Strix began to operate?'

'About then, yes,' Hanley agreed and then stared at Alleyn. 'Oh *no!*' he said. 'You're not suggesting? Or are you?'

'I'm not suggesting anything. Naturally I would like to hear more about Strix. Can you give me any idea of how many times the offensive photographs appeared?'

Hanley eyed him warily. 'Not precisely,' he said. 'There had been some on her European tour, before I joined the circus. About six I think. I've filed them and could let you know.'

'Thank you. And afterwards? After you and Marco had both arrived on the scene?'

'Now you'll be making *me* feel awkward. No, of course you won't. I don't mean that. Let me think. There was the one in Double Bay when he bounced round a corner in dark glasses with a scarf over his mouth. And the stage-door débâcle when he was in drag, and the one in Melbourne when he came alongside in a car and shot off before they could see what he was like. *And* of course the *really* awful one on the Opera House steps. There was a rumour then that he was a blond. That's only *four!*' Hanley exclaimed. 'With all the hullabaloo it seemed more like the round dozen. It certainly did the trick with Madame. The *scenes!*' He finished his brandy.

'Did Madame Sommita keep in touch with her family, do you know?'

'I don't think there is any family in Australia. I think I've heard they're all in the States. I don't know what they're called or anything, really, about them. The origins, one understood, were of the earth, earthy.'

'In her circle of acquaintances, are there many – or any – Italians?'

'Well – ' Hanley said, warming slightly to the task, 'let's see. There are the ambassadorial ones. We always make VIP noises about them, of course. And I understand there was a big Italian fan mail in Australia. We've a considerable immigrant population over there, you know.'

'Did you ever hear of anybody called Rossi?'

Hanley shook his head slowly. 'Not to remember.'

'Or Pepitone?'

'No. What an enchanting fun-name. Is he a fan? But, honestly, I don't have anything to do with The Lady's acquaintances or correspondents or on-goings of any sort. If you want to dig into *her* affairs,' said Hanley, and now a sneer was clearly to be heard, 'you'd better ask the infant phenomenon, hadn't you?'

'Bartholomew?'

'Who else? He's supposed to be her secretary. Secretary! My God!'

'You don't approve of Bartholomew?'

'He's marvellous to *look* at, of course.'

'Looks apart?'

'One doesn't want to be catty,' said Hanley, succeeding in being so pretty well, nevertheless, 'but what else is there? The opera? You heard that for yourself. And all that carry-on at the curtain call! I'm afraid I think he's a complete phoney. *And* spiteful with it.'

'Really? Spiteful? You surprise me.'

'Well, look at him. Take, take, take. Everything she could give. But *everything*. All caught up with the opera nonsense and then when it flopped, turning round and making a public fool of himself. *And* her. I could see *right* through the high tragedy bit, don't you worry: it was an act. He blamed her for the disaster. For egging him on. He was getting back on her.' Hanley had spoken rapidly in a high voice. He stopped short, swung round and stared at Alleyn.

'I suppose,' he said, 'I shouldn't say these things to you. For Christ's sake don't go reading something awful into it all. It's just that I got *so* bored with the way everyone fell for the boy-beautiful. *Everyone*. Even the Boss-Man. Until he chickened out and said he wouldn't go on with the show. That put a different complexion on the *affaire*, didn't it? Well, on everything, really. The Boss-Man was livid. Such a change!'

He stood up and carefully replaced his glass on the tray. 'I'm a trifle tiddly,' he said, 'but quite clear in the head. Is it true or did I dream it that the British press used to call you the Handsome Sleuth? Or something like that?'

'You dreamt it,' said Alleyn. 'Good night.'

II

At twenty to three Alleyn had finished his notes. He locked them away in his dispatch case, looked round the studio, turned out the lights and, carrying the case, went out into the passage, locking the door behind him.

And now how quiet was the Lodge. It smelt of new carpets, of dying fires and of the aftermath of food, champagne and cigarettes. It was not altogether silent. There were minuscule sounds suggestive of its adjusting to the storm. As he approached the landing there were Bert's snores to be heard, rhythmic but not very loud.

Alleyn had, by now, a pretty accurate knowledge, acquired on the earlier search, of the Lodge and its sleeping quarters. The principal bedrooms and the studio were all on this floor and opened on to two passages that led off, right and left, from the landing, each taking a right-angled turn after three rooms had been passed. The guests' names were inserted in neat little slots on their doors: à la Versailles, thought Alleyn; they might as well have gone the whole hog while they were about it and used the discriminating *pour*. It would be *Pour Signor Lattienzo*. But he suspected merely *Dr Carmichael*.

He crossed the landing. Bert had left the shaded table lamp on and it softly illuminated his innocent face. As Alleyn passed him he stopped snoring and opened his eyes. They looked at each other for a second or two. Bert said 'Gidday' and went back to sleep.

Alleyn entered the now dark passage on the right of the landing, passed his own bedroom door and thought how strange it was that Troy should be in there and that soon he would be able to join her. He paused for a moment and as he did so heard a door open somewhere beyond the turn of the passage.

The floor, like all floors in this padded house, was thickly carpeted; nevertheless he felt rather than heard somebody walking towards him.

Realizing that he might be silhouetted against the dimly glowing landing, he flattened himself against the wall and slid back to where he remembered seeing a switch for the passage lights. After some groping his hand found it. He turned it on and there, almost within touching distance, was Rupert Bartholomew.

For a moment he thought Rupert would bolt. He had jerked up his hands as if to guard his face. He looked quickly behind him, hesitated, and then seemed to pull himself together.

'It's you,' he whispered. 'You gave me a shock.'

'Wasn't Signor Lattienzo's pill any good?'

'No. I've got to get to the lavatory. I can't wait.'

'There isn't one along here, you must know that.'

'Oh God!' said Rupert loudly. 'Lay off me, can't you?'

'Don't start anything here, you silly chap. Keep your voice down and come to the studio.'

'No.'

'Oh yes you will. Come *on*.'

He took him by the arm.

Down the passage, back across the landing, back past Bert Smith, back into the studio, will this night never end? Alleyn wondered, putting down his dispatch case.

'If you really want the Usual Offices,' he said, 'there's one next door which you know as well as I do and I don't mind betting there's one in your own communicating bathroom. But you *don't* want it, do you?'

'Not now.'

'Where were you bound for?'

'I've told you.'

'Oh, come *on*.'

'Does it matter?'

'Of course it matters, you ass. Ask yourself.'

Silence.

'Well?'

'I left something. Downstairs.'

'What?'

'The score.'

'Of *The Alien Corn*?'

'Yes.'

'Couldn't it wait till daylight? Which is not far off.'

'No.'

'Why?'

'I want to burn it. The score. All the parts. Everything. I woke up and kept thinking of it. There, on the hall fire, burn it, I thought.'

'The fire will probably be out.'

'I'll blow it together,' said Rupert.

'You're making this up as you go along. Aren't you?'

'No. No. Honestly. I swear not. I want to burn it.'

'And anything else?'

He caught back his breath and shook his head.

'Are you *sure* you want to burn it?'

'How many times do I have to say!'

'Very well,' said Alleyn.

'Thank God.'

'I'll come with you.'

'*No*. I mean there's no need. I won't,' said Rupert with a wan attempt at lightness, 'get up to any funny business.'

'Such as?'

'Anything. Nothing. I just don't want an audience. I've had enough of audiences,' said Rupert and contrived a laugh.

'I'll be unobtrusive.'

'You suspect me. Don't you?'

'I suspect a round half-dozen of you. Come on.'

Alleyn took him by the arm.

'I've changed my mind,' Rupert said and broke away.

'If you're thinking I'll go to bed and then you'll pop down by yourself, you couldn't be more mistaken. I'll sit you out.'

Rupert bit his finger and stared at Alleyn. A sudden battering by the gale sent some metal object clattering across the patio down below. Still blowing great guns, thought Alleyn.

'Come along,' he said. 'I'm sorry I've got to be bloody-minded but you might as well take it gracefully. We don't want to do a cinematic roll down the stairs in each other's arms, do we?'

Rupert turned on his heel and walked out of the room. They went together, quickly, to the stairs and down them to the hall.

It was a descent into almost total darkness. A red glow at the far end must come from the embers of the fire and there was a vague, scarcely perceptible luminosity filtered down from the lamp on the landing. Alleyn had put Troy's torch in his pocket and used it. Its beam dodged down the stairs ahead of them.

'There's your fire,' he said. 'Now, I suppose, for the sacrifice.'

He guided Rupert to the back of the hall and through the double doors that opened into the concert chamber. When they were there he shut the doors and turned on the wall lamps. They stood blinking at a litter of discarded programmes, the blank face of the stage curtain, the piano and the players' chairs and music stands with their sheets of manuscript. How long, Alleyn wondered, had it taken Rupert to write them out! And then on the piano, the full score. On the cover *The Alien Corn* painstakingly lettered, 'by Rupert Bartholomew'. And underneath: 'Dedicated to Isabella Sommita.'

'Never mind,' Alleyn said. 'This was only a beginning. Lattienzo thinks you will do better things.'

'Did he say so?'

'He did indeed.'

'The duet, I suppose. He did say something about the duet,' Rupert admitted.

'The duet it was.'

'I rewrote it.'

'So he said. Greatly to its advantage.'

'All the same,' Rupert muttered after a pause, 'I shall burn it.'

'Sure?'

'Absolutely. I'm just going behind. There's a spare copy, I won't be a moment.'

'Hold on,' Alleyn said. 'I'll light you.'

'*No!* Don't bother. Please. I know where the switch is.'

He made for a door in the back wall, stumbled over a music stand and fell. While he was clambering to his feet, Alleyn ran up the apron steps and slipped through the curtains. He crossed upstage and went out by the rear exit arriving in a back passage that ran parallel with the stage and had four doors opening off it.

Rupert was before him. The passage lights were on and a door with a silver star fixed to it was open. The reek of cosmetics flowed out of the room.

Alleyn reached the door. Rupert was in there, too late with the envelope he was trying to stuff into his pocket.

The picture he presented was stagey in the extreme. He looked like an early illustration for a Sherlock Holmes story – the young delinquent caught red-handed with the incriminating document. His eyes even started in the approved manner.

He straightened up, achieved an awful little laugh, and pushed the envelope down in his pocket.

'That doesn't look much like a spare copy of an opera,' Alleyn remarked.

'It's a good luck card I left for her. I – it seemed so ghastly, sitting there. Among the others. *Good Luck!* You know?'

'I'm afraid I don't. Let me see it.'

'No. I can't. It's private.'

'When someone has been murdered,' Alleyn said, 'nothing is private.'

'You can't make me.'

'I could, very easily,' he answered and thought: And how the hell would *that* look in subsequent proceedings?

'You don't understand. It's got nothing to do with what happened. You wouldn't understand.'

'Try me,' Alleyn suggested and sat down.

'No.'

'You know you're doing yourself no good by this,' Alleyn said. 'If whatever's in that envelope has no relevance it will not be brought into the picture. By behaving like this you suggest that it has. You make me wonder if your real object in coming down here was not to destroy your work but to regain possession of this card, if that's what it is.'

'No. *No.* I *am* going to burn the script. I'd made up my mind.'

'Both copies?'

'What? Yes. Yes, of course. I've said so. Both.'

'And where is the second copy, exactly? Not in here?'

'Another room.'

'Come now,' Alleyn said, not unkindly. 'There is no second copy is there? Show me what you have in your pocket.'

'You'd read – all sorts of things – into it.'

'I haven't got that kind of imagination. You might ask yourself, with more cause, what I am likely to read into a persistent refusal to let me see it.'

He spared a thought for what he would in fact be able to do if Rupert *did* persist. With no authority to take possession forcibly, he saw himself spending the fag end of the night in Rupert's room and the coming day until such time as the police might arrive, keeping him under ludicrous surveillance. No. His best bet was to keep the whole thing in as low a key as possible and trust to luck.

'I do wish,' he said, 'that you'd just think sensibly about this. Weigh it up. Ask yourself what a refusal is bound to mean to you and for God's sake cough up with the bloody thing and let's go to bed for what's left of this interminable night.'

He could see the hand working in the pocket and hear paper crumple. He wondered if Rupert tried, foolishly, to tear it. He sat out the silence, read messages of goodwill pinned round the Sommita's looking glass and smelt the age-old incense of the make-up bench. He even found himself, after a fashion, at home.

And there, abruptly, was Rupert, holding out the envelope. Alleyn took it. It was addressed tidily to the Sommita in what looked to be a feminine hand and Alleyn thought had probably enclosed one of the greeting cards. It was unsealed. He drew out the enclosure: a crumpled corner, torn from a sheet of music.

He opened it. The message had been scrawled in pencil and the writing was irregular as if the paper had rested on an uneven surface.

> Soon it will all be over. If I were a Rossi I
> would make a better job of it. R.

Alleyn looked at the message for much longer than it took to read it. Then he returned it to the envelope and put it in his pocket.

'When did you write this?' he asked.

'After the curtain came down. I tore the paper off the score.'

'And wrote it here, in her room?'

'Yes.'

'Did she find you in here when she came for you?'

'I was in the doorway. I'd finished – that.'

'And you allowed yourself to be dragged on?'

'Yes. I'd made up my mind what I'd say. She asked for it,' said Rupert through his teeth, 'and she got it.'

'"Soon it will be all over",' Alleyn quoted. 'What would be over?'

'Everything. The opera. Us. What I was going to do. You heard me, for God's sake. I told them the truth.' Rupert caught his breath back and said: 'I was not planning to kill her, Mr Alleyn. And I did not kill her.'

'I didn't think that even you would have informed her in writing, however ambiguously, of your intention. Would you care to elaborate on the Rossi bit?'

'I wrote that to frighten her. She'd told me about it. One of those Italian family feuds. Mafia sort of stuff. A series of murders and the victim always a woman. She said she was in the direct line to be murdered. She really believed that. She even thought the Strix man might be one of them – the Rossis. She said she'd never spoken about it to anyone else. Something about silence.'

'*Omertà?*'

'Yes. That was it.'

'Why did she tell *you*, then?'

Rupert stamped his feet and threw up his hands. 'Why! Why! Because she wanted me to pity her. It was when I first told her that thing was no good and I couldn't go on with the performance: She – I think she saw that I'd changed. Seen her for what she was. It was awful. I was trapped. From then on I – well, you know, don't you, what it was like. She could still whip up – '

'Yes. All right.'

'Tonight – last night – it all came to a head. I hated her for singing my opera so beautifully. Can you understand that? It was a kind of insult. As if she deliberately showed how worthless it was. She was a vulgar woman, you know. That was why she degraded me. That was what I felt after the curtain fell – degraded – and it was then I knew I hated her.'

'And this was written on the spur of the moment?'

'Of course. I suppose you could say I was sort of beside myself. I can't tell you what it did to me. Standing there. Conducting, for Christ's sake. It was indecent exposure.'

Alleyn said carefully: 'You will realize that I must keep the paper for the time being, at least. I will write you a receipt for it.'

'Do you believe what I've said?'

'That's the sort of question we're not supposed to answer. By and large – yes.'

'Have you finished with me?'

'I think so. For the present.'

'It's an extraordinary thing,' said Rupert. 'And there's no sense in it but I feel better. Horribly tired but – yes – better.'

'You'll sleep now,' Alleyn said.

'I still want to get rid of that abortion.'

Alleyn thought wearily that he supposed he ought to prevent this but said he would look at the score. They switched off the backstage lights and went to the front-of-house. Alleyn sat on the apron steps and turned through the score, forcing himself to look closely at each page. All those busy little black marks that had seemed so eloquent, he supposed, until the moment of truth came to Rupert and all the strangely unreal dialogue that librettists put in the mouths of their singers. Remarks like: 'What a comedy!' and 'Do I dream?' and 'If she were mine.'

He came to the last page and found that, sure enough, the corner had been torn off. He looked at Rupert and found he was sound asleep in one of the VIP chairs.

Alleyn gathered the score and separate parts together, put them beside Rupert and touched his shoulder. He woke with a start as if tweaked by a puppeteer.

'If you are still of the same mind,' Alleyn said, 'it's all yours.'

So Rupert went to the fireplace in the hall where the embers glowed. Papers bound solidly together are slow to burn. *The Alien Corn* merely smouldered, blackened and curled. Rupert used an oversized pair of bellows and flames crawled round the edges. He threw on loose sheets from the individual parts and these burst at once into flame and flew up the chimney. There was a basket of kindling by the hearth. He began to heap it on the fire in haphazard industry as if to put his opera out of its misery. Soon firelight and shadows leapt about the hall. The pregnant woman looked like a smirking candidate for martyrdom. At one moment the solitary dagger on the wall flashed red. At another the doors into the concert chamber appeared momentarily and once the stairs were caught by an erratic flare.

It was then that Alleyn caught sight of a figure on the landing. It stood with its hands on the balustrade and its head bent, looking down into the hall. Its appearance was as brief as a thought, a fraction of a fraction of a second. The flare expired and when it fitfully reappeared whoever it was up there had gone.

Bert? Alleyn didn't think so. It had, he felt sure, worn a dressing gown or overcoat but beyond that there had been no impression of an individual among the seven men, any one of whom might have been abroad in the night.

At its end *The Alien Corn* achieved dramatic value. The wind howled in the chimney, blazing logs fell apart and what was left of the score flew up and away. The last they saw of it was a floating ghost of black thread-paper with 'dedicated to Isabella Sommita' in white showing for a fraction of a second before it too disintegrated and was gone up the chimney.

Without a word Rupert turned away and walked quickly upstairs. Alleyn put a fireguard across the hearth. When he turned away he noticed, on a table inside the front entrance, a heavy canvas bag with a padlock and chain: the mailbag. Evidently it should have gone off with the launch and in the confusion had been overlooked.

Alleyn followed Rupert upstairs. The house was now very quiet. He fancied there were longer intervals between the buffets of the storm.

When he reached the landing he was surprised to find Rupert still there and staring at the sleeping Bert.

Alleyn murmured: 'You've got a key to that door, haven't you?'

'Didn't you get it?' Rupert whispered.

'I? Get it? What do you mean?'

'She said you wanted it.'

'Who did?'

'Maria.'

'When?'

'After you and the doctor left my room. After I'd gone to bed. She came and asked for the key.'

'Did you give it to her?'

'Yes, of course. For you.' Alleyn drew in his breath. 'I didn't want it,' Rupert whispered. 'My God! Go into that room! See her! *Like that.*'

Alleyn waited for several seconds before he asked: 'Like what?'

'Are you mad?' Rupert asked. 'You've seen her. A nightmare.'

'So *you've* seen her too?'

And then Rupert realized what he had said. He broke into a jumble of whispered expostulations and denials. Of course he hadn't seen her. Maria had told him what it was like. Maria had described it. Maria had said Alleyn had sent her for the key.

He ran out of words, made a violent gesture of dismissal and bolted. Alleyn heard his door slam.

And at last Alleyn himself went to bed. The clock on the landing struck four as he walked down the passage to their room. When he parted the window curtains there was a faint greyness in the world outside. Troy was fast asleep.

III

Marco brought their breakfast at eight o'clock. Troy had been awake for an hour. She had woken when Alleyn came to bed and had lain quiet and waited to see if he wanted to talk but he had touched her head lightly and in a matter of seconds was dead to the world.

It was not his habit to use a halfway interval between sleep and wake. He woke like a cat, fully and instantly, and gave Marco good morning. Marco drew the curtains and the room was flooded with pallid light. There was no rain on the window-panes and no sound of wind.

'Clearing is it?' Alleyn asked.

'Yes, sir. Slowly. The lake is still very rough.'

'Too rough for the launch?'

'Too much rough, sir, certainly.'

He placed elaborate trays across them both and brought them extra pillows. His dark rather handsome head came close to theirs.

'It must be quite a sight – the lake and the mountains?' Alleyn said lightly.

'Very impressive, sir.'

'Your mysterious photographer should be there again with his camera.'

A little muscle jumped under Marco's olive cheek.

'It is certain he has gone, sir. But of course you are joking.'

'Do you know exactly how Madame Sommita was murdered, Marco? The details?'

'Maria is talking last night but she is excitable. When she is excitable she is not reasonable. Or possible to understand. It is all,' said Marco, 'very dreadful, sir.'

'They forgot to take the mailbag to the launch last night. Had you noticed?'

Marco knocked over the marmalade pot on Troy's tray.

'I am very sorry, madame,' he said. 'I am clumsy.'

'It's all right,' Troy said. 'It hasn't spilt.'

'Do you know what I think, Marco?' said Alleyn. 'I think there never was a strange photographer on the Island.'

'Do you, sir? Thank you, sir. Will that be all?'

'Do you have a key to the postbag?'

'It is kept in the study, sir.'

'And is the bag unlocked during the time it is in the house?'

'There is a posting-box in the entrance, sir. Mr Hanley empties it into the bag when it is time for the launchman to take it.'

'Too bad he overlooked it last night.'

Marco, sheet-white, bowed and left the room.

'And I suppose,' Troy ventured, 'I pretend I didn't notice you've terrified the pants off that poor little man.'

'Not such a poor little man.'

'Not?'

'I'm afraid not.'

'Rory,' said his wife. 'Under ordinary circumstances I never, *never* ask about cases. Admit.'

'My darling, you are perfection in that as in all other respects. You never do.'

'Very well. These circumstances are *not* ordinary and if you wish me to give my customary imitation of a violet by a mossy stone half hidden *from* the view you must also be prepared for me to spontaneously combust.'

'Upon my word, love, I can't remember how much you do or do not know of our continuing soap opera. Let us eat our breakfasts and you ask questions the while. When, by the way, did we last meet? Not counting bed.'

'When I gave you the powder and brush in the studio. Remember?'

'Ah yes. Oh, and thank you for the dispatch case. Just what I wanted, like a Christmas present. You don't know *how* she was killed, do you?

'Signor Lattienzo told me. Remember?'

'Ah yes. He came up to the studio, didn't he?'

'Yes. To see if I was all right. It was kind of him, really.'

'Very,' said Alleyn drily.

'Don't you like him?'

'Did he tell you in detail?'

'Just that she was stabbed. At first it seemed unreal. Like more bad opera. You know his flowery way of saying things. And then, of course, when it got real – quite appalling. It's rather awful to be wallowing between silken sheets, crunching toast while we talk about it,' said Troy, 'but I happen to be hungry.'

'You wouldn't help matters if you suddenly decided to diet.'

'True.'

'I think I'd better tell you the events of the night in order of occurrence. Or, no,' said Alleyn. 'You can read my file. While you're doing that I'll get up and see if Bert is still on duty, poor chap.'

'Bert? The chauffeur?'

'That's right. I won't be long.'

He gave her the file, put on his dressing gown and slippers and went out to the landing. Bert was up and slightly dishevelled. The chairs still barricaded the door.

'Gidday,' he said. 'Glad to see you.'

'I'm sorry I've left it so late. Did you have a beastly night of it?'

'Naow. She was good. Wee bit draughty but we mustn't grumble.'

'Anything to report?'

'Maria. At four-twenty. I'm right out to it but I reckon she must of touched me because I open my eyes and there she bloody is, hanging over me with a key in her hand looking as if she's trying to nut it out how to get the door open. Brainless. I say: "What's the big idea?" and she lets out a screech and drops the key. On me. Plonk. No trouble.'

'And did you – ?'

'Grab it. Kind of reflex action, really.'

'You didn't give it back to her, Bert?'

Bert assumed a patient, quizzical expression and produced the key from his trouser pocket.

'Good *on* you, boy,' said Alleyn, displaying what he hoped was the correct idiom and the proper show of enthusiasm. He clapped Bert on the shoulder. 'What was her reaction?' he asked and wondered if he too ought to adopt the present tense.

'She's moanin',' said Bert.

'Moaning?'

'This is right. Complainin'. Reckonin' she'll put my pot on with the boss. Clawin' at me to get it back. Reckonin' she wants to lay out the deceased and say prayers and that lot. But never raising her voice, mind. Never once. When she sees it's no dice and when I tell her I'll hand the key over to you she spits in my face, no trouble, and beats it downstairs.'

'That seems to be the Maria form. I'll take the key, Bert, and thank you very much indeed. Do you happen to know how many keys there are to the room? Four, is it?'

'That's right. To all the rooms. Weird idea.'

Alleyn thought: This one, which was Rupert Bartholomew's. The one already in my pocket which was Maria's, the housekeeper's key, and the Sommita's in her evening bag at the bottom of her dressing-table drawer.

He said: 'While I think of it. On the way over here you said something about a vet putting down Madame Sommita's dog. You said he chloroformed it before giving it the injection.'

'That's correct,' said Bert looking surprised.

'Do you remember by any chance what happened to the bottle?'

Bert stared at him. 'That's a hairy one,' he said. 'What happened to the bottle, eh?' He scratched his head and pulled a face. 'Hold on,' he said. 'Yeah! That's right. He put it on a shelf in the hangar and for-got to take it away.'

'And would you,' said Alleyn, 'know what became of it? Is it still there?'

'No, it is not. Maria come out to see if it was all OK about the dog. She'd been sent by the Lady. She seen the bottle. It was, you know, labelled. She reckoned it wasn't safe having it lying around. She took it off.'

'Did she indeed?' said Alleyn. 'Thank you, Bert.'

'Be my guest.'

Alleyn said: 'Well, you'd better get something to eat, hadn't you?'

'I don't mind if I do,' said Bert. 'Seeing you,' and went, in a leisurely manner, downstairs.

Alleyn returned to their bedroom. Troy was deep in the file and continued to read it while he shaved, bathed and dressed. Occasionally she shouted an enquiry or a comment. She had just fin-ished it and was about to get up when there was a tap on the door. Alleyn opened it and there was Mrs Bacon, trim and competent: the very epitome of the five-star housekeeper.

'Good morning, Mr Alleyn,' said Mrs Bacon. 'I've just come up to see if Mrs Alleyn has everything she wants. I'm afraid, in all this disturbance, she may have been neglected and we can't have that, can we?'

Alleyn said we couldn't and Troy called out for her to come in.

When she had been assured of Troy's well-being, Mrs Bacon told Alleyn she was glad of the opportunity to have a word with him. 'There are difficulties. It's very inconvenient,' she said as if the plumbing had failed them.

'I'm sure it is,' he said. 'If there's anything I can do – '

'It's Maria.'

'Is she still cutting up rough?'

'Indeed she is.' Mrs Bacon turned to Troy. 'This is all so unpleasant, Mrs Alleyn,' she apologized. 'I'm sorry to bring it up!'

The Alleyns made appropriate noises.

'Of course she *is* upset,' Mrs Bacon conceded. 'We understand that, don't we? But really!'

'What form is it taking now?' Alleyn asked.

'She wants to go – in there.'

'Still on that lay, is she? Well, she can't.'

'She – being a Catholic, of course, one should make allowances,' Mrs Bacon herself astonishingly allowed. 'I hope you're not – ?' she hurriedly added, turning pink. 'And, of course, being a foreigner should be taken into consideration. But it's getting more than a joke. She wants to lay Madame out. I was wondering if – just to satisfy her?'

'I'm afraid not, Mrs Bacon,' Alleyn said, 'the body must be left as it is until the police have seen it.'

'That's what they always say in the thrillers, of course. I know that, but I thought it might be an exaggeration.'

'Not in this instance at any rate.'

'She's worrying Mr Reece about it. He's spoken to me. He's very much shocked, you can sense that, although he doesn't allow himself to show it. He told me everything must be referred to you. I think he would like to see you.'

'Where is he?'

'In the study. That Italian gentleman, Mr Lattienzo, and Mr Ruby are with him. And then,' Mrs Bacon went on, 'there are the two ladies, the singers, who stayed last night, I must say what I can to them. They'll be wondering. Really, it's almost more than one can be expected to cope with.'

'Maddening for you,' said Troy.

'Well, it *is*. And the staff! The two housemaids are talking themselves into hysterics and refusing to come up to this landing and
the men are not much better. I thought I could depend on Marco
but he's suddenly gone peculiar and doesn't seem to hear when
he's spoken to. Upon my word,' said Mrs Bacon, 'I'll be glad to see
the police on the premises and I never thought to say *that* in my
occupation.'

'Can't Hanley help out?' asked Alleyn.

'Not really. They all giggle at him, or did when they had a giggle
left in them. I told them they were making a mistake. It's obvious
what he is, of course, but that doesn't mean he's not competent. Far
from it. He's very shrewd and very capable and he and I get on quite
well. I really don't know,' Mrs Bacon exclaimed, 'why I'm boring
you like this! I must be going off at the deep end, myself.'

'Small wonder if you did,' said Troy. 'Look, don't worry about the
rooms. How about you and me whipping round when they're all out
of them.'

'Oh!' cried Mrs Bacon. 'I couldn't dream of it.'

'Yes, you could. Or, I tell you what. I'll talk to Miss Dancy and
Miss Parry and see how they feel about a bit of bedmaking. Do us all
good instead of sitting round giving each other the jim-jams.
Wouldn't it, Rory?'

'Certainly,' said Alleyn and put his arm round her.

'Are they in their rooms? I'll ring them up,' Troy offered.

'If you don't mind my saying so, Mrs Alleyn, you're a darling.
Their breakfasts went up at eight-thirty. They'll still be in bed,
eating it.'

'One of them isn't,' said Alleyn who had gone to the window.
'Look.'

The prospect from their windows commanded the swimming
pool on the extreme left and the hangar on the right. In the centre,
Lake Waihoe swept turbulently away into nothing. The mountains
that rose from its far shore had been shut off by a curtain of ashen
cloud. The fringes of trees that ran out into the lake were intermittently wind-whipped. The waters tumbled about the shore, washed
over the patio and reared and collapsed into the brimming pool
which still overflowed its borders.

And down below on the bricked terrace, just clear of the water stood Rupert and a figure in a heavy mackintosh and sou'wester so much too big that it was difficult to identify as Miss Sylvia Parry.

Mrs Bacon joined Alleyn at the window. 'Well,' she said after a pause. 'If that's what it seems to be it's a pity it didn't develop when he was going away for days at a time for all those rehearsals.'

'Where was that?'

'On the other side – at a Canterbury seaside resort. The chopper used to take him over and he stayed the night. Mr Reece had them all put up at the Carisbrook. Luxury. Seven star,' said Mrs Bacon. 'They rehearsed in a local hall and gave concerts.'

Down below Rupert was speaking. The girl touched his arm and he took her hand in his. They remained like that for some moments. It had begun fitfully to rain again. He led her out of sight, presumably into the house.

'Nice girl,' said Mrs Bacon crisply. 'Pity. Oh well, you never know, do you?'

She made for the door.

Alleyn said: 'Wait a second, Mrs Bacon. Listen. Troy, listen.'

They listened. As always when an imposed silence takes over, the background of household sounds that had passed unnoticed and the voice of the wind outside to which they had grown inattentive, declared themselves. Behind them, very distant but thinly clear, was the sound of a bell.

'Les, by Heaven!' said Alleyn. 'Here! Mrs Bacon, have you got a bell in the house? A big bell?'

'No,' she said, startled.

'A gong?'

'Yes. We don't use it.'

'Bring it out on the terrace, please. Or get the men to bring it. And field glasses. I saw a pair in the hall, didn't I? But quick.'

He pulled the slips off two of their pillows and ran down the hall and out on the terrace to a point from which the jetty and boathouse could be seen across the lake. Out here the sound of the bell was louder and echoed in the unseen hills.

It was ringing irregularly: long-spaced notes mixed with quick short-spaced ones.

'Bless his heart he's signalling again,' said Alleyn. He got out his notebook and pen and set himself to read the code. It was a shortish sequence confused by its echo and repeated after a considerable pause. The second time round he got it. *Police informed*, Les signalled.

Alleyn, hoping he was a fairly conspicuous figure from the boatshed, had begun a laborious attempt at semaphoring with pillowcases when Bert and Marco piloted by Mrs Bacon staggered out of the house bearing an enormous Burmese gong on a carved stand. They set it up on the terrace. Alleyn discarded his pillowcases and whacked out a booming acknowledgement. This too set up an echo. *Received and understood thanks.*

It struck him that he had created a picture worthy of Salvador Dali – a Burmese gong on an island in New Zealand, a figure beating it – pillowslips on a wet shore and on the far shore another figure, waving. And in the foreground a string of unrelated persons strung out at intervals. For, in addition to trim Mrs Bacon, Dr Carmichael, Hanley, Ben Ruby, Signor Lattienzo and Mr Reece, in that order, had come out of the house.

Mrs Bacon gave Alleyn the binoculars. He focused them and Les, the launchman, jumped up before him. He was wearing a red woollen cap and oilskins. He wiped his nose with a mittened hand and pointed in the direction of the rustic belfry. He was going to signal again. He gesticulated, as much as to say 'Hold on', and went into the belfry.

'*Doyng!*' said the bell. ' '*oyng*, '*oyng*, '*oyng*,' said the echo.

This time Alleyn got it first time. *Launch engine crook* it read and was repeated. *Launch engine crook.*

'Hell!' said Alleyn and took it out on the gong.

Mr Reece, wearing an American sporting raincoat and hogskin gloves, was at his elbow. 'What's the message?' he asked.

'Shut up,' said Alleyn. 'Sorry. He's at it again.'

Les signalled: '*Hope temporary.*'

'*Bang!*' Alleyn acknowledged. ' '*ang*, '*ang*, '*ang*,' said the echo.

'*Over and out*,' signalled Les.

'Bang.'

Alleyn followed Les through the binoculars down to the jetty which was swept at intervals by waves. He saw Les dodge the waves, board the launch, jouncing at its moorings, and disappear into the engine room.

He gave Mr Reece a full account of the exchange.

'I must apologize for my incivility,' he said.

Mr Reece waved it aside. 'So if the lake becomes navigable,' he said, 'we are still cut off.'

'He did say he hopes the trouble's temporary. And by the time he's fixed it, surely the wind will have dropped and the helicopter will become a possibility.'

'The helicopter is in Canterbury. It took the piano-tuner back yesterday afternoon and remained on the other side.'

'Nobody loves us,' said Alleyn. 'Could I have a word with you, indoors?'

'Certainly. Alone?'

'It might be as well, I think.'

When they went indoors Alleyn was given an illustration of Mr Reece's gift of authority. Signor Lattienzo and Ben Ruby clearly expected to return with him to the study. Hanley hovered. Without saying a word to any of them but with something in his manner that was perfectly explicit Mr Reece gave them to understand that this was not to be.

Signor Lattienzo who was rigged out in a shepherd's cape and a Tyrolean hat said: 'My dear Ben, it is not raining. Should we perhaps, for the good of our digestions, venture a modest step or two abroad? To the landing and back? What do you say?'

Mr Ruby agreed without enthusiasm.

Mr Reece said to Hanley: 'I think the ladies have come down. Find out if there is anything we can do for them, will you? I shan't need you at present.'

'Certainly, sir,' said Hanley.

Dr Carmichael returned from outside. Alleyn suggested to their host that perhaps he might join them in the study.

When they were once more seated in the huge soft leather chairs of that singularly negative apartment, Alleyn said he thought that Mr Reece would probably like to know about the events of the previous night.

He went over them in some detail, making very little of Rupert's bonfire and quite a lot of Maria's on-goings and Bert's vigil. Mr Reece listened with his habitual passivity. Alleyn thought it quite possible that he had gone his own rounds during the night and wondered if it was he who had looked down from the landing. It would somehow be in character for Mr Reece not to mention his prowl but to allow Alleyn to give his own account of the bonfire without interruption.

Alleyn said: 'I hope you managed to get some sleep last night.'

'Not very much, I confess. I am not a heavy sleeper at normal times. You wanted to see me?'

'I'd better explain. I seem to be forever raising the cry that I am really, as indeed we all are, treading water until the police arrive. It's difficult to decide how far I can, with propriety, probe. The important thing has been to make sure, as far as possible, that there has been no interference at the scene of the crime. I thought perhaps you might be prepared to give me some account of Madame Sommita's background and of any events that might, however remotely, have some bearing on this appalling crime.'

'I will tell you anything I can, of course.'

'Please don't feel you are under any obligation to do so. Of course you are not. And if my questions are impertinent we'll make it a case of "No comment" and, I hope, no bones broken.'

Mr Reece smiled faintly. 'Very well,' he said, 'agreed.'

'You see, it's like this. I've been wondering, as of course we all have, if the crime ties up in any way with the Strix business and if it does whether the motive could be a long-standing affair. Based, perhaps, on some sort of enmity. Like the Macdonalds and the Campbells, for instance. Not that in this day and age they have recourse to enormities of that kind. Better perhaps to instance the Montagues and Capulets.'

Mr Reece's faint smile deepened.

He said, "You are really thinking more of the Lucianos and Costellos, aren't you?'

Alleyn thought: He's rumbled that one pretty smartly, and he said: 'Yes, in a way, I am. It's the Italian background that put it into my head. The whole thing is so shockingly outlandish and – well – theatrical. I believe Madame Sommita was born a Pepitone: a Sicilian.'

'You are very well-informed.'

'Oh,' Alleyn said, 'when we got your letter, asking me to come out with Troy and take a look at the Strix business, the Yard did a bit of research. It did seem a remote possibility that Strix might be acting as an agent of sorts. I was going to ask you if such an idea, or something at all like it, had ever occurred to you.'

With more animation than one might have supposed him to be capable of, Mr Reece gave a dismal little laugh and brought the palms of his hands down on the arms of his chair. He actually raised his voice.

'*Occurred to me!*' he exclaimed. 'You've got, as they say, to be joking, Mr Alleyn. How could it not have occurred to me when she herself brought it to my notice day in, day out, ever since this wretched photographer came on the scene.'

He paused and looked very hard at Alleyn who merely replied: 'She did?'

'She most certainly did. It was an obsession with her. Some family feud that had started generations ago in Sicily. She persuaded herself that it had cropped up again in Australia of all places. She really believed she was next in line for – elimination. It was no good telling her that this guy Strix was in it for the money. She would listen, say nothing, calm down and then when you thought you'd got somewhere simply say she *knew*. I made enquiries. I talked to the police in Australia and the USA. There was not a shred of evidence to support the idea. But she couldn't be moved.'

'Last night you said you were certain Strix was her murderer.'

'Because of what you told me about – the photograph. That seemed to be – still seems to be – so much in character with the sort of thing she said these people do. It was as if the man had signed his work and wanted to make sure it was recognized. As if I had been wrong and she had been right – right to be terrified. That we should have had her fully guarded. That I am responsible. And this,' said Mr Reece, 'is a very, very dreadful thought, Mr Alleyn.'

'It may turn out to be a mistaken thought. Tell me, how much do you know about Madame Sommita's background – her early life? Her recent associates?'

Mr Reece clasped his large well-kept hands and tapped them against his lower teeth. He frowned and seemed to be at a loss. At last he said: 'That is difficult to answer. How much do I know? In some ways a lot, in others very little. Her mother died in childbirth. She was educated at convent schools in the USA, the last being in New York where her voice was first trained. I got the impression that she saw next to nothing of her father, who lived in Chicago and died when Bella was twelve years old. She was brought up by an aunt of sorts who accompanied her to Italy and is now deceased. There used to be confused allusions to this reputed feud but in a way they were reticent – generalizations, nothing specific. Only these – these expressions of fear. I am afraid I thought they were little more than fairytales. I knew how she exaggerated and dramatized everything.'

'Did she ever mention the name Rossi?'

'Rossi? It sounds familiar. Yes, I believe she may have but she didn't, as a matter of fact, mention names – Italian names – when she talked about this threat. She would seem as if she was going to but if I asked her point blank to be specific in order that I could make enquiries, she merely crossed herself and wouldn't utter. I'm afraid I found that exasperating. It confirmed me in the opinion that the whole thing was imaginary.'

'Yes, I see.' Alleyn put his hand in his overcoat pocket, drew out the book from the library and handed it to Mr Reece. 'Have you ever seen this?' he asked.

He took it and turned it over distastefully.

'Not that I remember,' he said. He opened it and read the title, translating it. '*The Mystery of Bianca Rossi*. Oh, I see – Rossi. What is all this, Mr Alleyn?'

'I don't know. I hoped you might throw some light on it.'

'Where did you find it? In her room?' he asked.

'In the library. Have you noticed the name on the flyleaf?'

Mr Reece looked at it. 'M. V. Rossi,' he said. And then: 'I can't make any sense out of this. Do we assume it was hers?'

'It will be fingerprinted, of course.'

'Ah yes. Oh, I see. I shouldn't have handled it, should I?'

'I don't think you've done any damage,' Alleyn said, and took it from him.

'If it was Bella's she may have left it lying about somewhere and one of the servants put it in the library. We can ask.'

'So we can. Leaving it for the moment: did you ever hear of her association with the Hoffman-Beilstein group?'

It was curious to see how immediate was Mr Reece's return to his own world of financial expertise. He at once became solemn, disapproving and grand.

'I certainly did,' he said shortly and shot an appraising glance at Alleyn. 'Again,' he said, 'you seem to be well-informed.'

'I thought I remembered,' Alleyn improvised, 'seeing press photographs of her in a group of guests aboard Hoffman's yacht.'

'I see. It was not a desirable association. I broke it off.'

'He came to grief, didn't he?'

'Deservedly so,' said Mr Reece, pursing his mouth rather in the manner of a disapproving governess. Perhaps he felt he could not quite leave it at that because he added, stuffily, as if he was humouring an inquisitive child: 'Hoffman had approached me with a view to interesting me in an enterprise he hoped to float. Actually, he invited me to join the cruise you allude to. I did so and was confirmed in my opinion of his activities.' Mr Reece waited for a moment. 'As a matter of fact,' he said, 'it was then that I met one of his executives – young Ned Hanley. I considered he might well come to grief in that company and as I required a private secretary, offered him the position.' He looked much more fixedly at Alleyn. 'Has he been prattling?' he asked and Alleyn thought: He's formidable, all right.

'No, no,' he said. 'Not indiscreetly, I promise you. I asked him how long he'd been in your employ and he simply arrived at the answer by recalling the date of the cruise.'

'He talks too much,' said Mr Reece, dismissing him, but with an air of – what? Indulgence? Tolerance? Proprietorship? He turned to Dr Carmichael. 'I wanted to speak to you, Doctor,' he said. 'I want to hear from you exactly how my friend was killed. I do not wish, if it can be spared me, to see her again as she was last night and I presume still is. But I must know how it was done. I must *know*.'

Dr Carmichael glanced at Alleyn who nodded very slightly.

'Madame Sommita,' said Dr Carmichael, 'was almost certainly anaesthetized, probably asphyxiated, when she had become unconscious and, after death, stabbed. There will be an autopsy, of course, which will tell us more.'

'Did she suffer?'

'I think, most unlikely.'

'Anaesthetized? With what? How?'

'I suspect, chloroform.'

'But – chloroform? Do you mean somebody came here prepared to commit this crime? Provided?'

'It looks like it. Unless there was chloroform somewhere on the premises.'

'Not to my knowledge. I can't imagine it.'

Alleyn suddenly remembered the gossip of Bert the chauffeur. 'Did you by any chance have a vet come to the house?' he asked.

'Ah! Yes. Yes, we did. To see Isabella's Afghan hound. She was very – distressed. The vet examined the dog under an anaesthetic and found it had a malignant growth. He advised that it be put down immediately and it was done.'

'You wouldn't of course know if by any chance the vet forgot to take the chloroform away with him?'

'No. Ned might know. He superintended the whole thing.'

'I'll ask him,' said Alleyn.

'Or perhaps Marco,' speculated Mr Reece. 'I seem to remember he was involved.'

'Ah yes. Marco,' said Alleyn. 'You have told me, haven't you, that Marco is completely dependable.'

'Certainly. I have no reason to suppose anything else.'

'In the very nature of the circumstances and the development of events as we hear about them, we must all have been asking ourselves disturbing questions about each other, mustn't we? Have you not asked yourself disturbing questions about Marco?'

'Well, of course I have,' Mr Reece said at once. 'About him, and, as you say, about all of them. But there is no earthly reason, no conceivable motive for Marco to do anything – wrong.'

'Not if Marco should happen to be Strix?' Alleyn asked.

CHAPTER 7

Strix

When Alleyn and Dr Carmichael joined Troy in the studio rifts had appeared in the rampart of clouds and at intervals, shafts of sunlight played fitfully across Lake Waihoe and struck up patches of livid green on mountain flanks that had begun to reappear through the mist.

The landing stage was still under turbulent water. No one could have used it. There were now no signs of Les on the mainland.

'You gave Mr Reece a bit of a shake-up,' said Dr Carmichael. 'Do you think he was right when he said the idea had never entered his head?'

'What, that Marco was Strix? Who can tell? I imagine Marco has been conspicuously zealous in the anti-Strix cause. His reporting an intruder on the Island topped up with his production of the lens cap was highly convincing. Remember how you all plunged about in the undergrowth? I suppose you assisted in the search for nobody, didn't you?'

'Blast!' said Dr Carmichael.

'Incidentally the cap was a mistake, a fancy touch too many. It's off a mass-produced camera, probably his own, as it were, official toy and not at all the sort of job that Strix must use to get his results. Perhaps he didn't want to part with the Strix cap and hadn't quite got the nerve to produce it or perhaps it hasn't got a cap.'

'Why,' asked Troy, 'did he embark on all that nonsense about an intruder?'

'Well, darling, don't you think because he intended to take a "Strix" photograph of the Sommita – his *bonne bouche* – and it

157

seemed advisable to plant the idea that a visiting Strix was lurking in the underbrush. But the whole story of the intruder was fishy. The search party was a shocking-awful carry-on but by virtue of sheer numbers someone would have floundered into an intruder if he'd been there.'

'And you are certain,' said Dr Carmichael, 'that he is not your man?'

'He couldn't be. He was waiting in the dining room and busy in the hall until the guests left and trotting to and from the launch with an umbrella while they were leaving.'

'And incidentally in the porch, with me, watching the launch after they had gone. Yes. That's right,' agreed Dr Carmichael.

'Is Mr Reece going to tackle him about Strix?' Troy asked.

'Not yet. He says he's not fully persuaded. He prefers to leave it with me.'

'And you?'

'I'm trying to make up my mind. On the whole I think it may be best to settle Strix before the police get here.'

'Now?'

'Why not?'

Troy said: 'Of course he knows you're on to it. After your breakfast-tray remarks.'

'He's got a pretty good idea of it, at least,' said Alleyn and put his thumb on the bell.

'Perhaps he won't come.'

'I think he will. What's the alternative? Fling himself into the billowy wave and do a Leander for the mainland?'

'Shall I disappear?' offered Dr Carmichael.

'And I?' said Troy.

'Not unless you'd rather. After all, I'm not going to arrest him.'

'Oh? Not?' they said.

'Why would I do that? For being Strix? I've no authority. Or do you think we might borrow him for being a public nuisance or perhaps for false pretences? On my information he's never actually conned anybody. He's just dressed himself up funny-like and taken unflattering photographs. There's the forged letter in *The Watchman*, of course. That might come within the meaning of some act: I'd have to look it up. Oh yes, and makes himself out to be a gentleman's gent, with forged references, I dare say.'

'Little beast,' said Troy. 'Cruel little pig, tormenting her like that. And everybody thinking it a jolly joke. And the shaming thing is, it *was* rather funny.'

'That's the worst of ill-doing, isn't it? It so often has its funny side. Come to think of it, I don't believe I could have stuck my job out if it wasn't so. The earliest playwrights knew all about that: their devils more often than not were clowns and their clowns were always cruel. Here we go.'

There had been a tap at the door. It opened and Marco came in.

He was an unattractive shade of yellow but otherwise looked much as usual. He said: 'You rang, sir?'

'Yes,' Alleyn agreed. 'I rang. I've one or two questions to ask you. First, about the photograph you took yesterday afternoon through the window of the concert chamber. Did you put the print in the letter-bag?'

'I don't know what you mean, sir.'

'Yes, you do. You are Strix. You got yourself into your present job with the intention of following up your activities with the camera. Stop me if I'm wrong. But on second thoughts you're more likely to stop me if I'm right, aren't you? Did you see the advertisement for a personal servant for Mr Reece in the paper? Did it occur to you that as a member of Mr Reece's entourage you would be able to learn a lot more about Madame Sommita's programmes for the day? On some occasion when she was accompanied by Mr Reece or when Mr Reece was not at home and you were not required, you would be able to pop out to a room you kept for the purpose, dress yourself up like a sore thumb, startle her and photograph her with her mouth open looking ridiculous. You would hand the result in to the press and notch up another win. It was an impudently bold decision and it worked. You gave satisfaction as a valet and came here with your employer.'

Marco had assumed an air of casual insolence.

'Isn't it marvellous?' he asked of nobody in particular and shrugged elaborately.

'You took yesterday's photograph with the intention of sending it back to *The Watchman* and through them to the chain of newspapers with whom you've syndicated your productions. I know you did this. Your footprints are underneath the window. I fancy this was to be your final impertinence and that having knocked it off you would have given in your notice, claimed your money, retired to some inconspicuous retreat and written your autobiography.'

'No comment,' said Marco.

'I didn't really suppose there would be. Do you know where that photograph is now? Do you, Marco?'

'I don't know anything about any —ing photograph,' said Marco, whose Italian accent had become less conspicuous and his English a good deal more idiomatic.

'It is skewered by a dagger to your victim's dead body.'

'My victim! She was not my victim. Not – ' He stopped.

'Not in the sense of your having murdered her, were you going to say?'

'Not in any sense. I don't,' said Marco, 'know what you're talking about.'

'And I don't expect there'll be much trouble about finding your fingerprints on the glossy surface.'

Marco's hand went to his mouth.

'Come,' Alleyn said, 'don't you think you're being unwise? What would you say if I told you your room will be searched?'

'Nothing!' said Marco loudly. 'I would say nothing. You're welcome to search my room.'

'Do you carry the camera – is it a Strassman, by the way? – on you? How about searching *you*?'

'You have no authority.'

'That is unfortunately correct. See here, Marco. Just take a look at yourself. I shall tell the police what I believe to be the facts: that you are Strix, that you took the photograph now transfixed over Madame Sommita's heart, that it probably carries your fingerprints. If it does not, it is no great matter. Faced by police investigation, the newspapers that bought your photographs will identify you.'

'They've never seen me,' Marco said quickly and then looked as if he could have killed himself.

'It was all done by correspondence, was it?'

'They've never seen me because I'm not – I've never had anything to do with them. You're putting words in my mouth.'

'Your Strix activities have come to an end. The woman you tormented is dead, you've made a packet and will make more if you write a book. With illustrations. The only thing that is likely to bother you is the question of how the photograph got from your camera to the body. The best thing you can do if you're not the murderer of Isabella Sommita is help us find out who *is*. If you refuse, you remain a prime suspect.'

Marco looked from Troy to Dr Carmichael and back to Troy again. It was as if he asked for their advice. Troy turned away to the studio window.

Dr Carmichael said: 'You'd much better come across, you know. You'll do yourself no good by holding back.'

There was a long silence.

'Well,' said Marco at last and stopped.

'Well?' said Alleyn.

'I'm not admitting anything.'

'But suppose – ?' Alleyn prompted.

'Suppose, for the sake of argument, Strix took the shot you talk about. What *would* he do with it? He'd post if off to *The Watchman* at once, wouldn't he? He'd put it in the mailbox to be taken away in the bag.'

'Or,' Alleyn suggested, 'to avoid Mr Hanley noticing it when he cleared the box he might slip it directly into the mailbag while it was still unlocked and waiting in the study.'

'He might do that.'

'Is that what you'd say he did?'

'I don't say what he did. I don't know what he did.'

'Did you know the mailbag was forgotten last night and is still on the premises?'

Marco began to look very scary. 'No,' he said. 'Is it?'

'So if our speculation should turn out to be the truth: if you put the photograph, addressed to *The Watchman*, in the mailbag, the question is: who removed it? Who impaled it on the body? If, of course, you didn't.'

'It is idiotic to persist in this lie. Why do you do it? Where for me is the motive? Suppose I were Strix? So: I kill the goose that lays the golden egg? Does it make sense? So: after all, the man who takes the photograph does not post it. He is the murderer and he leaves it on the body.'

'What is your surname?'

'Smith.'

'I see.'

'It is *Smith*,' Marco shouted. 'Why do you look like that? Why should it not be Smith? Is there a law against Smith? My father was an American.'

'And your mother?'

'A Calabrian. Her name was Croce. I am Marco Croce Smith. Why?'

'Have you any Rossis in your family?'

'None. Again, why?'

'There is an enmity between the Rossis and Madame Sommita's family.'

'I know nothing of it,' said Marco and then burst out, 'How could I have done it? When was it done? I don't even know when it was done but all the time from when the opera is ended until Maria found her I am on duty. You saw me. Everybody saw me. I wait at table. I attend in the hall. I go to and from the launch. I have alibis.'

'That may be true. But you may also have had a collaborator.'

'You are mad.'

'I am telling you how the police will think.'

'It is a trap. You try to trap me.'

'If you choose to put it like that. I want, if you didn't do it, to satisfy myself that you didn't. I want to get you out of the way. I believe you to be Strix and as Strix I think your activities were despicable but I do not accuse you of murder. I simply want you to tell me if you put the photograph in the postbag. In an envelope addressed to *The Watchman*.'

There followed a silence. The sun now shone in at the studio windows on the blank canvas and the empty model's throne. Outside a tui sang: a deep lucid phrase, uncivilized as snow-water and ending in a consequential clatter as if it cleared its throat. You darling, thought Troy, standing by the window, and knew that she could not endure to stay much longer inside this clever house with its arid perfections and its killed woman in the room on the landing.

Marco said: 'I surmise it was in the postbag. I do not know. I do not say I put it there.'

'And the bag was in the study?'

'That is where it is kept.'

'When was the letter put in it? Immediately after the photograph was taken? Or perhaps only just before the postbox was emptied into it and it was locked.'

Marco shrugged.

'And finally – crucially – when was the photograph removed, and by whom, and stabbed on to the body?'

'Of that I know nothing. Nothing, I tell you,' said Marco, and then with sudden venom, 'But I can guess.'

'Yes?'

'It is simple. Who clears the postbox always? Always! Who? I have seen him. He puts his arms into the bag and rounds it with his hands to receive the box and then he opens the box and holds it inside the bag to empty itself. Who?'

'Mr Hanley?'

'Ah. The secretary. *Il favorito*,' said Marco and achieved an angry smirk. He bowed in Troy's direction. 'Excuse me, madam,' he said. 'It is not a suitable topic.'

'Did you actually see Mr Hanley do this, last evening?'

'No, sir.'

'Very well,' said Alleyn. 'You may go.'

He went out with a kind of mean flourish and did not quite bang the door.

'He's a horrible little man,' said Troy, 'but I don't think he did it.'

'Nor I,' Dr Carmichael agreed.

'His next move,' said Alleyn, 'will be to hand in his notice and wait for the waters to subside.'

'Sling his hook?'

'Yes.'

'Will you let him?'

'I can't stop him. The police may try to or I suppose Reece could simply deny him transport.'

'Do you think Reece believes Marco is Strix?'

'If ever there was a clam its middle name was Reece but I think he does.'

'Are you any further on?' asked the doctor.

'A bit. I wish I'd found out whether Marco knows who took his bloody snapshot out of the bag. If ever it was in the bloody bag, which is conjectural. It's so boring of him not to admit he put it in. If he did.'

'He almost admitted *something*, didn't he?' said Troy.

'He's trying to work it out whether it would do him more good or harm to come clean.'

'I suppose,' hazarded Dr Carmichael, 'that whoever it was, Hanley or anyone else, who removed the photograph, it doesn't follow he was the killer.'

'Not as the night the day. No.'

Troy suddenly said: 'Having offered to make beds, I suppose I'd better make them. Do you think Miss Dancy would be outraged if I asked her to bear a hand? I imagine the little Sylvia is otherwise engaged.'

'Determined to maintain the house-party tone against all hazards, are you, darling?' said her husband.

'That's right. The dinner-jacket-in-the-jungle spirit.'

Dr Carmichael gazed at Troy in admiration and surprise. 'I must say, Mrs Alleyn, you set us all an example. How many beds do you plan to make?'

'I haven't counted.'

'The round dozen or more,' teased Alleyn, 'and God help all those who sleep in them.'

'He's being beastly,' Troy remarked. 'I'm not all that good at bed-making. I'll just give Miss Dancy a call, I think.'

She consulted the list of room numbers by the telephone. Dr Carmichael joined Alleyn at the windows. 'It really is clearing,' he said. 'The wind's dropping. And I do believe the lake's settling.'

'Yes, it really is.'

'What do you suppose will happen first: the telephone be reconnected, or the launch engine be got going, or the police appear on the far bank, or the chopper turn up?'

'Lord knows.'

Troy said into the telephone, 'Of *course* I understand. Don't give it another thought. We'll meet at lunchtime. Oh. Oh, I see. I'm so sorry. Yes, I think you're very wise. No, no news. Awful, isn't it?'

She hung up. 'Miss Dancy has got a migraine,' she said. 'She sounds very Wagnerian. Well, I'd better make the best I can of the beds.'

'You're not going round on your own, Troy.'

'Aren't I? But why?'

'It's inadvisable.'

'But, Rory, I promised Mrs Bacon.'

'To hell with Mrs Bacon. I'll tell her it's not on. They can make their own bloody beds. I've made ours,' said Alleyn. 'I'd go round with you but I don't think that'd do either.'

'I'll make beds with you, Mrs Alleyn,' offered Dr Carmichael in a sprightly manner.

'That's big of you, Carmichael,' said Alleyn. 'I dare say all the rooms will be locked. Mrs Bacon will have spare keys.'

'I'll find out.'

Troy said: 'You can pretend it's a hospital. You're the matron and I'm a ham-fisted probationer. I'll just go along to our palatial suite for a moment. Rejoin you here.'

When she had gone Alleyn said: 'She's hating this. You can always tell if she goes all jokey. I'll be glad to get her out of it.'

'If I may say so, you're a lucky man.'

'You may indeed say so.'

'Perhaps a brisk walk round the Island when we've done our chores.'

'A splendid idea. In a way,' Alleyn said, 'this bedmaking nonsense might turn out to be handy. I've no authority to search, of course, but you two might just keep your eyes skinned.'

'Anything in particular?'

'Not a thing. But you never know. The skinned eye and a few minor liberties.'

'I'll see about the keys,' said Dr Carmichael happily and bustled off.

II

Alleyn wondered if he was about to take the most dangerous decision of his investigative career. If he took this decision and failed, not only would he make an egregious ass of himself before the New Zealand police but he would effectively queer the pitch for their subsequent investigations and probably muck up any chance of an arrest. Or would he? In the event of failure, was there no chance of a new move, a strategy in reserve, a surprise attack? If there was, he was damned if he knew what it could be.

He went over the arguments again: The time factor. The riddle of the keys. The photograph. The conjectural motive. The appalling conclusion. He searched for possible alternatives to each of these and could find none.

He resurrected the dusty old bit of investigative folklore: If all explanations except one fail, then that one, however outrageous, will be the answer.

And, God knew, they were dealing with the outrageous.

So he made up his mind and having done that went downstairs and out into the watery sunshine for a breather.

All the guests had evidently been moved by the same impulse. They were abroad on the Island in pairs and singly. Whereas earlier in the morning Alleyn had likened those of them who had come out into the landscape to surrealistic details, now, while still wildly anachronistic, as was the house itself, in their primordial setting, they made him think of persons in a poem by Verlaine or perhaps by Edith Sitwell. Signor Lattienzo in his Tyrolean hat and his gleaming eyeglass, stylishly strolled beside Mr Ben Ruby who smoked a cigar and was rigged out for the country in a brand new Harris tweed suit. Rupert Bartholomew, wan in corduroy, his hair romantically disordered, his shoulders hunched, stood by the tumbled shore and stared over the lake. And was himself stared at, from a discreet distance, by the little Sylvia Parry with a scarlet handkerchief round her head. Even the stricken Miss Dancy had braved the elements. Wrapped up, scarfed and felt-hatted, she paced alone up and down a gravel path in front of the house as if it were the deck of a cruiser.

To her from indoors came Mr Reece in his custom-built outfit straight from pages headed 'Rugged Elegance: For Him' in the glossiest of periodicals. He wore a peaked cap which he raised ceremoniously to Miss Dancy, who immediately engaged him in conversation, clearly of an emotional kind. But he's used to that, thought Alleyn, and noticed how Mr Reece balanced Miss Dancy's elbow in his dogskin grasp as he squired her on her promenade.

He had thought they completed the number of persons in the landscape until he caught sight out of the corner of his eye, of some movement near one of the great trees near the lake. Ned Hanley was standing there. He wore a dark green coat and sweater and merged with his background. He seemed to survey the other figures in the picture.

One thing they all had in common and that was a tendency to halt and stare across the lake or shade their eyes, tip back their heads and look eastward into the fast-thinning clouds. He had been doing this himself.

Mr Ben Ruby spied him, waved his cigar energetically and made towards him. Alleyn advanced and at close quarters found Mr Ruby looking the worse for wear and self-conscious.

"Morning, old man,' said Mr Ruby. 'Glad to see you. Brightening up, isn't it? Won't be long now. We hope.'

'We do indeed.'

'*You* hope, anyway, I don't mind betting. Don't envy you your job. Responsibility without the proper backing, eh?'

'Something like that,' said Alleyn.

'I owe you an apology, old man. Last evening. I'd had one or two drinks. You know that?'

'Well . . .'

'What with one thing and another – the shock and that. I was all to pieces. Know what I mean?'

'Of course.'

'All the same – bad show. Very bad show,' said Mr Ruby, shaking his head and then wincing.

'Don't give it another thought.'

'Christ, I feel awful,' confided Mr Ruby and threw away his cigar. 'It was good brandy, too. The best. Special cognac. Wonder if this guy Marco could rustle up a corpse-reviver.'

'I dare say. Or Hanley might.'

Mr Ruby made the sound that is usually written: 'T'ss' and after a brief pause said in a deep voice and with enormous expression: 'Bella! Bella Sommita! You can't credit it, can you? The most beautiful woman with the most gorgeous voice God ever put breath into. Gone! And how! And what the hell we're going to do about the funeral's nobody's business. I don't know of any relatives. It'd be thoroughly in character if she's left detailed instructions and bloody awkward ones at that. Pardon me, it slipped out. But it might mean cold storage to anywhere she fancied or ashes in the Adriatic.' He caught himself up and gave Alleyn a hard if bloodshot stare. 'I suppose it's out of order to ask if you've formed an idea?'

'It is, really. At this stage,' Alleyn said. 'We must wait for the police.'

'Yeah? Well, here's hoping they know their stuff.' He reverted to his elegiac mood. 'Bella!' he apostrophized. 'After all these years of taking the rough with the smooth, if you can understand me. Hell, it hurts!'

'How long an association has it been?'

'You don't measure grief by months and years,' Mr Ruby said reproachfully. 'How long? Let me see? It was on her first tour of Aussie. That would be in '72. Under the Bel Canto management in association with my firm – Ben Ruby Associates. There was a disagreement with Bel Canto and we took over.'

Here Mr Ruby embarked on a long parenthesis explaining that he was a self-made man, a Sydneysider who had pulled himself up by his own boot-strings and was proud of it and how the Sommita had understood this and had herself evolved from peasant stock.

'And,' said Alleyn when an opportunity presented itself, 'a close personal friendship had developed with the business association?'

'This is right, old man. I reckon I understood her as well as anybody ever could. There was the famous temperament, mind, and it was a snorter while it lasted but it never lasted long. She always sends – sent – for Maria to massage her shoulders and that would do the trick. Back into the honied-kindness bit and everybody loving everybody.'

'Mr Ruby, have you anything to tell me that might, in however far-fetched or remote a degree, help to throw light on this tragedy?'

Mr Ruby opened his arms wide and let them fall in the classic gesture of defeat.

'Nothing?' Alleyn said.

'This is what I've been asking myself ever since I woke up. When I got round, that is, to asking myself anything other than why the hell I had to down those cognacs.'

'And how do you answer yourself?'

Again the gesture. 'I don't,' Mr Ruby confessed. 'I can't. Except – ' He stopped, provokingly, and stared at Signor Lattienzo who by now had arrived at the lakeside and contemplated the water rather, in his Tyrolean outfit, like some poet of the post-Romantic era.

'Except?' Alleyn prompted.

'Look!' Mr Ruby invited. 'Look at what's been done and *how* it's been done. Look at that. If you had to say – you, with your experience – what it reminded you of, what would it be? Come on.'

'Grand opera,' Alleyn said promptly.

Mr Ruby let out a strangulated yelp and clapped him heavily on the back. 'Good on you!' he cried. 'Got it in one! Good on you, mate. And the Italian sort of grand opera, what's more. That funny business with the dagger and the picture! Verdi would have loved it. Particularly the picture. Can you see any of *us*, supposing he was a murderer, doing it that way? That poor kid Rupert? Ned Hanley, never mind if he's one of those? Monty? *Me? You?* Even if you'd draw the line at the props and the business. "No" you'd say "No". Not that way. It's not in character, it's impossible, it's not – it's not – ' and Mr Ruby appeared to hunt excitedly for the *mot juste* of his argument. 'It's not British,' he finally pronounced, and added: 'Using the word in its widest sense. I'm a Commonwealth man myself.'

Alleyn had to give himself a moment or two before he was able to respond to this declaration.

'What you are saying,' he ventured, 'in effect, is that the murderer must be one of the Italians on the premises. Is that right?'

'That,' said Mr Ruby, 'is dead right.'

'It narrows down the field of suspects,' said Alleyn drily.

'It certainly does,' Mr Ruby portentously agreed.

'Marco and Maria?'

'Right.'

During an uncomfortable pause Mr Ruby's rather bleary regard dwelt upon Signor Lattienzo in his windblown cape by the lakeside.

'And Signor Lattienzo, I suppose?' Alleyn suggested.

There was no reply.

'Have you,' Alleyn asked, 'any reason, apart from the grand opera theory, to suspect one of these three?'

Mr Ruby seemed to be much discomfited by this question. He edged with his toe at a grassy turf. He cleared his throat and looked aggrieved.

'I knew you'd ask that,' he said resentfully.

'It was natural, don't you think, that I should?'

'I suppose so. Oh yes. Too right it was. But listen. It's a terrible thing to accuse anyone of. I know that. I wouldn't want to say anything that'd unduly influence you. You know. Cause you to – to jump to conclusions or give you the wrong impression. I wouldn't like to do that.'

'I don't think it's very likely.'

'No? You'd *say* that, of course. But I reckon you've done it already. I reckon like everyone else you've taken the old retainer stuff for real.'

'Are you thinking of Maria?'

'Too bloody right I am, mate.'

'Come on,' Alleyn said. 'Get it off your chest. I won't make too much of it. Wasn't Maria as devoted as one was led to suppose?'

'Like hell she was! Well, that's not correct either. She was devoted all right but it was a flaming uncomfortable sort of devotion. Kind of dog-with-a-bone affair. Sometimes when they'd had a difference you'd have said it was more like hate. Jealous! She's eaten up with it. And when Bella was into some new "friendship" – know what I mean? – Maria as likely as not would turn plug-ugly. She was even jealous in a weird sort of way, of the artistic triumphs. Or that's the way it looked to me.'

'How did she take the friendship with Mr Reece?'

'Monty?' A marked change came over Mr Ruby. He glanced quickly at Alleyn as if he wondered whether he was unenlightened in some respect. He hesitated and then said quietly: 'That's different again, isn't it?'

'Is it? How, "different"?'

'Well – you know.'

'But I don't know.'

'It's platonic. Couldn't be anything else.'

'I see.'

'Poor old Monty. Result of an illness. Cruel thing, really.'

'Indeed? So Maria had no cause to resent him.'

'This is right. She admires him. They do, you know. Italians. Especially his class. They admire success and prestige more than anything else. It was a very different story when young Rupert came along. Maria didn't worry about letting everyone see what she felt about *that* lot. I'd take long odds she'll be telling you the kid done – did – it. That vindictive, she is. Fair go – I wouldn't put it past her. Now.'

Alleyn considered for a moment or two. Signor Lattienzo had now joined Rupert Bartholomew on the lakeside and was talking energetically and clapping him on the shoulder. Mr Reece and Miss Dancy still paced their imaginary promenade deck and the little Sylvia Parry, perched dejectedly on a rustic seat, watched Rupert.

Alleyn said: 'Was Madame Sommita tolerant of these outbursts from Maria?'

'I suppose she must have been in her own way. There were terrible scenes, of course. That was to be expected, wasn't it? Bella'd threaten Maria with the sack and Maria'd throw a fit of hysterics and then they'd both go weepy on it and we'd be back to square one with Maria standing behind Bella massaging her shoulders and swearing eternal devotion. Italians! My oath! But it was different, totally different – with the kid. I'd never seen her as far gone over anyone else as she was with him. Crazy about him. In at the deep end, boots and all. That's why she took it so badly when he saw the light about that little opera of his and wanted to opt out. He was dead right, of course, but Bella hadn't got any real musical judgement. Not really. You ask Beppo.'

'What about Mr Reece?'

'Tone deaf,' said Mr Ruby.

'Really?'

'Fact. Doesn't pretend to be anything else. He was annoyed with the boy for disappointing her, of course. As far as Monty was concerned the diva had said the opus was great, and what she said had got to be right. And then of course he didn't like the idea of throwing a disaster of a party. In a way,' said Mr Ruby, 'it was the Citizen Kane situation with the boot on the other foot. Sort of.' He waited for a moment and then said: 'I feel bloody sorry for that kid.'

'God knows, so do I,' said Alleyn.

'But he's young. He'll get over it. All the same, she'd a hell of a lot to answer for.'

'Tell me. You knew her as well as anybody, didn't you? Does the name "Rossi" ring a bell?'

'Rossi,' Mr Ruby mused. 'Rossi, eh? Hang on. Wait a sec.'

As if to prompt, or perhaps warn him, raucous hoots sounded from the jetty across the water, giving the intervals without the

cadence of the familiar singing-off phrase 'Dah dahdy dah-dah. Dah
dah.'

Les appeared on deck and could be seen to wave his scarlet cap.

The response from the islanders was instant. They hurried into a
group. Miss Dancy flourished her woollen scarf. Mr Reece raised his.
arm in a Roman salute. Signor Lattienzo lifted his Tyrolean hat high
above his head. Sylvia ran to Rupert and took his arm. Hanley
moved out of cover and Troy, Mrs Bacon and Dr Carmichael came
out of the house and pointed Les out to each other from the steps.
Mr Ruby bawled out, 'He's done it. Good on 'im, 'e's done it.'

Alleyn took a handkerchief from his breast pocket and a spare
from his overcoat. He went down to the lake edge and semaphored:
Nice Work. Les returned to the wheelhouse and sent a short toot of
acknowledgement.

The islanders chattered excitedly, telling each other that the signal *must* mean the launch was mobile again, that the lake was
undoubtedly calmer and that when the police did arrive they would
be able to cross. The hope that they themselves would all be able to
leave remained unspoken.

They trooped up to the house and were shepherded in by Mr
Reece who said, with sombre playfulness, that 'elevenses' were now
served in the library.

Troy and Dr Carmichael joined Alleyn. They seemed to be in
good spirits. 'We've finished our chores,' Troy said, 'and we've got
something to report. Let's have a quick swallow, and join up in the
studio.'

'Don't make it too obvious,' said Alleyn, who was aware that he
was now under close though furtive observation by most of the
household. He fetched two blameless tomato juices for himself and
Troy. They joined Rupert and Sylvia Parry who were standing a little apart from the others and were not looking at each other. Rupert
was still white about the gills but, or so Alleyn thought, rather less
distraught – indeed there was perhaps a hint of portentousness, of
self-conscious gloom in his manner.

She has provided him with an audience, thought Alleyn. Let's
hope she knows what she's letting herself in for.

Rupert said: 'I've told Sylvia about – last night.'

'So I supposed,' said Alleyn.

'She thinks I was right.'

'Good.'

Sylvia said: 'I think it took wonderful courage and artistic integrity and I do think it was right.'

'That's a very proper conclusion.'

'It won't be long now, will it?' Rupert asked. 'Before the police come?' He pitched his voice rather high and brittle with the sort of false airiness some actors employ when they hope to convey suppressed emotion.

'Probably not,' said Alleyn.

'Of course, I'll be the prime suspect,' Rupert announced.

'Rupert, *no*,' Sylvia whispered.

'My dear girl, it sticks out a mile. After my curtain performance. Motive. Opportunity. The lot. We might as well face it.'

'We might as well not make public announcements about it,' Troy observed.

'I'm sorry,' said Rupert grandly. 'No doubt I'm being silly.'

'Well,' Alleyn cheerfully remarked, 'you said it. We didn't. Troy, hadn't we better sort out those drawings of yours?'

'OK. Let's. I'd forgotten.'

'She leaves them unfixed and tiles the floor with them,' Alleyn explained. 'Our cat sat on a preliminary sketch of the Prime Minister and turned it into a jungle flower. Come on, darling.'

They found Dr Carmichael already in the studio. 'I didn't want Reece's "elevenses",' he said. And to Troy: 'Have you told him?'

'I waited for you,' said Troy.

They were, Alleyn thought, as pleased as Punch with themselves. 'You tell him,' they said simultaneously. 'Ladies first,' said the doctor.

'Come on,' said Alleyn.

Troy inserted her thin hand in a gingerly fashion into a large pocket of her dress. Using only her first finger and her thumb she drew out something wrapped in one of Alleyn's handkerchiefs. She was in the habit of using them as she preferred a large one and she had been known when intent on her work to confuse the handkerchief and her paint-rag, with regrettable results to the handkerchief and to her face.

She carried her trophy to the paint-table and placed it there. Then, with a sidelong look at her husband, she produced two clean hog-hair brushes and, using them upside down in the manner of chopsticks, fiddled open the handkerchief and stood back.

Alleyn walked over, put his arm across her shoulders and looked at what she had revealed.

A large heavy envelope, creased and burnt but not so extensively that an airmail stamp and part of the address was not still in evidence. The address was typewritten.

> The Edit
> *The Watchma*
> PO Bo
> NSW 14C
> SY
> Australia

'Of course,' Troy said after a considerable pause, 'it may be of no consequence at all, may it?'

'Suppose we have the full story?'

'Yes. All right. Here goes, then.'

Their story was that they had gone some way with their housemaiding expedition when Troy decided to equip herself with a box-broom and a duster. They went downstairs in search of them and ran into Mrs Bacon emerging from the study. She intimated that she was nearing the end of her tether. The staff, having gone through progressive stages of hysteria and suspicion, had settled for a sort of work-to-rule attitude and, with the exception of the chef who had agreed to provide a very basic luncheon and Marco who was, said Mrs Bacon, abnormally quiet but did his jobs, either sulked in their rooms or muttered together in the staff sitting room. As far as Mrs Bacon could make out, the New Zealand ex-hotel group suspected in turn Signor Lattienzo, Marco and Maria on the score of their being Italians and Mr Reece whom they cast in the role of *de facto* cuckold. Rupert Bartholomew was fancied as an outside chance on the score of his having turned against the Sommita. Maria had gone to earth, supposedly in her room. Chaos, Mrs Bacon said, prevailed.

Mrs Bacon herself had rushed round the dining and drawing rooms while Marco set out the elevenses. She had then turned her attention to the study and found to her horror that the open fire-place had not been cleaned nor the fire relaid. To confirm this, she had drawn their attention to a steel ashpan she herself carried in her rubber-gloved hands.

'And that's when I saw it, Rory,' Troy explained. 'It was sticking up out of the ashes and I saw what's left of the address.'

'And she nudged me,' said Dr Carmichael proudly, 'and I saw it too.'

'And he behaved *perfectly*,' Troy intervened. 'He said: "Do let me take that thing and tell me where to empty it." And Mrs Bacon said, rather wildly: "In the bin. In the yard," and made feeble protestations and at that moment we all heard the launch hooting and she became distracted. So Dr Carmichael got hold of the ashpan. And I – well – I – got hold of the envelope and put it in my pocket among your handkerchief which happened to be there.'

'So it appears,' Dr Carmichael summed up, 'that somebody typed a communication of some sort to *The Watchman* and stamped the envelope which he or somebody else then chucked on the study fire and it dropped through the grate into the ashpan when it was only half-burnt. Or doesn't it?'

'Did you get a chance to have a good look at the ashes?' asked Alleyn.

'Pretty good. In the yard. They were faintly warm. I ran them carefully into a zinc rubbish bin already half-full. There were one or two very small fragments of heavily charred paper and some clinkers. Nothing else. I heard someone coming and cleared out. I put the ashpan back under the study grate.'

Alleyn bent over the trophy. 'It's a Sommita envelope,' said Troy. 'Isn't it?'

'Yes. Bigger than the Reece envelope but the same paper: like the letter she wrote to the Yard.'

'Why would she write to *The Watchman*?'

'We don't know that she did.'

'Don't we?'

'Or if she did, whether her letter was in this envelope.' He took one of Troy's brushes and used it to flip the envelope over. 'It may have been stuck up,' he said, 'and opened before the gum dried. There's not enough left to be certain. It's big enough to take the photograph.'

Dr Carmichael blew out his cheeks and then expelled the air rather noisily. 'That's a long shot, isn't it?' he said.

'Of course it is,' agreed Alleyn. 'Pure speculation.'

'If *she* wrote it,' Troy said carefully, 'she dictated it. I'm sure she couldn't type, aren't you?'

'I think it's *most* unlikely. The first part of her letter to the Yard was impeccably typed and the massive postscript flamboyantly handwritten. Which suggested that she dictated the beginning or told young Rupert to concoct something she could sign, found it too moderate and added the rest herself.'

'But why,' Dr Carmichael mused, 'was this thing in the study, on Reece's desk? I know! She asked that secretary of his to type it because she'd fallen out with young Bartholomew. How's that?'

'Not too bad,' said Alleyn. 'Possible. And where, do you suggest, is the letter? It wasn't in the envelope. And, by the way, the envelope was not visible on Reece's desk when you and I, Carmichael, visited him last night.'

'Really? How d'you know?'

'Oh, my dear chap, the cop's habit of using the beady eye, I suppose. It might have been there under some odds and ends in his "out" basket.'

Troy said: 'Rory, I think I know where you're heading.'

'Do you, my love? Where?'

'Could Marco have slid into the study to put the photograph in the postbag before Hanley had emptied the mailbox into it and could he have seen the typed and addressed envelope on the desk and thought there was a marvellous opportunity to send the photograph to *The Watchman*, because nobody would question it. And so he took out her letter or whatever it was and chucked it on the fire and put the photograph in the envelope and – '

Troy, who had been going great guns, brought up short. 'Blast!' she said.

'Why didn't he put it in the postbag?' asked Alleyn.

'Yes.'

'Because,' Dr Carmichael staunchly declared, 'he was interrupted and had to get rid of it quick. I think that's a damn good piece of reasoning, Mrs Alleyn.'

'Perhaps,' Troy said, 'her letter had been left out awaiting the writer's signature and – no, that's no good.'

'It's a lot of good,' Alleyn said warmly. 'You have turned up trumps, you two. Damn Marco. Why can't he make up his dirty little mind that his best move is to cut his losses and come clean. I'll have to try my luck with Hanley. Tricky.'

He went out on the landing. Bert had resumed his guard duty and lounged back in the armchair reading a week-old sports tabloid. A homemade cigarette hung from his lower lip. He gave Alleyn the predictable sideways tip of his head.

Alleyn said: 'I really oughtn't to impose on you any longer, Bert. After all, we've got the full complement of keys now and nobody's going to force the lock with the amount of traffic flowing through this house.'

'I'm not fussy,' said Bert which Alleyn took to mean that he had no objections to continuing his vigil.

'Well, if you're sure,' he said.

'She'll be right.'

'Thank you.'

The sound of voices indicated the emergence of the elevenses party. Miss Dancy, Sylvia Parry and Rupert Bartholomew came upstairs. Rupert, with an incredulous look at Bert and a scary one at Alleyn, made off in the direction of his room. The ladies crossed the landing quickly and ascended the next flight. Mr Reece, Ben Ruby and Signor Lattienzo made for the study. Alleyn ran quickly downstairs in time to catch Hanley emerging from the morning room.

'Sorry to bother you,' he said, 'but I wonder if I might have a word. It won't take a minute.'

'But of *course*,' said Hanley. 'Where shall we go? Back into the library?'

'Right.'

When they were there Hanley winningly urged further refreshment. Upon Alleyn's declining, he said: 'Well, *I* will; just a teeny tiddler,' and helped himself to a gin-and-tonic. 'What can I do for you, Mr Alleyn?' he said. 'Is there any further development?'

Alleyn said: 'Did you type a letter to *The Watchman* some time before Madame Sommita's death?'

Hanley's jaw dropped and the hand holding his drink stopped half-way to his mouth. For perhaps three seconds he maintained this position and then spoke.

'Oh Christmas!' he said. 'I'd forgotten. You wouldn't credit it, would you? I'd entirely forgotten.'

He made no bones about explaining himself and did so very flu-
ently and quite without hesitation. He had indeed typed a letter
from the Sommita to *The Watchman*. She had been stirred up 'like a
hive of bees', he said, by the episode of the supposed intruder on the
Island and had decided that it was Strix who had been sent by *The
Watchman* and had arrived after dark the previous night, probably by
canoe, and had left unobserved by the same means, she didn't
explain when. The letter which she dictated was extremely abusive
and threatened the editor with a libel action. She had made a great
point of Mr Reece not being told of the letter.

'Because of course he'd have stopped all the nonsense,' said
Hanley. 'I was to type it and take it to her to sign and then put it in
the bag, all unbeknownst. She asked *me* to do it because of the row
with the Wonder Boy. She gave me some of her notepaper.'

'And you did it?'

'My dear! As much as my life was worth to refuse. I typed it out,
calming it down the least morsel, which she didn't notice. But when
she'd signed it I bethought me that maybe when it had gone *she'd*
tell the Boss-Man and he'd be cross with me for doing it. So I left the
letter on his desk meaning to show it to him after the performance.
I put it under some letters he had to sign.'

'And the envelope?'

'The envelope? Oh, on the desk. And then, I remember, Marco
came in to say I was wanted on stage to refocus a light.'

'When was this?'

'When? I wouldn't know. Well – late afternoon. After tea sometime, but well before the performance.'

'Did Marco leave the study before you?'

'*Did* he? I don't know. Yes, I do. He said something about making
up the fire and I left him to it.'

'Did Mr Reece see the letter, then?'

Hanley flapped his hands. 'I've no notion. He's said nothing to
me, but then with the catastrophe – I mean, everything else goes out
of one's head, doesn't it, except that nothing ever goes out of *his*
head. You could ask him.'

'So I could,' said Alleyn. 'And will.'

Mr Reece was alone in the study. He said at once in his flattest
manner that he had found the letter on his desk under a couple of

business communications which he was to sign in time for Hanley to send them off by the evening post. He did sign them and then read the letter.

'It was ill-advised,' he said, cutting the episode down to size. 'She had been over-excited ever since the matter of the intruder arose. I had told her Sir Simon Marks had dealt with *The Watchman* and there would be no more trouble in that quarter. This letter was abusive in tone and would have stirred everything up again. I threw it on the fire. I intended to speak to her about it but not until after the performance when she would be less nervous and tense.'

'Did you throw the envelope on the fire too?' Alleyn asked and thought: If he says yes, bang goes sixpence and we return to square one.

'The envelope?' said Mr Reece. 'No. It was not in an envelope. I don't remember noticing one. May I ask what is the significance of all this, Chief Superintendent?'

'It's really just a matter of tidying up. The half-burnt envelope stamped and addressed to *The Watchman* was in the ashpan under the grate this morning.'

'I have no recollection of seeing it,' Mr Reece said heavily. 'I believe I would remember if I had seen it.'

'After you burnt the letter, did you stay in the study?'

'I believe so,' he said and Alleyn thought he detected a weary note. 'Or no,' Mr Reece corrected himself. 'That is not right. Maria came in with a message that Bella wanted to see me. She was in the concert chamber. The flowers that I had ordered for her had not arrived and she was – distressed. I went to the concert chamber at once.'

'Did Maria go with you?'

'I really don't know what Maria did, Superintendent. I fancy – no, I am not sure but I don't think she did. She may have returned there a little later. Really, I do *not* remember,' said Mr Reece, and pressed his eyes with his thumb and forefinger.

'I'm sorry,' Alleyn said, 'I won't bother you any longer. I wouldn't have done so now but it just might be relevant.'

'It is no matter,' said Mr Reece. And then: 'I much appreciate what you are doing,' he said. 'You will excuse me, I'm sure, if I seem ungracious.'

'Good Lord, yes,' said Alleyn quickly. 'You should just hear some of the receptions we get.'

'I suppose so,' said Mr Reece heavily. 'Very likely.' And then with a lugubrious attempt at brightening up. 'The sun is shining continuously and the wind has almost gone down. Surely it can't be long, now, before the police arrive.'

'We hope not. Tell me, have you done anything about Marco? Spoken to him? Faced him with being Strix?'

And then Mr Reece made the most unexpected, the most remarkable statement of their conversation.

'I couldn't be bothered,' he said.

III

On leaving the study, Alleyn heard sounds of activity in the dining room. The door was open and he looked in to find Marco laying the table.

'I want a word with you,' Alleyn said, 'not here. In the library. Come on.'

Marco followed him there, saying nothing.

'Now, listen to me,' Alleyn said. 'I do not think, indeed I have never thought, that you killed Madame Sommita. You hadn't time to do it. I now think – I am almost sure – that you went into the study yesterday afternoon intending to put the photograph you took of her, in the mailbag. You saw on the desk a stamped envelope addressed in typescript to *The Watchman*. It was unsealed and empty. This gave you a wonderful opportunity, it made everything safer and simpler. You transferred the photograph from its envelope to this envelope, sealed it down and would have put it in the bag but I think you were interrupted and simply dropped it back on the desk and I dare say explained your presence there by tidying the desk. Now. If this is so, all I want from you is the name of the person who interrupted you.'

Marco had watched Alleyn carefully with a look, wary and hooded, that often appears on the faces of the accused when some telling piece of evidence is produced against them. Alleyn thought of it as the 'dock-face'.

'You *have* been busy,' Marco sneered. 'Congratulations.'

'I'm right, then?'

'Oh yes,' he said casually. 'I don't know how you got there, but you're right.'

'And the name?'

'You know so much, I'd have thought you'd know that.'

'Well?'

'Maria,' said Marco.

From somewhere in the house there came a sound, normally unexceptionable but now arresting. A door banged and shut it off.

'Telephone,' Marco whispered. 'It's the telephone.'

'Did Maria see you? See you had the envelope in your hands? Did she?'

'I'm not sure. She might have. She could have. She's been – looking – at me. Or I thought so. Once or twice. She hasn't said anything. We haven't been friendly.'

'No?'

'I went back to the study. Later. Just before the opera and it had gone. So I supposed someone had put it in the mailbag.'

There was a flurry of voices in the hall. The door swung open and Hanley came in.

'The telephone!' he cried. 'Working. It's the – ' He pulled up short, looking at Marco. 'Someone for you, Mr Alleyn,' he said.

'I'll take it upstairs. Keep the line alive.'

He went into the hall. Most of the guests were collected there. He passed through them and ran upstairs to the first landing and the studio where he found Troy and Dr Carmichael. He took the receiver off the telephone. Hanley's voice fluted in the earpiece: 'Yes. Don't hang up, will you? Mr Alleyn's on his way. Hold the line, please.' And a calm reply: 'Thank you, sir. I'll hold on.'

'All right, Hanley,' Alleyn said. 'You can hang up now,' and heard the receiver being cradled. 'Hullo,' he said. 'Alleyn speaking.'

'Chief Superintendent Alleyn? Inspector Hazelmere, Rivermouth Police, here. We've had a report of trouble on Waihoe Island and are informed of your being on the premises. I understand it's a homicide.'

Alleyn gave him the bare bones of the case. Mr Hazelmere repeated everything he said. He was evidently dictating. There were crackling disturbances on the line.

'So you see,' Alleyn ended, 'I'm a sort of minister without portfolio.'

'Pardon? Oh. Oh, I get you. Yes. Very fortunate coincidence, though. For us. We'd been instructed by head office that you were in the country, of course. It'll be an unexpected honour . . .' A crash of static obliterated the rest of this remark. '. . . temporary repair. Better be quick . . . should make it . . . chopper . . . hope . . . doctor . . .'

'There's a doctor here,' Alleyn shouted. 'I'd suggest a fully equipped homicide squad and a search warrant – can you hear? – and a brace and bit. Yes, that's what I said. Large. Yes, large. Observation purposes. Are you there? Hullo? Hullo?'

The line was dead.

'Well,' said Troy after a pause. 'This is the beginning of the end, I suppose.'

'In a way the beginning of the beginning,' Alleyn said wryly. 'If it's done nothing else it's brought home the virtues of routine. I'm not sure if they have homicide squads in New Zealand but whatever they do have they'll take the correct steps in the correct way and with authority. And you, my love, will fly away home with an untouched canvas.' He turned to Dr Carmichael. 'I really don't know what I'd have done without you,' he said.

Before Dr Carmichael could answer there was a loud rap at the door.

'Not a dull moment,' said Alleyn. 'Come in!'

It was Signor Lattienzo, pale and strangely unsprightly.

'I am *de trop*,' he said. 'Forgive me. I thought you would be here. I find the ambiance downstairs uncomfortable. Everybody asking questions and expressing relief and wanting above all to know when they can go away. And behind it all – fear. Fear and suspicion. Not a pretty combination. And to realize that one is in much the same state oneself, after all! That I find exceedingly disagreeable.'

Dr Carmichael said to Alleyn: 'They'll be wanting to know about the telephone call. Would you like me to go downstairs and tell them?'

'Do. Just say it *was* the police and they are on their way and the line's gone phut again.'

'Right.'

'That's a *very* nice man,' said Troy when he had gone. 'We never completed our bedmaking. I don't suppose it matters so much now but we ought at least to put our gear away, don't you think?'

She had managed to get behind Signor Lattienzo and pull a quick face at her husband.

'I expect you're right,' he said obediently and she made for the door. Signor Lattienzo seemed to make an effort. He produced a rather wan replica of his more familiar manner.

'Bedmaking! "Gear"?' he exclaimed. 'But I am baffled. Here is the most distinguished painter of our time whom I have, above all things, desired to meet and she talks of bedmaking as a sequence to murder.'

'She's being British,' said Alleyn. 'If there were any bullets about she'd bite on them. Pay no attention.'

'That's right,' Troy assured Signor Lattienzo. 'It's a substitute for hysterics.'

'If you say so,' said Signor Lattienzo and as an afterthought seized and extensively kissed Troy's hand. She cast a sheepish glance at Alleyn and withdrew.

Alleyn, who had begun to feel rather British himself, said he was glad that Signor Lattienzo had looked in. 'There's something I've been wanting to ask you,' he said, 'but with all the excursions and alarms, I haven't got round to it.'

'Me? But of course! Anything! Though I don't imagine that I can produce electrifying tidings,' said Signor Lattienzo. He sat down in the studio's most comfortable armchair and appeared to relax. 'Already,' he said, 'I feel better,' and took out his cigarette case.

'It's about Madame Sommita's background.'

'Indeed?'

'She was your pupil for some three years, wasn't she, before making her debut?'

'That is so.'

'You were aware, I expect, of her real name?'

'Naturally. Pepitone.'

'Perhaps you helped her decide on her professional name? Sommita, which is as much as to say "The Tops", isn't it?'

'It was not my choice. I found it a little extravagant. She did not and she prevailed. You may say she has been fully justified.'

'Indeed you may. You may also say, perhaps, that the choice was a matter of accuracy rather than of taste.'

Signor Lattienzo softly clapped his hands. 'That is precisely the case,' he applauded.

'Maestro,' Alleyn said. 'I am very ignorant in these matters, but I imagine that the relationship between pedagogue and pupil is, or at least can be, very close, very intimate.'

'My dear Mr Alleyn, if you are suggesting – '

'Which I am not. Not for a moment. There can be close relationships that have no romantic overtones.'

'Of course. And allow me to say that with a pupil it would be in the highest degree a mistake to allow oneself to become involved in such an attachment. And apart from all that,' he added with feeling, 'when the lady has the temperament of a wild cat and the appetite of a hyena, it would be sheer lunacy.'

'But all the same, I expect some kind of aseptic intimacy does exist, doesn't it?'

Signor Lattienzo broke into rather shrill laughter. ' "Aseptic intimacy",' he echoed. 'You are a master of the *mot juste*, my dear Mr Alleyn. It is a pleasure to be grilled by you.'

'Well, then: did you learn anything about a family feud – one of those vendetta-like affairs – between the Pepitones and another Sicilian clan: the Rossis?'

Signor Lattienzo took some time in helping himself to a cigarette and lighting it. He did not look at Alleyn. 'I do not concern myself with such matters,' he said.

'I'm sure you don't but did *she*?'

'May I first of all ask you a question? Do you suspect that this appalling crime might be traced to the Pepitone-Rossi affair? I think you must do so, otherwise you would not bring it up.'

'As to that,' said Alleyn, 'it's just a matter of avenues and stones, however unlikely. I've been told that Madame Sommita herself feared some sort of danger threatened her and that she suspected Strix of being an agent or even a member of the Rossi family. I don't have to tell you that Marco is Strix. Mr Reece will have done that.'

'Yes. But – do you think – '

'No. He has an unbreakable alibi.'

'Ah.'

'I wondered if she had confided her fears to you?'

'You will know, of course, of the habit of *omertà*. It has been remorselessly, if erroneously, paraded in works of popular fiction with a mafioso background. I expected that she knew of her father's alleged involvement with mafioso elements although great care had been taken to remove her from the milieu. I am surprised to hear that she spoke of the Rossi affair. Not to the good Monty, I am sure?'

'Not specifically. But it appears that even to him she referred repeatedly, though in the vaguest of terms, to sinister intentions behind the Strix activities.'

'But otherwise – '

Signor Lattienzo stopped short and for the first time looked very hard at Alleyn. 'Did she tell that unhappy young man? Is that it? I see it is. Why?'

'It seems she used it as a weapon when she realized he was trying to escape her.'

'Ah! That is believable. An appeal to his pity. That I can believe. Emotional blackmail.'

Signor Lattienzo got up and moved restlessly about the room. He looked out at the now sunny prospect, thrust his plump hands into his trouser pockets, took them out and examined them as if they had changed and finally approached Alleyn and came to a halt.

'I have something to tell you,' he said.

'Good.'

'Evidently you are familiar with the Rossi affair.'

'Not to say familiar, no. But I do remember something of the case.'

Alleyn would have thought it impossible that Signor Lattienzo would ever display the smallest degree of embarrassment or loss of *savoir-faire* but he appeared to do so now. He screwed in his eyeglass, stared at a distant spot somewhere to the right of Alleyn's left ear and spoke rapidly in a high voice.

'I have a brother,' he proclaimed. 'Alfredo Lattienzo. He is an *Avvocato*, a leading barrister, and he, in the course of his professional duties, has appeared in a number of cases where the mafioso element was – ah – involved. At the time of the Rossi trial, which as you will know became a *cause célèbre* in the USA, he held a watching brief on behalf of the Pepitone element. It was through him, by the way, that Isabella became my pupil. But that is of no moment. He was never called upon to take a more active part but he did – ah – he did learn – ah – from, as you would say, the horse's mouth, the origin and subsequent history of the enmity between the two houses.'

He paused. Alleyn thought that it would be appropriate if he said: You interest me, strangely. Pray continue your most absorbing narrative. However, he said nothing and Signor Lattienzo continued.

'*The origin*,' he repeated. 'The event that set the whole absurdly wicked feud going. I have always thought there must have been Corsican blood somewhere in that family. My dear Alleyn, I am about to break a confidence with my brother and one does not break confidences of this sort.'

'I think I may assure that whatever you may tell me I won't reveal the source.'

'It may, after all, not seem as striking to you as it does to me. It is this. The event that gave rise to the feud so many, many years ago, was the murder of a Pepitone girl by her Rossi bridegroom. He had discovered a passionate and explicit letter from a lover. He stabbed her to the heart on their wedding night.'

He stopped. He seemed to balk at some conversational hurdle.

'I see,' said Alleyn.

'That is not all,' said Signor Lattienzo. 'That is by no means all. Pinned to the body by the stiletto that killed her was the letter. That is what I came to tell you and now I shall go.'

CHAPTER 8

The Police

'From now on,' Alleyn said to Dr Carmichael, 'it would be nice to maintain a masterly inactivity. I shall complete my file and hand it over, with an anxious smirk, to Inspector Hazelmere in, please God, the course of a couple of hours or less.'

'Don't you feel you'd like to polish it off yourself? Having gone so far?'

'Yes, Rory,' said Troy. 'Don't you?'

'If Fox and Bailey and Thompson could walk in, yes, I suppose I do. That would be, as Noël Coward put it *"une autre paire de souliers"*. But this hamstrung solo, poking about without authority, has been damned frustrating.'

'What do you suppose the chap that's coming will do first?'

'Inspect the body and the immediate environment. He can't look at my improvised dabs-and-photographs because they are still in what Lattienzo calls the womb of the camera. He'll take more of his own.'

'And then?'

'Possibly set up a search of some if not all of their rooms. I suggested he bring a warrant. And by that same token did your bed-making exercise prove fruitful? Before or after the envelope-and-ashes episode?'

'A blank,' said Dr Carmichael. 'Hanley has a collection of bedside books with Wilde and Gide at the top and backstreet Marseilles at the bottom but all with the same *leitmotif*.'

'And Ben Ruby,' said Troy, 'has an enormous scrapbook of news-paper cuttings all beautifully arranged and dated and noted and with all the rave bits in the reviews underlined. For quotation in advance publicity, I suppose. It's got the Strix photographs and captions and newspaper correspondence, indignant and supportive. Do you know there are only seven European Strix photographs, one American, and four Australian, including the retouched one in *The Watchman*. Somehow one had imagined, or I had, a hoard of them. Signor Lattienzo's got a neat little pile of letters in Italian on his desk. Mr Reece has an enormous coloured photograph framed in silver of the diva in full operatic kit – I wouldn't know which opera except that it's not *Butterfly*. And there are framed photographs of those rather self-conscious, slightly smug walking youths in the Athens Museum. He's also got a marvellous equestrian drawing in sanguine of a nude man on a stallion which I could swear is a da Vinci original. Can he be as rich as all that? I really do swear it's not a reproduction.'

'I think he probably can,' said Alleyn.

'What a shut-up sort of man he is,' Troy mused. 'I mean, who would have expected it? Does he really appreciate it or has he just acquired it because it cost so much? Like the diva, one might say.'

'Perhaps not quite like that,' said Alleyn.

'Do you attach a lot of weight to Signor Lattienzo's observations. I don't know what they were, of course.'

'They were confidential. They cast a strongly Italian flavour over the scene. Beyond that,' said Alleyn, 'my lips are sealed.'

'Rory,' Troy asked, 'are you going to see Maria again? Before the police arrive?'

'I've not quite decided. I think perhaps I might. Very briefly.'

'We mustn't ask why, of course,' said Carmichael.

'Oh yes you may. By all means. If I do see her, it will be to tell her that I shall inform the police of her request to attend to her mistress and shall ask them to accede to it. When they've finished their examination of the room, of course.'

'You will?'

'That's the general idea.'

'Well, then . . . Are you going to explain why?'

'Certainly,' said Alleyn. And did.

When he had finished Troy covered her face with her hands. It was an uncharacteristic gesture. She turned away to the windows. Dr Carmichael looked from her to Alleyn and left the studio.

'I wouldn't have had this happen,' Alleyn said, 'for all the world.'

'Don't give it another thought,' she mumbled into his sweater and helped herself to his handkerchief. 'It's nothing. It's just the *fact* of that room along there. Off the landing. You know – behind the locked door. Like a Bluebeard's chamber. I can't stop thinking about it. It's kind of got me down a bit.'

'I know.'

'And now – Maria. Going in there. *Damn!*' said Troy and stamped. 'I'd got myself all arranged not to be a burden and now look at me.'

'Could it be that you've done a morsel too much self-arranging and I've done a morsel too much male chauvinism, although I must say,' Alleyn confessed, 'I'm never quite sure what the ladies mean by the phrase. Have a good blow,' he added as Troy was making gingerly use of his handkerchief. She obeyed noisily and said she was feeling better.

'What would Br'er Fox say to me?' she asked and answered herself. Alleyn joined in.

' "We'll have to get you in the Force, Mrs Alleyn",' they quoted in unison.

'And wouldn't I make a pretty hash of it if you did,' said Troy.

'You've done jolly well with the half-burnt envelope. Classic stuff that, and very useful. It forced Marco to come tolerably clean.'

'Well, come, that's something.'

'It's half an hour to lunchtime. How about putting a bit of slap on your pink nose and coming for a brisk walk.'

'Lunch!' said Troy. 'And Mr Reece's massive small talk. And *food*! More *food*!'

'Perhaps the cook will have cut it down to clear soup and a slice of ham. Anyway, come on.'

'All right,' said Troy.

So they went out of doors where the sun shone, the dark wet trees glittered, the lake was spangled and the mountains were fresh, as if, it seemed, from creation's hand. The morning was alive with birdsong, sounds that might have been the voice of the bush itself, its hidden waters, its coolness, its primordial detachment.

They walked round the house to the empty hangar and thence, across the landing ground, to the path through the bush and arrived at the lakeside.

'Wet earth and greenery again,' said Troy. 'The best smell there is.'

'The Maori people had a god-hero called Maui. He went fishing, and hauled up the South Island.'

'Quite recently, by the feel of it.'

'Geologically it was, in fact, thrust up from the ocean bed by volcanic action. I've no idea,' said Alleyn, 'whether it was a slow process or a sudden commotion. It's exciting to imagine it heaving up all of a sudden with the waters pouring down the flanks of its mountains, sweeping across its plains and foaming back into the sea. But I dare say it was a matter of aeons rather than minutes.'

'And you say there are now lots and lots of painters, busy as bees, having a go at – ' Troy waved an arm at the prospect – 'all that.'

'That's right. From pretty peeps to competent posters and from factual statements to solemn abstractions. You name it.'

'How brave of them all.'

'Only some of them think so.' Alleyn took her arm. 'Some have got pretty near the bones. If things had been different,' he said, 'would you have wanted to paint?'

'Not at once. Make charcoal scribbles, perhaps. And after a time make some more with paint. Bones,' said Troy vaguely. 'The anatomy of the land. Something might come of it.'

'Shall we see what happens if we follow round the shore?'

'If you like. We'll either fetch up in the front of the house or get ourselves bushed. After all we *are* on an island.'

'All right, smarty-pants. Come on.'

A rough track followed the margin of the lake, for the most part clear of the bush but occasionally cutting through it. In places stormwater poured across the path. They came to a little footbridge over a deep-voiced creek. Here the bush was dense but further on it thinned enough to allow glimpses, surprisingly close at hand, of the west wall of the house. They were walking parallel with the path that skirted the concert chamber. The ground here was soft under their feet.

They walked in single file. Alleyn stopped short and held up his hand. He turned and laid his finger on his lips.

Ahead of them, hidden by the bush, someone was speaking.

The voice was so low, so very quiet that it was almost toneless and quite without a personality. It was impossible to catch what was said or guess at who said it.

Alleyn signalled to Troy to stay where she was and himself moved soundlessly along the path. He was drawing closer to the voice. He remembered that at a point opposite the first window of the concert chamber there was a garden seat and he fancied the speaker might be sitting on it. He moved on and in another moment or two realized that he should be able to make out the sense of what was said and then that it was said in Italian.

Alleyn's Italian had been pretty fluent but it was several years since he had had occasion to use it and it had grown rusty. At first the phrases slid past incomprehensibly and then he began to tune in.

' – *I have acted in this way because of what is being – hinted – suggested by you. All of you. And because when these policemen come you may try –* '

Alleyn lost the next phrase or two. There were gaps as if the speaker paused for a reply and none was forthcoming. The voice was raised. ' *– this is why – I have anticipated – I warn you – can go further and if necessary I will. Now. How do you answer? You understand, do you not? I mean what I say? I will act as I have said? Very well. Your answer? Speak up. I cannot hear you.*'

Nor could Alleyn. There had been some sort of reply – breathy – short – incomprehensible.

'*I am waiting.*'

Into the silence that followed a bellbird, close at hand, dropped his clear remark ending with a derisive clatter. Then followed, scarcely perceptible, a disturbance, an intrusion, nowhere – somewhere – coming closer and louder: the commonplace beat of a helicopter.

Inside the house a man shouted. Windows were thrown open.

'*Il elicottero!*' exclaimed the voice. There was a stifled response from his companion and sounds of rapid retreat.

'Here are the cops, darling!' said Alleyn.

'Rapture! Rapture! I suppose,' said Troy. 'Will you go and meet them?'

'It may be a case of joining in the rush, but yes, I think I'd better.'

'Rory – what'll be the drill?'

'Unusual, to say the least. I suppose I introduce them to Reece unless he's already introduced himself and when that's effected I'll hand over my file and remain on tap for questioning.'

'Will you use the studio?'

'I'd prefer the study but doubt if we'll get it. Look, my love, after lunch will you take to the studio if it's available? Or if you can't stand that any more, our room? I know you must have *had* them both but perhaps you might suffer them again, for a bit. Carmichael will look in and so will I, of course, but I don't know – '

'I'll be as right as rain. I might even try a few tentative notes – '

'Might you? Truly? Marvellous,' he said. 'I'll see you round to the front of the house.'

Their path took a right turn through the bush and came out beyond the garden seat. On the gravel walk in front of the house stood Maria with her arms folded, a black shawl over her head, staring up at the helicopter, now close overhead and deafening.

'Good morning, Maria,' Alleyn shouted cheerfully. 'Here are the police.'

She glowered.

'I have been meaning to speak to you: when they have completed their examination I think you'll be permitted to perform your office. I shall recommend that you are.'

She stared balefully at him from under her heavy brows. Her lips formed a soundless acknowledgement. '*Grazie tante.*'

Hanley came running out of the house, pulling on a jacket over his sweater.

'Oh, hul-*lo*, Mr Alleyn,' he cried. 'Thank goodness. I'm the Official Welcome. The Boss-Man told me to collect you and here you are. *Ben' trovato,* if that's what they say. You *will* come, won't you? I thought *he* ought to be there in person, but no, he's receiving them in the library. You haven't seen the library, have you, Mrs Alleyn? My dear, *smothered* in synthetic leather. Look! That contraption's alighting! Do let us hurry.'

Troy went up the front steps to the house. Signor Lattienzo was there, having apparently stepped out of the entrance. Alleyn saw him greet her with his usual exuberance. She waved.

'Mr Alleyn, *please*!' cried the distracted Hanley and led the way at a canter.

They arrived at the clearing as the helicopter landed and were raked with the unnatural gale from its propeller. Hanley let out an exasperated screech and clutched his blond hair. The engine stopped.

In the silence that followed Alleyn felt as if he was involved in some Stoppard-like time-slip and was back suddenly in the middle of a routine job. The three men who climbed out of the helicopter wore so unmistakably the marks of their calling, townish suits on large heavily muscled bodies, felt hats, sober shirts and ties. Sharp eyes and an indescribable air of taking over. Their equipment was handed down: cases and a camera. The fourth man who followed was slight, tweedy and preoccupied. He carried a professional bag. Police surgeon, thought Alleyn.

The largest of the men advanced to Alleyn.

'Chief Superintendent Alleyn?' the large man said. 'Hazelmere. Very glad indeed to see you, sir. Meet Dr Winslow. Detective-Sergeant Franks, Detective-Sergeant Barker.'

Alleyn shook hands. The police all had enormous hands and excruciating grips and prolonged the ceremony with great warmth.

'I understand you've had a spot of bother,' said Inspector Hazelmere.

'If I *may* butt in,' Hanley said anxiously. 'Inspector, Mr Reece hopes – ' and he delivered his invitation to the library.

'Very kind, I'm sure,' acknowledged Hazelmere. 'You'll be his secretary, sir? Mr Hanley? Is that correct? Well now, if it's all the same to Mr Reece I think it might be best if we took a look at the scene of the fatality. And if the Chief Superintendent would be kind enough to accompany us he can put us in the picture, which will save a lot of time and trouble when we see Mr Reece.'

'Oh,' said Hanley. 'Oh yes. I see. Well – ' he threw a troubled glance at Alleyn – 'if Mr Alleyn will – '

'Yes, of course,' said Alleyn.

'Yes. Well, I'll just convey your message to Mr Reece. I'm sure he'll understand,' said Hanley uneasily.

'I suggest,' said Alleyn, 'that you might ask Dr Carmichael to join us. I'm sure Dr Winslow would be glad to see him.'

'Are you? Yes. Of course.'

'Thank you very much, Mr Hanley,' said Hazelmere, blandly dismissive.

Hanley hesitated for a second or two, said, 'Yes, well – ' again and set off for the house.

Alleyn said: 'I can't tell you how glad I am to see you. You'll understand what a tricky position I've been in. No official authority but expected to behave like everybody's idea of an infallible sleuth.'

'Is that a fact, sir?' said Mr Hazelmere. He then paid Alleyn some rather toneless compliments, fetching up with the remark that he knew nothing beyond the information conveyed by Les, the launchman, over a storm-battered telephone line that a lady had been, as he put it, made away with and could they now view the remains and would Alleyn be kind enough to put them in the picture.

So Alleyn led them into the house and up to the first landing. He was careful, with suitable encomiums, to introduce Bert who was laconic and removed his two armchairs from their barrierlike position before the door. Dr Carmichael arrived and was presented, Alleyn unlocked the door and they all went into the room.

Back to square one. Blades of cool air slicing in through the narrowly opened windows, the sense of damp curtains, dust, stale scent and a pervasive warning of mortality, shockingly emphasized when Alleyn and Dr Carmichael drew away the black satin sheet.

Hazelmere made an involuntary exclamation which he converted into a clearance of the throat. Nobody spoke or moved and then Detective-Sergeant Franks whispered, 'Christ!' It sounded more like a prayer than an oath.

'What was the name?' Hazelmere asked.

'Of course,' Alleyn said, 'you don't know, do you?'

'The line was bad. I missed a lot of what the chap was saying.'

'He didn't know either. We communicated by various forms of semaphore.'

'Is that a fact? Fancy!'

'She was a celebrated singer. In the world class. The tops, in fact.'

'*Not*,' exclaimed Dr Winslow, 'Isabella Sommita? It can't be!'

'It is, you know,' said Dr Carmichael.

'You better have a look, Doc,' Hazelmere suggested.

'Yes. Of course.'

'If you're thinking of moving her we'll just let Sergeant Barker and Sergeant Franks in first, Doc,' said Hazelmere. 'For photos and dabs.'

Alleyn explained that he had used his own professional camera and had improvised fingerprinting tactics. 'I thought it might be as well to do this in case of post-mortem changes. Dr Carmichael and

I disturbed nothing and didn't touch her. I dare say the results won't be too hot and I think you'd better not depend on them. While they're doing their stuff,' he said to Hazelmere, 'would you like to get the picture?'

'Too right I would,' said the Inspector and out came his notebook.

And so to the familiar accompaniment of clicks and flashes, Alleyn embarked on an orderly and exhaustive report, event after event as they fell out over the past three days including the Strix-Marco element, the puzzle of the keys and the outcome of the opera. He gave a list of the inmates and guests in the Lodge. He spoke with great clarity and care, without hesitation or repetition. Hazelmere paused, once, and looked up at him.

'Am I going too fast?' Alleyn asked.

'It's not that, sir,' Hazelmere said. 'It's the way you give it out. Beautiful!'

Succinct though it was, the account had taken some time. Franks and Barker had finished. They and the two doctors, who had covered the body and retired to the far end of the room to consult, now collected round Alleyn, listening.

When he had finished he said: 'I've made a file covering all this stuff and a certain amount of background – past history and so on. You might like to see it. I'll fetch it, shall I?'

When he had gone Dr Winslow said: 'Remarkable.'

'Isn't it?' said Dr Carmichael with a slightly proprietary air.

'You'll never hear better,' Inspector Hazelmere pronounced. He addressed himself to the doctors. 'What's the story, then, gentlemen?'

Dr Winslow said he agreed with the tentative opinion formed by Alleyn and Dr Carmichael: that on a superficial examination the appearances suggested that the deceased had been anaesthetized and then asphyxiated and that the stiletto had been driven through the heart after death.

'How long after?' Hazelmere asked.

'Hard to say. After death the blood follows the law of gravity and sinks. The very scant effusion here suggested that this process was well advanced. The post-mortem would be informative.'

Alleyn returned with the file and suggested that Inspector Hazelmere, the two doctors and he go to the study leaving Sergeants

Barker and Franks to extend their activities to the room and bath-room. They had taken prints from the rigid hands of the Sommita and were to look for any that disagreed with them. Particularly, Alleyn suggested, on the bottom left-hand drawer of the dressing table, the gold handbag therein and the key in the bag. The key and the bag were to be replaced. He explained why.

'The room had evidently been thoroughly swept and dusted that morning so anything you find will have been left later in the day. You can expect to find Maria's and possibly Mr Reece's but we know of nobody else who may have entered the room. The housekeeper Mrs Bacon may have done so. You'll find her very cooperative.'

'So it may mean getting dabs from the lot of them,' said Hazelmere.

'It may, at that.'

'By the way, sir. That was a very bad line we spoke on. Temporary repairs after the storm. Excuse me, but did you ask me to bring a brace and bit?'

'I did, yes.'

'Yes. I thought it sounded like that.'

'*Did* you bring a brace and bit, Inspector?'

'Yes. I chanced it.'

'Large-sized bit?'

'Several bits. Different sizes.'

'Splendid.'

'Might I ask – '

'Of course. Come along to the studio and I'll explain. But first – take a look at the fancy woodwork on the wardrobe doors.'

II

The conference in the studio lasted for an hour and at its conclusion Dr Winslow discussed plans for the removal of the body. The lake was almost back to normal and Les had come over in the launch with the mail. 'She'll be sweet as a millpond by nightfall,' he reported. The police helicopter was making a second trip bringing two uniform constables and would take Dr Winslow back to Rivermouth. He would arrange for a mortuary van to be sent out and the body would

be taken across by launch to meet it. The autopsy would be performed as soon as the official pathologist was available: probably that
night.

'And now,' said Hazelmere, 'I reckon we lay on this – er –
experiment, don't we?'

'Only if you're quite sure you'll risk it. Always remembering that
if it flops you may be in for some very nasty moments.'

'I appreciate that. Look, Mr Alleyn, if you'd been me would you
have risked it?'

'Yes,' said Alleyn. 'I would. I'd have told myself I was a bloody
fool but I'd have risked it.'

'That's good enough for me,' said Hazelmere. 'Let's go.'

'Don't you think that perhaps Mr Reece has been languishing
rather a long time in the library?'

'You're dead right. Dear me, yes. I'd better go down.'

But there was no need for Hazelmere to go down. The studio door
opened and Mr Reece walked in.

Alleyn thought he was probably very angry indeed.

Not that his behaviour was in any way exceptional. He did not
scold and he did not shout. He stood stock-still in his own premises
and waited for somebody else to perform. His mouth was tightly
closed and the corners severely compressed.

With his head metaphysically lowered to meet an icy breeze,
Alleyn explained that they had thought it best first to make an official survey and for Inspector Hazelmere, whom he introduced and
who was given a stony acknowledgement, to be informed of all the
circumstances before troubling Mr Reece. Mr Reece slightly inclined
his head. Alleyn then hurriedly introduced Dr Winslow who was
awarded a perceptibly less glacial reception.

'As you are now at liberty,' Mr Reece pronounced, 'perhaps you
will be good enough to come down to the library where we will not
be disturbed. I shall be glad to learn what steps you propose to take.'

Hazelmere, to Alleyn's satisfaction, produced his own line of
imperturbability and said blandly that the library would no doubt be
very convenient. Mr Reece then pointedly addressing himself to
Alleyn, said that luncheon had been postponed until two o'clock and
would be in the nature of a cold buffet to which the guests would
help themselves when so inclined. It was now one-twenty.

'In the meantime,' Mr Reece magnificently continued, 'I will take it as a favour if you will extend my already deep obligation to you by joining us in the library.'

Alleyn thought there would be nothing Hazelmere would enjoy less than having him, Alleyn, on the sideline, a silent observer of his investigatory techniques.

He said that he had promised to look in on Troy. He added (truthfully) that she suffered from occasional attacks of migraine and (less truthfully) that one had threatened this morning. Mr Reece expressed wooden regrets and hoped to see him as soon as it was convenient. Alleyn felt as if they were both repeating memorized bits of dialogue from some dreary play.

Mr Reece said: 'Shall we?' to Hazelmere and led the way out of the studio. Hazelmere turned in the doorway and Alleyn rapidly indicated that he was returning to the bedroom. The Inspector stuck up his vast thumb and followed Mr Reece to the stairs.

Alleyn shut the door and Dr Carmichael, who had continued his now familiar role of self-elimination, rose and asked if Hazelmere really meant to carry out The Plan.

'Yes, he does and I hope to God he'll do himself no harm by it.'

'Not for the want of warning.'

'No. But it was I who concocted it.'

'What's the first step?'

'We've got to fix Maria asking for or being given unasked permission to lay out the body. Hazelmere had better set it up that she'll be told when she may do it.'

'Suppose she's gone off the idea?'

'That's a sickening prospect, isn't it? But we're hoping the opportunity it offers will do the trick. I'm going along now to get those two chaps on to it.'

Dr Carmichael said: 'Alleyn, if you can spare a moment would you be very kind and go over the business about the keys. I know it, but I'd like to be reminded.'

'All right. There are three keys to the bedroom. Maria had one which I took possession of when I first was in the bedroom, the Sommita another, and young Bartholomew the third. Mrs Bacon held the fourth. When Reece and the Sommita went upstairs after the concert they found Maria waiting. If the door had been locked she had let herself in with her own key. The Sommita threw a violent temperament, gave them what for, kicked them out and locked the door after them. They have both said individually that they distinctly heard the key turn in the lock. Twenty minutes later Maria returned with a hot drink, let herself in with her own key and found her mistress murdered. There was no sight anywhere on any surface or on the floor or on the body of the Sommita's key. I found it subsequently in her evening bag neatly disposed and wrapped at the bottom of a drawer. Reece is sure she didn't have the bag when they took her upstairs. The people who fussed round her in her dressing-room say she hadn't got it with her and indeed in that rig it would have been an incongruous object for her to carry – even offstage. Equally it's impossible to imagine her at the height of one of her towering rages getting the key from wherever it was, putting it in the lock in the fraction of time between Reece or Maria closing the door behind them and them both hearing the turn of the lock, and then meticulously getting out her evening bag, putting her key in it and placing it in the drawer. It even was enclosed in one of those soft cloth bags women use to prevent gold mesh from catching in the fabric of things like stockings. That's the story of the keys.'

'Yes. That's right. That's what I thought,' said Dr Carmichael uneasily.

'What's the matter?'

'It's just – rather an unpleasant thought.'

'About the third key?'

'Yes!'

'Rupert Bartholomew had it. Maria came to his room very late in the night and said I'd sent her for it.'

'Did she, by God!'

'He gave it to her. Bert, asleep in the chairs across the doorway, woke up to find Maria trying to stretch across him and put the key in the lock.'

'She must have been dotty. What did she think she'd do? Open the door and swarm over his sleeping body?'

'Open the door, yes. It opens inwards. And chuck the key into the room? She was hell-bent on our finding it there. Close the door, which would remain unlocked: she couldn't do anything about that. And when, as is probable, Bert wakes, throw a hysterical scene with all the pious drama about praying for the soul of the Sommita and laying her out.'

'Actually what did happen?'

'Bert woke up to find her generous personal equipment dangling over him. She panicked, dropped the key on him and bolted. He collected it and gave it to me. So she is still keyless.'

'Could you ever prove all these theories?'

'If the plan works.'

'Maria, eh?' said Dr Carmichael. 'Well, of course, she does look – I mean to say – '

'We've got to remember,' Alleyn said, 'that from the time Maria and Reece left the room and went downstairs and he joined his guests for dinner, Maria was in the staff sitting room preparing the hot drink. Mrs Bacon and Marco and others of the staff can be called to prove it.'

Carmichael stared at him. 'An alibi?' he said. 'For Maria? That's awkward.'

'In this game,' Alleyn said, 'one learns to be wary of assumptions.'

'I suppose I'm making one now. Very reluctantly.'

'The boy?'

'Yes.'

'Well, of course, he's the prime suspect. One can turn on all the clichés: "lust turned to hatred", "humiliation", "breaking point" – the lot. He was supposedly in his room at the crucial time but could have slipped out and he had his key to her room. He had motive and opportunity and he was in an extremely unstable condition.'

'Do the rest of them think – ?'

'Some of them do. Hanley does, or behaves and drops hints as if he does. Maria, and Marco I fancy, have been telling everyone he's the prime suspect. As I dare say the rest of the domestic staff believe, being aware, no doubt, of the changed relationship between the boy and the diva. And of course most of them witnessed the curtain speech and the fainting fit.'

'What about Lattienzo?'

'Troy and I overheard the jocund maestro in the shrubbery or near it, and in far from merry pin, threatening an unseen person with an evidently damaging exposure if he or she continued to spread malicious gossip. He spoke in Italian and the chopper was approaching so I missed whole chunks of his discourse.'

'Who was he talking to?'

'Somebody perfectly inaudible.'

'Maria?'

'I think so. When we emerged she was handy. On the front steps watching the chopper. Lattienzo was not far off.'

'I thought Lattienzo was not in his usual ebullient form when he came up here just now.'

'You were right,' said Alleyn and gave an account of the interview.

'The Italian element with a vengeance,' said the doctor thoughtfully.

'I must go along and fix things up in that room and then hie me to the library and Mr Reece's displeasure. Look in on Troy, like a good chap, would you, and tell her this studio's free? Do you mind? She's in our bedroom.'

'I'm delighted,' said the gallant doctor.

And so Alleyn returned to the Sommita's death chamber and found Sergeants Franks and Barker in dubious consultation. A brace and a selection of bits was laid out on a sheet of newspaper on the floor.

'The boss said you'd put us wise, sir,' said Franks.

'Right,' said Alleyn. He stood with his back to one of the exuberantly carved and painted wardrobe doors, felt behind him and bent his knees until his head was on a level with the stylized sunflower which framed it like a formalized halo. He made a funnel of his hand and looked through it at the covered body on the bed. Then he moved to the twin door and went through the same procedure.

'Yes,' he said, 'it'll work. It'll work all right.'

He opened the doors.

The walk-in wardrobe was occupied but not crowded with dresses. He divided them and slid them on their hangers to opposite ends of the interior. He examined the inside of the doors, came out and locked them.

He inspected the bits.

'This one will do,' he said and gave it, with the brace, to Sergeant Franks. 'Plumb in the middle,' he said, putting his finger on the black centre of the sunflower. 'And slide that newspaper under to catch the litter. Very careful, now. No splintering whatever you do. Which of you's the joiner?'

'Aw heck!' said Franks to Barker, 'what about you having a go, Merv.'

'I'm not fussy, thanks,' said Barker, backing off.

They looked uncomfortably at Alleyn.

'Well,' he said, 'I asked for it and it looks as if I've bought it. If I make a fool of myself I can't blame anyone else, can I? Give it here, Franks. Oh God, it's one of those push-me-pull-you brutes that shoot out at you when you least expect it.' He thumbed a catch and the business end duly shot out. 'What did I tell you? You guide it, Franks, and hold it steady. Dead centre. Anyone'd think we were defusing a bomb. Come on.'

'She's new, sir. Sharp as a needle and greased.'

'Good.'

He raised the brace and advanced it. Franks guided the point of the bit. 'Dead centre, sir,' he said.

'Here goes, then,' said Alleyn.

He made a cautious preliminary pressure. 'How's that?'

'Biting, sir.'

'Straight as we go, then.' Alleyn pumped the brace.

A little cascade of wood dust trickled through the elaborate carving and fell on the newspaper.

'Nearly there,' he grunted presently and a few seconds later the resistance was gone and he disengaged the tool.

At the black centre of the sunflower was a black hole as wide as the iris of an eye and very inconspicuous. Alleyn blew away the remnants of wood dust that were trapped in curlicues, twisted a finger in the hole and stood back. 'Not too bad,' he said.

He opened the door. The hole was clean cut.

'Now for the twin,' he said and gave the companion door the same treatment.

Then he went into the wardrobe and shut the doors. The interior smelt insufferably of La Sommita's scent. He looked through one of the holes. He saw the body. Neatly framed. Underneath the black satin cover its arm, still raised in cadaveric spasm, seemed to point at him. He came out, shut and locked the wardrobe doors and put the key in his pocket.

'It'll do,' he said. 'Will you two clean up? Very thoroughly? Before you do that I think you should know why you've been called on to set this up and what we hope to achieve by it. Don't you?'

They intimated by sundry noises that they did think so and he then told them of the next steps that would be taken, the procedure to be followed and the hoped-for outcome. 'And now I think perhaps one of you might relieve poor old Bert on the landing and I'd suggest the other reports for duty to Mr Hazelmere who will probably be in the library. It opens off the entrance hall. Third on the right from the front. I'm going down there now. Here's the key to this room. OK?'

'She'll be right, sir,' said Franks and Barker together.

So Alleyn went down to the library.

It came as no surprise to find the atmosphere in that utterly neutral apartment tepid, verging on glacial. Inspector Hazelmere had his notebook at the ready. Mr Reece sat at one of the neatly laden tables with the glaze of boredom veiling his pale regard. When Alleyn apologized for keeping him waiting he raised his hand and let it fall as if words now failed him.

The Inspector, Alleyn thought, was not at the moment happy in his work though he put up a reasonable show of professional *savoir-faire* and said easily that he thought he had finished 'bothering' Mr Reece and believed he was now fully in the picture. Mr Reece said woodenly that he was glad to hear it. An awkward silence followed which he broke by addressing himself pointedly to Alleyn.

'Would you,' he said, 'be good enough to show me where you found that book? I've been wondering about it.'

Alleyn led the way to the remote corner of the library and the obscure end of a top shelf. 'It was here,' he said, pointing to the gap. 'I could only just reach it.'

'I would require the steps,' said Mr Reece. He put on his massive spectacles and peered. 'It's very badly lit,' he said. 'The architect should have noticed that.'

Alleyn switched on the lights.

'Thank you. I would like to see the book when you have finished with it. I suppose it has something to do with this family feud or vendetta or whatever that she was so concerned about?'

'I would think so, yes.'

'It is strange that she never showed it to me. Perhaps that is because it is written in Italian. I would have expected her to show it to me,' he said heavily. 'I would have expected her to feel it would give validity to her theory. I wonder how she came by it? It is very shabby. Perhaps it was second-hand.'

'Did you notice the name on the flyleaf? "M. V. Rossi"?'

'Rossi? *Rossi!*' he repeated, and stared at Alleyn. 'But that was the name she *did* mention. On the rare occasions when she used a name. I recollect that she once said she wished my name did not resemble it. I thought this very far-fetched but she seemed to be quite serious about it. She generally referred simply to the *nemico* – meaning the enemy.'

'Perhaps, after all, it was not her book.'

'It was certainly not *mine*,' he said flatly.

'At some time – originally, I suppose – it has been the property of the "enemy". One wouldn't have expected her to have acquired it.'

'You certainly would not,' Mr Reece said emphatically. 'Up there, was it? What sort of company was it keeping?'

Alleyn took down four of the neighbouring books. One, a biography called *La Voce*, was written in Italian and seemed from cover to cover to be an unmodified rave about the Sommita. It was photographically illustrated beginning with a portrait of a fat-legged infant, much be-frilled, be-ringleted and be-ribboned, glowering on the lap according to the caption, of '*La Zia Giulia*' and ending with La Sommita receiving a standing ovation at a royal performance of *Faust*.

'Ah yes,' said Mr Reece. 'The biography. I always intended to read it. It went into three editions. What are the others?'

One in English, one in Italian – both novels with a strong romantic interest. They were gifts to the Sommita, lavishly inscribed by admirers.

'Is the autobiography there?' asked Mr Reece. 'That meant a helluva lot to me. Yes, sir. A helluva lot.'

This piece of information was dealt out by Mr Reece in his customary manner: baldly as if he were citing a quotation from Wall Street. For the first time he sounded definitely American.

'I'm sure it did,' Alleyn said.

'I never got round to reading it right through,' Mr Reece confessed and then seemed to brighten up a little. 'After all,' he pointed out, 'she didn't write it herself. But it was the thought that counted.'

'Quite. This seems, doesn't it, to be a corner reserved for her own books?'

'I believe I remember, now I come to think of it, her saying something about wanting some place for her own books. She didn't appreciate the way they looked in her bedroom. Out of place.'

'Do you think she would have put them up there herself?'

Mr Reece took off his spectacles and looked at Alleyn as if he had taken leave of his senses. 'Bella?' he said. 'Up there? On the steps?'

'Well, no. Silly of me. I'm sorry.'

'She would probably have told Maria to do it.'

'Ah, apropos! I don't know,' Alleyn said, 'whether Mr Hazelmere has told you?' He looked at the Inspector who slightly shook his head. 'Perhaps we should – ?'

'That's so, sir,' said Hazelmere. 'We certainly should.' He addressed himself to Mr Reece. 'I understand, sir, that Miss Maria Bennini has expressed the wish to perform the last duties and Mr Alleyn pointed out that until the premises had been thoroughly investigated the *stattus*' (so Mr Hazelmere pronounced it) '*quow* must be maintained. That is now the case. So, if it's acceptable to yourself, we will inform Miss Bennini and in due course – '

'Yes, yes. Tell her,' Mr Reece said. His voice was actually unsteady. He looked at Alleyn almost as if he appealed to him. 'And what then?' he asked.

Alleyn explained about the arrangements for the removal of the body. 'It will probably be at dusk or even after dark when they arrive at the lakeside,' he said. 'The launch will be waiting.'

'I wish to be informed.'

Alleyn and Hazelmere said together: 'Certainly, sir.'

'I will – ' he hunted for the phrase – 'I will see her off. It is the least I can do. If I had not brought her to this house – ' He turned aside, and looked at the books without seeing them. Alleyn put them back on their shelf. 'I'm not conversant with police procedure in New Zealand,' Mr Reece said. 'I understand it follows the British rather than the American practice. It may be quite out of order, at this juncture, to ask whether you expect to make an arrest in the foreseeable future.'

Hazelmere again glanced at Alleyn who remained silent. 'Well, sir,' Hazelmere said, 'it's not our practice to open up wide, like, until

we are very, very sure of ourselves. I think I'm in order if I say that
we hope quite soon to be in a position to take positive action.'

'Is that your view, too, Chief Superintendent?'

'Yes,' Alleyn said. 'That's my view.'

'I am very glad to hear it. You wish to see Maria, do you not?
Shall I send for her?'

'If it's not putting you out, sir, we'd be much obliged,' said
Inspector Hazelmere who seemed to suffer from a compulsion to
keep the interview at an impossibly high-toned level.

Mr Reece used the telephone. 'Find Maria,' he said, 'and ask her
to come to the library. Yes, at once. Very well, then, find her. Ask
Mrs Bacon to deal with it.'

He replaced the receiver. 'Staff coordination has gone to pieces,'
he said. 'I asked for service and am told the person in question is
sulking in her room.'

A long silence followed. Mr Reece made no effort to break it. He
went to the window and looked out at the lake. Hazelmere
inspected his notes, made two alterations and under a pretence of
consulting Alleyn about them said in a slurred undertone: 'Awkward
if she won't.'

'Hellishly,' Alleyn agreed.

Voices were raised in the hall, Hanley's sounding agitated, Mrs
Bacon's masterful. A door banged. Another voice shouted something
that might have been an insult and followed it up with a raucous
laugh. Marco, Alleyn thought. Hanley, all eyes and teeth, made an
abrupt entrance.

'I'm terribly sorry, sir,' he said. 'There's been a little difficulty. *Just*
coming.'

Mr Reece glanced at him with contempt. He gave a nervous titter
and withdrew only to reappear and stand, door in hand, to admit
Maria in the grip of Mrs Bacon.

'I'm extremely sorry, Mr Reece,' said Mrs Bacon in a high voice.
'Maria has been difficult.'

She released her hold as if she expected her catch would bolt and
when she did not, left the arena. Hanley followed her, shutting the
door but not before an indignant contralto was heard in the hall:
'No,' it said, 'this is too much. I can take no more of this,' said Miss
Dancy.

'You handle this one, eh?' Hazelmere murmured to Alleyn.

But Mr Reece was already in charge.

He said: 'Come here.' Maria walked up to him at once and waited with her arms folded, looking at the floor.

'You are making scenes, Maria,' said Mr Reece, 'and that is foolish of you: you must behave yourself. Your request is to be granted, see to it that you carry out your duty decently and with respect.'

Maria intimated rapidly and in Italian that she would be a model of decorum, or words to that effect, and that she was now satisfied and grateful and might the good God bless Signor Reece.

'Very well,' said Mr Reece. 'Listen to the Chief Superintendent and do as he tells you.'

He nodded to Alleyn and walked out of the room.

Alleyn told Maria that she was to provide herself with whatever she needed and wait in the staff sitting room. She would not be disturbed.

'You found her. You have seen what it is like,' he said. 'You are sure you want to do this?'

Maria crossed herself and said vehemently that she was sure.

'Very well. Do as I have said.'

There was a tap on the door and Sergeant Franks came in.

Hazelmere said: 'You'll look after Miss Bennini, Franks, won't you? Anything she may require.'

'Sir,' said Sergeant Franks.

Maria looked as if she thought she could do without Sergeant Franks and intimated that she wished to be alone with her mistress.

'If that's what you want,' said Hazelmere.

'To pray. There should be a priest.'

'All that will be attended to,' Hazelmere assured her. 'Later on.'

'When?'

'At the interment,' he said flatly.

She glared at him and marched out of the room.

'All right,' Hazelmere said to Franks. 'Later on. Keep with it. You know what you've got to do.'

'Sir,' said Sergeant Franks and followed her.

'Up we go,' said Alleyn.

He and Hazelmere moved into the hall and finding it empty, ran upstairs to the Sommita's bedroom.

III

It was stuffy in the wardrobe now they had locked themselves in. The smell was compounded of metallic cloth, sequins, fur, powder, scent and of the body when it was still alive and wore the clothes and left itself on them. It was as if the Sommita had locked herself in with her apparel.

'Cripes, it's close in here,' said Inspector Hazelmere.

'Put your mouth to the hole,' Alleyn suggested.

'That's an idea, too,' Hazelmere said and began noisily to suck air through his peephole. Alleyn followed his own advice. Thus they obliterated the two pencils of light that had given some shape to the darkness as their eyes became adjusted to it.

'Makes you think of those funny things jokers on the telly get up to,' Hazelmere said. 'You know. Crime serials.' And after a pause: 'They're taking their time, aren't they?'

Alleyn grunted. He applied his eye to his peephole. Again, suddenly confronting him, was the black satin shape on the bed: so very explicit, so eloquent of the body inside. The shrouded limb, still rigid as a yardarm, pointing under its funeral sheet – at him.

He thought: But shouldn't the rigidity be going off now? And tried to remember the rules about cadaveric spasm as opposed to rigor mortis.

'I told Franks to give us the office,' said Hazelmere. 'You know. Unlock the door and open it a crack and say something loud.'

'Good.'

'What say we open these doors, then? Just for a second or two? Sort of fan them to change the air? I suffer from hay fever,' Hazelmere confessed.

'All right. But we'd better be quick about it, hadn't we? Ready?'

Their keys clicked.

'Right.'

They opened the doors wide and flung them to and fro, exchanging the wardrobe air for the colder and more ominously suspect air of the room. Something fell on Alleyn's left foot.

'Bloody hell!' said Hazelmere. 'I've dropped the bloody key.'

'Don't move. They're coming. Here! Let me.' Alleyn collected it from the floor, pushed it in the keyhole and shut and locked both doors. He could feel Hazelmere's bulk heaving slightly against his own arm.

They looked through their spyholes. Alleyn's was below the level of his eyes and he had to bend his knees. The bedroom door was beyond their range of sight but evidently it was open. There was the sound of something being set down, possibly on the carpet. Detective-Sergeant Franks said: 'There you are, then, lady. I'll leave you to it. If you want anything, knock on the door. Same thing when you've finished. Knock.'

And Maria: 'Give me the key. I let myself out.'

'Sorry, lady. That's not my orders. Don't worry. I won't run away. Just knock when you're ready. See you.'

The bedroom door shut firmly. They could hear the key turn in the lock.

Alleyn could still see, framed by his spyhole, the body and beyond it a section of the dressing table.

As if by the action of a shutter in a camera they were blotted out. Maria was not two feet away and Alleyn looked into her eyes. He thought for a sickening moment that she had seen the hole in the sunflower but she was gone only to reappear by the dressing table: stooping – wrenching open a drawer – a bottom drawer.

Hazelmere gave him a nudge. Alleyn remembered that he commanded a slightly different and better view than his own of the bottom left-hand end of the dressing table.

But now Maria stood up and her hands were locked round a gold mesh bag. They opened it and inverted it and shook it out on the dressing table and her right hand fastened on the key that fell from it.

Hazelmere shifted but Alleyn, without moving his eye from the spyhole, reached out and touched him.

Maria now stood over the shrouded body and looked at it, one would have said, speculatively.

With an abrupt movement, more feline than human, she knelt and groped under the shroud – she scuffled deep under the body, which jolted horridly.

The black shroud slithered down the raised arm and by force of its own displaced weight slid to the floor.

And the arm dropped.

It fell across her neck. She screamed like a trapped ferret and with a grotesque and frantic movement rolled away and scrambled to her feet.

'Now,' Alleyn said.

He and Hazelmere unlocked their doors and walked out into the room.

Hazelmere said: 'Maria Bennini, I arrest you on a charge – '

CHAPTER 9

Departure

The scene might have been devised by a film director who had placed his camera on the landing and pointed it downwards to take in the stairs and the hall beneath where he had placed his actors, all with upturned faces. For sound he had used only the out-of-shot Maria's screams, fading them as she was taken upstairs by the two detective-sergeants to an unoccupied bedroom. This would be followed by total silence and immobility and then, Alleyn thought, the camera would probably pan from face to upturned face: from Mr Reece halfway up the stairs, pallid and looking, if anything, scandalized, breathing hard, and to Ben Ruby immensely perturbed and two steps lower down, to Signor Lattienzo with his eyeglass stuck in a white mask. Ned Hanley, on the lowest step, held on to the banister as if in an earthquake. Below him Miss Dancy at ground level, appropriately distraught and wringing every ounce of star-quality out of it. Further away Sylvia Parry clung to Rupert Bartholomew. And finally, in isolation, Marco stood with his arms folded and wearing a faint, unpleasant smile.

Removed from all these stood Mrs Bacon in command of her staff who were clustered behind her. Near the door into the porch, Les and Bert kept themselves to themselves in close proximity to the pregnant nude whose smirk would no doubt be held in shot for a second or two providing an enigmatic note. Finally, perhaps, the camera would dwell upon the remaining stiletto and the empty bracket where its opposite number had hung.

Alleyn supposed this company had been made aware of what was going on by Hanley and perhaps Mrs Bacon and that the guests had been at their buffet luncheon and the staff assembled for theirs in their own region and that Maria's screams had brought them out like a fire alarm.

Mr Reece, as ever, was authoritative. He advanced up the stairs and Inspector Hazelmere met him at the top. He, too, in his professional manner was impressive and Alleyn thought: He's going to handle this.

'Are we to know,' Mr Reece asked at large, 'what has happened?'

'I was coming to see you, sir,' said Inspector Hazelmere. 'If you'll excuse me for a moment – ' he addressed the company – 'I'll ask everybody at the back, there, if you please, to return to whatever you were doing before you were disturbed. For your information, we have been obliged to take Miss Maria Bennini into custody – ' he hesitated for a moment – 'you may say protective custody,' he added. 'The situation is well in hand and we'll be glad to make that clear to you as soon as possible. Thank you. Mrs – er – '

'Bacon,' Alleyn murmured.

'Mrs Bacon – if you would be kind enough – '

Mrs Bacon was kind enough and the set was, as it were, cleared of supernumeraries.

For what, Alleyn thought, might well be the last time, Mr Reece issued a colourless invitation to the study and was at some pains to include Alleyn. He also said that he was sure there would be no objection to Madame's singing maestro for whom she had a great affection, Signor Lattienzo, and their old friend and associate, Mr Ben Ruby, being present.

'They have both been with me throughout this dreadful ordeal,' Mr Reece said drearily, and added that he also wished his secretary to be present and take notes.

The Inspector controlled any surprise he may have felt at this request. His glance which was of the sharp and bright variety rested for a moment on Hanley before he said there was no objection. In fact, he said, it had been his intention to ask for a general discussion. Alleyn thought that if there had been a slight juggling for the position of authority, the Inspector had politely come out on top. They all proceeded solemnly to the study and the soft leather chairs in front of the unlit fireplace. It was here, Alleyn reflected, that this case had taken on one of its more eccentric characteristics.

Inspector Hazelmere did not sit down. He took up his stance upon that widely accepted throne of authority, the hearthrug. He said:

'With your permission, sir, I am going to request Chief Superintendent Alleyn to set out the events leading up to this crime. By a very strange but fortunate coincidence he was here and I was not. Mr Alleyn.'

He stepped aside and made a very slight gesture handing over the hearthrug, as it were, to Alleyn, who accordingly took his place on it. Mr Reece seated himself at his desk which was an ultra-modern affair, streamlined and enormous. It accommodated two people facing each other across it. Mr Reece signalled to Hanley who hurried into the second and less opulent seat and produced his notebook. Alleyn got the impression that Mr Reece highly approved of these formalities. As usual he seemed to compose himself to hear the minutes of the last meeting. He took a leather container of keys from his pocket, looked as if he was surprised to see it, and swivelled round in his chair with it dangling from his fingers.

Alleyn said: 'This is a very unusual way to follow up an arrest on such a serious charge but I think that, taking all the circumstances which are themselves extraordinary, into consideration, it is a sensible decision. Inspector Hazelmere and I hope that in hearing this account of the case and the difficulties it presents you will help us by correcting anything I may say if you know it to be in the smallest degree, mistaken. Also we do beg you, if you can add any information that will clear up a point, disprove or confirm it, you will stop me and let us all hear what it is. That is really the whole purpose of the exercise. We ask for your help.'

He paused.

For a moment or two nobody spoke and then Mr Reece cleared his throat and said he was sure they all 'appreciated the situation'. Signor Lattienzo, still unlike his usual ebullient self, muttered 'Naturalmente' and waved a submissive hand.

'OK, OK,' Ben Ruby said impatiently. 'Anything to wrap it up and get shot of it all. Far as I'm concerned, I've always thought Maria was a bit touched. Right from the start I've had this intuition and now you tell me that's the story. She did it.'

Alleyn said: 'If you mean she killed her mistress single-handed, we don't think she did any such thing.'

Mr Reece drew back his feet as if he was about to rise but thought better of it. He continued to swing his keys.

Signor Lattienzo let out a strong Italian expletive and Ben Ruby's jaw dropped and remained in that position without his uttering a word. Hanley said 'What!' on a shrill note and immediately apologized.

'In that case,' Mr Reece asked flatly, 'why have you arrested her?'

The others made sounds of resentful agreement.

'For impaling the dead body with the stiletto thrust through the photograph,' said Alleyn.

'This is diabolical,' said Signor Lattienzo. 'It is disgusting.'

'What possible proof can you have of it?' Mr Reece asked. 'Do you know now, positively, that Marco is Strix and took the photograph?'

'Yes. He has admitted it.'

'In that case how did she obtain it?'

'She came into this room when he was putting it into an envelope addressed to *The Watchman* in typescript, on Madame Sommita's instructions, by Mr Hanley.'

'That's right – ' Hanley said. 'The envelope was meant for her letter to *The Watchman* when she'd signed it. I've told you – ' And then, on a calmer note. 'I see what you mean. Marco would have thought it would be posted without – anybody – *me* – thinking anything of it. Yes, I see.'

'Instead of which we believe Maria caught sight of Marco pushing the photograph into the envelope. Her curiosity was aroused. She waited until Marco had gone, and took it out. She kept it, and made the mistake of throwing the envelope into the fire. It fell, half-burnt, through the bars of the grate into the ashpan from where we recovered it.'

'If this is provable and not merely conjecture,' said Mr Reece, swinging his keys, 'do you argue that at this stage she anticipated the crime?'

'If the murder was the last in a long series of retributive crimes it would appear so. In the original case an incriminating letter was transfixed to the body.'

There followed a long silence. 'So she was right,' said Mr Reece heavily. 'She was right to be afraid. I shall never forgive myself.'

Ben Ruby said Mr Reece didn't want to start thinking that way. 'We none of us thought there was anything in it,' he pleaded. 'She used to dream up such funny ideas. You couldn't credit them.'

Signor Lattienzo threw up his hands. 'Wolf. Wolf,' he said.

'I've yet to be convinced,' Mr Reece said. 'I cannot believe it of Maria. I know they used to fall out occasionally but there was nothing in that. Maria was devoted. Proof!' he said still contemplating his keys. 'You have advanced no proof.'

'I see I must now give some account of the puzzle of the keys.'

'The keys? Whose keys?' asked Mr Reece, swinging his own.

Alleyn suppressed a crazy impulse to reply 'The Queen's keys' in the age-old challenge of the Tower of London. He merely gave as clear an account as possible of the enigma of the Sommita's key and the impossibility of her having had time to remove it from a bag in the bottom drawer of the dressing table and lock the bedroom door in the seconds that elapsed between her kicking out Mr Reece and Maria and them hearing it click in the lock.

Mr Reece chewed this over and then said: 'One can only suppose that at this stage her bag was not in the drawer but close at hand.'

'Even so: ask yourself. She orders you out, you shut the door and immediately afterwards hear it locked: a matter of perhaps two seconds.'

'It may have already been in her hand.'

'Do you remember her hands during the interview?'

'They were clenched. She was angry.'

'Well – it could be argued, I suppose. Just. But there is a sequel,' Alleyn said. And he told them of Maria's final performance and arrest.

'I'm afraid,' he ended, 'that all the pious protestations, all her passionate demands to perform the last duties were an act. She realized that she had blundered, that we would, on her own statement, expect to find her mistress's key in the room, and that she must at all costs get into the room and push it under the body where we would find it in due course.'

'What did she say when you arrested her?' Lattienzo asked.

'Nothing. She hasn't spoken except – '

'Well? Except?'

'She accused Rupert Bartholomew of murder.'

Hanley let out an exclamation. Lattienzo stared at him. 'You spoke, Mr Hanley?' he said.

'No, no. Nothing. Sorry.'

Ben Ruby said: 'All the same, you know – well, I mean, you *can't* ignore – I mean to say, there *was* that scene, wasn't there? I mean, she had put him through it, no kidding. And the curtain speech and the way he acted. I mean to say, he's the only one of us who you could say had motive and opportunity – I mean – '

'My good Ben,' Lattienzo said wearily, 'we all know in general terms what you mean. But when you say "opportunity" what *precisely* do you mean? Opportunity to murder? But Mr Alleyn tells us he does not as yet accuse the perpetrator of the dagger-and-photograph operation of the murder. And Mr Alleyn convinces me, for what it's worth, that he knows what he's talking about. I would like to ask Mr Alleyn if he links Maria, who has been arrested for the photograph abomination, with the murder and if so what that link is. Or are we to suppose that Maria, on re-entering the room, hot drink in hand, discovered the dead body and was inspired to go downstairs, unobserved by the milling crowd, remove the dagger from the wall, collect the photograph from wherever she'd put it, return to the bedroom, perform her atrocity and then raise the alarm? Is that, as dear Ben would put it, the story?'

'Not quite,' said Alleyn.

'Ah!' said Lattienzo. 'So I supposed.'

'I didn't say we don't suspect her for murder: on the contrary. I merely said she was arrested on the charge of mutilating the body, not on a charge of murder.'

'But that may follow?'

Alleyn was silent.

'Which is as much as to say,' Ben Ruby said, 'that you reckon it's a case of conspiracy and that Maria is half of the conspiracy and that one of us – I mean of the people in this house – was the principal. Yeah?'

'Yes.'

'Charming!' said Mr Ruby.

'Are we to hear any more?' Mr Reece asked. 'After all, apart from the *modus operandi* in Maria's case, we have learnt nothing new, have we? As, for instance, whether you have been able to clear any of us of suspicion. Particularly the young man – Bartholomew.'

'Monty, my dear,' said Lattienzo who had turned quite pale, 'how right you are. And here I would like to say with the greatest emphasis that I resist vehemently any suggestion, open or covert, that this unfortunate boy is capable of such a crime. Mr Alleyn, I beg you to consider! What does such a theory ask us to accept? Consider his behaviour.'

'Yes,' Alleyn said, 'consider it. He makes what amounts to a public announcement of his break with her. He puts himself into the worst possible light as a potential murderer. He even writes a threatening message on a greetings card. He is at particular pains to avoid laying on an alibi. He faints, is taken upstairs, recovers and hurries along to the bedroom where he chloroforms and asphyxiates his victim and returns to his own quarters.'

Lattienzo stared at Alleyn for a second or two. The colour returned to his face, he made his little crowing sound and seized Alleyn's hands. 'Ah!' he cried. 'You agree! You see! You see! It is impossible! It is ridiculous!'

'If I may just pipe up,' Hanley said, appealing to Mr Reece. 'I mean, all this virtuous indignation on behalf of the Boy-Beautiful! Very touching and all that.' He shot a glance at his employer and another at Lattienzo. 'One might be forgiven for drawing one's own conclusions.'

'That will do,' said Mr Reece.

'Well, all right, then, sir. Enough said. But I mean – after all, one would like to be officially in the clear. I mean: take me. From the time you escorted Madame upstairs and she turned you and Maria out until Maria returned and found her – dead – I was in the dining room and hall calming down guests and talking to Les and telling you about the lake and making a list for Les to check the guests by. I really could not,' said Hanley on a rising note of hysteria, 'have popped upstairs and murdered Madame and come back, as bright as a button, to speed the parting guests and tramp about with umbrellas. And anyway,' he added, 'I hadn't got a key.'

'As far as that goes,' said Ben Ruby, '*she* could have let you in and I don't mean anything nasty. Just to set the record straight.'

'Thank you very much,' said Hanley bitterly.

'To return to the keys,' Mr Reece said slowly, still swinging his own as if to illustrate his point. 'About the third key, *her* key.' He appealed to Hazelmere and Alleyn. 'There must be some explanation. Some quite simple explanation. Surely.'

Alleyn looked at Hazelmere who nodded very slightly.

'There is,' said Alleyn, 'a *very* simple explanation. The third key was in the bag in the bottom drawer where it had lain unmolested throughout the proceedings.'

Into the silence that followed there intruded a distant pulsation: the chopper returning, thought Alleyn.

Mr Reece said: 'But when Maria and I left – we – heard the key turn in the lock. What key? You've accounted for the other two. She locked us out with her own key.'

'We think not.'

'But Maria heard it too. She has said so. I don't understand this,' said Mr Reece. 'Unless . . . But no. No, I don't understand. Why did Maria do as you say she did? Come back and try to hide the key under – ? It's horrible. *Why* did she do that?'

'Because, as I've suggested, she realized we would expect to find it.'

'Ah. Yes. I take the point but all the same – '

'Monty,' Signor Lattienzo cried out. 'For pity's sake *do* something with those accursed keys. You are lacerating my nerves.'

Mr Reece looked at him blankly. 'Oh?' he said. 'Am I? I'm sorry.' He hesitated, examined the key by which he had suspended the others and, turning to his desk, fitted it into one of the drawers. 'Is that better?' he asked and unlocked the drawer.

Ben Ruby said in a voice that was pitched above its normal register: 'I don't get any of this. All I know is we better look after ourselves. And as far as our lot goes – you, Monty, and Beppo and me – we were all sitting at the dinner table from the time you left Bella alive and throwing a temperament, until Maria raised the alarm.' He turned on Alleyn. 'That's right, isn't it? That's correct? Come on – isn't it?'

'Not quite,' said Alleyn. 'When Mr Reece and Maria left Madame Sommita she was not throwing a temperament. She was dead.'

II

In the bad old days of capital punishment it used to be said that you could tell when a verdict of guilty was about to be returned. The jury always avoided looking at the accused. Alleyn was reminded now, obliquely, of this dictum. Nobody moved. Nobody spoke. Everyone looked at him and only at him.

Inspector Hazelmere cleared his throat.

The helicopter landed. So loud, it might have been on the roof or outside on the gravel. The engine shut off and the inflowing silence was intolerable.

Mr Reece said: 'More police, I assume.'

Hazelmere said: 'That is correct, sir.'

Somebody crossed the hall and seconds later Sergeant Franks walked past the windows.

'I think, Chief Superintendent Alleyn,' said Mr Reece, 'you must be out of your mind.'

Alleyn took out his notebook. Hazelmere placed himself in front of Mr Reece. 'Montague Reece,' he said, 'I arrest you for the murder of Isabella Sommita and I have to warn you that anything you say will be taken down in writing and may be used in evidence.'

'Hanley,' Mr Reece said, 'get through to my solicitors in Sydney.'

Hanley said in a shaking voice: 'Certainly, sir.' He took up the receiver, fumbled and dropped it on the desk. He said to Alleyn: 'I suppose – is it all right? I mean – '

Hazelmere said: 'It's in order.'

'Do it,' Mr Reece said. And then, loudly to Hazelmere: 'The accusation is grotesque. You will do yourself a great deal of harm.'

Alleyn wrote this down.

Mr Reece looked round the room as if he was seeing it for the first time. He swivelled his chair and faced his desk. Hanley, drawn back in his chair with the receiver at his ear, watched him. Alleyn took a step forward.

'Here *are* the police,' Mr Reece observed loudly.

Hazelmere, Lattienzo and Ruby turned to look.

Beyond the windows Sergeant Franks tramped past, followed by a uniform sergeant and a constable.

'*No!*' Hanley screamed. '*Stop him! No!*'

There was nothing but noise in the room.

Alleyn had not prevented Mr Reece from opening the unlocked drawer and snatching out the automatic but he had knocked up his arm. The bullet had gone through the top of a window-pane and two succeeding shots had lodged in the ceiling. Dust fell from the overhead lampshades.

Two helmets and three deeply concerned faces appeared at the foot of the windows, slightly distorted by pressure against the glass. The owners rose and could be heard thundering round the house.

Alleyn with Mr Reece's arms secured behind his back said, a trifle breathlessly: 'That was a very silly thing to do, Signor Rossi.'

III

'. . . almost the only silly thing he did,' Alleyn said. 'He showed extraordinary coolness and judgement throughout. His one serious slip was to say he heard the key turn in the lock. Maria set that one up and he felt he had to fall in with it. He was good at avoiding conflicts and that's the only time he told a direct lie.'

'What I *can't* understand,' Troy said, 'is his inviting you of all people to his party.'

'Only, I think, after the Sommita or perhaps Hanley told him about her letter to the Yard. It was dated a week before his invitations to us. Rather than un-pick her letter he decided to confirm it. And I'm sure he really did *want* the portrait. Afterwards it could have been, for him, the equivalent of a scalp. And as for my presence in the house, I fancy it lent what the mafiosi call "elegance" to the killing.'

'My God,' said Signor Lattienzo, 'I believe you are right.'

'There was one remark he made that brought me up with a round turn,' Alleyn said. 'He was speaking of her death to Ben Ruby and he said, "And now she no longer casts a shadow." '

'But that's – isn't it – a phrase used by – '

'The mafiosi? Yes. So I had discovered when I read the book in the library. It was not in Mr Reece's usual style, was it?'

Signor Lattienzo waited for a little and then said, 'I assure you, my dear Alleyn, that I have sworn to myself that I will not pester you but I immediately break my resolution to say that I die to know how you discovered his true identity. His name. "Rossi".'

'Have you ever noticed that when people adopt pseudonyms they are so often impelled to retain some kind of link with their old name? Often it is the initials, often there is some kind of assonance – Reece – Rossi. M. V. Rossi – Montague V. Reece. He actually had the nerve to tell me his Bella had confided that she wished his surname didn't remind her of the "enemy". The M. V. Rossi signature in the book bears quite a strong resemblance to the Reece signature, spiky letters and all. He seems to have decided very early in life to opt out of the "family" business. It may even have been at his father's suggestion. Papa Rossi leaves a hefty swag of ill-gotten gains which Monty Reece manipulates brilliantly and with the utmost propriety and cleanest of noses. I think it must have amused him to plant the book up there with the diva's bi- and autobi-ographies. The book has been instructive. The victim in the case it deals with was a Rossi girl – his sister. A paper was stabbed to her heart. She had a brother, Michele-Vittorio Rossi, who disappeared.'

'Our Mr Reece?'

'It's a good guess.'

'And Maria?'

'The widow Bennini? Who wouldn't tell me her maiden name. I wouldn't be surprised if it turns out to have been Rossi. He is said to have picked her up at the Italian Embassy. He may even have planted her there. Obviously they were in heavy cahoots. I imagine them enjoying a good gloat over the Strix on-goings.'

Signor Lattienzo said: 'Was Strix in Monty's pay?'

'So far there's no proof of it. It would fit in very tidily, wouldn't it? But all this is grossly speculative stuff. At best, merely Gilbertian "corroborative detail". The case rests on the bedrock fact that once you accept that the crime was committed at the earlier time, which the medical opinion confirms, everything falls into place and there are no difficulties. Nobody else could have done it, not even young Bartholomew who was being tended in his room by you and Dr Carmichael. The rest of us were at dinner. The doctors will testify that the stab was administered an appreciable time after death.'

'And – he – Monty, took Bella up to her room and – he – ?'

'With Maria's help, chloroformed and stifled her. I've been told that the diva, after cutting up rough, always without fail required Maria to massage her shoulders. Maria actually told me she offered this service and was refused, but perhaps it was Maria, ready and waiting, who seized the opportunity to grind away at Madame's shoulders and then use the chloroform while Mr Reece who – all inarticulate sympathy – had been holding the victim's hands, now tightened his grip and when she was insensible went in for the kill. He then joined us in the dining room as you will remember and told us she was not very well. Maria meanwhile prepared the hot drink and collected the dagger and photograph.'

'So that extra touch was all her own?'

'If it was I feel sure he approved it. It was in the mafioso manner. It had, they would consider, style and elegance.'

'That,' observed Signor Lattienzo, 'as Monty himself would say, "figures".'

Bert came into the hall. He said they were ready and opened the front doors. There, outside, was the dawn. Bellbirds chimed through the bush like rain distilled into sound. The trees, blurred in mist, were wet and smelt of honeydew. The lake was immaculate and perfectly still.

Troy said: 'This landscape belongs to birds: not to men, not to animals: huge birds that have gone now, stalked about in it. Except for birds it's empty.'

Bert shut the doors of the Lodge behind them.

He and Alleyn and Troy and Signor Lattienzo walked across the gravelled front and down to the jetty where Les waited in the launch.

Light Thickens

For James Laurenson who played The Thane
and for Helen Thomas (Holmes) who was his Lady,
in the third production of the play
by The Canterbury University Players.

Contents

PART ONE: CURTAIN UP

1	First Week	229
2	Second Week	257
3	Third Week	282
4	Fourth Week	308
5	Fifth Week. Dress Rehearsals and First Night	330

PART TWO: CURTAIN CALL

6	Catastrophe	345
7	The Junior Element	377
8	Development	399
9	Finis	418

Cast of Characters

Peregrine Jay	*Director, Dolphin Theatre*
Emily Jay	*His wife*
Crispin Jay	*Their eldest son*
Robin Jay	*Their second son*
Richard Jay	*Their youngest son*
Annie	*Their cook*
Doreen	*Her daughter*
Jeremy Jones	*Designer, Dolphin Theatre*
Winter Morris	*Business Manager*
Mrs Abrams	*Secretary*
Bob Masters	*Stage Director*
Charlie	*Assistant Stage Manager*
Ernie	*Property Master*
Nanny	*Miss Mannering's dresser*
Mrs Smith	*Mother of William*
Marcello	*A restaurateur*
The Stage-Door Keeper	

Chief Superintendent
  Roderick Alleyn
Detective-Inspector Fox   } *Of*
Detective-Sergeant Thompson   *Scotland*
Detective-Sergeant Bailey   *Yard*

Sir James Curtis   *Pathologist*

MACBETH

by
William Shakespeare

DUNCAN, KING OF SCOTLAND		*Norman King*
MALCOLM	HIS SONS	*Edward King*
DONALBAIN		*An Actor*
MACBETH	GENERALS OF THE	*Dougal Macdougal*
BANQUO	KING'S ARMY	*Bruce Barrabell*
MACDUFF		*Simon Morten*
LENNOX		
ROSS	NOBLEMEN OF SCOTLAND	*Actors*
MENTEITH		
ANGUS		
CAITHNESS		
FLEANCE, SON TO BANQUO		*An Actor*
SIWARD, EARL OF NORTHUMBERLAND		*Actors*
YOUNG SIWARD, HIS SON		
SEYTON, AN OFFICER ATTENDING ON MACBETH		*Gaston Sears*
BOY, SON TO MACDUFF		*William Smith*
A WOUNDED SERGEANT		
A PORTER		*Actors*
DOCTORS		
LADY MACBETH		*Margaret Mannering*
LADY MACDUFF		*Nina Gaythorne*
WAITING WOMEN		*Actresses*
THE WEIRD SISTERS		*Rangi*
		Wendy
		Blondie

Sundry soldiers, servants and apparitions
The Scene: Scotland and England
The play directed by PEREGRINE JAY
Setting and Costumes by JEREMY JONES

Part One: Curtain Up

CHAPTER 1

First Week

Peregrine Jay heard the stage door at the Dolphin open and shut and the sound of voices. His scenic and costume designer and lights manager came through to the open stage. They wheeled out three specially built racks, unrolled their drawings for the production of *Macbeth* and pinned them up.

They were stunning. A permanent central rough stone stairway curving up to Duncan's chamber. Two turntables articulating with this to represent, on the right, the outer façade of Inverness Castle or the inner courtyard with, on the left, a high stone platform with a gallows and a dangling rag-covered skeleton, or, turned, another wall of the courtyard. The central wall was a dull red arras behind the stairway and open sky.

The lighting director showed a dozen big drawings of the various sets with the startling changes brought about by his craft. One of these was quite lovely: an opulent evening in front of the castle with the setting sun bathing everything in splendour. One felt the air to be calm, gentle and full of the sound of wings. And then, next to it, the same scene with the enormous doors opened, a dark interior, torches, a piper and the Lady in scarlet coming to welcome the fated visitor.

'Jeremy,' Peregrine said, 'you've done us proud.'

'OK?'

'It's so *right*! It's so bloody *right*. Here! Let's up with the curtain. Jeremy?'

The designer went offstage and pressed a button. With a long-drawn-out sigh the curtain rose. The shrouded house waited.

'Light them, Jeremy! Blackout and lights on them. Can you?'

'It won't be perfect but I'll try.'

'Just for the hell of it, Jeremy.'

Jeremy laughed, moved the racks and went to the lights console.

Peregrine and the others filed through a pass-door to the front-of-house. Presently there was a total blackout and then, after a pause, the drawings were suddenly there, alive in the midst of nothing and looking splendid.

'Only approximate, of course,' Jeremy said in the dark.

'Let's keep this for the cast to see. They're due now.'

'You don't want to start them off with broken legs, do you?' asked somebody's voice in the dark.

There was an awkward pause.

'Well – no. Put on the light in the passage,' said Peregrine in a voice that was a shade too off-hand. 'No,' he shouted. 'Bring down the curtain again, Jeremy. We'll do it properly.'

The stage door was opened and more voices were heard, two women's and a man's. They came in exclaiming at the dark.

'All right, all *right*,' Peregrine called out cheerfully. 'Stay where you are. Lights, Jeremy, would you? Just while people are coming in. Thank you. Come down in front, everybody. Watch how you go. Splendid.'

They came down. Margaret Mannering first, complaining about the stairs in her wonderful warm voice with little breaks of laughter, saying she knew she was unfashionably punctual. Peregrine hurried to meet her. 'Maggie, *darling*! It's all meant to start us off with a bang, but I do apologize. No more steps. Here we are. Sit down in the front row. Nina! Are you all right? Come and sit down, love. Bruce! Welcome, indeed. I'm so glad you managed to fit us in with television.'

I'm putting it on a bit thick, he thought. Nerves! Here they all come. Steady now.

They arrived singly and in pairs, having met at the door. They greeted Peregrine and one another extravagantly or facetiously and all of them asked why they were sitting in front and not on stage or in the rehearsal room. Peregrine kept count of heads. When they got to seventeen and then to nineteen he knew they were waiting for only one: the Thane.

He began again, counting them off. Simon Morten – Macduff. A magnificent figure, six foot two. Dark. Black eyes with a glitter. Thick black hair that sprang in short-clipped curls from his skull. A smooth physique not yet running to fat and a wonderful voice. Almost too good to be true. Bruce Barrabell – Banquo. Slight. Five foot ten inches tall. Fair to sandy hair. Beautiful voice. And the King? Almost automatic casting – he'd played every Shakespearean king in the canon except Lear and Claudius, and played them all well if a little less than perfectly. The great thing about him was, above all, his royalty. He was more royal than any of the remaining crowned heads of Europe and his name was actually King: Norman King. The Malcolm was, in real life, his son – a young man of nineteen – and the resemblance was striking.

There was Lennox, the sardonic man. Nina Gaythorne, the Lady Macduff, who was talking very earnestly with the Doctor. And I don't mind betting it's all superstition, thought Peregrine uneasily. He looked at his watch: twenty minutes late. I've half a mind to start without him, so I have.

A loud and lovely voice and the bang of the stage door.

Peregrine hurried through the pass door and up on the stage.

'Dougal, my dear fellow, welcome,' he shouted.

'But I'm so sorry, dear boy. I'm afraid I'm a fraction late. Where is everybody?'

'In front. I'm not having a reading.'

'Not?'

'No. A few words about the play. The working drawings and then away we go.'

'Really?'

'Come through. This way. Here we go.'

Peregrine led the way. 'The Thane himself, everybody,' he announced.

It gave Sir Dougal Macdougal an entrance. He stood for a moment on the steps into the front-of-house, an apologetic grin transforming his face. Such a nice chap, he seemed to be saying. No upstage nonsense about him. Everybody loves everybody. Yes. He saw Margaret Mannering. Delight! Acknowledgement! Outstretched arms and a quick advance. 'Maggie! My dear! How too lovely!' Kissing of hands and both cheeks. Everybody felt as if the central heating had been turned up another five points. Suddenly they all began talking.

Peregrine stood with his back to the curtain, facing the company with whom he was about to take a journey. Always it felt like this. They had come aboard: they were about to take on other identities. In doing this something would happen to them all: new ingredients would be tried, accepted or denied. Alongside them were the characters they must assume. They would come closer and, if the casting was accurate, slide together. For the time they were on stage they would be one. So he held. And when the voyage was over they would all be a little bit different.

He began talking to them.

'I'm not starting with a reading,' he said. 'Readings are OK as far as they go for the major roles, but bit parts are bit parts and as far as the Gentlewoman and the Doctor are concerned, once they arrive they are bloody important, but their zeal won't be set on fire by sitting around waiting for a couple of hours for their entrance.

'Instead I'm going to invite you to take a hard look at this play and then get on with it. It's short and it's faulty. That is to say, it's full of errors that crept into whatever script was handed to the printers. Shakespeare didn't write the silly Hecate bits, so out she comes. It's compact and drives quickly to its end. It's remorseless. I've directed it in other theatres twice, each time I may say successfully and without any signs of bad luck, so I don't believe in the bad luck stories associated with it and I hope none of you do either. Or if you do, you'll keep your ideas to yourselves.'

He paused for long enough to sense a change of awareness in his audience and a quick, instantly repressed movement of Nina Gaythorne's hands.

'It's straightforward,' he said. 'I don't find any major difficulties or contradictions in Macbeth. He is a hypersensitive, morbidly imaginative man beset by an overwhelming ambition. From the moment he commits the murder he starts to disintegrate. Every poetic thought, magnificently expressed, turns sour. His wife knows him better than he knows himself and from the beginning realizes that she must bear the burden, reassure her husband, screw his courage to the sticking-point, jolly him along. In my opinion,' Peregrine said, looking directly at Margaret Mannering, 'she's not an iron monster who can stand up

to any amount of hard usage. On the contrary, she's a sensitive creature who has an iron *will* and has made a deliberate evil choice. In
the end she never breaks but she talks and walks in her sleep.
Disastrously.'

Maggie leant forward, her hands clasped, her eyes brilliantly fixed
on his face. She gave him a little series of nods. At the moment, at
least, she believed him.

'And she's as sexy as hell,' he added. 'She uses it. Up to the hilt.'

He went on. The witches, he said, must be completely accepted.
The play was written in James I's time at his request. James I
believed in witches. In their power and their malignancy. 'Let us
show you,' said Peregrine, 'what I *mean*. Jeremy, can you?'

Blackout, and there were the drawings, needle-sharp in their
focused lights.

'You see the first one,' Peregrine said. 'That's what we'll go up on,
my dears. A gallows with its victim, picked clean by the witches.
They'll drop down from it and dance widdershins round it. Thunder
and lightning. Caterwauls. The lot. Only a few seconds and then
they'll leap up and we'll see them in mid-air. Blackout. They'll fall
behind the high rostrum on to a pile of mattresses. Gallows away.
Pipers. Lighted torches and we're off.'

Well, he thought, I've got them. For the moment. They're caught.
And that's all one can hope for. He went through the rest of the cast,
noting how economically the play was written and how completely
the inherent difficulty of holding the interest in a character as seemingly weak as Macbeth was overcome.

'Weak?' asked Dougal Macdougal. 'You think him *weak*, do you?'

'Weak in respect of this one monstrous thing he feels himself
drawn towards doing. He's a most successful soldier. You may say
"larger than life". He "takes the stage", cuts a superb figure. The King
has promised he will continue to shower favours upon him.
Everything is as rosy as can be. And yet – and yet –'

'His wife?' Dougal suggested. 'And the witches!'

'Yes. That's why I say the witches are enormously important. One
has the feeling that they are conjured up by Macbeth's secret
thoughts. There's not a character in the play that questions their
authority. There have been productions, you know, that bring them
on at different points, silent but menacing, watching their work.

'They pull Macbeth along the path to that one definitive action. And then, having killed the King, he's left – a murderer. For ever. Unable to change. His morbid imagination takes charge. The only thing he can think of is to kill again. And again. Notice the imagery. The play closes in on him. And on us. Everything thickens. His clothes are too big, too heavy. He's a man in a nightmare.

'There's the break, the breather for the leading actor that comes in all the tragedies. We see Macbeth once again with the witches and then comes the English scene with the boy Malcolm taking his oddly contorted way of finding out if Macduff is to be trusted, his subsequent advance into Scotland, the scene of Lady Macbeth speaking of horrors with the strange, dead voice of the sleepwalker.

'And then we see him again; greatly changed; aged, desperate, unkempt; his cumbersome royal robes in disarray, attended still by Seyton who has grown in size. And so to the end.'

He waited for a moment. Nobody spoke.

'I would like,' said Peregrine, 'before we block the opening scenes to say a brief word about the secondary parts. It's the fashion to say they're uninteresting. I don't agree. About Lennox, in particular. He's likeable, down to earth, quick-witted but slow to make the final break. There's evidence in the imperfect script of some doubt about who says what. We will make Lennox the messenger to Lady Macduff. When next we see him he's marching with Malcolm. His scene with an unnamed thane (we'll give the lines to Ross) when their suspicion of Macbeth, their nosing out of each other's attitudes, develops into a tacit understanding, is "modern" in treatment, almost black comedy in tone.'

'And the Seyton?' asked a voice from the rear. A very deep voice.

'Ah, Seyton. There again, obviously, he's "Sirrah", the unnamed servant who accompanies Macbeth like a shadow, who carries his great claidheamh-mor, who joins the two murderers and later in the play emerges with a name – Seyton. He has hardly any lines but he's ominous. A big, silent, ever-present, amoral fellow who only leaves his master at the very end. We're casting Gaston Sears for the part. My Sears, as you all know, in addition to being an actor is an authority on medieval weapons and is already working for us in that capacity.' There was an awkward silence followed by an acquiescent murmur.

The saturnine person, sitting alone, cleared his throat, folded his arms and spoke. 'I shall carry,' he announced, basso-profundo, 'a claidheamh-mor.'

'Quite so,' Peregrine said. 'You are the sword-bearer. As for the – '

' – which has been vulgarized into "claymore". I prefer "claidheamh-mor" meaning "great sword", it being – '

'Quite so, Gaston. And now – '

For a time the voices mingled, the bass one coming through with disjointed phrases: '. . . Magnus's leg-biter. . . quillons formed by turbulent protuberance . . .'

'To continue,' Peregrine shouted. The sword-bearer fell silent.

'And the witches?' asked a helpful witch.

'Entirely evil,' answered the relieved Peregrine. 'Dressed like fantastic parodies of Meg Merrilies but with terrible faces. We don't see their faces until *"look not like the inhabitants of the earth and yet are on't,"* when they are suddenly revealed. They smell abominably.'

'And speak?'

'Braid Scots.'

'What about me, Perry? Braid Scots too?' suggested the porter.

'Yes. You enter through the central trap, having been collecting fuel in the basement. And,' Peregrine said with ill-concealed pride, 'the fuel is bleached driftwood and *most* improperly shaped. You address each piece in turn as a farmer, as an equivocator and as an English tailor, and you consign them all to the fire.'

'I'm a funny man?'

'We hope so.'

'Aye. A-weel, it's a fine idea, I'll give it that. Och, aye. A bonny notion,' said the porter.

He chuckled and mouthed and Peregrine wished he wouldn't, but he was a good Scots actor.

He waited for a moment, wondering how much he had gained of their confidence. Then he turned to the designs and explained how they would work and then to the costumes.

'I'd like to say here and now that these drawings and those for the sets – Jeremy has done both – are, to my mind, exactly right. Notice the suggestion of the clan tartans: a sort of primitive pre-tartan. The cloak is a distinctive check affair. All Macbeth's servitors and servitors of royal personages wore their badges and the livery of their masters. Lennox, Angus and Ross wear their own distinctive cloaks with the clan check. Banquo and Fleance have particularly brilliant ones, blood-red with black and silver borders. For the rest, thonged trousers, fur jerkins, and sheepswool chaps. Massive jewellery. Great jewelled bosses, heavy necklets and heavy bracelets, in Macbeth's case reaching up to the elbow and above it. The general effect is heavy, primitive but incidentally extremely sexy. Gauntlets, fringed and ornamented. And the crowns! Macbeth's in particular. Huge and heavy it must look.'

'*Look*,' said Macdougal, 'being the operative word, I hope.'

'Yes, of course. We'll have it made of plastic. And Maggie . . . do you like what you see, darling?'

What she saw was a skin-tight gown of dull metallic material, slit up one side to allow her to walk. A crimson, heavily furred garment was worn over it, open down the front. She had only one jewel, a great clasp.

'I hope I'll fit it,' said Maggie.

'You'll do that,' he said, 'and now – ' he was conscious of a tightness under his belt – 'we'll clear stage and get down to business. Oh! There's one point I've missed. You will see that for our first week some of the rehearsals are at night. This is to accommodate Sir Dougal who is shooting the finals of his new film. The theatre is dark, the current production being on tour. It's a bit out of the ordinary, I know, and I hope nobody finds it too awkward?'

There was a silence during which Sir Dougal with spread arms mimed a helpless apology.

'I can't forbear saying it's very inconvenient,' said Banquo.

'Are you filming?'

'Not precisely. But it might arise.'

'We'll hope it doesn't,' Peregrine said. 'Right? Good. Clear stage, please, everybody. Scene 1. The witches.'

II

'It's going very smoothly,' said Peregrine, three days later. 'Almost *too* smoothly. Dougal's uncannily lamblike and everyone told me he was a Frankenstein's Monster to work with.'

'Keep your fingers crossed,' said his wife, Emily. 'It's early days yet.'

'True.' He looked curiously at her. 'I've never asked you,' he said. 'Do you believe in it? The superstition business?'

'No,' she said quickly.

'Not the least tiny bit? Really?'

Emily looked steadily at him. 'Truly?' she asked.

'Yes.'

'My mother was a one hundred per cent Highlander.'

'So?'

'So it's not easy to give you a direct answer. Some superstitions – most, I think – are silly little matters of habit: a pinch of spilt salt over the left shoulder. One may do it without thinking but if one doesn't it's no great matter – that sort of thing. But – there are other ones. Not silly. I don't *believe* in them, but I think I avoid them.'

'Like the *Macbeth* ones?'

'Yes. But I didn't mind you doing it. Or not enough to try to stop you. Because I don't *really* believe,' said Emily very firmly.

'I don't believe at all. Not at any level. I've done two productions of the play and they both were accident-free and very successful. As for the instances they drag up – Macbeth's sword breaking and a bit of it hitting someone in the audience or a dropped weight narrowly missing an actor's head – if they'd happened in any other play nobody would have said it was an unlucky play. How about Rex Harrison's hairpiece being caught in a chandelier and whisked up into the flies? Nobody said *My Fair Lady* was unlucky.'

'Nobody dared to mention it, I should think.'

'There is that, of course,' Peregrine agreed.

'All the same, it's not a fair example.'

'Why isn't it?'

'Well, it's not serious. I mean, well . . .'

'You wouldn't say that if you'd been there, I dare say,' said Peregrine.

He walked over to the window and looked at the Thames: at the punctual late-afternoon traffic. It congealed on the south bank, piled up, broke out into a viscous stream and crossed by bridge to the north bank. Above it, caught by the sun, shone the theatre: not very big but conspicuous in its whiteness and, because of the squat mess of little riverside buildings that surrounded it, appearing tall, even majestic.

'You can tell which of them's bothered about the bad luck stories,' he said. 'They won't say his name. They talk about "the Thane" and "the Scots play" and "the Lady". It's catching. Lady Macduff – Nina Gaythorne, silly little ass – is steeped up to the eyebrows in it. And talks about it. Stops if she sees I'm about but she does all right, and they listen to her.'

'Don't let it worry you, darling. It's not affecting their work, is it?' Emily asked.

'No.'

'Well, then.'

'I know. I know.'

Emily joined him and they both looked out over the Thames to where the Dolphin shone so brightly. She took his arm. 'It's easy to say, I know,' she said, 'but if you *could* just not. Don't brood. It's not like you. Tell me how the great Scot is making out as Macbeth.'

'Fine. Fine.'

'It's his biggest role so far, isn't it?' Emily asked.

'Yes. He was a good Benedict, but that's the only other Shakespeare part he's played. Out of Scotland. He had a bash at Othello in his repertory days. He was a fantastic Anatomist in Bridie's play when they engaged him for the revival at the Haymarket. That started him off in the West End. Now, of course, he's way up there and one of our theatrical knights.'

'How's his love life going?'

'I don't really know. He's making a great play with Lady Macbeth at the moment but Maggie Mannering takes it with a tidy load of salt, don't worry.'

'Dear Maggie!'

'And dear you!' he said. 'You've lightened the load no end. Shall I tackle Nina and tell her not to? Or go on pretending I haven't noticed?'

'What would you say? "Oh, by the way, Nina darling, *could* you leave off the bad luck business, scaring the pants off the cast. Just a thought!"'

Peregrine burst out laughing and gave her a slap. 'I tell you what,' he said, 'you're so bloody sharp you can have a go yourself. I'll ask her for a drink here, and you can choose your moment and then lay into her.'

'Are you serious?'

'No. Yes, I believe I am. It might work.'

'I don't think it would. She's never been here before. She'd rumble.'

'Would that matter? Oh, I don't know. Shall we leave it a bit longer? I think so.'

'And so do I,' said Emily. 'With any luck they'll get sick of it and it'll die a natural death.'

'So it may,' he agreed, and hoped he sounded convincing. 'That's a comforting thought. I must return to the blasted heath.'

III

He wouldn't have taken much comfort from the lady in question if he could have seen her at that moment. Nina Gaythorne came into her minute flat in Westminster and began a sort of de-lousing ritual. Without even waiting to take off her gloves she scuffled in her hand-bag, produced a crucifix which she kissed, and laid on the table a clove of garlic and her prayer book. She opened the latter, put on her spectacles, crossed herself and read aloud the 91st Psalm.

'Whoso dwelleth under the defence of the Most High,' read Nina in the well-trained, beautifully modulated tones of a professional actress. When she reached the end she kissed her prayer book, crossed herself again, laid her cyclostyled part on the table, the prayer book on top of it, the crucifix on the prayer book, and, after a slight hesitation, the clove of garlic at the foot of the crucifix.

'*That* ought to settle their hash,' she said, and took off her gloves.

Her belief in curses and things being lucky or unlucky was not based on any serious study but merely on the odds and ends of gossip and behaviour accumulated by four generations of theatre people. In that most hazardous profession where so many mischances can occur, when so much hangs in the precarious balance on opening night, when five weeks' preparation may turn to ashes or blaze for years, there is a fertile soil indeed for superstition to take root and flourish.

Nina was forty years old, a good dependable actress, happy to strike a long run and play the same part for months on end, being very careful not to let it become an entirely mechanical exercise. The last part

of this kind had come to an end six months ago and nothing followed
it, so that this little plum, Lady Macduff, uncut for once, had been a
relief. And the child might be a nice boy. Not the precocious little horror that could emerge from an indifferent school. And the house! The
Dolphin! The enormous prestige attached to an engagement there. Its
phenomenal run of good luck and, above all, its practice of using the
same people, once they had gained an entry, whenever a suitable role
occurred: a happy engagement. Touch wood!

So, really, she must *not*, really *not*, talk about 'the Scots play' to
other people in the cast. It just kept slipping out. Peregrine Jay had
noticed and didn't like it. I'll make a resolution, Nina thought. She
shut her large faded eyes tight and said aloud:

'I promise on my word of honour and upon this prayer book *not*
to talk about you-know-what. Amen.'

IV

'Maggie,' shouted Simon Morten. 'Hold on. Wait a moment.'

Margaret Mannering stopped at the top of Wharfingers Lane
where it joined the main highway. A procession of four enormous
lorries thundered past. Morten hurried up the last steep bit. 'I got
trapped by Gaston Sears,' he panted. 'Couldn't get rid of him. How
about coming out for a meal? It won't take long in a taxi.'

'Simon! My dear, I'm sorry. I've said I'll dine with Dougal.'

'But – where *is* Dougal?'

'Fetching his car. I said I'd come up to the corner and wait for him.
It's a chance to talk about our first encounter. In the play, I mean.'

'Oh. I see. All right, then.'

'Sorry, darling.'

'Not a bit. I quite understand.'

'Well,' she said, 'I hope you do.'

'I've said I do, haven't I? Here comes your Thane in his scarlet
chariot.'

He made as if to go and then stopped. Dougal Macdougal – it was
his own given name – pulled in to the kerb. 'Here I am, sweetie,' he
declared. 'Hullo, Simon. Just the man to open the door for the lovely
lady and save me a bash on the bottom from oncoming traffic.'

Morten removed his beret, pulled on his forelock and opened the door with exaggerated humility. Margaret got into the car without looking at him and said, 'Thank you, darling.'

He banged the door.

'Can we drop you somewhere?' Dougal asked, as an afterthought.

'No, thank you. I don't know where you're going but it's not in my direction.' Dougal pulled a long face, nodded and moved out into the traffic. Simon Morten stood looking after them, six foot two of handsome disgruntlement, his black curls still uncovered. He said: 'Well, shit off and be damned to you,' crammed on his beret, turned into the lane and entered the little restaurant known as the Junior Dolphin.

'What's upset the Thane of Fife?' asked Dougal casually.

'Nothing. He's being silly.'

'Not by any chance a teeny-weeny bit jealous?'

'Maybe. He'll recover.'

'Hope so. Before we get round to bashing away at each other with Gaston's claymores.'

'Indeed, yes. Gaston really is more than a bit dotty, don't you think? All that talk about armoury. And he wouldn't *stop*.'

'I'm told he did spend a short holiday in a sort of halfway house. A long time ago, though, and he was quite harmless. Just wore a sword and spoke Middle English. He's a sweet man, really. He's been asked by Perry to teach us the fight. He wants us to practise duels in slow motion every day for five weeks, building up muscle and getting a bit faster very slowly. To the Anvil Chorus from *Trovatore*.'

'Not really?'

'Of course not, when it comes to performance. Just as rehearsals to get the rhythm. They are frightfully heavy, claymores are.'

'Rather you than me,' said Maggie, and burst out laughing.

Dougal began to sing very slowly. '*Bang*. Wait for it. *Bang*. Wait again. And Bangle-bangle-*bang*. Wait. *Bang*.'

'With two hands, of course.'

'Of course. I can't lift the thing off the floor without puffing and blowing. Gaston brought one down for us to try.'

'He's actually *making* the ones you're going to use, isn't he? Couldn't he cheat and use lighter material or *papier-mâché* for the hilt or something?'

'My dear, no good at all. It would upset the balance.'

'Well, do be careful,' said Maggie vaguely.

'Of course. The thing is that the blades won't be sharp at all. Blunt as blunt. But if one of us was actually hit, it would break his bones.'

'Really?'

'To smithereens,' said Dougal. 'I promise you.'

'I think you're going to look very silly, the two of you, floundering about. You'll get laughs. I can think of all sorts of things that might go wrong.'

'Such as?'

'One of you making a swipe and missing and the claymore getting stuck in the scenery.'

'It's going to be *very* short. In time. Only a half-minute or so. He backs away into the OP corner and I roar after him. Simon's a very powerful man, by the by. He picked the claymore up in a *dégagée* manner and then he spun round and couldn't stop and got a way on, hanging on to it, looking absolutely terrified. That *was* funny,' said Dougal. 'I laughed like anything at old Si.'

'Well, don't, Dougal. He's very sensitive.'

'Oh, pooh. Listen, sweetie. We're called for eight-thirty, aren't we? I suggest we go to my restaurant on the Embankment for a light meal and we'll be ready for the blood and thunder. How does that strike you? With a dull thud or pleasurably?'

'Not a large, sinking dinner before work? And nothing to drink?'

'A dozen oysters and some thin brown bread and butter?'

'Delicious.'

'Good,' said Dougal.

'By "settle our relationship" you refer exclusively to the Macbeths, of course.'

'Do I? Well, so be it. For the time being,' he said coolly, and drove on without further comment until they crossed the river, turned into a tangle of little streets emerging finally in Savoy Minor, and stopped.

'I've taken the flat for the duration. It belongs to Teddy Somerset who's in the States for a year,' said Dougal.

'It's a smashing façade.'

'Very Regency, isn't it? Let's go inside. Come on.'

So they went in.

It was a sumptuous interior presided over by a larger-than-life nude efficiently painted in an extreme of realism. Maggie gave it a quick look, sat underneath it and said: 'There are just one or two things I'd like to get sorted out. They've discussed the murder of Duncan before the play opens. That's clear enough. But always it's been "if" and "suppose", never until now, "He's coming here. It's now or never." Agreed?'

'Yes.'

'It's only been something to talk about. Never calling for a decision. Or for anything real.'

'No. And now it does, and he's face to face with it, he's appalled.'

'As she knows he will be. She knows that without her egging him on he'd never do it. So what has she got that will send him into it? Plans. Marvellous plans, yes. But he won't go beyond talking about plans. Sex. Perry said so the first day. Shakespeare had to be careful about sex because of the boy actor. But we don't.'

'We certainly do not,' he said. He moved behind her and put a hand on her shoulder.

'Do you realize,' Maggie said, 'how short their appearances together are? And how *beaten* she is after the banquet scene? I think, once she's rid of those damned thanes and is left with her mumbling, shattered lion of a husband and they go dragging upstairs to the bed they cannot sleep in, she knows that all that's left for her to do is shut up. The next and last time we see her she's talking disastrously in her sleep. Really it's quite a short part, you know.'

'How far am I affected by her collapse, do you think?' he asked. 'Do I notice it? Or by that time am I determined to give myself over to idiotic killing?'

'I think you are.' She turned to look at him and something in her manner of doing this made him withdraw his already possessive hand. She stood up and moved away.

'I think I'll just ring up the Wig and Piglet for a table,' he said abruptly.

'Yes, do.'

When he had done this she said: 'I've been looking at the imagery. There's an awful lot about clothes being too big and heavy. I see Jeremy's emphasizing that and I'm glad. Great walloping cloaks that can't be contained by a belt. Heavy crowns. We have to consciously fill them. You much more than I, of course. I fade out. But the whole picture is nightmarish.'

'How do you see *me*, Maggie?'

'My dear! As a falling star. A magnificent, violently ambitious being, destroyed by his own imagination. It's a cosmic collapse. Monstrous events attend it. The Heavens themselves are in revolt. Horses eat each other.'

Dougal breathed in deeply. Up went his chin. His eyes, startlingly blue, flashed under his tawny brows. He was six feet one inch in height and looked more.

'That's the stuff,' said Maggie. 'I think you'll want to make it very, *very* Scots, Highland Scots. They'll call you The Red Macbeth,' she added, a little hurriedly. 'It *is* your very own name, sweetie, isn't it – Dougal Macdougal?'

'Oh, aye. It's ma' given name.'

'That's the ticket, then.'

They fell into a discussion of whether he should, in fact, use the dialect, and decided against it as it would entail all the other lairds doing so too.

'Just porters and murderers, then,' said Maggie. 'If Perry says so, of course. You won't catch me doing it.' She tried it out. '"Come tae ma wummen's breasts and tak' ma milk for gall." Really, it doesn't sound too bad.'

'Let's have one tiny little drink to it. Do say yes, Maggie.'

'All right. Yes. The merest suggestion, though.'

'OK. Whisky? Wait a moment.'

He went to the end of the room and pressed a button. Two doors rolled apart, revealing a little bar.

'Good Heavens!' Maggie exclaimed.

'I know. Rather much, isn't it? But that's Teddy's taste.'

She went over to the bar and perched on a high stool. He found the whisky and soda and talked about his part. 'I hadn't thought big enough,' he said. 'A great, faulty giant. Yes. Yes, you're right about it, of course. *Of course.*'

'Steady. If that's mine.'

'Oh! All right. Here you are, lovey. What shall we drink to?'

'Obviously, *Macbeth.*'

He raised his glass. Maggie thought: He's a splendid figure. He'll make a good job of the part, I'm sure. But he said in a deflated voice: 'No, no, don't say it. It might be bad luck. No toast,' and drank quickly as if she might cut in.

'Are you superstitious?' she asked.

'Not really. It was just a feeling. Well, I suppose I am, a bit. You?'

'Like you. Not really. A bit.'

'I don't suppose there's one of us who isn't. Just a bit.'

'Peregrine,' Maggie said at once.

'He doesn't seem like it, certainly. All that stuff about keeping it under our hats even if we do fancy it.'

'Still. Two successful productions and not a thing happening at either of them,' said Maggie.

'There is that, of course.' He waited for a moment and then in a much too casual manner said: 'They were going to do it in the Dolphin, you know. Twenty years or so ago. When it opened.'

'Why didn't they?'

'The leading man died or something. Before they'd come together. Not a single rehearsal, I'm told. So it was dropped.'

'Really?' said Maggie. 'What are the other rooms like? More nudes?'

'Shall I show you?'

'I don't think so, thank you.' She looked at her watch. 'Shouldn't we be going to your Wig and Piglet?'

'Perry's taking the witches first. We've lots of time.'

'Still, I'm obsessively punctual and shan't enjoy my oysters if we're cutting it short.'

'If you insist.'

'Well, I do. Sorry. I'll just tidy up. Where's your bathroom?'

He opened a door. 'At the end of the passage,' he said.

She walked past him, hunting in her bag as she went, and thought: If he pounces I'll be in for a scene and a bore.

He didn't pounce but nor did he move. Unavoidably she brushed against him and thought: He's got more of what it takes, Highland or Lowland, than is decent.

She did her hair, powdered her face, used her lipstick and put on her gloves in a bathroom full of mechanical weight-reducers, pot plants and a framed rhyme of considerable indecency.

'Right?' she asked briskly on re-entering the sitting room.

'Right.' He put on his overcoat and they left the flat. It was dark outside now. He took her arm. 'The steps are slippery,' he said. 'You don't want to start off with a sprained ankle, do you?'

'No. That I don't.'

He was right. The steps glimmered with untimely frost and she was glad of his support. His overcoat was Harris tweed and smelt of peat fires.

As she got into the car, Maggie caught sight of a tall man wearing a short camel overcoat and a red scarf. He was standing about sixty feet away.

'Hullo,' she exclaimed. 'That's Simon. Hi!' She raised her hand but he had turned away and was walking quickly into a side street.

'I thought that was Simon Morten,' she said.

'Where?'

'I made a mistake. He's gone.'

They drove along the Embankment to the Wig and Piglet. The street lights were brilliant: snapping and sparkling in the cold air and broken into sequins on the outflowing Thames. Maggie felt excited and uplifted. When they entered the little restaurant with its huge fire, white tablecloths and shining glasses, her cheeks flamed and her eyes were brilliant. Suddenly she loved everybody.

'You're fabulous,' Dougal said. Some of the people had recognized them and were smiling. The *mâitre d'hôtel* made a discreet fuss over them. She was in rehearsal for a superb play and opposite to her was her leading man.

She began to talk, easily and well. When champagne was brought she thought: I ought to stop him opening it. I *never* drink before rehearsals. But how dreary and out-of-tune with the lovely evening that would be.

'Temperamental inexactitude,' she said quite loudly. 'British Constitution.'

'I beg your pardon, Maggie?'

'I was just testing myself to make sure I'm not tiddly.'

'You are not tiddly.'

'I'm not used to whisky and you gave me a big one.'

'No, I didn't. You are not tiddly. You're just suddenly elevated. Here come our oysters.'

'Well, if you say so, I suppose I'm all right.'

'Of course you are. Wade in.'

So she did wade in and she was not tiddly. In the days to come she was to remember this evening, from the time when she left the flat until the end of their rehearsals, as something apart. Something between her and London, with Dougal Macdougal as a sort of necessary ingredient. But no more.

V

Gaston Sears inhabited a large old two-storey house in a tiny cul-de-sac opening off Alleyn Road in Dulwich. It was called Alleyn's Surprise and the house and grounds occupied the whole of one side. The opposite side was filled with neglected trees and an unused pumping-house.

The rental of such a large building must have been high and among the Dulwich College boys there was a legend that Mr Sears was an eccentric foreign millionaire who lived there, surrounded by fabulous pieces of armour, and made swords and practised black magic. Like most legends, this was founded on highly distorted fact. He *did* live among his armour and he did very occasionally make swords. His collection of armour was the most prestigious in Europe, outside the walls of a museum. And certainly he *was* eccentric.

Moreover, he was comfortably off. He had started as an actor, a good one in far-out eccentric parts, but so inclined to extremes of argumentative temperament that nobody cared to employ him. A legacy enabled him to develop his flair for historic arms and accoutrements. His expertise was recognized by all the European collectors and he was the possessor of honorary degrees from various universities. He made lecture tours in America for which he charged astronomical fees, and extorted frightening amounts from greedy, ignorant and unscrupulous buyers which more than compensated for the opinions he gave free of charge to those he decided to respect. Of these Peregrine Jay was one.

The unexpected invitation to appear as sword-bearer to Macbeth had been accepted with complacency. 'I shall be able to watch the contest,' he had observed. 'And afterwards correct any errors that may creep in. I do not altogether trust the Macbeth. Dougal Macdougal indeed!'

He was engaged upon making moulds for his weapons. From one of these moulds would be cast, in molten steel, Macbeth's claidheamh-mor. Gaston himself, as Seyton, would carry the genuine claidheamh-mor throughout the performance. Macbeth's claymore he would wear. A second claymore, less elaborate, would serve to make the mould for Macduff's weapon.

His workshop was a formidable background. Suits of armour stood ominously about the room, swords of various ages and countries hung on the walls with drawings of details in ornamentation. A life-size effigy of a Japanese warrior in an ecstasy of the utmost ferocity, clad in full armour, crouched in warlike attitude, his face contorted with rage and his sword poised to strike.

Gaston hummed and occasionally muttered as he made the long wooden trough that was to contain clay from which the matrix would be formed. He made a good figure for a Vulcan, being hugely tall with a shock of black hair and heavily muscled arms.

'*"Double, double toil and trouble,"*' he hummed in time with his hammering. And then:

> '*"Her husband's to Aleppo gone, master o'th' Tiger,*
> *But in a sieve I'll thither sail*
> *And like a rat without a tail*
> *I'll do, I'll do and I'll do."*'

And on the final 'I'll do' he tapped home his nail.

VI

Bruce Barrabell who played Banquo was not on call for the current rehearsal. He stayed at home and learned his part and dwelt upon his grievances. His newest agent was getting him quite a bit of work but nothing that was likely to do him any lasting good. A rather dim supporting role in another police series for Granada TV. And now, Banquo. He'd asked to be tried for Macbeth and been told the part was already cast. Macduff: same thing. He was leaving the theatre when some whippersnapper came after him and said would he come to read Banquo. There'd been some kind of a slip-up. So he did and he'd got it. Small part, actually. Lot of standing around with one foot up and the other down on those bloody

steps. But there was one little bit. He flipped his part over and
began to read it:

'*There's husbandry in Heaven. Their candles are all out.*'

He read it aloud. Quietly. The slightest touch of whimsicality. Feel
the time-of-night and the great empty courtyard. He had to admit it
was good. 'There's *housekeeping* in Heaven.' The homely touch that
somehow made you want to cry. Would a modern audience understand that housekeeping was what was meant by husbandry?
Nobody else could write about the small empty hours as this man
did. The young actor they'd produced for Fleance, his son, was nice:
unbroken, clear voice. And then Macbeth's entrance and Banquo's
reaction. Good stuff. *His* scene, but of course the Macbeth would
overact and Perry let him get away with it. Look at the earlier scene.
Although Perry, fair's fair, put a stop to that little caper. But the
intention was there for all to see.

He set himself to memorize but it wasn't easy. Incidents out of the
past kept coming in. Conversations.

'*Actually we are not quite strangers. There was a* Macbeth *up in
Dundee, sir. I won't say how many years ago.*'

'*Oh?*'

'*We were witches.*' Whispering it. Looking coy.

'*Really? Sorry. Excuse me. I want to –* Perry, Perry, dear boy, just a
word – '

Swine! Of course he remembered.

VII

It was the Angus's birthday. He, Ross, and the rest of the lairds and
the three witches were not called for the evening's rehearsal. They
arranged with other free members of the cast to meet at the Swan in
Southwark, and drink Angus's health.

They arrived in twos and threes and it was quite late by the time
the witches, who had been rehearsing in the afternoon, came in.
Two girls and a man. The man (First Witch) was a part-Maori called
Rangi Western, not very dark but with the distinctive short upper lip
and flashing eyes. He had a beautiful voice and was a prize student
from LAMDA. The second witch was a nondescript thin girl called

Wendy possessed of a remarkable voice: harsh, with strange unexpected intervals. The third was a lovely child, a white-blonde, delicate, with enormous eyes and a babyish high-pitched voice. She was called Blondie.

Their rehearsal had excited them. They came in talking loudly. 'Rangi, you were *marvellous*. You sent cold shivers down my spine. Truly. And that movement! I thought Perry would stop you but he didn't. The stamp. It was super. We've got to do it, Wendy, along with Rangi. His tongue. And his eyes. Everything.'

'I thought it was fabulous giving us the parts. I mean the *difference*! Usually they all look alike and are too boring for words – all masks and mumbles. But we're *really* evil.'

'Angus!' they shouted. 'Happy birthday, love. Bless you.'

Now they had all arrived. The witches were the centre of attention. Rangi was not very talkative but the two girls excitedly described his performance at rehearsal.

'He was standing with us, listening to Perry's description, weren't you, Rangi? Perry was saying we have to be the *incarnation* of *evil*. Not a drop of goodness anywhere about us. How did he put it, Wendy?'

'"Trembling with animosity",' said Wendy.

'Yes. And I was standing by Rangi and I *felt* him tremble, I swear I did.'

'You did, didn't you, Rangi? Tremble?'

'Sort of,' Rangi mumbled. 'Don't make such a thing about it.'

'No, but you were marvellous. You sort of grunted and bent your knees. And your *face*! Your tongue! And eyes!'

'Anyway, Perry was completely taken with it and asked him to repeat it and asked us to do it – not too much. Just a kind of ripple of hatred. It's going to work, you know.'

'Putting a curse on him. That's what it is, Rangi, isn't it?'

'Have a drink, Rangi, and show us.'

Rangi made a brusque dismissive gesture and turned away to greet the Angus.

The men closed round him. They were none of them quite drunk, but they were noisy. The members of the company now far outnumbered the other patrons, who had taken their drinks to a table in the corner of the room and looked on with ill-concealed interest.

'It's my round,' Angus shouted. 'I'm paying, all you guys. No arguments. Yes, I insist. *"That which hath made them drunk hath made me bold,"'* he shouted.

His voice faded out and so, raggedly, did all the others. Blondie's giggle persisted and died. A single voice – Angus's – asked uncertainly: 'What's up? Oh. Oh hell! I've quoted from the play. Never mind. Sorry, everybody. Drink up.'

They drank in silence. Rangi drained his pint of mild and bitter. Angus nodded to the barman, who replaced it with another. Angus mimed pouring in something else and laid an uncertain finger on his lips. The barman winked and added a tot of gin. He pushed the drink over towards Rangi's hand. Rangi's back was turned but he felt the glass, looked round and saw it.

'Is that mine?' he asked, puzzled.

They all seized on this. They said confusedly that of course it was his drink. It was something to make a fuss about, something that would make them all forget about Angus's blunder. They betted Rangi wouldn't drink it down then and there. So Rangi did. There was a round of applause.

'Show us, Rangi. Show us what you did. Don't *say* anything, just show.'

'E-e-e-*uh*!' he shouted suddenly. He slapped his knees and stamped. He grimaced, his eyes glittered and his tongue whipped in and out. He held his umbrella before him like a spear and it was not funny.

It only lasted a few seconds.

They applauded and asked him what it meant and was he 'weaving a spell'. He said no, nothing like that. His eyes were glazed. 'I've had a little too much to drink,' he said. 'I'll go, now. Good night, all of you.'

They objected. Some of them hung on to him but they did it half-heartedly. He brushed them off. 'Sorry,' he said, 'I shouldn't have taken that drink. I'm no good with drinking.' He pulled some notes out of his pocket and shoved them across the bar. 'My round,' he said. 'Good night, all.'

He walked quickly to the swing doors, lost his balance and regained it.

'You all right?' Angus asked.

'No,' he answered. 'Far from it.'

He walked into the doors. They swung out and he went with
them. They saw him pull up, look stiffly to right and left, raise his
umbrella in a magnificent gesture, get into the taxi that responded
and disappear.

'He's all right,' said one of the lairds. 'He's got a room round here.'

'Nice chap.'

'Very nice.'

'I've heard, I don't know who told me, mark you,' said Angus,
'that drink has a funny effect on Maori people. Goes straight to their
heads and they revert to their savage condition.'

'Rangi hasn't,' said Ross. 'He's gone grand.'

'He did when he performed that dance or whatever it was,' said
the actor who played Menteith.

'You know what I think,' said the Ross. 'I think he was upset
when you quoted.'

'It's all a load of old bullshit, anyway,' said a profound voice in the
background.

This provoked a confused expostulation that came to its climax
when the Menteith roared out: 'Thass all very fine but I bet you
wouldn't call the play by its right name. Would you do that?'

Silence.

'There you are!'

'Only because it'd upset the rest of you.'

'Yah!' they all said.

The Ross, an older man who was sober, said: 'I think it's silly to
talk about it. We feel as we do in different ways. Why not just accept
that and stop nattering?'

'Somebody ought to write a book about it,' said Wendy.

'There *is* a book called *The Curse of Macbeth* by Richard Huggett.'

They finished their drinks. The party had gone flat.

'Call it a day, chaps?' suggested Ross.

'That's about the strength of it,' Menteith agreed.

The nameless and lineless thanes noisily concurred and gradually
they drifted out.

Ross said to the Angus: 'Come on, old fellow, I'll see you home.'

'I'm afraid I've overstepped the mark. Sorry. *"We were carousing till
the second cock."* Oh dear, there I go again.' He made a shaky attempt
to cross himself. 'I'm OK,' he said.

'Of course you are.'

'Right you are, then. Good night, Porter,' he said to the barman.

'Good night, sir.'

They went out.

'Actors,' said one of the guests.

'That's right, sir,' the barman agreed, collecting their glasses.

'What was that they were saying about some superstition? I couldn't make head or tail of it.'

'They make out it's unlucky to quote from this play. They don't use the title either.'

'Silly sods,' remarked another.

'They take it for gospel.'

'Probably some publicity stunt by the author.'

The barman grunted.

'What is the name of the play, then?'

'Macbeth.'

VIII

Rehearsals for the duel had begun and were persisted in remorselessly. At 9.30 every morning Dougal Macdougal and Simon Morten, armed with weighted wooden claymores, sloshed and banged away at each other in a slow dance superintended by a merciless Gaston.

The whole affair, step by step, blow by blow, had been planned down to the last inch. Both men suffered agonies from the remorseless strain on muscles unaccustomed to such exercise. They sweated profusely. The Anvil Chorus, out of tune, played slowly on a gramophone, ground out a lugubrious, a laborious, a nightmare-like accompaniment, made more hateful by Gaston humming, also out of tune.

The relationship between the three men was, from the first, uneasy. Dougal tended to be facetious. 'What ho, varlet. Have at thee, miscreant,' he would cry.

The Macduff – Morten – did not respond to these sallies. He was ominously polite and glum to a degree. When Dougal swung at him, lost his balance and ran, as it were, after his own weapon, wild-eyed, an expression of great concern upon his face, Morten allowed himself a faint sneer. When Dougal finally tripped and fell in a sitting position with a sickening thud, the sneer deepened.

'The balance!' Gaston screamed. 'How many times must I insist? If you lose the balance of your weapon you lose your own balance and end up looking foolish. As now.'

Dougal rose. With some difficulty and using his claymore as a prop.

'No!' chided Gaston. 'It is to be handled with respect, not dug into the floor and climbed up.'

'This is merely a dummy. Why should I respect it?'

'It weighs exactly the same as the claidheamh-mor.'

'What's that got to do with it?'

'Again! We begin at the beginning. Again! Up! Weakling!'

'I am not accustomed,' said Dougal magnificently, 'to being treated in this manner.'

'No? Forgive me, Sir Dougal. And let me tell you that I, Gaston Sears, am not accustomed to conducting myself like a mincing dancing master, Sir Dougal. It is only because this fight is to be performed before audiences of discrimination, with weapons that are the precise replicas of the original claidheamh-mor, that I have consented to teach you.'

'If you ask me we'd get on a lot better if we faked the whole bloody show. Oh, all right, all right,' Dougal amended, answering the really alarming expression that contorted Gaston's face. 'I give in. Let's get on with it. Come on.'

'Come on,' echoed Morten. '*"Thou bloodier villain than terms can give thee out."*'

Whack. Bang. Down came his claymore, caught on Macbeth's shield. 'Te-*tum*. *Te-tum*. *Te* – Disengage,' shouted Gaston. 'Macbeth sweeps across. Macduff leaps over the blade. Te-tum-tum. This is better. This is an improvement. You have achieved the rhythm. We take it now a little faster.'

'Faster! My God, you're killing us.'

'You handle your weapon like a peasant. Look. I show you. Here, give it me.'

Dougal, using both hands, threw the claymore at him. With great dexterity, he caught it by the hilt, twirled it and held it before him, pointed at Dougal.

'Hah!' he shouted. 'Hah and hah again.' He lunged, changed his grip and swept his weapon up – and down.

Dougal leapt to one side. 'Christ Almighty!' he cried. 'What are you doing?'

Grimacing abominably, Gaston brought the heavy claymore up in a conventional salute.

'Handling my weapon, Sir Dougal. And you will do so before I have finished with you.'

Dougal whispered.

'I beg your pardon?'

'You've got the strength of the devil, Gaston.'

'No. It is a matter of balance and rhythm more than strength. Come, we take the first exchange *a tempo*. Yes, *a tempo*. Come.'

He offered the claymore ceremoniously to Dougal, who took it and heaved it up into a salute.

'Good! We progress. One moment.'

He went to the gramophone and altered the timing. 'Listen,' he said, and switched it on. Out came the Anvil Chorus, remorselessly truthful as if rejoicing in its own restoration. Gaston switched it off. 'That is our timing.' He turned to Simon Morten. 'Ready, Mr Morten?'

'Quite ready.'

'The cue, if you please.'

'*"Thou bloodier villain than terms can give thee out."*'

And the fight was a fight. There was rhythm and there was timing. For a minute and a quarter all went well and at the end the two men, pouring sweat, leaning on their weapons, breath less, waited for his comment.

'Good. There were mistakes but they were comparatively small. Now, while we are warm and limbered up we do it once more but without the music. Yes. You are recovered? Good.'

'We are not recovered,' Dougal panted.

'This is the last effort for today. Come. I count the beats. Without music. The cue.'

'*"Thou bloodier villain than terms can give thee out."*'

Bang. Pause. *Bang*. Pause. And *Bangle-bangle-bang*. Pause. They got through it but only just and they were really cooked at the end.

'Good,' said Gaston. 'Tomorrow. Same time. I thank you, gentlemen.'

He bowed and left.

Morten, his black curls damp and the tangled mat of hair on his chest gleaming, vigorously towelled himself. Sir Dougal, tawny, fair-skinned, drenched in sweat and breathing hard, reached for his own towel and feebly dabbed at his chest.

'We did it,' he said. 'I'm flattened but we did it.'

Morten grunted and pulled on his shirt and sweater.

'You'd better get something warm on,' he said. 'Way to catch cold.'

'Night after night after night. Have you thought of that?'

'Yes.'

'Why do I do it! Why do I submit myself! I ask myself: Why?'

Morten grunted.

'I'll speak to Perry about it. I'll demand insurance.'

'For which bit of you?'

'For all of me. The thing's ridiculous. A good fake and we'd have them breathless.'

'Instead of which we're breathless ourselves,' said Morten and took himself off. It was the nearest approach to a conversation that they had enjoyed.

So ended the first week of rehearsals.

CHAPTER 2

Second Week

Peregrine had blocked the play up to the aftermath following the murder of King Duncan. The only break in the performance would come here.

Rehearsals went well. The short opening scene with the witches scavenging on the gallows worked. Rangi, perched on the gibbet arm, was terribly busy with the head of the corpse. Blondie, on Wendy's back, ravaged its feet. A flash of lightning. Pause. Thunder. They hopped down, like birds of prey. Dialogue. Then their leap. The flash caught them in mid-air. Blackout and down.

'Well,' said Peregrine, 'the actions are spot-on. Thank you. It's now up to the lights: an absolute cue. Catch them in a flash before they fall. You witches must remember to keep flat and then scurry off in the blackout. OK?'

'Can we keep well apart?' asked Rangi. 'Before we take off. Otherwise we may fall on each other.'

'Yes. Get in position when you answer the caterwauls. Blondie, you take the point furthest away when you hear them. Wendy, you stay where you are, and Rangi, you answer from under the gallows. Think of birds . . . ravens . . . That's it. Splendid. Next scene.'

It was their first rehearsal in semi-continuity. It would be terribly rough but Peregrine liked his cast to get the feeling of the whole as early as possible. Here came the King. Superb bearing. Lovely entrance. Pause on steps. Thanes moved on below him. Bloody Sergeant on ground level, back to audience. The King – magnificent.

Up to his tricks again, thought Peregrine, and stopped them.

'Sorry, old boy,' he said. 'There's an extra move from you here. Remember? Come down. The thanes wheel round behind you. Bloody Sergeant moves up and we'll all focus on him for the speech. OK?'

The King raised a hand and slightly shook his head. 'So sorry. Of course.' He graciously complied. The Bloody Sergeant, facing front and determined to wring the last syllable from his one-speech part, embarked upon it with many pauses and gasps.

When it was over Peregrine said: 'Dear boy, you are determined *not* to faint or *not* to gasp. You can't quite manage it but you do your best. You keep going. Your voice fades out but you master it. You even manage your little joke, *"As sparrows eagles or the hare the lion,"* and we cut to: *"But I am faint, my gashes cry for help."'* You make a final effort. You salute. Your hand falls to your side and we see the blood on it. You are helped off. Don't *do* so much, dear boy. *Be!* I'll take you through it afterwards. On.'

The King returned magnificently to his place of vantage. Ross made an excitable entrance with news of the defeat of the faithless Cawdor. The King established his execution and the bestowal of his title upon Macbeth. Peregrine had cut the scene down to its bones. He made a few notes and went straight on to the witches again.

Now came the moment for the first witch and the long speech about the sailor to Aleppo gone. Then the dance. Legs bent. Faces distorted. Eyes. Tongues. It works, thought Peregrine. The drums and pipes. Offstage with retreating soldiers. Very ominous. Enter Macbeth and Banquo. Witches in a cluster, floor level. Motionless.

Macbeth was superb. The triumphant soldier – a glorious figure: ruddy, assured, glowing with his victories. Now, face to face with evil itself and hailed by his new title. The hidden dream suddenly made actual; the unwholesome pretence a tangible reality. He wrote to his wife and sent the letter ahead of his own arrival.

Enter the Lady. Maggie was still feeling her way with the part, but there were no doubts about her intention. She had deliberately faced the facts and made her choice, rejected the right and fiercely embraced the wrong. She now braced herself for the monstrous task of *'screwing her husband to the sticking-point'*, knowing very well that there was no substance in their previous talks although his morbidly vivid imagination gave them a nightmarish reality.

The play hurried on: the festive air, Macbeth's piper, servants scurrying with dishes of food and flagons of wine, and all the time Macbeth was crumbling. The great barbaric chieftain who should outshine all the rest made dismal mistakes. He was not there to welcome the King, was not in his place now. His wife had to leave the feast, find him, tell him the King was asking for him, only to have him say he would proceed no further in the business and offer conventional reasons.

There was no time to lose. For the last assault she laid the plot before her husband (and the audience) – quickly, urgently and clearly. He caught fire, said he was 'settled' and committed himself to damnation.

Seyton, with the claymore, appeared in the shadows. He followed them off.

The lights were extinguished by a servant, leaving only the torch in a wall-bracket outside the King's door. A pause during which the stealthy sounds of the night were established. Cricket and owl. The sudden crack of expanding wood. A ghostly figure, who would scarcely be seen when the lighting was finalized, appeared on the upper level, entered the King's rooms, waited there for a heartbeat or two, re-entered and slipped away into the shadows. The Lady.

An inner door at ground level opened to admit Banquo and Fleance, and the exquisite little night scene followed.

Bruce Barrabell had a wonderful voice and he knew how to use it, which is not to say he turned on the Voice Beautiful. It was there, a gift of nature, an arrangement of vocal cords and resonators that stirred the blood in the listener. He looked up, and one knew it was at the night sky where husbandry was practised and the candles were all out. He felt the nervous, emaciated tension of the small hours and was startled by the appearance of Macbeth attended by the tall shadow of Seyton.

He says he dreamt of the three Sisters. Macbeth replies that he thinks not of them and then goes on, against every nerve in the listener's body, to ask Banquo to have a little talk about the Sisters when he has time. Talk? What about? He goes on with sickening ineptitude to say the talk will 'make honour' for Banquo, who at once replies that as long as he loses none he will be 'counselled' and they say good night.

Peregrine thought: *Right.* That was *right.* And when Banquo and Fleance went off he clapped his hands softly, but not so softly that Banquo didn't hear him.

Now Macbeth was alone. The ascent to the murder had begun. Up and up the steps, following the dagger that he knew was hallucination. A bell rings. *'Hear it not, Duncan.'*

Dougal was not firm on his lines. He started off without the book but depended more and more on the prompter, couldn't pick it up, shouted *'What!'*, flew into a temper and finally started off again with his book in his hand.

'I'm not ready,' he shouted to Peregrine.

'All right. Take it quietly and read.'

'I'm *not ready.*'

Peregrine said: 'All right, Dougal. Cut to the end of the speech and keep your hair on. Give your exit line and off.'

'"Summons thee to heaven or to hell,"' Dougal snapped, and stamped off through the mock-up exit at the top of the stair.

The Lady re-entered at stage level.

Maggie was word-perfect. She was flushed with wine, over-strung, ready to start at the slightest sound but with the iron will to rule herself and Macbeth. When his cue for re-entry came he was back inside his part. His return to stage level was all Peregrine hoped for.

'I have done the deed. Didst thou not hear a voice?'
'I heard the owl scream and the crickets cry. Did not you speak?'
'When?'
'Now.'
'As I descended?'
'Ay.'
'Hark! Who lies i' th' second chamber?'
'Donalbain.'
'This is a sorry sight.'
'A foolish thought, to say a sorry sight.'

She glances at him. He stands there, blood-bedabbled and speaks of sleep. She sees the two grooms' daggers in his hands and is horrified. He refuses to return them. She takes them from him and climbs up to the room.

Macbeth is alone. The cosmic terrors of the play roll in like breakers. At the touch of his hands the multitudinous seas are incarnadined, making the green one red.

The Lady returns.

Maggie and Dougal had worked together on this scene and it was beginning to take shape. The characters were the absolute antitheses of each other: he, every nerve twanging, lost to everything but the nightmarish reality of murder, horrified by what he has done. She, self-disciplined, self-schooled, logical, aware of the frightful dangers of his unleashed imagination. *'These deeds must not be thought after these ways: so, it will make us mad.'*

She says a little water will clear them of the deed, and takes him off, God save the mark, to wash himself.

'We'll stop here,' said Peregrine. 'I've a lot of notes, but it's shaping up well. Settle down please, everybody.'

They were in the theatre, the current piece having gone on tour. The stage was lit by working lights and the shrouded house waited, empty, expectant, for whatever was to be poured into it.

The assistant stage manager and his assistant shifted chairs on stage for the principals and the rest sat on the stairs. Peregrine laid his notes on the prompter's table, switched on the lamp and sat down.

He took a minute or two, reading his notes and seeing they were in order.

'It's awfully stuffy in here,' said Maggie suddenly. 'Breathless, sort of. Does anybody else think so?'

'The weather's changed,' said Dougal. 'It's got much warmer.'

Blondie said: 'I hope it's not a beastly thunderstorm.'

'Why?'

'They give me the willies.'

'That comes well from a witch!'

'It's electrical. I get pins and needles. I can't help it.'

Ascendant thunder, startling, close, everywhere, rolled up to a sharp definitive crack. Blondie screamed.

'Sorry!' she said. She put her fingers in her ears. 'I can't help it. Truly. Sorry.'

'Never mind, child. Come over here,' said Maggie. She held out her hand. Blondie, answering the gesture rather than the words, ran across and crouched beside her chair.

Rangi said: 'It's true, she can't help it. It affects some people like that.'

Peregrine looked up from his notes. 'What's up?' he asked and then, seeing Blondie: 'Oh. Oh, I see. Never mind, Blondie. We can't see the lightning, can we, and the whole thing'll be over soon. Brace up, there's a good girl.'

'Yes. OK.'

She straightened up. Maggie patted her shoulder. Her hand checked and then closed. She looked at the other players, made a long face, and briefly quivered her free hand at them.

'Are you cold, Blondie?' she asked.

'I don't think so. No. I'm all right. Thank you. Ah!' she gave a little cry.

There was another roll of thunder; not so close, less precipitant.

'It's moving away,' said Maggie.

It died out in an indeterminate series of three or four thuds and bumps. Then, without warning, the sky opened and the rain crashed down.

'Overture and Beginners, please,' Dougal quoted and got his laugh.

By the time, about an hour later, Peregrine had finished his notes and recapped the faulty passages, the rain had stopped almost as abruptly as it began and the actors left the theatre on a calm night with stars shining: brilliant, above the rain-washed air. London glittered. A sense of urgency and excitement was abroad and when Peregrine whistled the opening phrase of a Brandenburg Concerto it might have been a whole orchestra giving it out.

'Come back to my flat for an hour, Maggie,' said Dougal. 'It's too lovely a night to go home on.'

'No, thank you, Dougal. I'm tired and hungry and I've ordered a car and here it is. Good night.'

Peregrine saw them all go their ways. Still whistling, he walked downhill and only then noticed that a little derelict shed on the waterfront lay in a heap of rubble.

I hadn't realized it had been demolished, he thought.

Next morning, a workman operating a scoop-lift pointed to a black scar on one of the stones.

'See that,' he said cheerfully to Peregrine. 'That's the mark of the Devil's thumb, that is. You don't often see it. Not nowadays you don't.'

'The Devil's thumb?'

'That's right, Squire. Lightning.'

II

Simon Morten had taken the part of Macduff by storm. His dark good looks and dashing, easy mockery of the porter on his first entrance with Lennox, his assertion of his hereditary right to wake his king, his cheerful run up the stairs whistling as he went into the bloodied chamber while Lennox warmed himself at the fire and talked cosily about the wild intemperance of the night, all gave him an easy ascendancy.

Macbeth listened, but not to him.

The door opened. Macduff stumbled on stage, incoherent, ashen-faced, the former man wiped out as if by the sweep of the murderer's hand. The stirred-up havoc, the alarum bell, the place alive suddenly with the horror of assassination. The courtyard filled with men roused from their sleep, nightgowns hastily pulled on, wild and dishevelled. The bell jangling madly.

The scene ends with the flight of the King's sons. Thereafter, in a short final scene, Macduff, already suspicious, decides not to attend Macbeth's coronation but to retire to his own headquarters at Fife. It is here that he will make his fatal decision to turn south to England, where he will learn of the murder of his wife and children. From then on he will be a man with a single object: to return to Scotland, find Macbeth and kill him.

Once Banquo has been murdered, Macduff moves forward and the end is now inevitable.

Morten had now become enamoured of the fight, which he continued to rehearse with Dougal. At Gaston's suggestion they both began to exercise vigorously, apart from the actual combat, and became expert in the handling of their weapons, twirling and slashing with alarming dexterity. The steel replicas were ready and they used them.

Peregrine came down to the theatre early one morning for a discussion on costumes and found them hard at it. Blue sparks flew, the claymores whistled. The actors leapt nimbly from spot to spot. Occasionally they grunted. Their shields were tightly strapped to their left forearms, leaving the hand free for the double-handed weapon. Peregrine gazed upon them with considerable alarm.

'Nimble, aren't they?' asked Gaston, looming up behind him.

'Very,' Peregrine agreed nervously. 'I haven't seen them for a fortnight or more. I – I suppose they are safe. By and large. *Safe*,' he repeated on a shriller note, as Macduff executed a downward sweep which Macbeth deflected and dodged by the narrowest of margins.

'Absolutely,' Gaston promised. 'I stake my reputation upon it. Ah. Excuse me. Very well, gentlemen, call it a morning. Thank you. Don't go, Mr Jay. Your remark about safety has reminded me. There will, of course, be no change in the size and position of the rostra? They are precisely where they will be for the performance?'

'Yes.'

'Good. To the fraction of an inch, I hope? Their footwork has been rehearsed with the greatest care, you know. Like a dance. Let me show you.'

He produced a plan of the stage. It was extremely elaborate and was broken up into innumerable squares.

'The stage is marked – I dare say you have noticed – in exactly the same way. Let me say I am asking the Macduff to deliver a downward sweep from right to left and the Macbeth is to parry it and leap to the lower level. I shall say – ' and here he raised his voice and shrieked: 'Mac-d. Right foot at 13b. Raise claidheamh-mor – move to 90 degrees. Sweep to 12. Er-one. Er-two. Er-three. Meanwhile . . .'

He continued in this baffling manner for some seconds and then resumed in his normal bass: 'So you will understand, Mr Jay, that the least inaccuracy in the squares might well lead to – shall we say? – to the bisection of the opponent's foot. No. I exaggerate. The crushing would be more appropriate. And we would not want that to happen, would we?'

'Certainly not. But my dear Gaston, please don't misunderstand me. I think the plan is most ingenious and the result – er – breathtaking, but would it not be just as effective, for instance – '

He got no further. He saw the crimson flush rise in Gaston's face.

'Are you about to suggest that we employ a "fake"?' Gaston demanded, and before Peregrine could reply said: 'In which case I leave this theatre. For good. Taking with me the weapons and writing to *The Times* to point out the ludicrous aspects of the charade that will inevitably be foisted upon the audience. Well? Yes or no?'

'Yes. No. I don't know which I mean but I implore you not to go waltzing out on us, Gaston. You tell me it's safe and I accept your authority. I'll get the insurance people to cover us,' he added hurriedly. 'You've no objection to that, I hope?'

Gaston waved his hand grandly and ambiguously. He went up on stage and collected the weapons which the users had put into felt containers.

'I wish you good morning,' he said. And, as an afterthought: 'I will take charge of the claidheamh-mors, and will return them tomorrow. Again, good morning.'

'Good morning, Gaston,' Peregrine said thankfully.

III

Peregrine had to admit, strictly to himself, that a change had come over the atmosphere in the theatre. It was not that rehearsals went badly. They went, on the whole, very well, with no more than the expected clashes of temperament among the actors. Barrabell, the Banquo, was the most prominent where these were concerned. He had only to appear on stage for an argument to begin about the various movements of the actors. But Peregrine was, for the most part, a patient and sagacious director and he never let loose a formidable display of anger without considering that the time had come for it and the result would be salutary. He had never encountered Barrabell before but it didn't take him long to suspect a troublemaker and this morning he had confirmation of it. Barrabell and Nina Gaythorne arrived together. He had dropped his beautifully controlled voice to its lowest level, he had taken her arm, and in her faded, good-natured face there appeared an expression that reminded Peregrine of a schoolchild receiving naughty but absorbing information upon a forbidden subject.

'*Most* unexpected,' the Voice confided. 'I wasn't here, of course, but I happened to look out . . .' It sank below the point of audibility. '. . . concentrated . . . *most* extraordinary . . .'

'Really?'

'. . . Blondie . . . rigor . . .'

'No!'

'I promise.'

At this point they came through the scenic archway and saw Peregrine. There was a very awkward silence.

'Good morning,' said Peregrine happily.

'Good morning, Perry. Er – good morning. Er.'

'You were talking about last night's storm.'

'Ah. Yes. Yes, we were. I was saying it was a heavy one.'

'Yes? But you were not here.'

'No. I saw it from a window. In Westminster: well, Pimlico.'

'I didn't see it,' said Nina. 'Not really.'

'Did you notice that old shed on the waterfront has collapsed?' Peregrine asked.

'Ah!' said Barrabell on a full note. '*That's* what it is! The difference!'

'It was struck by lightning.'

'Fancy!'

'The centre of the storm.'

'Not the theatre.'

'No,' they both fervently agreed. 'Not our theatre.'

'Did you hear about Blondie?'

They made noises.

'She was here,' said Peregrine. 'So was I. Blondie has this thing about lightning. Electricity in the air. My mother has it. She's seventy and very perky.'

'Oh yes?' said Nina. 'How lovely.'

'Very fit and well but gets electrically disturbed during thunderstorms.'

'I see,' said Barrabell.

'It's quite a common occurrence. Like cat's fur crackling. Nina darling,' said Peregrine, putting his arm around her, 'I've got three little boys coming this morning to audition for the Macduff kid. Would you be an angel and go through the scene with them? Here are their photographs. Look.'

He opened a copy of *Spotlight* at the child-actors' section. Three infant phenomena were displayed. Two were embarrassingly overdressed and bore an innocent look that only just failed to conceal an awful complacency. The third had sensible clothes and a cheeky face.

'*He's* got something,' said Nina. 'I would feel I could bear to cuddle him. When was the photo taken, I wonder.'

'Who can tell? He's called William Smith, which attracts one. The others, as you'll see, are called Wayne and Cedric.'

'Little horrors.'

'Probably. But one never knows.'

'We'll have to see, won't we?' said Nina, who had recovered her poise and was determined not to get involved with Barrabell-Banquo again.

A girl from the manager's office came through to say the juveniles had arrived, each with its parent.

'I'll see them one by one in the rehearsal room. Nina, would you come, dear?'

'Yes, of course.'

They went together.

For a little while Barrabell was alone. He had offered his services as the obligatory Equity Representative for this production. It is not a job that most actors like very much. It's not pleasant to tell a fellow player that his subscription is overdue or to appeal against an infringement, imagined or genuine, by the management, though the Dolphin in its integrity and strong 'family' reputation was not likely to run into trouble of that sort.

Barrabell belonged to a small, extreme leftist group called The Red Fellowship. Nobody seemed to know what it wanted except that it didn't want anything that was established or that made money in the theatre. Dougal Macdougal was equally far on the right and wanted, or so it was believed, to bring a Jacobite pretender to the throne and restore capital punishment.

Barrabell kept his ideas to himself. Peregrine was vaguely aware of his extreme leftist views but being himself hopelessly uncommitted to anything other than the theatre, gave it no more consideration than that.

The rest of the cast were equally vague.

So when the business of appointing a representative came up and Barrabell said he'd done it before and if they liked he'd do it again,

they were glad to let him be their Eq. Rep. Equity is an apolitical
body and takes in all shades of opinion.

But if they were indifferent to him, he was far from being indifferent to them. He had a cast list with little signs against quite a
number of names. As rehearsals went on he hoped to add to it.
Dougal Macdougal's name was boxed in. Barrabell looked at it for
some time with his head on one side. He then put a question mark
beside it.

The rest of the cast for the morning's rehearsal arrived. Peregrine
and Nina returned with a fresh-faced child in tow.

'Quickest piece of casting in our records,' said Peregrine. 'This is
William Smith, everybody. Young Macduff to you.'

The little boy's face broke into a delightful smile. Delighted and
delightful. It was transformed.

'Hal-lo, William,' said Dougal.

'Hallo, sir,' said William. Not a vowel wrong and nothing forced.

'His mama is coming back for him in an hour,' said Peregrine. 'Sit
over there, William, and watch rehearsal.'

He sat by Nina.

'This morning we're breaking new ground,' said Peregrine.
'Banquet scene with ghost of Banquo. I'll explain the business with
the ghost. You, Banquo, will wear a mask. A ghastly mask. Open
mouth with blood running. You'll have time to change your clothes.
You will have doubles. The table will have a completely convincing
false side with heavily carved legs and the black space painted
between them. You and your double will be hidden behind this side.
Your stool is at the head of the table.

'Now. The Macbeths' costumes. The Lady has voluminous sleeves,
attached all the way down to her costume. When she says "*Meeting
were bare without it,*" she holds out her hands. She is standing in front
of the stool and masks it. Macbeth goes up to her and on his own
"*Sweet remembrancer*" takes and kisses her hands. They form, momentarily, a complete mask to the stool. Banquo, from under the table,
slides up on to the stool. The speed with which you do this is all-
important. Banquo, you sit on the stool with your back to Macbeth
and your head bent down. The Macbeths move off to his right.

'On Macbeth's "*Where?*" Banquo turns. Recognition. Climax. He's
a proper job. Bloody hair, throat cut, chest stabbed, blood all over it.

On *"Feed and regard him not"* the thanes obey the Lady but rather self-consciously. They eat and mumble. Keep it quiet. Macbeth shrinks back and to the right. She follows.

'On Macbeth's *"What care I,"* Banquo lets his head go back and then fall forward. He rises and exits left. This is going to take a lot of work. You thanes, all of you, can *not* see him. Repeat: you can *not* see him. He almost touches you but for you he is *not there.* You all watch Macbeth. Have you all got that? Stop me if I'm going too fast.'

'Just a moment,' said Banquo.

Here we go, thought Peregrine. 'Yes, Bruce?' he said.

'How much room will there be under this thick-table affair?'

'Plenty, I hope.'

'And how do I see?'

Peregrine stopped himself saying 'With your eyes.' 'The mask,' he explained, 'is being very carefully designed. It is attached to the headpiece. The eye-holes are big. Your own eyes will be painted out. Gaston has done an excellent drawing for us. They will take a mould of your face.'

'Oh my God.'

'A bloodied cloak will be firmly fixed to the neck and ripped up in several places.'

'I'll want to see all these things, Perry. I'll want to rehearse in them.'

'So you shall. Till the cows come home.'

'Thank you very much,' said the beautiful voice silkily.

'Any more questions? No? Well, let's try it.'

They tried it slowly and then faster. Many times.

'I think it'll work,' Peregrine said at last to Nina who was sitting behind him.

'Oh *yes*, Perry. Yes. Yes.'

'We'll move on to the next "appearance". Dougal, you have this distraught, confused, self-betraying speech. You pull yourself together and propose a health. You stand in front of the stool, masking it, holding out the cup in your left hand. Ross fills it. The understudy is in position. Under the table. Is he here? Yes, Toby. You've moved up to the end. You can see when Macbeth's arm and hand, holding the goblet, are in place and you slip up on the stool. Macbeth proposes the toast. He moves away, facing front. He does what we all hope he will not do:

he names Banquo. The thanes drink. He turns to go upstage and there is the Ghost. On "*unreal mockery, hence*" the Ghost rises. He moves to the stairs, passing between Menteith and Gaston and past the soldiers on guard, up into the murder chamber. Everyone watches Macbeth who raves on. Now, inch by inch, we'll walk it.'

They did so, marking what they did in their scripts, gradually working through the whole scene, taking notes, walking the moves, fitting the pieces together. Peregrine said: 'If ever there was a scene that could be ruined by a bit-part actor, this is it. It's all very well to say you must completely ignore the Ghost, that for you it's not there; but it calls for a damn good actor to achieve it. We've got to make the audience accept the reality of the Ghost and be frightened by it. The most intelligent of you all, Lennox, has the line: "*Good night, and better health attend His Majesty.*" When next we see Lennox he's speaking of his suspicions to Ross. The actor will, ever so slightly, not a fraction too much, make us aware of this. A hair's-breadth pause after he says good night, perhaps. You've got your moves. Take them once more to make sure and go away and think through the whole scene, step by step, and then decide absolutely what you are feeling and doing at every moment.'

When they had gone Peregrine took Macbeth's scene with the murderers. Then the actual murder of Banquo.

'Listen!' Peregrine said. 'Just listen to the gift this golden hand offers you. It's got everything. The last glint of sunset, the near approach of disaster.

> "*The West yet glimmers with some streaks of day.*
> *Now spurs the lated traveller apace*
> *To gain the timely inn.*"

'And now we hear the thud of horses' hooves. Louder and louder. They stop. A pause. Then the horses go away. Enter Banquo with a lanthorn. I do want a profoundly deep voice for this speech. I'm sorry,' he said to the First Murderer. 'I'm going to give it to Gaston. It's a matter of voice, dear boy, not of talent. Believe me, it's a matter of voice.'

'Yes. All right,' said the stricken murderer.

They read the scene.

'That's exactly what I want. You will see that Seyton is present in both these scenes and indeed is never far from Macbeth's business from this time on. We are very lucky to have Mr Sears to take the part. He is the sword-bearer. He looms over the play and so does his tremendous weapon.'

'It is,' Gaston boomingly explained, 'the symbol of coming death. Its shadow grows more menacing as the play draws inexorably towards its close. I am reminded – '

'Exactly,' Peregrine interrupted. 'The play grows darker. Always darker. The relief is in the English scene. And now – ' He hurried on, while Gaston also continued in his pronouncements of doom. For a short time they spoke together and then Gaston, having attained his indistinguishable climax, stopped as suddenly as a turned-off tap, said 'Good morning' and left the theatre.

Peregrine opened his arms and let them flop. 'One puts up with the unbelievable,' he said. 'He's an actor. He's a paid-up member of Equity. He spoke that little speech in a way that sent quivers up and down my spine and he's got Sir Dougal Macdougal and Simon Morten banging away at each other with a zeal that makes you sweat. I suppose I'm meant to put up with other bits of eccentricity as they occur.'

'Is he certifiable?' asked Maggie.

'Probably.'

'I wouldn't put up with it,' said Bruce Barrabell. 'Get him back.'

'What do I say when he comes? He's perfect for the part. Perfect.'

Nina said: 'Just a quiet word in private? Ask him not to?'

'Not to what?'

'Go on talking while you are talking?' she said doubtfully.

'He hasn't done it since the first day until now. I'll leave it for this time.'

'Of course, if one's afraid of him . . .' sneered Barrabell, and was heard.

'I *am* afraid. I'm afraid he'll walk out and I don't mind admitting it. He's irreplaceable,' said Peregrine.

'I agree with you, dear boy,' said Sir Dougal.

'So do I,' said Maggie. 'He's too valuable.'

'So be it,' said Peregrine. 'Now, William, let's see how you shape up. Come on, Nina. And Lennox. And the murderers.'

They shaped up well. William was quick and unobjectionable. The young Macduff was cheeky and he showed spirit and breeding. His mama returned, a quietly dressed woman from whom he had inherited his vowels. They completed the financial arrangements and left. Nina, delighted with him, also left. Peregrine said to Dougal and Maggie: 'And now, my dears, the rest of the day is ours. Let's consolidate.'

They did. They too went well. Very well. And yet there was something about the rehearsal that made Peregrine almost wish for ructions. For an argument. He had insisted upon the Lady using the sexual attributes she had savagely wrenched away from herself. Maggie agreed. Dougal responded. He actually shivered under her touch. When they broke for discussion, she did so absolutely and was at once the professional actress tackling a professional detail. He was slower, resentful almost. Only for a second or two and then all attention. Too much so. As if he was playing to an audience; in a way, as if he showed himself off to Maggie – 'I'm putting on an act for you.'

Peregrine told himself he was being fanciful. It's this play, he thought. It's a volcano. Overflowing. Thickening. And then: Perhaps that's why all these damn superstitions have grown up round it.

'Any questions?' he asked them.

'It's about her feeling for Macbeth,' said Maggie. 'I take it that from the beginning she has none. She simply uses her body as an incentive.'

'Absolutely. She turns him on like a tap and turns him off when she gets her response. From the beginning she sees his weakness. He wants to eat his cake and keep it.'

'Yes. She, on the other hand, dedicates herself to evil. She's not an insensitive creature but she shuts herself off completely from any thought of remorse. Before the murder she takes enough wine to see her through and notes, with satisfaction, that it has made her bold,' said Maggie.

'She asks too much of herself. And pays the penalty. After the disastrous dinner party, she almost gives up,' Peregrine said. 'Macbeth speaks disjointedly of more crimes. She hardly listens. Always the realist, she says they want sleep! When next we see her she *is* asleep and saying those things that she would not say if she were awake. She's driven herself too hard. Now, the horror finds its way out in her sleep.'

'And what about her old man all this time?' asked Dougal loudly. 'Is she thinking about him, for God's sake?'

'We're not told but – no. I imagine she still goes on for a time stopping up the awful holes he makes in the façade but with no pretence of affection or even much interest. He's behaving as she feared he might. She has no sympathy or fondness for him. When next we see him, Dougal, he's half mad.'

'Thank you very much!'

'Well, distracted. But what words! They pour out of him. Despair itself. *"To the last syllable of recorded time."* You know, it always amazes me that the play never becomes a bore. The leading man is a hopeless character in terms of heroic images. It's the soliloquies that work the magic, Dougal.'

'I suppose so.'

'You know so,' said Maggie cheerfully. 'You know exactly what you're doing. Doesn't he, Perry?'

'Of course he does,' Peregrine said heartily.

They were standing on stage. There were no lights on in the auditorium but a voice out there said: 'Oh, don't make any mistake about it, Maggie, he knows what he's doing.' And laughed.

It was Morten: the Macduff.

'Simon!' Maggie said. 'What are you doing down there? Have you been watching?'

'I've only just come in. Sorry I interrupted, Perry. I wanted to see the Office about something.'

The door at the back of the stalls let in an oblong of daylight and shut it out again.

'What's the matter with *him*?' Dougal asked at large.

'Lord knows,' said Peregrine. 'Pay no attention.'

'It's nothing,' Maggie said. 'He's being silly.'

'It's not exactly silly, seeing that baleful face scowling at one and him whirling his claymore within inches of one's own face,' Dougal pointed out. 'And if I catch your meaning, Maggie love, all for nothing. I'm as blameless as the Bloody Child. Though not, I may add, from choice.'

'I'll have a word with him.'

'Choose your words, darling. You may inflame him.'

'Maggie dear,' Peregrine begged her, 'calm him down if you can. We're doing the English scene this week and I *would* like him to be normal.'

'I'll do my best. He's so *silly*,' Maggie reiterated crossly. 'And I'm so busy.'

Her opportunity occurred the next afternoon. She had stayed in the theatre after working at the sleepwalking scene, while Peregrine worked with Simon on the English scene.

When they had finished and Morten was about to leave, she crossed her fingers and stopped him.

'Simon, that's a *wonderful* beginning. Come home with me, will you, and talk about it? We'll have a drink and a modest dinner. Don't say no. Please.'

He was taken aback. He looked hard at her, muttered sulkily and then said, 'Thank you, I'd like that.'

'Good. Put on your overcoat. It's cold outside. Have you got your part? Come on, then. Good night, Perry dear.'

'Good night, lovely lady.'

They went out by the stage door. When he heard it bang, Peregrine crossed himself and said 'God bless her.' He turned off the working lights, locked the doors and used his torch to find his way out by the front-of-house.

They took a taxi to Maggie's flat. She rang the bell and an elderly woman opened the door. 'Nanny,' said Maggie, 'can you give two of us dinner? No hurry. Two hours.'

'Soup. Grilled chops.'

'Splendid.'

'Good evening, Mr Morten.'

'Good evening, Nanny.'

They came in. A bright fire and comfortable chairs. Maggie took his coat and hung it in the hall. She gave him a pretty robust drink and sat him down. 'I'm breaking my own rule,' she said, pouring a small one for herself. 'During rehearsal period, no alcohol, no parties, and no nice gentlemen's nonsense. But you've seen that for yourself, of course.'

'Have I?'

'Of course. Even supposing Dougal was a world-beater sex-wise, which I ain't supposing, it'd be a disaster to fall for him when we're playing The Tartans. Some people could do it. Most, I dare say, but not this lady. Luckily, I'm not tempted.'

'Maggie?'

'No.'

'Promise?'

'Of course.'

'*He* doesn't share your views?'

'I don't know how he feels about it. Nothing serious,' said Maggie lightly. She added, 'My dear Si, you can see what he's like. Easy come, easy go.'

'Have you – ' he took a pull at his drink – 'have you discussed it?'

'Certainly not. It hasn't been necessary.'

'You had dinner with him. The night there was a rehearsal.'

'I can have dinner with someone without falling like an over-ripe apple for him.'

'What about *him*, though?'

'Simon! You're being childish. He did not make a pass at me and if he had I'd have been perfectly well able to cope. I told you. During rehearsals I don't have affairs. You're pathologically jealous about nothing. Nothing at all.'

'Maggie, I'm sorry. I'm terribly sorry. Forgive me, Maggie darling.'

'All right. But no bedroom scenes. I told you, I'm as pure as untrodden snow while I'm rehearsing. Honestly.'

'I believe you. Of course.'

'Well then, do stop prowling and prowling around like the hosts of whoever-they-were in the hymn book. "Lor'," as Mrs Boffin said, "let's be comfortable."'

'All right,' he said, and a beguiling grin transformed his face. 'Let's.'

'And clean as a whistle?'

'So be it.'

'Then give yourself another drink and tell me what you think about the young Malcolm.'

'The young Malcolm? It's a difficult one, isn't it? I think he'll get there but it'll take a lot of work.'

And they discussed the English scene happily and excitedly until dinner was ready.

Maggie produced a bottle of wine, the soup was real and the chops excellent.

'How nice this is,' said Maggie when they had finished.

'It's perfect.'

'So what a Silly Simon you were to cut off your nose to spite your face, weren't you? We'll sit by the fire for half an hour and then you must go.'

'If you say so.'

'I do, most emphatically. I'm going to work on the sleepwalking scene. I want to get a sleepwalking voice. Dead. No inflections. Metallic. Will it work?'

'Yes.'

She looked at him and thought how pleasant and romantic he seemed and what a pity it was that he was so stupidly jealous. It showed in his mouth. Nothing could cure it.

When he got up to go she said, 'Good night, my dear. You won't take it out on Dougal, will you? It would be so silly. There's nothing to take.'

'If you say so.'

He held her by her arms. She gave him a quick kiss and withdrew.

'Good night, Simon.'

'Good night.'

When she had shut the door and he was alone outside, he said: 'All the same, to hell with Sir Dougal Macdougal.'

IV

On Monday morning there was a further and marked change in the atmosphere. It wasn't gloomy. It was oppressive and nervous. Rather like the thunderstorm, Peregrine thought. Claustrophobic. Expectant. Stifling.

Peregrine finished blocking. By Wednesday they had covered the whole play and took it through in continuity.

There were noticeable changes in the behaviour of the company. As a rule, the actor would finish a scene and come off with a sense of anxiety or release. He or she would think back through the dialogue, note the points of difficulty and re-rehearse them in the mind or, as it were, put a tick against them as having come off successfully.

Then he would disappear into the shadows, or watch for a time with professional interest or read a newspaper or book, each according to his temperament and inclination.

This morning it was different. Without exception the actors sat together and watched and listened with a new intensity. It was as though each actor continued in an assumed character, and no other reality existed. Even in the scenes that had been blocked but not yet developed there was a nervous tension that knew the truth would emerge and the characters march to their appointed end.

The company were to see the fight for the first time. Macduff now had something of a black angel's air about him, striding through the battle on the hunt for Macbeth. He encountered men in the Macbeth tartan, and mistook them for him, but it must be Macbeth or nobody. Then Macduff saw him, armoured, helmeted, masked, and cried out: *'Turn, hell-hound. Turn!'*

Macbeth turned.

Peregrine's palms were wet. The thanes, waiting offstage now, stood aghast. Steel clashed on steel or screamed as one blade slid down another. There was no other sound than the men's hard breathing.

Macduff swung his claymore up, then swiftly down. Macbeth caught it on his shield and lurched forward.

Nina, in the audience, screamed.

The boast while they both fought for breath that no man of woman born should harm Macbeth, Macduff's reply that he was *'from his mother's womb untimely ripped'* and then the final exit, Macduff driving him backwards and out. Macbeth's scream, cut short, offstage. An empty stage for seconds, then trumpets and drums and re-enter Malcolm, old Siward and the thanes, in triumph. Big scene. Old Siward on his son's death. Re-enter Macduff and Seyton with Macbeth's head grinning on the point of his claymore. *'Behold where stands the usurper's cursed head,'* shouts Macduff.

Malcolm is hailed King of Scotland and the play is over.

'Thank you, everybody,' said Peregrine. 'Thank you very much.'

And in the sounds of relief that answered him the clearly articulated treble of William Smith spoke the final word:

'He got his comeuppance, didn't he, Miss Gaythorne?'

V

When Peregrine had taken his notes and the mistakes had been corrected the cast stayed for a little while as if reluctant to break the bond that united them.

Dougal said: 'Pleased, Perry?'

'Yes. Very pleased. So pleased, I'm frightened.'

'Not melodramatic?'

'There were perhaps three moments when it slid over. None of them involved you, Dougal, and I'm not even sure about them. Will they laugh when the head comes on? Its face is seen only for a moment. Seyton's downstage and its back's to the audience.'

'It's taking a risk, of course. Seyton's become a sort of Fate, hasn't he? Or like Macbeth's alter ego.'

'Yes,' Peregrine said gratefully. 'Or his shadow. By the way, Gaston's making the head.'

'Good. *Maggie* darling,' Dougal cried as she joined them. 'You are wonderful. Satanic and lovely and baleful. I can't begin to tell you. Thank you, thank you.' He kissed her hands and her face and seemed unable to stop.

'If I can get a word in,' said Simon. He was beside them, his hair damp with sweat stuck to his forehead and a line of it glinted on his upper lip. Maggie pushed herself free of Dougal and held Simon by his woollen jacket. 'Si!' she said and kissed him. 'You're *fantastic.*'

They'll run out of adjectives, Peregrine thought, and then we'll all go to lunch.

Simon looked over the top of Maggie's head at Dougal. 'I seem to have won,' he said. 'Or do I?'

'We've all won or hope we will have in three weeks' time. It's too early for these raptures,' said Peregrine.

Maggie said: 'I've got someone in a car waiting for me and I'm late.' She patted Simon's face and freed herself. 'I'm not wanted this afternoon, Perry?'

'No. Thank you, lovely.'

''Bye, everyone,' she cried, and made for the stage door. William Smith ran ahead of her and opened it.

'Ten marks for manners, William,' she said.

There was nobody waiting for her. She hailed a taxi. That's settled *their* hashes, she thought as she gave her address. And the metallic voice will work wonders if I get it right. She made an arrangement in her vocal cords and spoke.

'*"Who would have thought the old man to have' so much blood in him."*'

'What's that, lady?' asked the startled driver.

'Nothing, nothing. I'm an actress. It's my part.'

'Oh. One of them. Takes all sorts, don' it?' he replied.

'It certainly does.'

Ross, Lennox, Menteith, Caithness and Angus were called for three o'clock, so had time to get a good tuck-in at the Swan. They walked along the Embankment and the sun shone upon them: four young men with a fifth – the Ross – who was older. They had a certain air about them. They walked well. They spoke freely and clearly and they laughed loudly. Their faces had a pale smoothness as if seldom exposed to the sun. When they were separated by other pedestrians they raised their voices and continued their conversation without self-consciousness. Lennox, when not involved, sang tunefully:

> '*"Not a flower, not a flower sweet,'*
> *On my black coffin let there be strown."*

'Wrong play, dear boy,' said Ross. 'That's from *Twelfth Night*.'

'Bloody funny choice for a comedy.'

'Strange, isn't it?'

Lennox said: 'Do any of you find this play . . . I don't know . . . oppressive? Almost too much. I mean, we can't escape it. Do you?'

'I do,' Ross confessed. 'I've been in it before. Same part. It does rather stick with one, doesn't it?'

'Well,' Menteith said reasonably, 'what's it *about*? Five murders. Three witches. A fiendish lady. A homicidal husband. A ghost. And the death of the name-part with his severed head on the end of a claymore. Rather a bellyful to shake off, isn't it?'

'It's melodrama pure and simple,' said Angus. 'It just happens to be written by a man with a knack for words.'

Lennox said: 'What a knack! No. That doesn't really account for the thing I mean. We don't get it in the other tragedies, do we? Not in *Hamlet* or *Lear* or *Antony and Cleopatra*.'

'Perhaps it's the reason for all the superstitions.'

'I wonder,' Ross said. 'It may be. They all say the same thing, don't they? Don't speak his name. Don't quote from it. Don't call it by its title. Keep off.'

They turned into a narrow side street.

'I tell you what,' Caithness said. 'I don't mind betting anyone who's prepared to take up that Perry's the only one of the whole company who *really* doesn't believe a word of it. I mean that – *really*. He doesn't *do* anything but that's so that our apple-carts won't be upset.'

'You sound bloody sure of yourself, little man, but how do you know?' asked Menteith.

'You can tell,' said Caithness loftily.

'No, you can't. You just kid yourself you can.'

'Oh, do shut up.'

'OK, OK. Look, there's Rangi. What's *he* think of it all?'

'Ask him.'

'Hullo! Rangi!'

He turned, waved at the Swan and pointed to himself.

'So are we,' Angus shouted. 'Join us.'

They caught up with him and all entered the bar together.

'Look, there's a table for six. Come on.'

They slipped into the seats. 'I'll get the beer,' Ross offered. 'Everybody want one?'

'Not for me,' said Rangi.

'Oh! Why not?'

'Because I do better without. Tomato juice. A double and nothing stronger with it.'

Menteith said: 'I'll have that too.'

'Two double tomatoes. Four beers,' Ross repeated and went to the bar.

'Rangi,' Lennox said, 'we've been arguing.'

'Oh? What about?'

Lennox looked at his mates. 'I don't know exactly. About the play.'

'Yes?'

Menteith said: 'We were trying to get to the bottom of its power. On the face of it, it's simply what a magical hand can do with a dose of blood-and-thunder. But that doesn't explain the atmosphere it churns up. Or does it?'

'Suppose – ' Caithness began. 'You won't mind, Rangi, will you?'

'I've not the faintest idea what you're going to ask, but I don't suppose I will.'

'Well, suppose we were to offer a performance of the play on your – what do you call it – ?'

'The marai?'

'Yes. How would you react?'

'To the invitation or to the performance?'

'Well – to the performance, I suppose. Both, really.'

'It would depend upon the elders. If they were sticklers, really orthodox people, you would be given formal greetings, the challenge and the presentation of the weapon. It is possible . . .' He stopped.

'Yes?'

'It would have been possible, I believe, that the tahunga – that's what you'd call a wise man – would have been asked, because of the nature of the play, to lay a tapu on the performance. He would do this. And then you would go away and dress and the performance would take place.'

'You don't mind about using – well, you know – eyes, tongue and everything in the play?'

'I am not entirely orthodox. And we take the play seriously. My great-grandfather was a cannibal,' said Rangi in his exquisite voice. 'He believed he absorbed the attributes of his victims.'

A complete silence fell upon the table. Perhaps because they had been rather a noisy party before, their silence affected other patrons and Rangi's declaration, quite loudly made, was generally heard. The silence lasted only for a second or two.

'Four beers and two tomato juices,' said Ross, returning with the drinks. He laid the tray on the table.

CHAPTER 3

Third Week

In the third week the play began to consolidate. The parts that were clearly spurious had of course been taken out; the structure was fully revealed. It was written with economy: the remorseless destiny of the Macbeths, the certainty from the beginning that they were irrevocably cursed, their progress, at first clinging to each other, then separated and swept away downstream to their damnation: these elements declared themselves in every phase of this destructive play.

Why, then, was it not dreary? Why did it excite rather than distress?

'I don't know,' Peregrine said to his wife. 'Well, I do, really. It's because it's wonderfully well written. Simple as that. It's the atmosphere that it generates.'

'When you directed it before, did you feel the same way about it?'

'I think so. Not so marked though. It's a much better company, of course. Really, it's a perfect company. If you heard Simon Morten in the English scene, Emily. Saying: "*My wife killed too?*" Then when Malcolm offers his silly conventional bit of advice, Simon looks at Ross and says: "*He has no children.*"'

'I know.'

'Come down to rehearsal one of these days and see.'

'Shall I?'

'Yes. Do. At the end of next week.'

'All right. How about the superstitions? Is Nina Gaythorne behaving herself?'

'She's trying to, at least. I don't mind betting she's taking all sorts of precautions on the side, *but* as long as she doesn't *talk* about it . . .

Barrabell – he's the Banquo – feeds her stories, I'm quite sure. I caught him at it last week. The scrap shed down by the river was struck by lightning last week.'

'No! You never told me.'

'Didn't I? I suppose I've clapped locks on anything that looks like superstition and don't unfasten them even for you. I caught Barrabell nicely and gave poor old Nina the shock of her life.'

'What were they saying?'

'He was on about one of the witches – Blondie – making a scene and getting the willies during the storm. Some people do get upset, you know – it's electrical. They always say they're sorry and they can't help it.'

'Was Blondie all right?'

'Right as rain when the lightning stopped.'

'How unfortunate.'

'What?'

'That there should be a thunderstorm.'

'You don't mean – '

'Oh, *I* don't believe all the nonsense. Of course I don't. I just thought how unfortunate from the point of view of the people who do.'

'The silly fatheads have got over it. The theatre wasn't struck by lightning. Being fixed up with a good conductor, it wouldn't have felt it anyway.'

'No.' After a short silence Emily said: 'How's the little boy behaving?'

'William Smith? Very well. He's a good actor. It'll be interesting to see what happens to him after adolescence. He may not go on with the theatre but I hope he does. He's doubling.'

'The Bloody Child?'

'And the Crowned Child. They're one and the same. You should hear him wail out his *"Great Birnam Wood to high Dunsinane Hi-i-ill shall come against him."'*

'Golly!'

'Yes, my girl. That's the word for it.'

'How are you working the scene? The apparitions?'

'The usual things. Dry ice. A trap door. A lift. Background of many whispering voices: *"Double, double."* Strong rhythm. The show of Kings are all Banquo's descendants. The scene ends with "*And points at them for his.*" The next bit in the script is somebody's incredibly silly addition – I should think the stage manager's for a fourth-rate company in the sticks. It's a wonder he didn't give the witches red noses and slapsticks.'

'So you go on with – what?'

'There's a blackout and great confusion. Crescendo. Noises. Macbeth's voice. Sounds, possibly drums. I'm not sure. Macbeth's voice again, strongly, calling: 'Lennox!' Sound of footfalls. Lights dim up with Lennox knocking on the door. Macbeth comes out. Rest of scene as written.'

'Smashing.'

'Well, I hope so. It's going to need handling.'

'Yes. Of course.'

'It's the only tricky one left from the staging point of view.'

'Could Gaston be a help? About witchcraft?'

'I daren't risk asking him. He could, of course, but he does so – go off the deep end. He is a teeny bit mad, you know. Only on his own lay, but he is. He'd God's gift when it comes to claidheamh-mors. What will you think of the fight? It terrifies me.'

'Is it *really* dangerous, Perry?'

He waited for a minute.

'Not according to Gaston, always making sure the stage is right. He'll keep a nightly watch on it. The two men have reached an absolute perfection of movement. They're getting on together a bit better, too, man to man. Maggie had a go at Simon, bless her, and he's less crissy-crossy when they are not fighting, thank God.'

'Well,' said Emily, 'nobody can accuse you of being superstitious, I'll say that for you.'

'Will you? And you'll come next week when we'll take it in continuity with props?'

'You bet I will,' said Emily.

'I don't know what you'll think of Gaston. I mean, of what I'm doing with him. He's the bearer of the great ceremonial sword – the claidheamh-mor – we're making a harness for him to take the haft. It's the real weapon and weighs a ton. He's as strong as a bull. He follows Macbeth everywhere like a sort of judgement. And at the end he'll carry the head on it. He is watching Jeremy's drawings for his costume with the eye of a hawk.'

'What's it like?'

'Like all the other Macbeth ménage. Embryo tartan, black woollen tights, thonged sheepskin leggings. A heavy belt to take the sword-hilts. A mask for the fights. In his final appearance with the head on the sword – er – he suggested a scarlet tabard.'

'Oh, for heaven's sake, Perry!'

'I know. Where would he change, and why? With fighting thanes milling all round. I pointed this out and for once he hadn't an answer. He took refuge in huffy grandeur, said it was merely an idea and went into a long thing about colour and symbolism.'

'I feel I must meet him.'

'Shall I invite him for tea?'

'Do you *like* him?' she asked incredulously.

'Oh, one couldn't exactly do that. Or I don't think one could. *Collect* him, perhaps. No, he might just turn into a bore and not go home.'

'In that case we won't ask him here.'

'Or bring the Macbeth's head with him to show you. He did that to me. When we'd finished afternoon rehearsal. It was in the shadows of the wardrobe room. I nearly fainted.'

'Frightful?'

'Terrifying. It's sheet white and so *like* Dougal. With a bloody gash, you know. He wondered if I had any suggestions to make.'

'Had you?'

'Just to cover it up quick. Fortunately the audience only sees it momentarily. He turns it to face Malcolm who is up on the steps at the back. It'll be back to audience.'

'They'll laugh,' said Emily.

'If they laugh at that they'll laugh at anything.'

'What do you bet?'

'Well, of course they have in the past always laughed at a head and the management always says it's a nervous reaction. So it may be but I don't think so. I think they know it isn't, and can't be, Macbeth's or anybody else's head and they laugh. It's as if they said: "This is a bit too thick. Come off it." All the same I'm going to risk it.'

'You jolly well do and more power to your elbow.'

'The final words are cut. The play ends with the thanes all shouting: "*Hail, King of Scotland*," and pointing their swords at Malcolm.
He's in a strong light. I hope the audience will go away feeling, well –
relieved, uplifted, as if Scotland stands free of a nightmare.'

'I hope so too. I think they will.'

'May you think so when you've seen it.'

'I bet I will,' said Emily.

'I'll push off. So long, Em, wish me luck.'

'With all my heart,' she said, and gave him a kiss and a packet
and a Thermos. 'Your snack,' she said.

'Thanks, love. I don't know when I'll be home.'

'OK. Always welcome.'

She watched him get into his car. He gave her a toot and
was off.

II

He was taking the witches' scenes. Mattresses had been placed on the
stage behind the gallows rostrum. The body on the scaffold moved
slightly in its noose, turned by one of the mysterious draughts that
steal about backstage regions. When Peregrine walked in Rangi stood
beside it and peered into the void beneath.

'See anything?' he asked.

A muffled voice from the void said something indistinguishable.

'If you can't see the back of the gallery they can't see you.'

'Too dark.'

'He'll put a light on for you. Anyone up there?' Rangi called and
was answered by an affirmative.

'Light yourself up.'

'Hang on.' A pause. A lighter flickered over a hirsute face. 'See
that?' asked Rangi.

'I can't see nothing.'

'Fair enough. OK,' Rangi yelled. 'You can come down from up
there.'

''Morning, Rangi,' said Peregrine. 'Joined the Scene-shifters' Union?'

Rangi grinned. 'We wanted to make sure we were masked from
up there.'

'You want to watch it. The right way is to ask me and I'll check with the SM.' He put his arm across Rangi's shoulders. 'You're not in the land of Do-It-Yourself now,' he said.

'I'm sorry. I didn't *do* anything. Just yelled.'

'All right. You need to watch it. We might have the whole stage staff going out on strike. Is Bruce Barrabell here?'

'I don't think so.'

'Good. Your part's shaping up nicely. Do you like it?'

'Oh, sure. Sure.'

'We'll give you a skirt for rehearsals.'

'A sort of lady-tohunga, uh? Except that tohungas are always men.'

'You'll look like three disreputable old women until Macbeth sees your faces, and they are terrible and know everything. In the opening scene we see them, birdlike, as they are; almost ravens. Busy on the gallows collecting from the corpse what's left of the *"grease that's sweaten from the murderer's gibbet"*. In the second scene when Macbeth first meets them they've put on a sort of caricature of respectability: hats, filthy aprons, dirty mutches that hold up their chins like grave-cloths. Blondie is the sexy one. One breast hangs out. Brown and stringy. They are *not* like female tohungas, really.'

'Not in the least,' said Rangi cheerfully.

Dougal Macdougal arrived. He never 'came in'. There was always the element of an event. He could be heard loudly greeting the more important members of the company who had now assembled and not forgetting to say "Morning. 'Morning,' to the bit parts. He arrived on stage, hailed Peregrine as if they hadn't encountered each other for at least a month, saw the witch-girls – 'Good morning, dear. Good morning, dear – ' and fetched up face to face with Rangi. 'Oh. Good morning – er – Rainy,' he said loftily.

'Settle down, everyone,' said Peregrine. 'We are taking the witches' scenes. I've got the lights manager to come down and the effects man: I'd like them to sit beside me, take notes and go away after this rehearsal to map out their plots. The message I plan to convey depends very much upon dead cues for effects and I hope that between us we'll cook up something that'll raise the pimples on the backs of the audiences' necks. Right.'

He waited while the witches took up their positions and the others sat in the front-of-house.

'No overture,' he said, 'in the usual sense. The house darkens and there's a muffled drumbeat. Thud, thud, thud. Like a heart. Curtain up, flash of lightning. We get a fleeting look at the witches. Dry ice.'

Rangi on the arm of the gibbet reaching down at the head. Wendy doubled up, and Blondie on Wendy's back clawing the feet. Busy. Hold for five seconds. Blackout. Thunder. Fade up to half-light concentrated on witches who are now all on the ground. Dialogue.

'*When shall we three meet again?*'

Blondie's voice was a high treble, Wendy's gritty and broken, Rangi's full and quivering.

'*There to meet with –* ' A pause. Silence. Then they all whisper: '*Macbeth.*'

'Flash of lightning,' said Peregrine. 'And two caterwauls. Dry ice – lots of it.'

' *– hover through the fog and filthy air.*'

'Blackout! Catch them in mid-air still going up. Split-second cue. Hold blackout for scenic change. Witches! Ask them to come on, will you, someone.'

'We heard you,' said a voice, Rangi's. 'We're coming.' He and the two girls came on from behind the rostrum.

'There'll have to be means for a quick exit from behind in the blackout. OK? Charlie there?'

'OK,' said the ASM coming on stage.

'Got it?'

'Got it.'

'Good. Any questions? Rangi, are the mattresses all right?'

'I was all right. What about you two?'

'All right that time,' said Wendy. 'We *might* sprain an ankle.'

'Fall soft, lie flat and crawl off,' said Peregrine.

'Yes.'

'Wait a bit.' He used his makeshift steps to the stage and ran up on to the rostrum. 'Like this,' he said, and jumped high. He fell out of sight with a soft thud.

'We'll have to deal with that,' said the effects man. 'How about the muffled drum again?'

There followed a complete silence. Wendy on the edge of the rostrum looked over. Perry lying on his back looked up at her.

'All right?' she asked.

'Perfectly,' he said in a strange voice. 'I won't be a moment. Next scene. Clear stage.'

They moved away. Peregrine gingerly explored his right side. Below the ribs. Above the hip. Nothing broken but a hellishly sore bruise. He crept up into a kneeling position on the tarpaulin-covered mattress and from there saw what had happened. Under the tarpaulin was an unmistakable shape, cruciform, bumpy, with the hilt tailing out into the long blade. He felt it: undoubtedly the claymore. The wooden claymore, discarded since they had begun using the steel replicas of the original.

He got to his feet and, painfully holding his bruise, stumped on to the clear stage. 'Charlie?'

'Here, sir.'

'Charlie, come here. There's a dummy claymore under the cover. Don't say anything about it. I don't want anyone to know it's there. Mark the position with chalk and then move it out and tuck the cover back in position. Understand?'

'I get you.'

'If they know it's there, they'll start talking a lot of nonsense.'

'Are you all right, sir?'

'Perfectly,' said Peregrine. 'Just a jolt.'

He straightened up and drew in his breath. 'Right,' he said, and walked on stage and down into the auditorium to his desk.

'Call Scene Three,' he said and sank into his seat.

'Scene Three,' called the Assistant Stage Manager. 'Witches. Macbeth. Banquo.'

III

Scene Three was pretty thoroughly rehearsed. The witches came in from separate spots and met on stage. Rangi had his speech about the sailor to Aleppo gone, and contrived an excretion of venom in voice and face, egged on by moans of pleasure from his sisters. Enter Macbeth and Banquo. Trouble. Banquo's position. He felt he should be on a higher level. He could not see Macbeth's face. On and on in his beautiful voice. Peregrine, exquisitely uncomfortable and feeling rather sick, dealt with him, only just keeping his temper.

'The ladies will vanish as they did before. They get up to position on their *"Banquo and Macbeth, all hail."'*

'May I interrupt?' fluted Banquo.

'No,' said Peregrine over a vicious stab of pain. 'You may not. Later, dear boy. On, please.'

The scene continued with Banquo, disconcerted, silver-voiced and ominously well-behaved.

Macbeth was halfway through his soliloquy. *'Present fears,'* he said, *'are less than horrible imaginings* and if the gentleman with the fetching laugh would be good enough to shut his silly trap *my thought whose murder yet is but fantastical* will probably remain so.'

He was removed by the total width and much of the depth of the stage from Banquo, who had been placed in tactful conversation with the other lairds as far away as possible from the soliloquist and had burst into a peal of jolly laughter and slapped the disconcerted Ross on his shoulders.

'Cut the laugh, Bruce,' said Peregrine. 'It distracts. Pipe down. On.'

The scene ended as written by the author and with the barely concealed merriment of Ross and Angus.

Dougal went into the auditorium to apologize to Peregrine. Banquo affected innocence. 'Cauldron Scene,' Peregrine called.

Afterwards he wondered how he got through the rest of the rehearsal. Luckily the actors and apparitions were pretty solid and it was a matter of making the electrician and effects man acquainted with what would be expected of them.

The cauldron would be in the passage under the steps up to what had been Duncan's room. A door, indistinguishable when shut, *would* shut at the disappearance of the cauldron and witches amidst noise, blackout and a great display of dry-ice-fog and galloping hooves. Full lighting and Lennox tapping with his sword hilt at the door.

'You've seen our side of it,' Peregrine said to the effects man. 'It's up to you to interpret. Go home, have a think. Come and tell me. Right?'

'Right. I say,' said the electrician, 'that kid's good, isn't he?'

'Yes, isn't he?' said Peregrine. 'If you'll excuse me, I want a word with Charlie. Thank you so much. Goodbye till we three meet again. Sooner the better.'

'Yes indeed.' A chorus of goodbyes.

The men left. Peregrine mopped his face. I'd better get out of this, he thought, and wondered if he could drive.

It was not yet four-thirty. Banquo was not in sight and the traffic had not thickened. His car was in the yard. To hell with everything, thought Peregrine. He said to the ASM: 'I want to get off, Charlie. Have you fixed it up? The sword?'

'It's OK. Are you all right?'

'It's just a bruise. No breakages. You'll lock up?'

'Sure!'

He went out with Peregrine, opened the car door and watched him in.

'Are you all right? Can you drive?'

'Yes.'

'Saturday tomorrow.'

'That's the story, Charlie. Thank you. Don't talk about this, will you? It's their silly superstition.'

'I don't talk,' said Charlie. '*Are* you all right?'

He was, or nearly so, when he settled. Charlie watched him out of the yard. Along the Embankment, over the bridge and then turn right and right again. When he got there he was going to sound his horn.

To his surprise, Emily came out of their house and ran down the steps to the car. 'I thought you'd never get here,' she cried. And then: 'Darling, what's wrong?'

'Give me a bit of a prop. I've bruised myself. Nothing serious.'

'Right you are. Here we go, then. Which is the side?'

'The other. Here we go.'

He clung to her, slid out and stood holding on to the car. She shut and locked the door.

'Shall I get a stick or will you use me?'

'I'll use you, love, if you don't mind.'

'Away we go, then.'

They staggered up the steps. Emmy got the giggles. 'If Mrs Sleigh next door sees us she'll think we're tight.'

'You needn't help me, after all. Once I've straightened up I'm all right. My legs are absolutely OK. Let go.'

'Are you sure?'

'Of course,' he said. He straightened up and gave a short howl. 'Absolutely all right,' he said, walked rather quickly up the steps

into the house and fell into an armchair. Emily went to the telephone.

'What are you doing, Em?'

'Ringing up the doctor.'

'I don't think – '

'I do,' said Emily. She had an incisive conversation. 'How did it
happen?' she broke off.

'I fell on a sword. On the wooden hilt.'

She repeated this into the telephone and hung up. 'He's looking
in on his way home,' she said.

'I'd like a drink.'

'I suppose it won't do you any harm?'

'It certainly will not.'

She fetched him a drink. 'I'm not sure about this,' she said.

'I am,' said Peregrine. He swallowed it. 'That's better. Why did
you come running out of the house?'

'I've got something to show you but I don't know that you're in
a fit state to see it.'

'Bad news?'

'Not directly.'

'Then show me.'

'Here, then. Look at this.'

She fetched an envelope from the table and pulled out a cutting
from one of the more lurid Sunday tabloids. It was a photograph of
a woman and a small boy. They were in a street and had obviously
been caught unawares. She was white-faced and stricken; the little
boy looked frightened. 'Mrs Geoffrey Harcourt-Smith and William,'
the caption read. 'After the Verdict.'

'It's three years old,' said Emily. 'It came in the post this morning.
It was a murder. Decapitation. Last of six, I think. The husband was
found guilty but insane and he got a life sentence.'

Peregrine looked at it for a minute and then held it out. 'Burn it?'
he said.

'Gladly.' She lit a match and he held the cutting over an ashtray.
It turned black and disintegrated.

'This too?' Emily asked, holding up the envelope. It was addressed
in capital letters.

'Yes. No. No, not that. Not yet,' said Peregrine. 'Put it in my desk.'

Emily did so. 'You're quite sure? It was William?'

'Three years younger. Absolutely sure. And his mother. Damn.'

'Perry, you've never seen the thing. Put it out of your mind.'

'I can't do that. But it makes no difference. The father was a schizo-phrenic monster. Life sentence in Broadmoor. They called him the Hampstead Chopper.'

'You don't think – it's – anybody in the theatre who sent this?'

'No!'

Emily was silent.

'They've no cause. None.'

After a pause he said: 'I suppose it might be a sort of warning.'

'You haven't told me how you came to fall on the claymore.'

'I was showing the girls and Rangi how to fall soft. They don't know what happened. They've each got a special place. The sword was halfway between two places.'

'It was there – under the cover when they fell?'

'Must have been.'

'Wouldn't they have seen it? Seen the shape under the cover?'

'No. I didn't. It's very dark down there.'

They were silent, for a moment. The sound of London swelled into the gap. On the river a solitary craft gave out its lonely call.

'Nobody knew,' Emily ventured, 'that you were going to make that jump?'

'Of course not. I didn't know myself, did I?'

'So it being you that got the jab in the wind was just bad luck.'

'Must have been.'

'Well, thank God for that, at least.'

'Yes.'

'Where was it? Before he hid it.'

'I don't know. Wait a sec. Yes, I do. The two wooden claymores were hung up on nails. On the back wall. They were very much the worse for wear, in spite of having cloth shields on the blades. One was split. Being Gaston's work, they were carefully made: the right weight and balance and grip but they were really only makeshift. They were no good for anything except playing soldiers.' He stopped and then said hurriedly: 'I won't elaborate on the sword to the doctor. I'll just say it'd been left lying there and nobody cleared it up.'

'Yes. All right. True enough as far as it goes.'

'And as for William, beyond taking care what we talk about, we ignore the whole thing.'

'The play being what it is – ' Emily began. And stopped.

'It's all right. He was shouting out "He got his comeuppance, didn't he?" just like any other small boy. At rehearsal, I mean.'

'How old was he when it happened?'

'Six.'

'He's nine now?'

'Yes. He looks much younger. He's a nice boy.'

'Yes. Does it hurt much? Your side?'

'If I move it's unpleasant. I wonder if for the cast there's some chronic affliction I could have had at odd times? The result of something that happened long before *Macbeth*.'

'Diverticulitis?'

'Why diverticulitis?'

'I don't know why,' said Emily, 'but it seems to me it's something American husbands have. Their wives say mysteriously to one: "My dear! He has *diverticulitis*." And one nods and looks solemn.'

'I think I'd be safer with a growling gall bladder. Whereabouts is one's gall bladder?'

'We can ask the doctor.'

'So we can.'

'Shall I have a look at you?'

'No, we'd better leave well alone.'

'What a dotty remark that is. After all,' said Emily, 'the bit in question is the bit of you that is *not* well so how can we leave it alone? I'll get our dinner instead. It'll be a proper onion soup and then an omelette. OK?'

Emily made up their fire, gave Peregrine a book to read and went to the kitchen. The onion soup was prepared and only needed heating. She cut up bread into snippets and heated butter in a frying pan. She opened a bottle of burgundy and left it to breathe.

'Emily!' called Peregrine.

She hurried back to the study.

'What's up?'

'I'm all right. I've been thinking. Nina. She won't be satisfied with the chronic gallstones or whatever. She'll just think my chronic thing's coming back now is another stroke of bad luck.'

They had their dinner on trays. Emily tidied them away and they sat with modest glasses of burgundy over their fire.

Peregrine said: 'The sword and the photograph? Are they connected?'

'Why should they be?'

'I don't know.'

The doctor came. He made a careful examination and said there were no bones broken but there was severe bruising. He made Peregrine do painful things.

'You'll survive,' he said facetiously. 'I'm leaving something to help you sleep.'

'Good.'

'Don't go prancing about showing actors what to do.'

'I'm incapable of even a teeny-weeny prance.'

'Jolly good. I'll look in again tomorrow evening.'

Emily went to the front door with the doctor. 'He'll be down at the theatre on Monday come hell or high water,' she said. 'He doesn't want the cast to know he fell on a sword. What could he have? Something chronic.'

'I really don't know. Stomach cramp? Hardly.' He thought for a moment. 'Diverticulitis?' he suggested. And then: 'Why on earth are you laughing?'

'Because it's a joke word.' Emily put on a grave face, raised her eyebrows and nodded meaningfully. '*Diverticulitis,*' she said in a sepulchral voice.

'I don't know what you're on about,' said the doctor. 'Is it something to do with superstitions?'

'That's *very* clever of you. Yes. It is. In a way.'

'Good night, my dear,' said the doctor, and left.

IV

Rehearsals went well during the first four days of the next week. The play had now been completely covered and Peregrine began to polish, dig deeper and make discoveries. His bruises grew less painful. He had taken a high hand and talked about his 'tiresome tum' in a vague, brief and lofty manner and, as far as he could make out, the cast did not pay an enormous amount of attention to it. Perhaps they were too busy.

Macbeth, in particular, made a splendid advance. He gained in stature. His nightmarish descent into horror and blind, idiotic killing was exactly what Peregrine asked of him. Maggie, after they had worked at their scenes, said to him: 'Dougal, you are playing like the devil possessed. I didn't know you had it in you.' He thought for a moment and then said: 'To tell you the truth, nor did I.' And burst out laughing. 'Unlucky in love, lucky in war,' he said. 'Something like that, eh, Maggie?'

'Something like that,' she agreed lightly.

'I suppose,' he said, turning to Peregrine, 'it is absolutely necessary to have Marley's Ghost haunting me? What's he meant to signify?'

'Marley's Ghost?'

'Well – whoever he is. Seyton. Gaston Sears. What's he meant to be, silly old fool?'

'Fate.'

'Come off it. You're being indulgent.'

'I honestly don't think so. I think he's valid. He's not intrusive, Dougal. He's just – there.'

Sir Dougal said: 'That's what I mean,' and drew himself up, holding his claymore in front of him. 'His tummy rumbles are positively deafening,' he said. 'Gurgle, gurgle. Rumble. Crash. A one-man band. One can hardly hear oneself speak.'

'Nonsense,' Peregrine said, and laughed. Maggie laughed with him. 'You're very naughty,' she said to Dougal.

'You've heard him, Maggie. In the banquet scene. Standing up by your throne rumbling away. You do know he's a bit off-pitch in the upper register, Perry, don't you?' He touched his own head.

'You're simply repeating a piece of stage gossip. Stop it.'

'Barrabell told me.'

'And who told him? And what about your fight?' Peregrine made a wide gesture and swept his notes to the floor. 'Damn,' he said. 'Nothing dotty about that, is there?'

'We'd have been just as good if we'd faked it,' Dougal muttered.

'No, you wouldn't and you know it.'

'Oh well. But he does rumble. Admit.'

'I haven't heard him.'

'Come on, Maggie. I'm wasting my time with this chap,' Dougal said cheerfully. Peregrine heard the stage door shut behind them.

He had begun painfully to pick up pages of the notes he had dropped when he heard someone come on stage and cross it. He tried to get up but the movement caught him. By the time he had hauled himself up the door had opened and closed and he never saw who had crossed the stage and gone out of the theatre.

Charlie had replaced the wooden claymore with its fellow on the back wall. Peregrine, having put his papers in order, laboured up on to the stage and made his way through pieces of scenery and book wings that had been set up as temporary backing. Only the working light had been left on and it was dark enough in this no-man's-land for him to go carefully. He was quite startled to see the figure of a small boy with its back towards him. Looking up at the claymore.

'William!' he said. William turned. His face was white but he said, 'Hullo, sir,' loudly.

'What are you doing here? You weren't called.'

'I wanted to see you, sir.'

'You did? Well, here I am.'

'You hurt yourself on the wooden claymore,' the treble voice stated.

'What makes you think that?'

'I was there. Backstage. When you jumped, I saw you.'

'You had no business to be there, William. You come only when you are called and stay in front when you are not working. What were you doing backstage?'

'Looking at my claymore. Mr Sears said I could have one of them after we opened. I wanted to choose the one that was least knocked about.'

'I see. Come here. Where I can see you properly.'

William came at once. He stood to attention and clenched his hands.

'Go on,' said Peregrine.

'I took it down: it was very dark. I brought it into the better light. It was still pretty dark but I examined it. Before I could get back there and hang it up, the witches came and started rehearsing. Down on the main stage. I hid it under the canvas. I was very careful to hide it where I thought nobody would fall. And I hid, too. I saw you fall. I heard you say you were all right.'

'You did?'

'Yes.'

After a considerable pause, William went on. 'I knew you weren't really all right because I heard you swear. But you got up. So I sneaked off and waited till there was only Charlie left and he was whistling. So I bolted.'

'And why did you want to see me today?'

'To tell you.'

'Has something else happened?'

'In a way.'

'Let's have it, then.'

'It's Miss Gaythorne. She keeps on about the curse.'

'The curse?'

'On the play. Now she's on about things happening. She makes out the sword under the cover is mixed up with all the things that go wrong with *Macbeth*, with – ' William corrected himself – 'the Scots play. She reckons she wants to sprinkle holy water or something and say things. I dunno. It sounds like a lot of hogwash to me but she goes on and on and of course the claymore's all my doing, isn't it? Nothing to do with this other stuff.'

'Nothing in the wide world.'

'Anyway, I'm sorry you've copped one, sir. I am really.'

'So you ought to be. It's much better. Look here, William: have you spoken to anyone else about this?'

'No, sir.'

'Word of a gentleman?' said Peregrine, and wondered if it was comically snobbish.

'No. I haven't – not a word.'

'Then don't. Except to me, if you want to. If they know I'm hurt because of the claymore they'll go weaving all sorts of superstitious rot-gut about the play and it'll get about and be bad for business. Mum's the word. OK? But *I* may say something. I'm not sure.'

'OK.'

'And you'll get your claymore but no funny business with it.'

William looked blankly at him.

'No swiping it round. Ceremonial use only. Understood?'

'I've understood all right.'

'Agreed?'

'I suppose so,' William muttered.

Peregrine reminded himself that William was certainly unable to raise the weapon more than waist high, if that, and decided not to insist. They shook hands and paid a visit to the Junior Dolphin at a quarter to six, where William consumed an unbelievable quantity of crumpets and fizzy drink. He seemed to have recovered his sangfroid.

Peregrine drove him home to a minute house in a tidy little street in Lambeth. The curtains were not yet drawn but the room was lit and he could see a pleasant picture, a fully stocked bookcase and a good armchair. Mrs Smith came to the window and looked out before shutting the room away.

William invited him in.

'I'll deliver you but I won't come in, thank you. I'm due at home. Overdue, in fact.'

A brisk knock brought William's mother to the door, a woman who was worn down to the lowest common denominator. She was dressed in a good but not new coat and skirt and spoke incisively.

'I've got a call to make in this part of the world so I've brought William home,' said Peregrine. 'He's aged nine, isn't he?'

'Yes. Only just.'

'In that case I'm afraid we'll have to find a second boy for alternate nights. It's not going to be easy but that's the rule. I'll try and bend it. You don't know of one, I suppose, do you?'

'I'm afraid not. I expect his school would provide.'

'I expect so. I've got their address. We'll just have to go to the usual sources,' Peregrine said. He took off his hat. 'Goodbye, Mrs Smith. The boy's doing very well.'

'I'm glad. Goodbye.'

''Bye, William.'

'Goodbye, sir.'

Peregrine drove home in a state of some confusion. He was glad the hidden sword mystery was solved, of course, but uncertain how much, if anything, of the explanation should be passed on to the company. In the end he decided to say something publicly to Gaston about his promising to give the wooden sword to William and

William hiding it. But, according to William, Nina Gaythorne knew about the sword. How the hell had the silly old trout found out? Charlie? Perhaps he'd let it out. Or more likely Banquo. He was there. He could have seen. And pretty well satisfied that this was the truth, he arrived home.

Emily heard the story of William.

'Do you think he'll keep his word?' she asked.

'Yes, I do. I'm quite persuaded he will.'

'What was it like? The house. And his mother?'

'All right. I didn't go in. Tiny house. Their own furniture. She's as thin as a lath and definitely upper-class. I don't remember if her circumstances came out at the trial but my guess would be that after the legal expenses were settled there was enough to buy the house or pay the rent and furnish it from what they had after the sale. He had been a well-heeled stockbroker. Mad as a hatter.'

'And William's at a drama school.'

'The Royal Southwark Theatre School. It's good. They get the whole works, all school subjects. Registered as a private school. There must have been enough for William's fees. And she's got some secretarial job, I fancy.'

'I've been trying to remember what it was like when I was six. What was he told and how much does he retain?'

'At a guess, I'd say he was told his father was mentally very ill and committed to an asylum. Probably he was sent abroad until it was all over.'

'Poor little man,' said Emily.

'He'll be a good actor. You'll see.'

'Yes. How's your bruised tum?'

'Better every day.'

'Good.'

'In fact everything in the garden is – ' He pulled up. Emily saw that he had crossed his first and second fingers. 'That really would be asking for it,' he said.

The next day shone brightly. Peregrine and Emily drove happily along the Embankment, over Blackfriars Bridge and turned right for Wharfingers Lane and the theatre. The entire company had been called and had nearly all arrived and were assembled in the auditorium.

It was to be a complete run-through of the play with props. This week would be the last one entirely for the actors. After that would come the mechanical effects and lights rehearsals with endless stops, adjustments and repositionings. And then, finally, two dress rehearsals.

Emily knew a lot of the company. Sir Dougal was delighted that she had come down to rehearsal. Why did they not see more of her in these days? Sons? How many? Three? All at school? Wonderful!

It struck her that he was excited. Keyed up. Not attending to the answers she gave him. She was relieved when he strolled away.

Maggie came up to her and gave her a squeeze. 'I'll want to know what you think,' she said. 'Really. What you think and feel.'

'Perry says you're wonderful.'

'Does he? Does he really?'

'Really and truly. Without qualifications.'

'Too good. Too soon. I don't know,' she muttered.

'All's well.'

'I hope so. Oh, this play. This *play*, Emmy, my dear.'

'I know.'

She wandered distractedly away and sat down, her eyes closed, her lips moving. Nina Gaythorne came in, draped, as always, in a multiplicity of hand-woven scarves. She saw Emily and waved the end of one of them, at the same time making a strange grimace and raising her faded eyes to contemplate the dome. It was impossible to interpret; some kind of despair, Emily wondered? She waved back conservatively.

The man with Miss Gaythorne was unknown to Emily. Straw-coloured. Tight mouth, light eyes. She guessed he was the Banquo. Bruce Barrabell. They sat together, apart from the others. Emily had the uncomfortable feeling that Nina was telling him who she was. She found herself momentarily looking into his eyes, which startled her by their sharpness and the quick furtive withdrawal of his gaze.

Macduff, Simon Morten, she recognized from Peregrine's description. He was physically exactly right; dark, handsome and reckless; at the moment, nervous and withdrawn but a swashbuckler nevertheless.

Here came the three witches, two girls gabbling nervously, and Rangi, aloof, indrawn and anxious. Then the Royals: King Duncan, magnificent, portentous, and his two sons to whom he seemed to lend a condescending ear. Two Murderers. The Gentlewoman and the Doctor. Lennox and Ross. Menteith. Angus. Caithness. And, with Nina Gaythorne, a small boy. So that's William, she thought. Last, solemn, brooding, his claymore held upright in its harness, Gaston, the sword-bearer.

I'm thinking about them as they are in the play, Emily told herself. And they are behaving as they do in the play. No. Not behaving. How absurd of me. But they are keeping together in their groups.

The front curtains parted and Peregrine came through.

'This,' he said, 'is an uninterrupted run-through, with props and effects. It will be timed. I'll take notes at the end of the first half. There has been a slight tendency to drag. We'll watch that, if you please. Right. Act I, Scene 1. The witches.'

They went up through the box.

Peregrine came down the temporary steps into the house and to his improvised desk across the stalls. His secretary was beside him and the mechanical people behind.

He had given Emily a typed scene sequence each with a hint of what went on in it.

'You don't need it,' he said. 'I just thought you might like to be reminded of the sequence of events.'

'Yes. Thank you.'

Act I	Scene 1	The Witches.
	2	The Camp near Forres. Bleeding Sergeant.
	3	The Witches. Blasted Heath. Gallows. News for Macbeth. Ross. Lennox. Banquo.
	4	The camp near Forres. King Duncan presents Malcolm.
	5	Inverness. Macbeth's Castle. Letter. Interior.
	6	Inverness Exterior. Arrival of King.
	7	Inverness Interior. Decision.
Act II	Scene 1	Inverness. Macbeth's Court. Banquo. Fleance. Macbeth. Dagger Soliloquy. Murder.
	2	Inverness. Discovery. Aftermath.

'Right,' Peregrine called.

Emily's heart thumped. Thud, thud, thud. A faint, wailing cry, a gust of crying wind and the curtain rose.

There are times – rare but unmistakable – in the theatre when, at rehearsal, the play flashes up into a life of its own and attains a reality so vivid that everything else fades into threadbare inconsequence. These startling transformations happen when the play is over halfway to achievement: the actors are not in costume, the staging is still bare bones. Nothing intervenes between the characters and their projection into the void. This was such a day.

Emily felt she was seeing *Macbeth* for the first time. She was constantly taken by surprise. Perfect. Wonderful. Terrible, she thought.

Duncan arrived at the castle. The sound of wings fluttering in the evening air. Peaceful. Then the squeal of pipes, the rumble of the great doors, the opening and the assembly of servants. Seyton. Lady Macbeth a scarlet figure at the top of the stairs. *Don't go in, don't go in.*

But she welcomed him. They all went in and the doors rumbled and closed on them.

Afterwards Emily could not remember if the sounds Shakespeare introduces were actually heard; the cricket, the owl, the usual domestic sounds that continue in an old house when the guests are all asleep in bed. The other ambiguous sounds the Macbeths think they hear . . .

It was accomplished. The 'terrible imaginings' were real, now, and they went to wash the blood from their hands.

Now came the knocking at the south entry. Enter from below the drunken porter with his load of obscenely shaped driftwood. He committed it to the fire, piece after piece, staggered to the south entry and admitted Macduff and Lennox.

Simon Morten looked as fit as a fiddle. He and Lennox brought the fresh morning air in with them as he ran upstairs to Duncan's bedroom. The door shut behind him.

Macbeth stood very still, every nerve in his body listening, Lennox went to the fire, warmed his hands and gossiped about the wildness of the night.

The door upstairs opened and Macduff came out.

Extraordinary! He was as white as a sheet. He whispered: '"*Horror. Horror. Horror.*"'

Now disaster broke: the alarm bell, the disordered guests, Lady Macbeth's 'fainting' when her husband's speech threatened to get out of hand, the appearance of the two frightened sons, their decision to flee. And the little front scene when Macduff, an Old Man and Ross speak an ominous afterword and the first part closes.

V

Peregrine finished his notes. Macbeth and Macduff waited behind. They were on stage.

'Come on,' said Peregrine. 'What was the matter? You're both good actors but you don't turn sheet-white out of sheer artistry. What went wrong?'

Sir Dougal looked at Simon. 'You went up before I did,' he said. 'You saw it first.'

'Some idiot's rigged a bloody mask in the King's Chamber. One of those Banquo things of Gaston's. Open mouth, blood running out of it. Bulging eyes. I don't mind telling you it shocked the pants off me.'

'You might have warned me,' said Sir Dougal.

'I tried, didn't I? Outside the door. You and Lennox. After I said "*Destroy your sight with a new Gorgon.*"'

'You muttered something. I didn't know what you were on about.'

'I could hardly yell: "There's a bloody head on the wall," could I?'

'All right, all right.'

'When you went up the first time, Sir Dougal, was it there?'

'Certainly not. Unless . . .'

'Unless what?'

'What's the colour of the cloak attached to it?'

'Dark grey,' said Peregrine.

'If it was covered by the cloak I might have missed it. It was dark up there.'

'Who could have uncovered it?'

'The grooms?'

'What grooms? There are no grooms,' said Simon. 'Are you crazy?'

'I was making a joke,' said Sir Dougal with dignity.

'Funny sort of joke, I must say.'

'There's some perfectly reasonable explanation,' Peregrine said. 'I'll talk to the Property Master. Don't let a damn silly thing like this upset you. You're going very well indeed. Keep it up.'

He slapped them both on the shoulders, waited till they had gone and climbed the stairs to the room.

It *was* extremely dark: an opening off the head of the stairs with a door facing them. The audience saw only a small inside section of one wall when this door was open. The wall which would have a stone finish faced the audience and ran down to stage-level and the third wall, unseen by the audience, was simply used as a brace for the other two. It was a skeleton. A ladder was propped against the floor leading down to the stage. A ceiling, painted with joists, was nailed to the structure.

And looming in the darkest corner, facing the doorway, the murdered head of Banquo.

Peregrine knew what to expect but even so he got a jolt. The bulging eyes stared into his. The mouth gaped blood. His own mouth was dry and his hands wet. He walked towards it, touched it and it moved. It was fixed to a coat-hanger. The ends of the hanger rested on the corner pieces of the walls. The grey shroud had a hole, like a poncho, for the head. He touched it again and it rocked towards him and, with a whisper, fell.

Peregrine started back with an oath, shut the door and called out 'Props!'

'Here, guv.'

'Come up, will you. Put the working light on.'

He picked the head up and returned it to its place. The working light took some of the horror out of it. Props's head came up from below. When he arrived he turned and saw it.

'Christ!' he said.

'Did you put that thing there?'

'What'd I do that for, Mr Jay? Gawd, no.'

'Did you miss it?'

'I didn't know how many there was, did I? Its mates are all laid out in the walking gents' room. Gawd, it'd give you the willies, woon' it? Seeing it unexpected, like.'

'Take it down and put it with the others. And Ernie?'

'Guv?'

'Don't mention this. Don't say you've seen it. Not to anyone.'

'OK.'

'I mean it. Hope to die.'

'Hope to die.'

'Cross your heart, Ernie. Go on. Do it. And say it.'

'Aw, hell, guv.'

'Go on.'

'Cross me 'art. 'Ope to die.'

'That's the style. Now. Take this thing and put it with the others. Half a jiffy.'

Peregrine was wrapping the head in the shroud. He turned back the hem and found a stick of green wood about two feet long slotted at either end into the hem of the shroud. The string was knotted halfway across into another and very much longer piece. He took it to the edge of the floor and let the loose end fall. It reached to within three feet of the stage.

Peregrine coiled it up, detached it and put it in his pocket. He gave Ernie the head, neatly parcelled. He looked at the place where the head had rested and, above it, saw a strut of rough wood.

'Preposterous!' he muttered.

'OK,' he said. 'We push on.' He went downstairs.

'Second part,' he called. 'Settle down, please.'

VI

The second part opened with Banquo alone, suspecting the truth yet not daring to cut and run. Next, Macbeth's scene with the murderers and Seyton nearer, ever present, and then the two Macbeths together. This is perhaps the most moving scene in the play and reveals the most about them. It opens up, in extraordinary language, the nightmare of guilt, their sleeplessness, and when at last they sleep the terrifying dreams that beset them. She fights on but knows now, without any shadow of doubt, that her power over him is less than she had bargained for, while he is acting on his own, hinting at what he plans but not telling. There follows the coming of darkness and night and the release of night's creatures. It ends with self-dedication to the dark. Now comes the murder of Banquo and the escape of Fleance. And now the great banquet.

It opens as a front scene before curtains. Macbeth, crowned and robed, seems for the moment in command as if he actually thrives on the shedding of blood. He is a little too loud, too boisterous in his welcome. He is sending his guests through the curtains and is about to follow when he sees Seyton in the downstage entrance. He waits for the last guest to pass through and then goes to him.

> *'There's blood upon thy face.'*
> *''Tis Banquo's then.'*

Nothing is perfect: Fleance has escaped. Macbeth gives Seyton money and signals for the curtains to be opened. And they open upon the opulence of the banquet. The servants are filling glasses. Lady Macbeth is on her throne. And the Ghost of Banquo, hidden, waits.

It was going well. The masking of the stool as rehearsed. The timing. The nightmarish efforts of Macbeth to recover something of his royalty. Every cue observed. Thank God! Peregrine thought. It's working. Yes. Yes.

> *'Our duties and the pledge.'*

The servants swept the covers off the main dishes.

The head of Banquo was in pride of place: outrageous and glaring on the main dish.

'What the bloody hell is this!' Sir Dougal demanded.

CHAPTER 4

Fourth Week

The time for concealment was past. Strangely enough, Peregrine felt a sort of relief. He would no longer be obliged to offer unlikely explanations, beg people not to talk, feel certain that they would talk. Shuffle. Pretend.

He said 'Stop,' and stood up. 'Cover that thing.'

The servant who still had the oval dish-cover in his hand clapped it back over the head. Peregrine walked down the aisle. 'You may sit if you want to but remain in your positions. Any staff who are here, on stage, please.'

The Assistant Stage Manager, Charlie, two stagehands and Props came on and stood in a group on the Prompt side.

'Somewhere among you,' said Peregrine, 'there is a funny man. He has been operating intermittently throughout rehearsals, his object, if he can be said to have one, being to support the superstitious theories that have grown up round this play. *This* play. *Macbeth.* You hear me? *Macbeth.* He put the Banquo mask on the wall of Duncan's room. He's put another one in this serving dish. In any other context these silly tricks would be dismissed but here they are reprehensible. They've upset the extremely high standard of performance. And that is lamentable. I ask the perpetrator of these tricks to let me know by whatever means he chooses that he is the – comedian.

'I remind you,' he said, 'of the arrangement of this scene. It opens as a front scene with the curtains closed. They are held open by servitors while the Macbeths welcome the guests and closed again when they have all gone through. The servitors go off. Macbeth has his scene with the Third Murderer who is Gaston. At the end Gaston goes off. Macbeth claps his hands and the servitors from the sides open the curtains completely.

'For the good of the production I undertake not to reveal the trickster's name. Nor will I sack the man or refer to the matter again. It shall be as if it had never happened. Is this understood?'

He stopped.

They stared at him rather like children, he thought, brought together for a wigging and not knowing what would come next.

Bruce Barrabell came next, the silver-tongued Banquo.

'No doubt I shall be snubbed,' he said, 'but I really feel I must protest. If this person is among us, I think we should all know who he is. He should be publicly exposed and dismissed. By us. As the Equity Representative I feel I should take this stand.'

Peregrine had not the faintest notion of what if any stand the Equity Representative was entitled to take.

He said grandly: 'Properties belonging to the theatre have been misused. Rehearsal time interrupted. This is my affair: I propose to continue. The time for Equity to butt in may or may not arise in due course. If it does I shall advise you of it. At this stage I must ask you to sit down, Mr Barrabell.'

If he won't sit down, he wondered, what the hell do I do?

'Hear, hear,' said Sir Dougal helpfully.

There was an affirmative murmur. Nina was heard to say she felt faint. Peregrine said: 'Props, when did you last look under the lid of that dish?'

'I never looked under it,' said Props. 'It was in place on the table which was carried on as soon as the curtains closed. The dish would have a plastic boar's head for performance but not until the dress rehearsal.'

'Was anyone there? A scene-shifter or an actor?'

'The two scene-shifters who carried the table on. They went off on the other side. And him,' said Props, jerking his head at Barrabell, 'and the other ghost. The double. They got down under the table just before the curtains re-opened.'

'Familiar business for Banquo,' said Sir Dougal, and laughed.

'What do you mean by that, may I ask?' said Barrabell.

'Oh, nothing. Nothing.'

'I insist on an explanation.'

'You won't get one.'

'Quiet, *please*,' Peregrine shouted. He waited for a second or two and then said 'Anyone else?'

'Certainly,' said a sepulchral voice. 'I was there. But very briefly. I simply informed Macbeth of the murder. I came off downstage, prompt. Somebody was there with my claidheamh-mor. I seized it. I ran upstage, engaged it into my harness and entered near the throne as the curtains were re-opened. The previous scene,' reminisced Gaston, 'was that of the murder of Banquo. The claidheamh-mor would never have been used for that affair. It is too large and too sacred. An interesting point arises . . .'

He settled into his narrative style.

'Thank you, Gaston,' said Peregrine. 'Very interesting,' and hurried on. 'Now, Banquo, you were there during this scene. At what stage did you actually get under the table, do you remember?'

'When I heard Macbeth say *"Thou art the best of the cut-throats."* The curtains were shut and the scene between Macbeth and Gaston, the murderer, was played in front of them. The head and cloak were stuffy and awkward and I always delay putting them on and getting down there. They are made in one and it takes only seconds to put them on. Angus and Caithness popped the whole thing over my head. I gathered up the cloak round my knees and crouched down.'

'And the ghost double? Toby?'

A youth held up his hand. 'I put my head and cloak on in the dressing room,' he said, 'and I got under the table as soon as it was there. The table has no upstage side and there was lots of room, really. I waited at the rear until Bruce got under and crawled forward.'

'When was the dish put on the table?'

Props said: 'It's stuck down. All the props not used are stuck down, aren't they? I put the lid on it after I got it ready, like.'

'Before the rehearsal started?'

'That's right. And if there's anybody thinks I done it with the head, I never. And if there's any doubts about that I appeal to my Union.'

'There are no doubts about it,' said Peregrine hurriedly. 'Where *was* the head? Where are all the heads? Together?'

'In the walking gents' dressing room. All together. Waiting for the dress rehearsal nex' week.'

'Is the room unlocked?'

'Yes. And if you arst 'oo 'as the key, I 'as it. The young gents arst me to unlock it and I unlocked it, din' I?'

'Yes. Thank you.'

'I got me rights like everybody else.'

'Of course you have.'

Peregrine waited for a moment. He looked at the familiar faces of his actors and thought: This is ridiculous. He cleared his throat. 'I now ask,' he said, 'which of you was responsible for this trick.'

Nobody answered.

'Very well,' Peregrine said. 'I would beg you not to discuss this affair among yourselves but,' he added acidly, 'I might as well beg you not to talk. One point I do put to you. If you think of linking these silly pranks with the *Macbeth* superstitions you will be doing precisely what the perpetrator wants. My guess is that he or she is an ardent believer. So far no ominous sights have occurred. So he or she has planted some. It's as silly and as simple as that. Any comments?'

'One asks oneself,' announced Gaston, 'when the rumours began and whether, in fact, they go back to some pre-Christian Winter Solstice ritual. The play being of an extremely sanguinary nature – '

'Yes, Gaston. Later, dear man.'

Gaston rumbled on.

Sir Dougal said: 'Oh, for pity's sake will somebody tell him to forget his claddy-mor and to shut his silly old trap.'

'How dare you!' roared Gaston suddenly. 'I, who have taught you a fight that is authentic in every detail except the actual shedding of blood! How dare you, sir, refer to my silly old trap?'

'I do. I do dare,' Sir Dougal announced petulantly. 'I'm still in great pain from the physical strain I've been obliged to suffer and all for something that would be better achieved by a good fake and if you won't shut up, by God, I'll use your precious techniques to make you. I beg your pardon, Perry, dear boy, but *really*!'

Gaston had removed his claidheamh-mor from his harness and now, shouting insults in what may have been early Scots, performed some aggressive and alarming exercises with the weapon. The magnificent Duncan, who was beside him, cried out and backed away. 'I say!' he protested. 'Don't! No! Too much!'

Gaston stamped, and rotated his formidable weapon.

'Put that damn silly thing away,' said Sir Dougal. 'Whatever it's called: "Gladtime Saw". You'll hurt yourself.'

'Quiet!' Perry shouted. 'Gaston! Stop it. At once.'

Gaston did stop. He saluted and returned the weapon to its sheath, a leather pouch which hung by straps from his heavy belt and occupied the place where a sporran would have rested. The hilts being established there, the monstrous blade rose in front of his body and was grasped by his gloved paws. It passed within an inch of his nose, causing him to squint.

Thus armed, he retired and stood to attention, squinting hideously and rumbling industriously by Maggie's throne. She gave one terrified look at him and then burst out laughing.

So after a doubtful glance did the entire company and the people in the stalls, including Emily.

Gaston stood to attention throughout.

Peregrine wiped the tears from his face, walked up to Gaston, put his arm round his shoulders and took the risk of his life.

'Gaston, my dear boy,' he said, 'you have taught us how to meet these ridiculous pranks. Thank you.'

Gaston rumbled. 'What did you say?'

'*Honi soit qui mal y pense.*'

'Exactly,' agreed Peregrine, and wondered if it was really an appropriate remark. 'Well, everybody,' he said, 'we don't know who played this trick and for the time being we'll let it rest. Will you all turn your backs for a moment.'

They did so. He whipped off the lid, wrapped the head in its cloak, took it backstage to the property table and returned.

'Right!' he said. 'From where we left off, please.'

'"*Our duties and the pledge,*"' said the prompter.

'Yes. Places, everybody. Are you ready, Sir Dougal, or would you like to break?'

'I'll go on.'

'Good. Thank you.'

And they went on to the end of the play.

When it was all over and he had taken his notes and gone through the bits that needed adjustment, Peregrine made a little speech to his cast.

'I can't thank you enough,' he said. 'You have behaved in a civilized and proper manner like the professionals you are. If, as I believe, the perpetrator of these jokes – there have been others that came to nothing – is among you, I hope he or she will realize how silly they are and we'll have no more of them. Our play is in good heart and we go forward with confidence, my dears. Tomorrow morning. Everybody at ten, please. In the rehearsal room.'

II

Peregrine had a session with the effects and lights people which lasted for an hour, at the end of which they went off, satisfied, to get their work down on paper.

'Come on, Em,' he said. 'You've had more entertainment than we bargained for, haven't you?'

'I have indeed. You handled them beautifully.'

'Did I? Good. Hullo, here's William. What are you doing, young man? Emily, this is William Smith.'

'William, I very much enjoyed your performance,' said Emily, shaking his hand.

'Did you? I thought I might be called for this afternoon, Mr Jay, and I brought my lunch. My mum's coming in later for me.'

'There's no rehearsal this afternoon. We're handing over to the staff. They're moving in, as you see.'

The stage was patched with daylight. Sheets of painted plywood were being carried in from the workshop. Workmen shouted and whistled.

'I'll just wait for her,' said William.

'Well – I don't think you can quite do that. It's one of those rules. You know?'

In the silence that followed a vivid flush mounted in William's face. 'Yes. I think I do,' he said. 'I wanted to speak to you about it, but . . .' He looked at Emily.

'About what?' Peregrine asked.

'About the head. About the person who's done it. About every-one saying it's the sort of thing kids do. I didn't do it. Really, I didn't. I think it's silly. And frightening. Awfully frightening,' William whis-pered. The red receded and a white-faced boy stared at them. His eyes filled with tears. 'I can't look at it,' he said. 'Much less touch it. It's awful.'

'What about the other one?' asked Peregrine.

'What other one, sir?'

'In the King's room.'

'Is there one there too? Oh gosh!'

'William!' Emily cried out. 'Don't worry. They're only plastic mock-ups. Nothing to be afraid of. Pretence ghosts. William, never mind. Gaston made them.' She held out her arms. He hung back and then walked, shamefaced, into her embrace. She felt his heart beat and his trembling.

'Thank you very much, Mrs Jay,' he muttered, and sniffed.

Emily held out her hand to Peregrine. 'Hankie,' she mouthed. He gave her his handkerchief.

'Here you are. Have a blow.' William blew and caught his breath. She waggled her head at Peregrine, who said: 'It's all right, William. You didn't do it.' And walked away.

'There you are! Now you're in the clear, aren't you?'

'If he means it.'

'He never, *never* says things he doesn't mean.'

'Doesn't he? Super,' said William and fetched a dry sob.

'So that's that, isn't it?' He didn't answer. 'William,' Emily said. 'Are you frightened of the head? Quite apart from anyone thinking you did it. Just between ourselves.'

He nodded.

'Would you be if you'd made it? You know? It's a long business. You take a mould in plaster of Mr Barrabell's face and he makes a fuss and says you're stifling him and he won't keep his mouth open. And at last, when you've got it and it's dried, you pour a thin layer of some plastic stuff into it and wait till that dries and then the hardest part comes,' said Emily, hoping she'd got it vaguely right. 'You've got to separate the two and Bob's your uncle. Well – something like that. Broadly speaking.'

'Yes.'

'And you see it in all its stages and finally you've got to paint it and add hair and red paint for blood and so on and it's rather fun and *you* made *it*, frightening but you know it's just *you* being rather clever with plaster and plastic and paint.'

'That's like the chorus of a song, *"With plaster and plastic and paint,"*' said William.

'*"I'm producing a perfect phenomenon,"*' said Emily. 'So it is. You go on.'

'*"I'm making things look what they ain't,"*' said William. 'Your turn. I bet you won't get a rhyme for "phenomenon",' and gave another dry sob.

'You win. When's your mama coming for you?'

'About four, I should think. She's buying our supper. It's her afternoon off.'

'Well, you can wait here with me. Perry's got stuck into something up there. Have you heard how he came to restore this theatre?'

'No,' said William. 'I don't know anything about the theatre except it's meant to be rather grand to get a job in it.'

'Well,' said Emily, 'come and sit down and I'll tell you.'

And she told him how Peregrine, a struggling young author-director, came into the wrecked Dolphin and fell into the bomb hole on the stage and was rescued from it and got the job of restoring the theatre and being made a member of the board.

'Even now, it's a bit like a fairy-tale,' she said.

'A nice one.'

'Very nice.'

They sat in companionable silence, watching the men working on the stage.

'You go to a drama school, don't you?' Emily said after a pause.

'The Royal Southwark Theatre School. It's a proper school. We learn all the usual things and theatre as well.'

'How long have you been going to it?'

'Three years. I was the youngest kid there.'

'And you like it?'

'Oh yes,' he said. 'It's OK. I'm going to be an actor.'

'Are you?'

'Of course.'

The door at front-of-house opened. His mother looked in. He turned and saw her. 'Here's my mum,' he said. 'I'd like you to meet her if that's all right. Would it be all right?'

'I'd like to meet her, William.'

'Super,' he said. 'Excuse me.' He edged past her and ran up the aisle. Emily stood up and turned round. Apparently Mrs Smith had expostulated with him. 'It's all right, Mum,' he said. 'Mrs Jay says it is. Come on.'

Emily said: 'Hello, Mrs Smith. Do come in. I am so pleased to meet you,' and held out her hand. 'I'm Emily Jay.'

'I'm afraid my son's rather precipitate,' said Mrs Smith. 'I've just called to collect him. I do know outsiders shouldn't walk into theatres as if they were bus stations.'

'William's your excuse. He's our rising actor. My husband thinks he's very promising.'

'Good. Get your overcoat, William, and what's happened to your face?'

'I don't know. What?' asked William unconvincingly.

'Same as what's the matter with all our faces,' Emily explained. 'One of Gaston Sears's dummy heads for the parade of Banquo's successors got on to the banquet table and gave us the fright of our lives. Run and get your coat, William. It's over the back of your seat.'

He said: 'I'll get it,' and wandered down the aisle.

Emily said: 'I'm afraid it frightened him and made him jump and he became a very little boy but he's quite recovered now. It did look *very* macabre.'

'I'm sure it did,' said Mrs Smith. She had gone down the aisle and met William. She put him into his coat with her back turned to Emily.

'Your hands are cold,' he said.

'I'm sorry. It's icy out of doors.' She buttoned him up and said, 'Say good night to Mrs Jay.'

'Good night, Mrs Jay.'

'Good night, old boy.'

'Good night,' said Mrs Smith. 'Thank you for being so kind.'

They shook hands.

Emily watched them go out. A lonely little couple, she thought.

'Come along, love,' said Peregrine. He had come up behind her and put his arm round her. 'That's settled. We can go home.'

'Right.'

He wanted a word in the box office so they went out by the front-of-house.

The lifesize photographs were there being put into their frames. Sir Dougal Macdougal. Margaret Mannering. Simon Morten. The Three Witches. Out they came, one after another. Only ten days left.

Emily and Peregrine stood and looked at them.

'Oh, darling!' she said. 'This is your big one, isn't it? So big. So *big*.'

'I know.'

'Don't let these nonsense things worry you. They're silly.'

'Yes. I know. You're talking to me as if I'm William.'

'Come along, then. Home.'

So they went home.

III

The final days were, if anything, less hectic than usual. The production crew had the use of the theatre and the actors worked in the rehearsal room on a chalked-out floor. Gaston insisted on having the stage to rehearse the fight, pointing out the necessity for the different levels and insisting on the daily routine being maintained. 'As it will be,' he said, 'throughout the season.'

Macbeth and Macduff made routine noises of protest but by this time they had become proud of their expertise and had gradually speeded up to an unbelievable pace. The great cumbersome weapons swept about within inches of their persons, sparks literally flew, inarticulate cries escaped them. The crew, overawed, knocked off and watched them for half an hour.

The end of the fight was a bit of a problem. Macbeth was beaten back to the OP exit which was open but masked from the audience by an individual Stonehenge-like piece, firmly screwed to the floor. Macbeth backed down to it and crouched behind his shield. Macduff raised his claymore and swept it down. Macbeth caught it on his shield. A pause. Then with an inarticulate, bestial sound he leapt aside and backwards. He was out of sight. Macduff raised his claymore high above his head and plunged offstage. There was a scream cut short by an unmistakable sound: an immense thud.

For three seconds the stage was empty and silent.

'Rata-tat-rata-tat-rata-tat-RATA-TAT and bugles. Crescendo! Crescendo! and enter Malcolm *et al*,' roared Gaston.

'How about it?' asked Macbeth. 'It's a close call, Gaston. He missed the scenery but only by a hair's-breadth, you know. These claymores are so bloody long.'

'He missed. If you both repeat where you were and what you do to a fraction of an inch he'll always miss. If not – *not*. We'll take it again, if you please. The final six moves. Places. Er-one. Er-two. Er-three.'

'We're at hellish close quarters at the side there,' said Simon when they had finished. 'And it's as dark as hell, too. Or will be.'

'I'll be there with the head on my claidheamh-mor. Don't go hunting for me. Simply take up your place and I'll fall in behind you. Macbeth will have gone straight out.'

'I'll scream and scramble off, don't you worry,' said Sir Dougal.

'All right.'

'Until tomorrow. Same time. I thank you, gentlemen,' said Gaston to the stagehands. He saluted and withdrew.

'Proper caution, in't 'e?' said a stagehand.

'Well, gentlemen,' said the foreman, doing a creditable bit of mimicry, 'shall we resume?'

They set about nailing the sanded and painted wallboard facing to the set. The stairs curved up to the landing and the door to Duncan's room. The red arras was hung and dropped in above the stairway. Below the landing a tunnel pierced the wall, making a passage to the south entry.

Peregrine on his way to the rehearsal room saw this and found it all good. The turntables, right and left, presented outside walls. The fireplace appeared. The gallows came into view and was anchored.

It was all smooth, he thought, and moved on into the rehearsal room. He had called the scene – he thought of it as the Aleppo scene – when the witches greet Macbeth. He was a little early but most of them were there. Banquo was there.

If they had been the crew of a ship, he thought, Banquo would have been the sea lawyer. He knew what Banquo had been like as a schoolboy. Always closeted with other smaller boys who listened furtively to him, always behind the dubious plan but never answerable. Always the troublemaker but never openly so. A boy to be dreaded.

Peregrine said: 'Good morning, everybody.'

'Good morning, Perry.'

Yes. There he was with two of the witches. Silly little things listening to his nonsense, whatever it was. The first witch, Rangi, hadn't arrived yet. He would not listen to Banquo, Peregrine thought. He goes his own way. He too is an actor and a good one. For that I respect him.

Banquo detached himself from the witches and made for him.

'Happy, Perry?' he asked, coming close to him. 'Sorry! I shouldn't ask, should I? It's not done. Unlucky.'

'Very happy, Bruce.'

'We haven't got the Boy Beautiful this morning?'

'Do you mean William Smith? He'll be here.'

'He's dropped the hyphen, of course. Poor little chap.'

Peregrine, inside himself, did what actor's call a double take. His heart skipped a beat. He looked at Barrabell, who smiled at him. *Damn!* Peregrine thought. He knows. Oh damn, damn, damn.

Rangi came in and glanced at the clock. Just in time.

'Second witches scene,' Peregrine said. 'Witches on from the three points of the compass. There will be a rumble of thunder. Just a hint. You arrive at exactly the same time and at dead centre. Rangi through the passage. Each with a dishevelled marketing bag. Blondie Prompt. Wendy OP. It wasn't together last time. You'll have to get a sign. Rangi's got the farthest to walk. The other two are equal. Perhaps you should all have sticks? I don't want any hesitation. Wait for the thunder and start when it stops. Try that. Ready. Rumble, rumble. Now.'

The three figures appeared, hobbled on, met. 'Much better,' said Peregrine. 'Once more. This time greet each other. Rangi centre. A smacking kiss on each of his cheeks simultaneously by each of you. Close up. In front. Together. Right. Dialogue.'

They used their natural, well-contrasted voices. The rhymes were stressed. The long speech about the hapless sailor gone to Aleppo, was a curse.

> '"Though his bark cannot be lost.
> Yet it shall be tempest-tossed.
> Look what I have."'

And Rangi scuffled in his marketing bag.

'"*Show me. Show me*,"' slavered the greedy Wendy.

But Rangi's hand in his bag was stilled. He himself was still. Frozen. And then he suddenly opened the bag and peered inside. He withdrew his clenched hand.

> '"*Here I have a pilot's thumb*
> *Wrecked as homeward he did come.*"'

He opened his hand very slightly.

'What's wrong?' Peregrine asked. 'Haven't they given you something for the thumb?'

Rangi opened his hand. It was empty.

'I'll speak to Props. On you go.'

'"*A drum, a drum*,"' said Wendy, '"*Macbeth doth come.*"'

And now their dance, about, about, turn and twist, bow, raise their joined hands. All very quick.

'"*Peace! The charm's wound up.*"'

'Yes,' Peregrine said. 'The Aleppo speech has improved enormously. It's *really* alarming now. One feels the wretched sailor in his doomed ship, tossing and turning, not dying and not living. Good. We'll go on. Banquo and Macbeth. One moment, though. Banquo, the whole scene has been very carefully ordered so that Macbeth, the convention of the soliloquy having changed over four centuries, will not seem to be within hearing distance of his brother-officers. You and Ross and Angus are talking together. Way upstage. But very quietly and with virtually no movement. Shakespeare himself seems to have felt the usual convention not really good enough. His "*thank you, gentlemen*" is a dismissal. We'll make it so. They bow and move as far away as they can get. The soliloquy, I needn't tell you, is of great importance. So no loud laughter, if you please. OK?'

'I took the point the first time you made it,' said Banquo.

'Good. That will save me the fatigue of making it a third time. Are you ready? "*The earth hath bubbles.*"'

The scene went forward. The messages of favours to come were delivered. The golden future opened out. Everything was lovely and yet . . . and yet . . .

Presently they embarked on the cauldron scene. Peregrine developed the background of whispering. *'Double, double toil and trouble . . .'* Would it be heard? He tried a murmur: *'Double, double toil and trouble . . .'* 'We'll try it whispered when the whole company is here,' he said. 'Six groups each beginning after "trouble". I think that'll work.'

The witches were splendid. Clear and baleful. Their movements were explicit. They were real. But Peregrine was conscious that Rangi was troubled by something. He did not fumble a cue or muddle a movement or need a prompt but he was unhappy. Unwell? Sickening for something? Oh God, please not, thought Peregrine. Why is he looking at me? Am I missing something?

'And points at them for his.'

Thunder and fog. Blackout, and then the door will be shut and Lennox knocking on it as the scene ends.

'All right,' said Peregrine. 'I've no notes specifically for you. It will need adjustments, no doubt, when we get the background noise settled. Thank you all very much.'

They all left the rehearsal, except Rangi.

'Is something amiss? What's the matter?'

He held out his marketing bag. 'Will you look in it, sir?' Peregrine took the bag and opened it.

Out of it a malignant head stared up at him. Mouth open, eyes open, teeth bared. Pinkish paws stretched upwards.

'Oh God!' said Peregrine. 'Here we go again. Where was this bag?'

'With the other two on the props table. Since yesterday.'

'Anyone look in it?'

'I shouldn't think so. Only to put the rat in. There was no means of telling which bag belonged to whom. It might have been Blondie's. She'd have fainted or gone into high-powered hysterics,' said Rangi.

'She wouldn't have looked in. Nor would Wendy. Their bags are filled with newspaper and fastened with thongs, tightly knotted. Yours isn't because you're meant to open it and produce the pilot's thumb.'

'So I was meant to find it,' said Rangi.

'It wouldn't have worked with the other two.'

'There's an obvious man to have played all these silly tricks.'

'Props?' said Peregrine.

'Ask yourself.'

'I do, and I don't believe it. Did you hear his outcries and threats to appeal to his Union over the Banquo's head business? Was that all my eye? We'd have to say we've got a bloody star actor on the books. No. We've had him as Props for years. I simply cannot wear him for the job.'

'Can't you narrow down the field? Where everyone was at the different times? Who could have gone up to Duncan's room with the head, for instance?'

There was a long silence.

'Duncan's room?' said Peregrine at last. 'With the head?'

'That's right. What's wrong with you?'

'How do you know about the head in that room?'

'Props told me. I ran into him with it. Coming down the ladder from Duncan's chamber. Now I think of it,' said Rangi, 'his manner was odd. I said: "What are you doing with that thing?" and he said he was putting it where it ought to be. I'm sorry, Perry. I really think he's your man, you know. He must have put it under the dish-cover, mustn't he?'

'He was taking it back to the other heads in the walking men's room. I told him to.'

'Did you see him do it?'

'No.'

'Ask him if he did it.'

'Of course I will. But I'm sure he didn't put it in the dish. I admit he doesn't look too good but I'm sure of it.'

'That blasted rat. Where did it come from?'

'Oh God!'

'Have we been using traps?'

'And who sets them? All right. Props. He put one up a narrow passage where Henry couldn't squeeze in.' (Henry was the theatre cat.) 'Props told me so himself. He was proud of his cunning.'

Rangi said: 'We'll have to look at it.'

He opened the bag and turned it upside down. The rat's forequarters fell with a soft plop on the floor.

'There's the mark of the bar across its neck. It's deep. And wet. Its neck's broken. It's bled,' said Rangi. 'It doesn't smell. It's recently killed.'

'We'll have to keep it.'

'Why?'

Peregrine was taken aback. 'Why?' he said. 'Upon my word I don't know. I'm treating it like evidence for a crime and there's no crime of that sort. Nor any sort, really. All the same . . . Wait a bit.'

Peregrine went to a rubbish bin backstage, found a discarded brown paper bag and turned it inside out. He brought it back and held it open. Rangi picked the rat up by the ear and dropped it in. Peregrine tied it up.

'Horrible beast,' he said.

'We'd better – Ssh!'

A padded footfall and the swish of a broom sounded in the passage.

'Ernie!' Peregrine called. 'Props!'

The door opened and he came in. How many years, Peregrine asked himself, had Ernie been Props at the Dolphin. Ten? Twenty? Dependable always. A cockney with an odd quirky sense of the ridiculous and an over-sensitive reaction to an imagined slight. Thin, sharp face. Quick. Sidelong grin.

'Hello, guv,' he said. 'Fought you'd of gawn be now.'

'Just going. Caught any rats?'

'I never looked. 'Old on.'

He went to the back of the room behind a packing case. A pause and then Props's voice. "Ullo! What's this, then?' A scuffling and he appeared with a rat-trap on a long string.

'Look at this,' he said. 'I don't get it. The bait's gawn. So's the rat's head. There's *been* a rat. Fur and gore and hindquarters all over the trap. Killed. Somebody's been and taken it. Must of.'

'Henry?' asked Peregrine.

'Nah! Cats don't eat rats. Just kill 'em. And 'Enery couldn't get up that narrer passage. Nah! It's been a man. 'E's pulled out the trap, lifted the bar and taken the rat's forequarters!'

'The caretaker?'

'Not 'im. They give 'im the willies, rats do. It ought to be 'im that sets the trap, not me, but 'e won't.'

'When did you set it then, Ernie?'

'Yesterday morning. They was all collected in 'ere waiting for rehearsal, wasn't they?'

'Yes. We did the crowd scenes,' said Peregrine. He looked at Rangi. 'You weren't here,' he said.

'No. First I've heard of it.'

Peregrine saw an alert, doubtful look on Props's face. 'We've been wondering who knew all about the trap. Pretty well the whole company seems to be the answer,' he said.

'That's right,' Props said. He was staring at the brown paper parcel. 'What's that?' he asked.

'What's what?'

'That parcel. Look. It's mucky.'

He was right. A horrid wetness seeped through the paper. 'It's half your rat, Props,' said Peregrine. 'Your rat's in the parcel.'

''Ere. What's the game, eh? You've taken it off of the trap and made a bloody parcel of it. What for? Why didn't you say so instead of letting me turn myself into a blooming exhibition? What's all this about?' Props demanded.

'We didn't remove it. It was in Mr Western's bag.'

Props turned and looked hard at Rangi. 'Is that correct?' he asked.

'Perfectly correct. I put my hand in to get the pilot's thumb and – ' he grimaced – 'I touched it.' He picked up his bag and held it out. 'Look for yourself. It'll be marked.'

Props took the bag and opened it. He peered inside. 'That's right,' he said. 'There's marks.' He stared at Peregrine and Rangi. 'It's the same bloody bugger what did the other bloody tricks.'

'Looks like it,' Peregrine agreed. And after a moment: 'Personally I'm satisfied that it wasn't you, Props. You're not capable of such a convincing display of bewilderment. Or of thinking it funny.'

'Ta very much.' He jerked his head at Rangi. 'What about him?' he asked. 'Don't 'e fink I done it?'

'I'm satisfied. Not you,' said Rangi.

There was a considerable pause before Props said: 'Fair enough.'

Peregrine said: 'I think we say nothing about this. Props, clear up the wet patch in the witch's bag, would you, and return it to its place on the table with the other two. Drop the rat in the rubbish bin. We've overreacted, which is probably exactly what he wanted us to do. From now on, you keep a tight watch on all the props right up to the time they're used. And not a word to anyone about this. OK?'

'OK,' they both said.

'Right. Go ahead then. Rangi, can I give you a lift?'

'No, thanks. I'll take a bus.'

They went out through the stage door.

Peregrine unlocked his car and got in. Big Ben tolled four o'clock. He sat there, dog-tired suddenly. Drained. Zero hour. This time on Saturday: the opening night and the awful burden of the play: of lifting the cast. Of hoping for the final miracle. Of being, within himself, sure, and of conveying that security somehow to the cast.

Why, why, *why*, thought Peregrine, do I direct plays? Why do I put myself into this hell? Above all, why *Macbeth*? And then: It's too soon to be feeling like this; six days too soon. Oh God, deliver us all.

He drove home to Emily.

'Do you have to go out again tonight?' Emily asked.

'I'm not sure. I don't think so.'

'How about a bath and a zizz?'

'I ought to be doing something. I can't think.'

'I'll answer the telephone and if it's important I swear I'll wake you.'

'Will you?' he said helplessly.

'Come on, silly. You haven't slept for two nights.'

She went upstairs. He heard the bath running and smelt the stuff she used in it. If I sit down, he thought, I won't get up.

He wandered to the window. There was the Dolphin across the river, shining in the late afternoon sun. Tomorrow they'll put up the big poster. *Macbeth*. Opening April 23! I'll see it from here.

Emily came down.

'Come on,' she said.

She helped him undress. The bath was heaven. Emily scrubbed his back. His head nodded and his mouth filled with foam.

'Blow!'

He blew and the foam floated about, a mass of iridescent bubbles.

'Stay awake for three minutes longer,' said her voice. She had evidently pulled out the plug. 'Come on. Out.'

He was dried. The sensation was laughable. He woke sufficiently to fumble himself into his pyjamas and then into bed.

'"*Sleep*,"' he said, '"*that knits up the ravelled sleave of care.*"'

'That's right,' said Emily, a thousand miles away.

He slept.

IV

Across the river, not very far away as the crow flies, the theatre trembled with the rebirth of the play. The actors were gone but Winter Morris and his staff worked away in the front-of-house. Telephones rang. Bookings were made. Royalty were coming and someone from Buck House would soon appear to settle the arrangements. The police and Security people would make decisions. Chief Superintendent Alleyn was coming. The Security pundits thought it a good idea if he were to be put in the next box to Royalty. Chief Superintendent Alleyn received the order philosophically if not jubilantly and asked for a second seat later in the season when he could watch the play rather than the house.

'Of course, of course, my dear chap,' Winty gushed. 'Any time. Anywhere. Management seat. Our pleasure.'

Flower shop. Cleaners. Press. Programmes. Biographical notes. Notes on the play. Nothing about superstitions.

Winter Morris read through the proofs and could find nothing to crack the eggshell sensitivity of any of the actors. Until he came to the piece on Banquo.

'Mr Bruce Barrabell, too long an absentee from the West End.' He won't relish that, thought Winty, and changed it to '. . . makes a welcome return to . . .'

He went through the whole thing again and then rang up the printers and asked if the Royal Programme was ready and when he could see a copy.

Winter Morris's black curls were now iron-grey. He had been Business Manager at the Dolphin ever since it was restored and he remembered the play about Shakespeare by Peregrine Jay that twenty years ago was accompanied by a murder.

Seems a long time ago now, thought Winty. Things have gone rather smoothly since then. He touched wood with his plump white finger. Of course we're in a nice financial position, permanently endowed by the late Mr Conducis. Almost *too* secure, you might think. *I* don't, he added with a fat chuckle. He lit a cigar and returned to his work.

He had dealt with his in-tray. There was only an advertisement left from a wine merchant. He picked it up and dropped it in his WPB, exposing a folded paper at the bottom of his tray.

Winty was an extremely tidy man and liked to say he knew exactly where everything lay on or in his desk and what it was about. He did not recognize this folded sheet. It was, he noted, a follow-up sheet of his office letter-paper. He frowned and opened it.

The typed message read: 'murderers sons in your co.'

Winter Morris sat perfectly still, his cigar in his left hand and in his right this outrageous statement.

Presently he turned and observed on a small table the typewriter sometimes used by his secretary for taking down dictated letters. He inserted a sheet of paper and typed the statement.

This, he decided, corresponds exactly. The monstrous truth declared itself. It had been executed in his office. Somebody had come in, sat down and infamously typed it. No apostrophes or full stop and no capital letter. Because the writer was in a hurry? Or ignorant? And the motive?

Winty put both typed messages into an envelope and wrote the date on it. He unlocked his private drawer, dropped the envelope in and re-locked it.

The son of a murderer?

Winty consulted his neatly arranged, fabulous memory. Since the casting-list was completed he mentally ticked off each player until he came to William Smith. He remembered his mother, her nervous manner, her hesitation, her obvious relief. And diving backwards, at last he remembered the Harcourt-Smith case and its outcome. Three years ago, was it? Six victims, and all of them girls! Mutilated, beheaded. Broadmoor for life.

If that's the answer, Winty thought, I've forgotten the case. But, by God, I'll find out who wrote this message and I won't rest till I've faced him with it. Now then!

He thought very carefully for some time and then rang his secretary's room.

'Mr Morris?' said her voice.

'Still here, are you, Mrs Abrams? Will you come in, please?'

'Certainly.'

Seconds later the inner door opened and a middle-aged lady came in, carrying her notebook.

'You just caught me,' she said.

'I'm sorry.'

'It's all right. I'm in no hurry.'

'Sit down. I want to test your memory, Mrs Abrams.'

She sat down.

'When,' he asked, 'did you last see the bottom of my in-tray?'

'Yesterday morning, Mr Morris. Ten-fifteen. Teatime. I checked through the contents and added the morning's mail.'

'You saw the *bottom*?'

'Certainly. I took everything out. There was a brochure from the wine people. I thought you might like to see it.'

'Quite. And nothing else?'

'Nothing.' She waited for a moment and then said incredulously: 'There's nothing *lost*?'

'No. There's something found. A typed message. It's on our follow-up paper and it's typed on that machine over there. No envelope.'

'Oh,' she said.

'Yes. Where was I? While you were in here?'

'On the phone. Security people. First night arrangements.'

'Ah yes. Mrs Abrams, was this room unoccupied at any time, *and* unlocked, between then and now? I lunched at my club.'

'It was locked. You locked it.'

'Before that?'

'Er – I think you went out for a few minutes. At eleven.'

'I did?'

'The toilet,' she said modestly. 'I heard the door open and close.'

'Oh yes. And later?'

'Let me think. No, apart from that it was never unoccupied *and* unlocked. Wait!'

'Yes, Mrs Abrams.'

'I had put a sheet of our follow-up paper in the little machine here in case you should require a memo.'

'Yes?'

'You did not. It is not there now. How peculiar.'

'Yes, very.' He thought things over for a moment and then said: 'Your memory, Mrs Abrams, is exceptional. Do I understand that the only time it could have been done was when I left the room for – for at least five minutes? Would you not have heard the typewriter?'

'I was using my own machine in my own room, Mr Morris. No.'

'And the time?'

'I heard Big Ben.'

'Thank you. Thank you very much.' He hesitated. He contemplated Mrs Abrams doubtfully. 'I'm very much obliged. I – thank you, Mrs Abrams.'

'Thank *you*, Mr Morris.'

She closed the door behind her. I wonder, she thought, why he doesn't tell me what was in the message.

On the other side of the door he thought: I would have liked to tell her but – no. The fewer the better.

He sat before his desk and thought carefully and calmly about this disruptive event. He was unaware of the previous occurrences: Peregrine's accident; the head in the King's room; the head in the meat-dish; the rat in Rangi's bag. They were not in his department. So that he had nothing to relate the message to. A murderer's son in the cast! he thought. Preposterous! What murderer? What son?

He thought of the Harcourt-Smith case. He remembered that the sensational papers made a great thing of the wife's having no inkling of Harcourt-Smith's second 'personality' and, yes, of his little son, who was six years old.

It's our William, he thought. Blow me down flat but it's our William that's being got at. And after a further agitation: I'll do nothing. It's awkward, of course, but until the show's been running for some time it's better not to meddle. If then. I don't know who's typed it and I don't want to know. Yet.

He looked at his day-to-day calendar. A red ring neatly encircled April 23. Shakespeare's birthday. Opening night. Only a week left, he thought.

He was not a pious man but he caught himself wondering for the moment about the protective comfort of a phylactery and wishing he could experience it.

CHAPTER 5

Fifth Week.
Dress Rehearsals and First Night

The days before the opening night seemed to hurry and to darken. There were no disasters and no untoward happenings, only a rushing immediacy. The actors arrived early for rehearsals. Some who were not called came to the last of the piecemeal sessions and watched closely and with a painful intensity.

The first of the dress rehearsals, really a technical rehearsal, lasted all day with constant stoppages for lights and effects. The management had a meal sent in. It was set up in the rehearsal room: soup, cold meat, potatoes in their jackets, salad and coffee. Some members of the cast helped themselves when they had an opportunity. Others, Maggie for one, had nothing.

The props for the banquet were all there: a boar's head with an apple in its jaws and glass eyes. Plastic chickens. A soup tureen that would exude steam when a serving-man removed the lid. Peregrine looked under the covers but the contents were all right: glued down. Loose: wine jugs; goblets; a huge candelabrum in the centre of the table.

The stoppages for lights were continual. Dialogue. Stop. 'Catch them going *up*. Re-focus it. Is it fixed? This mustn't happen again.'

The witches had each a tiny blue torch concealed in her clothes. They switched these on when Macbeth spoke to them. They had to be firmly sewn and accurately pointed at their faces.

Plain sailing for a bit but still the feeling of pressure and anxiety. But that, after all, was normal. The actors played 'within themselves'. Or almost. They got an interrupted run. The tension was extreme. The theatre was full of marvellous but ominous sounds. The air was thick with menace.

The arrival at Macbeth's castle in the evening was the last seen of daylight for a long time. Exquisite lighting: a mellow and tranquil scene. Banquo's beautiful voice saying *'the air nimbly and sweetly recommends itself unto our gentle senses.'* The sudden change when the doors rolled back and the piper skirled wildly and Lady Macbeth drew the King into the castle.

From now on it is night, for the dawn, after the murder, was delayed and hardly declared itself and before the murder of Banquo it is dusk: *'The West yet glimmers with some streaks of day,'* says the watchful assassin.

Banquo is murdered.

After the banquet the Macbeths are alone together, the last time the audience sees them so, and the night is *'almost at odds with morning, which is which'*. Otherwise, torchlight, lamplight, witchlight, right on until the English scene, out-of-doors and sunny with a good King on the throne.

When Macbeth reappears he is aged, dishevelled, half-demented, deserted by all but a few who cannot escape. Dougal Macdougal would be wonderful. He played these last abysmal scenes now well under their final pitch, but with every wayward change indicated. He was a wounded animal with a snarl or two left in him. *'Tomorrow and tomorrow and tomorrow . . .'* The speech tolled its way to the end like a death knell. Macduff and Malcolm, the lairds and their troops arrived. Now, at last, Macbeth and Macduff met. The challenge. The fight. The exit and the scream cut short.

The brief scene in which Old Siward speaks the final conventional merciless word on his son's death, and then Macduff enters, downstage, and behind him, Seyton with Macbeth's head on his claidheamh-mor.

Malcolm, up on the stairway among his soldiers, is caught by the setting sun. They turn their heads and see The Head.

'Hail gobbledy-gook,' shout the soldiers, avoiding the tag. Superstitious, thought Peregrine.

'Curtain,' he said. 'But don't bring it down. Hold it. Thank you. Lights. I think they're a little too juicy at the end. Too pink. Can you give us something a bit less obvious? Straw perhaps. It's too

much: "Exit into sunset." You know? Right. Settle down, everybody. Bring some chairs on. I won't keep the actors very long.
Settle down.'

He went through the play. 'Witches, *all* raise your arms when you
jump.

'Details. Nothing of great importance except on the Banquo's ghost
exit. You were too close to Lennox. Your cloak moved in the draught.'

'Can they leave a wider gap?' Banquo asked.

'I can,' said Lennox. 'Sorry.'

'Right. Any more questions?' Predictably, Banquo had. His scene
with Fleance and Macbeth. The lighting. 'It feels false. I have to
move into it.'

'Come on a bit further on your entrance. Nothing to stop you, is
there?'

'It feels false.'

'It doesn't give that impression,' said Peregrine very firmly. 'Any
other questions?'

William piped up. 'When I'm stabbed,' he said. 'I kind of hold the
wound and then collapse. Could the murderer catch me before I fall?'

'Certainly,' said Peregrine. 'He's meant to.'

'Sorry,' said the murderer. 'I missed it. I was too late.'

They ploughed on. Attention to details. Getting everything right,
down to the smallest move, the fractional pause. Changes of pace
building towards a line of climax. Peregrine spent three-quarters of
an hour over the cauldron scene. The entire cast were required to
whisper the repeated rhythmic chant as in a round. *'Double, double
toil and trouble, fire burn and cauldron bubble.'*

At last they moved on. There were no more questions. Peregrine
thanked them. 'Same time tomorrow,' he said, 'and I *hope* no stops.
You've been very patient. Bless you all. Good night.'

II

But again next day there were stops. A number of technical hitches
occurred during the final dress rehearsal, mostly to do with the
lights. They were all cleared up. Peregrine had said to the cast: 'Keep
something in the larder. Don't reach the absolute tops. Play within

yourselves. Conserve your energy. Save the consummate thing for the performance. We know you can do it, my dears. Don't exhaust yourselves.'

They obeyed him but there were one or two horrors.

Lennox missed an entrance and arrived looking as if the Devil himself was after him.

Duncan lost his lines, had to be prompted and was slow to recover. Nina Gaythorne dried completely and looked terror-stricken. William went straight on with his own lines. *'And must they all be hanged that swear and lie?'* and she answered like an automaton.

'It was a dose of stage fright,' she said when they came off. 'I didn't know where I was or what I said. Oh, this play. This play.'

'Never mind, Miss Gaythorne,' said William, taking her hand. 'It won't happen again. I'll be with you.'

'That's something,' she said, half-laughing and half-crying.

At the end they rehearsed the curtain call. The 'dead' characters on the OP side and the live ones on the Prompt. Then the Macbeths alone and finally the man himself. Alone.

Peregrine took his notes and thanked his cast. 'Change but don't go,' he said. *'Bad dress. Good show,'* quoted the stage director cheerfully. 'Are we getting them down tomorrow?'

'No. They'll be right. We'll make it a technical rehearsal now,' said Peregrine. 'We'll run through the lighting and effects without the actors tomorrow.'

He put this to the company.

'If we get it rotten-perfect now, you can sleep in tomorrow morning. It's just a matter of working straight on from cue to cue with nothing between. All right? Any objections? Banquo?'

'I?' said Banquo who had been ready to make one. 'Objections? Oh no. No.'

They finished at five to two in the morning. The management had provided beer, whisky and sherry. Some of them left without taking anything. William was dispatched in a taxi with Angus and Menteith who lived more or less in the same direction. Maggie slipped away as soon as her sleepwalking scene was over and she had seen Peregrine. Fleance went after the murder, Banquo after the cauldron scene and Duncan on his arrival at the castle. There were not many hold-ups. A slight re-arrangement of the company-fights at the end. Macbeth and Macduff went like clockwork.

Peregrine waited till they were all gone and the nightwatchman was on his rounds. The theatre was dark except for the dim working light. Dark, coldly stuffy. Waiting.

He stood for a moment in front of the curtain and saw the care-taker's torch moving about the circle. He felt empty and deadly tired. Nothing untoward had happened.

'Good night,' he called.

'Good night, guv'nor.'

He went through the curtain into backstage and past the menac-ing shapes of scenery, ill-defined by the faraway working light. Where was his torch? Never mind, he'd got all his papers under his arm fastened to a clapperboard and he would go home. Past the masking pieces, cautiously along the Prompt side.

Something caught hold of his foot.

He fell forward and a jolt wrenched at his former injury and made him cry out.

'Are you all right?' asked the scarcely audible voice in the circle.

He was all right. He still had hold of his clapperboard. He'd caught his foot in one of the light cables. Up he got, cautiously. 'All serene,' he shouted.

'Are you *quite* sure?' asked an anxious voice close at hand.

'God! Who the hell are you?'

'It's me, guv.'

'Props! What the blazes are you doing? Where are you?'

'I'm 'ere. Thought I'd 'ang abaht and make sure no one was up to no tricks. I must of dozed off. Wait a tick.'

A scrabbling noise and he came fuzzily into view round the corner of a dark object. A strong smell of whisky accompanied him. 'It's the murdered lady's chair,' he said. 'I must have dropped off in it. Fancy.'

'Fancy.'

Props moved forward and a glassy object rolled from under his feet.

'Bottle,' he said coyly. 'Empty.'

'So I supposed.'

Peregrine's eyes had adjusted to the gloom. 'How drunk are you?' he asked.

'Not so bad. Only a few steps down the primrose parf. There wasn't more'n three drinks left in the bottle. Honest. And nobody got up to no tricks. They've all vanished. Into thin air.'

'You'd better follow them. Come on.'

He took Props by the arm, steered him to the stage door, opened it and shoved him through.

'Ta,' said Props. 'Goo'night,' and made off at a tidy shamble. Peregrine adjusted the self-locking apparatus on the door and banged it. He was in time to see Props being sick at the corner of Wharfingers Lane.

When he had finished he straightened up, saw Peregrine and waved to him.

'That's done the trick,' he shouted, and walked briskly away.

Peregrine went to the car park, unlocked his car and got in. Emily, in her woolly dressing gown, let him in.

'Hullo, love,' he said, 'you shouldn't have waited up.'

'Hullo.'

He said: 'Just soup,' and sank into an armchair.

She gave him strong soup laced with brandy.

'Golly, that's nice,' he said. And then: 'Pretty bloody awful but nothing in the way of practical jokes.'

'Bad dress. Good show.'

'Hope so.'

And in that hope he finished his soup and went to bed and to sleep.

III

Now they were all in their dressing rooms, doors shut, telegrams, cards, presents, flowers, the pungent smell of greasepaint and wet white and hand lotion, the close, electrically charged atmosphere of a working theatre.

Maggie made up her face. Carefully, looking at it from all angles, she drew her eyebrows together, emphasized the determined creases at the corners of her mouth. She strained back her flattened mane of reddish hair and secured it with pins and a band.

Nanny, her dresser and housekeeper, stood silently holding her robe. When she turned there it was, opened, waiting for her. She covered her head with a chiffon scarf: Nanny skilfully dropped the robe over it, not touching it.

The tannoy came to life. 'Quarter hour. Quarter hour, please,' it said.

'Thank you, Nanny,' said Maggie. 'That's fine.' She kissed a bedraggled bit of fur with a cat's head. 'Bless you, Thomasina,' she said and propped it against her glass.

A tap on the door. 'May I come in?'

'Dougal! Yes.'

He came in and put a velvet case on her table. 'It was my grandma's,' he said. 'She was a Highlander. Blessings.' He kissed her hand and made the sign of the cross over her.

'My dear, thank you. Thank you.'

But he was gone.

She opened the case. It was a brooch: a design of interlaced golden leaves with semi-precious stones making a thistle. 'It's benign, I'm sure,' she said. 'I shall wear it in my cloak. In the fur, Nanny. Fix it, will you?'

Presently she was dressed and ready.

The three witches stood together in front of the looking glass, Rangi in the middle. He had the face of a skull but his eyelids glittered in his dark face. Round his neck on a flax cord hung a greenstone tiki, an embryo child. Blondie's face was made ugly and was grossly over-painted: blobs of red on the cheeks and a huge scarlet mouth. Wendy was bearded. They had transformed their hands into claws.

'If I look any longer I'll frighten myself,' said Rangi.

'Quarter hour. Quarter hour, please.'

Gaston Sears dressed alone. He would have been a most uncomfortable companion, singing, muttering, uttering snatches of ancient rhymes and paying constant visits to the lavatory.

He occupied a tiny room that nobody else wanted but which seemed to please him.

When Peregrine called he found him in merry mood. 'I congratulate you, dear boy,' he cried. 'You have undoubtedly hit upon a valid interpretation of the cryptic Seyton.'

Peregrine shook hands with him. 'I mustn't wish you luck,' he said.

'But why not, perceptive boy? We wish each other luck. *A la bonne heure.*'

Peregrine hurried on to Nina Gaythorne's room.

Her dressing table was crowded with objects of baffling inconsistency and each of them must be fondled and kissed. A plaster Genesius, patron saint of actors, was in pride of place. There were also a number of anti-witchcraft objects and runes. The actress who played the Gentlewoman shared the dressing room and had very much the worst of the bargain. Not only did Nina take three-quarters of the working bench for her various protective objects, she spent a great deal of time muttering prophylactic rhymes and prayers.

These exercises were furtively carried out with one scary eye on the door. Whenever anyone knocked she leapt up and cast her make-up towel over her sacred collection. She then stood with her back to the bench, her hands resting negligently upon it, and broke out into peals of unconvincing laughter.

Macduff and Banquo were in the next-door room to Sir Dougal and were quiet and businesslike. Simon Morten was withdrawn into himself, tense and silent. When he first came he did a quarter of an hour's limbering-up and then took a shower and settled to his make-up. Bruce Barrabell tried a joke or two but, getting no response, fell silent. Their dresser attended to them.

Barrabell whistled two notes, remembered it was considered unlucky, stopped short and said, '*Shit.*'

'Out,' said Simon.

'I didn't know *you* were one of the faithful.'

'Go on. Out.'

He went out and shut the door. A pause. He turned round three times and then knocked.

'Yes?'

' – humbly apologize. May I come back? Please.'

'Come in.'

'Quarter hour. Quarter hour, please.'

William Smith dressed with Duncan and his sons. He was perfectly quiet and very pale. Malcolm, a pleasant young fellow, helped him make up. Duncan, attended by a dresser, magnificently looked on.

'First nights,' he groaned comprehensively. 'How I hate them.' His glance rested upon William. 'This is your first First Night, laddie, is it not?'

'There've been school showings, sir,' said William nervously.

'School showings eh? Well, well, well,' he said profoundly. 'Ah well.'

He turned to his ramshackle part propped up against his looking glass and began to mutter. '"*So well thy words become thee as thy wounds.*"'

'I'm at your elbow, Father. Back to audience. I'll give it to you if needs be. Don't worry,' said Malcolm.

'You will, my boy, won't you? No, I shan't worry. But I can't imagine *why* I dried like that yesterday. However.'

He caught his cloak up in a practised hand and turned round: 'All right behind?' he asked.

'Splendid,' his son reassured him.

'Good. Good.'

'Quarter hour, please.'

A tap on the door and Peregrine looked in. 'Lovely house,' he said. 'They're simmering. William – ' he patted William's head – 'you'll remember tonight through all your other nights to come, won't you? Your performance is correct. Don't alter anything, will you?'

'No, sir.'

'That's the ticket.' He turned to Duncan. 'My dear fellow, you're superb. And the boys. Malcolm, you've a long time to wait, haven't you? For your big scene. I've nothing but praise for you.'

The witches stood in a tight group. The picture they presented was horrendous. They said 'Thank you' all together and stood close to one another, staring at him.

'You'll do,' said Perry.

He was going his rounds. It wasn't too easy to find things to say to them all. Some of them hated to be wished well in so many words. They liked you to say facetiously, 'Fall down and break your leg.' Others enjoyed the squeezed elbow and confident nod. The ladies were kissed – on the hands or in the air because of make-up. Round he went with butterflies busily churning in his own stomach, his throat and mouth dry as sandpaper and his voice seeming to come from someone else.

Maggie said: 'It's your night tonight, Perry dear. All yours. Thank you.' And kissed him.

Sir Dougal shook both his hands. '"*Angels and ministers of grace defend us*,"' he said. 'Amen,' Perry answered and welcomed the *Hamlet* quotation.

Simon, magnificently dark and exuding a heady vitality, also shook his hands. 'Thank you,' he said, 'I'm no good at this sort of thing but blessings and thank you.'

'Where's Banquo?'

'He went out. Having a pee, I suppose.'

'Give him my greetings,' said Peregrine, relieved.

On and on. Nina, 'discovered' leaning back against her dressing table and laughing madly. A strong smell of garlic.

The thanes nervy and polite. The walking gents delighted to be visited.

Finished at last. Front-of-house waiting for him: Winty's assistant.

'All right,' he said. 'We're pushing the whole house in. Bit of a job. There are the royalty-hunters determined to stay in the foyer but we've herded them all in. Winty's dressed up like a sore thumb and waiting in the entrance. The house is packed with security men and Bob's your uncle. They've rung through to say the cars have left.'

'Away we go?'

'Away we go.'

'*Beginners, please. Beginners*,' said the tannoy.

The witches appeared in the shadows, came on stage, climbed the rostrum and grouped round the gallows. Duncan and his sons and thanes stood offstage waiting for the short opening scene to end.

An interval of perhaps five interminable minutes. Then trumpets filled the air with their brazen splendour and were followed by the sound of a thousand people getting to their feet. Now the National

Anthem. And now they settled in their seats. A peremptory buzzer. The stage manager's voice.

'Stand by. House lights. Thunder. Curtain up.'

Peregrine began to pace to and fro, to and fro. Listening.

IV

After the fourth scene he knew. It was all right. Their hearts are in it, he thought, and he crept into the Prompt-side box. Winty squeezed his arm in the darkness and said, 'We'll run for months and months. It's a wow.'

'Thank God.'

He'd been right. They had left themselves with one more step to the top and now they took it.

You darling creatures, he thought, suddenly in love with all of them. Ah, you treasures. Bless you. Bless you.

The rest of the evening was unreal. The visit to the royal box and the royal visit to the cast. The standing ovation at the end. Everything to excess. A multiple Cinderella story. Sort of.

He didn't go to the opening night party. He never did. Emily came round and hugged him and cried and said: 'Oh *yes*, darling. Yes. Yes.'

The company collected round him and cheered. And finally the critic whose opinion he most valued astonishingly came round; he said he was breaking the rule of a lifetime but it had undoubtedly been the best Macbeth since Olivier's and the best Lady Macbeth in living memory and he must do a bolt.

'We'll get out of this,' Peregrine said. 'I'm hungry.'

'Where are we going?'

'The Wig and Piglet. It's only minutes away and they stay open till the papers come in. The manager's getting them for me.'

'Come on, then.'

They edged through the milling crowd of shouting visitors and out of the stage door. The alley was full of people waiting for actors to appear. Nobody recognized the director. They turned into the theatre car park, managed to edge their way out and up the lane.

At the corner of the main street stood two lonely figures, a thin and faintly elegant woman and a small boy.

'It's William and his mum,' said Emily.

'I want to speak to the boy.'

He pulled up beside them. Emily lowered her window. 'Hullo, Mrs Smith. Hullo, William. Are you waiting for a bus?'

'We *hope* we are,' said Mrs Smith.

'You're not doing anything of the sort,' said Peregrine. 'The management looks after getting you home on the first night,' he lied. 'Didn't you know? Oh, good luck: there's a taxi coming.' Emily waved to it. 'William,' Peregrine said. William ran round to the driver's side. Peregrine got out. 'You can look after your mother, can't you? Here you are.' He pushed a note into William's hand. 'You gave a thoroughly professional performance. Good luck to you.'

The taxi pulled up. 'In you get, both of you.' He gave the driver the address.

'Yes – but – I mean – ' said Mrs Smith.

'No, you don't.' They were bundled in. 'Good night.' He slammed the door. The taxi made off.

'Phew! That was quick,' Emily said.

'If she'd had a moment to get her second wind she'd have refused. Come on, darling. How hungry I am. You can't think.'

The Wig and Piglet was full. The head waiter showed them to a reserved table.

'A wonderful performance, sir,' he said. 'They are all saying so. My congratulations.'

'Thank you. A bottle of your best champagne, Marcello.'

'It awaits you.' Marcello beamed and waved grandly at the wine bucket on their table.

'Really? Thank you.'

'Nothing,' said Peregrine when he had gone, 'succeeds like success.' He looked at Emily's excited face. 'I'm sorry,' he said gently. 'On a night like this one should not think forward or back. I found myself imagining what it would have been like if we'd flopped.'

'Don't. I know what you mean but don't put the stars out.'

'No husbandry in our Heaven tonight?' He reached out a hand. 'It's a bargain,' he said.

'A bargain. It's because you're hungry.'

'You may be right.'

An hour later he said she was a clever old trout. They had a cognac each to prove it and began to talk about the play.

'Gaston,' Peregrine said, 'may be dotty but he's pretty good where he is tonight, wouldn't you say?'

'Exactly right. He's like death itself, presiding over its feast. You don't think we've gone too far with him?'

'Not an inch.'

'Good. Winty says it'll run for as long as Dougal and Maggie can take it.'

'That's a matter of temperament, isn't it?'

'I suppose so. For Maggie, certainly. She's rock calm and perfectly steady. It's Dougal who surprises me. I'd expected a good, even a harrowing, performance but not so deeply frightening a one. He's got that superb golden-reddish appearance and I thought: We must be very clever about make-up so that the audience will see it disintegrate. But, upon my soul, he *does* disintegrate, he *is* bewitched, he *has* become the Devil's puppet. I even began to wonder if it was all right or if it might be embarrassing, as if he'd discarded his *persona* and we'd come face to face with his naked, personal collapse. Which would be dreadful and wrong. But no. It hasn't happened. He's come near the brink in the last scene but he's still Macbeth. Thanks to Gaston, he fights like a man possessed but always with absolute control. And so – evilly. For Macduff, it's like stamping out some horror that's lain under a stone waiting for him.'

'And his whole performance?'

'If I could scratch about for something wrong I would. But no, he's going great guns. The straightforward avenger. And I think he plays his English scene beautifully. I'm sorry,' said Emily. 'I wish I could find something wrong and out-of-key or wanting re-adjustment somewhere, but I can't. Your problem will be to keep them up to this level.'

They talked on. Presently the door into the servery opened and their waiter came in with an armful of Sunday papers.

Peregrine's heart suddenly thumped against his ribs. He took up the top one and flipped over the pages.

'AT LAST! A FLAWLESS MACBETH'

And two rave columns.

Emily saw his open paper trembling in his hands. She went through the remaining ones, folding them back at the dramatic criticisms.

'This is becoming ridiculous,' she said.

He made a strange little sound of agreement. She shoved the little pile of papers over to him. 'They're all the same, allowing for stylistic differences.'

'We'll go home. We're the only ones left. Poor Marcello!'

He lowered his paper and folded it. Emily saw that his eyes were red. 'I can't get over it,' he said. 'It's too much.'

He signed his bill and added an enormous tip. They were bowed out.

The Embankment was being washed down. Great fans of water swept to and fro. In the east, buildings were silhouetted against a kindling sky. London was waking up.

They drove home, let themselves in and went to bed and a fathomless sleep.

The first member of the company to wake on Sunday was William Smith. He consulted his watch, dragged on his clothes, gave a lick to his face and let himself out by the front door. Every Sunday at the end of their little lane on a flight of steps in a major traffic road, a newsman set up his wares. He trustfully left his customers to put the right amount in a tin, helping themselves to change when required. He kept an eye on them from the 'Kaff on the Korner'.

William had provided himself with the exact sum. Mr Barnes, he recollected, had said something about the 'Quality' papers being the ones that mattered. He purchased the most expensive and turned to the headlines.

'AT LAST! A FLAWLESS MACBETH'

William read it all the way home. It was glorious. At the end it said: 'The smallest parts have been given the same loving attention. A pat on the head is here awarded to Master William Smith for totally avoiding the Infant Phenomenon.'

William charged upstairs shouting: 'Mum! Are you awake? Hi, Mum! What's an Infant Phenomenon? Because I've avoided one.'

By midday they had all read the notices and by evening most of them had rung somebody else in the company and they were all delighted but feeling a sort of anticlimactic emptiness. The only thing left to say was: 'Now we must keep it up, mustn't we?'

Barrabell went to a meeting of the Red Fellowship. He was asked to report on his tasks. He said the actors had been too much occupied to listen to new ideas but that now they were clearly set for a long run he would embark on stage two and hoped to have more to report at the next meeting. It was a case of making haste slowly. They were all, he said, steeped to their eyebrows in a lot of silly superstitions that had grown up around the play. He had wondered if anything could be made of this circumstance but nothing had emerged other than a highly wrought state of emotional receptivity. The correct treatment would be to attack this unprofitable nonsense.

Shakespeare, he said, was a very confused writer. His bourgeois origins distorted his thought-processes.

Maggie stayed in bed all day and Nanny answered the telephone.

Sir Dougal lunched at the Garrick Club and soaked up congratulations without showing too blatantly his intense gratification.

Simon Morten rang Maggie and got Nanny.

King Duncan spent the afternoon cutting out notices and pasting them in his fourth book.

Nina Gaythorne got out all her remedies and good luck objects and kissed them. This took some time as she lost count and had to begin all over again.

Malcolm and Donalbain got blamelessly drunk.

The speaking thanes and the witches all dined with Ross and his wife, bringing their own bottles, and talked shop.

The Doctor and the Gentlewoman were rung up by their friends and were touchingly excited.

The non-speaking thanes dispersed to various unknown quarters.

And Gaston? He retired to his baleful house in Dulwich and wrote a number of indignant letters to those papers whose critics had referred to the weapons used in the duel as swords or claymores instead of claidheamh-mors.

Emily answered their telephone and by a system they had perfected, either called Peregrine or said he was out but would be delighted to know they had rung up.

So the day passed and on Monday morning they pulled themselves together and got down to the theatre and to the business of facing the second night and a long run of *Macbeth*.

Part Two: Curtain Call

CHAPTER 6

Catastrophe

The play had been running to full houses for a month. Peregrine no longer came down to every performance but on this Saturday night he was bringing his two older boys. There had been no more silly tricks and the actors had settled down to a successful run. The boys came home for half-term and Peregrine had a meeting with the management about how long the season should run and whether, for the actors' sakes, after six months they should make a change and, if so, what that change should be.

'We don't need to worry about it if we decide to have a Shakespeare rep season: say *Twelfth Night* and *Measure for Measure* with *Macbeth*,' said Peregrine. 'We'll just keep it in mind. You never know what may turn up, do you?'

They said no, you didn't, and the discussion ended.

The day turned out to be unseasonably muggy and exhausting. Not a breath of wind, the sky overcast and a suggestion of thunder. 'On the left,' said Gaston as he prepared to supervise the morning's fight. 'Thunder on the left meant trouble in Roman times. The gods rumbling, you know.'

'They ought to have heard *you*,' said Dougal rudely. 'That would have pulled them up in their tracks.'

'Come *on*,' said Simon. 'Let's press on with it. We've got a matinée, remember.'

They shaped up and fought.

'You are dragging. *Dragging!*' Gaston shouted. 'Stop. It is worse than not doing it at all. Again, from the beginning.'

'Have a heart, Gaston. It's a deadly day for these capers,' said Simon.
'I am merciless. Come. Begin. *A tempo*. Er-one. Er-two – '

They finished their fight and retired, sweating heavily and sulking, to the showers.

Peregrine was taking his two elder sons, Crispin and Robin, aged fifteen and nine, to the evening performance. Richard was going to a farce with his mother, being thought a little young for *Macbeth*.

'Is it bloody?' Richard asked ruefully.

'Very,' Peregrine replied firmly.

'Extra special bloody?'

'Yes.'

'I'd like that. Is it going to run a long time?'

'Yes.'

'Perhaps I'll grow up into it.'

'Perhaps you will.'

Emily took a taxi and she and Richard sailed off together, looking excited. Peregrine and his two boys took their car. Crispin's form at school was working on *Macbeth* and he asked a great many questions that Peregrine supposed were necessary and that he answered to the best of his ability. Presently Crispin said: 'Old Perky says you ought to feel a great weight's been shifted off your shoulders at the end. When Macduff sort of actually lifts Macbeth's head off and young Malcolm comes in for King.'

'I hope you'll feel like that.'

'Does the lights man have to allow an *exact* time-lag between cue and performance?' asked Robin, who at the moment wanted to become an electrical engineer.

'Yes.'

'How long?'

'I've forgotten. About one second, I think.'

'Gosh!'

The foyer was crowded and the House Full notice displayed.

'We're in a box,' said Peregrine. 'Come on. Up the stairs.'

'Super,' said the boys. The usher at the door into the circle said, 'Good evening, sir,' and smiled at them. He wagged his head. Peregrine and the boys left the queue and slipped behind him into the circle.

They passed round the back of the circle into the middle box. Peregrine bought them a programme each. The programme girl smiled upon them. The house was almost full. A tall man, alone, came down the centre aisle and made for a management seat in the stalls. He looked up, saw Peregrine and waved his programme. Peregrine answered.

'Who are you waving to, Pop?'

'Do you see that very tall man just sitting down, in the third row?'

'Yes. He looks super,' said Crispin. 'Who is he?'

'Chief Superintendent Alleyn. CID. He was here on our opening night.'

'Why's he come again?' asked Robin.

'Presumably because he likes the play.'

'Oh.'

'Actually he didn't get an uninterrupted view on the first night. There were royals. He was helping the police look after them.'

'So he had to sit watching the audience and not the actors?'

'Yes.'

A persistent buzzer began ringing in the foyer. Peregrine looked at his watch. 'We're ten minutes over time,' he said. 'Give them five minutes more and then the latecomers'll have to wait until Scene 2. No, it's OK. Here we go.'

The house lights dimmed very slowly and the audience was silent. Now it was dark. There was a flash of lightning and a distant roll of thunder and the faint sound of wind. The curtain was up and the witches at their unholy work on the gallows.

The play flowed on. Peregrine looked at the backs of his sons' heads and wondered what was going on in them. He had been careful not to rub their noses in Shakespeare's plays and had left it to them whether or not they would read them. As far as he could make out, Mr Perkins was not sickening Crispin with over-insistence on notes and disputed passages but had interested him first in the play itself and in the magic and strength of its language.

Robin at six years old had seen a performance of the *Dream* and enjoyed it for all the wrong reasons. The chief comic character, in his opinion, was Hippolyta and he laughed very heartily at all her entrances. When Emily asked why, he said: 'At her legs.' He thought Bottom a very good actor and the 'audience' extremely rude to laugh at him.

At nine years old he would be less surprising in his judgements.

Now they were both very still and attentive. Peregrine sat behind Robin. When Banquo and Fleance came in for their little night scene, Robin turned in his seat and looked at him. He bent down. 'Nice,' Robin whispered and they nodded to each other. But later, when Macbeth began to climb the stairs, Robin's hand moved round behind him and felt for his father's. Peregrine held it tightly until the end of the scene when the Porter came on. Both the boys laughed loudly at the bawdy-looking pieces of driftwood and the Porter's description of the aggravating effects of drinking too much.

In the interval Robin visited the lavatories. Crispin said he might as well go with him and their father had a drink with the management. They arranged to meet in the foyer. Under the photo of Macbeth.

Winty came out to welcome Peregrine. They went into his office. 'Still goes on,' Winty said. 'Booked solid for the next six months.'

'Odd,' said Peregrine, 'when you think of the superstitions. There's a record of good business and catastrophe going back hand in hand for literally centuries.'

'Not for us, old boy.'

'Touch wood.'

'You too?' asked Winty, giving him his drink.

'No. No way. But it's rife in the company.'

'Really?'

'Old Nina's got the bug very badly. Her dressing table's like a second-hand charm shop.'

'No signs of catastrophe, though,' Winty said. And when Peregrine didn't answer he said sharply: 'Are there?'

'There are signs of some half-wit planting them. Whoever it is hasn't got the results he may have hoped for. But it's very annoying, for all that. Or *was*. They seem to have died out.'

Winty said slowly: 'I fancy we had a sample.'

'You had? A sample? What sort of sample?'

'I haven't mentioned it to anybody except Mrs Abrams. And she doesn't know what was typed and anyway she's a clam of clams. But since you've brought it up – '

The buzzer started.

'I'm sorry,' said Peregrine. 'I'll have to go. I promised my young son. He'll be having kittens. Thank you, Winty. I'll come in tomorrow morning.'

'Oh. Well . . . I think we'd better have a talk.'

'So do I. Tomorrow. Thank you.'

Out in the foyer he found Robin under the photograph of Macbeth.

'Oh, hullo,' he said casually when Peregrine reached him. 'There's the bell.'

'Where's Cip?'

Crispin was over in the crowd by the bookstall. He was searching his pockets. Peregrine, closely followed by Robin, worked his way over to him.

'I've got it all but twenty p.,' said Crispin. He clutched a book, *Macbeth Through Four Centuries*.

Peregrine produced a five-pound note. 'For the book,' he said, and they returned to their box. The interval ended, the house darkened and the curtain rose.

On Banquo. Alone and suspicious. Macbeth questions him. He is going out? Riding? He must return. For the party. Does Fleance go with him? Yes. Yes to all those questions. There is a terrible smile on Macbeth's face, the lips stretch back. *'Farewell.'*

Seyton is at once sent for the murderers. He has them ready and stands in the doorway and hears the wooing. Macbeth is easier, almost enjoys himself. They are his sort. He caresses them. The bargain is struck, they go off.

Now Lady Macbeth finds him: full of strange hints and of horror. There is the superb invocation to night and he leads her away. And the scene changes. Seyton joins the murderers and Banquo is dispatched.

Back to the banquet.

Seyton tells Macbeth that Fleance escaped.

The bloodied Ghost of Banquo appears among the guests.

And now the play begins to swell towards its appointed ending. After the witches, the apparitions, the equivocal promises, the murder of Macduff's wife and child, comes Lady Macbeth. Asleep and talking in that strange metallic nightmare voice. Macbeth again, after a long interval. He has degenerated and shrunk. He beats about him with a kind of hectic frenzy and peers hopelessly into the future. These are the death-throes of a monster. Please let Macduff find him and finish it.

Macduff has found him.

'Turn, hell-hound. Turn.'

Now the fight. The leap, clash, sweep as Macbeth is beaten backwards, Macduff raises his claymore and they plunge out of sight. A
scream. Silence. Then the distant approach of pipe and drums.
Malcolm and his thanes come out on the upper landing. The rest of
his troops march on at stage level and up the steps with Old Siward,
who receives the news of his son's death.

Macduff comes on downstage, OP followed by Seyton.

Seyton carries his claidheamh-mor and on it, streaming blood,
the head of Macbeth.

He turns it upstage, facing Malcolm and the troops.

Macduff has not looked at it.

He shouts, '"*Behold where stands the usurper's cursed head. Hail, King
of Scotland."*'

The blood drips into Seyton's upturned face.

And being well-trained, professional actors, they respond and
with stricken faces and shaking lips repeat, '"*Hail, King of Scotland."*'

The curtain falls.

II

'Cip,' Peregrine said, 'you'll have to get a cab home. Here's the cash.
Take care of Robin, won't you? Do you know what's happened?'

'It seems – some sort of accident?'

'Yes. To the Macbeth. I've got to stay here. Look, there's a cab.
Get it.'

Crispin darted out and ran towards the taxi, holding up his hand.
He jumped on the platform and the taxi-driver drew up. Peregrine
said: 'In you get, Rob.'

'I thought we were going backstage,' Robin said.

'There's been an accident. Next time.'

He gave the driver their address and Crispin some money and
they were gone. Someone tapped his arm. He turned and found it
was Alleyn.

'I'd better come round, hadn't I?' he said.

'*You!* Yes. You've seen it?'

'Yes.' They found a crowd of people milling about in the alley.

'My God,' said Peregrine. 'The bloody public.'

'I'll try and cope,' Alleyn said.

He was very tall. There was a wooden box at the stage door. He made his way to it and stood on it facing the crowd. 'If you please,' he said, and was listened to.

'You are naturally curious. You will learn nothing and you will be very much in the way if you stay here. Nobody of consequence will be leaving the theatre by this door. Please behave reasonably and go.'

He stood there, waiting.

'Who does he think he is?' said a man next to Peregrine.

'He's Chief Superintendent Alleyn,' said Peregrine. 'You'd better do what he says.'

There was a general murmur. A voice said: 'Aw, come on. What's the use.'

They moved away.

The doorkeeper opened the door to the length of the chain, peered out and saw Peregrine. 'Thank Gawd,' he said. 'Hold on, sir.' He disengaged the chain and opened the door wide enough to admit them. Peregrine said: 'It's all right. This is Chief Superintendent Alleyn,' and they went in.

To a silent place. The stage was lit. Masking pieces rose up; black masses, through which the passage could be seen running under the landing in front of the door to Duncan's chamber. At the far end of this passage, strongly lit, was a shrouded object, a bundle, lying on the stage. A dark red puddle had seeped from under it.

They moved round the set and the stage director came offstage.

'Perry! Thank God,' he said.

'I was in front. So was Superintendent Alleyn. Bob Masters, our stage director; Mr Alleyn.'

'Have you rung the Yard?' Alleyn asked.

'Charlie's doing it,' said Masters, 'now. Our ASM. He's having some difficulty getting a line out.'

'I'll have a word with him,' said Alleyn, and went into the Prompt corner.

'I'm a policeman,' he told Charlie. 'Shall I take over?'

'Ah? Are you? Yes. Hullo? Here's a policeman.' He held out the receiver. Alleyn said: 'Superintendent Alleyn. At the Dolphin. Homicide. Decapitation. That's what I said. I imagine that as I was here I'll be expected to take it on. Yes, I'll hold on while you do.' There was a short interval and he said, 'Bailey and Thompson. Yes. Ask for Inspector Fox to come down. My case is in my room. He'll bring it. Get the doctor. Right? Good.'

He hung up. 'I'll take a look,' he said and went on stage.

Four stagehands and the Property Master were on stage, keeping guard.

'Nobody's gone,' Bob Masters said. 'The company are in their dressing rooms and Peregrine's gone back to the office. There's a sort of conference.'

'Good,' said Alleyn. He walked over to the shrouded bundle. 'What happened after the curtain fell?'

'Scarcely anybody *really* realized it was – not a dummy. The head. The dummy's a very good head. Blood and everything. I didn't realize. I said "Picture" and they took up the final picture and the curtain went up and down. And then Gaston, who carried it on the end of his claidheamh-mor – the great claymore thing he carries throughout the play – that thing – ' He pointed at the bundle.

'Yes?'

'He noticed the blood on his gloves and he looked at them. And then he looked up and it dripped on his face and he screamed. The curtain being down.'

'Yes.'

'We all saw, of course. He let the – the head – on the claymore – fall. The house was still applauding. So I – really I didn't know what I was doing. I went out through the centre break in the curtain and said there'd been an accident and I hoped they'd forgive us not taking the usual calls and go home. And I came off. By that time,' said Mr Masters, 'panic had broken out in the cast. I ordered them all to their rooms and I covered the head with that cloth – it's used on the props table, I think. And Props sort of tucked it under. And that's all.'

'It's very clear indeed. Thank you, Mr Masters. I think I'll look at the head now, if you please. I can manage for myself.'

'I'd be glad not to.'

'Yes, of course,' said Alleyn.

He squatted down, keeping clear of the puddle. He took hold of the cloth and turned it back.

Sir Dougal stared up at him through the slits in his mask. The eyes were bloodshot and glazed. The steel guard over his mouth had fallen away and the mouth was stretched in a clown's grin. Alleyn saw that he had been struck from behind: the wound was clean and the margin turned outward. He covered the face.

'The weapon?' he asked.

'We think it must be this,' Masters said. 'At least, I do.'

'This is the weapon carried by Seyton?'

'Yes.'

'It's bloodied, of course.'

'Yes. It would be anyway. *And* with false blood too. There's false blood over everything. But – ' Masters shuddered – 'they're mixed.'

'Where's the false head?'

'The false –? I don't know. We haven't looked.'

Alleyn walked into the OP corner. It was encircled with scenery masking pieces and very dark. He waited for his eyes to adapt. In the darkest corner, on the stage, a man's form slowly assembled itself, its head face down. Its *head*?

He moved towards it, stooped down and touched the head. It shifted under his fingers. It was the dummy. He touched the body. It was flesh – and blood. And dead. And headless.

Alleyn moved back and returned to the stage.

There was a loud knocking on the stage door.

'I'll go,' said Masters.

It was the Yard. Inspector Fox and Sergeants Bailey and Thompson. Fox was the regular, old-style, plain-clothes man: grizzled, amiable and implacable.

He said: 'Visiting your old haunts, are you, sir?'

'Nearly twenty years ago, isn't it, Br'er Fox? And you two. I want you to give the full treatment, photos, prints, the lot, to that head on stage there, covered up, and the headless body in the dark corner over there. They parted company just before the final curtain. All right? And the dummy head in the corner. The assumed weapon is the claymore on which the real head's fixed, so include that in the party. Any more staff coming?'

'Couple of uniform coppers. Any moment now.'

'Good. Front doors and stage door for them. On guard.'

He turned to Masters. 'We'll need to know who to inform. Can you help?'

'There's his divorced wife. No children. Winty may know. Mr Winter Morris.'

'He's still here?' Alleyn exclaimed.

'In the office. With Peregrine Jay. Discussing what we're to do.'

'Ah yes. You've got tomorrow, Sunday, to make up your minds.'

He looked at the stage crew. 'You've had a bit of a job. Which of you is responsible for the properties?'

Props made an awkward movement.

'You are? I'm afraid I must ask you to wait a little longer. The foreman? I'm sorry but you and you three men will have to wait, too. There's no need for you to remain on stage any longer. Thank you.' The men moved off into the shadows.

Bailey and Thompson assembled their gear.

'You'll want the lights man, won't you?' Alleyn said. 'Is he here?'

'Here,' said the lights man, who was with Charlie, the assistant stage manager.

'Right! I'll leave you to it. Don't touch anything.' And to Masters: 'Where does Mr Gaston Sears dress?'

'I'll show you,' said Masters.

He led Alleyn into the world of dressing rooms. They walked down a passage with doors on either side and the occupants' names on them. It was very, very quiet until they came to Nina Gaythorne's room. Her voice, high-pitched and hysterical, sounded incomprehensibly beyond the closed door.

Gaston's room was not much more than a cubicle at the end of the passage. Masters tapped on the door and the deep voice boomed: 'Come in.' Masters opened the door.

'These two gentlemen would like a word with you, Gaston,' he said, and made his way back pretty quickly.

There was only just room for Alleyn and Fox. They edged in and with difficulty shut the door.

Gaston had changed into a black dressing gown and had removed his make-up. He was sheet-white but perfectly composed. He gave his name and address before being asked to do so.

Alleyn exclaimed: 'Ah, I was right. You won't remember me but I called on you several years ago, Mr Sears, and asked you to give us the date and value of a claidheamh-mor, part of a burglar's haul we had recovered.'

'I remember it very well. It was of no great antiquity but it was, as far as that went, not a fake.'

'That's the one. Tragically enough, it's about a claidheamh-mor that I'd like to ask you a few questions now.'

'I shall be glad to offer an opinion, particularly as you use the correct term correctly pronounced. It is my own property and it is an authentic example of the thirteenth-century fighting tool of the Scottish nobleman. In our production I carry it on all ceremonial occasions. It weighs . . .'

He sailed off into a catalogue of details and symbolic significance and from thence into a list of previous owners. The further he retreated into history the murkier did his anecdotes become. Alleyn and Fox stood jammed together. Fox had with difficulty drawn his notebook from his breast pocket and had opened it in readiness, when Alleyn nudged him, to record anything that seemed to be of interest.

'. . . as with many other such tools – Excalibur is one – there has grown up with the centuries the belief that the weapon, whose name (I translate "Gut-ravager") is engraved in a Celtic device on the hilts, is possessed of magic powers. Be that as it may . . .' he paused to draw breath and take thought.

'You would not wish to let it out of your grasp,' Alleyn cut in and nudged Fox. 'Naturally.'

'Naturally. But also I was obliged to do so. Twice. When I joined the murderers of Banquo and when I came off in the last scene. After Macbeth said "*A time for such a word*," the Property man took it from me in order to affix the head. I *made* the head. I could be thought to have the ability to place it on the claidheamh-mor but unfortunately when I did so the first time, I made a childish error and the weapon, which is extremely sharp, pierced the top of the head and it swung about in a ludicrous fashion. So it was thought better to mend the hole and let Props fix it. He had to ladle blood on it.'

'And he returned it to you?'

'He put it in the OP corner, on the left as you go in. Nobody else was allowed to go into the corner because of Macbeth and Macduff coming off after their fight, straight into it. I should have said, perhaps, that it is not *pitch* dark all the time. It was made so for the end of the fight to guard against anyone in front at the extreme right or in the Prompt boxes seeing Macbeth recover himself. A curtain, upstage of it, was closed by a stagehand as soon as their fight was engaged.'

'Yes. I've got that.'

'Props put the claidheamh-mor in the corner some time before the end of the fight. I took it up at the last moment before Macduff and I re-entered.'

'So Macbeth came off, screamed, was decapitated by the claidheamh-mor from which the dummy's head had been pulled. The real head now replaced it.'

'I – yes, I confess I had not worked it out so carefully but – yes, I suppose so. I *think* there would be time.'

'And room? To swing the weapon?'

'There is always room. Macduff, under my instruction, swung his weapon up while still in view of the audience and brought it down when he was just out of view in the OP corner. There was room. I was up at the back talking to the King and Props and others. I saw Macduff come off. I have grown more and more certain,' said Gaston, 'that there is a malign influence at work, that the claidheamh-mor has a secret life of its own. It is satisfied now. We hope. We hope.'

He gazed at Alleyn. 'I am extremely tired,' he said. 'It has been an alarming experience. Horrifying, really. It must be something I have done. I didn't look up at first. It was dark. I took it and engaged the hilts in my harness and entered behind Macduff. And when I looked up it dropped blood on my face. What have I done? How have I, who bought and treasured it, committed an offence? Is it because I have allowed it to be used in a public display? True, I *have* done so. I have carried it.' His piercing eyes brightened. He re-assumed his commanding posture. 'Can it have been the accolade?' he asked. 'Was I being admitted to some esoteric comradeship and baptized with blood?' He made a helpless gesture. 'I am confused.'

'We won't worry you any more just now, Mr Sears. You've been very helpful.'

They found their way back to the stage where Bailey and Thompson squatted, absorbed, over their unspeakable tasks.

'Not much doubt about the weapon, Mr Alleyn,' said Bailey. 'It's this thing it's stuck on. Sharp! Like a razor. And there's the marks, see. Done from the back when the victim's bending over. Clean as a whistle.'

'Yes, I see. Prints?'

'He was wearing gloves. Gauntlets. Whoever he was. They all were.'

'Thompson, have you got all the shots you want?'

'Yes, thanks. Close up. All round. And the whole thing.'

There was the sound of the stage door being opened and a quick, incisive voice. 'All right. Dark, isn't it? Where's the body?'

'Sir James,' Alleyn called. 'Here!'

'Hullo, Rory. Up to your old games, are you?'

Sir James Curtis appeared, immaculate in dinner jacket and black overcoat and carrying his bag. 'I was at a party at St Thomas's. What have you got – Good God, what is all this?'

'All yours at the moment,' said Alleyn.

Bailey and Thompson had stepped aside. Macdougal's head on the end of the claidheamh-mor stared up at the pathologist. 'Where's the body?' he asked.

'In the dark corner over there. We haven't touched it.'

'What's the story?'

Alleyn told him. 'I was in front,' he said.

'Extraordinary. I'll look at the body.'

It lay face down. The rudimentary Macbeth tartan was wrapped around the left arm and tucked under the shield-fastening and the other end secured by a brooch to the shoulder. Sir James looked at the wound. The lip was turned in and a piece of the collar was sliced across it into the gash.

'One blow,' he said. He bent over the body. 'Better get the remains to the mortuary. If your men have finished.'

They went back on stage.

'You may separate them,' said Alleyn.

Bailey produced a large plastic bag. He then laid hold of the head. Thompson with both hands on the hilts grasped the claidheamh-mor. They faced each other, their feet apart and the blade parallel with the stage: a parody of artisans sweating it out in hell.

'Right?'

'Right.'

'Go.'

The sound was the worst part of it. It resembled the drawing of an enormous cork. It was effective. Bailey put the head in the bag, wrote on a label and tied it up. He put the bag in a canvas container. 'I'll stow this away,' he said and went out to the police car with it.

'What about the weapon?' asked Thompson.

'There's a sort of cardboard thing for it,' said Alleyn. 'On the props table. It'll lie from end to end along the backs of the seats or on the floor. Then the body and the dummy head. You'll go straight to the mortuary, I suppose?'

'Yes. And you'll be here for some time to come?' said Sir James.

'Yes.'

'I'll ring you if anything turns up.'

'Thanks.'

The ambulance men came in and put the body into a plastic bag and the bag on a stretcher and covered it. They carried it out and drove away. Sir James got into his car and followed them.

Alleyn said, 'Come on, Fox. We'll find the Property man.'

Masters was waiting offstage for them.

'I thought you might use the greenroom as an office,' he said. 'I'll show you where it is.'

'That's very thoughtful. I'll see the Property man there.'

The greenroom was a comfortable place with armchairs, books, a solid table and framed photographs and pictures on the walls. They settled themselves at the table.

'Hullo, Ernie,' said Alleyn when he came in. 'We don't know your surname, I'm afraid. What is it?'

'James, sir.'

'Ernest James. We won't keep you long, I hope. This is a pretty grim business, isn't it?'

'Bloody awful.'

'You've been on the staff for a long time, haven't you?'

'Fifteen year.'

'Long as that? Sit down, why don't you?'

'Aw. Ta,' said Ernie and sat.

'We're trying at the moment to sort out when the crime was committed and then when the heads were changed. Macbeth's last words are "*Hold, enough.*" He and Macduff then fight and a marvellous fight it was. He exits and we assume was killed at once. There's a pause. Then pipe and drums coming nearer and nearer. Then a prolonged entry of everyone left alive in the cast. Then dialogue between

Malcolm and Old Siward. Macduff comes in with Gaston Sears following him, the head on his giant weapon.'

'Was you in front, then, guv'nor?'

'Yes, as it happened.'

'Gawd, it was awful. Awful.'

'It was indeed. Tell me, Props. When did you put the dummy head on the claymore and when did you put them in the OP corner?'

'Me? Yeah, well. I got hold of the bloody weapon – it's sharp as hell – off 'is Lordship when he came off after the Chief said "*There'd 'ave been a time for such a word*," whatever that may mean. I took it up to the props table, see, and I put the dummy on it. That took a bit of time and handling, like. What with the sharpness and the length, it was awkward. The 'ed's stuffed full of plaster except for a narrer channel and I had to fit it into the channel and shove it home. It kind of locked. And then I doused it with "blood" rahnd the neck and put it in the corner.'

'When?'

'I got faster with practice. Took me about three minutes, I'd say. Simon Morten was shouting "*Make all our trumpets speak.*" Round about then.'

'And there it remained until Gaston collected it and carried it on – with a different head – at the very end.'

'Correct.'

'Right. We'll ask you to sign a statement to that effect later on. Can you think of anything at all that could help us? Anything out of the ordinary? Superstitions, for instance.'

'Nuffink,' he said quickly.

'Sure of that?'

'Yer.'

'Thank you, Ernie.'

'Fanks, guv. Can I go home?'

'Where do you live?'

'Six Jobbins Lane. Five minutes' walk.'

'Yes. All right.' Alleyn wrote on a card. *Ernest James. Permission to leave. R. Alleyn.* 'Here you are. Show it to the man at the door.'

'You're a gent, guv. Fanks,' Ernie repeated and took the card.

But he did not go. He shuffled towards the door and stood there, looking from Alleyn to Fox who had put on his steel-rimmed glasses and now contemplated him over the tops.

'Is there something else?' Alleyn asked.

'I don't fink so. No.'

'Sure?'

'Yer,' said Ernie and was gone.

'There *was* something else,' Fox observed tranquilly.

'Yes. We'll leave him to simmer.'

There was a sharp rap at the door.

'Come in,' Alleyn called. And Simon Morten came in.

III

He had changed, of course, into his street clothes. Alleyn wondered if he was dramatically and habitually pale or if the shock of the appalling event had whitened him out of all semblance to normality.

'Mr Morten?' Alleyn said. 'I was just going to ask if you would come in. Do sit down. This is Inspector Fox.'

'Good evening, sir. May I have your address?' asked Fox, settling his glasses and taking up his pen.

Simon had not expected this bland reception. He hesitated, sat down, and gave his blameless address as if it was that of an extremely disreputable brothel.

'We are trying to get some sort of pattern into the sequence of events,' Alleyn said. 'I was in front tonight, which may be a bit of a help but not, I'm afraid, very much. Your performance really is wonderful: that fight! I was in a cold sweat. You must be remarkably fit, if I may say so. How long has it taken you to bring it up to this form?'

'Five weeks' hard rehearsal and we've still –' He stopped. 'Oh God!' he said. 'I actually forgot what has happened – I mean that – ' He put his hands over his face. 'It's so incredible. I mean . . .' He dropped his hands and said: 'I'm your prime suspect, aren't I?'

'To be that,' said Alleyn, 'you would have to have pulled off the dummy head and used the claidheamh-mor to decapitate the victim. *He* would have to have waited there and suffered his own execution without raising a finger to stop you. Indeed, he would have obligingly stooped over so that you could take a fair swipe at him. You would have dragged the body to the extreme corner and put the dummy head on it. Then you would have put the real head on the end of the claidheamh-mor and placed them both in position for Gaston to take them up. All in about three minutes.'

Simon stared at him. A faint colour crept into his cheeks.

'I hadn't thought of it like that,' he said.

'No? Well, I may have slipped up somewhere but that's how it seems to me. Now,' said Alleyn, 'when you've got over your shock, do you mind telling me exactly what did happen when you chased him off.'

'Yes, certainly. Nothing.'

'Nothing?'

'Well, he screamed and fell as usual and I ran out. Then I just hung around with all the others who'd been called until I got my cue and re-entered. I said my final speech ending *"Hail, King of Scotland."* I didn't turn to look at Seyton carrying – that thing. I just pointed my sword at it while facing upstage. I thought some of them looked and sounded – well – peculiar, but they all shouted and the curtain came down.'

'Couldn't be clearer. What sort of man was Macdougal?'

'Macdougal? Sir Dougal? Good-looking, if you like the type.'

'In himself?'

'Typical leading man, I suppose. He was very good in the part.'

'You didn't go much for him?'

He shrugged. 'He was all right.'

'A bit too much of a good thing?'

'Something like that. But, really, he *was* all right.'

'De mortuis nil nisi bonum?'

'Yes. Well, I didn't know anything that was *not* good about him. Not really. He was fabulous in the fight. I never felt in danger. Even Gaston said he was good. You couldn't fault him. God! I'm the understudy! If it's decided we go on.'

'Will it be so decided, do you think?'

'I don't know. I daren't think.'

'"The show must go on"?'

'Yes. I suppose,' Simon said after a pause, 'it may depend on the press.'

'The *press*?'

'Yes. If they've got a clue as to what happened they could make such a hoo-hah we couldn't very well go on as if Macbeth was ill or dying or dead or anything of that sort, could we? But if they only get a second-hand account of there having been an "accident", which is what Bob Masters said in his curtain speech, they may decide it's not worth a follow-up and do nothing. Tomorrow. One thing is certain,' said Simon, 'we don't need a word of publicity.'

'No. Has it occurred to you,' said Alleyn, 'that it might strike someone as a good moment to revive all the superstitious stories about *Macbeth*?'

Simon stared at him. 'Good God! No, it hadn't. But you're dead right. As a matter of fact – well, never mind about all that. But Perry, our director, had been on at us about the idiot superstitions and not to believe any of it and – and – well, all that.'

'Really? Why?'

'He doesn't believe in any of it,' said Simon, looking extremely ill at ease.

'Has there been an outbreak of superstitious observances in the cast?'

'Well – Nina Gaythorne rather plugs it.'

'Yes?'

'Perry thinks it's a bad idea.'

'Have there been any occurrences that seemed to bolster up the superstitions?'

'Well – sort of.'

'What, for instance?'

'If you don't mind I'd rather not go into details.'

'Why?'

'We said we wouldn't talk about them. We promised Perry.'

'I'll ask Jay to elucidate.'

'Yes. Well, don't let him think I blew the gaff, will you?'

'No.'

'If you don't want me any more . . .?'

'I don't think I do. We'll ask you to sign a typed statement later on.'

'I see. Well, thank you,' said Simon and got up. 'You did mean what you said? About it being impossible for me to have – done it?'

'Yes. Unless some sort of crack appears, I mean it.'

'Thank God for *that*, at least,' said Simon. 'Good night.'

'Good night, Mr Morten.'

He went to the door, hesitated and spoke.

'If I'd wanted to kill him,' he said, 'I could have faked it during the fight. And been "terribly sorry". You know?'

'Yes,' said Alleyn. 'There's that, too, isn't there? Good night.'

When he had gone, Fox said: 'That's one we can tick off, isn't it?'

'At this point, Fox.'

'He doesn't seem to have liked the deceased much, does he?'

'Not madly keen, no. But very honest about it as far as it went. He was on the edge of talking about the superstitions but pulled himself up short and said Jay extracted promises not to gossip about the aspect.'

'That's right. So who do you see next?'

'Obviously, Peregrine Jay.'

'He was here twenty years ago, at the time of the former case. Nice young chap he was then.'

'Yes. He's in conference. Up in the offices,' said Alleyn.

'Shall I pluck him out?'

'Would you?'

Fox removed his spectacles, put them in his breast pocket and left the room. Alleyn walked about, muttering to himself.

'It *must* have been then. After the fight. Say, one minute for the pause and the pipe and drums coming nearer, two at the outside. The general entry: say a quarter of a minute, Siward's dialogue about his son's death. Another two minutes. Say three to four minutes all told. Macbeth exits and yells. Macduff says something that makes him stoop or – no – he *did* fall forward to give the thud. The man, having removed the dummy head, decapitates him, gathers up the real head and jams it on the claidheamh-mor. That's what takes the time. Does he wedge the hilts against the scenery and then push the head on? He lugs the body into the darkest corner and stands the claidheamh-mor in its place ready for Gaston to grasp it. He puts the dummy head by the body. And that's it. Where does he go now? What does he look like?'

He stopped short, closed his eyes and recalled the fight. The two figures. The exchange of dialogue and Macbeth's hoarse final curse.

'And damned be him that first cries, "Hold, enough!"'

'It must have been done after the fight. There's no other way. Or is there? Is there? Nonsense.'

The door opened. Fox, Winter Morris and Peregrine came in.

'I'm sorry to drag you away,' said Alleyn.

'It's all right. We'd come to a deadlock. To go on. Or not.'

'A difficult decision?'

'Yes. As a matter of fact I was going to ask you how much longer . . .' said Morris.

'We'll have finished here tomorrow. Possibly tonight. The body has been removed to the mortuary and the *op* corner is now being examined. We'll clean up.'

'I see. Thank you.'

'How will the actors feel?'

'About going on? Not very happy but they'll do it.'

'And the new casting?'

'There's the rub,' said Peregrine. 'Simon Morten is Macbeth's understudy and the Ross is Simon's. We'll have to knock up a new, very simple fight, a new Macduff can't possibly manage the present one. Simon's good and ready. He'll give a reasonable show, but the whole thing's pretty dicey.'

'Yes. What sort of actor is Gaston Sears?'

Peregrine stared at him. 'Gaston? *Gaston?*'

'He knows – or rather he invented – the fight. He's an arresting figure. It's a very far-fetched notion but I wondered.'

'It's – it's a frightening thought. I haven't seen him acting but I'm told he was good in an unpredictable sort of way. He's a *very* unpredictable person. A bit on the dotty side, some of them think. It – it certainly would solve a lot of problems. We'd only need to find a new Seyton and he's a tiny part as far as lines go. He's only got to look impressive. There's a tall, dark chap . . . My God, I wonder . . . No. *No,*' repeated. And then: 'We may decide to cut our losses and rehearse a new play. Probably the best solution.'

'Yes. I think I should remind you that – it's a dazzling glimpse of the obvious – the murderer (and who he is I've not the faintest notion) must be one of your actors or else a stagehand. If the latter, I suppose you can go ahead, but if the former – well, the mind boggles, doesn't it?'

'I can feel mine boggling anyway.'

'In the meantime I'd like to know what the story is, about the *Macbeth* superstitions and why Props and Simon Morten go all peculiar when I ask them.'

'It doesn't matter, now. I'd asked them not to talk to each other or to anyone else about these – happenings. You've got to consider the general atmosphere.'

And he told Alleyn, sparingly, about the dummy heads and the rat's head in Rangi's marketing bag.

'Have you any idea who the practical joker was?'

'None. Nor do I know if there is any link with the subsequent horror.'

'It sounds like an unpleasant schoolboy's nonsense.'

'It certainly isn't our young William's nonsense,' said Peregrine quickly. 'He was scared as hell at the head on the banquet table. He's a very nice small boy.'

'He'd have to be an infant Goliath to lift the claidheamh-mor two inches.'

'Yes. He would, wouldn't he?'

'Where is he?'

'Bob Masters sent him home. Straight away. He didn't want him to see it. Gaston dropped the claidheamh-mor and head on the stage. The boy was waiting to go on for the curtain call. Bob told him there'd been a hitch and there wasn't to be a call and to get into his own clothes quick and go home.'

'Yes. William Smith, Fox. In case we want him. Has he got a telephone number?'

'Yes,' said Peregrine. 'We've got it. Shall I – ?'

'I don't think we want it tonight. We'll ask the King and Props to confirm that Gaston Sears stood with the boy offstage. And that Macduff came straight off. If this is so, it completely clears Macduff. And Gaston, of course.'

'Yes.'

'During the fight, Malcolm and Old Siward with Ross and Caithness assembled on the Prompt upper landing, out of sight, waiting for their final entrance. The rest of the forces waited on the OP side. The "dead" characters – the King, Banquo, Lady Macduff and her son were also waiting OP for the second curtain call. The witches were alone upstage.'

'Yes.'

'Therefore he *must* have been decapitated in the interval between his and Macduff's exit, fighting, and Macduff and Gaston's re-entry with his head.'

'Yes,' said Peregrine wearily. 'And it's three and a half minutes at the most.'

'We'll now summon the rest of the company and get them, if they can, to give each other alibis for that period.'

'Shall I call them?'

'In here, if you would. I don't want them on stage just yet. Nor, I think, do they want it. Thank you, Jay. It'll be a squash but never mind.'

Peregrine went out. Winter Morris, who had stood inside the door without speaking, came to Alleyn's table and put a folded paper on it.

'I think you should see this,' he said. 'Perry agrees.'

Alleyn opened it.

The tannoy boomed out: 'Everyone in the greenroom, please. Company and staff call. Everyone in the greenroom.'

Alleyn read the typed message: '*murderers sons in your co.*'

'When did you get it? And how?' Winty told him.

'Is it true?'

'Yes,' said Winty miserably.

'Does anyone else know?'

'Perry thinks Barrabell does. The Banquo.'

'Spiteful character?'

'Yes.'

'It refers to the little Macduff boy, William Smith. I represented the police in the case,' Alleyn said. 'He was a little chap of six then but I recognized him. He's got a very distinctive face. One of the victims was named Barrabell. Bank clerk. She was beheaded,' said Alleyn. 'Here come the actors.'

IV

By using a considered routine they managed to extract the information wanted in reasonable time.

The alibis of Gaston Sears, Props and Macduff were secured. Alleyn read the names out from his programme and each in turn was remembered as being offstage in the group of waiting actors. The King and Nina Gaythorne were whispering to Gaston. Her dress was caught up.

'I want you to be very sure how you answer the next question. Does anyone remember any movement among you all that could have meant someone had slipped into the OP corner after Macduff came out?'

'We were too far upstage to do it,' said Simon. 'All of us.'

'And does anyone remember Macbeth *not* coming off?'

There was a pause and then Nina Gaythorne said: 'William said: "Where's Sir Dougal? He's still in there." Or something like that. Nobody paid much attention. Our cue was coming and we were getting into position to go on for the second call.'

'Yes,' Alleyn said. 'Now, I wonder if you would all go to your rooms and come out when you are called, as far as you can remember, exactly in the order you observed tonight. From the start of the fight until the end I want you all to do *exactly* what you did then. Is that understood?'

'Not very pleasant,' said Barrabell.

'Murder and its consequences are never very pleasant, I'm afraid. Mr Sears, will you read Macbeth's lines, if you please?'

'Certainly. I know them, I think, by heart.'

'Good. You had better have a look, though. The timing must be exact.'

'Very well.'

'There's a book on the prompt table.'

'Thank you.'

'Do you know the moves?'

'Certainly. I also,' he said loftily, 'know the fight.'

'Good. Are we ready? Will those of you who were in their dressing rooms please go to them?'

They trooped off. Alleyn said to Peregrine: 'You take over, will you?'

'Very well.' He raised his voice: 'From:

'"*Blow wind, come wrack,*
At least we'll die with harness on our back."'

'We'll go out on stage. It's tidied up, I hope,' Alleyn said.

'I hope so,' said Peregrine devoutly.

'Come on, then. Fox, you watch the stage. The OP side in particular, will you?'

'Right.'

'Is the effects man here? He is. With his assistants? I think mechanical effects were overlaid by live voices. Good. We want the whole thing exactly timed as for performance. Right? Can you manage?'

They walked down the dressing-room passages and suddenly the theatre was alive with the presence of actors waiting behind closed doors for the play to begin. Thompson and Bailey had been tidy. They left the patch of stage where the bundle had been covered over with a mackintosh sheet weighted down. In the OP corner, they had outlined the body in chalk before removing it. There was a bucket of 'blood' beside it.

'Right,' said Alleyn who had moved into the house front. Peregrine called: 'Macbeth. Macduff. Young Siward. You're on, please. Malcolm, Old Siward and the Forces. Called and waiting.' There was the sound of movements offstage. Malcolm and Siward spoke and went off.

Gaston entered and spoke. The others had given their lines automatically and not played up to performance pitch but he went the whole hog. His fatigue vanished and he was good.

'"*At least we'll die with harness on our back,*"' he ended and went off into the OP area and through it. He waited offstage.

They played through the battle scenes to the point where Macbeth entered on the platform OP and Macduff entered from Prompt corner.

'*Turn, hell-hound. Turn.*'

The fight. Gaston was perfect. Macduff, who looked exhausted and tried to go through it at token speed, was forced to respond fully.

Exeunt. Macbeth's scream, cut off. Macduff ran straight through and out. Alleyn set his watch.

There followed the long triumphant entry and final scene with Old Siward. Macduff re-entered OP corner. Gaston reverted to Seyton and came on, without the claidheamh-mor, behind him. He proclaimed in his natural tones: 'I assume my claidheamh-mor is not to be found. I presume it has been seized by the police. I take this opportunity,' he went on, pitching his considerable voice into the auditorium, 'of warning them that they do so at their peril. There is strength in the weapon.'

'The claidheamh-mor is perfectly safe in our keeping,' said Alleyn.

'It may be, and doubtless is, safe. It is the police who should be trembling.'

Before addressing the actors Alleyn allowed himself a moment to envisage this situation.

'Thank you, gentlemen,' Alleyn said. 'It was asking a lot of all of you to re-enact the last scene but I think I can tell you that you have really helped us. Now, if you will do the same thing again with the scene immediately before it, from "*brandished by man that's of a woman born*" up to "*Enter, sir, the castle,*" I think you will then be free to go home. It's Macduff's soliloquy. I want you all in your given places. With offstage action and noises, please. Jay, would you?'

Peregrine said: 'It's where the group of Macduff's soldiers run across and upstairs. Right? Simon?'

'Oh God. Yes. All right,' said the exhausted Simon.

'Ready, everybody. "*Brandished by man that's of a woman born.*"'

The speech was broken by offstage entries, excursions and alarms. Alleyn timed it. Three minutes. Macbeth entered on OP rostrum.

'Right. Thank you very much, Mr Morten. And Mr Sears. We've not established your own movements, Mr Sears, as you've been kind enough to impersonate Macbeth's. Can you now tell us where you were over this period?'

'Certainly. On the OP side but not in the darkened corner. I remained there throughout, keeping out of the way of the soldiers who entered and exited in some disorder. I may say their attempts at soldierly techniques during these exercises was pitiful. However, I was not consulted and I kept my opinions to myself. I spoke, I believe, to several fellow players during this period. Those who were called for the final curtain – Miss Gaythorne, I recall – advanced some astonishing claptrap about garlic as a protection against bad luck. Duncan was one. Banquo was another. He complained, I recollect, that he was called too soon.'

Duncan and Banquo agreed. Several other actors recalled seeing Gaston there, earlier in the action.

'Thank you very much,' said Alleyn. 'That's all, ladies and gentle-men. You may go home. Leave your dressing-room keys with us. We'd be grateful if you would arrange to be within telephone call. Good night.'

They said good night and left the theatre in ones and twos. Gaston wore his black cloak clutched histrionically above his chest in an actor's hand. He bowed to Alleyn and said: 'Good night, sir.'

'Good night, Mr Sears. I'm afraid the fight was a severe ordeal: you are still breathless. You shouldn't have been so enthusiastic.'

'No, no! A touch of asthma. It is nothing.' He waved his hand and made an exit.

The stagehands went at once and all together. At last there was only Nina Gaythorne and one man left, a pale, faintly ginger, badly dressed man with a beautiful voice.

'Good night, Superintendent,' he said.

'Good night, Mr Barrabell,' Alleyn returned and became immersed in his notebook.

'A very interesting treatment, if I may say so.'

'Thank you.'

'If I may say so, there was no need, really, to revive anything before Macbeth's exit and from then up to the appearance of his head. About four minutes, during which time he was decapitated.'

'Quite so.'

'So I wondered.'

'Did you?'

'Poor dotty old Gaston,' said the beautiful voice, 'having to labour through that fight. Why?'

Alleyn said to Fox: 'Just make sure the rooms are all locked, will you, Mr Fox?'

'Certainly, sir,' said Fox: He walked past Barrabell as if he was not there, and disappeared.

'One of the old type,' said Barrabell. 'We don't see many of them nowadays, do we?'

Alleyn looked up from his notebook. 'I'm very busy,' he said.

'Of course. Young Macduff is not with us, I see.'

'No, Mr Barrabell. They sent him home. Good night to you.'

'You know who he is, of course?'

'Of course.'

'Oh? Oh well, good night,' said Barrabell. He walked away with his head up and a painful smile on his face. Nina went with him.

'Br'er Fox,' said Alleyn when that officer returned, 'let us consider. Is it possible for the murder to have been performed after the fight?'

'Just possible. Only just. But it *was*.'

'Shall we try? I'll be the murderer. You be Macbeth. Run into the corner. Scream and drop down. Hold on.' He went into the dark area, OP. 'We'll imagine the Macduff. He runs after you and goes straight on and away. Ready? I'm using my stopwatch. Three, two, one, zero. Go.'

Mr Fox was surprisingly agile. He imitated swordplay, backed off-stage, yelled and fell at Alleyn's feet. Alleyn had removed the imaginary dummy head from the imaginary claidheamh-mor. He raised the latter above his shoulder. It swept down. Alleyn let go, stooped and seized the imaginary head. He fixed it on the point of the claymore and rammed it home. He propped it in its corner, dragged the body (Mr Fox weighing fourteen stone) into the darkest corner, and clapped the dummy head down by it. And looked at his watch.

'Four and a third minutes,' he panted. 'And the cast made it in three. It's impossible.'

'You don't seem as disappointed as I'd have expected,' said Fox.

'Don't I? I – I'm not sure. I may be going dotty. I *am* going dotty. Let's check the possibles, Fox. Which is Number One?'

'Macduff? He killed Macbeth as we were meant to think. Duel. Chased him off. Killed him. Fixed the head on the weapon and came on with Seyton carrying it behind him. Sounds simple.'

'But isn't. What was Macbeth doing? Macduff chased him in and then had to dodge about, take the dummy head off the claidheamh-mor, raise it and do the fell deed.'

'Yerse.'

'Did Macbeth lie there and allow him to get on with it? And how about the time? If I couldn't do it in three minutes, nobody else could.'

'Well, no. No.'

'Next?'

'Banquo?' Fox suggested.

'He could have done it. He was hanging about in that region after he was called. He could have slipped in and removed the dummy head. Waited there for the end of the duel. Done it. Fixed the head. And walked out in plenty of time for the second curtain call. He was wearing his bloodied cloak, which would have accounted for any awkward stains. Next?'

'Duncan and/or one of his sons. Well,' said Fox apologetically, 'it's silly, I know, but they *could* have. If nobody was watching them. And they could have come out just when nobody was there. If it wasn't so beastly it would be funny. The old boy rolling up his sleeves and settling his crown and wading in. *And*, by the way, if there were two of them the time thing vanishes. The King beheads him and drags the body over and puts the dummy head by it while his son puts the real head on the weapon and places them in the corner. However,' said Mr Fox, 'it *is* silly. How about one of the witches? The man-witch?'

'Rangi? Partly Maori. He was wonderful. Those grimaces and the dance. He was possessed. He was also with his girls, and you noted it, all through the crucial time.'

'All right then. The other obvious one. Gaston,' said Fox moodily.

'But *why* obvious? Well, because he's a bit dotty – but that's not enough. Or is it? And again: time. We've got to face it, Fox. For all of them. Except for the royal family, Banquo, and the witches – time! Rangi could have taken a girl in to fix the head on the claidheamh-mor and thus saved about a minute. It's impossible to imagine anybody collaborating with the exuberant Gaston.'

'Anyway,' said Fox, 'we've got to face it. They were all too busy fighting and on-going.'

'It's all approximate. Counsel for the defence, whatever the defence might be, would make mincemeat of it.'

'They talked during the fight. Here.' He flattened out his Penguin copy of the play. 'I got this out of a dressing room,' he said. 'Look. The dialogue was cut pretty severely but there's enough left. Macbeth gets the last word. "*And damned*,"' quoted Mr Fox who read laboriously through his specs, '"*be him that first cries, 'Hold, enough!'*" and with that they set to again. And within the next three minutes, whoever did it, his head was off his shoulders and on the stick.'

'Our case in a nutshell, Br'er Fox.'

'Yerse.'

'And now, if you will, let me examine what may or may not be the side issues in evidence. Where's Peregrine Jay? Has he gone with the others?'

'No,' said Peregrine, 'I've been here all the time.' And he came down the centre aisle into the light. 'Here I am,' he said. 'Not as bright as a button, I fear, but here.'

'Sit down. Did you hear what I said?'

'Yes. I'm glad you said it. I'm going to break my own rule and tell you more fully of what may be, as you've hinted, side issues.'

'I'll be glad to hear you.'

Peregrine went on. He described the unsettling effect of the tales of ill-luck that had grown up round the play of *Macbeth* and his own stern injunctions to the company that they should ignore them.

'The ones most committed, of course, like Nina Gaythorne, didn't obey me but I think, though I can't be sure, that on the whole they were more or less obeyed. For a time, at any rate. And then it began. With the Banquo mask in the King's room.'

He described it. 'It was extraordinarily effective. Glaring there in the shadow. It's like all Gaston's work, extremely macabre. You remember the procession of Banquos in the witches' scene?'

'I do indeed.'

'Well, to come upon one suddenly! I was warned but even then – horrid!'

'Yes.'

'I examined it and I found the arrangement of string connected with the slate-coloured poncho. The head itself was fixed on a coat-hanger and the poncho hung from that. The long end of string reached down to the stage. There is a nail in the wall above the head. The string passed over it and down. To stage level. Now it seemed to me, it still seems to me, that if I'm on the right track this means that the cloak was pulled up to cover the head and the cord fastened down below. I've had a look and there's a crosspiece in the back of the scenery in exactly the right place.'

'It could be lowered from stage level?'

'Yes. The intention being that it remained hidden until Macduff went in.'

'Macduff saw it first. He tried to warn Macbeth.'

'What did you do with it?'

'I called Props and wrapped it up in its cloak and told him to put it with its mates on the property table.'

'And then?'

'The next thing that happened was a servant at the banquet swept off the dish-cover and there underneath was the man's head again. Grinning at Macbeth. It was – well, *awful*. You know?'

'What did you do?'

'I addressed the actors. All of them. I said – the expected things, I suppose. That it was a rather disgusting trick but as none of them was prepared to own up to being the perpetrator I thought the best thing we could do was ignore it. Something like that.'

'Yes. It must have thrown a spanner in your works, didn't it?'

'Of course. But we rose above. Actors are resilient, you know. They react to something with violence and they talk a great deal but they go on. Nobody walked out on us, though there was a nasty feeling in the air. But I really think Rangi's rat's head was the worst.'

'Rangi's rat's head?' Alleyn repeated.

'Well, it was the head that mattered. In his marketing bag. That's what we called their bags – a sort of joke. For the things they collected for their spell, you know – some of them off the corpse on the gallows. Did you know the items they enumerate are really authentic?'

'I didn't know that.'

'Well, they are. *"For a charm of powerful trouble."* There's no mention of a rat's head, though.'

'Have you got your own ideas about the author of these tricks?'

'I have, yes. But they are not supported by any firm evidence. Merely unsecured ideas. They couldn't be vaguer. They arise from a personal distaste.'

'Can we hear them? We won't attach too much importance to them.'

Peregrine hesitated. Mr Fox completed his notes and looked benevolently at him, his vast hand poised over the notebook.

'Have you spoken to Barrabell? The Banquo.'

'Not really,' said Alleyn. 'Only to get his name and address and a very few bits of information about the other people's positions.'

'He's a strange one. Beautiful voice, well managed. A mischief-maker. He belongs to some way-out society, the Red Fellowship, I think it's called. He enjoys making sneaky little underhand jokes about other actors. I find myself thinking of him as a sea-lawyer. He's always making objections to "business" in the play, which doesn't endear him to me, of course.'

'Of course not.'

'I think he knows about young William.'

Alleyn took the folded paper from his pocket, opened it and showed it to Peregrine.

'This was left in Winter Morris's office and typed on the machine there?'

Peregrine looked at it. 'Yes,' he said. 'Winty told me.'

'Did you guess who did it?'

'Yes. I thought so. Barrabell. It was only a guess but he was about. In the theatre at that time. The sort of thing he'd do, I thought.'

'Did you say so to Winter?'

'I did, yes. Winty says he went to the loo. It was the only time the room was free. About five minutes. There's a window into the foyer. Anybody there could look in, see it was empty and – do it.'

'One of the Harcourt-Smith victims was called Barrabell. Muriel Barrabell. A bank clerk. She was beheaded.'

'Do you think – ?'

'We'll have to find out,' Alleyn said. 'Even so, it doesn't give him a motive to kill Macbeth.'

'And there's absolutely no connection that we know of with poor Sir Dougal.'

'No.'

'Whereas with Simon Morten – ' Perry stopped.

'Yes?'

'Nothing. That sounds as if I was hiding something. I was only going to say Simon's got a hot temper and he suspected Dougal of making passes at the Lady. She put that right with him.'

'He hadn't got the opportunity to do it. He must have chased Macbeth off with his own blunt weapon raised. He'd have to change his weapon for the real claidheamh-mor, from which he had to remove the dummy head while his victim looked on, did nothing and then obligingly stooped over to receive the stroke.'

'And Gaston?'

'First of all, time. I've done it in dumb show myself, all out and way over the time. And what's even more convincing, Gaston was seen by the King and Nina Gaythorne and, as they came out, by people going on for the call. He actually spoke to them. This was while the murder was taking place. He went into the OP corner and collected the claidheamh-mor at the last moment when Macduff came round and he followed him on.'

Peregrine raised his arms and let them drop. 'Exit Gaston Sears,' he said. 'I don't think I ever really thought he'd done it but I'm glad to have it confirmed. Who's left?'

'Without an alibi? Barrabell. The stagehands. Various thanes. Lady Macbeth. Old Uncle Tom Cobbleigh and all.'

'I'd better go back to the boys in the office. They're trying to make up their minds.'

Alleyn looked at his watch. 'It's ten past two,' he said. 'If they haven't made up their minds I suggest they sleep on it. Are the actors called?'

'For four o'clock this afternoon, poor dears.'

'It's none of my business, of course, but I don't think you should go on with *Macbeth*.'

'No?'

'It's only a matter of time before the truth is known. A very short time probably. You'll get a sort of horror-reaction, a great deal of morbid speculation, and, I should think, the kind of publicity that will be an insult to a beautiful production.'

'Oh.'

'There will be a trial. We hope. Your actors will be pestered by the press. Quite possibly the Harcourt-Smith case will be revived and young William cornered by the tabloids and awful interpretations put on his reactions. He and his mother will be hunted remorselessly.'

'This may happen whatever we do,' said Peregrine unhappily.

'Certainly. But to nothing like the same extent if you don't do this play.'

'No. No, nothing like.' Peregrine got up and walked to the door. 'I'll speak to them,' he said. 'Along those lines. Good night, Alleyn.'

'Good night, my dear chap.'

CHAPTER 7

The Junior Element

It was a quarter past three when Peregrine let himself into his house and gave himself a very stiff whisky and a sandwich and then crept upstairs to bed.

'Hullo,' said Emily. 'You needn't creep about, I waked when you opened the front door.'

He turned on his bedside lamp.

'What's happened?' she said when she saw his face.

'Didn't Cip tell you?'

'Only that there'd been an accident. He said, privately, that Robin didn't understand. Not properly and he wasn't sure that *he* did.'

'Is Robin upset?'

'You know what he's like.'

'Has he gone silent?'

'Yes.'

'I'd better tell you,' said Peregrine. And did.

'Oh, Perry,' she whispered. 'How *awful*!'

'Isn't it?'

'What will you do? Go on?'

'I think not. It's not decided. Alleyn pointed out what would happen.'

'Not the same Mr Alleyn?' she exclaimed.

'Yes. The very same. He was in front last night. He's a Chief Superintendent now. Very grand.'

'Nice?'

'Yes. There's nobody arrested or anything like that. Shall I take a look at the boys?'

'They were both asleep an hour ago. Have a look.'

Peregrine crept along the landing and opened their doors. Steady regular breathing in each room.

He came back to his wife and got into bed.

'Sound asleep,' he said.

'Good.'

'God, I'm tired,' he said. He kissed her and fell asleep.

Maggie Mannering with Nanny was driven home in her hired car. She was in a state of bewilderment. She had heard the cast go by on their way for the second curtain call, the usual storm of applause and the rest of the company's movement forward for the second curtain when everyone except herself and Macbeth went on. She heard Gaston cry out: 'No! For God's sake, no!' and Bob Masters's 'Hold it! Hold everything.' There had been a sudden silence while someone held the curtain back and he went out and then came his voice: 'Ladies and Gentlemen, I regret to tell you there has been an accident . . .'

And then the confused sound of the audience leaving and Masters again, saying 'Clear, please. Everybody off and to their dressing-rooms. Please.' And hurrying figures stumbling past her and asking each other: 'What accident? What's happened?' and Malcolm and the soldiers saying: 'It's him. Did you see? Christ Almighty!'

There was a muddle of human beings, Nanny taking her to her dressing-room and she removing her make-up and Nanny getting her into her street clothes.

'Nanny, what's *happened*? Is it Sir Dougal? *What* accident?'

'Never you mind, dear. We'll be told. All in good time.'

'Go out, Nanny. Ask somebody. Ask Mr Masters. Say I want to *know*.'

Nanny went out. She ran into somebody, another woman, in the passage and there was a gabble of voices. There was no mistaking the high-pitched, nicely articulated wail.

'Nina!' Maggie had called. 'Come in. Come in, darling.'

Nina was in disarray but had changed and had pulled on a tam-o'-shanter of the kind that needs careful adjustment and had not received it. There were traces of mascara under her eyes.

'Maggie!' she cried. 'Oh, Maggie, isn't it awful?'

'Isn't *what* awful? Here. Sit down and pull yourself together, for pity's sake, and tell me. Is somebody dead?'

Nina nodded her head a great many times.

'*Who?* Is it Dougal? Yes? For heaven's sake pull yourself together. Has everybody lost their heads?'

Nina produced a shrill cackle of laughter.

'What *is* it?' Maggie demanded.

'He has,' shrieked Nina. 'Dougal has.'

'Has *what?*'

'Lost his head. I'm telling you. *Lost his head.*'

And while Maggie took in the full enormity of this, Nina broke into an extraordinary diatribe.

'I told you. I told lots of you. You wouldn't listen. It's the *Macbeth* curse, I said. If you make a nonsense of it, it'll strike back. If Perry had listened to me, this wouldn't have happened. You ask Bruce Barrabell, he'll tell you. He knows. Those tricks with heads. They were warnings. And now – look.'

Maggie went to her little drinks cupboard. She was an abstemious woman and it was stocked for visitors rather than herself, but she felt she now needed something, actually to prevent her fainting. The room was unsteady. She poured out two large brandies and gave one to Nina. Both their hands were shaking horridly.

They drank quickly, shuddered and drank again.

Nanny returned. She took one look at them and said: 'I see you know.'

'Sort of,' said Maggie. 'Only what's happened. Not how, or why or anything else.'

'I saw Mr Masters. The first anybody knew was the head carried on by Mr Sears. Mr Masters said that was absolutely all and he's coming to see you as soon as he can. While we were talking a very distinguished-looking gent came up who said he was the Yard. And that's all *I* know,' said Nanny. 'Except that Mr Masters said I could give them your telephone number and after a word with Mr Masters the gentleman said I could take you home. So we'll go home, love, won't we?'

'Yes. What about you, Nina? You could ask to go and I could take you.'

'I said I'd go with Bruce. I'm on his way and he'll drop me. I've finished my drink, thank you all the same, dear Maggie, and I feel better.'

'Come on, then. So do I. I think,' said Maggie. 'Lock up, Nanny. We'll go home. They want our keys, don't they?'

They left their key with Mr Fox. Masters was in deep conference with Alleyn but he saw Maggie and hurried towards her.

'Miss Mannering, I am *so* sorry. I *was* coming. Did Nanny explain? Is your car here? This is appalling, isn't it?'

He went out with them. Their car was waiting and there was still a small crowd in the alleyway. Maggie turned up her collar but was recognized.

'It's Margaret Mannering,' shouted a man. 'What's happened? What was the accident? Hi!'

'I don't know,' she said. Nanny scrambled in beside her and the driver sounded his horn.

The car began to back down the alleyway. Greedy faces at the windows. Impudent faces. Curious, grinning faces. A prolonged hooting and they were in Wharfingers Lane and picking up speed.

'Horrible people,' she said. 'And I thought I loved them.'

She began, helplessly, to cry.

Gaston Sears walked up the path to his front door and let himself in. He was, by habit, a night owl and a lonely bird, too. Would it have been pleasant to have been welcomed home by a tender little woman who would ask him how the day, or rather, the night had gone? And would it have been a natural and admirable thing to have told her? He went into his workroom and switched on the light. The armed Japanese warrior, grimacing savagely, leapt up, menacing him, but he was not alarmed. He found, as he expected, the supper tray left by his Chinese housekeeper. Crab salad and a bottle of a good white wine.

He switched on his heater and sat down to it.

He was hungry but worried. What would be done to his claidheamh-mor? The distinguished-looking policeman had assured him that great care would be taken of it but although he called it by its correct name he did not, he could not, understand. After all, he himself did not fully understand. As things had turned out it had fulfilled its true function but there was no telling, really, if it was satisfied.

He had enjoyed playing Macbeth for the police. He had a most phenomenal memory and years ago had understudied the part. And of course, once memorized, it was never forgotten. It struck him, not for the first time, that if they decided to go on they might ask him to play the part instead of the understudy. He would have played it well.

By Heaven! he thought. They will offer it to me! It would be a good solution. I could wear my own basic Macbeth clothes for the garments. Any personable extra can go on for Seyton. And I invented and know the fight. It went well in their reconstruction. I would have been a success. But it would not be a gracious thing to do. It would be an error in taste. I shall tell them so.

He fell to his crab salad with an appetite and filled his Waterford glass to the brim.

Simon Morten lived in Fulham on the borders of Chelsea. He thought he would walk to St James's and on by way of Westminster where he would probably pick up a cab.

Mentally he went over the fight. Gaston played it all out and backed into the OP. He yelled and fell with a plop. I couldn't have done it, thought Simon. Not in the time. Found the claith-something. Removed the dummy head. Placed it by the body. Two-handed grip on the pommel. Swing it up and what's he doing all the time? For Gaston had gone. He walked off and found him standing with Nina Gaythorne and the King and William. He waited for his re-entrance. Gaston came down and followed him on.

There was the repeat and then the Yard men with their notes and inaudible discussions and then they were told they could all go home.

In a way Simon was actually sorry. There hadn't been time to think coherently. He went to Maggie's dressing-room but she was gone. He went to his own room and found Bruce Barrabell there, putting on his rather dreary overcoat.

'We have to suppose these Yard people think they know what they're doing,' he said. 'I take leave to doubt it.'

Simon got his own coat and put it on.

'Our Mr Sears had himself a marvellous party, didn't he?'

'I thought he was very good.'

'Oh yes. Marvellous. If you were in the mood.'

'Of course. Good night.'

'Good night, Morten,' said Barrabell and Simon took himself off.

He was deadly tired. He had thought the fresh air would revive him but he was beyond that point. He walked quickly but his legs were like logs and each stride took an intense mental effort. Not a soul about and St James's Street a thousand miles away. Big Ben tolled three. The Thames slapped against the embankment. A taxi came out of a side street.

'Taxi! Taxi!'

It wasn't going to stop. '*Taxi!*' cried Simon in despair.

He forced himself to run. It pulled in to the kerb.

'Oh, thank God,' he said. He got into it and gave the address. 'I'm stone-cold sober,' he said, 'but, my God, I'm tired.'

Bruce Barrabell fastened his awful overcoat and pulled on his black beret.

He was going to drop Nina on his way home. She was coming to the Red Fellowship meeting next Sunday and would probably become a member. Not much of a catch but he supposed it was something to have a person from the Dolphin company. He must try to keep her off her wretched superstitious rigmaroles, poor girl.

He lit a cigarette and began to think of the killing of Dougal Macdougal. Just how good was this Alleyn? A hangover from the old school tie days, of course, but probably efficient in his own way. He looked in his drawer and removed a paper. After a moment's hesitation he burnt it with his lighter over an ashtray and then emptied the ash into the wastepaper tin.

We shall see, thought Barrabell. He went along to Nina's dressing-room. She was alone in it, dressed and ready to go.

'This is so kind of you, Bruce,' she said. 'I don't really know quite what's happened to me. It's knocked the stuffing out of me, this awful business. I mean, one keeps asking oneself why. *Why* poor Sir Dougal, I mean, who was so friendly and nice and full of fun always. Who would *want* to do it? And one thinks it must be someone possessed of a devil. Truly, a *devil*. That's what I think, what I firmly believe. A devil.'

'Come on, I'll take you home. You'll feel better when you've had a sleep. We all will.'

'Yes. Perhaps we will. We don't know what the Management will do, do we? You go on and I'll lock up.'

He went out. Nina scrabbled in her handbag and extracted a key.

'We were told to give our keys to those policemen.'

'That's right. I'll hand yours in with mine, if you like.'

She gave it to him. They went out to the desolate stage. The massive Mr Fox sat writing at a little prompter's table. Alleyn wandered about with his hands in his pockets.

'Hullo, Miss Gaythorne,' he said. 'You're late getting away, aren't you? Will you be all right?'

'Yes, thank you. Mr Barrabell is very kindly dropping me. I'm on his way home.'

'Ah yes. I'm afraid all this has been very tiring and confusing for you. The Scots play coming home with a vengeance, isn't it?'

'Oh, if only you believed it! There's so much, so *many* indications. It's so clearly *that*. You know?' she asked. 'They none of them want to face up to it. But I *know*. Sign after sign. Warning after warning. All to do with *heads*. If only they'd listened to me.'

Barrabell was behind her. He put his head on one side and made a long comic face. 'Come along, dear,' he said, 'you'll feel better when you've had a nice sleep, won't you?'

'How do I know I'll get a nice sleep? I'm terrified.'

'Do you live alone, Miss Gaythorne?' Alleyn asked.

'Yes, I do. Quite alone.'

'Well, I'll tell you what to do. When you get home have a very hot bath, make yourself a very hot drink with lots of alcohol in it, get into bed and take two aspirins. Start to write an account of all the warning signs in their right order and exact time and place and I bet you a pound you'll drop off before you've finished. Do you take me?'

She looked at him with a kind of dim relish.

'You're not much like a copper, are you?' she said doubtfully, and then: 'I always enjoy a little flutter. Yes. I take you.'

'Splendid. Fox is our witness. Away you go. Good night and God bless.'

'Oh! Thank you. God bless,' she said carefully.

'Here we go!' said Barrabell in his beautiful voice. He put their keys on the table and then his arm round Nina. 'Come along, Ninie,' he fluted and for the first time he sounded well off-key. 'Beddy-byes.'

The stage door closed behind them.

'That's the last of them, isn't it, Fox?' Alleyn asked.

'The last,' said Mr Fox.

'What's emerged definitely from it all?'

They opened their notebooks. Alleyn also opened his programme.

'We can wipe out most of the smaller parts,' he said. 'They were too active. All the fighting men. When they were offstage they were yelling and bashing away at each other like nobody's business.'

'I stood over by the dark corner and I'll take my oath none of them got within coo-ee of it,' Fox said.

'Yes. They were very well-drilled and supposing one of them got out-of-step-on-purpose, the others would have known and been down on him at once. It may have looked like an Irishman's picnic but they were worked out in inches.'

'You can scratch the lot,' said Fox.

'Gladly,' said Alleyn, and did so.

'Who's left?' he asked.

'Speaking parts. It's easier than it looks. The old Colonel Blimpish chap and his son. Never had a chance. The son was "dead" and lying on the stage, hidden from the audience, and the old boy was stiff-upper-lipping on the stairs while the murder was done.'

'So much for the Siwards. And Malcolm was on stage and speaking. Now I'm going to reiterate. Not for the first and I'm afraid not for the last time. Gaston Sears was offstage at the crucial moment and talking in a whisper to the King and Miss Gaythorne. Young William was with them.

'The witches had come on for the curtain call and were waiting upstage on the rostrum. Macduff, now. Let's look a bit closer at Macduff. At first glance he seemed a possibility. He's a man with a temper and there's been some sort of trouble between him and Macbeth. He ended the fight by chasing Macbeth off. His story is that Macbeth screamed and fell down as usual and he went straight off and was seen to do so by various actors. Confirmed by the actors. By which time Macbeth was dead. I tried it out with you, Br'er Fox, and I was well over four minutes. We played the scene with Gaston as

Macbeth and the cast and it was three. Moreover, Morten – Macduff – would have had to get the dummy head off the claidheamh-mor before killing Macbeth with it while Macbeth – I've said this ad nauseam – stood or lay there waiting to be beheaded. It does *not*, Br'er Fox, make sense. As Macduff himself pointed out, it would have been a whole lot easier for him to have done a Lizzie Borden on Macbeth during their fight and afterwards say he didn't know how he'd gone wrong.'

'His weapon's blunt.'

'It weighs enough for a whack on the head to fix Macbeth.'

'Yerse. But it didn't.'

'No. We'll move on. Banquo. Banquo is a very rum fellow. He's devious, is Banquo, and he was "dead" all this long time and free, up to the second curtain call, to go wherever he liked. He could have gone into the OP corner and waited there in the dark with the claidheamh-mor when Gaston left it there for the stagehand to put the dummy head on it. The stagehand did put it there. Banquo removed it and did the deed. There's no motive that I can see but he's a possibility.'

'And are you going to tell me that Banquo is the perpetrator of the funny business with the dummy heads? And the typed message?'

'I rather think so. I'm far from happy with the idea, all the same.'

'Humph,' said Fox.

'We'll knock off now and go home.' He looked into the dark house. 'It was a wonderful production, Fox,' he said. 'The best I've seen. Almost too good. I don't think they can carry on.'

'What do you suppose they'll do in its place?'

'Lord knows. Something quite different. *Getting Gertie's Garter,*' said Alleyn angrily.

II

'I wonder,' said Emily, 'what the Smiths are doing.'

'The *Smiths*?' asked Crispin. 'What Smiths? Oh, you mean William and his mum,' he said, and returned to his book.

'Yes. Your father sent him home as soon as he realized what had happened. I think he just said there'd been an accident. He may have said: "to Sir Dougal". There's nothing they could have read in the Sunday papers. It'll be an awful shock for them.'

'How old is he?' asked Robin, who lay on his back on the window-seat, vaguely kicking his feet in the air.

'Who? William?'

'Yes.'

'Nine.'

'Same as me.'

'Yes.'

'Is he silly and wet?'

'He's certainly not silly and I don't know what you mean by "wet".'

'Behind the ears. Like a baby.'

'Not at all like that. He can fight. He's learning karate and he's a good gymnast.'

'Does he swear?'

'I haven't heard him but I dare say he does.'

'I suppose,' said Robin, bicycling madly, 'he's very busy on Sundays.'

'I've no information. Shall I ask him to come to lunch? You could go over in a taxi to Lambeth where he lives and fetch him. Only an idea,' said Emily very casually.

'Oh yes. You could do that,' shouted Robin and leapt to his feet. 'Please ask him. Thrice three and double three. Two for you and three for me. Please.'

'Right you are.'

Emily consulted the cast list that Peregrine kept pinned up by the telephone and dialled a number.

'Mrs Smith? It's Emily Jay. I've got two sons home for half-term and we wondered if by any chance William would like to pay us a visit today. Robin, who's William's age, could come and collect him for lunch and we'd promise to return him after an early supper here . . . Yes . . . Yes, would you?'

She heard Mrs Smith's cool voice repeating the invitation: 'You'd like that, wouldn't you?' she added and William's voice: 'I think so. Yes. Thank you.'

'Yes, he'd like to come, thank you *very* much.'

'Robin will be there in about half an hour depending on a cab . . . Lovely . . . Mrs Smith, I suppose William told you what happened last night at the theatre? . . . Yes . . . Yes, I see. I'm afraid they were all in a great state. It's Sir Dougal. He's died . . . Yes, a fearful blow to us all . . . I don't know. They'll tell the company what's been decided at four this afternoon. I don't think William need go down. He'll be here and we'll tell him . . . Yes, tragic. It's hard to believe, isn't it? . . . Yes. Goodbye.'

She hung up and said to Robin, 'Go and get ready,' and to Crispin: 'Do you want to go, Cip? Not if you don't.'

'I think I'd like to.'

'Sure?'

'Yes. I can see the infant's on his best behaviour, can't I?' Robin from the doorway gave a complicated derisory noise and left the room.

'There's always that,' said their mother. 'There's just one thing, Cip. Do you know what happened last night? Sir Dougal died – yes. But how? What happened? Did you see? Have you thought?'

'I'm not sure. I saw – it. The head. Full-face but only for a split second.'

'Yes?'

'Lots of people in the audience saw it but I think they just thought it was an awfully good dummy, and lots didn't see it at all, it was so quick.'

'Did Robin?'

'I'm not sure. I don't think he's sure either but he doesn't say. He doesn't want to talk about it.'

'The thing is, young William didn't see *anything*. He was waiting offstage. He only knows Macbeth is dead. So don't say anything to upset that, will you? If you can, keep right off the whole subject. OK?'

'Yes.'

'That's fine. Here he comes.'

Crispin went out to the hall and Emily thought: He's a nice boy. Old for his years but that's rather nice too. She went up to the ex-nursery and hunted out a game of Chinese Checkers, one of Monopoly, a couple of memo pads.

Then she went downstairs and looked out of the window. No sign of her sons so they must have picked up a cab. She went to the kitchen and found her part-time cook making a horseradish sauce. There was a good smell of beef in the air.

'Richard's spending the day with friends but we've got an extra small boy for lunch, Annie.'

'That's OK,' said Annie, whose manner was very free and easy.

'I'll lay the table.'

'Doreen's obliging. *Doreen*,' screamed Annie and her daughter came in, a lanky girl of fifteen with a simper.

'Say good morning to Mrs Jay, Dor, and lay an extra place.'

Emily shook hands with Doreen, who giggled.

'Will the boss be in?' asked Annie.

'If he can make it. We're not to wait.'

'Right you are,' said Annie. 'No problem.'

Emily couldn't settle to anything. She wandered downstairs and into the living room. It was a sunny morning and across the river the Dolphin stood out brightly from its setting in the riverside slums. Peregrine would be there, and all the important people in the Dolphin, trying to reach a conclusion on the immediate future.

I hope they decide against carrying on, she thought. It would be horrible. And, remembering a half-hearted remark of Peregrine's to the effect that Gaston would be good: It wouldn't be the same, I hope they won't do it.

She tried to think of a revival. There was Peregrine's own play about the Dark Lady and the delicate little Hamnet and his glove. The original glove was now in the Victoria and Albert Museum. They had discussed a revival, and it seemed to fill the bill. The child they had used in the original production had been, as far as she recollected, an odious little monster, but William would play him well. In her mind she began to cast it from the present company, leaving herself out.

It being Sunday, there was very little traffic in their part of the world. The boys decided to walk to the main street. They set out and almost at once a cruising taxi came their way. Crispin held up his first finger as his father always did and Robin pranced, waved his arms and imitated a seagull's cry. In no time they were in Lambeth and the taxi stopped in a narrow lane off Stangate Street in front of a tidy little house.

'Will you wait for us, please,' said Crispin to the driver. 'You wait in the car, Rob.' He went up the flight of three steps to the front door. Before he could ring the door opened and William came out.

'I'm Crispin Jay,' said Crispin. 'That's Robin in the cab.'

'I'm William Smith. Hullo. Hullo, Robin.'

'Hullo,' Robin muttered.

'Get in, William,' Crispin said. And to the driver: 'Back to Bankside, please.'

They set off. Robin said he bet he knew all the streets they would go through before they got to Bankside. Crispin said he wouldn't and won. William laughed infectiously and got a number of the early ones right. 'I walk down them every day when I go to school,' he said, 'so it's not fair.'

'I go to the Blue Caps,' said Robin. 'When I'm the right age I'll go to Winchester if I pass the entrance exam.'

'I went to the Blue Caps when I was six but only for a term. I wanted to be an actor so I got a scholarship to the Royal Southwark Theatre School. It's a special school for actors.'

'Do you like it?'

'Yes,' said William. 'I do like it, very much.'

'Do you like being in the play?'

'Gosh, yes.'

The taxi made a sharp turn to the right. Crispin took the opportunity to kick his brother who said: 'Hi! Watch your great feet where you put them. Oh! Sorry.'

'There's the river,' said Crispin, 'we're nearly home.'

'Gosh, I'm starving. Are you starving, William?' Robin enquired.

'You bet,' said William.

They drew up and stopped.

The two little boys tumbled out and ran up the steps while Crispin paid off the taxi.

Emily opened the door and the boys went in, Robin loudly asking if it was time for lunch and saying that he and William were rattling-empty. William shook hands and was not talkative. Peregrine came out to the hall and ran his fingers over William's hair. 'Hullo, young fellow,' he said. 'Nice to see you.'

'Hullo, sir.'

'I'm afraid I've got disturbing news for you. You know Sir Dougal died very unexpectedly last night, don't you?'

'Yes, sir.'

'Well, we've been trying to decide what to do: whether to continue with someone else in the part or close down for a week and then rehearse and re-open with a revival. We have almost decided on the latter policy, in which case the play will have to be chosen. There are signs of a return to popularity of the sophisticated romantic drama. Christopher Fry, for instance. Your immediate future depends, of course, on our choice which will have to be made tonight. There has been one suggestion of a play we used years ago for the gala opening of this theatre. It's a small cast and one of the characters is a boy. I wrote it. If we choose that play, we will suggest you read for the part. You die at the end of Act I but it is an extremely important part while you're with us.'

William said: 'Could I do it?'

'I think so. But we'd have to try you, of course. You may not suit.'

'Of course.'

'The character is Hamnet Shakespeare, Shakespeare's son. I thought I might as well tell you what we're thinking about. You're a sensible chap.'

'Well,' said William dubiously, 'I hope I am.'

'Lunch,' cried Emily.

Peregrine found in his place at table a sheet of paper and on it in her handwriting a new casting for *The Glove* by Peregrine Jay. He looked from it to her. 'Extraordinary,' he said. 'Two minds with but a single thought. Or something like that. Thank you, darling.'

'Do you like the idea? Or have you grown out of your play?'

'We're in such a state I don't know what I think. I've been reading it, and I fancy I still quite like it.'

'It wouldn't matter that it was running years ago at the Dolphin at the time of that other messy business?'

'Only you and I and Jeremy and Winty would know. It was a long run, which is all the Management considers.'

'Yes.'

Peregrine looked at her notes. 'Maggie: The Dark Lady. Yes. Shakespeare – Simon Morten? Do you think?'

'Yes, I do. He's got a highly-strung manner, a very quick temper and a sense of humour. And with a Shakespeare wig he'd look marvellous.'

'Better than Barrabell?'

'I think so, but then I don't like Barrabell. What little I've seen of him.'

'He'd succumb to the Voice Beautiful, I fear. He doesn't as Banquo but the Bard himself would be too much for him. He'd begin to sing.'

'He's a meanie.'

'Yes.'

'I've got a riddle,' Robin shouted.

'I'm no good at riddles,' William said doubtfully.

'Look – ' Crispin began.

'Shut up, Cip. Your mother and I are talking. Pipe down. Who wants more beef? Anybody? Clear away the plates and tell Doreen we're ready for her delicious pudding.'

'*Doreen! Pud!*' Robin yelled.

'That's *really* rude,' said Emily. 'Crispin, go into the kitchen and ask her properly. And if she doesn't throw a pot at you it's because she's got much nicer manners than any of us. Honestly, Perry, I sometimes wonder where these boys were lugged up.'

'William, will you have a look at this part and I'll get you to read it for me before I go down to the theatre.'

'Yes, sir.'

'You can read it in my study. The boys are not allowed in there.'

And so, for about an hour after lunch William read the first act. There were passages he did not understand and other passages which, though clear enough as far as the words went, seemed meant to convey another meaning from that usually attached to them. But the boy, Hamnet, was plain sailing. He was ill; he was lonely; his mother was too much occupied with a personal resentment to do more than attend impersonally to him, and his father was a star-like marvellous creature who came and went and was adored and vilified.

He began to read the boy's lines, trying them one way and another until the sound of them seemed right or nearly so.

Peregrine came in, so quietly that William did not hear him. He sat down and listened to the treble voice. Presently he opened his copy of the play and began to feed out the lines. William looked up at him and then returned to his task and they finished the act together.

'Well,' said Peregrine, 'that was a good beginning. It's three o'clock. Let's go up to the nursery and see what the others are doing.'

So they went to the ex-nursery and found Emily and Robin playing with Robin's train and Crispin, oblivious of the noise, deep in his
book. It was all about the play of *Macbeth* and the various productions through the past four centuries. There was a chapter on the
superstitions.

'You're not going on with this play, are you?' asked Crispin.

'No,' said his father. 'It's tempting, but I don't think we are.'

'Why, tempting?'

'I think Gaston would be exciting as Macbeth.'

'Yes?'

'But terribly risky.'

'Ah.'

The telephone rang.

'I'll answer it, Mummy. May I?' asked Robin.

'If you're polite.'

'Of course.' He ran out of the room, leaving the door open. They
all waited to hear what he would say.

'Hello?' said the treble voice. 'This is Mr Peregrine Jay's house . . .
Yes . . . If you don't mind waiting for a moment, I'll find out if he
can speak to you. Hold on, please. Thank you.'

He reappeared. 'It's Mr Gaston Sears, Pop,' he said. 'And he
sounds very sonky-polly-lobby.'

'I'll speak to him,' said Peregrine and went out to the telephone,
shutting the door behind him.

Crispin said: 'I dare say, William, you are wondering what
"sonky-polly-lobby" means. It's a family word and it means –
"Happy with yourself and a bit self-conscious, with it."'

'Oh.'

The little boys returned to their train. Emily and Crispin waited.
When he came back Peregrine looked disturbed.

'Gaston,' he said, 'has the same idea as we have. He thinks that if
we did decide to go on with *Macbeth* he would be good in the name
part, but would have to decline out of feelings of delicacy. He said it
would be an error of taste if he accepted. He said he knew we all
thought him a heartless kind of fellow but he was not. He felt we
should be told at once of this decision.'

'He – oh *dear*! He took it as a matter of course he would be cast?'

'Yes. And he was perfectly right. He would have been.'

'What did you say?'

'That we have for many reasons almost decided against it but that, had the many reasons not existed, I agreed. I thought he would have been good. So did the Management. With reservations that I didn't mention.'

'And he took it?'

'He said "So be it" in a grand voice and hung up. Poor old boy. He would be good, I do believe, but an awful nuisance nevertheless.'

'I'm sure you're right, Perry.'

'*Hoo, hoo*,' shouted William. 'Clear the line. The midnight express is coming straight through.'

Emily looked at him and then at Peregrine who gave her a thumbs-up signal. 'Very much so,' he said.

'Really? That's quite something.'

'All aboard. All aboard,' said Robin. 'All seats, please.'

He blew a piercing blast on a tin whistle. William rang the minute station bell and pressed a button. The toy train lit up and moved out of the station.

'Now I take over till we reach Crewe,' said Robin. He and William changed places and the train increased its speed. William answered a toy telephone.

'Midnight express. Urgent call. Yes?' he panted and blew. 'Gaston Sears speaks,' he gasped. 'Stop the train at Crewe. He's hurt and he's due at the theatre at seven.'

'Coming into Crewe. Clear the line.'

William produced a white van with a red cross and placed it on a side line. 'Ready for Mr Sears,' he said.

'Where is Sears?'

William emptied out a box of toy soldiers: Army, Navy, Highlanders and Crusaders. He cried out triumphantly and displayed a battered Crusader with an enormous sword and full mask and black cloak. 'Look! Perfect,' he cried. 'In every detail.'

'Hooray! Put him in the van.'

The game proceeded with the preposterous illogic of a child's dream and several changes of plot, but the train arrived conveniently at Euston Station, 'Gaston Sears' was pushed on to a battered car and, remarking that he'd got his 'second wind', was sent to the Dolphin Theatre. End of game.

'That was fun,' said Robin, 'wasn't it?'

'Yes,' his father agreed. 'Why did you have Gaston Sears in it?'

'Why not?' Robin replied with a shrug. He walked away. He was no longer interested.

'Because he was breathless and tried not to be?' William suggested vaguely. 'It's asthma but he pretends it isn't now he's an actor again.'

'I see,' Peregrine lied. 'Show it to me. The toy Sears.'

William took the battered little figure out of the car. A shrewd whack in some past contest had disposed of the cross on its cloak. The sword, bent but intact, was raised above its shrouded head in gloved hands. It was completely black and in its disreputable way quite baleful. 'Thank you,' said Peregrine. He put it in his pocket.

'Have you finished with the train?' asked Emily.

'We might want it later,' Robin said quickly.

'I don't think you will. It's *The Duke* on telly in a quarter of an hour and then teatime.'

'Oh, *Mummy*!'

The train was carefully put away and the toy soldiers swept into their box pell-mell. All except the 'Mr Sears' which was still in Peregrine's pocket when he looked at his watch and prepared to leave.

'I must be off,' he said. 'I don't know when I'll get home, my love. Cip says he'll come down with me and walk back, so I'll leave you to take William home. OK? Good evening, William. Come again soon, won't you? We've enjoyed having you here.'

'Thank you, sir,' said William, shaking hands. 'It's been a lovely day. The nicest day I've ever had.'

'Good. Cip! Ready?'

'Coming.'

They banged the front door and ran down the steps to the car.

'Pop,' said Crispin when they got going, 'that book you paid for last night. About *Macbeth*.'

'Yes?'

'It's jolly good. It's got quite a lot about the superstitions. If you don't mind, I would just like to ask if you *totally* dismiss that aspect of the play.'

'I think,' said Peregrine very carefully, 'that the people who do so put the cart before the horse. Call a play "unlucky" and take any mishap that befalls the rehearsals or performances, on stage or in the dressing-rooms or offices, and immediately everyone says: "There you are. Unlucky play." If the same sort of troubles occur with other plays nobody counts them up or says anything about them. Until, perhaps, there are rather more misfortunes than with other contemporary shows and someone like poor old maddening Nina says, "It's an unlucky piece, you know," and it's got the label tied round its neck for keeps.'

'Yes, I see that. But in this instance – I mean that business with the heads. It's a bit thick, isn't it?'

'There you go! Cart before the horse. They may have been planted to make us believe in the unlucky play story.'

'I see what you mean, of course. But you can't say it applies to this final tragedy. Nobody in his right senses is going to cut off a harmless actor's head – that's what happened, Pop, isn't it? – just to support the unlucky play theory?'

'Of course not. No. And the only person who might be described as being a bit dotty, apart from Nina, is old Gaston who was chatting away to the King and William and Nina and several others at the time the murder was committed.'

There was a longish silence. 'I see,' said Crispin at last.

'I don't want you to – to – '

'Get involved?'

'Certainly not.'

'Well, I won't. But I can't help *wondering*,' said Crispin. 'Seeing you're my papa and seeing the book I'm reading. Can I?'

'I suppose not.'

'Are you going on with *Macbeth*?'

'I don't think so. I think it'll probably be a revival of my own play.'

'*The Glove*?'

'Yes.'

'That *will* be fun. With William, of course?'

'He gave a very promising reading.'

They crossed Blackfriars Bridge and turned left and left again into Wharfingers Lane. There were three cars ahead of them.

'Winty's car and two of the board,' Peregrine noted. 'As usual, I don't know when I'll be home. Goodbye, old boy.'

''Bye, Pop.'

Peregrine watched him walk away up Wharfingers Lane. He went in by the stage door.

Most of the cast were there in groups of three and four. The stage had been scrubbed down and looked the same as usual. He wondered what would be its future. The skeleton hung from the gallows and swung in the draught. Bob Masters and Charlie greeted him and so did a number of the actors. They gathered round him.

He said at once: 'No absolute news but it will, I imagine, be out before long. The pundits are gathering in front-of-house. I think, my dears, it's going to be the end of *Macbeth*. I hope the new play will be announced tonight. I'd like to say now that it will almost certainly be a much, much smaller cast, which means that for a number of you the prospect of a long season comes to an abrupt end. I'd like to thank you from a very full heart for your work and say that, no matter what may befall in the years to come, you will be known – every bit part of you – for having played in, to quote several of the reviews, the "flawless *Macbeth*".'

'Under flawless direction, Perry,' said Maggie and the others after a murmured agreement clapped him: a desultory sound in the empty Dolphin. It died away. A throat was cleared. Gaston stepped forward.

Somebody said: 'Oh no.'

'I may *not*,' Gaston proclaimed with an air of infinite conceit, 'be considered the appropriate figure to voice our corporate approval of the style in which the play has been presented. However, as no one else has come forward, I shall attempt to do so.' He spread his feet and grasped his lapels. 'I have been glad to offer my assistance in matters of production and to have been able to provide the replicas for the weapons used by Macbeth and Macduff. I made them,' he said, with a modest cough. 'I do, however, now frankly deplore the use of the actual, historical claidheamh-mor. At the time I felt that since no hands but mine own would touch it, there would be no desecration. I was utterly mistaken and take this opportunity of admitting as much. The claidheamh-mor is possessed of a power – '

'For God's sake, somebody stop him,' muttered Simon.

' – it moves in its own appointed way – '

The doors at the back of the stalls opened and Alleyn came into the house and walked down the centre aisle.

Gaston paused, his mouth open. Peregrine said: 'Excuse me, Gaston. I think Mr Alleyn wants to speak to me.' The actors, intensely relieved, set up a buzz of affirmation.

'It's to say that we've just about finished our work in the theatre,' Alleyn said, 'and the dressing-rooms are now open for use. I understand that the production of *Macbeth* will be discontinued and that the Management will make an announcement, now, to the company. I must ask you all to remain at your present addresses or, if any of you change your address, to let us know. If this is inconvenient for any of you I am very sorry. It will not, I hope, be for long.'

He turned to Peregrine. 'I think the Management would like a word with you,' he said.

Bruce Barrabell said importantly, 'I am the Union's representative in this production. I will have to ask for a ruling on the situation.'

'No doubt,' said Alleyn politely, 'they will be glad to advise you. There is a telephone in the Prompt corner.' And to the company: 'Mr Fox has the keys. He's in the greenroom.'

'I suppose,' said Barrabell, 'you've been through our private possessions like the proverbial toothcomb.'

'I'm not sure how proverbial toothcombs work but I expect you're right.'

'And retired to your virtuous bed to sleep the sleep of the just, no doubt?'

'I didn't go to bed last night,' said Alleyn mildly. He surveyed the company. 'The typescripts of your statements are in the greenroom,' he said. 'We'd be grateful if you'd be kind enough to read them and, if they're correct, sign them before you go. Thank you all very much.'

In the boardroom, Peregrine faced his fellow guardians and Winter Morris. Mrs Abrams was secretary.

'In the appalling situation in which we find ourselves,' he said, 'the immediate problem is how we conduct our policy. We've been given twenty-four hours in which to decide. One: we can go dark and advertise that money for advance bookings will be refunded at the box office. Two: we can continue with the presentation with Simon Morten in the lead and his understudy playing Macduff. The fight at the end would be replaced by a much simpler routine. *Or*, and this is an unorthodox decision, Gaston Sears would play the lead. He tells me he is in a fair way to being word-perfect and of course he knows the fight, but he adds that he feels he would have to decline. Three: we can take a fortnight off and re-open with the revival of one of our past successes. *The Glove* has been mentioned. As the author, I feel I can't speak for or against the play. I can, however, say that I have heard William Smith read the very important part of the young Hamnet Shakespeare and he promised extremely well. We can cast it from the present company. Maggie would be splendid as the Dark Lady and I fancy Simon as the Bard and Nina as Anne.'

He was silent for a second or two and then went on: 'This is a terrible thing that has happened. One would have said that our dear Sir Dougal had no enemies. I still can't get myself round to – to – facing it and I dare say you can't either. Of one thing we may all be sure: he would have wanted us to do what is best for the Dolphin.'

He sat down.

For a time nobody spoke. Then one bald and stout guardian whispered to another and a little pantomime of nods and portentous frowns passed round the table. The senior guardian, who was thin and had a gentle air, stood up.

'I move,' he said, 'that we leave the matter in Mr Peregrine Jay's hands and do so with our complete trust in his decision.'

'Second that,' said an intelligent Jewish guardian.

'Those in favour? Unanimous,' said the chairman.

CHAPTER 8

Development

'I suppose I ought to be feeling all glowing and grateful,' said Peregrine, 'but I'm afraid I don't. They are nice old boys all of them but they're dab hands at passing the buck and making it look like a compliment.'

'You've been given a completely free hand and if it turns out a dead failure you'll find yourself out on a limb and all of them saying, ever so delicately, that they felt at the time the decision was a mistaken one,' Alleyn observed.

'That's right.'

'If it's any comfort, which it isn't, I'm familiar with these tactics.'

'Why don't we leave them to make the decision? Why don't I say I feel it would be better, in the circumstances, for somebody less intimately concerned with the Dolphin to produce the next show? God knows, it'd be true.'

'Yes?'

'But I'd feel I was ratting.' He dug his hands into his pockets. 'I'm fond of them. We've taken a journey together and come out on the golden sands. We've found *Macbeth*. It's a marvellous feeling. Or was. Are *you* any further on?'

'A little, I think. Not enough, not anything like enough, to think of an arrest.'

Peregrine's fingers had been playing with something in his pocket. They closed round it and fetched it out, a dilapidated little figure, jet black, flourishing a bent weapon behind its shoulder.

'Where did you find that?' Alleyn asked.

'It's one of my boy's toy soldiers – a Crusader. William found it.'

'William?'

'Smith. He spent the day with us. He's the same age as young Robin. They got on like a house on fire playing with the boys' electric train. This thing was a passenger, picked up at Crewe. He said he was hurt but he had to get to the theatre at seven. It gave me quite a shock – all black and with a claymorish thing – like Sir Dougal. Only they called him Sears. Extraordinary, how children behave. You know? William didn't know what had happened in the theatre but he guessed Sir Dougal was dead. Robin didn't know, or wasn't certain about the decapitation, though he'd been very much upset when it happened. I'd realized that, but he didn't ask any questions and now there he was making a sort of game of it.'

'Extraordinary,' said Alleyn. 'May I see it? The Crusader?'

Peregrine handed it over. 'It might be Sir Dougal or Barrabell or Sears or nobody,' he said. 'It doesn't look tall enough for Simon Morten. It's masked, of course.'

'*He* wasn't masked. And in any case – '

'No. In any case the whole thing's a muddle and a coincidence.' William fished this thing out of a box full of battered Crusaders.'

'And called it – what? Sears?'

'Not exactly. I mean it became Sears. They picked him up at Crewe. Before that, William – being Sears at the moment when he used the telephone – rang up the station for an emergency stop. He said – what the hell *did* he say? That he was hurt and had to get to the Dolphin by seven. That's when William took this thing from the box and they put it in the train. It was a muddle. They hooted and whistled and shouted and changed the plot. William gasped and panted a lot.'

'Panted? As if he'd been running?' Alleyn asked.

'Yes. Sort of. I think he said something about trying not to. I'm not sure. He said it was asthma but Sears wouldn't let on because he was an actor. One thing I am sure about, though.'

'What's that?'

'They got rid of whatever feelings they had about the real event by turning it all into a game.'

'That sounds like good psychology to me,' said Alleyn. 'But then I'm no psychologist. I can understand Robin calling this thing Sears, though.'

'Why?'

'He was here, wasn't he? In the theatre. He saw the real Sears carry the head on. Associated images.'

'I *think* I see what you mean,' said Peregrine doubtfully. 'Oh well, I'll have to go up to the offices and get an audition notice typed out. What about you?'

'We'll see them out of here,' said Alleyn.

'Good luck to you,' said Peregrine. He vaulted down into the orchestral well and walked away up the centre aisle. The doors opened and shut behind him.

Alleyn went over his notes.

Is there a connection or isn't there? he asked himself. Did the perpetrator of these nasty practical jokes have anything to do with the beheading of an apparently harmless star actor or was he practising along his own beastly self-indulgent lines? Who is he? Bruce Barrabell? Why are his fellow actors and – well, Peregrine Jay – so sure he's the trickster? Simply because they don't like him and he seems to be the only person in the company capable of such murky actions? But *why* would he do it? I'd better take a pot-shot and try to find out. He looked at his notes. Red Fellowship. H'm. Silly little outfit but they're on the lists and so's he, so here goes.

He walked down the dressing-room corridor until he came to the one shared by Barrabell and Morten. He paused and listened. Not a sound. He knocked and a splendid voice said 'Come'. They always made such a histrionic thing of it when they left out the 'in', Alleyn thought.

Bruce Barrabell was seated in front of his looking glass. The lights were switched on and provided an unmotivated brilliance to the dead room. The make-up had all been laid by in the old cigar-box fastened by two rubber bands and put into a suitcase. The dirty grease-cloths were neatly rolled up in a paper bag, the dull red dressing gown folded and in the bottom of the same battered suitcase with Russian labels stuck on it. On the top of his belongings was a programme, several review pages and a small collection of cards and telegrams. Crumpled tissues lay about the dressing table.

Simon Morten's possessions were all packed away in his heavily labelled suitcase which was shut and waited on the floor, inside the door. The indescribable smell of greasepaint still hung on the air and the room was desolate.

'Ah. Mr Alleyn!' said Barrabell expansively. 'Good evening to you. Can I be of any help? I'm just tidying up, as you see.' He waved his hand at the disconsolate room. 'Do sit down,' he invited.

'Thank you,' said Alleyn. He took the other chair and opened his file. 'I'm checking all your statements,' he said.

'Ah yes. Mine is quite in order, I hope?'

'I hope so, too,' Alleyn said. He turned the papers slowly until he came to Mr Barrabell's statement. He looked at his man and saw two men. The silver-voiced Banquo saying so beautifully, *'There's husbandry in Heaven. Their candles are all out,'* and the unnaturally pale actor with light eyes whose hands trembled a little as he lit a cigarette.

'I'm sorry. Do you?' Barrabell asked winningly and offered his cigarettes.

'No, thank you. I don't. About these tricks that have been played during the rehearsal period. I see you called them "schoolboy hoaxes" when we asked you about them.'

'Did I? I don't remember. It's what they were, I suppose. Isn't it?'

'Two extremely realistic severed heads? A pretty case-hardened schoolboy. Had you one in mind?'

'Oh no. No.'

'Not the one in Mr Winter Morris's "co." for instance?'

There was a pause. Barrabell's lips moved, repeating the words, but no sound came from them. He shook his head slightly. 'There was somebody,' Alleyn went on, 'a victim, in the Harcourt-Smith case. Her name was Muriel Barrabell, a bank clerk.' He waited. Somewhere along the corridor a door banged and a man's voice called out: 'In the greenroom, dear.'

'Was she your sister?'

Silence.

'Your wife?'

'No comment.'

'Did you want the boy to get the sack?'

'No comment.'

'He was supposed to have perpetrated these tricks. And all to do with severed heads. Like his father's crimes. Even the rat's head. A mad boy, we were meant to think. Like his father. Get rid of him, he's mad, like his father. It's inherited.'

There was another long silence.

'She was my wife,' said Barrabell. 'I never knew at the time what happened. I didn't get their letter. He was charged with another woman's murder. Caught red-handed. I was doing a long tour of Russia with the Leftist Players. It was all over when I got back. She was so beautiful, you can't think. And he did that to her. I made them tell me. They didn't want to but I kept on and on until they did.'

'And you took it out on this perfectly sane small boy?'

'How do you know he's perfectly sane? Could you expect me to be in the same company with him? I wanted this part. I wanted to work for the Dolphin. But do you imagine I could do so with that murderer's brat in the cast? Not bloody likely,' said Barrabell and contrived a sort of laugh.

'So you came to the crisis. All the elaborate attempts to incriminate young William came to nothing. And then suddenly, inexplicably, there was the real, the horrible crime of Sir Dougal's decapitation. How do you explain that?'

'I don't,' he said at once. 'I know nothing about it. Nothing. Apart from his vanity and his accepting that silly title, he was harmless enough. A typical bourgeois hero, which maybe is why he excelled as Macbeth.'

'You see the play as an anti-heroic exposure of the bourgeois way of life, do you? Is that it? *Can* that be it?'

'Certainly. If you choose to put it like that. It's the Macbeths' motive. Their final desperate gesture. And they both break under the strain.'

'You really believe that, don't you?'

'Certainly,' he repeated. 'Of course, our reading was, as usual, idiotic. Take the ending: "*Hail, King of Scotland.*" In other words: "Hail to the old acceptable standards. The old rewards and the old dishing out of cash and titles." We cut all that, of course. And the bloody head of Macbeth stared the young Malcolm in the face. Curtain,' said Barrabell.

'Have you discussed the play with your political chums at the Red Fellowship meetings?'

'Yes. Not in detail. More as a joke, really.'

'A *joke*,' Alleyn exclaimed. 'Did you say a *joke*?'

'A bit on the macabre side, certainly. There's a meeting every Sunday morning. You ought to come. I'll bring you in on my ticket.'

'Did you talk about the murder?'

'Oh yes. Whodunnit talk. You know.'

'Who *did* do it?'

'Don't ask me. *I* don't know, do I?'

Alleyn thought: He's not so frightened, now. He's being impudent.

'Have you thought about the future, Mr Barrabell? What do you think of doing?'

'I haven't considered it. There's talk of another Leftist Players Tour but of course I thought I was settled for a long season here.'

'Of course. Would you read this statement and, if it's correct, sign it? Pay particular attention to this, will you?'

The forefinger pointed to the typescript.

'You were asked: where were you between Macbeth's last speech and Old Siward's epitaph for his son? It just says: "*Dressing-room and OP centre waiting for call.*" Could you be a little more specific?' Alleyn asked.

'I really don't see quite how.'

'When did you leave the dressing-room?'

'Oh. We were called on the tannoy. They'll give you the time. I pulled on my ghost's head and the cloak and went out.'

'Did you meet anybody in the passage?'

'*Meet* anyone? Not precisely. I followed the old King and the Macduffs, mother and son, I remember. I don't know if anyone followed me. Any of the other "corpses".'

'And you were alone in the dressing-room?'

'Yes, my dear Chief Superintendent. Absolutely alone.'

'Thank you.' Alleyn made an addition and offered his own pen. 'Will you read and sign it, please? There.'

Barrabell read it. Alleyn had written: 'Corroborative evidence: none.'

He signed it.

'Thank you,' Alleyn said and left him.

In the passage he ran into Rangi. 'Hullo,' he said, 'I'm getting statements signed. Would it suit you to do yours now?'

'Sure.'

'Where's your room?'

'Along here.'

He led the way to where the passage turned left and the rooms were larger.

'I've got Ross and Lennox and Angus in with me,' Rangi said. He came to the correct door and opened it. 'Nobody here. It's a bit of a muddle, I'm afraid.'

'Doesn't matter. You've packed up, I see.'

He cleared a chair for Alleyn and took one himself.

'Yours was a wonderful performance,' said Alleyn. 'It was a brilliant decision to use those antipodean postures: the whole body working evil.'

'I've been wondering if I should have done it. I don't know what my Elders would say: the strict ones. It seemed to be right for the play. Mr Sears approved of it. I thought maybe he would think it all nonsense but he said there are strong links throughout the world in esoteric beliefs. He said all or anyway most of the ingredients in the spell are correct.'

'I'm sure you're right,' Alleyn said. He saw that round his neck on a flax cord Rangi wore a tiki, a greenstone effigy of a human foetus. 'Is that a protection?' Alleyn asked.

'In my family for generations.' The brown fingers caressed it.

'Really? You're a Christian, aren't you? Forgive me: it's rather confusing – '

'It is really. Yes. I suppose I am. The Mormon Church. It's very popular with my people. They don't "Mormonize", you know, only one wife at a time and they're not all that fussy about our old beliefs. I suppose I'm more pakeha than Maori in ordinary day-to-day things. But when it comes to this – what's happened here – it – well, it all comes rolling in like the Pacific, in huge waves, and I'm Maori through and through.'

'That I understand. Well, all I want is your signature to this statement. You weren't asked many questions but I wonder if you can give me any help over this one. The actual killing took place

between Macbeth's exit fighting and Malcolm's entrance. Those of
you who were not on stage came out of your dressing-rooms. There
were you three witches and the dead Macduffs and the King and
Banquo under his ghost mask and cloak. Is that correct?'

Rangi shut his large eyes. 'Yes,' he said, 'that's right. And Mr Sears.
He was with the rest of us but as the cue got nearer he moved away
into the OP corner with Macduff, ready for their final entrance.'

'Was anyone following you?'

'The other two witches. We were in a bunch.'

'Anyone else?'

'I don't think so.'

'Sure?'

'Yes,' said Rangi firmly. 'Quite sure. We were last.'

He read the statement carefully and signed it. As he returned it to
Alleyn he said: 'It doesn't do to meddle with these things. They are
wasps' nests that are better left alone.'

'We can't leave a murder alone, Rangi.'

'I suppose not. All the same. He made fun of things that are tapu –
forbidden. My great-grandfather knew how to deal with that.'

'Oh?'

'He cut off the man's head,' said Rangi cheerfully. 'And ate him.'

The tannoy broke the silence that followed. 'Members of the
company are requested to assemble in the greenroom for a managerial announcement. Thank you,' it said.

II

Alleyn found Fox in the greenroom. 'Finished?' he asked.

'I've got all the statements. Except, of course, your lot. They're
not conspicuously helpful. There's one item that the King noticed.
He says – hold on – here we are. He says he noticed that Sears was
wheezing while he waited with them before the final entry. He said
something about it and Sears tapped his own chest and frowned. He
made a solemn thing with his eyebrows. "Asthma, dear boy, asthma.
No matter." Can't you see him doing it?'

'Yes. Vincent Crummles stuff. He must have found that massive
claidheamh-mor a bit of a burden.'

'What I thought. Poor devil. Here comes the Management. We'll hand over.'

They put the statements in a briefcase and settled themselves inconspicuously at the back of the room.

The Management came through the auditorium and on stage by way of the Prompt-box and thence to the greenroom. They looked preternaturally solemn. The senior guardian was in the middle and Winter Morris at the far side. They sat down behind the table.

'I'm afraid,' said the senior guardian, 'there are not enough chairs for everybody but please use the ones that are available. Oh, here are some more.'

Stagehands brought chairs from the dressing-rooms. There was a certain amount of politeness. Three ladies occupied the sofa. Simon Morten stood behind Maggie. She turned to speak to him. He put his hand on her shoulder and leant over her with a possessive air. Gaston Sears stood apart with folded arms, pale face and dark suit, like a phoney figurehead got up for the occasion. William and his mother had appeared and were at the back of the room. Bruce Barrabell occupied an armchair. Rangi and his girls were together by the doorway.

And in the back of the room, quietly side by side, sat Alleyn and Fox, who would sooner or later, it must be assumed, remove one of the company, having charged him with the murder by decapitation of their leading man.

The senior guardian said his piece. He would not keep them long. They were all deeply shocked. It was right that they should know as soon as possible, what had been decided by the Management. The usual procedure of the understudy taking over the leading role would not be followed. It was felt that the continued presentation of the play would be too great a strain on actors and on audiences. This was a difficult decision to take when the production was such a wonderful success. However, after much anxious consideration it had been decided to revive *The Glove*. The principals had been cast. If they looked at the board they would see the names of the actors. There were four good parts still uncast and Mr Jay would be pleased to see anyone who wished to apply. Rehearsals would begin next week, that was to say on tomorrow week. Mr Morris would be glad to settle *Macbeth* salaries this evening if the actors would kindly call at the office. He thanked them all for being so patient and said he would ask them to stand in silence for one minute in remembrance of Sir Dougal Macdougal.

They stood. Winter Morris looked at his watch. The minute seemed interminable. Strange little sounds – sighs; a muffled thump; a telephone bell; a voice, instantly silenced – came and went and nobody really thought of Sir Dougal except Maggie, who fought off tears. Winter Morris made a definitive movement and there was no more silence.

'Excuse me, Mr Chairman. Before we break up.'

It was Bruce Barrabell.

'As representative of Equity I would just like to convey the usual messages of sympathy and to say that I will make suitable enquiries on your behalf as to the correct action to be taken in these very unusual circumstances. Thank you.'

'Thank you, Mr Barrabell,' replied the flustered senior guardian.

He and his colleagues left in a discreet procession by the stage door. The actors went out to the empty stage and collected round the noticeboard.

Winter Morris said: 'The office is now open, ladies and gentlemen,' and hurried back to it.

The green board carried a typed notice on company paper.

MACBETH

ALL PERSONNEL
ANNOUNCEMENT EXTRAORDINARY

Owing to an unforeseen and most tragic circumstance the season will, as from now, be closed. The play *The Glove* by Peregrine Jay will replace it. Four of the leading parts are cast from the existing company. The remainder are open for auditions which will be held this evening and tomorrow and, if necessary, the next two days. Rehearsals will begin next week.

The Management thanks the company for its outstanding success and deeply regrets the necessity to close.

Signed:

Dolphin Enterprises,   Samuel Goodbody.
31st May, 1982.   *Chairman*.

At a respectable distance was a second announcement.

CURRENT PRODUCTION

The Glove Auditions: This afternoon and two following days
11 a.m.–1 p.m. 2 p.m.–5 p.m.

Shakespeare	Mr Simon Morten
Anne Hathaway	Miss Nina Gaythorne
Hamnet Shakespeare	Master William Smith
The Dark Lady	Miss Margaret Mannering
Dr Hall	
Joan Hart	
The Rival	
Burbage	

Books of the Play obtainable at office.

Peregrine stood in front of the board and copied the casting into his own book. The actors read the notices and by ones and twos moved into the auditorium and through the stalls into the foyer.

He moved chairs on to the stage, placing them back to back to mark the doorways into Shakespeare's parlour and leaving a group of six as working props. He went into the stalls and sat down.

I must pull myself together, he thought, I must go on as usual and I must whip up from somewhere enthusiasm for my own play.

Bob Masters came on stage and peered into the auditorium.

'Bob,' Peregrine said, 'we'll hold auditions in the usual way when everyone is ready.'

'Right. Give us half an hour while Winty settles the treasury.'

'OK.'

The last of the actors had gone into the foyer. A lonely couple emerged from the shadows and appeared on stage: William and his mother, she tidy in a dark grey suit and white blouse, William also in dark grey, white shirt and dark blue tie. He walked over to the board, looked at it and turned to his mother. She joined him and put her hands on his shoulders. 'I'm not sure,' he said clearly. 'Don't I have to audition?'

'Hullo, William,' Peregrine called out. 'You don't, really. We're taking a gamble on you. But I see you've got your book. Go and collect your treasury and come back here and we'll see how you shape up. All right?'

'Yes, thank you, sir.'

'I'll come back and wait for you outside,' said his mother. She had gone out by the stage door before Peregrine realized what she was up to.

William went through the house to the offices, and for a short time Peregrine was quite alone. He sat in the stalls and supposed that people like Nina had begun to say that the Dolphin was an unlucky theatre. And suddenly time contracted and the first production of his play seemed to have scarcely completed its run. He could almost hear the voices of the actors . . .

William came back. He went through the opening scenes and Peregrine thought: I was right. The boy's an actor.

'You'll do,' he said. 'Go home and learn your lines and come down for rehearsals in a week's time.'

'Thank you, sir,' said William and went out by the stage door.

'"Yes, sir. No, sir. Three bags full, sir," said an unmistakable voice. It was Bruce Barrabell, sitting up at the back. In the dark.

Peregrine peered at him. 'Barrabell?' he said. 'Are you going to audition?'

'I thought so. For Burbage.'

He doesn't come on until the second act, Peregrine thought. He would be good. And he felt a sudden violent dislike of Barrabell. I don't want him in the cast, he thought. I can't have him. I don't want to hear him audition. I don't want to speak to him.

The part of Burbage was of a frantically busy man of affairs and an accomplished actor in the supposed Elizabethan manner. Silver-tongued, blast it, thought Peregrine. He's ideal, of course. Oh damn and blast!

The actors began to trickle in from the offices and Mrs Abrams came down to take notes for Peregrine and say, 'Thank you, darling. We'll let you know.' The Ross auditioned for Dr Hall. He read it nicely with a good appreciation of the medical man of his day and his anxious and lethal treatment of young Hamnet. The Gentlewoman tried for Joan Hart, the poet's sister. That had been Emily's part and Peregrine tried not to let himself be influenced by this. If he suggested she came back and played it she would say she was too old now.

They plodded on. Someone came and sat behind Peregrine. He felt a hand on his arm.

'Has Barrabell read for you?' the voice murmured.

'No.'

'I wouldn't cast him.' The hand was withdrawn and Alleyn left quietly.

III

Before he left the theatre, Alleyn had a short talk with Peregrine and told him of Barrabell's confession, if confession it could be called.

Back at the Yard he went through the statements and put the regulation conclusion before himself and Mr Fox, who remained, as it were, anonymous.

'If all reasonable explanations fail, the investigation must consider the explanation which, however outlandish, is not contradicted?'

'And what in this case is the outlandish explanation that is not contradicted?'

'There is not time for the murder to be accomplished between the end of the fight and the appearance of Macbeth's head on the claidheamh-mor so it must have been done before the fight.'

'But Macbeth spoke during the fight. True, his voice was hoarse and breathless.'

Alleyn took his head in his hands and did his best to listen to the past. *'Get thee back. My soul is too much charged with blood of thine already.'* Sir Dougal had had the slight but unmistakable burr of Scots in his voice. He had given it a little more room for the Thane: *'too much charrged'.* A grievous sound. It drifted through his memory, but his recollection held no personality behind it. Just the broken despair of any breathless, beaten fighter.

He must look for a new place in the play where the murder could have been committed. It was Sir Dougal who fought and killed Young Siward. He wore his visor up, displaying his full face. His speech ended with his desperate recollection of the last of the witches' equivocal pronouncements:

> ' – *weapons laugh to scorn,*
> *Brandished by man that's of a woman born'*

and there, suddenly, in his imagination, stood the actor. Up went the
gauntleted hand and down came the visor. He went off into the OP
corner – and was murdered? Macduff came on. He had a soliloquy,
broken by skirmishes and determined searches. Outbursts of fighting
occurred now here, now there. The Macbeth faction were dressed
alike: black, gauntleted, some masked, others not. The effect was
nightmarish. What if Macduff encountered a man uniformed like
Macbeth but not Macbeth? Pipes. Malcolm with a group of soldiers
marched on. Old Siward greeted him and welcomed him to the
castle. He made a ceremonial entry. Cheering within. The masked
'Macbeth' entered. Macduff came on. Saw him. Challenged him.
They fought.

'Yes,' Alleyn said, 'it's possible. It's perfectly possible but does it
throw a spanner in all our calculations and alibis! None of the
"corpses" are in position for the curtain call. The Macduff, Simon
Morten, could *just* have done it, but he'd have got a nasty shock
when the dead man turned up to fight him. On the other hand, as
Macbeth's understudy he would know the fight. But he was already
engaged in the fight himself. Damn. Barrabell? Gaston? Props?
Rangi? All possible. But wait a bit: all but one *im*possible. Unless we
entertain the idea of a collaborator who understood the fight. Let's
take any one of them regardless and see how it works out. Rangi.'

'Rangi,' said Fox without enthusiasm.

'He would do the murder at the earlier time. He'd wait till the last
minute. Then rush round to Gaston and say Sir Dougal's fainted and
he, Gaston, will have to go on for the fight with Macduff. All right
so far?'

'It's all right,' said Fox, 'as far as you've got. Motive, though?'

'Ah, motive. His great-grandfather knew how to deal with this
sort of nonsense. He told me in the nicest way imaginable. He cut off
the other chap's head and ate him.'

'Really!' said Fox primly. 'How very unpleasant. But I suppose he
could have done a return to his great-grandfather's state of mind and
killed Macbeth. You know, reverted to the Stone Age, sort of.'

'Any of the others could have done the same thing.'

'You don't mean – '

'I don't mean the chopper and cooking-pot bit, and I'll thank you
not to be silly. I mean could have gone to Gaston at the last moment

and asked him to fight. The catch in that is, it'd be a damnable bit of evidence against him, later on.'

'Yerse,' said Mr Fox. 'And whoever he was, he didn't do it.'

'I *know* he didn't do it. I'm simply trying to find a way out, Fox. I'm trying to eliminate and I *have* eliminated.'

'Yes, Mr Alleyn. You have. When do we book the gentleman?'

'I doubt if we've got a tight enough case, you know.'

'Do you?'

'Blast the whole boiling of them,' said Alleyn. He got up and walked about the room. 'Do you know what they're doing now? At this precise moment? Holding auditions for the replacement. A good play by Jay built round the death of Shakespeare's young son and the arrival of the Dark Lady. So far they haven't cast the murderer but there's no guarantee they won't. What's more, it's the play they were doing with great success when this theatre re-opened. There was a mess then and one of the company was guilty.'

'God bless my soul!' said Fox. 'That's right. I remember. Proper turn-up for the books, that one was.'

'And a right proper young monster the boy was. This is altogether a different story. D'you know who this kid is?'

'No. Ought I to? Not anything in our line of business, I suppose?'

'No – well, that's not quite true. He's a nice well-brought-up little chap and he's the son of the Hampstead Chopper. He doesn't know that and I'm extremely anxious that he shan't find out, Fox.'

'Harcourt-Smith, wasn't it?'

'It was. His mother dropped the Harcourt. He knows his father's in a loony-bin but not why.'

'Broadmoor?'

'Yes. A lifer.'

'Fancy that, now,' Fox said, shaking his head.

'One of his father's earlier victims was a Mrs Barrabell.'

'You're not telling me – '

'Yes, I am. Wife. Barrabell put those practical jokes together. All to do with heads. He hoped the Management would think the boy was responsible and give him the sack.'

'Has he told you? Barrabell?'

'Not in so many words.'

'He's a member of some potty little way-out group, isn't he?'

'The Red Fellowship. Yes.'

'What do we know about them?'

'The usual. Meeting once a week on Sunday mornings. Genuine enough. No real understanding of the extraordinary and extremely complicated in-fighting that goes on at sub-diplomatic levels. A bit dotty. He and his mates iron everything out to a few axioms and turn a blind eye to all that doesn't fit. The terrible reality of Bruce Barrabell rests in the fact that his wife was beheaded by a maniac. I think he believes, or has brooded himself into believing, that the child has inherited the father's madness and that sooner or later it'll emerge and then it'll be too late.'

'I still don't know where Sir Dougal fits in. If he does.'

'Nor do I. Except that he was a far from subtle funster and Bruce came in for his share of the ragging. He was forever making snide references to leftish groups and so on.'

'Hardly enough to make Bruce cut his head off.'

'Not if we were dealing with anything like normal people. I'm beginning to believe there's a stepped-up abnormality about the whole thing, Fox. As if the actors had become motivated by the play. That leads one to the proposition that no play should be as compulsive as *Macbeth*. Which is ridiculous.'

'All right. So what, to get down to our weekly pay packet, do we do to earn it?'

'Find a conclusive reason that will give us the time of the murder as being immediately after "*brandished by man that's of a woman born*". Find alibis for all but one of the company at that time and then face him with it. That's the ideal, of course.'

'Yes. All right. Let's tackle the alibis and see if we can do it with both feet on the ground. Now, the troops and all the extras and doubles are already engaged in battle: all the thanes; the Doctor, disguised as one of Macbeth's soldiers; Malcolm; Siward. That leaves Rangi, Gaston and Banquo. Macduff's out. The King. Where was Props?'

'In and out of the OP corner fixing the claidheamh-mor. And that's all,' said Fox.

'We can cut out the King.'

'Why?'

'Too silly,' said Alleyn. 'And too elderly.'

'All right. No King. How about Props? Any motive at all?'

'Not unless something turns up. In a way he's tempting, though. Nobody would pay any attention to him slipping into or out of the OP corner. He'd be there with the naked claidheamh-mor when Macbeth came off and could kill him and put his head on it.'

'Like Rangi, he'd have to give the phoney message to Gaston, but I think it would hold up,' said Fox. 'Gaston's hanging about there and Props says to him, "For Gawd's sake, sir, he's fainted. You've got this one speech of Macduff's and the fight. You know it. You can do it." And later on when the body's found he says it was so dark he just saw it lying there and, realizing there was only a matter of minutes before Macbeth's entrance for the fight, he rushed out, found Gaston and asked him. It hangs together. Except – '

'No motive? Bloody hell, Fox,' shouted Alleyn. 'We've lost our touch. We've gone to pieces. Gaston being told Macduff's fainted doesn't work. It doesn't work with anyone asking him to do it. He'd have told us. Of course he would. Back to square one.'

There was a long silence.

'No,' said Alleyn at last. 'There's only one answer. We'd better get a warrant, old chap.'

'I suppose we had,' said Fox heavily.

IV

The auditions were nearly over and the play fully cast from the present company. In the office, announcements for the Press were being telephoned and Peregrine actually felt better. Whatever the outcome and whoever was arrested, they were doing their own thing. In their own theatre. They were doing what they were meant to do: getting on with a new piece.

The discordant note was sounded, needless to say, by Gaston. He had not, of course, auditioned but nor had he left the theatre. No sooner had an audition finished than he began. He buttonholed one nervous actor after another and his subject was the claidheamh-mor. He wanted it back. Urgently. They tried to shut him up but he kept recurring like a decimal and complaining in an audible rumble that he would not be held responsible for anything that happened to anyone into whose care it had been consigned.

He asked to see Alleyn and was told he and Fox had left the theatre. Where had they gone? Nobody knew.

At last Peregrine stopped Rangi's audition and said he could not allow Gaston into the auditorium while they were working. What did he want?

'My claidheamh-mor,' he roared. 'How often must I say it? Are you an idiot, have you not been given sufficient evidence of what it can do if a desecrating hand is laid upon it? It is my fault,' he shouted. 'I allowed it to become involved in this sanguinary play. I released its power. You have only to study its history to realize – '

'Gaston! Stop! We are busy and it is no affair of ours. We have not time to listen to your diatribe and it is not within my sphere of activities to demand the thing's return. In any case I wouldn't get it. Do pipe down like a good chap. The weapon is perfectly safe in police custody and will be returned in due course.'

'Safe!' Gaston cried, swinging his arms about alarmingly. 'Safe! You will drive me demented.'

'Not far to go,' remarked a splendid voice in the back stalls.

'Who made that repulsive observation?'

'I did,' said Barrabell. 'In my opinion you're certifiable. In any correctly ordered state – '

'Shut up, both of you,' Peregrine cried. 'Good Lord! Haven't we had enough to put up with! If you two can't pipe down, at least go out of earshot and get on with it in the yard.'

'I shall bring this up with Equity. It is not the first time I have been insulted in this theatre – '

' – my claidheamh-mor. I implore you to consider – '

'Gaston! Answer me. Are you here to audition? Yes or no.'

'I am here – No.'

'Barrabell, are you here to audition?'

'I was. I now see that it would be useless.'

'In that case neither of you has any right to stay. I must ask you both to go. Go, for pity's sake, both of you.'

The doors into the foyer opened. Winty Morris's voice said: 'Oh, sorry. I didn't realize – '

'Mr Morris, wait! I must speak with you. My claidheamh-mor, Mr Morris! Please!'

Gaston hurried down the aisle and out into the foyer. The doors swung to behind him and he became a distant rumpus.

Peregrine said: 'I'm extremely sorry, Rangi. We'll go on when I've settled this idiotic affair. Now then, Bruce.'

He took Barrabell's elbow and led him aside. 'My dear chap,' he said, forcing his voice into a warmth he did not feel, 'Alleyn has told me of your tragedy. I couldn't be sorrier for you. But I must ask you this: don't you feel that with young William in the company you would be most unhappy? I do. I – '

Barrabell turned deadly white. He stared at Peregrine.

'You little rat,' he said. He turned on his heel, picked up his case and left the theatre.

'Phew!' said Peregrine. 'OK, Rangi. We'll have an audition.'

CHAPTER 9

Finis

By Monday morning the theatre was almost rid of *Macbeth*. The units, that from the auditorium had seemed solid but had silently revolved showing different aspects of the scenery, had been taken apart and stacked against the walls.

The skeleton dangling from its gallows had been cut down and put in the property room, still decked out in its disreputable rags.

The stage, every inch of it, was scrubbed and smelt of disinfectant. In front-of-house, advertisements for the new play replaced the old *Macbeth* posters and in the foyer the giant photograph frames were empty. The lifesize photograph of Macbeth was rolled up and slid into a cardboard cylinder. It disappeared into the basement.

The bookstall had its display for the most part taken down and stacked in cartons; the programmes had been cleared out and stuffed into rubbish bags awaiting the collectors.

Going, going, gone, thought little Winter Morris. It was a lovely show.

The dressing-rooms were empty and scrubbed. All except the star-room which was locked and untouched, except by the police, since Sir Dougal Macdougal walked out of it for the last time. His solicitors had given notice of sending persons in to collect his possessions. His name had been removed from the door.

The first rehearsal for the new play was set down for Tuesday morning. The cast took the day off, trying to cope with delayed shock.

Nina in her diminutive flat told herself that the malign influence of *Macbeth* was now satisfied and made a solemn promise to herself that she would not talk about it inside the theatre. She was greatly distressed, of course, and she wondered avidly who had done the murder, but she was sustained and even excited by being so overwhelmingly right in all her pronouncements.

They've not got a leg to stand on, she thought triumphantly.

Simon Morten rang up Maggie Mannering and asked her to lunch with him at the Wig and Piglet. She said she would and invited him to come early for her so that they could have a good talk in private. He arrived at noon.

'Maggie,' he said, holding her hands, 'I wanted to ask you last night but you've been so *remote*, darling. I thought perhaps . . . I didn't know how you felt or . . . well, I even thought you might have your doubts about me. And I thought I'd better find out, one way or another. And so – here I am.'

Maggie stared at him. 'Do you mean,' she said, 'that you thought I wondered if you decapitated Dougal? Is that it?'

'Well, I know it's idiotic but – well, yes. Don't laugh at me Maggie, *please*. I've been in hell.'

'I'll try not to,' she said. 'I'm sure you have. But why? Why would I think you'd done it? What motive could you have had for it?'

'Haven't you even noticed?'

'What haven't I noticed?'

'I'm horribly jealous,' he muttered, turning dark red. 'And you did the sex thing with him so awfully well. Just looking at you and listening, I – well, I'm sorry.'

'Now just you look here, Simon,' said Maggie vigorously. 'We're both going to play in *The Glove*. You're going to be tormented by me and it is not going to be all muddled up with the real thing: that way it'll go wrong. The audience will sense there's another reality intruding on the dramatic reality and they'll feel uncomfortable. Won't they?'

'I know how *you* feel about the mask an actor wears,' he said.

'Yes, I do. And you take yours off at your peril. Right?'

'All right.'

'Shake?' she said, holding out her hand.

'All right, shake,' he said and took it.

'Now we can go and have our blameless luncheon,' said Maggie. 'Come on. For the first time since it happened, I'm nervous. Let's talk about The Bard in love.'

So they went to the Wig and Piglet.

To everyone's relief Gaston retired to his own premises. Presumably to lick his incomprehensible wounds. On Monday evening he renewed his assault on the Yard. Mr Fox was called to the telephone which was switched through to Alleyn's room. 'Hullo?' he said.

'First of all,' roared the intemperate man, 'I intimated that I wished to communicate with Chief Superintendent Alleyn. You do not sound like the Chief Superintendent.'

'This is his room, sir, but I am not the Chief Superintendent. He is unable to come to the telephone and authorizes me to speak for him. What seems to be the trouble, sir?'

'Nothing *seems* to be the trouble. The trouble IS. I *demand* – repeat *demand* – the instant return of my claidheamh-mor under police armed guard, to my personal address. Tonight. Now.'

'If you'll hold on for a minute, sir, I'll just write a note to that effect and leave it here in a prominent position on the Chief Superintendent's desk.'

Fox clapped his enormous paw over the receiver and said: 'Sears.'

'So I supposed.'

'Here we are, sir. What was the message?'

'Odds boddikins, fellow – '

'I beg your pardon, sir?'

A stream of abuse, or what seemed to be abuse, was followed by a deathly silence and then a high-pitched female voice.

'Master not velly well, please. Sank you. Good evening,' and the telephone was disconnected.

'The housekeeper is Chinese,' said Alleyn.

Monday was the day the Jay boys returned to school after half-term. Crispin left by train in a dignified manner with a number of young men of equal status, an array of noisy smaller boys, and a little group of white-faced new ones.

Robin and Richard behaved with the eccentricity that the household had come to expect of them on these occasions. Peregrine, coming home to lunch, found he still had the toy figure of the Crusader in his pocket.

'I forgot about you,' he said and took it out. 'Your sword has made a little hole in my pocket.'

'May I have him back?' asked Robin. He took the mannikin and went to the telephone.

'Who are you ringing up?' asked Peregrine.

'A boy.'

He consulted the list and dialled the number. 'Hullo, Horrible,' he said. 'What d'you think I've got? Three guesses . . . No . . . No . . . Yes! Good for you . . . What are you doing? . . . Oh, *Daddy's* play. Well, I thought you'd like to know we're going back to school today so we'll be half-starved.'

He hung up and immediately dialled again.

'It's me again,' he announced. 'I forgot to mention that I knew all along the fighter wasn't Macbeth. I'll give you three guesses who it was . . . One – no . . . Two – no . . . Three – no. I'll give you till next Sunday.' He replaced the receiver.

'Out of the mouths of babes and sucklings,' muttered Peregrine. 'Robin! Come here. You must tell me. How did you know?'

Robin looked at his papa and saw that he meant business. He adopted a defiant attitude: feet apart, hands on hips, slightly nervous smile. 'Three guesses?' he invited.

But Peregrine only needed one.

He rang Alleyn up at the Yard.

II

The company of Dolphins at the Swan was diminished but Rangi and Ross and Lennox were still regulars and on Monday they met there for lunch. Rangi was quiet and withdrawn. His dark eyes and brilliant teeth dominated his face and it struck the others that he looked more 'native' than he had before. But he was pleased with his new part, that of The Rival, an ambiguous gentleman from Italy, overdressed and wearing a single earring.

'We start rehearsals tomorrow,' said Ross. 'Thank God without the ineffable Sears *or* dreary old Banquo. The whole tragedy as far as the Dolphin's concerned is finished.' He made a dismissive gesture with both hands.

'It won't be finished, my dear chap,' said Lennox, 'until somebody's under lock and key.'

'The stigma remains,' said Rangi. 'It must.'

'I looked in this morning. It's as clean as a whistle and smells of Jeyes' Fluid everywhere.'

'No policemen?'

'Not then, no. Just the offices clicking over merrily. There's a big notice out in front saying people can use their tickets for the new play or get their money back at the box office. And a board with nothing but rave notices from the former production of *The Glove*.'

'Any reasons given?'

'"Owing to unforeseen circumstances."'

'There's a piece in the papers. I suppose you saw.'

Lennox said yes, he had read it.

'I haven't seen the papers,' said Rangi.

'It just says that Dougal died on Saturday night very suddenly in the theatre. And there's the usual obituary: half a column and photographs. The Macbeth one's very good,' said Ross.

'It said that "as a mark of respect" the theatre would be dark for three weeks,' Ross added.

Rangi said, as if the words were dragged out of him: 'It's tapu. We all are tapu and will be until the murderer is found. And who will whakamana?'

There was an awkward silence.

'I don't know what you mean,' Lennox said.

'Better that you don't,' said Rangi. 'You wouldn't understand.'

'Understand *what*?' asked Lennox.

'Maoritanga.'

'Maori how much?'

'Shut up,' said Ross, and kicked him underneath the table.

Lennox looked at Rangi and found something in his face that made him say hurriedly: 'Sorry. Didn't mean to pry.'

'Not at all,' said Rangi. He stood up. 'I must get back. I'm late. Excuse me.'

He went to the counter, paid his bill and left.

'What's biting him?' Lennox asked.

'Lord knows. Something to do with the case, I imagine. He'll get over it, whatever it is.'

'I didn't mean to be rude or anything. Well, I wasn't, was I? I apologized.'

'Perhaps you said something that upset his mana.'

'Oh to hell with him and his mana. Where did you pick up the word anyway?'

'In conversation with him. It means all sorts of things but pride is the principal one.'

They ate their lunch in silence. Rangi had left a copy of *The Stage* on the bench. Ross looked at it. A small paragraph at the bottom of the page caught his eye. 'Hi,' he said. 'This would interest Barrabell. This is the lot he went abroad with. Take a look.'

Lennox bent over the table. He read:

'The Leftist Players are repeating their successful tour of Soviet Russia. They are now about to go into rehearsal with three contemporary plays. Ring club number for auditions.'

'That's the gang he went with before,' said Ross.

'He wouldn't be let go. Not while nobody's been caught.'

'I suppose not.'

'I wonder if he's seen this,' said Lennox without interest.

They finished their lunch without much conversation.

Barrabell had seen it. He read it carefully and consulted his notebook for the club number.

His bed-sitting room carried the absolute negation of any personal characteristics whatever. It was on the large side, tidy and clean. Its two windows looked across an alleyway at the third-storey shutters of an equally anonymous building.

He opened his wardrobe and took out a battered suitcase with old Aeroflot labels pasted on it. On opening, some tidily folded garments – pyjamas, underclothes and shirts – were revealed and under these a package of press-cuttings and the photograph of a rather good-looking young woman.

The press-cuttings were mainly of productions that he had appeared in but there were also relics of the trial of Harcourt-Smith. A photograph. The man himself, handcuffed between two policemen, entering the Old Bailey and looking blankly at nothing, one of Mr

Justice Swithering, and one of William and his mother taken in the street. There were accounts of the trial.

Barrabell read the cuttings and looked at the photographs. He then put them one by one into the dead fireplace and burnt them to ashes. He went to the bathroom on the landing and washed his hands. Then he replaced all the theatrical reviews in the suitcase and looked for a long time at the photograph which was signed 'Muriel'. His hands trembled. He hid it under the others, shut and locked the case and put it back in the wardrobe.

Now he consulted his copy of *The Stage* and rang the number given for enquiries about auditions.

He made a quick calculation, arrived at the amount he owed his landlady and put it in a used envelope with a Cellophane window. He wrote her name on the outside and added: 'Called away very unexpectedly. B.B.'

Whistling almost inaudibly, he re-opened the case and packed into it everything else that he owned in the room. He double-checked every drawer and shelf, put his passport in the breast pocket of his jacket and, after a final look round, picked up his case and left the room. The landlady's office was locked. He pushed the envelope under the door and walked out.

He was on a direct route for his destination and waited at the bus stop, dumping his case on the ground until the right bus came along. He climbed aboard, sat near the door, tucked his case under his legs and paid his fare.

The man who had been behind him in the queue heard him give the destination and gave the same one.

At twenty-six minutes to six a message came through to Alleyn.

'Subject left lodging house carrying suitcase with old Aeroflot labels. Followed to address suggested and is still there.'

To which he received a reply. 'Keep obbo. No arrest but don't lose him.'

III

'It's one thing,' said Alleyn that evening, 'to have the whole case wrapped up in the copper's mind and to be absolutely sure, as I am, who's responsible; and it's an entirely different matter to get a jury to believe it. God knows it's a tangle, and can't you hear counsel for the defence? "Ladies and Gentlemen of the jury, you have listened very patiently to this – this impudent tarradiddle," and so on. I've been hoping for something to break – the man himself, perhaps – but there's nothing. Nothing.'

Fox made a long sympathetic rumbling sound.

'I've read and re-read the whole case from the beginning, and to me it's as plain as the nose on your old face, Br'er Fox, but I'm damned if it will be to anybody else. It's too far removed from simple, short statements although, God knows, they *are* there. *I* don't know. You've got the warrant. Shall we walk in and feel his collar or shan't we?'

'We're not likely to pick up anything else if we don't.'

'No. No, we're not, I suppose.'

His telephone rang.

As Alleyn listened and made notes, his face cleared.

'Thank you,' he said, 'I think so. I freely confess I didn't notice . . . It may be considerable . . . I see . . . Thank you, Peregrine,' he said again and hung up, pushing the paper over to Fox who had assumed his spectacles in preparation. 'This helps,' he said.

'Certainly does,' Fox agreed.

'I never noticed.'

'You didn't know there was going to be a murder.'

'Well, no. But nor did young Robin. Lay on a car and a couple of coppers, will you, Fox?'

He took a pair of handcuffs from a drawer in his desk.

'Think he'll turn ugly?' asked Fox.

'I don't know. He might. Come on.'

They went down in the lift.

It was a warm early summer's night. The car was waiting for them and Alleyn gave the address to the driver. He and Fox sat in front and the two uniform police in the back.

'It's an arrest,' Alleyn said. 'I don't expect much trouble but you never know. The *Macbeth* murder.'

The traffic streamed past in a world of lights, hurrying figures, incalculable urgencies proclaiming the warmth and excitability of London at night. In the suburbs the traffic thinned out. In Dulwich they slowed down and pulled up. The cul-de-sac off Alleyn Road was a dark entry with no lights in the front of the house. A man was waiting for them and came up to the car.

'Hullo,' said Alleyn. 'Nobody stirring?'

'He hasn't left the place, sir. There's another of our chaps by the back entrance.'

'Right. Ready?'

'Yes, sir.' The other three men spread out behind him.

Alleyn pressed a bellpush. Footsteps. A dim light behind glass panels and a fine voice, actor-trained, called out: 'I'll go.' Footsteps sounded and the clank of a chain and turn of a key.

The door opened. The tall figure was silhouetted against the dimly lit hall.

'I was expecting you,' the man said. 'Come in.'

Alleyn went in, followed by Fox. The two constables followed. One of them locked the door and pocketed the key.

'Gaston Sears,' said Alleyn, 'I am about to charge you with the murder of Dougal Macdougal. Do you wish to say anything? You are not obliged to say anything unless you wish to do so, but whatever you say will be taken down and may be given in evidence.'

'Thank you. I wish to say a great deal.'

Fox took out his notebook and pen. Alleyn said: 'I will search you, if you please, before you begin.'

Gaston turned and placed his hands against the wall.

He wore his black cloak; there were letters and papers of all kinds in every pocket. Alleyn handed them to Fox who noted their contents and tied them together. They seemed for the most part to be concerned with ancient weaponry and in particular with the claidheamh-mor.

'Please do not lose them,' Gaston said. 'They are extremely valuable.'

'They will be perfectly safe.'

'I am relieved to receive your assurance, sir. Where is my claidheamh-mor?'

'Locked up at the Yard.'

'Locked up? *Locked up?* Do you know what you are saying? Do you realize that I, who know more about the latent power of the claidheamh-mor than anyone living, have so disastrously aroused it that I am brought to this pass by its ferocity alone? Do you know – '

On and on went the great voice. Ancient documents, the rune on the hilts, the history of bloodshed, formal executions, decapitation in battle, what happened to the thief of the sixteenth century (decapitation), its effect on people who handled it (lunacy). 'I, in my pride, in my arrogance, supposed myself exempt. Then came the fool Macdougal and his idiot remarks. I felt it swell in my hands.

'And what do you suppose inspired the practical joker? Decapitated heads. But how do you account for them? You cannot. I could not until I discovered Barrabell's wife had suffered decapitation at the hands of the so-called Hampstead Chopper. Wherever the claidheamh-mor turns up, it is associated with decapitation. And I, its demented agent, I in my vanity – '

On and on. Sometimes fairly logical reasoning, sometimes high-flown nonsense, until at last Gaston stopped, wiped his brow, said he was rather warm, and asked for a glass of water, which the Chinese servant brought.

'Before you go on again,' said Alleyn, 'you have just said – ' he consulted his notes – '"I, its demented agent, I in my vanity". What were you about to say?'

'Let me think. "Demented agent" did I say? "In my vanity"? But it's as clear as may be, surely. It came alive in my hands. I was the appointed man.'

'You mean you killed Dougal Macdougal?'

'Certainly. If holding the claidheamh-mor can be *called* "killing", I killed him.' He drew himself up. He might have been an eccentric professor about to address his class. He grasped the lapels of his cloak, raised his chin and pitched his voice on a declamatory level.

'It was after the servant put the false head on my claidheamh-mor. He carried it into the appointed corner and left it there and went away. I removed the belt of my tunic. I held the claidheamh-mor in my hands and it was alive and hot and desirous of blood.

'I stood there in the shadows. Very still. I heard him declaim:

". . . weapons laugh to scorn,
Brandished by man that's of a woman born."

I heard him cross the stage. I raised the claidheamh-mor. He came in, shielding his eyes in the comparative dark. He said, "Who's there?" I said, "Sir Dougal, there's a thong loose on your left foot. You will trip," and he said, "Oh, it's you, is it. Thank you." He stooped down and the claidheamh-mor leapt in my hands and decapitated him. I put the head on it and left it in the corner. The coronet had fallen off it and I put it on my own head. I could hear Macduff's soliloquy and his encounters with the other figures that he mistook for Macbeth and I was ready. I heard Old Siward say, "*Enter, sir, the castle*," and I pulled down my visor and adjusted my cloak and I went on and fought as Macbeth and Macduff chased me off and ran on past me. I replaced my heavy belt. That is how it was. I was the avenger. I was proud as Lucifer.'

IV

A sunny Sunday and sightseeing craft plied up and down the Thames on their trips to the Tower. The Jays with Alleyn were drinking their after-lunch coffee on the terrace outside their house and across the river the Dolphin, having had its outside washed down, sparkled in the sunshine. William, whose Sunday visit had become a fixture, was being noisily entertained upstairs in the ex-nursery by Robin and Richard.

'Gaston's saved us a lot of trouble by confessing,' said Alleyn. 'Though I can't think of a more *mot injuste* for his manner of doing it. He sticks to his story and I can't make up my mind, to my own satisfaction, whether the plea's altogether genuine. Luckily I don't have to. The defence, if he allows it, will be guilty but insane. His past history will support it though he'll fight it tooth and nail. But he was very cunning, you know. He cooked up an alibi for himself by committing the crime earlier. He was talking away to the covey of "corpses" when the murder was supposed to be done, and alleging he suffered from asthma which he kept quiet about for professional reasons to conceal the fact that he was out of breath from the fight. In reality he's as strong as an ox with the wind of a bellows. There's no question of it being an unrehearsed impulse. All the same – '

'All the same?' said Emily.

'Whatever the verdict is, I've an idea it won't upset him as much as it would anyone else. He'll write a book, I dare say. And he'll adore the trial.'

'What about Barrabell?'

'Horrid little man with his tricks and manners and anonymous messages. But we won't let him go to Russia. He's required to give evidence. I shouldn't talk like this about him, he's had an appalling experience, God knows, but it's not fair to be such a good actor and such a crawler. In a way he's a link in the whole business. He started the decapitation business and he got Gaston thinking about it and about the claidheamh-mor. Upon my word, I wouldn't be surprised if he planted the idea in Gaston's wild imagination. How's your play going? You've started rehearsals, haven't you?'

'Yes. All right. Too early to predict. Young William's an actor. Maggie's shaping well. And – Good Lord, I've forgotten. It's why I asked you to lunch in the first place. Wait a moment.'

Peregrine went indoors. There was a wild shriek from above and the three little boys came tumbling downstairs. They fell into a scrum and out of it and rushed round the house, William shouting, '"*The devil damn thee black, thou cream-faced loon.*"'

Alleyn called out, 'Robin! May I interrupt?'

'Yes, sir?' said Robin warily.

'It's about you knowing the fighter wasn't Macbeth.'

'Did you guess?' said Robin, rallying.

'Only after you gave the hint. Macbeth and all his men wore black lambskin tunics, didn't they?'

'Yes.'

'And Seyton wore a heavy belt to support the claidheamh-mor?'

'That's right.'

'And when he took it off it showed the wear – the lambskin all flattened and worn?'

'Yes. Only when his cloak-thing shifted for a second.'

'I should have noticed and I didn't. You've been a great help, Robin.'

'Will I have to give evidence?' Robin asked hopefully.

'Not if he confesses.'

'Oh.'

'I just wanted to thank you.'

'You didn't notice at the time, sir. I expect you would have,' said Robin kindly. 'When you got round to it.'

'I hope so,' Alleyn said meekly.

'Hi!' Robin shouted. *'William!'* And tore off round the house.

Peregrine reappeared. He carried a long package carefully wrapped in brown paper. 'Do you know what's in here?' he asked.

Alleyn took it, passed his hands over it and weighed it. 'Dummy swords?' he asked.

'Right. The wooden swords used for rehearsing the fight while Gaston made the steel ones. Being Gaston, they are needlessly ornate and highly finished. Now look at this.'

He gave Alleyn an open envelope addressed to 'Master William Smith'. 'Read it,' he said.

Alleyn took it out.

Master William Smith.

   I regret that I, having been much engaged of late, forgot the promise I made you at the beginning of the season. I have, as some compensation, included both weapons. You will be anxious to learn their correct usage. Treat them with the utmost care and respect. Regrettably, I shall not be at liberty to teach you but Mr Simon Morten will no doubt be glad to do so. You will be a good actor.

I remain,

Your obedient servant,
Gaston Sears

'Shall I give them to the boy? And the letter?'

After a long pause, Alleyn said: 'I don't know William. If he is a sensible boy and respects the tools of his trade – yes. I think you should.'

Black Beech
and Honeydew

An Autobiography

In remembrance of my mother

Contents

1	'All Kind Friends and Relations'	435
2	The Hills	461
3	School	482
4	Mountains	501
5	The Coast	521
6	Winter of Content	535
7	Enter the Lampreys	558
8	Northwards	575
9	Turning Point	596
10	New Ways	613
11	Exercise Heartbreak and Recovery	641
12	Second Wind	678
13	A Last Look Back	704
	Bibliography	722

CHAPTER 1

'All Kind Friends and Relations'

In 1912, on a midsummer morning in the foothills of the Southern Alps, I experienced a moment of absolute happiness: bliss, you might call it, only I don't want to kill the recollection with high words.

Whenever I travel backwards, as of course one inclines to do as one grows older, it is at this point that I find an accent, a kind of halt, as emphatic as one of those little stations that interrupt the perspective of railway lines across the Canterbury Plains in New Zealand. I am almost afraid to stop there because, as everybody knows, one may return too often to past delights; to the smell of a book, of a crushed geranium leaf, of a box-tree hedge, hot with sunshine: or of honeydew in summertime.

This was a morning that would soon grow very warm. At that early hour – about half-past six – one could already smell the honeydew. It is exuded by a tiny insect and sweats in transparent globules through a black, mossy parasite that covers the trunks of native beech trees in New Zealand. Chip-dry twigs snapped under my feet. Bellbirds, exactly named, absent-mindedly prolonging their dawn-song, tinkled in the darker reaches of the bush. From our hidden tents, the smell of woodsmoke and frying bacon drifted through the trees. Someone climbed down to the river for water and a bucket clanked pleasantly. I came to a halt and there at once was the voice of the river filling the air in everlasting colloquy with its own wet stones.

It was then abruptly that I was flooded by happiness. In an agony of gratitude, I flung my arms round the nearest honeyed tree and hugged it. I was fourteen years old.

An impressionable age, of course, but, if this was a moment of typical adolescent rapture, I can only say that for me it was unique. One anticipates or remembers happiness; one feels but does not define, responds but does not pause to say, of the present delighted moment: 'How astonishing! I am perfectly happy.'

I have recorded this sensation because I recognized it when it happened. For that reason it might be said to have been a moment of truth. With this trip to an isolated station I move down the parallel lines of my backward journey until they meet at the point where remembrance seems to begin.

In the first decade of this century, Fendalton was a small, genteel suburb on the outskirts of Christchurch in the South Island of New Zealand. Large Edwardian houses stood back in their own grounds masked by English trees. Small houses hid with refinement behind high evergreen fences. Ours was a small house. There was a lawn in front and an orchard behind. To me they were extensive but I don't suppose they amounted to more than a quarter of an acre. I remember the trees: a pink-flowering, glossy, sticky-leafed shrub that overhung the garden gate, a monkey-puzzle which I disliked and a giant (or again so it seemed to me) wellingtonia that I was able to climb. From its branches I looked south across rooftops and gardens to a plantation of oaks with a river flowing through it where we kept our rowing-boat. Behind that was Hagley Park with a lake, sheep and playing fields, then the spire of Christchurch Cathedral and in the far distance, the Port Hills. I might have been an English child looking across a small provincial city except that when I turned to the north, there, on a clear day, forty miles across the plains, shone a great mountain range.

Outside my bedroom window stood a lilac bush, a snowball tree and a swing. In the orchard I remember only a golden pippin, currant bushes, a throbbing artesian well, hens and a rubbish heap. The rubbish heap is appallingly clear because in it one afternoon, when I was about six years old, I buried a comic song which I had previously stolen from the drawing room and torn to pieces. It was called 'Villikins and His Dinah' and the last line was 'a cup of cold poison lay there by her side'. My father, who had an offhand, amused talent in such matters, used to sing this song in Dickensian cockney with mock heroics and whenever he did so struck terror to my heart.

The paper-chase fragments of this composition must have been found, I think, that same evening. I remember my mother's very beautiful troubled face and her saying rather despairingly, 'But why? Why did you?' I must have shown, or tried to express, my fear because I was not in deep disgrace and only had to say I was sorry to my father and promise to tell my mother about things that frightened me. In the end, but it seems to me it must have been a long time afterwards, I did manage to tell her of my terror of poison and how, without believing them, I constantly made up fantasies about it being spread like invisible butter on handtowels or inserted slyly into the porridge one was made to eat for breakfast.

'But do you think I put it there?' asked my gentle mother.

'Not truly,' I wept. 'Not really and truly.'

With her arm sheltering me, she said profoundly, to herself, not to me: 'It must have been *The Fool's Paradise*.'

This, I should explain, was a play. Was it by Sutro or perhaps a translation from Sardou? My parents, who were gifted amateurs, had recently played in the piece and had, I imagine, rehearsed their scenes together in my hearing, never supposing that I understood a word of them. The theme was that of a *femme fatale* who slowly poisoned her husband and was suspected and finally accused of her crime by the family doctor. I have no idea whether it ended in her arrest or suicide but rather think the latter. I am sure my mother was right and that it was this highly coloured drama that engendered the terror which obsessed me, in the validity of which I did not believe and which took so long to evaporate. To this day, on the rare occasions that I use poison in a detective story, I am visited by a ludicrous aftertaste of my childish horrors.

It may be seen from this episode that I supported the theme, so indefatigably explored by psycho-novelists, of the anguish of the only child. I was, I am afraid, a morbid little creature.

For all this, there were raptures, delights and cosy satisfactions.

Here are my parents, standing before the range in an old-fashioned colonial kitchen. My father, an amateur carpenter, has been building a boat. He carries his pipe in his hand and wears a red tam-o'-shanter on his head. His arm is round my mother. They are smiling at me. I am in a sort of fenced baby swing that has been slung from the ceiling. I swoop towards them and my father says delightfully, 'We don't want you.' He gives me a shove and I am swung away from them, shouting with laughter. He has me on his shoulders. The doors have been shut and we are in a dark passage but perfectly secure. He gives a leap and we are in the roof. He is talking to the friendly house-pixies who reply in falsetto voices. Do I know that it's an act? I think I do, but am enchanted all the same. He tells me, for the hundredth time, his original story of Maria and John who bought a piglet called Grunter which, in trickery, was replaced by a terrier pup. If he changes a word I correct him. He tries *Alice in Wonderland* but is too dramatic with 'Off With Her Head' and frightens me. He reads *Pickwick Papers* and *The Ingoldsby Legends*. I am enraptured, particularly with Mr Winkle with whom, for some reason, I feel I have much in common: timidity perhaps. Even the discovery, when I look into the book myself, of the awful picture of a dying clown in a four-poster, although it appals me, doesn't put me off *Pickwick Papers*. Worse than this is the cut of the Dead Drummer in *Ingoldsby*. The book is in our Edwardian drawing room, a tiny peacock-blue and white place. I sneak in there, and for the sheer compulsive horror of it, turn the pages until the ghastly lamps of the dead drummer's eyes are turned up at me. Further on and still worse is the Nun of Netley Abbey being walled up by smug-faced monks. Yet neither of these diminishes my relish of the Witches Frolic, of the macabre, the really ghastly, but strangely enjoyable reiterations of 'The Hand of Glory' or the rollicking wholesale slaughters of Sir Ingoldsby Bray. I am enchanted by the legend of The Leech of Folkestone and gratified when my father points out that the description of Thomas Marsh's Arms correspond with our own. These, with the Teutonic brutalities of the brothers Grimm, leave me engaged but unmoved – yet a story of Hans Andersen is so dreadful that even now I don't enjoy recalling it. Who can tell what will frighten or delight a child, or why?

II

It seems to me now that in those early days my father was a kind of a treat: that I enjoyed him enormously without being involved with him. It was my mother who had the common but appalling task of 'bringing me up' and who had to steer an uncharted course between the nervous illogic of a delicate child, prone to fear, and the cunning obstinacy of a little girl determined to give battle in matters of discipline. Here she is, suddenly, running in a preoccupied manner across the lawn from the garden gate where she has said goodbye to a caller. She runs with a graceful loping stride, unhampered by her long skirt: brown stuff with brown velvet endorsements. I watch her from the dining-room window and twiddle the acorn end of the blind cord. She looks up and sees me and a smile, immensely vulnerable, breaks over her face. How dreadfully easy it is to love and hurt her. I adored, defied and finally obeyed my mother and believed that she understood me better than anyone else in my small world.

It was a very small world indeed: a nurse called Alice, whom I don't remember and who must have left me when I was still a baby, a maid called May who had a round red face and was considered a comic, my maternal grandparents, my parents and their circle of friends. A cat called Susie and a spaniel called Tip.

Quite early in the day I learned to laugh at my father: not unkindly but because it was impossible to know him well and not to think him funny. He thought himself funny when his oddities were pointed out to him. 'I didn't!' he would say to my mother. 'How you exaggerate! I did *not*, Betsy.' And break out laughing. It was, in fact, impossible to exaggerate his absent-mindedness or the strange fantasies that accompanied this comic-opera trait in his character.

'My saddle-tweed trousers have gone!' he announced, making a dramatic entrance upon my mother and a luncheon guest.

'They can't have gone.'

'Completely. You go and look. Gone! That's all.'

'How can they have gone?'

My father made mysterious movements of his head in the direction of the dining room and May.

'Taken them to give that chap,' he whispered. May had a follower.

'Oh, no, Lally. Nonsense.'

'All right! Where are they? Where are they?'

'You haven't looked properly.'

He stared darkly at her and retired. Doors and drawers could be heard angrily banging. Oaths were shouted.

'*Are* they gone, do you suppose?' asked our visitor who was a close friend.

'No,' said my mother composedly.

My father returned in furious triumph. 'Well,' he sneered, 'that's that. That's the end of my saddle-tweed trousers.' He laughed shortly. 'You won't get cloth like that in New Zealand.'

'They must be somewhere.'

He stamped. His eyes flashed. 'They are *not* somewhere,' he shouted. 'That damn' girl's stolen them.'

'Ssh!'

My father's nostrils flared. He opened his mouth.

'What are those things on your legs, my dear chap?' asked our guest.

My father looked at his legs. 'Good Lord!' he said mildly, 'so they are.'

Early one morning he met Susie, our cat, walking in the garden. He carried her to my mother who was not yet up.

'Look, Betsy,' he said. 'I found this cat walking in the garden. Isn't she like Susie?'

'She is Susie,' said my mother.

'I thought you'd say that,' he rejoined, delightedly. Susie purred and rubbed her face against his. 'She's awfully tame. You'd think she knew me, wouldn't you?' asked my father.

'It is Susie,' said my mother on a hysterical note.

He smiled kindly at her and put Susie down. 'Run along, old girl,' he said. 'Go home to your master.'

My mother was now laughing uncontrollably.

'Don't be an ass, Betsy,' said my father gently and left her.

It must not be supposed that he was an unintelligent man. He was widely read, particularly in biology and the natural sciences, was an enthusiastic rationalist and a member of the Philosophical Society. He was also an avid reader of fiction. Of the Victorians, he most enjoyed Dickens and Scott. My mother disliked Scott because of his historical inaccuracies and bias. None of his novels was in the house. She deeply admired Hardy and once told me that after reading the end of *Tess*, she sat up all night, imprisoned in distress and unable to free herself. In later years we all three read and discussed the Georgian novelists. My mother's favourites were Galsworthy (with reservations: she thought Irene a stuffed dummy) and Conrad.

Almayer's Folly she read over and over again. Somehow her copy of this novel has been lost. I would like to discover why it so held her. My father's favourite was Aldous Huxley though he often remarked that the chap was revolting for the sake of being revolting and that *Point Counter Point* gained nothing by its elaborate form. He was more gregarious in his reading than my mother and would sometimes devour a 'shilling shocker'. His hand trembled and his pipe jigged between his teeth as he approached the climax. 'Frightful rot!' he would say. 'Good Lord! Regular Guy Boothby stuff,' and greedily press on with it.

When I was about four years old, I was given a miniature arm-chair made of wicker and a children's annual. I remember dragging the chair on to the lawn, seating myself, opening the book and thinking furiously, 'I *will* read. I *will* read.' After some boring, but I fancy, brief, struggles with *The Dog Has Got a Bone* and a beastly poem about reindeer, I went forward under my own steam and became an avid bookworm.

My parents never stopped me reading a book though I believe my mother was at pains to see that nothing grossly 'unsuitable' was left in my way. The criterion was style: 'He *could* write well,' my mother said of the forgotten William J. Locke, 'but he pot-boils. Very second-rate.' I became something of an infant snob about books, and, like my father, felt a bit below par when I read *Chums* and *Buffalo Bill*, but continued, at intervals, to do so.

My father was English and my mother a New Zealander. She was the one, however, who doggedly determined that I should not acquire the accent. 'The cat,' I was obliged interminably to repeat, 'sat on the mat and the mouse ran across the barn.' 'The cart,' my father would interrupt in a falsetto voice, 'sart on the mart arnd the moose rarn across the bawn.' I thought this excruciatingly witty and so did my mother but by these means the accent was held at bay.

In spite of his anti-religious views my father can have made no objection to my being taken to our parish church or taught to say my prayers. These I found enjoyable. 'Jesustender. Shepherdhearme.' 'Our Fatherchart' and a monotonous exercise beginning 'God bless Mummy and Daddy and All Kind Friends and Relations. God bless Gram and Gramp and – ' It was prolonged for as long as my mother could take it. 'Susie – and Tip – ' I would drone, desperate for more objects of beatitude to fend off the moment when I would be left to set out upon the strange journeys of the night. These were formidable and sometimes appalling. There was one uncouth and recurrent dream in which everything Became Too Big. It might start with one's fingers rubbing gigantically together and with a sickening three-penny piece that swelled horrifically between forefinger and thumb. Then everything swelled to become stifling and I awoke sobbing in my mother's embrace. With a strangely logical determination, I learned to recognize this nightmare while I was experiencing it and trained my sleeping self to force the strangulated dream-scream that would deliver me.

'I know,' my father said. 'I used to have it. Beastly, isn't it, but only a dream. One grows out of it.'

My cot with its wooden spindle sides was brought into my parents' room. In it, on more propitious nights, I sailed and flew immense distances into slowly revolving lights, rainbow chasms and mountainous realms of incomprehensible significance, through which my father's snores surged and receded. Asleep and yet not asleep, I made these nightly journeys: acquiescent, vulnerable, filled with a kind of wonder.

There were day dreams, too, some of them of comparable terror and wonder, others cosy and familiar. I cannot remember a time when I was not visited occasionally, and always when I least expected it, by an experience which still recurs with, if anything, increasing poignancy. It is a common experience and for all I know there may be a common scientific explanation of it. It comes suddenly with an air of truth so absolute that one feels all other times must be illusion. It is not a sensation but a confrontation with duality. One moves outside oneself and sees oneself as a complete stranger and this is always a shock and an astonishment although one recognizes the moment and can think: 'Here we go again. This is it.' It is not self-hypnotism, because there is no loss of awareness as far as everyday surroundings are concerned: only the removal of oneself from the self who observes them and the overwhelming sensation of strangeness. It seems that if one held on to this moment and extended it one would make an enormous discovery but, for me, at least, this is impossible and I always return. Is this, I wonder, what was meant originally by being 'beside oneself'. It is an odd phenomenon and as a child I grew quite familiar with it.

My grandmother considered that my religious observances were inadequate. When she came to stay with us she brought a Victorian manual which had been the basis of my mother's and aunts' and uncles' dogmatic instruction. It was called *Line Upon Line* and was in the form of dialogue, like the catechism: Q. and A.

' "Who," ' asked my grandmother, beginning at the beginning, ' "is God?" '

I shook my head.

' "God," ' said my grandmother, taking both parts, ' "is a Spirit." '

Reminded of the little blue methylated flame on the tea tray I asked: 'Can you boil a kekkle on Him, Gram?'

She turned without loss of poise to Bible Stories: to Balaam and his ass. I suggested cooperatively that this was probably a circus donkey. My father was enchanted.

My grandmother told my mother that it was perhaps rather too soon to begin religious instruction and, instead, read me the Peter Pan bits out of *The Little White Bird*.

When I was about twelve my father brought home the collected works of Henry Fielding. 'Jolly good stuff,' he said. 'You'd better read it.'

I began with the plays and was at once nonplussed by many words. 'What is a "wor"?' I asked my father who said I knew very well what a war was and mentioned South Africa. 'This is spelt differently,' I said, nettled. 'It seems to be some sort of girl.' My father quickly said it was a 'fast' sort of girl. This was good enough. I had heard girls stigmatized as being 'fast' and certainly these ladies of Fielding's seemed to behave with a certain incomprehensible alacrity. My father suggested that I try *Tom Jones*. I did so: I read it all and also, since Smollett turned up at this juncture, *Roderick Random*. It bothered me that I could not greatly enjoy these works since David Copperfield, whom I adored, had at my age or earlier, relished them extremely. I, on the contrary, still doted upon Little Lord Fauntleroy.

We were, as I now realize, hard up. On both sides I came from what Rose Macaulay called 'have-not' families. My father was the eldest of ten. When he was still a schoolboy his own father (the youngest of three) died, leaving his widow in what were called reduced circumstances. He was a tea broker in the days of the clippers. This was considered OK socially for a younger son but then 'an upstart called Thomas Lipton' came along with his common retail packets and instead of following suit like a sensible man and going into 'trade' my grandfather remained genteelly aloof and his affairs went into a decline. His elder brother, William, was in the Colonial Service and became a Vice Admiral and Administrator of Hong Kong. Upon him, a childless man, the hopes of my grandmother depended.

Having begun in a prep school at Harrow and been destined, I suppose, for the public school, my father declined, with the family fortune, upon a number of private establishments but finally was sent to Dulwich College. He used to tell me how it was founded in Elizabethan times by a wonderful actor called Alleyn. The name stuck in my memory. My grandmother had inherited a small Georgian house near Epping and there she coped vaguely with her turbulent sons and three docile daughters with whose French governess one of my great-uncles soon eloped. This was Uncle Julius, a 'wag' as his contemporaries would have said and an original: much admired by his nephews, especially by my father. His wife had a markedly Gallic disposition, according to her legend, and unfortunately went mad in later life and used to send flamboyant Christmas cards to my father addressed to H. E. Marsh Esq., General Manager, The Bank of New Zealand, New Zealand. This, as will appear, was a gross overstatement. My father, who had a deep and passionate love of field sports, used to poach with his Uncle Julius on the game preserves of his more richly possessed second cousin. I still have the airgun he bought for this purpose. It is made to resemble a walking-stick. Perhaps his propensity for firearms led him into joining the Volunteers who preceded the New Zealand Army. Before he married he had already received a commission from Queen Victoria in which he was referred to as her 'trusty and well-beloved Henry Edmund'. He continued with his martial activities until the Volunteers dissolved into a less picturesque organization. I used to think he looked perfectly splendid in his uniform.

The family is supposed to derive from the reprobate de Mariscos of Lundy. Whether this is really so or not, the legend is firmly implanted in all our bosoms. When, as a girl, I read of Geoffrey de Marisco who had the effrontery to stab a priest in the presence of the

King, I asked myself if my father's anticlerical bias was perhaps hereditary. By the reign of Charles II we are on firm historical ground for there is Richard Stephen Marsh, an Esquire of the Bedchamber, a direct forebear and almost the only really interesting character, apart from the de Mariscos, that the family has thrown up. He concerned himself with the trials and misfortunes of Fox, the Quaker, and actually persuaded the King so far out of his chronic lethargy as to intercede very mercifully between Fox and his savage persecutors. It is a curious and all too scantily documented affair. Apparently not only Esquire Marsh, as he is invariably called, but Charles himself responded to the extraordinary personality of this intractable Quaker. Although Marsh died an Anglican and an incumbent of the Tower (or should it be 'Constable') there seems to have been some sort of Foxian hangover because his descendants became Quakers and remained so until my great-great-grandfather married out of the Society of Friends and returned to the Church of England. My father was never rude about the Society of Friends.

In Uncle William's day, the Governor of Hong Kong – a Pope-Hennessey – was often absent and twice, for long stretches, Uncle William was called upon to administer the government of the Colony. Yellowing photographs portray him in knickerbockers and sola topee, seated rather balefully under a marquee among ADCs in teapot attitudes and ladies with croquet mallets. One of his nieces ('Imported,' my father used to say, 'for the purpose.') was married to Thomas Jackson, the founder of the Hong Kong & Shanghai Bank. ('Good Lord! They've stuck up a statue to Tom Jackson!')

These connections were supposed to settle my father's future. On leaving school he was sent to learn Chinese at London University and banking at the London office of the Hong Kong-Shanghai. From here, aided perhaps by nepotic shoves, he was to mount rapidly into the upper reaches of Head Office. Instead, he went, as the saying then was, into a consumption and was sent to South Africa where, after a stay on the bracing veldt, he came out of it again. What was to be done with him?

Uncle William, now in retirement, visited New Zealand where his brother-in-law had founded the Colonial Bank. Indefatigable in good works, he sent for my father. The pattern was to be repeated in a more favourable climate. No sooner were my father's feet planted on the ladder than, owing to political machinations, the Colonial Bank broke. Uncle William returned to England. My father got a clerkship in the Bank of New Zealand and there remained until he retired. I can imagine nobody less naturally suited to his employment. He might have been a good man of science where absence-of-mind is tolerantly regarded: in a bank clerk it is a grave handicap. When I was about ten years old, very large sums of money were stolen from my father's desk and from that of his next-door associate. I can remember all too vividly the night he came home with this frightful news. Sensible of my parents' utter misery I tried to cheer them up by playing 'Nights of Gladness' very slowly with the soft pedal down. I was not musical and in any case it is a rollicking waltz.

It was an inside job and the thief was generally known but there was not enough evidence to bring him to book and the responsibility was my father's. Uncle William, always helpful, died at this juncture and left him a legacy from which he was able to replace the loss. The amount that remained was frivolously invested for him in England and also lost. He was a have-not.

His rectitude was enormous: I have never known a man with higher principles. He was thrifty. He was devastatingly truthful. In many ways he was wise and he had a kind heart, and a nice sense of humour. He was never unhappy for long: perhaps, in his absent-mindedness, he forgot to be so. I liked him very much.

III

My mother's maiden name was Rose Elizabeth Seager. Her paternal grandfather was completely ruined by the economic disturbances that followed the emancipation of slaves in the West Indies. As the Society of Friends was in a considerable measure responsible for this admirable reform, it is not too fanciful, perhaps, to suggest that one great-grandfather may have had a share in the other's undoing. There is a parallel in the later history of the two families. Among the Seagers also, there appears briefly an affluent and unencumbered uncle to whom my great-grandfather was heir. The story was that this uncle took his now impoverished nephew to Scotland to see the estates he would inherit and on the return journey died intestate in the family chaise. His fortune was thrown into Chancery and my great-grandfather upon the world. He got some extremely humble job in the Middle Temple and my grandfather went to the choir school of the Temple Church. None of the family fortunes was ever recovered.

These misadventures sound like the routine opening of a dated and unconvincing romance and I think were so regarded by my mother and her brothers and sisters. Perhaps they grew tired of hearing their father talk about the fortune lost in Chancery and more than a little sceptical of its existence. Indeed stories of 'riches held in Chancery' have a suspect glint over them, as if the narrator had looked once too often into Bleak House. Moreover, my grandfather – Gramp – had a reputation for embroidery. He was of a romantic turn, and extremely inventive and he had a robust taste in dramatic narrative. The story of the lost fortune was held to be one of Gramp's less successful excursions into fantasy and his virtuoso performance of running back at speed through his high-sounding ancestry to the Conquest was tolerated rather than revered.

He died when I was about eighteen. My mother and aunts went through his few possessions and discovered a trunkful of letters which turned out to be a correspondence between his own father and a firm of London solicitors. They were chronologically assembled. The earlier ones began with references to ancient lineage and ended with elaborate compliments. The tone grew progressively colder and the last letter was short.

'Dear Sir: We are in receipt of your latest communication which we find impertinent and hostile. We have the honour to be your obedient servants . . .'

They were all about estates in Scotland, a death in a family chaise and monies in Chancery. The sums mentioned were shatteringly large.

Even then my mother was incredulous and I think would have remained so had not she and I, sometime afterwards, gone to stay with friends in Dunedin. Our host was another victim of the courts of Chancery and, like my great-grandfather, had written to his family solicitors in England to know if there was the smallest chance of recovery. They had replied extremely firmly that there was none but, for his information, had enclosed a list of the principal – is the word heirs? – to monies in Chancery. There, almost at the top of the list, which was a little out of date, was Gramp. For once, he had not exaggerated.

He had come as a youth to the province of Canterbury in New Zealand in the early days of its settlement. He too was a 'have-not' and also a spendthrift but he enjoyed life immensely. He met my grandmother – Gram – in Christchurch. They went for their honeymoon in a bullock wagon. Canterbury in the 1850s was still a swamp.

One of my grandfather's acquaintances of the early days was Samuel Butler who had taken up sheep-country in a mountainous region which is now sometimes called after his Utopian romance – *Erewhon*. 'Odd chap, Sam Butler,' Gramp used to say and then he would tell us of the occasion when he went to stay with Butler who met him at the railhead somewhere out on the Canterbury Plains and drove him over many miles of very rough country, through water-races and a dangerous river up into Mesopotamia which is the true name of this part of the Alps.

While Gramp was staying there, Butler received a letter from an acquaintance, inviting himself as a guest. Butler took this in very bad part and did nothing but grumble. He would not allow Gramp to relieve him of the long and tedious journey to the rendezvous but settled angrily on their both going. Hour after hour their gig bumped and jolted over pleistocene inequalities. When they achieved the railhead and the train arrived with the self-invited guest, Gramp proposed to transfer to the backward-looking rear seat of the gig.

'No you don't, Seager!' Butler shouted, irritably slamming his guest's valise under the seat. 'Stay where you are, God damn it.' His wretched guest climbed up behind.

They set off for Mesopotamia. Butler became excited by some topic and talked and drove vigorously. He touched up the mare and they staggered through a watercourse at an inappropriate pace and drove rapidly on over Turk's heads and boulders. My grandfather felt sorry for the guest. He turned to include him in the conversation and found that he was no longer there.

'Butler – your visitor! He has fallen off. That last water-race – '

Butler broke out in a stream of vituperation, and could scarcely be persuaded to turn back. He did so, however, and presently they met the guest, wet and bruised and plodding desperately towards the Southern Alps. Butler abused him like a pickpocket and could scarcely wait for him to climb back on his perch.

Like all Gramp's stories this should, I suppose, be taken with a pinch of salt but he used to laugh so heartily when he told it and stick so closely to the one version that I feel it must have been, like the blue blood and monies in Chancery, substantially true.

Of Gram's family I know next to nothing except that they lived in Gloucestershire and that her great-grandparents were friends of Dr Edward Jenner. Gram's great-grandmother kept a journal which a century after it was written Gram showed to my mother. It set out how Dr Jenner became interested in the West Country belief that persons who had had cowpox never developed smallpox and he asked my great-to-the-fourth-power grandmother if she would have a record kept of her own dairymaid's health. She became as interested as he and the journal was full of his theories. Finally, between them, they persuaded a dairymaid called Sarah Nelmes to let Dr Jenner take lymph from a cow poxvesicle on her finger. With this, on 14th May, 1775, he vaccinated a boy called Phipps and from then onwards his advances were excitedly recorded by his friends. My mother did not know what became of her great-great-grandmother's journal and indeed the only other piece of information she had about Gram's people was that some of them are buried in Gloucester Cathedral where she looked them up when she was in England. Gram was rather austere and extremely conventional but she had a twinkle.

On Gramp's immigration papers he appeared as a 'schoolmaster' but never practised as one. Instead, he gave his romantic streak full play. He joined the newly formed police force, took a hand in designing a dashing uniform which he wore when he made a number of exciting arrests including those of a famous sheep-stealer and a gigantic Negro murderer. He was put in charge of the first gaol built in the Province but left this job to become superintendent of the new mental asylum: Sunnyside. He was not, of course, a doctor (I imagine there were not enough to go round), but he was strangely advanced in his methods, playing the organ to his 'children' as he called the patients, whom he loved, and using a form of mesmerism on some of the more violent ones. If any of his own family had a headache my grandmother would say crisply: 'Go to your father and be mesmerized.' Gramp would flutter his delicate hands across and across their foreheads until the headache had gone. He did this with the full approval of the visiting medical superintendent, Dr Coward, who was very interested in Gramp's therapeutic methods.

He had a good stage built in the hall at Sunnyside, no doubt as part of the treatment but also, I suspect, because theatre was his ruling passion. Here he produced plays, using his children, his friends and some of the more manageable patients as actors. He also performed conjuring tricks, spending far too much of his own money on elaborate and costly equipment. His patter was magnificent. One by one as each of my aunts grew to the desirable size, she was crammed into a tortuous under-suit of paper-thin jointed steel, and, so attired, walked on the stage, seated herself on a high stool at an expensive trick-table, adopted a pensive attitude, her elbow on the table, her finger on her brow and, like Miss Bravassa, contemplated the audience. A spike in the elbow of her armour engaged with a slot in the table. 'Hey presto!' Gramp would say, waving his wand and turning a secret key in his daughter's back. The armour locked. Puck-like, Gramp snatched the stool from under her and there she was: suspended. My Aunt Madeleine, at the appropriate age, was plump. The armour nipped her and she often wept but as the next-in-order was still too small, she was squeezed into service until Gram forbade it. Gramp busily sawed his daughters in half, shut them up in magic cabinets and caused them to disappear. The patients adored it.

I can just remember him doing some of his sleight-of-hand tricks at his grandchildren's birthday parties and playing 'See Me Dance the Polka' while we held out our skirts and bounced.

Of all his children, only my mother inherited his love of theatre and she did so in a marked degree. I know I am not showing partiality when I say that she was quite extraordinarily talented. From the time I first remember her acting it was never in the least like that of an amateur: her approach to a role, her manner of rehearsing, her command of timing and her personal impact were all entirely professional. My grandfather used to organize productions in aid of charities and his daughter became so well known that when an American Shakespearean actor, George Milne, brought his company to New Zealand he asked my mother, then nineteen years old, to play Lady Macbeth with him in Christchurch. She did so with such success that he urged her to become an actress. I cannot imagine what Gram thought of all this. One would suppose her to have been horrified but perhaps her built-in Victorianism worked it out that her husband knew best. There can be little doubt that Gramp was all for the suggestion. The real objections appear to have come from my mother. Strangely, as it seems to me, she had no desire to become a professional actress. The situation was repeated when the English actor Charles Warner, famous for his role in *Drink*, visited New Zealand. He was a personal friend of my grandfather who, I supposed, caused my mother to perform before him. Warner offered to take her into his company and launch her in England. She declined. He and his wife suggested that she should come as their guest to Australia and get the taste of a professional company on tour. In the event, she did cross the Tasman Sea under Mrs Warner's wing. She stayed with family friends in Melbourne, and saw a good deal of the company while she was there. This adventure, though she seemed to have enjoyed it, confirmed her in her resolve. The life, she once said to me, 'was too messy'. I have an idea that the easy emotionalism and 'bohemian' habits of theatre people, while they appealed to her highly developed sense of irony, offended her natural fastidiousness. In many ways a pity, and yet, such is one's egoism, I get a peculiar feeling when I reflect that if she had been otherwise inclined I would have been – simply, *not*. She returned to New Zealand and after an interval of a year or two met and married my father.

It seems to me that almost always a play was toward in our small family and that my nightmare, *The Fool's Paradise*, was only one of a procession. As a child I did not really enjoy hearing my mother rehearse. She became a stranger to me. If the role was a dramatic or tragic one, I was frightened and curiously embarrassed. When as a very small girl, she asked me if I would like to walk on for a child's part in – I think – a Pinero play, I was appalled. Yet I loved to hear all the theatre-talk, the long discussions on visiting actors, on plays and on the great ones of the past. When I was big enough to be taken occasionally to the play my joy was almost unendurable.

One was made to rest in the afternoon. Blinds were drawn and one lay in a state of tumult for the prescribed term, becoming quite sick with anticipation. When confronted with food at an unusual hour, one could eat nothing.

'Good Lord!' said my father. 'Look at the child. She'd better not go if she gets herself into such a stink over it.'

Frightful anxieties arose. Suppose the tickets were lost, suppose we were late? Suppose, from sheer excitement, I were to be sick? In the earliest times, I seem to remember hansom-cabs, evening dress, long gloves and a kind of richness about the arrival but later on, when economy ruled, we waited in queues for the early doors. It was all one to me. There I was, sitting between my parents, in an expectant house. It was no matter how long we waited: the time came when the lights were dimmed and a band of radiance flooded the curtain fringe, when the air was plangent with the illogic of tuning strings, when my heart was either in my stomach or my throat, when a bell rang in the prompt corner and the play was on.

Which came first: *Sweet Nell of Old Drury* or *Bluebell in Fairyland*? Perhaps *Bluebell*. To this piece I was escorted by my great friend, Ned Bristed: a freckled child, perhaps a year my senior. We were taken to the theatre by his mother who saw us into our seats in the dress circle and then left us there, immensely important, and collected us at the end when we returned in a rapturous trance to Ned's house where I spent the night. Ned and I were in perfect accord. Some twenty years later, long after he had been killed in action, it fell to my lot to produce *Bluebell in Fairyland*. I stood in the circle and watched a dress rehearsal and was able for a moment to put into the front row the shadows of a freckled boy and a small girl: ecstatic and feverishly wolfing chocolates.

My mother took me to a matinée of *Sweet Nell of Old Drury*. I saw the whole thing in terms of a fairy tale and fell madly in love with Charles II in the person of Mr Harcourt Beatty. How kindly he shone upon the poor orange girl (Miss Nellie Stewart), how beastly was the behaviour of the two witches, Castlemaine and Portsmouth, how menacing and how superbly outsmarted was the evil Jeffreys. The company returned, we went again and I became even more deeply committed. Later on, when I began to do history, it was irritating to find so marked a note of disapproval in the section on Charles II: Mr Harcourt Beatty, I felt, and not the pedagogue Oman, had the correct approach.

Our visits to the play were not always so successful. When Janet Achurch came, with Ibsen, I was not taken to see her and wish that

I had been but, unless I have confused the occasions, her company, or one that came soon after it, also played *Romeo and Juliet*. To this my mother and I went one afternoon. She was immensely stimulated: too much so, for once, to notice my growing alarm. When the Montagues and Capulets began to set about each other in the streets of Verona I asked nervously: 'They aren't really fighting, are they?'

'Yes, yes!' she replied excitedly. I dived into her lap, surfaced at long intervals and upon finding that people seemed to be dreadfully unhappy, hurriedly submerged again. Worst of all, of course, there was Poison and a girl was Taking It. I vividly remember one final appalled glance at the Tomb of the Capulets and what was going on there and then a shaken return to Fendalton.

'I expect I should have brought you away,' my mother used to say long afterwards, 'but it was a good company. The Mercutio was wonderful.' I know exactly how she felt: it couldn't have been expected of her. She was always very loving and patient over my fears and a constant refuge from them.

She read aloud quite perfectly: not with the offhand brio of my father but with a quiet relish that was immensely satisfying. One was gathered into the book as if into a lap and completely absorbed by it. Her voice was unforced and beautiful.

Whatever I may write about my mother will be full of contradictions. I think that as I grew older I grew, better perhaps than anyone else, to understand her. And yet how much there was about her that still remains unaccounted for, like odd pieces of a jigsaw puzzle. Of one thing I am sure: she had in her an element of creative art never fully realized. I think the intensity of devotion which might have been spent upon its development was poured out upon her only child, who, though she returned this love, inevitably and however unwisely, began at last to make decisions from which she would not be deflected.

IV

It so happened that my two constant companions when I was very small and before I met Ned, were also boys: another only child called Vernon, and my cousin Harvey. They were both older than I and good-naturedly bossed me: always I was the driven horse, obediently curvetting and prancing, always the seeker and never the hider. I accepted their attitude and listened with the deepest respect to their stories of other little boys to whom they 'owed a hiding'. On a seaside holiday with our parents, Harvey and I discovered a religious affinity. We built a sand-castle and on the top moulded a cross. This gave us an extremely complacent and holy feeling.

Of all my parents' circle I loved best the friend who was present on the occasion of the saddle-tweed trousers. His name was Dundas Walker. He acted in most of their plays and made a great success of 'Cis', the precocious youth in Pinero's farce *The Magistrate*. Finding Dundas rather difficult to say I called him by this Victorian nickname but afterwards changed it to 'James'. Destined by his people for the church, he became instead a professional actor. In this choice he was egged on by my mother: was this one of her contradictions or did she realize, quite correctly, that he would be happy in no other sphere?

He invented the most entrancing games: 'Visiting', for instance, when he was always Mrs Finch-Brassy and I, Mrs Boolsum-Porter. 'Forgive me, my dear,' he would say, 'if I borrow your poker. A morsel of your delicious cake has lodged in a back tooth and I must positively rid myself of it.' I always handed him the poker and he then engaged in an elaborate pantomime. 'Ah!' he would say, 'there's nothing like a poker for picking one's teeth. Do you agree?'

I agreed so heartily that on observing an elderly uncle engaged in a furtive manoeuvre behind his napkin I said loudly and confidently: 'Uncle Ellis, Cis says there's nothing like a poker for picking one's teeth.'

'I think, Rose,' my grandmother said to my mother, 'that Mr Walker goes too far with the child.'

He gave me my nicest books, made me laugh more often than anybody except my father and never spoiled me. When he found me trying to dragoon one of Susie's kittens into being harnessed to a shoe box he was so severe that I was stricken with misery and while being bathed that evening burst into tears, tore myself from my mother's hands and fled, roaring my remorse, to the drawing room where I flung myself, dripping wet, into his astonished embrace.

Nothing could exceed the admiration he inspired.

'When I am grown up,' I said warmly, 'I shall marry you.'

'Very well, my dear, and you shall have the family pearls.'

He went on the stage and to England. My mother and I met him in London twenty years later and the friendship was taken up as if it had never been interrupted. I don't think he was ever a very wonderful actor – he always had great difficulty in remembering his lines – but he was fortunate in that he played the leading role in a farce called *A Little Bit of Fluff* that broke all records by running for about eight years up and down the English, Scottish and Irish provinces, so that he had plenty of time to make sure of the lines. He was entirely a man of the theatre and was, I believe, the happiest human being I have ever known and one of the best loved. When he retired in the 1930s he came out to New Zealand and lived with his unmarried sister and brother in a rambling house full of family treasures. The pearls, he once told me, were kept in a newspaper parcel, on the top of his wardrobe.

In 1943, when I began to produce Shakespeare's plays for the University of Canterbury, James helped in all of them, sometimes playing small parts. As he grew older and memorizing became more and more of a difficulty, he concentrated upon make-up for which he had a wonderful gift. He was like a gentle spirit of good luck and was much loved by my student-players. When he died, which he did at an advanced age, and with exquisite tact and the least possible amount of fuss, a group of undergraduates asked to carry him and that must have pleased him very much if he was aware of it.

Our other close friend was Mivvy, daughter of that family with monies in Chancery who lived in Dunedin. In age she was almost midway between my parents and me: old enough to be slightly deferred to and young enough to confide in and to cheek. She has told how I burst in upon her privacy with a howl, having committed some misdemeanour. Tears poured from my eyes into my open mouth.

'Mummy's cross of me!' I bawled. 'But I don't care, Mivvy, do I?'

Mivvy was the kind of friend whose visits can never be long enough and to whom everyone turns at moments of distress without feeling that they ask too much of her. I hope we didn't ask too much: I don't think we did. She was very easy to tease and she was also extremely and comically obstinate. During one of her visits, which we all so much liked, my mother sprained her ankle. Mivvy

was determined to administer fomentations, my mother, equally formidable on such issues, was adamant that she should do no such
thing. Mivvy set her jaw. The siege of the fat ankle, to my infinite
enjoyment, lasted all through one day. Suddenly, at nightfall, my
mother yielded. Mivvy, triumphant, became businesslike. Saucepans
were set to boil. Linen was torn into strips. Lint and aromatic
unguents were displayed. A footbath was prepared. For about an
hour my mother suffered her extremity to be alternately seethed
and chilled while Mivvy, neatly aproned, bustled vaingloriously.
Finally, the ankle was anointed and elaborately bound.

'There!' she cried. 'Now! Doesn't it feel better?'

'It feels perfectly all right, thank you, Mivvy dear,' said my mother
and from beneath the hem of her Edwardian skirt displayed the
other ankle: still swollen.

'If there had been any scalding water left,' Mivvy said, 'I would
have hurled it at you.'

Of all the other grown-up friends and relations who came and
went during my earliest childhood the outlines are blurred. There
were facetious gentlemen who pretended to be staggered by my
voice which was rather deep, and an offensive musical gentleman
who insisted, like Svengali, on looking at my vocal cords. Luckily he
was not possessed of Svengali's expertise. Nothing short of deep and
remorseless hypnosis would ever have induced me to sing in tune.
There was Captain Sykes who became famous, and Mr Parkinson
who collected china and committed suicide, there were numbers of
ladies who came to my mother's 'day' and to whose 'days' I was bor-
ingly taken, since I could not be left at home. One of them kept
swans on an ornamental pond and these arrogant birds rushed, hiss-
ing, at me, when I was sent to play in the garden.

Across the lane in a very big house with a long drive, a lodge at the
gates, a horse-paddock, carriages and gigs, a motor, grooms, servants
and a nanny, lived a boy and girl with whom I loved to play when
my mother visited there. It seemed to me to be a magical place filled
with the scent of flowers. The boy, who was asthmatic and often confined to a wheeled chair, was some three or four years my senior: his
sister about my own age. This was the beginning of an established
friendship. Into the dawn of it, floatingly recollected, come the Duke
and Duchess of York (afterwards King George V and Queen Mary) to

stay at this house. I remember being lifted on a high evergreen fence to watch my friend's uncle wire-jumping his horse for the Duke's entertainment and I remember my parents making ready for a royal reception. Was it on that occasion or a later one that I so laboriously picked violets, bound them, limp and intractable, with a piece of fencing wire out of the gardening shed and presented them to my mother? I see them, wilted, slithering from their confine and weighty to a degree and I see my mother anchoring them in the black lace of her corsage. They must have all disappeared, this way and that, long before the ducal assemblage and I suppose that by some means or other, she rid herself of an embarrassment of stout wire.

I am convinced that recollections of childhood go much further back than we are accustomed to suppose. I realise that mine are based in some measure upon what my parents and friends afterwards told me but for all this I know that many of them have stayed in my conscious memory and that these are the most vivid. The smell, for instance, of newly shot game birds and the glossy slide of their feathers: with this, a shooting hut near the shores of a lake, the song of larks, dry cowpats that were burned in the open fire and, especially, some domestic pigs whose personal hygiene, for some reason, I determined to improve. I remember perfectly well the indignant screams of one of these creatures and the difficulty of retaining my hold on its ear, the depths of which I explored with my own soapy bath-flannel. I have a snapshot taken at the time: it displays my mother graceful and long-skirted, Mivvy and my father in oilskins and sou'westers with shotguns under their arms, the spaniel, Tip, and a stout truculent child of four who is myself.

I have grown, in theory at least, to dislike blood sports but how superb were those sunny mornings when I was allowed to walk behind my father and Tip through the plantation where he and his friends went quail-shooting. On these occasions he was completely and explicitly himself. He would imitate the cry of a Californian cock-quail, make little clucking noises to Tip and even quiver very slightly as Tip did. One had to keep perfectly silent and walk lightly behind the guns. The click of the hammer when he cocked his gun, the sudden whirr of wings, the deafening report and the heady cordite reek of the ejected cartridge-case: these were the ingredients of pure happiness.

When we had followed the guns as far as our picnic place my mother and I would stay there, make a fire of heaven-smelling dry bluegum, and await their return for luncheon. Every now and then we would hear the guns. Shockingly, as one may now feel, my father loved the creatures he shot. Once he described to me very vividly the flight of an English pheasant and the heavy, dark abruptness of its fall. He thought for a moment. 'Awful, really,' he said in a surprised voice, 'isn't it? Awful, I suppose.' As a boy, he saw Ellen Terry play Beatrice and of course fell in love with her. 'When she had to run "like a lapwing, close to the ground" she did it like a hen-partridge, trailing her wing to draw attention away from her nest. Beautiful!' It was the highest praise he could have given Miss Terry.

He was a purist in the management of field sports. When I stumped behind him with a heeled stock in the crook of my arm I had to behave exactly as if it was a real gun: 'uncocking' it at fences or gates, 'unloading' it before I put it down and never pointing it at anybody. To do otherwise was 'loutish'. He was dealt one of those strokes of malevolent ill-fortune that so punctually overtook him when he loaded his walking-stick air gun to shoot a fruit-robbing blackbird, was called away and put it in a corner unfired and, for once, forgotten. Weeks later, my mother, who was alone in the house, knocked the gun sideways and it discharged into her middle finger. We had no telephone then and no near neighbours. She bound it up as best she could and waited all day for us to come home. A dreadful episode.

When I was still a small girl I was given a Frankfurt single-bore rifle. I practised, under stern supervision, on suspended tins and cardboard targets until I was a good shot and allowed to go out with the guns. This was wonderful. To kill rabbits was an honourable procedure. And then, on an autumn morning, I wounded a hare. The landscape blackened and cried out against me and that was the end of my active part in field sports.

These expeditions alternated with boating on the quiet river where one glided through unknown people's gardens, under willows and between the spring-flowering banks of our curiously English antipodean suburbs. The oars clunked rhythmically in their rowlocks, weeping willows dipped and brushed across our faces. If you nibbled the pale young leaves they were surprisingly bitter.

Sometimes our keel grated on shingle or sent up a drift of cloudy mud. One trailed one's fingers and felt grand and opulent. It seems to me that it was always late afternoon on the river.

Until my schooldays came and, with them, camping holidays in the mountains, the great adventure, undertaken on several occasions by my mother and me, was a journey to Dunedin. It lasted all day. Up before dawn, we dressed by lamplight while cocks crew in the darkness beyond the window-pane. We seemed to have taken our house by surprise while it was still leading a night life of its own. In the hall stood our corded boxes and the coats we would wear. Breakfast was a strange hurried business eaten by the light of an oil lamp with a clock on the table. Presently the front door had banged behind us.

My father took us to the station and put us into our carriage (second-class after the financial setbacks). It had wooden benches running lengthways and spittoons along the floor. Now began a period of frightful anxieties. Suppose we stayed too long on the platform and the train suddenly went away without us? Suppose, as I was getting in, my mother should be left behind, mouthing after me on the platform while I was carried rapidly south? Suppose we were in the wrong train and would be swept up through the mountains to Westland or that my father, having established us in our seats, foolishly dallied and was borne away in the train with us and financially ruined.

When we were on our way these apprehensions faded, most of them recurring when my mother decided that we should stretch our legs at the longer stops. The journey became fascinating. We racketed across the Canterbury Plains while in the world outside the Southern Alps advanced, retired and slowly looked over each other's snowy shoulders, and mad loops of telephone wires dipped and leapt in front of them. 'Dun-e-DIN. Dun-e-DIN' said the hurrying train and 'No-you-DON'T. No-you-DON'T,' sometimes breaking out into a violent excitable clatter as we roared through a cutting: 'Rackety-plan. Rackety-plan.' We crossed great rivers and saw men and vast mobs of sheep on lonely roads. A long day.

There were three little parcels to be opened at appropriately spaced stations. They were always books. There were the lurching hazards of an endless stagger through other carriages and over-shifting footplates in a roaring wind, to the dining car. There were Other People to speculate upon and at evening when one was very tired indeed there was a final treat: my mother's dressing case to be explored. It was lined with deliciously-smelling leather and fitted with crystal, silver-topped bottles. Soap, eau-de-Cologne with which one's face was cleaned and freshened. A tiny phial of real attar-of-roses sent out by my grandmother from England. *Papier-poudré*, which was a little book of leaflets that my mother rubbed over her eau-de-Cologned nose and chin. An ivory-backed brush and comb. A looking glass from which one's face stared back like a ghost in the murky lamplight. Now we were hurtling round the high cliffs of the Otago coast. If there was a moon outside it shone on the Pacific, far below. Lonely patches of bushland and ranges of hills moved against the sky behind cadaverous nodding reflections of Other People's faces.

At last, at the end of a lifetime and late at night: Dunedin, the smell of Mivvy's fur coat and the familiar sound of her voice. The platform heaved under one's legs. I cannot remember, on any occasion, the drive out to St Clair and suppose I must always have fallen asleep. One entered the house through a conservatory smelling of wet fern. We were near the sea and the last thing one heard was the roar of surf on a lonely coast.

One day, at St Clair, it rained so heavily that I was not allowed to put my nose out-of-doors. Under the dining-room bay-window seat was a system of lockers. Mivvy said they were full of old magazines and suggested that I might like to explore them. They were of two kinds. *The Windsor*, which was lettuce green with the Castle, I think, in brown, and *The Strand* with a picture of that thoroughfare on the cover. All day I hunted and devoured, tracing the enchanting series from one edition to the next. The rain beat down, not on the windows of a New Zealand house but across those of a gas-lit upstairs room in a London street. It glistened on the roofs of hansom-cabs and bounced off cobblestones. It mingled with the cries of newsboys and eccentric improvisations upon the fiddle. A solitary visitor was approaching: there was a peremptory double-knock at the street door. Someone came up the stairs and entered.

'Hullo,' said Mivvy, looking over my shoulder, 'you've discovered Sherlock Holmes.'

CHAPTER 2

The Hills

Miss Sibella E. Ross was a gentlewoman of Highland descent. She was also a cousin of my adored Dundas. Her shape was firm, her bust formidable, her eyes blue and, like her face, surprisingly round. Her teeth were slightly prominent. She lived with her highly respected family in a large house generally known, though not I think to the Rosses, as 'The Tin Palace', since it had been constructed in pioneering days from galvanized iron and had a tower. In premises conveniently adjacent, Miss Ross kept school: a select dame school for about twenty children between the ages of six and ten years. Miss Ross's family and immediate friends called her Tibby and her ex-pupils referred to her school as Tib's.

To this establishment I was sent when I was, I suppose, six years old. I have no doubt whatever that it was a wise decision but the experience in its initial stages was hellish.

In the morning I was put into a horse-drawn bus where there were already three fellow pupils. We were met at the other end by Miss Irving, the governess at Miss Ross's, and escorted to school.

'Good morning, children.'

'Good morning, Miss Ross. Good morning, Miss Irving.'

For the first time I found myself one of a group of children and, for the first time, I was conscious of being tall for my age. This made the simple business of standing up to answer questions an embarrassing ordeal. Miss Ross had invented an 'honour' system which decreed that at the end of the morning each child must stand up and proclaim how many times he or she had spoken unlawfully in class. When my

immediate neighbours discovered, with the terrible prescience of children, that this observance frightened me, they determined, gleefully, to
enhance its terrors by forcing me to talk. They would hiss questions. If
I didn't answer, they would make jabs at me, for all the world as hens
peck at a sick bird. They would peck and jab until I made some kind of
response and then stare accusingly at me when the moment for public
confession arrived. One could not always ask to 'leave the room' at the
crucial moment. I cannot think that this was a good practice: it engendered, in a single operation, elements of guilt, fear, loneliness and in-
feriority, and, indeed, provoked a sort of Freudian extravaganza in the
reactions of a little girl who was unprepared for it. The follow-up treatment took place in playtime and was set in hand by the nine-year-olds.
They organized themselves and their juniors into something that was
called a 'secret army' and from it excluded two stalwart little boys and
myself. The boys were called Charles and Roderick and were kind.
Roderick became a soldier and Charles a man of letters. Both of them
left New Zealand. When, on separate occasions and about thirty years
afterwards, I met them again, something of the intense gratitude I had
felt for them returned. We talked about our first term at Tib's.

I did not say anything at all about these miseries to my parents
but I think my mother must have known that all was not well and
decided that I should stick it out. Very properly so, I expect. After all,
she was up against the problem of the only child. It is true that by
some process of adaptation the picture gradually changed. I was no
longer bullied. I formed heartening friendships with other small
girls. I toughened.

As time went on I was even given certain responsibilities at Tib's.
When Ian, a fighting boy in a kilt, was brought at eleven o'clock every
morning by his nanny, I was one of two sent to take delivery of him
in the porch. He yelled, bit and kicked, while his nurse recommended
that he should go with the nice young ladies to his lesson. We led him,
roaring, to his desk, rather impressed than otherwise by the extremity
of his passion. Dick, a fat boy, was more vulnerable and wept sometimes. He was jeered at by my former tormentors and I'm glad to
remember that I was sorry for him and didn't join in. I was out of the
wood by that time. Rightly or wrongly, however, I still think that my
first term at Tib's was far from being all to the good. It does not
improve the character to be bullied. Children are microcosms of

people. Treat them badly for long enough and then give them a little power and they will punctually repeat with greater emphasis the behaviour to which they have been subjected. Fear is the most damaging emotion that can be inflicted on the character of any child and on one already as morbidly prone to inexplicable terrors as I was, the early torments I underwent at Tib's were pretty deadly. When they moderated and I was no longer in thrall, I reacted predictably. I don't think that on the whole I was all that much more obnoxious than any other little girl of my age but for a time I became so: bossy, bullying, and secretive, paying back however unconsciously, I am sure, for what had been dealt out to me. I don't think it lasted very long but it happened and in my old age I still remember and am sorry about it.

Fear can be perhaps the most corrupting of our basic emotions and fear without the possibility of release, the worst of all. The child who has been overtaken by it is a microcosm of the mob. If you rule a people by fear and treat them as an inferior race and then give them power, don't expect them to use it like angels. You have corrupted them and many of them will abuse it.

One day, while I and other Fendaltonians waited for Miss Irving to put us on the bus, we heard a clatter of hooves in the quiet street and mounted policemen rode splendidly by, followed by a carriage with a crown on the door.

'The Governor,' gabbled Miss Irving in a fluster. 'Girls curtsey and boys bow. Off with your caps. Quick.'

We bobbed and nodded, eyeing each other sideways and then looked up to see the Governor smiling and bowing very pointedly to us. With him was his wife and unless I am at fault, a little girl of about my own age of whom there will be much more to say.

Away rolled the carriage and up came the bus.

One other incident sticks in my memory. Miss Ross, rather ominously smiling, asks her pupils what they wish to be when they grow up. She concentrates upon the boys since the girls are destined for matrimony: an employment not to be examined in detail with propriety. I, however, hold up my hand. 'I want,' I venture, 'to be an artist.' 'Ho!' Miss Ross atrociously says, 'you'll never do that, my dear. Your hand shakes.'

I suppose I had attended Miss Ross's school for about a year when the great change came. We went to live on the hills.

II

When I looked south from the higher branches of my wellingtonia tree in suburbia, I saw, above park, roofs and Cathedral spire, the Port Hills. They were only four miles away but to me they seemed as romantically distant as those snowy Alps that stood to the north beyond the Canterbury Plains. The hills were rounded and suave in outline with occasional craggy accidents. They would be called mountains in England. The tussock that covered them gave them a bloomy appearance as blonde hair does to a living body. I was told that a long time ago they had moved gigantically and heaved themselves into their present form and then grown hard, being the overflow of a volcano.

The crater of this volcano is now a deep harbour into which a hundred and fifteen years ago, sailed the First Four Ships: *Sir George Seymour*, *Randolph*, *Cressy* and *Charlotte Jane*, bringing the founders of the Canterbury Settlement. These intrepid emigrants landed at the port of Lyttelton, wearing stovepipe hats, heavy suits, crinolines and bonnets. They climbed the Port Hills and reached the summit where, with a munificent gesture, their inheritance was suddenly laid out before them. Whenever I return to New Zealand I like to come home by the hills and still think that an arrival at the pass on a clear dawn is the most astonishing entry one could make into any country. There, as abruptly as if one had looked over a wall, are the Plains, spread out beyond the limit of vision, laced with early mist, and a great river, bounded on the east by the Pacific, on the west by mere distance, and from east to west by a lordly sequence of mountains, rose-coloured where they receive the rising sun.

Gramp came this way in, I think, 1853 and looked down at swamps and a little group of huts and wooden buildings. When he was eighty he still used to go for a Sunday walk on the Port Hills and glare sardonically at the city of Christchurch.

In our Fendalton days there was only a scatter of about twenty houses on the hills. We were lent one of these for a summer holiday – a house amidst tussock with nothing but clear air between it and the foothills of the Alps, forty miles away on the other side of the Plains. It was this visit, I think, that decided our move. My father bought the nose of the same hill; some three-quarters of an acre of ground, already fenced, partly cultivated and set about with baby trees – pinus radiata and limes, not much higher than the surrounding tussock. A sou'-wester is blowing this morning and I look anxiously at the tops of my pines, a hundred feet tall, and hope they have enough sap in their old bodies to withstand the gale.

As soon as the momentous decision was taken, it was communicated to an architect cousin of my mother's. He at once caused to be set aside a stack of seasoned timber and exposed it to further weathering. It had come out of the mountains, horse-drawn through virgin forest to a bush tramway, or had been floated across a lake and broken down in Westland timber mills. When I made some alterations in this house, the carpenters were unable to drive a nail into the old joists; the wood, they said, was like iron rather than timber.

Perhaps the lease of our house in Fendalton expired before the new one could be built or perhaps there was a delay in the building. For whatever the reason, it was decided that we should camp in tents near the site of our future home and stay there until it was completed. I fancy that we adopted this hardy adventuresome procedure partly because my father considered it would be an advantage if he were at hand to keep an eye on the workmen.

'You never know,' he said darkly, 'with those chaps.'

It was on an early summer's day that we left Fendalton, seated on top of our tents and boxes in a spring-wagon. My father's closest friend of those times had a motor-car, one of the first in Christchurch, and had offered to drive us to the hills, but I think the recollection of innumerable breakdowns and hour-long unproductive explorations of its less accessible mysteries decided my mother against this vehicle. She felt that the important thing was to arrive.

So, on what seems to me to have been an interminable journey, we plodded through the borders of Fendalton, round the parks, past a region of drafting-yards and sheep pens where, once a week, livestock was sold, down a long highway and into Wilderness Road, an endless stretch between gorse hedges. It is now a main suburban street. This brought us at last to the hills; to a winding lane, a rough track and our destination. I remember that a hot nor'wester raged across the plains and when we tried to pitch our bell tents, got inside them and threatened to blow them away like umbrellas. We settled at last upon the sheltered end of a valley, below our section and within sight of the scaffolding that had already been set up.

There we lived throughout the summer. It was the beginning of a new life for all of us.

I continued at Tib's. Every morning, with my father, I left our tents, climbed up and over a steep hill, or as an alternative, walked a mile round the foot of it to the terminus of a steam-tramway and was carried into Christchurch. In winter I was dressed in a blue serge sailor suit with braid on the collar and skirt and an anchor on the dicky. I also wore a sailor's cap with HMS Something on it. In summer this nautical motif was carried out in cotton or piqué and the hat was of straw. We had friends living near us in a large house with plantations and a rambling garden – the Walkers: mother, sister and four enormously tall brothers of Dundas, who was now on the stage in Australia. Three of the brothers were bearded, which in those days was unusual, and they were all extremely handsome: Graham, Colin, Alexander, Cecil. I transferred much of my devotion to them, particularly to Colin. Although they were cousins of Miss Ross, they held her so little in awe that on one occasion, finding me alone on the top of the double-decker steam-tram, they rifled my satchel and extracted an exercise book. Alexander gripped my arms while Colin wrote on a virgin page:

> Kids may come and kids may go
> But Tib goes on forever.

We were not permitted to tear leaves out of our books.

'You can say we did it,' they told me. 'It won't be splitting. We'd like you to.'

We had to lay our exercises on Miss Ross's desk. I watched her work her way down the pile until she came to mine. For the first time in my life I saw a woman turn red with anger.

'Who,' she asked with classic economy, 'has done this? Ngaio?'

'The Boys,' I faltered, for so I called these bearded giants, and she knew who I meant. With a magnificent gesture she ripped out the page. She then strode to the fire, committed the couplet to the flames and returned to her desk.

'The hymn,' she said in a controlled but unnatural voice, '*We are but little children weak.* Open your books.'

Soon after this incident I became ten and had grown out of Tib's.

By that time our house was almost built. We struck camp, climbed our hill and moved into it.

'This,' said my father, referring to the workmen, 'will hurry them up,' and indeed I think it must have done so, for they disappeared quite soon.

The new house smelt of the linseed oil with which the panelled walls had been treated and of the timber itself. It was a four-roomed bungalow with a large semi-circular verandah. The living room was biggish. There were recesses in its bronze wooden walls and there was a pleasant balance between them and the windows. My mother had a talent for making, out of undistinguished elements, a kind of harmony in a room. At once it became an expression of herself and the warmth she always lent to human relationships: newcomers used to exclaim on this and often said that they felt as if they had been there before.

At a little distance below the house was a big bicycle shed which, by a heroic concerted effort made by my father and his friends, had been actually hauled up the hill on sleds and then turned over and over until it was brought into position. It was then floored and lined and fitted with bunks like a cabin and became a guest room. From the beginning we loved our house. It was the fourth member of our family and for me, who still lives in it, has retained that character: it has been much added to but I think its personality has not changed. A city has spread across the open country where sheep and cows were grazed: the surrounding hills where I and my friends tobogganed and rode our ponies, are richly encrusted with bungaloid or functional dwellings. An enormous hospital covers the old mushroom-paddock: Cashmere, which is our part of the Port Hills, is now a 'desirable suburb'. But no skyscraper out on the plains can ever be tall enough to hide the mountains and, strangely enough, the little river Heathcote, where we used to sail on rafts that we built ourselves, has scarcely changed. Children still paddle about on it in home-made craft.

A few miles away from us, round the hills, there lived a horse-coper called Mr McGuinnes. For him my father conceived an admiration ('Decent fellow, McGuinnes') and with him, soon after we arrived, a bargain was struck. Mr McGuinnes would keep me supplied with a pony which would be grazed in the Top Paddock to which we had access. The pony would be changed from time to time and the outgoing mount sold, I now realize, as having been used by a child. I, who had never bestridden anything but my rocking horse, was madly excited.

In due course the first pony arrived. Dolly, she was called: a pretty, mettlesome little creature who sidled up the lane showing the whites of her eyes. When my father put the new slithery pad on her back she kicked him. This unsettled his temper. Mr McGuinnes, who held her firmly with both hands near the bit, made the classic observation that it was only her fun. I was put up. Before my feet could be set in the stirrups, Dolly went into a series of humpbacked bucks. Like Mr Winkle before me, I clung to her neck while Mr McGuinnes and my father shouted at each other. I would have liked to show the intrepid spirit of Little Lord Fauntleroy who, it may be remembered, gallantly trotted and cantered at his first venture. But the Earl of Dorincourt's stables did not produce half-broken buckjumpers for the little heir to learn upon, nor did the Earl and his groom scream instructions at each other not to let her bolt.

'I'm getting off,' I said.

'No, you're not,' shouted my father.

But somehow or another I did, and we had a row.

'It doesn't matter if you do fall off,' roared my father. 'It'd only be like falling off the kitchen table. You wouldn't think anything of that. Get up again.'

Dolly snorted, reared and backed, and Mr McGuinnes fought with her head.

'I don't want to,' I said. 'It's not a bit like the kitchen table.'

'Good Lord!' said my father in disgust. 'Here. I'll show you, you ass.' He leapt into the saddle. 'Let her go,' he said sternly.

Dolly made a complicated bound and broke into a gallop. Halfway down the lane she threw him and the rest of the afternoon was spent in recapturing her.

My nerve, if not completely shattered, was far from secure. However, there were further equestrian attempts. Dolly was again ridden by my father and, after bolting with him for a considerable distance, came lathering back in what was held to be a chastened mood. I was led up and down the lane, whitely attempting to ride in my stirrups and hating it.

I doubt if I would ever have become a horsey child if we had not, at this juncture, paid one of our visits to Dunedin. Here, under the guidance of a very old and almost stone-deaf gardener-groom, I became acquainted with two elderly ponies, Tasman and Tommy. I fed them over the paddock rails, learnt to bridle them, climbed on them of my own accord and when nothing untoward occurred, began to bump bareback around the paddock. It seems to me, now, that there was no interval between this tentative experiment and early morning rides when I cantered along the sea front, a hardened but far from technically accomplished equestrienne. The Pacific thundered and crashed along the beach, seagulls screamed over the island they had whitened, and sometimes I rode up a steep and winding road to Cargill's Castle. Up this same road my father, when he first came to New Zealand, had been driven with Uncle William and his wife to balls the Cargills gave in their antipodean highland castle. He told me how the lights of the carriages had glowed and turned in the night, how gay life was in the Eighties and Nineties. Sometimes on my early morning rides I remembered his stories.

On our return to Christchurch came Frisky, from whom I should have learned the facts of life.

She was a little chestnut mare, part Arab, and she stayed with me until my feet were a few inches from the ground. Other ponies and horses came and went ('Ridden by a child. Very quiet.') but Frisky remained. I adored and bossed her, sometimes flinging my arms round her neck and burying my face in her celery-smelling hide, sometimes cramming her into prolonged gallops. After a time she was removed for a short period by Mr McGuinnes. When she returned, I was told that she was in a delicate state of health and must be taken quietly until further orders. I obeyed these injunctions tenderly and without question. My mother afterwards told me that, encouraged by this ready-made exemplar, she attempted to use it as a basis for biological instruction but that I paid no attention whatever to her carefully chosen phrases. I rode Frisky quietly, my legs spreading wider and wider apart, and concluded that as she was getting fatter she must be getting better. My father suggested, one morning, that I should accompany him to the Top Paddock. Nothing could have exceeded my astonishment when I found that Frisky was attended by a foal that wobbled round her like a sort of animated diagram. Delighted, I was: enlightened as to the facts of life, not at all.

To this day I cannot understand my idiocy in this respect; I behaved like a Goon. When one of my little girl friends from Miss Ross's who was called Merta, told me that her mummy was fat because she was going to have a baby I thought she was spinning an extremely unconvincing yarn and didn't believe a word of it. An intelligent and amiable child, Merta took no offence but merely said: 'Well, anyway, that's why she's fat. You'll see,' and did not reopen the discussion. When another little girl confided specific, if not altogether accurate, information imparted by her brother, I was interested but never for one moment did I apply it to anybody I knew. When my mother asked me if I'd like a brother or sister because Dr Dick had said she might have one now, I merely said I wouldn't and continued to think that our family physician concocted babies in his surgery. What is the psychiatrist's explanation of such booby-like obstinacy? I have noticed it in other children whose mothers, spurred on by contemporary attitudes, have lost no opportunity to point the moral, if not adorn the procreative tale. In each case the reaction was unrewarding.

'You see, darling, Mummy is keeping the new baby warm under her heart until it is ready – '

'Yes, Mummy. Mummy, if I kept a penny for every day for a million years could it buy a bicycle?'

'I expect it could, don't you? And you see, darling, Daddy is really like a gardener – '

'Can I have a garden of my own to grow mustard and cress?'

'We'll see. And it was just the same when you were born – '

'When's my birthday? Can I have a gun for my birthday?'

Heavy going.

III

After I left Tib's, my mother struggled for a short time with my lessons and then I had a governess: Miss Ffitch. The capital F was used, I imagine, as a concession to colonial prejudice. Nowhere in the English-speaking world are proper names more arrogantly misused than in New Zealand. In retrospect, my heart bleeds for Miss Ffitch who, I am sure, would have been much happier with a conventional and nicely comported little girl. Invigorated by the fresh air of the hills, toughened by the companionship of neighbouring children and reacting, perhaps, from the complicated terrors that had beset my first decade, I had become a formidable, in some ways an abominable, child. My dear friend Ned, who in all other respects never led me into mischief, had taught me to smoke. We bought a tin of ten 'Three Castles Yellow (strong)', divided them equally, retired into a wigwam we had built among some gorse-bushes, and chain-smoked the lot without evil results. Encouraged by this success, we carved ourselves pipes from willow wood into which we introduced bamboo stems and in which we smoked tea. We also smoked red-hot cigars made of pine needles and newspaper.

Lessons ended at noon. On one occasion I retired into the trees outside my bedroom and lit my pipe. I had forgotten that Miss Ffitch adjusted her hat at a glass in the window. Wreathed in smoke and glancing hardily about me, I encountered her gaze: transfixed, blank, appalled, incredulous. For a second or two we stared at each other and then her face withdrew into the shadows. I awaited her displeasure but she said nothing, having decided, I suppose, like a sensible woman, that this sort of thing lay outside the pale of her authority and was better cut dead.

I tied an alarm clock under her chair, and set it for noon. On one occasion only, I blatantly cribbed to see if she would spot it, which of course she did, and very properly made me feel that I had been extremely unfunny. These were isolated acts of insubordination. As a general rule I think I was reasonably tractable but the overall effect of Miss Ffitch was positive only in respect of the amount of information she managed to inject.

Why, I wonder, did Miss Ffitch decree that my introduction to the plays of Shakespeare should be through *King Lear*? Remembering her mild exterior, her unexceptionable deportment, her ladylike constraint: why, I ask myself, did she so placidly launch a small girl upon that primordial, that cataclysmic, work? One would have said she was a sitter for the Forest of Arden or the Wood Near Athens. *Hamlet* or *Macbeth* would have been much less surprising: children are extremely responsive to both these tragedies. But *Lear*?

I cannot remember that Miss Ffitch uttered a word of exposition or drew my attention to anything but the notes. Upon these she laid great emphasis. The version was an expurgated one. No lechery. No civet. No small gilded flies. Just torture, murder and madness. Yet, as far as I could understand it, I lapped it up, and was, I remember, greatly surprised by its beauty. Kent's speech in the stocks, the theadbare Fool. The recognition scene:

> 'Do not laugh at me
> For, as I am a man, I think this lady
> To be my child, Cordelia.'
> 'And so I am. I am.'

This lovely grief was understandable. When told to read the scene aloud, my voice trembled. Perhaps after all Miss Ffitch was on the right lines.

For Christmas, Miss Ffitch very kindly gave me Carlyle's *French Revolution*. I tried hard but failed. All that turgid, and at the same time bossy, excitability was too much for me. Nor did I respond with marked enthusiasm to the *Lays of Ancient Rome* or to a poem which maundered, in lachrymose pentameters, over Mary, Queen of Scots, or to another that said:

> Watch where ye see my helmet shine amid the tanks of wah
> And be your oriflamme today the White Plume of Navarre

Kipling, however, got under my tender diaphragm. I was already deeply committed to the *Just So Stories* which my father read superbly and to their end-poems which, with those of the *Jungle Books*, I learnt by heart without knowing I had done so. I still think them almost flawless for readers of seven to thirteen years.

> Now Chil the Kite brings home the Night
> That Mang, the Bat sets free
> The herds are shut in byre and hut
> For loosed till dawn are we.

and:

> Oh hush thee, my baby, the night is behind us.

What is to be said of the taste of a child reader? From what half-formed preferences, what unrecognized instincts is it shaped? Why did the opening phrase of the *Jungle Stories* so captivate me that I must read it over and over again with such deep satisfaction? *'It was seven o'clock of a very warm evening in the Seeonee hills –'*

This was magic.

Then came *The Brushwood Bay*, which I shall never dare to read again lest the recollection should crumble into disillusion, and some of the sea poems, particularly *The Coast-Wise Lights of England*.

Our brows are bound with spindrift and the weed is on our knees
And our loins are battered 'neath us by the swinging, smoking seas.

By these I was ravished.

Unfortunately I found that I myself was capable of some morsels in Kiplingesque pastiche.

'*Up*,' I wrote with my tongue firmly gripped between my teeth:

Up from the rolling plains, up where the blue mist lies

and a little further on and even more regrettably

We must be nothing weak, Vallies and hills are ours
From the last lone mountain creek to where the rata flowers.

I really believe that in my heart I knew what dreadful stuff this was and can distinctly remember that on completing it I was discomforted by a sensation of embarrassment. I don't think I ever showed it to my mother. At ten years, however, according to a note she made on it, I had presented her with a poem.

The sun is sinking in the west
The stars begin to shine
The birds are singing in their nest
And I must go to mine.

These lines preceded my Kipling period and are, I think, greatly to be preferred to it. Oddly enough, although it reads like a direct pinch from Blake, I had not, at that time, been introduced to the *Songs of Innocence* and therefore may be held, I suppose, to have perpetrated an infantile literary coincidence.

For one odd preference in reading I can find no explanation. This was a book by an, at that time, popular journalist called John Foster Fraser. It was about the trans-Siberian railway and it completely fascinated me. Perhaps my love of trains had something to do with this but I think that I had made some strange association between the word 'Russia' and an idea of the quintessence of adventure. This strange feeling was to reach a kind of climax after many years by the wharves of Odessa.

In addition to lessons with Miss Ffitch I went twice a week to Miss Jennie Black, Mus. Bac., for the piano. She was dark and incisive with flashing eyes behind her spectacles. She taught Mathey's method and she stood no nonsense. I rode Frisky and my mother rode her bicycle as far as the tram stop. She sat on a grassy bank and read. Frisky often dropped off to sleep, resting her chin rather heavily on my mother's hat and slightly dribbling. There they would be on my return, with Tip, now an old dog, panting in the shade of Frisky's belly.

I must have been an infuriating pupil for the piano. I had a poor ear, little application and fluctuating interest, but I was not bad enough to be given the sack and even passed some Trinity College examinations. My mother, winning a perpetual series of rearguard actions, insisted on regular practice which I loathed. Yet every now and then I would suddenly become engaged by the current piece and work quite hard on it.

'But you played that well. You played it quite well. Tiresome little wretch!' exclaimed Miss Jennie Black, Mus. Bac., in an extremity of irritation.

We almost always referred to her by her full title because of its snappy rhythm. Indeed, I once absent-mindedly replied to one of her demands: 'Yes, Miss Jennie Black, Mus. Bac.,' and got an awful rocket for impertinence. It was impossible to explain.

In spite of Miss Ross's stricture and with a hand that has always been slightly tremulous, I continued to draw and paint with great assiduity but not, I think, very marked talent. I had come upon one of the repellent soft leather booklets that people used to give each other in those days: *The Rubáiyát of Omar Khayyám*. Instantly enthralled, I tried to illustrate it, using a birthday box of pastels, a drawing board and an easel that made me feel very grown-up. The figure stealing at dusk through the marketplace, the potter moulding his wet clay, the Sultan's turret in a noose of light – it was frustrating to a degree that, with such enthusiasm, I was able to express so little.

Watching my struggles, my mother asked me if I would like to have lessons and I said I would. I was too young to be a junior student at the Canterbury University College Art School but, after she had seen the Director, he allowed me to go twice a week for instruction in the Antique Room where I struggled with charcoal and Michelet paper, confronted by blankly explicit plaster casts. I also was permitted to slosh about with watercolours and rather depressing still-life arrangements. My drawing began to improve a little.

It seems to me that in our early years on the hills I was never at a loose end, that there was always something to do, and that these were halcyon days. Sometimes I would wake at dawn, steal from the sleeping house and climb up through the mist, chilling my bare legs in tussock that bent earthwards under its veil of dew. Frisky, hearing me call, would whinny, look over the hilltop and come to meet me. She shared the Top Paddock with Beauty and Blazer, two cows belonging to our nearest neighbour, Mr Evans. Jack Evans, a quiet self-contained boy who did three hours' hard work before going to school, would plod up the hill, softly chanting.

'C'mon, Beauty. C'mon, Blazer.

C'mo-on, c'mo-on.'

And we would all go down the track together, I to my dawn-ride and Jack to his milking.

Sometimes one or the other of my two particular friends from Tib's would come to stay: Mina and Merta. Mina was an extremely witty and articulate little girl who wore grey dresses and immaculately starched pinafores. 'O Ngaio, fool that I am, I have forgotten my book!' she dramatically exclaimed when we were still at Tib's and she about seven years old. Mina shared my passion for reading, but was cleverer and much more discriminating than I. When we were a little older, she confirmed my suspicions of Kipling in his extroverted manner. 'I understand it,' Mina said, 'and I don't care for poetry that I understand.' She had a grand manner and for that reason, I suppose, we called her Dutchy.

On wet days we wrote stories and illustrated them. My mother would set a competition to last through the holidays and give us each a fat little book with delectable blank pages. Two days before Mina was to leave, we handed over our completed works and my mother retired to deliberate. The following day she gave a very detailed judgement with marks for every story and illustration and stringent comments. The result was a tie. My mother presented each of us with a book, explaining that if the contest had not been drawn the winner would have received both of them. We were, I suppose, rather precocious little girls but we were completely taken in by this transparent device. Our mutual admiration was extreme.

Merta lived near us and we met frequently. I think it must have been on the occasion of her mother's confinement, which Merta generously refrained from throwing in my teeth, that she came to stay with us. I have a vivid recollection of the day her father arrived to fetch her. By some mischance Merta and I got ourselves locked in the lavatory and in a state of rising panic, hammered and roared until we made ourselves heard by my mother, who was entertaining Mr Fisher, a shy man, to tea. She was unable to effect our release and was obliged, in the end, to ask for help. Through the keyhole, Mr Fisher begged us to keep our heads and follow his instructions, which we did at last, and emerged to find him scarlet in the face and walking rapidly away.

On my tenth birthday I had a party.

For many years my father had boasted about the excellence of the ginger beer brewed by their gardener and his assistant at Woodside, Essex.

'Jolly good stuff, Old Jo's and The Boy's ginger beer. Totally different from the rotgut they sell out here.'

He wrote to my grandmother about it and she sent out the recipe. My father bought half a used brandy cask and a great many ingredients and set himself up in the cellar under our verandah. It was a long and elaborate process and for many days the house was suffused with pungent fumes. Occasionally, muffled oaths could be heard beneath the floorboards and my mother made remarks like: 'Well said, Old Mole, cans't work i' the earth so fast' and 'You hear this fellow in the cellarage.' She also asked him if Old Jo and The Boy had sent any incantations or runes to be muttered in the Essex dialect over his seething cauldron.

'Don't be an ass, Betsy,' said my father, grinning happily. He had reached the bottling phase. On my birthday the proper time had elapsed for the brew to be mature.

The party was in full swing. Gramp played 'Sir Roger de Coverley' on the piano and gaily shouted instructions. My mother and aunts and uncles sedately chasséd and swanned down the dance while we children hopped, linked arms and became hot and excited. Some of the little boys went mad and made exhibitionist faces. The moment had arrived for refreshment.

My father had retired to the kitchen from whence presently there came a formidable explosion. He appeared briefly, looking rather like a mythical sea-god, being wreathed, bearded and crowned with foam.

'Is it Old Father Christmas?' an awestruck child asked. 'Is it Christmas-time?'

My father went into the garden. A *feu de joie* of reports rang out and we eyed each other in wild surmise. He returned triumphant with a great trayload of buzzing drinks.

The response was immediate and uproarious. In next to no time my aunts and uncles and acquaintances were screaming with laughter in each other's faces while their children, unreproved, tacked about the room, cannoned into each other, fell, threw cream cakes or subsided on the floor in a trance. I remember particularly a nicely mannered boy called Lewis who zig-zagged to and fro and offered a tilted plate of sandwiches to wild little girls. The sandwiches, one by one, slid to the floor but Lewis continued to present the empty plate. I must have been quite overcome because I have no recollection whatever of how the party ended.

'Can't make it out,' my father said the next day. 'It's no good you thinking it was my ginger beer, Betsy. Absolute rot! Jolly wholesome stuff.'

Some weeks later we were visited by a hot nor'wester, a very trying and enervating wind in our part of New Zealand.

'Shall we,' my mother limply suggested, 'have some of Daddy's ginger beer?'

She poured out two small glasses. We spent the rest of the morning lying quietly side-by-side on the carpet, looking at the ceiling. In the afternoon I had a bilious attack.

My father, concerned, said: 'It might be the brandy I suppose.'

And so, of course, it was. The fermenting ginger beer had drawn into itself the overproof spirits with which the cask was saturated. In future, this heavily fortified beverage was offered only to grown-ups and, at that, it was dynamite.

'Damn' good stuff,' my father would say. 'Ginger beer. Old Essex recipe you know. M'mother's gardener – '

To this day I cannot bear the smell, much less the taste of ginger beer.

IV

I think the greatest difference in convention between the children of my time and those of today may be seen in the amount of money spent on their entertainment and this, I believe, was a consideration not only of necessity but of principle. Books and toys were a fraction of their present cost but they were not casually bestowed. Gifts were largely restricted to special occasions and to open a parcel was a matter of burning excitement.

I am glad my friends and I were less indulged than children are nowadays. Even if my parents could have afforded to give me lots of expensive presents I am sure they would not have done so. If birthdays and Christmas had brought a succession of grand parties with everybody getting a great many impersonal gifts at each of them, I really do not believe these occasions would have held the same enchantment. There were very few formal parties. In the early affluent days in Fendalton, there had been journeys in hansom-cabs to fancy-dress balls in large houses. At one of these, I, dressed as a tiny Marion de Lorne, walked in procession with a fairy whose face fascinated me by growing more and more scarlet with each promenade. A day or two later I developed measles.

On the hills there were, for the most part, only impromptu festivities. My mother and her sisters and my father were superb in charades. One of my uncles (Unk), a distinguished geologist, also liked to take part. He always insisted, regardless of subject matter, on being dressed up and on carrying their parrot in its cage. This odd piece of business struck Unk as being exquisitely comical.

Even at Christmas our celebrations were of a casual family kind, except for the Tree, for which I made elaborate preparations.

There was a little black japanned cabinet in my room with painted figures on the doors. Into this I put the Christmas presents I assembled for my friends, starting early in the year and gradually adding to the collection. Pink sugar pigs, I can remember, a pin-cushion and wooden Dutch dolls costing from fourpence to tenpence according to size. These I sometimes attempted to clothe but I had and have, rather less aptitude than a bricklayer for sewing. The result was lamentable. I bought shiny fairy tales at threepence a book, a Jacko, which was a tin monkey that climbed a string, a jack-in-the-box, and a thumb-sized china fairy for the top of the tree. I would squat, absorbed, in front of my cabinet, arranging these presents under stuck-on-labels bearing the names of my friends. My pocket-money was sixpence a week. The English grandmother sent me a sovereign and an English godmother half-a-sovereign. These were saved in a scarlet tin postbox.

In the mind of a small New Zealander, Christmas was a strange mixture of snow and intense heat. All our books in those days were English. Christmas annuals were full of middle-class sleighs and children. Reindeer, coach horns, frozen roads, muffled boys coming home from boarding school, snapdragons and blazing fires were strongly featured. These were Christmas. But so, too, were home-made toboggans that shot like greased lightning down glossy, mid-summer tussock: hot, still evenings, the lovely smell of cabbage-tree blossom, open doors and windows and the sound, far away, down on the flat, of boys letting off crackers. I settled this contradiction in my own way. For as long as I thought I still believed in Father Christmas, I climbed a solitary pine tree that stood on the hillside and put a letter in a box that I had tied near the top. Being a snow-minded person, Father Christmas, I thought, probably lived in the back country, out on the main range where there were red deer, and he would know about my letter and pause in his night-gallop through the sky to collect it. I suppose my father climbed up and retrieved the letters. They always disappeared.

On Christmas Eve, I sat under this tree and wrote in a book that was kept secretly for that one occasion. It was started, I think, when I was about seven years old and the first entry was in a round, unsteady hand. I tried to put down the enchanted present and this was my first attempt at descriptive writing. I also gave a morbidly accurate summary of my misdeeds and tribulations throughout the year. These portions should perhaps count as a first attempt at sub-jective analysis. The entries always ended with a quotation: *'The time draws near the birth of Christ.'* The last one was made when I was thirty-five years old and unhappy. After that I burnt the book.

In the summer I slept on the verandah and on Christmas Eve went to bed in ecstasy. The door into the living room was open. Mixed with the smell of sweet-scented tobacco, night-flowering stocks, freshly watered earth and that cabbage-tree blossom, was the drift of my father's pipe. I could hear the crackle of his newspaper and the occasional quiet murmur of my parents' voices. At the head of my bed hung one of my long black stockings. I fingered its limpness two or three times before I went to sleep. Sometime during the night I would wake for a bemused second or two, to reach out. On the last of these occasions there would be a glorious change. My hand closed round the fat rustling inequalities of a Christmas stocking. When dawn came, I explored it.

I remember one stocking in particular. A doll, dressed, as I now realize, by my mother, emerged from the top. She had a starched white sun-hat, a blue gingham dress and a white pinafore. Her smirk differed slightly from that of Sophonisba whom she replaced. Sophonisba was a wax doll sent by my English grandmother in the Fendalton days and so christened by my mother. Her end had been precipitate and hideous: I left her on the seat of the swing and her face melted in the New Zealand sun. Under my new doll were books making tightly stretched rectangles in the stocking and farther down – beguiling trifles: a pistol, a trumpet, crayons, a pencil box and an orange in the toe. Placed well away from the stocking were books from my parents, grandmother and Mivvy.

I have no idea when I left off believing in Father Christmas. It was a completely painless transition. The pretence was long kept up between my father and me as a greatly relished joke. He would come out to the verandah in the warm dark when I was still awake and would growl in a buffo voice: 'Very c-o-o-o-ld in the chimney tonight. Who have we here? A good little girl or a bad little girl? I must consult my notes.'

I would lie with my eyes tight shut, rejoicing, while he hung up my stocking.

At some appallingly early hour, I took their presents into my parents' bedroom. The only ones I can remember were an extremely fancy paua-shell napkin ring engraved with a fisherman's head, which I gave my mother, and a pipe (it must have been a cheap one!) which my father obligingly put in his mouth before going to sleep again.

The morning ripened to distant squeaks and blasts from tin trumpets in the house at the foot of the hill where my friends, the Evanses, had opened their stockings. My mother and I trudged up and over a steep rise to an Anglican Service held in the Convalescent Home, the first building of any size to be built in these parts. Soon after our return came The Boys, walking up the garden path in single file: tall, and with the exception of Alexander, bearded: sardonic and kind. How well they chose their presents: books, when they could get them, that were reprints of ones they had liked when they were really boys: Jules Verne, *Uncle Remus*, the *Boys' Own Paper*. Colin, after a visit to England, brought back the complete works of Juliana Horatia Ewing, producing them one by one from a Gladstone bag. On the following Christmas he gave me *The Scarlet Pimpernel* and my mother began reading it aloud that same afternoon. It was decreed that we should go for a walk and the interruption at a crucial juncture when M. Chauvelin contemplated the sleeping Sir Percy Blakeney, was almost unendurable.

This, I think, was the Christmas when I wrote and produced my first play, *Cinderella*, in rhymed couplets with a cast of six. It was performed before an audience of parents by three of my cousins, two friends and myself on a large dining-room table in a conveniently curtained bay window of my cousins' house. I remember the opening scene: Cinderella, discovered in rags before the fire, soliloquized.

> *O dear, O dear, what shall I do,*
> *Of balls I've been to such a few*
> *Just once I've seen that handsome Prince*
> *And I have never seen him since.*

Her predicament having been thus established, the Ugly Sisters made a brief and brutal appearance and I came on as The Fairy Godmother, croaking offstage:

> *Knock at the door and lift the latch*
> *And cross the threshold over.*

The rest of the dialogue escapes me.

I am conscious that I am vague about dates and the order of events during these early years and have dodged backwards and forwards between my tenth and thirteenth birthdays. The passage of time had not the same significance in those days. The terrors of childhood receded. Other people became more complicated and the firm blacks and whites of human relationships mingled and developed passages of grey. One grew taller. Frisky went into retirement and was replaced by a large rawboned horse called Monte. And then, one day in 1910, Miss Ffitch said goodbye and bicycled down the lane for the last time. I was to go to school.

CHAPTER 3

School

St Margaret's College was only six months old when I became a pupil there. It was one of a group of schools established in the Dominions by the Kelburn Sisters of the Church, an Anglo-Catholic order of nuns. These ladies already conducted St Hilda's College in Dunedin. With funds raised by their Colonial exertions they supported their work amongst the poor in the East End of London.

On the face of it, the choice of St Margaret's would seem to have been an odd one on the part of my parents. My mother certainly respected and subscribed to the Anglican faith but she was not an ardent churchwoman. Occasionally she would let fall a remark that suggested not doubt so much as a sort of ironical detachment. 'Apparently,' she once said, 'the Almighty can see everything except a joke.'

This was not the sort of quip that would have gone down well at St Margaret's.

As for my father, he seldom missed an opportunity of pointing out the devastation wrought by 'religion' (usually undefined) upon the progress of mankind. He would invite my mother and me to look at the Crusades. 'Bloodiest damn' business in history. Look at Evolution! You want to read. Read Haeckel!' he would shout. 'Or Darwin. Or Winwood Reade. They'll show you.'

My mother had hidden Haeckel's *Evolution of Man* in the lockers under the living-room windows, mainly, I suppose, because of its rather surprising illustrations. There it lay, cheek-by-jowl with *Three Weeks*. These were the only books that were ever withdrawn from my attention, and I found them both in due course. I was but mildly engaged by the first, thought the second pretty silly and didn't get farther than the first chapter of either. She needn't have bothered.

It does seem strange that, holding such rationalistic views, my father should have sent me to a school where every possible emphasis was placed upon high-church dogma and orthodox observances. Moreover his attitude to the Sisters, although he occasionally referred to them as Holy-Bolies, was one of amused respect. He did their banking for them and knew their real names. Once, in an absent-minded moment, he let fall to my mother that one of them was a lady of title in her own right. He caught sight of me and was disconcerted.

'Pay no attention,' he said, 'that sort of thing doesn't matter. I shouldn't have said anything.'

He made less of class distinctions than anybody I have ever known, not self-consciously, I think, but because they were of no interest to him and he had a talent for forgetting anything that bored him. My mother, nowadays, would probably have been thought of as an 'inverted snob', a term which, if it means anything at all, indicates, I imagine, somebody who is inclined to suspect and give battle to snobbish attitudes where none exist. It is true, however, that they both intensely disliked what they considered vulgar turns of speech, oafish manners or slipshod utterance. They came down remarkably crisply if I showed any signs of backsliding in these respects. 'Rude,' said my mother, 'is Never Funny.' The aphorism was shortened into 'R is Never F' and constantly employed.

'Jump up,' she would mutter when grown-ups approached, and when they left: 'Up. Run and open the door.'

'I was *going* to!' I would furiously mutter back, but I jumped to it.

Such was her authority that it involved a trigger-reaction. It was not enough to rise. One leapt.

Perhaps it was because of their views on civilized behaviour that they made what must have been a great sacrifice to send me to St Margaret's. I took it all as a matter of course but remember now, with something like heartache, how long my mother's coats and skirts lasted her.

I now realize that she refused many invitations because she had no appropriate dress for the occasion. My father thought she looked beautiful, as indeed she did, but he was vague to a degree about clothes and it never entered his head that she was hypersensitive in matters of economy.

'Good Lord!' he would ejaculate on being told the probable cost of some painfully rare necessity. '*Thirty bob!* It can't be as much as that, can it? Are you sure, Betsy?'

He would grin incredulously at her and she would shrink inside herself and do without. He was far from being ungenerous, but he was singularly blind to certain forms of vulnerability and so, alas, at that time, was his daughter.

Economies that would have seemed irksome to other children were unnoticed by me. I remember how we used to leave the tram (now on an extended route) a half-mile stop before our own because it was the end of a section. My mother was not very robust. She must have often longed for the extra lift. We were, because we had to be so, a thrifty family, and if my parents had been content, as many parents in their circumstances were, to send me to a high school, there would have been a much wider margin for those small luxuries which their friends enjoyed without thinking about the cost.

Having made their decision, they might have settled on one of the other private schools less extreme in their religious attitudes than St Margaret's and, one would have thought, more acceptable to my father if not to both my parents. Perhaps they considered that the, as it were, personified focus given by a Church school to pure ethics, would be salutary. If so, I think they were right. The fervour, the extremes and the uncertainties of adolescence must find some sort of channel. I took mine out in Anglo-Catholic observance.

II

'Good morning, girls.'

'Good morning, Sister. Good morning, Miss Fleming.'

Every morning after prayers we performed this ritual, bobbing first to Sister Winifred, our headmistress, and then, on a half-turn, to our form mistress who, with a sort of huffy grandeur, returned our greeting.

From the first day, I loved St Margaret's. All the observances that had terrified and haunted me at Tib's were now enthusiastically embraced. It was superb to be one of a crowd. Appeals to Honour produced a reaction as instantly responsive as a knee jerk under a smart tap.

Several of my schoolfellows at Tib's were now at St Margaret's and turned out to be so unalarming that one wondered why they had ever seemed formidable. And here, after a long interval, was the friend of that magic house in Fendalton. She asked me to stay with her and the old enchantment was revived; the delight, quite untouched by envy, of a visit to another world.

Among my closest friends was Friede Burton. She was one of four daughters of a newly arrived English vicar at the Highest of Anglican churches in Christchurch. The eldest of these girls, Aileen, who had been at the Slade school, made sensitive drawings of birds and painted miniatures. The second, Helen, had been a student at Tree's School, afterwards The Royal Academy of Dramatic Art. Friede came third and Joanie fourth. There were two older sisters in England.

All the Burtons were knowledgeably interested in the theatre and as soon as they were established in their father's parish began to organize plays. He was himself an extremely good actor both in and out of the pulpit. His sermons were *tours-de-force*. In a darkened church he would thunder doctrinal anathemas and blinded by the very knowledgeably placed light that shone upwards into his face, would point accusingly at some unseen trembling old lady or startled vestryman. '*You* know what I mean. Yes, *You!*'

'Even a little child – ' he would say and single out some gratified infant. 'Even a little child – Friede, Helen, Ngaio, I have left my spectacles on my desk. Go and fetch them.'

Whichever of us was nearest to the aisle would then rise, hurriedly bob to the east and bolt over to the vicarage. On our return we would hand the spectacles up to him. Though I would not have put it like that, he was a great loss to the stage.

For the first time I found myself among contemporaries who shared my own enthusiasms and from whom I could learn. I stayed with them often, tumbling out of bed when the huge bell of St Michael's in its separate belfry shook the vicarage windows with a summons to seven o'clock Mass. My memory of those mornings is so vivid that I can almost smell the drift of incense mingled with coir matting and the undelicious aftermath of Sunday School children. Candles shone like gold sequins above the altar, dawn mounted behind the east window, the celebrant's level but immensely significant monotone was punctuated with imperative interjections from – the analogy though instantly rejected was inescapable – something rather like a giant bicycle bell. We were rapt. From this it will be seen that I had become an ardent Anglo-Catholic.

To say that I took to Divinity as a duck to water is a gross understatement. I took to it with a sort of spiritual whoop and went in, as my student-players would say, boots and all.

I was still at school when the first volume of Sir Compton Mackenzie's *Sinister Street* appeared. The other day, after almost half a century, I took down my copy of this novel and re-read it. The book, tattered and stained, is encased in a dust jacket that I made for it. Michael Fane is seated on the top of a library stepladder with Lily and the appalling Meates peering over his shoulders. It is not a very good drawing but it does express something of the extraordinary attraction this romance of adolescence held for adolescents. It never occurred to me to draw a parallel between Michael's Anglo-Catholic raptures and my own but, in point of fact, there was an extremely close one. To revisit the book was to look again at a faded photograph of myself, at the wraiths of impressions that had once been most strongly defined, to catch at the memory of evaporated emotions and remain gently, regretfully, unmoved by them.

In retrospect it is impossible not to smile at many of the excesses and solemnities of one's behaviour during those intensely awkward years. How illogical, how dogmatic, how comically arrogant, one mutters, and how vulnerable! Perhaps the Roman Catholic Church is wise to offer its members for confirmation while they are still children and so avoid the complications of later transitional years. This church believes, no doubt, that calm, thorough and early saturation is better than a delayed-action plunge and the illogical anticlimax of experiencing nothing in particular except the firm pressure of the bishop's hands on one's head.

'I didn't feel *anything*,' the honest girl next to me whispered. 'Not *anything*.'

I, less honest, would not allow myself to say, 'Nor did I'.

All the same, at the very moment when the intemperances and egoism of those years are most vividly recollected there follows an acknowledgement: the failures and blind spots were often one's own, the exalted teaching, even if one no longer can accept it, remains exalted.

I felt other things: longueurs, unheralded gusts of joy that arose out of nothing and drove one to run the length of the room and launch oneself, exultant, face downwards, on one's bed. Onsets of love that were for some undefined object – the world, a flower: a storm of tears, unexpected and agonizing, when my mother asked me what I would like for my fifteenth birthday.

'I don't know, I don't want anything, I don't know.'

'What's the matter? Just crying? For nothing in particular?'

'For nothing at all.'

'Never mind. It doesn't matter. It won't last,' said my mother.

Here are three persons to whom I owe a debt of gratitude. The first is Canon Jones. He was precentor at Christchurch Cathedral and a man of learning. Once a week he lectured on Church History to the fifth and sixth forms at St Margaret's. He was a white-faced Welshman with rich curls, burning, pitch-ball eyes and an excitable manner. He wore decent black canonicals and a shovel hat, tilted forward as he himself was tilted, being usually burdened with an armful of books. He was reputed to have the most distinguished private library in New Zealand. Canon Jones walked with a feverish pace and would enter our formroom abruptly, almost at a run.

'Morning, Sister,' (we were, of course, chaperoned), 'Morning, girls,' he would pant, and dump his books on the desk. On one occasion, he then screamed: '*Sister! Spiders!*' and Sister Winifred composedly removed a suspended creature while Canon Jones, grinning desperately, backed into a corner.

He lectured to us as if we were adults and we learned more secular history from him than from any of our history mistresses. We followed him avidly, took frenzied notes, since he was very fast in his delivery, and were always chagrined when his period came to an end. He led us down many rococo byways of history.

'A rooster!' he ejaculated, 'a cock, a barndoor chanticleer! Solemnly excommunicated, girls, and I quote, "for the heinous and unnatural offence of laying an egg.' " And Canon Jones gave a

crowing laugh appropriate to his subject. He spent an entire period
over the death of William the Conqueror, dwelling on its horrors
with the utmost relish and baring his splendid teeth at us in a final
triumphant grimace. In spite of these excursions he was extremely
thorough and searchingly critical of our essays. 'Padding!!!' he
would write in an irritable neo-gothic script in the margin. 'Not
lucid. The line of argument is not sustained.' Thus from Canon
Jones I learned that things which are thought of together should be
written together and that they should be stated with becoming
economy.

In his cassock, seated to one side of the altar in our chapel during
Lenten instruction, he was a different being. He spoke quietly then,
without emphasis and with wisdom. He was a person of authority.

Miss Hughes was an Englishwoman with round, rather staring
and indignant eyes and pouting lips. She taught English and mathe-
matics and she taught them very well. With her we read *Julius
Caesar*, *Hamlet*, *The Faerie Queene*, *The Prologue to the Canterbury Tales*,
and a certain amount of English Augustan prose. She did not drama-
tize like Canon Jones, she was not excitable, and she had a cool
voice. Everything we read with her was firmly and at the same time
vividly examined. I do not remember that she ordered us to learn
great chunks of the plays and poems we studied but somehow or
another one found that they were there in one's memory and they
remain there to this day. She was a dragon on the notes and introduced us to considerably more scholarship than they embraced but
there was no hardship in this: we hunted after her like falconers, flying at anything we saw. Eng. Lit. with Miss Hughes was exacting,
and absorbing, an immensely rewarding adventure. I don't think she
particularly liked me and indeed, during the first onset of devotional
fervour, I must have been hard to suffer. Moreover it was a matter
of understandable irritation for Miss Hughes that, when I won a
Navy League Empire Prize, I did so with an essay containing thirty-
one spelling mistakes. For all the time I was at school I think Miss
Hughes scarcely spoke three sentences to me out of class and yet she
gave me a present that I value more than any other: an abiding passion for the plays and sonnets of Shakespeare.

Sister Winifred, our headmistress, was a tiny woman with blue
eyes, a large, pink, inquisitive nose, a wide mouth and excellent

large teeth. I think her age could have been little over forty. It may have been less: the veil and wimple are great levellers in this respect. On a single occasion, a short wisp of hair showed itself briefly under the cambric that bound her forehead. It was ginger. Her manner was extremely austere but her smile engaging and rather boyish. Her voice was clear and her style patrician. She had immense authority and a highly developed sense of humour. The only daughter in a long family of boys, she had been brought up in France where her father held a diplomatic post. She told me that when she announced her intention of taking vows her brothers all laughed till they cried and said she'd be back in a fortnight. Her French was exquisite. If she had taken us in this subject we would have undoubtedly gained a much more civilized notion of the language than the extraordinary jargon that emerged from unruly classes held by poor Monsieur Malequin who had no discipline and a most baffling squint.

I had arrived at the age for hero-worship and upon Sister Winifred, in the ripeness of time, did I lavish my homage. It is easy enough to laugh at 'schoolgirl crushes' and it is easier still, in these days, to overburden with heavy psychological implications an essentially fleeting, often delicate and always tenuous emotion. No doubt disturbing undertones sometimes appear but when the child's bewildered devotion meets with a temperate and uncomplicated response there is nothing to regret.

By the time I had begun to admire Sister Winifred so ardently, I had been made head prefect and my duties sent me quite often to her office. It was during those visits that she occasionally told me something of her childhood, discussed school affairs, received my own stumbling and difficult confidences and spoke, once or twice, of the aims and hopes of her Order.

Out of these brief conversations there was to arise, in my final term, a great embarrassment. I called at her office on some prefectorial errand. When it had been dispatched, I tried to express my desire to do something specific for the Church after I left school. I suspect that in doing this I was as much moved by the hope of pleasing Sister Winifred as I was by a devotional intention: if so, I was most effectively hoist on my own petard. Her response was immediate and alarming. To my amazement, she opened wide her arms and, with a delighted smile, exclaimed 'You are coming to us!'

Nothing could have been farther from my thoughts. Never in my
most exalted moments had I imagined myself to have a vocation for
the Sisterhood. Immersed in the folds of her habit, I was appalled
and utterly at a loss. It was impossible to extricate myself saying:
'Not at all. Nothing of the sort. No, no!' I listened aghast to her
expressions of joy and left in a state of utmost confusion. It was an
appalling predicament.

During the next two or three days, I managed to snarl up an
already sufficiently complicated situation. I began to wonder if I was
right in thinking it was all a hideous misunderstanding. Suppose
that, all unknown to myself, I was indeed called to take the veil and
Sister Winifred had been elected as a sort of harbinger and prologue
to the omens coming on. Perhaps, after all, she had made no mistake
and this acutely embarrassing moment had been one of divine rev-
elation. Which? It was a nice dilemma and I made no attempt to
resolve it. I trod water and continued to do so until my last term
expired.

My adolescence, as I have suggested, was taken out in religious fervour rather than in any abrupt onset of boy-consciousness. I did not,
however, escape the awakening of those emotions proper to my age.

When I was fourteen I fell in love.

The object of my passion was a retired Dean. He was remarkably
handsome with the profile of a classic hero. His voice was deep and
harsh, his manner abrupt and his conversation rather like that of the
Duke of Wellington as recorded by Mr Phillip Guedella though, of
course, without the expletives. He also reminded me of Mr
Rochester; I cannot imagine why, as there was but little correspondence. He was in the habit of taking a Saturday afternoon walk on
the Hills and would call on my mother for tea. My heart thumped
obstreperously when I saw him approach. If he missed a Saturday I
was desolate. I cannot remember that we ever conversed at great
length but may suppose that he was not positively averse to my
company since he sometimes came out of the Deanery which was in
the same street as St Margaret's and accompanied me as far as the
school gate, actually carrying my satchel. These were tremendous
occasions.

I was not alone in my obsession. The Dean was hotly pursued by
members of a Ladies' Guild who were said by my mother to lie in

ambush for him on the Port Hills and so irritated him that he sought refuge in our house where he spoke in anger against them. She had many stories about him. When he was a parish priest she had been asked by his wife to luncheon at the vicarage. He was late and they did not wait for him. Just as they were about to help themselves from a side table, he strode in and without a word snatched up the cold joint and went away through the french windows.

'That,' said his wife, 'is the third time this week. Will you have some ham?'

It was a poor parish and there was, in those days, a financial depression in New Zealand. The joint had gone to one of his flock.

By the time I adored him, the Dean had retired and become a widower. He was a great admirer of my grandmother and was, I think, 73 years old. At the very height of my passion he married Miss Tibby Ross.

On his honeymoon he encountered an acquaintance in the upstairs corridor of the hotel.

'This is a rum go,' he was reputed to have said.

III

For two afternoons a week I went to the School of Art and it was understood that when I left St Margaret's I would become, not a full-time student, but at least a daily one. I would have to get a morning job of some sort and, if possible, a scholarship to pay for my fees. In the meantime, through the Burton sisters, the smell of greasepaint had entered into my system never to be expelled.

They turned St Michael's parish hall into a workable theatre with an old-fashioned raked stage, an overhead grille and adequate lighting. Here they produced 'costume' comedies, rather nebulous miracle plays and fairy pieces garnished with mediaeval songs and ballets of the gay flat-footed kind. Nothing could point more sharply the difference in theatrical attitudes and taste between those days and the present time than these blameless entertainments. Nowadays my friends would no doubt have chosen plays by Harold Pinter, even Ionesco, even Beckett and would perhaps, by diligent application, have discovered in such works undertones of religious significance that would have astonished their authors if they had ever heard about them. With us all was sweetness, tabards, and tights.

The first of these productions was called *Isolene*. My father unkindly referred to it as 'Vaseline' . I was cast as the Prince. Aileen, the artist sister, designed and made the clothes and did so with imagination and ingenuity. I wore a white tabard, heavily emblazoned in great detail, and white ostrich plumes on my head. I have not the smallest recollection of the plot but can recall, as if it had been last evening, the wave of intoxication that came over me when I made my first entrance on to any stage. There is no experience to be compared with this: the call, the departure from an overheated room reeking of greasepaint and wet white, the arrival backstage into a world of shadows, separated only by stretched canvas from a world of light: a region of silence and stillness attentive to a region of sound and movement. Here the player waits, suspended between preparation and performance. He stares absently at a painted legend on the back of a canvas door through which he must enter. 'Act II, Scene I, p. 2', or into the prompt corner where a shaded lamp casts its light on a book and on a hand that follows the dialogue. He may look up at the perch. There is the switchboard man into whose watchful face is reflected light from the unseen stage. On the other side of the door they are building to his own entrance. The voices are pitched larger than life and respond to each other in a formal pattern. Beyond them, like an observant monster in a black void, is the audience. The player listens and with a sick jolt may ask himself, 'Why, why, why did I subject myself to this terror?' Then he steps back a pace or two and on his cue moves up to the door and enters.

This is his moment of truth. Even though the role he plays is insignificant, the play worthless and the actor himself of no great account, this first crossing of a threshold from one reality to another will stand apart from anything else that he does.

My introduction to the working half of a theatre was thus by way of an insipid little piece in a converted parish hall. Luckily I never thought of myself as, potentially, a dynamic actress. If I had cherished any such illusion my mother would very promptly have disabused me of it. It was the whole ambience of backstage that I found so immensely satisfying: the forming and growth of a play and its precipitation into its final shape. That wonderful phrase 'the quick forge and working-house of thought' was unknown to me then: I would have leapt at it as an exact expression of the living theatre.

I don't know when I first realized that I wanted to direct rather than to perform: at this early stage I was equally happy painting scenery, mustering props, prompting or going on for a speaking-part. I was at home.

At school, also, there was dramatic endeavour. *Antigone* (in English), excerpts from *A Midsummer Night's Dream* and, every year, a play in French composed and produced by M. Malequin. M. Malequin was an ardent monarchist and was rumoured to have been tutor to a scion of the Bourbons. His plays, mimeographed in purple from his own spidery hand, tended to reflect his opinions. One was about the Little Dauphin of the Terror, un-murdered and in durance. I was his gaoler – inevitably, since my voice and height always prompted M. Malequin to cast me for the 'heavies'. I was very brutal and brought the Dauphin a meat pie. I think I had doctored it but that somehow or another a blameless pie had been substituted by a virtuous hand.

'Eh bien!' I rasped as the Dauphin attacked it. 'Bon appetit!'

Monsieur was, of course, anti-Bonapartist and in another piece I was a servile and sinister agent.

'Excusez-moi, Madame la Duchesse, mais je suis ici envoyé de l'Empereur, mon maître.'

There was nobody on the staff of St Margaret's who had the slightest acquaintance with stage-production. My parents suffered these performances annually at the prize-giving and I cannot recall that either of them ever offered an opinion. In this they showed superhuman forbearance.

There was a Lower School at St Margaret's. After I became head prefect, I went there twice a week in the luncheon break to amuse the very small girls: I read to them and began to write and illustrate stories for their entertainment. Then I wrote a play and rehearsed it with them. This was a popular move and our effort, having been passed by Sister Winifred, was introduced into the prize-giving ceremonies at the end of the year. The play was called *Bundles* and the title is all I can remember about it. A New Zealand authoress of those days – Miss Colburn-Veale – saw it and wrote to my mother, offering to show it to her English publisher for an opinion. He wrote back very kindly and sent me a book: *Tristie's Quest* by Dr Greville Macdonald, the son of George Macdonald whose stories my father, having delighted in them as a child, had tried in vain to get for me. *Tristie's Quest* was a wonderful children's novel and I wish very much that I had not lent it to the little girl who never returned it.

Encouraged by these events, I now wrote a full-length piece based on one of George Macdonald's fairy tales as related by my father. It was called *The Moon Princess*. There were long chunks of very torrid blank verse and a good deal of theeing and thouing. For songs, I wrote new verses to old music and got very worked up over the whole affair. When it was finished I showed it to my friends, the Burtons, and they bravely decided to produce it on quite an imposing scale at St Michael's.

'I hear, Ngaio,' said Miss Hughes, shouting down the length of the luncheon table, 'you have written a play.' Her manner was friendly but I was seized with embarrassment and muttered churlishly at my plate: 'Yes, Miss Hughes.'

I would have done much better to show it to her and take what no doubt would have been a devastating opinion.

In the event, it went quite well and drew good audiences. Perhaps, after all, it was not too bad since my mother agreed to play the witch. She made a splendidly frightening thing of the curse:

'In the dark nights that follow the old moon – '

Her big scene was with Helen Burton, the director and star of the production, and they both let fly with everything they had, lifting my dialogue into a distinction that it certainly did not possess. This feat, it occurs to me, illustrates in miniature one of the strange paradoxes of the Victorian, Edwardian and Georgian theatres. It can be seen at all levels from our remote New Zealand amateurism up to the great actor-managers. Irving's most successful roles were in pieces that today reveal themselves as unbelievable fustian. These strange monsters of the theatre poured the charged stream of their personality and technique into dialogue which, by its very mediocrity, gave them the freedom which they needed. Irving was an intelligent man with a strong vein of irony but he seems to have been quite uncritical of his material except in so far as it provided him with a vehicle. Ellen Terry was different. 'A twopenny-ha'penny play,' she said of their enormously successful travesty on *Faust*. If there were adequate recordings or a film of Irving I wonder what we would think of them. Grotesque helpings of ham and corn? Or would some tingle of the electricity he generated in a theatre still make itself felt? Ellen Terry lived to a great age and people who remember her performance as the Nurse in *Romeo and Juliet* tell us that it was timeless in its perfection. But Irving?

'I went to the Lyceum for Ellen Terry,' my father said. 'Irving's mannerisms – ' He thought for a moment. 'All the same,' he said, 'there was something – ' He gave a little chuckle. 'Yes. There was something.'

And he went on to relate how Irving as Mephistopheles, in a scene with Martha, the character-woman played as a tiresome old village body, had an aside to the audience.

'I don't know where *she'll* go when she dies. *I* won't have her,' which always brought the house down. It is hardly enough to set us falling about in the aisles nowadays but my father insisted that Irving gave out the line in such a droll, unexpected manner that it always 'went' tremendously in the Lyceum.

Irving's mannerisms of course inspired every drawing-room entertainer of the day. In the Grossmiths' *Diary of a Nobody* there is the egregious Burwin-Fosselton who, without being asked, insisted on giving his repertoire of Irving imitations after a meat-tea at the wretched Pooter's house and to their dismay invited himself for the following evening to present the second half of his repertoire.

As for Irving's extraordinary vocal eccentricities: 'gaw' for go and 'god' for good, and all the rest of them, they were meat and drink for his mimics.

It was while I was stemming the full tide of my devotional convictions that Irving's son, H. B., visited New Zealand with an English company giving *Hamlet*, *The Lyons Mail*, *Louis XIth* and *The Bells*. This was an acid test, since the visit to Christchurch came in Lent and during those forty days and nights I had forsworn entertainment. The Burtons, very reasonably, decided that such an event, never to be repeated, might be granted an exemption. My parents were agog. Whether my decision was rooted in devotion, exhibitionism or sheer obstinacy I do not know but whatever the underlying motive, it was a difficult one to take and I can only hope I wasn't insufferably smug about it. I listened avidly to their enraptured reports. My mother described in detail the 'business' of the play scene in *Hamlet*, the protracted death of Louis, the gasp of relief from the audience when he finally expired, the tap of Lesourque's foot as the tumbrels rolled by. It seems probable that H. B. Irving suffered, in England, from inevitable comparison with his father. New Zealand audiences found him dynamic. I wish I had seen him.

It was not very long after this visit, I think, that Ellen Terry, now in her old age, came on a recital tour. It was said that her memory, always an enemy, had grown so faulty that the performance was riddled with prompts that often had to be repeated. My father preferred to remember Beatrice running like a lapwing close to the ground and my mother also felt that this might be a painful experience. So we missed Ellen Terry, and this was a mistake for she was so little troubled by her constant 'dries' that her audiences, also, were quite unembarrassed.

'What?' she would call out to her busy prompters: 'What is it? Ah, yes!' and would sail away again, sometimes on a ripple of laughter that my father used to say was never matched by any other actress.

A friend of ours called Fred Reade Wauchop played Friar John and stage-managed in the *Romeo and Juliet* of her Indian summer. He used to call for Miss Terry at her dressing-room, carry her lanthorn for her and see her on for her entrance as the Nurse. The production was by her daughter, Edith Craig, and the star was an American actress very young and beautiful but not deeply acquainted with Shakespeare. Miss Craig thought it best to spare her mother the early rehearsals but when the play was beginning to take shape, asked her to come down to the theatre. Miss Terry had taken a great liking to Freddie Reade Wauchop and invited him to sit with them in the stalls.

Juliet, alone, embarked upon the wonderful potion speech:

> *Farewell. God knows when we shall meet again.*
> *I have a faint, cold fear thrills through my veins –*

It is a long speech. The star had enunciated but half a dozen lines when a scarcely audible moaning sound began in the stalls. Ellen Terry rocked to and fro and gripped her daughter's hand.

'O Edy! Edy! Tell her she mustn't. Tell her she mustn't.'

In the event, it was the Nurse whom the audiences went to see in this production.

Stories of these and the more remote days of the Victorian actor-managers turned my interest to the past rather than to the contemporary theatre and this inclination was encouraged by Gramp. After the final performance of *The Moon Princess* he gave me two parcels. One was a book called *Actors of the Century*. It began with Kean and ended with *The Second Mrs Tanqueray* and was nobly illustrated. Almost every page was enriched by marginal notes in Gramp's handwriting. '*My father recollected this performance.*' '*I saw him as an old man.*' '*Drank.*' '*No good in comedy.*' '*Mannered and puerile.*' '*Drank himself to death.*' '*Noble as Coriolanus.*' The most exciting of these remarks appeared in the chapter on Edmund Kean. '*Old Hoskins*' it read '*gave me Kean's coat.*'

The second parcel contained the coat. It was made of tawny-coloured plush-velvet and lined with brown silk that had worn to threadpaper and torn away from its handsewn stitching. Pieces of tarnished gold braid dangled from the collar and cuffs. It was tiny.

'It's very kind of Gramp,' my mother said, 'to give you Kean's coat. You must take care of it.'

I wish we had asked him to write down the story of its coming into his hands. As far as I have been able to piece it together from memory, conjecture and subsequent reading, it should run something like this. 'Old Hoskins', who as I remember them, appears frequently in Gramp's marginal comments, was a family acquaintance. He was the son of a Devonshire squire and became an actor of merit, often playing with Samuel Phelps. When a stuttering West Country lad called John Brodribb first came to London, Mr Hoskins, having seen him in an amateur performance, very kindly gave him lessons in speechcraft and technique and a letter of introduction to an actor-manager. In 1853 when Hoskins sailed for Australasia, young Brodribb changed his name to Henry Irving and went on the stage.

A few years later Mr Hoskins turned up in New Zealand and renewed his acquaintance with Gramp. It is in my mind that much of this was in the notes but they were so copious and diffuse and often so difficult to make out that I skipped a great many of them. Kean's coat had been passed on to Mr Hoskins by somebody – Phelps? – and he gave it to my grandfather in gratitude for an obligation that he was unable to repay in any other way. It was an heirloom.

About thirty years after Gramp gave me the coat, Sir Laurence Olivier played Richard III in Christchurch. There are few, a very few, actors of today in whom there is a particular quality that is not a sport of personality or even, however individual in character, exclusively their own. Rather, one feels, it is a sudden crystallization, a propitious flowering of an element that is constant in the history of the English theatre: it appeared in Alleyn, no doubt, and in Garrick, in Siddons and in Edmund Kean. When the door on the prompt side opened in a New Zealand theatre and Crookback came on with his face turned away from his audience, this witness to the thing itself, the truth about great acting, was at once evident. When the final curtain had been taken I said to myself: 'He shall have Kean's coat.' And so he did. Gramp was a good judge of acting: he would certainly have approved.

Vivien Leigh tried it on. She was small, slight and delicately shaped and it fitted her enchantingly.

As for the book, I shall relate what happened to it at the appropriate time.

One other of Gramp's theatre stories sticks in my memory. When he was a very small boy he was taken with his father to call upon William Charles Macready in his dressing room. The production included a big crowd scene. Macready took the little boy by the hand and led him up to one of the bit-part actors who carried him onstage. All he could remember of this experience was being told by his father not to forget it. Stories about Macready abound, many of them authenticated by his own hectic diaries. Actors, perhaps obeying some kind of occupational chemistry, are frequently obstreperous but Macready takes, as we used to say, the buttered bun, for throwing ungovernable tantrums. I like best the stories that collected round his frightful rows in America. These culminated in a pitched battle with his audience during a performance of *Macbeth*. Articles of furniture were thrown about, armed troops were called in. People were shot. At the centre of this gigantic rumpus, Macready continued in his role but selected suitable lines (and there were many) to hurl in the teeth of one or another of his tormentors. One can see him advance to the footlights, squinting hideously at the audience and beside himself with rage, point a trembling finger at a jeering face and yell 'The devil damn thee black thou cream-faced loon'. Speaking of buns, it is worth noting that his unfortunate manager in London was called Mr Bunn, a sort of Happy Family name that accorded ill with the insults Macready tended to throw at him.

In his old age Gramp was both energetic and cantankerous. After Gram died he stayed with each of his daughters in rotation. He still took long walks over the hills and on his return would sit on the verandah apostrophizing the city on the plains with as much energy as if it had been Gomorrah itself. His hat was tilted over his astonishingly blue eyes, his pince-nez was perched halfway down his formidable nose, his head was thrown back and his very moustache sneered.

'Generation of vipers!' he would groan. 'Sycophantic dolts! Perfidious beasts! Bah!'

Nobody knew why he had taken up this attitude towards the city of his adoption. My mother said he merely enjoyed the sound of the phrases. Perhaps his elevated position reminded him of Mount Horeb and the mantle of the prophets fell across his shoulders or perhaps he was merely giving a final airing to his undoubtedly strong histrionic inclinations. At last he became very old and silent and it was not possible to guess at his thoughts or know if he listened to anything that was said to him. He died when he was over ninety years old and left behind him the trunk full of documents that I have already described and a great deal of material for the performance of conjuring tricks.

IV

'*Lord Dismiss Us With Thy Blessing* – ' I had expected to be torn with emotion when, for the last time and well off-pitch, I joined in this valedictory hymn. It was annoying to find oneself relatively unmoved. Perhaps if it had been a rather more inspiring composition – 'Jerusalem', for instance, or 'Ye Watchers and Ye Holy Ones' – I might have risen to the occasion with a poignant throb or two but as it was, the final break-up passed off quite calmly and we faced the world with equanimity.

It was a world on the brink of war and that seemed very odd to my schoolfellows and me. We had been taught by Miss Fleming, who took us in history, to look upon war between civilized peoples as an anachronism. It could never happen again, Miss Fleming had crisply decided. The appalling potential of modern weapons of destruction was a safeguard: no nation, she assured us, not even Germany, would dare to invoke it. In that cosy belief we went forward with our plans for growing up. One of my best friends was to have a coming-out ball. There were endless consultations.

In the meantime we went into the mountains for our fourth summer camp. I find I have caught up with the beginning of this book.

CHAPTER 4

Mountains

Glentui is a bush-clad valley running up into the foothills of the Southern Alps between Burnt Hill and Mount Thomas. The little Glentui river churns down this valley, icy-cold and swift among its boulders. The summit of Mount Richardson from which it springs is called Blowhard and from here one looks across a wide hinterland, laced by the great Ashley river, to the main range. The Alps are the backbone of the South Island. When, in comparatively recent geological times, New Zealand was thrust up from the bed of the Pacific, this central spine must have monstrously emerged while the ocean divided and its waters streamed down the flanks of the heaving mountains and across the plains until they found their own level and the coastline was defined in a pother of foam. Ours is a young country. Everything you see in the South Island leads up to the mountains. They are the *leitmotif* of a landscape for full orchestra.

Glentui is about thirty miles crow's-flight from our hills. On winter mornings when the intervening plains are often blanketed in mist, it seems much closer and on a nor'west evening in summer when a strange clarity, an intensity of colour, follows the sudden lapse of the wind, one can see in detail patches of bush and even isolated trees. So that we were, in a sense, familiar with Glentui long before we camped there in the first summer of my schooldays at St Margaret's. We were a large party: two of the middle-aged Walker Boys – Colin and Cecil – Mivvy, the four Burtons, Aileen's and Helen's fiancés, who were called John and Kennedy, and Sylvia, another schoolfriend. To reach Glentui was an all-day business. We had to go roundabout: by train to Rangiora, a mid-plains town, and then by a meandering branch line to Oxford, where we lunched at a country pub. Here, in sweltering midsummer heat, we picked up two farm carts loaded with stores, tents, shooting equipment, and hay for our sleeping-sacks. Then came an eight-mile plod round the foothills and across the great bridge over the Ashley. The air, as clean as mountain water, smelt of sun-baked tussock and our load of hay. On hilly stretches we climbed down and walked to ease the horses. Tuis sang in the hills. Is the song of our native birds really as beautiful as we think? The tui, black-coated with a white jabot, has a deep voice and changes his tune with the seasons, often interrupting himself with a consequential clearing of his throat. Sometimes he sings the opening phrase of 'Home to our Mountains' and sometimes two liquid notes, a most melodious shake and a final question. I tried to suit words to his song: 'Remote. Remote. Alone and fordone. Gone,' but they didn't really fit and I was left with that aftertaste of an acute pleasure that always resembles pain.

In the late afternoon we reached Glentui and turned up the valley to find a camping ground. The carts jolted down a rough track and we ran ahead of them into the bush.

On our side of the ranges the bush is hardy: not gigantic and lush like the Westland forests but tenacious and resistant to sun and wind. Most of the trees are native 'beech' with an undergrowth of flowering-creepers, mosses and fern. The smell is glorious. As we entered, we heard the little Glentui river. It flowed through the silence like some cool and preoccupied conversation. We found a clearing and below it, at the base of a steep bank, the stream itself, emergent from a small gorge.

The men cut poles for the tents. We unpacked the stores, stuffed the mattresses, cut pegs for guy ropes, made a temporary fireplace and collected wood. Presently a spiral of aromatic smoke rose like a thank-offering for pleasures to come. I climbed down the bank with a clanking kerosene-tin bucket and now the mingled voices of the river were loud. Talk, talk, talk and always one significant insistent voice that muttered beneath the multiple colloquy. I squatted at the water's edge, leaned out, and felt the tug of the stream as it filled my bucket. When I returned, the first tent was hanging from its ridge pole and we began to drive in the pegs. My mother hung a billy from a forked green stick over the fire and prepared to make tea. My father was magnificent on these occasions. He was in his natural element and seemed to give off a glow of profound satisfaction. If one caught his eye he would grin or make a droll grimace.

'Good. Splendid. We'll be shipshape before sunset. Get all the gear under canvas: that's the first thing. Always make sure you've got a dry camp.'

Indoors, doing the accounts or arranging some matter of business, he was a fusspot and used to drive us into a frenzy with his antics but out in the open, his natural element, he was peaceful and, as one might say, came to himself.

There is, of course, no such thing as a norm in human behaviour: inside every conventional man there's an eccentric refusing to come out. The real eccentric – the 'character' – is the person whose other self doesn't sulk but comes out boldly and lets fly. Such a one, to some extent, was my father. When he was cross he shouted and kicked things. When he was gripped by a book he read it, under the very nose of his visitors. When he was happy, his whole person bore witness to his satisfaction.

Such a one too, though in an entirely different vein, was Cecil Walker, the youngest of the bearded Boys. He was, in common with his brothers, possessed of a private income, a family house and servants. He, therefore, did not seek employment of any kind and this, in New Zealand, was already extraordinary. He was extremely ingenious and of a mechanical and inventive turn of mind and he spent a great deal of his time in a little workshop in the garden where he made, among other curiosa, a clockwork egg-beater which he presented to my mother. Like my father's ginger beer, it went off with a bang and in its brief frenzy covered them both with agitated albumen.

'There has been a miscalculation,' Cecil said coldly. 'I shall have to revise my original conception.'

In our Glentui days the preoccupation of the year for Cecil was the construction of a camper's stove. He began making it in the winter, using the ubiquitous kerosene tin as raw material. It was his *oeuvre*: his triumph. We all recognized that in setting up camp he must be excused from any other job than the installation of his stove. Slowly and with infinite care, he dug out the emplacement in a meticulously chosen bank. The stove was unpacked and displayed in all its splendour of chimney, oven, flues and shining trays. It was packed round with earth. Kindling of exactly the correct length was arranged by Cecil as if for a votive offering. We all attended the lighting of the stove except my father who could be heard singing at the top of his voice in the bush as he chopped down another tent pole.

The stove worked superbly. In it my mother would bake scones and cakes and roast wild suckling pig. Cecil did not openly exult in his achievement but when we congratulated him gave a series of little sniffs which were his substitute for laughter.

There was a kind of dedication about his stoves, a purity of intention and an artist's disregard for the fugitive nature of his work. Each stove would serve its purpose nobly for eight weeks and at the end, already showing signs of decay, would be given decent burial. In six months' time he would begin to make another stove.

He was an oddity in looks as well as in character. As a model, he would have been a *trouvaille* for an illustrator of Don Quixote. The long narrow head, the beard, the height and sparseness of frame and above all, the glint of fanaticism in the eyes: they were all there. He was argumentative and shouted a good deal when roused. His brothers found him rather trying in this respect. They were men with a gift of irony and great reserve. They came of an old and, I suspect, rather inbred Scottish family to which they seldom referred. One of their aunts was a duchess with whom Colin and his mother stayed during a trip to England. Colin, on his return, spoke dryly of the experience. There had been a dinner party for which he wore his new tails and white tie. On this occasion he had behaved, for the only time on record, rather in the manner of my father. At seven o'clock he appeared in a state of agitation at his mother's door. 'Some bastard,' he said, 'has pinched my pants.'

Mrs Walker said: 'They are being pressed. And don't speak like that.'

He raised his eyebrows and withdrew.

The men at this party, he related, had only one thing to say to him. It was: 'By Jove! Come a long way!'

His aunt sent him out in the mornings for some 'rough shooting'. Colin was used, in New Zealand, to no other kind and he was a brilliant shot. Accustomed to the rigours of the high country, his stroll with an attendant gamekeeper through his aunt's well-kept preserves made him feel foolish. 'I didn't know what to do with the damn' chap,' he said.

'What did you shoot?' asked my mother.

'Bunnies,' said Colin, bitterly.

Cecil refused to go on this jaunt to England.

Cecil had a number of stock observations which became catch phrases in my own family. 'They didn't ask me,' and 'I should have to look it up,' were two of the most familiar. He pronounced his a's as in 'lack'. 'They didn't âsk me.' When the war came he did not enlist but waited huffily for his name to be drawn in the ballot. 'When they want me they can âsk for me.' He was wounded in the ankle and suffered himself to be anaesthetized, probed and manipulated.

'They wanted to find out whether it was broken. I could have told them it wasn't, for I ran a couple of chains after I was hit. But they didn't âsk me.'

He had one, to me, very endearing trait: he loved stories for children. Every Christmas until he died at an advanced age, I gave him one. He never pronounced upon them. Once, pleased with my choice, I ventured to ask him if he had enjoyed it. He sniffed three times. 'I return to it,' he said, 'upon an average, once every two months.' Success!

Cecil met with a strange adventure at Glentui. The men had been out all day on a wild pig hunt and were returning empty-handed to camp, their rifles already unloaded. With Cecil some distance in the van, they plodded in single file along a narrow track above a cliff-face. Cecil turned a corner and approached an outcrop of rock. A gigantic boar walked round it and confronted him. It was an old-man-tusker, a most formidable and dangerous creature. For a second or two they glared at each other. Cecil's pig-hunting weapon was slung behind his shoulder but he carried a small .22 bore rifle which was still loaded. The boar made an uncompromising noise. Its eyes glowed, it lowered its head and prepared to attack. Cecil madly discharged his pea-rifle. He heard the bullet ricochet off his opponent's hide and spatter on the rock face. The boar gave an ejaculation of the utmost savagery, launched itself full at him and fell down dead.

No wound was found upon the carcass. There was no explanation.

'Unless, my dear chap,' my father said, 'you frightened him to death.'

Cecil removed the tusks and returned to camp flushed with his ambiguous victory.

'It is,' he said haughtily, 'a perfectly well-recognized phenomenon. The details escape me. I should have to look it up.'

When the nights were warm, we girls dragged our hay-stuffed mattresses out of the hot canvas-smelling tent and slept under the trees. Starlight darted and winked behind the branches and when the moon was high it looked as if it had been crackle-glazed with twigs. The open fire alongside Cecil's stove pulsed and faded. Inside the glowing tents quiet voices exchanged a few desultory remarks, wished each other goodnight and went out with the candles. Then the bush and hills possessed the night. Moreporks called to each other across the valley, sounding very lonely in a silence that was compounded of small rustling movements, unnoticed by day, and the undertone of hurrying water.

During the night, wekas, flightless and inquisitive birds who in those days lived in the foothills, would explore the camp looking for anything bright they might steal. They would go off with a spoon or tin lid making a strange mumbling noise and when they were safe in the bush would give a vainglorious screech. One of them stole my confirmation cross from beside my pillow. My mother, who happened to be awake, saw him hurdling over our sleeping bodies with the chain dangling from his beak.

In the bush everything stirs at the first light and we too would wake and hear the bellbirds. Their dawn-song is, in fact, exactly like the tinkle of a very small melodious bell: '*Tink. Ding.*' Native pigeons, fat and unwieldy, whirred and flopped about over the tents. 'Morning is beginning to happen' one would think with satisfaction and go to sleep again.

We dammed the river with turf and boulders and made a swimming pool. We had a private glade downstream where the girls could rid themselves of their neck-to-knee bathing clothes and receive exultantly the sun and the springing pleasure of young grass. One day we climbed the mountain to Blowhard and looked across a great valley into the back country: range after naked range with a glitter of snow on the big tops.

'My country,' I thought.

And yet, so young and at the same time so primordial was this landscape, that the sense of belonging to it was disturbed by a doubt that, for all our adoptive gestures, our presence here was no more than a cobweb across the hide of a monster, that in spite of our familiarity with its surface we had made no mark upon our country and were still newcomers. I do not know if other New Zealanders are visited by this contradictory feeling of belonging and not-belonging but it came upon me very vividly when I first looked into the high country from the top of Blowhard and it has returned many times since then. It is a feeling that deepens rather than modifies one's attachment to New Zealand.

Cecil was at his most pontifical on Blowhard. When he saw us making a fire for the billy, he put his head on one side and gave the three-sniff laugh.

'Judging by the general configuration of the country and the overall appearance of the scrub I am afraid I must tell you that you are wasting your time. Unless' (sniff-sniff-sniff) 'you are prepared to climb down a thousand feet for it, you won't find any water.'

'Here you are, old feller,' said my father coming through the stunted manuka scrub with a billy-full of spring water.

It was maddening for Cecil. He glanced coldly at my father and said: 'Well I was wrong,' in a loud and angry voice. For a little while he was greatly put out, especially, I think, because his brother Colin made no comment and avoided looking at him.

Colin, who had the appearance of a Velázquez grandee, was gentle but quietly sardonic. I loved and respected him more, I think, than anyone else and, although he never criticized or scolded I would have hated to do anything that he might have thought shabby. It was clear to us all that he and Mivvy had fallen in love and we were delighted. I don't know if he told her of the, by that time, incurable disease from which he suffered. During the year after our first camp he became very ill. I visited him in hospital one hot, windy afternoon. My school uniform, my shoes and my satchel were powdered with dust. I sat by his bed and wondered what to say to him, so beautiful and strange did he look with the bones of his face precariously veiled by his olive skin; his eyes and beard, dark and exotic against the pillows. He seemed glad to see me but for the first

time I experienced that sense of exclusion which removes us from
the dying. One morning, a few weeks later, Cecil came to our house
with a black band on his arm. I ran to my room and refused to come
out and was unable to cry.

II

Aileen and Helen Burton had firmly announced that whoever in the
ripeness of time they married, it would never be a 'curick'. They
occasionally employed and I picked up from them, a cockney dialect.
In those days it was not considered arrogant or reactionary to think
of cockney as a comic form of expression. The Burtons, who politically inclined to the left, were brilliant mimics of the women in their
father's English parish. Their impersonations were not patronizing
exaggerations, but authentic and extremely funny. They also had a
private town called Burleyrap which they inhabited as consistent
though fantastic characters about whom they had made an epic
poem. These alter egos were so firmly defined and had such distinctive voices and mannerisms that they were instantly recognizable.
'She's in Burleyrap' they would say and at once follow suit.

In spite of their determination not to do so, both Aileen and Helen,
in the event, married their father's curates. John, Helen's husband, was
an Englishman: a delicate and scholarly young man who at Oxford had
become an ardent member of the High Church group and a devoted
and active adherent of the Labour Party. He had a bookish wit and was
a poet of distinction. Kennedy, Aileen's husband, was a New Zealander;
an athletic giant with a slow smile. When he was first ordained he had
been sent by his bishop to a very tough parish in a gold-prospecting and
lumbering district of the West Coast. On Saturday nights he used to
walk down the railway track, pick up the drunks and dump them on
their doorsteps. He would haul them out of the pub and if they showed
fight placidly knock them senseless. When he came to Glentui he
walked from the railhead carrying his pack. He was the gentlest and
simplest of men, and I don't think a doubt about anything except the
control of alcohol on the Coast ever crossed his mind.

Strangely as it may seem, my father got on quite happily with
these two young parsons. He did not refer them to Winwood Reade

or to Draper's *Intellectual Development of Europe* and when, during the critical General Strike, he became a special constable, this circumstance made no difference to his friendly relations with John who was actively associated with the Unions. When, on the first Christmas Eve at Glentui, he learned that John would celebrate Holy Communion next morning at dawn, my father cut down some more poles and built an altar in a little glade above the river, placing it in an eastward position between two trees so that the sky would brighten behind it. He made a very good job of this and slept peacefully in his tent throughout the celebration.

As soon as dawn was established we got up and washed in the cold river. Then we walked through bush to the glade. There was not a breath of wind. The candle flames stood as still as spearheads on the altar and John's vestments glinted in the half-light. We knelt on dry leaves, crumbling earth and little twigs. The bellbirds, detached and silvery, tinkled in the bush. Afterwards John wrote a very scholarly sonnet about it.

For each Christmas, while I was at St Margaret's, we went for a long summer camp and the recollection of those days is of pure delight. And then Helen and Aileen married and left Christchurch. Friede and Joan returned to England and we followed new ways.

I believe Glentui is now a popular resort with a car park and barbecues and that on public holidays an ice-cream and Coca-Cola van fills to overflowing the trippers' cup of happiness. I have never revisited the valley.

III

Canterbury University College School of Art was conducted on an established pattern. An antique room smelling of mice and Michelet paper, a still-life room smelling of stale vegetables, a modelling room smelling of clay, an architectural room and, exclusively at the top of its own flight of stairs, the life room, smelling very strong indeed of paint, turpentine and hot stoves. To the life room, on most afternoons and nights of the week, I now penetrated. Here we drew and painted from the head, the draped figure and the nude. The classes were mixed, the male students, because of the war, being over forty or under eighteen or not up to army medical standards. There were no entirely fit young men in New Zealand. Those who survived Gallipoli, the Middle East and Passchendaele did not return on leave. Those who came back (and they seemed very few) were too badly injured to be any more use in the army. My partners at school-age dances and my particular young men all vanished in turn and there were no coming-out balls after all.

Ned came to say goodbye, looking strange in his uniform. He had missed Gallipoli. He sent his photograph when he was commissioned in Flanders, wrote that he felt depressed and uneasy and was killed in action a few days later. My mother worked in the Red Cross rooms and my father trained strenuously with the Citizen Defence Corps and wondered if the war would catch up with his age group. At the art school we made patriotic posters. The Casualty lists filled many pages of the newspapers.

It had never occurred to me that I would attempt to be anything else in life but a serious painter: there was no question of looking upon art as a sort of obsessive hobby – it was everything. I knew hope and despair, hesitancy, brief certitude and very occasionally that moment when one thinks: 'How did the fool, who is I, do this?' I trained myself to become so conscious of the visual element that I could scarcely look at anything without seeing it in terms of line, mass or colour. I find it impossible, now, to form any idea of my work as a whole. I think that perhaps it had a kind of vigour which may have been an unconscious expression of my sense of theatre. It was good enough to keep me going on scholarships and to reach exhibition level, but it seems to me, now, that I never drew or painted in the way that was really my way: that somehow I failed to get on terms with myself. I may be quite wrong about this: perhaps I had no more in me than the works that emerged but there will always be a kind of doubt about this. Our training at the art school was strictly academic. The instructors who sought to find a different approach were, unfortunately, not very articulate and I found their hesitancies and half-expressed generalizations frustrating. I wanted to be told flatly whether things I had drawn were too big or too small, too busy or too empty. I wanted to know, when I failed completely, exactly where I had gone wrong and how I might have avoided doing so. I didn't mind how brutally I was told as long as the instruction was valid and specific. Richard Wallwork, the life master, was extremely specific and a dedicated teacher. I did not want to paint as he painted and I think I realized that his attitudes were those of a vigorous but conventional London school. Nevertheless, his students learned the fundamental elements of drawing and the necessity for exhaustive self-criticism. There was no chance, with that uncompromising little man, of disguising ineptitude under the cloak of artistic sensibility. The student who raised the protest: 'But that's how I see it' was often left with the dismal suggestion that what had been seen had not been communicated. I think that even those who rebelled against his taste, his pronouncements and his instruction, afterwards came to realize their great debt to him. He was a most generous man and gave much of his own spare time to his students, staying behind after each class to teach one or two of us advanced anatomy and artistic perspective and taking us with him to paint out-of-doors.

I enjoyed best the nights when we made time studies from the nude. The model, for a long period, was Miss Carter, a dictatorial but good-tempered girl who came to us from show business. She had been the subject of a Professor Psycho's expertise and during the rests liked to talk about her ordeal. The professor performed in a tent at agricultural fairs and in obscure halls. He used to wave his hands at Miss Carter and say 'Sleep. Sleep.' She would then shut her eyes and, faintly smiling, sustain an appearance of peaceful oblivion while he ran pins into her shoulders. She was exhibited in a shop window for three days with a notice beside her to say she was in a cataleptic trance; she was stealthily nourished by the professor in the small hours of the morning. We found the undoubted scars on her shoulders a great bore. A legend about the model related that during a series of sharp earthquakes in Christchurch she had lectured the students in a superior manner about the foolish behaviour of people who ran out into the street during a shock. They ought, she said, to remain indoors, standing quietly under doorways. While she was posing, a particularly sharp jolt shook the life room. The students, as usual threw down their palettes and rushed into the fairly busy street where they were joined by Miss Carter in the nude and quite unaware of it.

On time-study nights, the life room was crowded. The students, with the exception of one girl who acted as chaperone, stayed outside while Mr Wallwork set the pose. Miss Carter slid out of her kimono and with a sort of bovine good nature, eased herself into position. She was a big fair creature. If a twist of the torso or pelvis was asked of her she would grumble professionally and then grin. The gas heaters roared and the great lamp above the throne held the motionless figure in a pool of light. When the door was opened the students hurried in to manoeuvre for places. In a semi-circle round the throne sat people on 'donkeys' and behind them easels jockeyed for vantage points. 'Have you seen it from over there?' Mr Wallwork would mutter, with a jerk of his head, and one would hurriedly shift into the gap he indicated. The room looked like a drawing from Trilby: timeless, oddly dramatic, sweltering-hot and alive with concentration.

Each pose was maintained for three-quarters of an hour. It was a matter of catching hold of the movement and feeling and getting it down eloquently, rapidly and decisively: a feverish, hit-or-miss business that was enormously exciting.

Conventionally brought up though most of the girl students had been, I am sure it never occurred to one of us that there was anything remarkable, still less embarrassing, in these mixed classes for the nude. Nor can I suppose that the men were disturbed by frissons other than those associated with the technical problems offered by Miss Carter's bones, muscles and skin and Mr Wallwork's aphorisms upon them. These were pronounced in an incisive voice with the short vowels of the English midlands.

'A câst shadow is influenced by the object which câsts it and the surface upon which it is câst.'

'There are no concavities in the living body. All apparent concavities are built up by a series of convexities. Is that too big or too small?'

'Too big,' one bleated, suddenly aware of this.

'Reduce it. Is the lower leg foreshortened or is it not?'

'It is.'

'Then why don't you make it so? You have drawn what you know, not what you see. Look at the shape of the space between the legs.'

'Unless you understand the structure – '

The white, muscular hand would make an anatomical drawing on the edge of the paper while Mr Wallwork's firmly closed lips twitched convulsively.

His methods were academic but there was no nonsense about them. He was an instructor with a vocation.

At the end of the year there were examinations upon which the chance of a scholarship, and there were not many of these, largely depended. To me the examinations were anathema. The hand that had trembled under Miss Ross's sardonic glance, shook again and most persistently.

'Put it under the cold tap,' said Mr Wallwork observing it before we started.

The anatomy and perspective papers gave no trouble and I usually did reasonably well in drawing from life but painting from the head and figure under these circumstances was diabolical: I veered about and produced works that were occasionally above and far more often a long way below my normal form. At half-past nine at night, dog-tired and either exalted or in the depths, with my paintbox slung over my shoulder, I trudged a half-mile to the tram stop in Cathedral Square and (after a wearisome ride) another half-mile along a dark road and up the lane to our house on the hills. 'How did it go?' my mother used to say and my father would look up from his book and listen.

In the mornings I had teaching jobs: first of all with Colin, a little boy who had been ill and of whom I grew very fond, and then, when he went to school, with Bet, a girl who was about four years my junior and whose brother and I had been schoolmates at Tib's. She became one of my greatest friends. We 'did lessons' in her father's library, and while she laboured at arithmetic and composition I read greedily through a pretty comprehensive field. It felt rather odd, after so short a time, to have turned into a sort of Miss Ffitch myself.

Colin's father, one of New Zealand's most distinguished surgeons, was the son of an early Canterbury pioneer. Their family sheep station lies between a great and turbulent river and the alpine approaches to the West Coast. At that time it ran far back into the high country, embracing two mountains. The house and little church are built of bricks made from local clay and in some sort reflect the character of the family estates in Devonshire. When the men went out to muster the back country on the far side of Big Mount Peel, they were accompanied by a mule-train carrying their stores. In this house, while I was a student, I spent very happy holidays struggling to get down in paint the strange ambiguities presented by English trees mingled with native bush against the might of those fierce hills.

It was while I was at Art School that I made one of those satisfying friendships that crop up at rare intervals and have a lifelong vitality. Phyllis and I exchanged all the usual confidences about our young men, shared the same iconoclastic views of our contemporaries and at the end of a day's work, glared in companionable silence at what we had done.

She lived in South Canterbury near a settlement in the foothills that was so English in character that visitors from England couldn't get over it. Here was the antipodean equivalent set in an uncompromising landscape almost without history, of county and village, of Sunday morning service, of tennis parties, calls, house parties and neatly defined class-distinctions, and overall a kind of feudalism that I think could have had no exact equivalent anywhere else in New Zealand.

I first went to stay with Phyllis in midwinter. She met me at the railway station in a gig and we drove some ten miles up into the frosty hills. It was dark before we got there and the stars burnt above the snowy ranges. From the moment I went into the house I loved it: the smell of a pinewood fire and the indefinable character of rooms that had grown quietly around the people who lived in them. This house, too, was on the fringe of the mountains and to me, therefore, on the edge of adventure.

Until now the country beyond the Southern Alps – Westland, or the Coast as it is often called – was unknown to me. The very name held overtones of romance. It had all the ingredients: it lay beyond the mountains that were often in my mind and, from our windows at home, before my eyes. It was remote. It had a history of gold rushes, bushrangers, unexplored forests, glaciers, hidden lakes of unplumbed depths and ghost towns. People who had been there came back with stories of its strangeness and fascination. I would look, on clear days, across our plains at the entry to the great Waimakariri Gorge through which the West Coast train was pulled by two engines, deep into the ranges as far as Arthur's Pass. I knew that beyond the Gorge was the great divide and the road into Westland.

After I had been for a year at Art School, Mr Wallwork suggested that we should accompany him and his wife, also a painter, to the West Coast.

IV

My mother, a schoolboy cousin called Robin and the two Wallworks made up the party.

The train left at 8 o'clock on a midsummer morning. For a short distance it followed the familiar Dunedin route and then, at a junction out on the plains, curved away to the west and bucketed towards the mountains. At noon their foothills closed about us and we began to climb in earnest: up into the outer ramparts of the Main Divide, shingle-scarred and drained of colour by the noonday glare. Place names were hard and explicit. Craigieburn. Castle Hill. The Cass. Broken River.

'The tunnels are coming,' Robin said. 'Let's go out on the platform.'

The platform jerked and bucked under our feet. There was a sooty rail to cling to and one was glad of it. Out here, the clamour of our progress was deafening.

We hurtled through a kaleidoscopic world. Tunnels blinked on and off like shutters. We were suspended for an unreal second or two high above Staircase Gulley with the river no more than a thread beneath us. It was gone and the next picture bore no kinship to it.

There are many tunnels on the railroad to the Coast but at that time the greatest of them was still under construction. The railhead was at Arthur's Pass.

Here we walked out of the stale-smelling train into the mountain air: we were over three thousand feet up in the world and for all the heat, you could fancy you smelt snow and the ice of the Rolleston Glacier.

Arthur's Pass was a group of railway sheds, tunnel-workers' galvanized iron huts and a pub where we ate cold meat and yellow pickles and drank black tea in a room buzzing with flies. We came out, hung round our baggage in the blazing sun and looked about us.

This was the true high country; above and far beyond the foothills and the middle ramparts that I had seen from Blowhard and from the windows of our house. I was visited again by an ambiguous ache of separation and belonging. Not for long, however.

We heard a clatter before we saw the first sign of it beyond a bend in the road: a moving cloud of dust. Then the first one swung into view, scarlet and superb, and was followed by five others: Cobb and Co.'s Royal Mail coaches.

In a little while the tunnel would go through and the coaches would be gone for ever from the Pass. One or two would turn up in museums or be brought out for historical pageants with people dressed-up, old-fashioned, to ride in them. We were only just in time.

They wheeled in the yard and pulled up. The reek of horseflesh and leather was on the air and the horny, ugly smell of hot brakes. Passengers from the Coast climbed down and presently we moved in to take their places.

There was a tendency to put the ladies inside and the gentlemen on top. By dint of asking first one driver and then another, I was allowed a box-seat on the nearside and clambered up by small iron discs on curved legs. Once precariously established up there, the world was ours. Our driver returned from the pub and nodded to his mate.

The leading coach was ready and away it went with its passengers looking self-important and superior: then the second and third. The driver, a lean man, mounted to the box and gathered the reins. He sat easily, his right foot handy to a lever that controlled the curved shoe of the brake. His mate looked over the horses and their harness. There were five: two wheelers and three leaders. They were half-clipped rangy animals: not at all smart but tough-seeming. The nearside leader showed the white of its eyes, laid back its ears and fidgeted.

'She'll be right,' said the driver.

His mate climbed up to his seat. 'G'dap,' said the driver and with a scrape, a strain and a rattle we were off.

The road climbed steadily to the Pass. The bush grew more stunted and finally petered out in a grey mottle of low-growing scrub. The country is now as it was then – a sun-bleached hinterland: arid and down to its bones. We clattered through it at a fine clip and soon reached the top. The road flattened out and then, suddenly, dived into a new world.

We were plunged into a region of wet forest and dark mountains. We looked into a chasm where treetops were no bigger than green fungi and the great Otira river, a cold shimmer. Heavy rain had fallen on this side and the blue zinc skies of Canterbury were gone. Loaded clouds hung over the tops and waterfalls jetted from the bush. We splashed across shallow races and slowly bumped and ground through deep ones. The air was cool on our faces as we began the descent into Otira Gorge.

It opens with a series of hairpin bends. I am badly affected with height vertigo. Edges are anathema to me and I find it difficult to believe those psychiatrists who tell us that people who think: 'If I should leap!' never do so. I am firmly persuaded that for tuppence, I would.

Being so constituted, I was not an ideal subject for the notorious zig-zag in the Otira Gorge.

The technique in approaching the bends was to drive straight at them as if we were about to launch ourselves into Wagnerian flight. At the last second, the driver braked and swung his team. The leaders seemed, to my transfixed gaze, to wheel at right angles. Then we were around the bend and never was a colloquialism more vividly illustrated. So sharp were the turns that the coaches on the reaches above and below us looked, when we caught sight of them through the bush, as if they drove towards us.

On the outside seat one seemed, literally, to overhang the edge. I gripped a ridiculously small curved rail with my left hand and watched the horses. The nearside leader pulled away from her companions and her feet were so close to the lip that they induced a feeling of sickening incredulity. Once, her forefoot actually dislodged a stone into the gulf. The man who sat next to me kept giving little coughs. Nobody spoke. From time to time the brakes screamed and stank.

I have forgotten how many bends there were in the zig-zag. When we had completed them we were already sunk deep in the gorge, unmenaced by knife edges and chasms. The passengers began to tell each other how enraptured they had been by the scenic beauties of the descent. With this relief came a sense of exhilaration, and awareness of the smell of wet earth, moss and fern and of the voices of bellbirds. The valley had filled with shadow like a cup with wine and the thunder of the river was loud in our ears. Soon we

were beside it and, the road now being level, the drivers whipped up
their horses. With a clatter, a flourish and a drumming of hooves,
Cobb and Co.'s Royal Mail coaches bowled into Otira.

V

It lies at the bottom of the Gorge as if in a well and even in midsummer sees little of the sun. It is always possessed by the voice of the river,
the shadow of mountains and the smell of wet bush. All the ramshackle, casual flavour, the beauty and the human raffishness of the
Coast, is there at Otira. Again, we found a straggle of huts, a large pub
and a little station: the terminus of the West Coast railroad. A string of
the oddest looking carriages stood alongside the platform: little boxes
on wheels that dated back to the beginning of rail on the Coast.

We had a long wait before we left and went into the pub which,
evening being now advanced, was coming to life. The reek of beer met
us in the doorway. Nobody was about but a great noise issued from
the bar. Presently a door opened at the end of the passage and the
publican's wife came through, a handsome, casual woman. The voices
in the bar swung in and out with the door. She showed us into a parlour that looked as if it staggered under her colossal indifference, and
lit a pile of brushwood in the fireplace. We sat on a broken-down
horsehair sofa and two chairs. Presently the inevitable cold mutton,
yellow pickles, cruet, loaf and butter were brought in with a pot of
black tea. We had no idea when we would reach our destination and
it seemed a long time back to Arthur's Pass. We drew up to the table.

When we had eaten this odd meal we went to the station. Evening
comes early in the Gorge and the air was cold. One or two of our fellow travellers who were going through to Greymouth sat in the little
waiting room by a wonderful log fire. Perhaps the long day with its
changes of landscape, its alarms and excitements had made me rather
sleepy. The glow from the fire, the multiple voices of the river, and
occasional cascade of song from the bush and the murmur of conversation: I remember it all vividly, and yet rather as if it were a dream.

Presently an elderly engine was backed up to the little row of carriages. We got into the train and in a casual sort of way, were pulled
out of Otira.

Now, I began to see how beautiful this country was. Our train ambled through the valley between Otira and Lake Brunner at the best part of the day; the hour when its extreme darkness is briefly visited by shafts of horizontal light and by explicit colour. The mantled hills that at midday oppress one by their heaviness and uniformity, are now articulate. Their bones show through the forests which, themselves swept by wings of sunlight above translucent wells of shadow, start up in a new and emphatic brilliance. As for the sky: it would make sails for Cleopatra's barge.

We had been told that at Te Kinga, fifteen to twenty miles down the line, there was a sawmill, a store, a pub and a number of unoccupied huts. The train would stop there but we could leave it at Moana, the next station but one along the line, spend the night there at the pub and return to Te Kinga by slow train in the morning. As the train approached Te Kinga there came a break in the trees and we saw Lake Brunner: a looking glass sunk in the mountains. Two narrow arms forming a lagoon carried ranks of delicate trees. Far out on the waters, suspended between incandescent skies, a launch towed a flotilla of logs. Behind them, like some accomplished calligraphist, they traced their progress on the surface of the lake.

Moana turned out to be less entrancing than Te Kinga and the pub looked and sounded rather forbidding.

My mother said: 'Let's walk. It's not far. I'm game.'

She sometimes used schoolboy colloquialisms and they always came oddly from her. 'Don't kid yourself,' she would say when she found me out in some gloss over a misdeed. She had a lovely voice quite at variance with these occasional essays in slang.

Richard Wallwork compounded for a railroad jigger whose crew he ran to earth in the bar. They would bring our luggage to Te Kinga sometime during the evening.

The sun was behind the mountains when we set out and dusk had fallen when we trudged round the last bend and made Te Kinga. Lights shone in the windows of the pub and the store.

'You girls go up to the huts,' Richard said. 'Robin and I will find out if it's all right.'

'How?'

'At the pub.'

The huts stood in a row on the hillside above the railway and between the sawmill and a slag heap. They were one-room shacks built of raw wood that had weathered grey. They had galvanized iron chimneys serving enormous open fireplaces. Several of them were unoccupied. We inspected one of these. It contained two bunks, a table and some benches, all made of offcuts from the mill. It smelt of old woodsmoke. We found a broom, a bucket, a shovel and a cloth like a dead rat. Two half-consumed candles had guttered over the shoulders of beer bottle containers.

In the light that remained, I fetched dry bracken from the hillside, filled the bunks and collected firewood from the slag heap. Elizabeth Wallwork and my mother swept out three of the huts.

They overlooked a railway bridge spanning the Brunner River. Presently, in the half-light, we saw Robin sickeningly negotiating a loaded wheelbarrow over loose footplanks that lay between the rails. He was followed by Richard, heavily laden, and a tall sloping figure who, when they arrived, turned out to be the foreman at the mill. He shook hands all round and in the slow, guarded manner of the Coasters, told us we were welcome to the huts. There was a rent, he said. Five bob a week. He looked at our painting gear. 'You'll be taking pictures,' he said. 'There was another bloke done that. Paid his way at the pubs, like. Well, anything I can do.' We thanked him effusively. 'She'll be right,' he said. 'Hooray, all. Be seeing you.'

We began to unload the barrow.

The foreman turned away and paused. Into a silence broken only by the high-pitched reiterations of tree frogs, there entered a metallic and continuous sound. A light moved on the railroad and faintly illuminated two figures that faced each other and swayed rhythmically, in the manner of oarsmen, propelling the driving bar of a jigger.

'This'll be your gear, I reckon,' said the foreman.

The men went down the hill to collect it.

At about half-past ten we had set our three houses in order and gone to bed in a trance of fatigue. The bracken crackled and snapped under my blanket. I had begun to wonder if it would make, after all, an uncomfortable bed, when a road slid towards me in a cloud of dust. The driver had fallen asleep; his horses mended their pace and instead of wheeling, sped to the lip of the gorge. We leapt outwards and, after a sickening jolt, fell into oblivion.

CHAPTER 5

The Coast

At Te Kinga we were woken at dawn by timber men leaving by horse-tramway for their camp, seven miles away in the virgin bush. When we got to know them they suggested that we should spend a day in-back and this was a compliment.

The bush behind Te Kinga was heavy and very tall. It closed round and above us and shut out everything but itself and its immense indifference. The man on our truck was called Sandy: a red blond with a singing drawl in his voice. The boles of great trees moved by against a backdrop of dense, cluttered green. We passed deep through a valley and across a forester's bridge. There was no sky.

She was lonely, all right, in-back, Sandy agreed in answer to a question from my mother. Some jokers, he said, couldn't seem to stand it. Take him and his mate. They was sent in to prospect, like. Look out the timber: pick where the tramway'd be drove in. They took a couple of packhorses and was meant to stay in-back for three weeks. 'You wouldn't credit it, lady, but after four days we turned it in and come out. It was the quiet. Dead quiet it is, barring the birds. Some jokers reckon it's haunted. Call it what you like: we was satisfied: it was no good to us. We wasn't the only jokers got that reaction. It's well-known.'

And easy to believe, we thought, when we reached the tramway head. Here, in the green dark were a winch, a loco-driven circular saw and, close to the ground, a steel cable that ran inconsequently into the forest. As we watched it, it quivered. From a hidden and remote distance a human voice gave a drawn-out, beautiful and incredibly desolate cry.

'That's the snigger,' Sandy said. The winch started up with a falsetto blast on its whistle. Sandy told us that if we followed the cable we would come to where they were felling. We would meet the snigger and he would stop us from going in too far. His name was Jock.

The cable jerked and moved towards us. The ground was muddy but the going not too bad because on either side of the cable, undergrowth had been smashed and flattened. It was strange, though, when the bush closed behind us and stifled the sound of the winch. The cable quietly poured itself past us, an endless and incongruous interloper. Presently the call was repeated, nearer at hand now, astonishing in its strength and purity of sound. The cable stopped until the voice started it on its way again. For a time there was no sound beyond that of our own squelching progress. Then we saw a disturbance in the forest, a shudder among tops of saplings. We heard sounds of breaking wood and a heavy drag and at last saw the log. It came lurching towards us, bleeding and chained to the end of the cable. It slowly passed us by, quivering and destructive.

It was followed by a man and a one-eyed horse. This was Jock the snigger and his snig-mare. He had evidently been told that we were coming. He described how he chained the log and escorted it to the winch. Then the mare carried the end of the unwinding chain back to the place where they were felling. When a log jammed, he and the mare cleared it. 'That's how she lost an eye. Sapling got it. You see a lot of that with snig-horses.'

My mother said something about his voice.

'Some jokers carry a whistle,' Jock said. 'I don't seem to fancy it.'

He had halted the felled tree in order to talk to us and now said he must be getting on. His ribs expanded under his singlet and the great sound, 'Oh-hoy', was released again. The chain quivered and took up and the log began to move.

Guided by the chunk-chunk of axe-blows, we went as far as Jock had said we might and, at a distance, saw two men, stripped to the waist, poised on either end of a plank that was set in a wound across the bole of a giant tree whose top, far above the tangle of undergrowth, trembled under their blows. They changed to a two-handed saw, swaying in a superb rhythm. We saw the death of the tree. The plumed top swept down with a great whiffling sound, a crescendo of splitting timber and a thud that jolted the ground under our feet.

In the late afternoon we rode back to Te Kinga on chained logs, still bleeding sap. The next morning we saw them thunder down skids to a breaking-down bench in the mill. I did a painting of this and would have liked to call it 'Too Bloody Big', for that was what the millhands said repeatedly of the giant we had seen felled. They defeated it in the end. It passed on to the sawyer's screaming bench and finally in planks, to a rail truck and so down to the coast or up to Otira.

We made great friends with the people at the little farm. The family consisted of the farmer and his wife and four sons between the ages of eight and seventeen. They were all very fair with clear skins and the luxuriant glossy hair that one sees so often on the Coast. Their physique was magnificent. They were splendid young men and their mother was very proud of them. She confided in my mother that she had dreaded the time when the eldest would be old enough to enlist and was thankful when the Armistice came. Richard persuaded the youngest, Ernie, to sit for him. He was apple-cheeked and blue-eyed. Renoir would have liked to paint him. It was Ernie who told us that his eldest brother was to fight another joker. Fights took place in the evening outside the pub and were, it seemed, formal affairs. Richard and Robin would have liked to see it but decided that they might not be welcome. The next day Ernie said his brother had laid the other joker out cold. They were all very gentle in their manner and used to arrive, speechless and grinning, with offerings of vegetables from their farm.

On a return visit to Te Kinga we met again as old friends and spent New Year's Eve at the farm playing round games. There were three girls in our party on this occasion and the boys paid us decorous attention. Several days later, the elder brothers went wild-goat shooting on a mountain across Lake Brunner. We saw them go down to their boat. That afternoon one of the local storms, called – I don't know why – Brucers, got up over the lake. For a time it was very rough but it soon died out and the evening was beautiful. The boys were to have returned at five. At seven their father and some of the millhands crossed the lake in launches. My mother went down to the farm and watched with the boys' mother. We could see the flares and hear the gunshots fired by the searchers. At dawn they found the three boys quite close in-shore under a few feet of clear water. They were brought back and we saw a railway truck being pushed up the line to the farm with a tarpaulin covering its load.

They were taken by train to Greymouth and their mother remained there for some time after the funeral. Their father came back to the farm and Ernie helped him.

II

During my Art School days we returned three times to Westland. These were all painting holidays: mornings and evenings of immense concentration, afternoons when we explored the country or merely glowered at our work. We learned about the behaviour of trees, about the anatomy of mountains, how to lay out the ghost of a subject and then, at the fleeting hour of sunset, seize upon it as if, in fact, one was making another kind of time-study. In the afternoons there were expeditions and from these a patchwork memory recalls disjointed incidents.

In some ways the most vivid recollection is of the first Easter holidays after the war ended.

Here we are, my great friend and fellow student, Phyllis, and I. Our skirts are down to our shins and our hair is coiled about our heads. We are far from being hard-boiled and would, I think, seem singularly vulnerable to our modern contemporaries. We are setting out for Westland and neither of us has ever before taken so considerable an excursion unaccompanied by elders. We are, therefore, elevated and feel hardy and independent. Our journey is enlivened by a hoard of repatriated and demobilized soldiers returning to the Coast. They roar, sing and brandish beer bottles but mysteriously maintain a state of suspended inebriety. When we leave the train at Jackson's, the first stop down the Otira line, they cheer and wish us luck.

Jackson's consists, simply, of a pub on the edge of the bush. It is a one-storeyed wooden building, patronized by tunnel-workers, prospectors, swaggers and bushmen, and is run by Mr and Mrs

Clancy and their extremely pretty daughter. The other resident guests are two railwaymen and a foreman from the tunnel. We think they are a little nonplussed by our arrival but seem friendly and pleasant. When Mrs Clancy hears that we are painters she asks us, on an afternoon when we are housebound by rain, if we would touch up a screen which is very dear to her and which has become a little tashed with wear. It turns out to be the most remarkable *meuble* we have ever seen. Handpainted by a cousin in a convent, it presents to our incredulous gaze, pink flamingoes wading in a bog infested by floating kidneys. A lolly-pink-and-chrome sunset is repeated in these waters. Lilies, there are, amidst emerald green reeds and, over all, an oleaginous lustre. We tinker gingerly with scratches and abrasions and at last satisfy Mrs Clancy. It is the screen which she displays to her guests, not our paintings.

Easter Saturday. We have been 'down the line' all day, painting, and have caught The Night Train From Grey, back to Jackson's. With Miss Clancy and one or two weary ladies who have spent the day in Greymouth, we are the only sober passengers in the train, this being the night for revelry on the Coast. Through the carriage stagger at intervals a company of gentlemen paying tribute to Miss Clancy. They chant in chorus that she is 'the pr'eest girl from Greymouth to Otira BAR NONE.' Miss Clancy tosses her head and they break into song:

> Have you ever seen the devil with his little pick and shovel,
> Digging of pertaters with his tail cocked up?

We hear them as they progress through the train to the leading carriage. They live at Inchbonnie and when we stop there are ejected with difficulty by the guard. This takes some time as he also hangs sacks of meat along the fence for householders who have ordered them from down the line. When the last reveller has been detrained the guard blows his whistle and we move on. Presently, from the rear carriage but drawing nearer, comes another verse of their song.

> Have you ever seen his son with his daddy's gun
> Shooting little bunnies with their tails cocked up?

The procession re-enters. Miss Clancy bridles.

– *pr'eest girl from Greymouth to Otira* BAA-AR NONE

They do not pause by, or even look at, Miss Clancy but continue on their way. The guard appears.

'They got in at the bloody rear,' he says distractedly, 'while I was hanging up the bloody meat.'

At Jackson's they leave the train voluntarily and follow Miss Clancy and Phyllis and me up the hill.

> *Have you ever seen his wife with a carving knife*
> *Cutting up pertaters with her tail cocked up?*

They effect an entry into the pub and we are now enthusiastically included in their tributes. Phyllis comes into my room and we lock the door and sit on the bed. The noise in the bar is formidable. After a time Mr Clancy's voice and boots are heard in the passage and a chucking out process begins, accompanied by fearful language and a great deal of thumping and scuffling. A door bangs and Mr Clancy returns.

Outside our window in the moonlight they are quarrelling among themselves. A dominant voice says smugly: 'You oughter be ashamed of yerselves cursing and swearing in front of them two bloody girls.' There is a general gloomy assent and they retire down the hill.

> *. . . ever seen his daughter with a bucket gettin' water*
> *From the well that's in the garden with her tail cocked up?*

The voices fade. The last thing we hear is a prolonged 'BAA-AR NONE' followed by a howl of vague approbation.

When I returned to Christchurch I wrote an account of this experience. It was accepted by the *Sun*. 'The Night Train From Grey', was my first venture in professional writing.

III

When I think about the Coast, many pictures return, some of them with great clarity, others a little blurred and elusive.

Here are my mother, a fellow painter called Bill and I in a farm cart drawn by Tim, an elderly white horse, and hung about with camping and painting impedimenta. We are embarked on a ten-days' journey along the coast itself from Hokitika to the Franz Josef Glacier. In 1920, Hokitika, founded in the days of the big gold rush, still carries some rags of its former raffishness: deserted dance halls, derelict pubs and, at dawn, a few beachcombers panning the black sand at low tide for gold dust.

The Wallworks were to join us on this expedition but were prevented at the last moment so here we are, an odd little party, camping out at night and following at a walk, since Tim knows no other gait, the convolutions of the lonely coastal road: up and over Mount Hercules, down to Lake Ianthe, in and out of water-races until we find one of them in spate and a row of frustrated motorists on the near side. With a great jangling of billy and frying pan and a grinding over boulders, Tim walks us into the ford. The cart lurches and tilts, water churns about its axles. Tim plunges and veers but knows his job and we emerge triumphant on the far side. We camp in the bush beside a lake but are tormented in the daytime by sandflies that, sated with our blood, blunder on to our wet canvases and stick in the paint. At night, mosquitoes take over. We move on and at last arrive at the Franz Josef where there is an empty hut. We stay here in preference to the tourists' hotel.

The rata is in flower. It splashes the lower slopes of the forest with washes of incredible scarlet and overhangs the green caverns of the glacier. Bill and I, who have both started big canvases, paint steadily day after day. Tim meets a wall-eyed mare as elderly as himself and bolts with her into the bush from which after an exhausting search we extract him, very much above himself, leaving his decrepit minion to flaunt round in circles with her tail up, giving broken-winded whinnyings.

We spend a day on the glacier with a famous guide, Peter Graham. He is a man of immense charm and tells us in a plain unaffected manner that sometimes he hears voices in the deep crevasses. It is a misty day and the going is slippery. A woman in the party who has been to Switzerland wails continuously that there, on much less tricky ice, we would have been roped. 'They rope you for anything in Switzerland,' Peter Graham says. My mother, who is immediately behind him, unobtrusively holds a strap of his rucksack. 'It made me feel surprisingly better,' she says afterwards. We have to jump over a crevasse. It is no more than a long stride but very deep and green. Rendered lopsided by the heavy paintbox I have been foolish enough to bring, I am secretly appalled. On the return trip we find hot springs a few feet from the lateral moraine of the glacier. If you want to bathe in the big one, Peter Graham says, you cool it with lumps of ice.

At night we walk into the bush. The banks alongside our track are hung with glow-worms and we speak in whispers as they incline to take alarm at the sound of human voices and put out their lamps.

People still say of Westland: 'It's different on the Coast. It's another country,' and although nearly forty years had gone by since our last camping holiday there, I found, when I revisited it with a theatre company not so long ago, that outside the main towns it felt and looked and smelt the same. The Otira Pass was still hazardous going in a car and there was only one other route through the mountains from east to west. Ghost towns with their shells of gold-rush pubs have not yet been smothered by bush or cleared to make roads. There is still gold in the rivers and hills but so remote that only a handful of lone prospectors look for it and the dredges, once some of the biggest in the world, have all shut down. The tracts of devastation they left in their wake will I suppose be slowly re-captured by the bush. Native timber is carefully protected nowadays and behind the few railroads and highways lie vast tracts of virtually unexplored forests. It is still the same Coast.

I daresay, if one should turn away from the main routes of the tourist and explore those inconsequent little tracks that lead to nowhere in particular, one might come upon such another recluse as the lady we visited near the shore of Lake Kaniere.

She lived in a deserted lumberman's shack in a bush-clearing. We had been hunting for subjects to paint when we saw the smoke from her chimney and found her chopping wood for her fire. She was white-haired and very thin and wore a sacking apron over her ramshackle grey dress. Her working-men's boots were broken across the insteps. She asked us, in the modulated, clear voice of an accomplished hostess, if we would come to tea with her.

Her single room was scrubbed and airy. A piece of threadbare patchwork covered the bunk. Apart from the usual bush bench and table and a single broken armchair there was no furniture. A goatskin served as a rug before the fire. The cups we drank from were exquisite. One or two ghostly photographs – a very pretty woman in full Victorian evening dress and a group of three children, the boy in an Eton suit – were pinned to the walls. On the unplaned plank over the open fireplace stood a dim Edwardian photograph of a garden party: the ladies in picture hats trailed parasols and the top-hatted, frock-coated gentlemen stood about attentively in heroic attitudes. The façade of the first Government House at Wellington formed their background.

Our hostess, smiling indulgently, asked about our painting and made poised conversation with my mother. When we left we shook hands with her and she hoped we would meet with good weather for the rest of our holiday.

'It rains a great deal on the Coast,' she said. 'A bore, of course, but one can't have everything.'

She waited for the prescribed time while we walked away and then we heard the door of her shack close.

'Did you recognize the photograph on the wall?' my mother said. 'She must have been lovely as a girl.'

I think I see, now, after nearly half a century, that although, during those long visits to Westland, my whole intent was to translate what I felt about it in terms of paint, the more valid but scarcely recognized impulse was towards words. I had a small success with a short story about a ghostly stagecoach which was, I am afraid, a bastard offspring of E. M. Forster's *Celestial Omnibus*. I made a tentative approach to a novel of which I shall have something to say later on. I think I was aware of the danger of writing a book that would turn out to be – not, alas, a rattling good yarn but merely a chunk of pseudo-colonial romanticism and much too long. There was, and is, room for a rattling good yarn about the Coast but I was not and am not the one to write it. A gap waited and still waits for a penetrating and aesthetically satisfying novel born of that formidable landscape. Our contemporary writers are, I think, too solemn and not grave enough to achieve it. In New Zealand letters of today there is a wearisome dread of superficiality that inspires the dragging in backwards through a native thornbush of an all too easily anticipated symbol. That sort of writing would be no good for the Coast.

I find that in retrospect the figures of the drunken seranaders, the boys who drowned in Lake Brunner and the lady of quality in the shack near Lake Kaniere seem like the shadows of my own shortcomings. Perhaps that is why I often think of revisiting the Coast but, though it lies within a day's journey, never do so.

The summer holidays of 1920 were the last I was to spend camping in Westland. The coming year was to bring a change.

IV

One of the greatest events of my student days had been the visit of the Allan Wilkie Shakespeare Company to New Zealand. The first intimation we had of this was the sight of one or two shop windows in Christchurch draped in black velvet with a skull and a crown in the centre. Then there were the advance notices and posters. Allan Wilkie and Frediswyde Hunter-Watts in *Hamlet* to be followed by *Twelfth Night, As You Like It, Macbeth* and *A Midsummer Night's Dream.* Apart from the disastrous matinée of *Romeo and Juliet* (which in any case I could not be said to have seen) I had witnessed, while still at school, two performances of Shakespeare: *Othello* and *The Merry Wives of Windsor* by the Oscar Ashe Company. *Othello* had harrowed me so much that my memory of it is one of unnerving details: black hands tearing lilies to pieces: a black face convulsed and animal-like, the same hands putting out candles, closing round an arched throat, striking down and inward with a sword of Spain: with these, an incredulous sense of looking, appalled, into an unsuspected chasm of human suffering and knowing it was true. I still have a feeling that a perfect performance of this play would be insupportable.

Of *The Merry Wives*, I remember that Mr Ashe wolfed an entire chicken and that for the last scene the stage was covered, a foot deep, in horticultural salt.

The Wilkie Company gave me my first real joy in Shakespearean acting. The opening night of *Hamlet* was the most enchanted I was ever to spend in the theatre. We waited from four o'clock in the afternoon, in an open passageway at the top of an outside iron stair-case. By half-past six the stairs were crammed and the crowd, as seven approached, began to stamp with a ringing rhythm that shook the whole structure like a thunder-sheet. We were next to the doors and heard the rattle of the metal ticket box and the sound of the bolts being drawn. In those days, early-door theatre queues in New Zealand were not decorously mannered as they are in London. When the gallery was opened the crowd surged forward. By a pre-arranged manoeuvre I (an old hand) having gained an entry, plunged down the steeply-raked wooden seats as if they were giant steps, flung myself into the front row and spread myself. My mother descended by the centre stairs and was soon beside me while the

mob thundered in behind us. We had achieved the best seats: plumb
in the middle, beside the two arc-lights. An hour to wait with the
excitement piling up on itself. Not far above our heads was the
painted cupola, imported from Paris, with its lavish Hippolita, Indian
Puck, capering lovers, bearded Theseus (who looks like an Athenian
gendarme) and any number of airy fairies all capering about a mild
Bottom and a singularly nubile Titania. Programmes were bought
from a man who came down the rows asking us to move up a little,
if you please, so that more people could be crammed in. I can see the
programme now. Gertrude – Miss Lorna Forbes. Claudius, King of
Denmark – Mr Augustus Neville. Polonius – Mr Edward Landor.
Ophelia – Miss Frediswyde Hunter-Watts. Hamlet – Mr Allan Wilkie.
All new names to us and little did I think how familiar they were to
become before 1920 was out.

At a quarter-to-eight the first reserved stalls and circle patrons
began to come in. One heard the thump-thump of turned down
seats and caught sight of acquaintances who sometimes, in edging to
their places, would look up at us in the gods and wave. The fire
curtain – The Iron as I would learn to call it – crept upwards and
there at last was the peacock-blue velvet curtain.

There is much to be said, and perhaps later on I may try to say it,
for theatre in the round, for the open stage and for the Elizabethan
plan. But I think I am glad that the theatre of my youth was that of
footlights and the curtained proscenium. I cannot believe I would
have felt the same delight, endured the same rapturous agony of
anticipation, if I had stared for an hour at an acting area made commonplace by unfocused light from the auditorium. A performance
was 'a mystery' in those days, a happening that bided its time in concealment and though 'they' could look at us, and sometimes might
be detected doing so through their spy-hole in the curtain, we must
be denied everything until the appointed time.

At last the orchestra came in, then the conductor, Mr Bradshaw
Major. Then the house rose for 'the King'. The lights dimmed and
there were drums.

The live orchestra may often have produced sounds of extreme
vulgarity, though in this case it did not, but it also engendered and
wound up to its quivering extreme, the joy of anticipation. My state
of mind, while I awaited my first Hamlet was, I concede, scarcely

more grown-up than that of the little girl who, with Ned, frantically devoured chocolates while she waited for *Bluebell in Fairyland*. Except that I knew what was coming.

Who's there?

Nay, answer me. Stand and unfold yourself.

Long live the king!

Bernardo?

He.

You come most carefully upon your hour.

'Tis now struck twelve. Get thee to bed, Francisco.

For this relief much thanks: 'Tis bitter cold and I am sick at heart.

Have you had quiet guard?

Not a mouse stirring.

Well – goodnight.

The best opening scene, I swear, in dramatic literature.

I wonder what I would think if I saw that performance again to-night. Allan Wilkie was in the direct line of the English actor-managers and this was an actor-manager's production. Of his performance, I remember best the climax to the play-scene when Hamlet, exultant, flung the Gonzago script high in the air and the leaves fluttered down in an arc as the curtain fell. Frediswyde Hunter-Watts, his wife, was a Pre-Raphaelite Ophelia: delicate, gen-tle, with a cloud of bronze hair and a strangely moving little break in her voice. The Polonius was excellent. Of the others I remember little. Strange that the effect of this Hamlet should be so vividly rec-ollected and the details of the performance so vaguely retained.

My mother and I sat up till all hours talking it over: she, I suspect, taking pleasure in my delight and perhaps a little subduing any stric-tures she may have felt disposed to make.

The Wilkie Company played for about a fortnight in Christchurch. For the first time, I, with some of my fellow students, cut evening life classes to go to the theatre. The plays that, under Miss Hughes, I had learned to read with a growing sense of wonder, I now saw in their native climate. I may have realized then, however dimly, the essential difference between those often jarring opposites: Shakespearean scholarship and Shakespearean production.

The Wilkie Company paid, I think, two return visits to New Zealand during my student days. They were our gods. In the excess of our devotion, I remember, several of us sent Miss Hunter-Watts (Mrs Wilkie) a weighty sheaf of spring blossom tied with pink ribbon. 'From five art students', we wrote on one of my mother's visiting cards and left it at the stage door. Can we possibly have stolen this token of our esteem from an ornamental island, civically maintained on the river Avon? I am inclined to think that our parents' gardens not being equal to our design, we did so augment our offering. I seem to remember one of the boys climbing down from a conveniently situated bridge after nightfall. We had the gratification of seeing Mrs Wilkie take her curtain call, heavily burdened with our massive tribute and of receiving a note from her saying that she herself had been an art student before she went on the stage.

Between the first and third visits of this company I wrote a play. It was called *The Medallion*.

The plot escapes me. It was a Regency piece with a central scene in which a number of high-stomached blades caroused together in a manner derived without prejudice from Shakespeare, Sheridan, Wilde and the Baroness Orczy. I think it ended with an insult and a duel and am sure a Lady's Name was in question, although at that time I had no idea just how or why the situation I had concocted should tarnish it, being still largely uninformed of the facts of life. I think my play must have been very bad in a slightly promising way. It still puzzles me that my mother suggested I should send it to Mr Wilkie.

For a few shillings I had bought an old and faulty typewriter and, with many dreary setbacks and repetitions, at last produced a stuttering copy. Before I could lose my nerve I left it at the theatre with a note (rewritten not more than half a dozen times) saying that if he could spare the time I would be very grateful indeed for Mr Wilkie's opinion. I begged him not to trouble himself to read my play if disinclined to do so and said that I would collect it at the office after the company had left. This was in case Mr Wilkie should think I manoeuvred for a meeting. It is the only time I have ever asked for a completely outside criticism of anything I have written.

I was astounded, stimulated and terrified when Mr Wilkie wrote asking me to call at his hotel when he would return the play and tell me what he thought of it.

My mother said that it would not be suitable for me to go alone to the hotel and she would accompany me. This was a great relief.

To this day I cannot walk into the Clarendon Hotel in Christchurch without remembering that call. I have no doubt I was white to the lips though why I was so agitated I would have been at a loss to explain. It had nothing to do with my play. I remember that after she had sent up our names and we waited in the lounge, my mother gave me a look and said I'd better buck up. Then Mr and Mrs Wilkie came in and, little as I dreamed of such a thing, the foundation of a long friendship was laid.

I have scarcely any recollection of the meeting. Mr Wilkie seemed immensely tall and his wife extremely beautiful. He said, I fancy, that my central scene showed some appreciation of actable dialogue and that I would no doubt write another play. My mother spoke about the pleasure their season had given us and presently I was floating home on a pink cloud.

The company left Christchurch and I returned in a peculiar state of mind to the Art School.

With a group of fellow students, I shared at this time a small, scantily furnished room at the top of an old office block near the school. We gave it the courtesy title of a studio and in it we had meals between classes, worked at anatomy, perspective and composition, talked and talked and sometimes sat to each other as models for the head. My parents would meet me there on nights when we went to the cinema or the theatre and the room became a rendezvous for our friends. Late on a summer afternoon with my paintbox slung on my shoulder I climbed the stairs alone and walked in.

Mr and Mrs Wilkie were sitting in the studio.

'I obtained the address,' Mr Wilkie said in his resonant actor's voice, 'from your father. I have a suggestion to make.'

To this day I have no idea how he found my father and at the time was much too dumbfounded to ask. My bewilderment was, I suppose, comically apparent and the reason why they both seemed so amused.

I was speechless. Beyond an open window, somewhere down the street a gramophone blared out the final duet from *Trovatore*. I have only to think of those plangent exchanges and at once I am back in the studio and Mr Wilkie is smiling at my astonishment.

'How,' he says, 'would you like to be an actress?'

CHAPTER 6

Winter of Content

They were passing through Christchurch on their way to the North Island and had only two hours to spare before they left. In a trance I heard that Miss Lorna Forbes was obliged to return to Australia for domestic reasons and that her absence would leave a gap in the company. If, said Mr Wilkie, I intended, as of course I did, to write for the professional theatre, it would be of advantage to me to learn something about it from the inside. He planned to make a return tour of New Zealand with four modern plays. He offered me a part in each of them. My father, he said, had not rejected the idea out-of-hand. How did I feel about it?

On the whole I felt as if the heavens had opened and Mr and Mrs Wilkie had descended in a chariot to the sound of trumpets. I felt wonderful. I felt as I had never felt in my life before. I suppose I contrived to say something to this effect and that my rapture was in any case self-evident. Mr Wilkie stood looking down at me with his hands in his pockets.

'You haven't asked me what your salary is to be,' he said.

'Oh. Er – '

'What do you demand?'

I didn't know.

'Pound a week and all travelling expenses?'

I think I said that would do very nicely, I expected, and he burst out laughing. 'Nine pounds,' he said. 'Ruin stares me in the face.'

A very sobering thought occurred. 'How,' I said, 'about Mummy?'

'Will Mrs Marsh not care for the idea?'

Recollections of my mother's lack of enthusiasm when a similar chance had come her way were not encouraging.

We had no telephone and there were no means of communicating with her. My father, I realized, was now on his way home, vaguely freighted with his momentous tidings. It was arranged that the decision would be communicated to Mr Wilkie within the week.

They went away and a shutter clicks down upon the sequel. Strangely enough I can remember nothing of the long discussion that must have followed this unnerving visit. Only the upshot remains: the offer was to be accepted.

I have said that whatever I may write about my mother will be full of contradictions. This episode might well be thought to illustrate the contention. My mother was an exceptionally gifted amateur, she dearly loved the theatre and enjoyed the company and conversation of actors. Although she was, I think, fundamentally an unconventional woman she had, nevertheless, a distaste for many forms of unconventional behaviour and a contempt for anything that suggested easy promiscuity. Above all, she despised humbug and self-deception. During her brief acquaintance with the Charles Warner Company she had discovered these elements in the offstage life of actors and had found them disagreeable. This fastidiousness was very much to the fore in my upbringing. When, in the process of growing up, my attitude to my boy friends changed and theirs to me, my mother, always loving and discerning, grew more watchful. Anything remotely provocative on my part or physically demonstrative on theirs was, in the most economical manner possible, condemned as second-rate behaviour. It was, I understood, a matter of taste. I accepted her ruling and continued in a state of unbelievable naïveté, to wonder why such demonstrations of physical attraction as came my way should have the bad taste to be agreeable.

It is not my intention to dwell upon emotional engagements that have naturally cropped up with varying intensity over the years, but in this instance, if my mother's non-resistance to Mr Wilkie's offer is to make any kind of sense, I shall have to recall two of them.

The first appears in the person of a man about whom it will be difficult to write without extravagance. He was a Little Russian, the son of a merchant father and an aristocratic mother. I shall call him

Sasha since that was the name of a part he played opposite my mother in a production of George Calderon's *The Little Stone House*.

He was a lawyer and had come out to New Zealand before the Russian Revolution to escape from political complications. These had followed his defence of two peasants who had offered violence to an unscrupulous landshark. Sasha's intention was to discover a Tolstoyian fulfilment on the land and his first step towards this end was to enter himself as a student – he was about thirty-five years old – at an Agricultural University College. He had little English and no understanding of New Zealand youth. When, on his first night, he was subjected to a certain amount of student ragging, he wrenched an iron batten off his bed, laid about him with the utmost vigour, causing anguish among the hefty sons of run-holders, and then shook, as it were, the fertilizer from his boots. He next became an art, and later on a medical, student.

After the Russian Revolution and the extermination of his family, his ample remittances vanished and he was obliged to go back to the land in sober necessity. He became a ploughman and expected the hands on back-country farms to converse with beautiful peasant simplicity, about immortal longings, European literature and Grand Opera. When they responded but rudely to his overtures, he fought them. He was a powerful man.

He went from one job to another, sometimes becoming involved in lawsuits and always in quarrels. 'I am insult,' was an ejaculation with which his friends were all too familiar. He was a comic and a tragic person: subject to fits of the blackest depression, immensely lonely, very disturbing and destined for unhappiness.

The producer for *The Little Stone House* was a friend of Sasha's and asked him to undertake the leading male role. Calderon's play is a tragedy. For the first and last time I saw my mother play opposite someone of her own mettle. Sasha – her son in this piece – was a dynamic actor and she always said that at some point in his turbulent past he must have been a professional. During rehearsals he came often to our house and she helped him with his English.

In a scene in which the son, whom she had long supposed to be dead, returned from Siberia, he had to say: 'I have seen my mother weeping on my tomb.' They rehearsed it. He had a superb voice, very deep and vibrant.

'I haff seen my mosser veepink on my tum.'

'No – no. Tomb.'

'Ah. Sank you. Toom-ber.'

But his accent improved very quickly, and his performance developed an extraordinary intensity. My mother enjoyed herself enormously and between them they created a sensation. The production is still remembered in Christchurch. After it was over Sasha continued to visit us and indeed, for a long time we were the only friends with whom he did not quarrel or by whom he did not fancy he had been insulted. He became very much attached to my mother and, adopting what he thought to be the correct and respectful English equivalent of 'mamushka', he continued their make-believe relationship and called her 'Mum'. With me he fell in love.

Difficult to a degree, and impossibly touchy in all other respects, in this he was gentle and delicate. He knew very well that nothing could come of his attachment and when he declared himself, added at once: 'But Mum would never permit.' I agreed, but I was – and the Victorian phrase is exactly appropriate to my flustered reaction – not insensible of his attractions. Nor, in a different mode, were my parents. Without anything specific being said, I was steered past this strange and, as I now see it, oddly lyrical encounter. For a time, and at long intervals, Sasha would appear unexpectedly, usually in the evening. He would sing at the top of his formidable bass voice as he climbed the hill. My father, who found him noisy, would look up from his book and say mildly: 'Good Lord, the Russian.' The song of toiling peasants (in those days the Volga boatmen were unknown in New Zealand) would grow louder and he would arrive with some passionate account of his latest row. Shouting his tragic laughter, he would exhaust us with his need for an indefinable agreement, a wholesale acquiescence.

At last the inevitable happened: he became insulted over an imagined affront and never returned. We did not know what he was doing or where he lived until, after many months, we heard that, following a violent fracas with two drunken soldiers who had baited him, he had spent a night alone in an open park and at dawn, almost casually as it seemed, had ended his inexplicable life.

This interlude dropped like a meteorite into the field of my inexperience. Incongruous and completely alien, it lay spent in the cavity it had made. Nobody had behaved really badly, unless it was the soldiers who were in any case irresponsible. The happening was terrible most of all because Sasha's thoughts, during his vigil, were so tragically beyond our conjecture. We had, I think, come as near to understanding him as any foreigners could and we were haunted by the thought that if only he had not taken umbrage he might, in whatever desolation of spirit possessed him, have come to us that night.

In one of the many letters he wrote, letters to which his imperfect English lent a false air of quaintness, he said that I was 'encased in transparent enwellop'. It was, I think, an accurate observation but perhaps only another way of saying I was very young.

Remote and transparently enveloped I may have been but this did not prevent me some time later from foolishly getting myself involved in a very different and a wildly incongruous predicament. The trouble was that when I found myself the object of a violent attachment it seemed to me that it was, in the first place, astonishing and also extremely obliging of my admirer, whom I liked personally, to get himself into such a state about me and, in the second place, that perhaps all this vehemence and agitation could not, as it were, exist in a vacuum and rage away without any reciprocal justification. The situation was, in fact, a more explosive instance of the kind of muddle that had arisen out of Sister Winifred's mistake. Badgered and bewildered, I shrank inside my transparent envelope and wondered if perhaps I was after all destined to marry a middle-aged Englishman simply because he so ardently desired me to do so. I became frightened and so miserable that at last, in answer to a question from my mother, I confided the whole story to her. Once again my unfortunate parents came to my rescue.

'How could you,' my poor mother asked, 'be such an ass?'

'I don't know.'

'You've plenty of sense but you've no *common* sense.'

'But he's in such a taking-*on*. You can't think.'

She made an exasperated noise and gave me a hug.

'Your father,' she said, 'will speak to him.'

And so he did and to some effect. 'I felt damn' sorry for the fellow,' said my father. 'He made such a thing of it.'

'There you are, you see!' I cried.

'Well, never mind, old girl,' said my father, vaguely discomforted. 'He'll get over it, no doubt.'

He didn't do so as quickly as I could have wished. He took to haunting me at a distance. One night, when I was alone in the studio, he came up the stairs and stood (I knew it was he) in utter silence on the landing while I sat petrified and sick, on the other side of the door. After a long time I heard him creak away and the front door slammed. I was appalled by this incident and said nothing about it.

It was at this juncture that Mr Wilkie made his astonishing offer.

No doubt my mother felt that after these upheavals a change was the thing and I daresay my incredulous rapture did something to forward her decision, but, most of all, I think, she was influenced by the Wilkies themselves to whom she had taken a great liking. Never for one moment did she make the mistake of supposing me to have any more than an adequate talent for acting. For one thing, as she rightly said, I was too tall and for another I hadn't the basic ingredients. She may have suspected that I might become a producer. My father was amiably detached and rather amused.

'So you're off,' he said, 'with the raggle-taggle-gypsies, O,' and we grinned happily at each other.

II

It was to be a winter tour. Autumn – March with us – never comes round without its reminder of the enchanted weeks of anticipation that I now enjoyed. I would wake early in my bed on the verandah and look at the mountains, savouring my bliss before I remembered its cause. The Southern Alps were not more rosy in the dawnlight than were my thoughts. In a few weeks I would be on the other side of the curtain, behind the stage door: an initiate.

My part in the first play arrived: old-fashioned typed 'sides' in which only the dead cues were given and made, practically speaking, no sense. I appeared to be a German maid masquerading as a French maid and up to no good. I had to speak broken English and snatches of French with lapses into German ejaculations and I opened the second act with a polyglot conversation on the telephone. Seduced, I had evidently been, and the dupe of a powerful group of spies. There were, I think, about twelve sides. The piece was called *The Luck of the Navy*. My name was Anna. I would have the benefit of seeing Miss Forbes in this role for two performances in Christchurch before she left for Australia and then I would replace her. Under these circumstances, of course, it was well to memorize, but had I been in for three weeks' solid rehearsal I would, in my zeal, have come down to the first one word-perfect and prepared to act the boots off my feet.

By this time I had become a fairly regular contributor to the *Sun*, an evening newspaper that 'featured' short stories, special articles and verse. The editor suggested that during the four weeks' absence on leave of the lady-editor I should take over her job. When the autumn term began I did not return to the Art School but, instead, reported parties, lectures and entertainments. I described clothes, sifted material provided by hostesses who yearned for the social column and concocted paragraphs to fill in the gaps on my page. I would take my copy down to the sub-editor's tray and have my leg pulled by senior reporters. One of them, from the far end of the immensely long room, would telephone for the lady-editor and, in full view, would squeak fictitious and libellous gossip into the receiver. I spent my earnings on books, and on clothes for an actress.

April came and with it the advance notices of the Allan Wilkie Company in *The Luck of the Navy*, *Hindle Wakes*, *The Rotters* and *A Temporary Gentleman*. On a warm autumn morning I reported at the Theatre Royal, walked under the ringing iron stairs I had so often climbed and went in at the Stage Door. The world of glue-size, canvas, dust and shadows engulfed me.

On the empty stage under a single working light, Mr Wilkie took me through the part of Anna.

He gave me the moves, checked my mistakes and was patient with them, being aware, I have no doubt, of my extreme nervousness. I gathered that he thought I would do. There would be a rehearsal next morning at 10.30 and I should report to the Stage Director. I had become a professional actress.

It was strange beyond words, at that first call, to meet the actors and actresses that we had applauded and criticized and discussed during the Shakespeare seasons. The splendid Polonius turned out to be a scholarly and pleasant Englishman who had had a distinguished career in the theatre, 'creating' parts in several Galsworthy plays and also his present role in *Hindle Wakes*. Unhappily he was subject to heroic drinking bouts which Mr Wilkie fended off by making bets with him that he would refrain from alcohol for a given time and then renewing them, not always successfully, at its expiration. He was in the middle of such a period of abstinence when I joined the company.

It was unbelievable to find myself kneeling at the feet of the quondam Claudius and reminding him (tri-lingually, while he breathed garlic and scorn all over my protestations) how often he had lavished endearments upon me in our questionable past.

And there, in lace-up boots and a fur tippet, was Miss Vera St John whose laughter as Maria had so entranced us. The first gravedigger turned out to be a pale, sardonic and raffish personage with heavy eyebrows, a seedy blue suit and yellow boots and the second, a quiet conscientious young actor whose only characteristic seemed to be a complete lack of what I would learn to call star quality. The juvenile was Henri Doré. He was an excellent comedian: how is it that I cannot more clearly remember his performance in Shakespeare? He was leaving the company in Auckland to take up another engagement and would be replaced by Reginald Long who, with his wife Dorothy, joined us in Christchurch. Dorothy was the pianist with our orchestra. The 'heavy' woman, my employer in *The Luck of the Navy*, seemed to me extremely old and formidable. She was a completely instinctive actress who, in character parts, could score point after subtle point with rather less notion of their implication than a child of seven. Imported from Sydney for the tour was an actor who had fought with the Thirteenth Australian Light Horse throughout the war. His name was John Castle-Morris. Our other ex-officer was the stage director, Kingston Hewett.

The tone and character of the Wilkie Company were perhaps most clearly shown in the Scullys: Pat and Addie. Pat was our stage manager. He was a gentle and elderly Irishman who played decrepit old men – Adam in *As You Like It*, for instance – with a great deal of toothless quavering and head-wagging: '*Cheerily, marshter, cheerily.*' He prompted, took routine rehearsals, called the actors and minded his own business which was multifarious. I hear his voice rumbling down the dressing-room passages. 'Overture and beginners, please. Overture and beginners.'

Addie, his wife, was an Australian. She played bit parts and was dresser to Mrs Wilkie whom she adored. Addie had progressed from child-actress, through the chorus, to her present authoritative position. In the programmes, she appeared as Miss Mona Duval. When I got to know her I ventured to ask why she had chosen this name.

'Nothing to do with me, dear. When I was in me first shop in the chorus the management came in to get us girls' names for the programme. "What's yours?" he asked me. "Addie Jenkins," I said. "Mona Duval for you, dear," he said, quick as lightning, and Mona Duval it was. It's a funny old world, though, isn't it, dear?'

Addie was full of such Mowcher-like generalizations. She was jealously protective of Mrs Wilkie, who was really fond of her, and between them there had developed a sort of abigail-patroness relationship that was peculiar to the theatre. Pat accorded Mr Wilkie a complimentary devotion.

The Scullys had one child, Phyllis, at present in a convent school but formerly an actress. She had played Myl-tyl in *The Bluebird* and, with the Wilkies, Young Macduff, The Bloody Child, Mamillius and any number of pages. She was a strictly brought up child and very polite. On one occasion, as Young Macduff, she bounced her leather ball too zealously and it struck Lady Macduff smartly in the bosom. 'I beg your pardon, Miss Forbes,' Phyllis piped in her well-projected voice.

The final member of the company was also a child, engaged to play the newsboy and shout 'Dunton Evening Echo' in *The Luck*. He was placed under the care of the Scullys: B. Briggs, aged about twelve but born elderly. He wore an overcoat with a false astrakhan collar and had his own visiting cards: 'Mr Bernard Briggs. Allan Wilkie Company.' 'That child will come to no good,' Addie said darkly.

This was the Company that assembled in the Theatre Royal on my first morning. They were kindly people but they threw me into a fever when they began to rehearse *The Luck of the Navy*. It was a run-through for words. They skidded and rattled over their lines, cut the long speeches or muttered them at breakneck speed, raising their voices suddenly as they came down to the cue. They sketched their gestures and walked through their moves like automata. When the first act was over I still had no idea of what the play was about.

'Second Act beginners,' called Pat Scully. This was it. 'Beginner' was indeed the *mot juste* for Anna, the Franco-Teutonic spy. For as long as I was on, they considerately played out but between my brief appearances, back they went to their gabbling. I waited by the door in a ferment until my entrance cue was suddenly thrown up and I was on again as if the devil was after me. At one point I had to scream offstage. It seemed an indecent act to do it all alone and unheralded.

Mr Hewett shepherded me about. At one juncture Mr Wilkie came up. 'Rather confusing,' he said. 'You'll know more about it when you've seen it from the front.' I hoped so.

The play turned out to be a well-constructed thriller of the *Bulldog Drummond* genre and I am sorry that I cannot remember its author. It built to a meticulously engineered climax in the third act with Mr Wilkie (Lieut. Stanton) tied up in a chair by German spies. When the heavy lady (now a self-confessed Gauleiter-hausfrau) came on to taunt him, he convulsed the audience by remarking with the utmost sangfroid: 'Ah! Here is mütter.' It was somewhere about then that I screamed and an aeroplane (two motorcycles in the yard) took off. The *dénouement* was effected by Henri Doré (Midshipman Something) who entered through french windows asking jauntily: 'Anyone aboard?' and getting a round for it.

It may seem strange that a dedicated, scholarly and distinguished Shakespearean, which Mr Wilkie undoubtedly is, should have lent himself and his company to these somewhat off-Shakespearean capers. It was not at all strange as I shall now try to show.

Until his retirement, Allan Wilkie, like Sir Donald Wolfit, was one of the last in line of British actor-managers. Such men of the theatre stem directly from Burbage and his contemporaries: it is an unbroken sequence, merely going underground during the Protectorate. The actor-managers reached their highest point of affluence and display with Irving and his Edwardian successors. They were overwhelmed at last by show biz and the 'prestige' managements.

Theirs was always a precarious calling and to follow it a man needed a good lacing of fanaticism in his make-up. This element was not lacking in Allan Wilkie. He was, and in his sunny retirement, still is, a dedicated, an unquenchable Shakespearean.

Throughout the Far East, across Canada and for fifteen years in Australasia, on a multiplicity of stages and under every shade of theatrical environment, he mounted the battlements of Elsinore and Dunsinane, the Forests of Arden and Windsor, the wood near Athens, blasted heaths, palaces of Plantagenet and Old Nile, the road to Dover, the seaboards of Illyria and Prospero's unnamed island. Sometimes the coffers were full and then Mr Wilkie bought new and exciting scenery and wardrobes and engaged highly salaried actors; sometimes they were all but empty and he would tour melodrama in the mining towns of Australia and our own West Coast. Sometimes, as now, when I joined the company, he would present a mixed bag of one box-office draw and three intelligent contemporary pieces while he gathered his forces for a new Shakespearean assault.

He was known throughout the world of theatre for his scrupulous integrity and his fixed determination to play under no banner but his own. He had a kindly and generous regard for his actors and was an extremely strict disciplinarian. He called none of his company by their Christian names and it is impossible – it is even terrifying – to imagine him using the word 'darling' when directing an actress. His manner was punctilious and his flow of blasphemy when something went amiss during a performance, startling and inventive. On *Macbeth* nights he was unapproachable; a looming and a lowering menace crowned with a headdress made of coffin-plates. This morbid but enormously impressive item was conceived and carried out by a designer of conspicuous merit who also played bit parts with frenetic enthusiasm and finally went mad. 'I could,' said Mr Wilkie, 'have better spared a saner man.'

How, as they say nowadays in the theatre, was Mr Wilkie's acting? I cannot write of it with detachment. It was in the grand, declamatory manner. My impression is that the Macbeth was terrific and the Bottom certainly the funniest I have ever seen. Between these extremes there were excellencies and, no doubt, lapses. 'After all,' as he himself once remarked with a Micawber-like roll in his voice – he is not unlike a more personable Micawber – 'After all, I have played in thirty-four of the works. You can't expect me to be good in all of them. Indeed, I think I may say I am the *worst* Mercutio to have trod the boards in living memory.' He will, I know, forgive me for quoting him in this context. Later on he changed to Friar Lawrence. Advisedly.

It is for himself that he is remembered in these antipodes and for his achievement in making the plays a series of living adventures for hordes of Australians and New Zealanders who, without his productions, would never have returned to Shakespeare after they left their schools and universities.

Here I must recount an incident that seemed to reflect, however ambiguously, on a reaction to his presentation of the plays. In a town in Western Australia, after a performance of *The Merchant of Venice*, Mr and Mrs Wilkie were walking back to their hotel. It was a very warm night and the time being close on twelve, the shops and houses were dark and the street lamps not very explicit. Their way had taken them into a particularly dark passage, when out of nowhere something dropped with a thud at their feet. Mr Wilkie stopped, groped and picked up a small object which his fingers, rather than his eyes, suggested was a figurine.

They arrived at their hotel and there discovered their find to be indeed the four-inch primitive head and shoulders of a bearded man wearing what might have been an Elizabethan ruff. The effigy had been pierced with a diagonal hole. All the edges and surfaces were greatly worn and eroded. But to the Wilkies there was no mistaking the personage; it was William Shakespeare. They asked themselves: was it a strangely presented tribute from some diffident admirer in an otherwise sleeping household or was it a cast-off from a disgusted patron who had stayed up in order to drop it on their heads?

The company in due course came to New Zealand and the Wilkies couldn't wait to show us their strange treasure-trove. At that time Professor MacMillan Brown was our great, if controversial, pundit on the plays of Shakespeare and also on the islands of the South Pacific which he had explored and written about profusely. He was an old acquaintance of our family and his daughter, Viola, and I were and still are close friends. So we took the Wilkies and their figurine to the Professor for a pronouncement.

He held it on the palm of his hand and without a moment's hesitation discoursed. The figurine, said the Sage, was of South American West Coast origin and had been hung from the prow of a canoe. The ruff was evidence of Spanish influence and the worn and eroded surface, of its antiquity.

All of which was fascinating news but did not explain why someone dropped it from a dark window at midnight *almost* on Mr Allan Wilkie's head.

One feels that Mr Thor Heyerdahl, not yet so busy at that distant time, would have had something to say about the little man with the ruff and might have liked to pass a fibre cord through the diagonal hole and hung him from the prow of the *Kon-Tiki*.

I have kept myself waiting in the wings for my initiation into the Wilkie Company. My only recollection is, in fact, of doing exactly this in an indescribable condition; of being wished well by Mrs Wilkie and the company and of finding Mr Wilkie standing beside me at the zero minute. 'You'll be all right,' he said, and I can only hope that it was so.

III

During the next three weeks we rehearsed H. F. Maltby's savage little post-war comedy: *A Temporary Gentleman*. In this piece, Mr Maltby takes a number of shrewd swipes at a particular form of snobbery afflicting demobilized lower-middle-class officers of the First War. On the way he also has a jaundiced look at the officer-private relationship. It is a play that is in tune with present-day attitudes and I should think might very well be revived.

I was given the part of an ex-WAAF, now a maid in the demobilized officer's house, who tells him a number of stinging home truths and ends by engaging his affection. I didn't appear until the last act and my principal scene was with Mr Wilkie. It was a very rewarding little part: I learned a lot from it and even more from watching rehearsals. I learned how actors work in consort, like musicians, how they shape the dialogue in its phrases, build to points of climax, mark the pauses and observe the tempi. There was a passage in the first act that looked insignificant to the point of banality. It went something like this.

'Good morning, Mrs Hope.'
'Good morning, Mrs Jack.'
'Good morning, Mr Jack.'
'Good morning, Miss Hope.'
'Good morning.'
'Good morning.'

Mr Wilkie took it again and again, insisting on a specific cadence. It was wonderful to see how it took shape and suddenly became as satisfying as a Mozartian interchange of voices. I had seen my mother working like this at rehearsals but not with the knowledgeable support of everybody else on the stage. Thus, I discovered how actors must listen to the dramatic shape of sound. When, in after years, I became a producer and when, at last, the plays I directed were Shakespeare's, I remembered, most clearly of all the lessons I had been given, this commonplace exchange of 'Good mornings' and how the final word had fallen so sweetly and justly into its appointed resolution.

If I gave a tolerably good account of myself in this play, I made an astonishing hash of my role in *The Rotters*, a Maltby farce that was as acidulous as it was funny. Again it was a third act appearance but this time as a weather-beaten harridan of sixty. I lined my face like a gridiron, I padded, I shrieked, but all to no avail. The performance was a vain mockery and I knew it. Luckily it was confined to a single scene but the entrance was important and climactic and I hated making such a botch of it. But still I learned. I learned that the techniques for farce were unlike and in many ways more exacting than for those of comedy, that the timing of a laugh-line was a most delicate matter of finesse, that an actor could score better by alighting on a point than by clambering up to it. I saw that the open-handed action carrying *The Luck of the Navy* through its *Boys' Own Paper* situations, needed an entirely different treatment from that of either of the Maltby plays. And when we came to rehearse *Hindle Wakes* for the newcomers in the company: here was a fourth and marked difference – that of the *genre* play with its dialect, for which Mr Wilkie was a stickler, and its harsh regional attitudes. I had a tiny bit – another maid – in this admirable and, at that time, daringly outspoken piece. In the course of playing it I made yet another discovery. A minimal, a half-minute scene with Mr Wilkie, the overbearing mill-owner, ended when he turned his back and dismissed me with a short 'Good night'. After one or two performances it occurred to me to smile when I replied 'Good night, sir', and there was a murmur, like a reflection, from the house. One may learn much from bit parts in the theatre.

'What did you do on your exit line?'

'I – I think I smiled.'

Mr Wilkie made the sound that is written 'Humph'. After a hazardous pause he said: 'Building your mighty role up, I suppose,' and walked away.

'Only I,' he remarked on another occasion, 'am at liberty to take six-foot strides on this stage.'

I hobbled my legs above the knees with a stocking.

I didn't get off so lightly on the dreadful night when, the offstage area being cold, I wore an overcoat and left it across a chair while I was on. Mr Wilkie had a quick change into a dressing gown which was carefully laid out for him. During the blackout I heard a stream of shattering profanity. He had put on my overcoat.

I apologized at the end of the show. By that time the edge of his fury had a little blunted. I think he said something about being trussed up like a sacrificial rooster.

The Christchurch season came to its end. Our family friendship with the Wilkies had ripened. Mr Wilkie had been shown Kean's coat and had made a cautious attempt to fit his arms in the sleeves which did not reach his elbows. He had also been shown Gramp's book and asked to see it on each successive visit. On Sundays we had taken long walks on the hills, returning to our house for an improvised supper. Jack Castle-Morris had come to tea. The dates for the tour were posted up and I began rapturously to smother my luggage with the white and red labels of the Allan Wilkie Company.

I had never been out of the South Island. At seven o'clock on a blustery evening I attended my first train call as an actress. We had our own carriage. To reach Lyttelton one passed through our Port Hills by the longest and smokiest tunnel in New Zealand.

Our head mechanist arrived at the last minute, extremely drunk. He sat opposite me and turned out to be in the oncoming stage of his cups. Nothing could illustrate more precisely the difference between young persons of that generation and this than the circumstance of his being the first inebriate with whom I experienced a personal encounter and nothing could point more exactly the social attitudes of the actors in this old-fashioned company than the immediate intervention of two who happened to be at hand. A 'young girl' was placed between inverted commas in the theatre of those days. She was 'sweet' by definition and without irony, the word being used in its Elizabethan sense. I really don't think she was any the smugger for this rather nauseating addition. The adjective was understood if not specifically attached and when, as now, the occasion arose, her status was protected. If she chose to relinquish her sweetness she moved, I imagine, into another category.

I was much too excited to be more than momentarily perturbed by this incident. The train emerged from its tunnel into the port and there were ships riding at anchor with lights along their decks and mastheads moving against the stars. Cranes made wide, grandiloquent gestures, sailors leaned over taffrails and winches rattled. The train ran past a murky little station and then back down the wharves until we were alongside the night ferry to the North Island.

To me she looked enormous. Her tiers of portholes glowed, there were cars on her afterdeck and white-coated stewards at the gangways. An offshore wind blew strongly in our faces as we went aboard and then was lost in the hot rubber-and-soup smell of the ship's inside.

I was to share a cabin with Vera St John and I had the top bunk. I left my suitcase and went up on deck. The port withdrew into itself and became a lonely arrangement of lights with an illuminated sign, 'Lane's Emulsion', standing on the cliff-face above them. A lamp at the end of a mole slid past. The ship moved under my feet and the night wind was cold.

Mr and Mrs Wilkie were taking a walk round the deck. They paused for a moment.

'Singularly distasteful trip, this, I always think, don't you?' Mr Wilkie remarked with that roll in his voice that I associated with Mr Micawber.

I looked at the black shapes of the Port Hills, the pinpoint lights of Lyttelton, the rough, cold sea and the harbour heads with Godley Lighthouse beaming across them.

'It's wonderful,' I said.

'You don't mean to say this is your first trip?'

'Yes. I can hardly believe it's true.'

I heard Mrs Wilkie's warm laugh. They moved away. 'Youth!' the Micawber voice rolled out in a generalized comment. 'My God! Youth!'

I went below and presently, in company with Miss Vera St John, was seasick.

IV

We came into Wellington at seven the next morning and late the same afternoon caught the Express to Auckland where we were to open in three days' time.

In this year the Prince of Wales visited New Zealand and our tour was arranged to follow hard in his wake before the enormous crowds had dispersed. The train journey to Auckland would take about fourteen hours and with or without a sleeper was, and still is, one of considerable discomfort and few amenities. I, however, persisted in my rapture. It was the first of many such occasions and I was to grow familiar with the look of my fellow players in transit: the ones who read, the ones who stared out of the window, the ones who slept, the cheerful, the morose and the resigned. Mr Wilkie and Pat Scully, their shoulders hunched and their heads nodding with the motion of the train, played endless games of two-handed whist. Mrs Wilkie read. Jack Castle-Morris told me stories of his experiences as an actor in Africa and as a soldier in the mud and carnage of Flanders. I had a sketchbook with me and made drawings of many of the company. The world outside darkened and night had fallen when we reached Palmerston North where the train waited for half an hour while we hurtled into an eating room and had plates of food slammed down in front of us. Dining cars had long since been abandoned by New Zealand Railways. Mr Wilkie was nowhere to be seen.

Here, at Palmerston, our child-actor, B. Briggs, having alighted to refresh himself with pork pies entered the wrong train and was borne rapidly back to Wellington. This mischance did not call up any particular consternation in the company. Mrs Wilkie murmured that there were no doubt other infant phenomena in Auckland. Henri Doré stuck his head round the door of our compartment and shouted 'Dunton Evening Echo' in a falsetto voice. Addie Scully said: 'Never stops eating: that's the root of his trouble. He'll turn up, don't worry, if he has to charter a special.' Remembering my own childish terrors I was alarmed for B. Briggs: unnecessarily as it turned out. He presented himself and his professional card at the Station Master's Office in Wellington and was, by what precise means I have forgotten, speeded north again.

Mr Wilkie had been brought a sheaf of telegrams at Palmerston. He stood at the far end of the swaying carriage in what appeared to be a portentous discussion with Kingston Hewett. The guard came through and joined them. Everybody settled down and after a timeless interval we prepared for the night. The train had worked itself into its accustomed uproar. The guard came through again and turned down the lights to a cadaverous blue. I tipped back my seat, arranged my hired pillow and twisted myself into a series of unpromising postures. The clamour of our progress swelled and faded, became grotesque and was lost in a scurrying flight of images.

I opened my eyes. Kingston Hewett and Pat Scully were lurching down the corridor. They leant over the occupants of the seats and shook them. Because one could not hear what they were saying they seemed to behave secretively. They left behind them a wave of consternation and bemused activity. As they came near I heard their message. The Company would leave the train at Frankton Junction. A general strike was coming into force on New Zealand Railways and the Auckland season would be delayed. We had *The Luck* scenery on board and would fill in by playing at Hamilton and Cambridge.

I had only just crammed my oddments into a suitcase and scrambled into my overcoat when we drew into Frankton Junction. It was now, I think, about two o'clock in the morning.

When the train had gone and we were left in a huddle on the silent and deserted station, it seemed to me that now we were displayed, for nobody to see, in our irreducible element. Our rugs and suitcases might have been bundles of swords, goblets, tinselled doublets and a tarnished crown or two. Nothing of moment had altered since the days of the strolling players: we were on the road.

I remember that this notion seemed to be confirmed by Henri Doré who croaked sardonically:

'*For us and for our traged-eye.*'

The porter lit a fire in the waiting room and we sat round it on hard benches. Somebody – could our touring manager have met us there? – said that before morning a vehicle of sorts would pick us up and take us into Hamilton. It was only about three miles away. One or two of the men, I think Mr Wilkie was among them, decided to walk. We heard them tramp off down the frosty road. I slid to the floor and leant my head against the bench.

Time passed in a blur of half-sleep, aching bones and a feeling of immense satisfaction. At dawn a motor-lorry came. The cocks were crowing when I stumbled into a bedroom in a sleeping hotel.

My first two nights on tour had not been without incident.

V

All through that winter we moved up and down New Zealand with our four plays. The places changed, the routine was constant. One arrived and, in the jargon of actors, 'found a home'. One went down to the theatre, collected one's mail, saw the familiar set mounted on a new stage and attended the run-through for words. Somewhere or another I have a sketch in oils that I made one morning from the stalls. In the foreground, looming over the footlights, is the rearward aspect of the actor-manager. His overcoat makes a dark rectangle, his hands are in his pockets and a trace of cigarette smoke rises above his bullet-shaped head. He watches rehearsal, picks up any bits that have lost tone and will move into the action when his cue comes. Pat Scully sits at his table on the prompt side. The actors are dabbed in with broad touches. The play is *A Temporary Gentleman*.

More evocative than this sketch was the tune broadcast the other day, and heard after a forty years' interval, of a raucous song the men used to bawl offstage during the second act.

> *Après la guerre fin-ee*
> *Soldats anglais par-tee*
> *Maddymazelle, O what will she say*
> *When she finds all 'er best customers gawn away?*

> *What 'ave they left be'ind?*
> *Souvenir for Yvonne.*
> *They spent all their pay and they alleyed away*
> *Beaucoup zig-zag très bong.*

Yes, I feel sure *A Temporary Gentleman* would revive, given the right treatment: say, by Miss Joan Littlewood.

In the afternoons I sometimes went for a walk with Mrs Wilkie who was indefatigable in such exercise. How very unlike she was to the actress gay of popular imagination! Both she and her husband loathed parties from the bottom of their souls, dressed quietly, read widely and were happiest in each other's company and that of a few close friends. If every human being has an affinitive creature, Mrs Wilkie's was the gazelle. She was delicately in accord with Viola and Rosalind and alighted on their comedy lines with a warmth and sureness of touch that surprised and delighted by its freshness. As Ophelia she solved, without excess, the problem of reconciling 'distraction' with lyricism. When she first studied this part she used to visit a mental hospital where the resident psychiatrist was a personal friend of the Wilkies. He told her that from a professional point of view the characteristics were most accurately observed by Shakespeare and he arranged that she should meet parallel cases: adolescent girls whose behaviour, she said, was uncannily evocative of the part. She discovered their colour preferences: magenta and a morbid dull blue and these she wore in the mad scene. When they played *Hamlet* in Christchurch, my mother used to make Ophelia's crazy bouquets, going to infinite pains over them. Mrs Wilkie said they were the most demented flowers she ever had and they delighted her.

One of my clearest remembrances of her is on the nights when she played the errant mill-girl in *Hindle Wakes*. When she was made-up, she liked to murmur through her lines in the first scene, a demanding one, and asked me to go to her dressing-room and feed her the cues while she held her hands, which were delicate, in a basin of almost scalding water. It was better, she said, than making them up. She used to keep them there until she was called: they emerged scarlet and swollen. She was very good indeed in this part, the only one of any real significance that she played during that tour.

I am not a great hoarder. The fragment of a scarlet and white stick-on-label still clings to the lid of an old suitcase in my cellar but if it was opened I doubt if I should find any forgotten programmes or press notices or photographs of the Wilkie Company on Tour and I don't know where the sketchbook can be in which I made drawings of the actors. But on my bookshelves there is a copy of Maeterlinck's *Monna Vanna* with an inscription in Mrs Wilkie's hand on the flyleaf.

'I had an idea that a man might pass a very pleasant life in this manner: – Let him on a certain day read a certain page full of poetry or distilled prose, and let him wander with it and muse upon it and reflect from it and dream upon it . . . Any one grand and spiritual passage serves him as a starting-post towards all "the two-and-thirty Palaces". How happy is such a voyage of conception, what delicious, diligent indolence!'

The quotation is from Kcats.

In her continuous travels through the Far East, North America and Australasia, Mrs Wilkie could not be said to have a golden opportunity for the enjoyment of this delicious indolence but in general terms the excerpt does express something of her temperament.

But how strange that forty years ago an intelligent, highly civilized and deeply read woman could have thought so well of *Monna Vanna* and that I could have so eagerly concurred in her opinion. Literary criticism of the time supported this view: Maeterlinck was a seriously regarded dramatist and *Monna Vanna* not the least respected of his works. It is true that the central act (the 'great love scene' it was inevitably called) was held to be superior to the others and I can see that even now its lily-fingered swoonery might be rewarding material in the hands of two romantic players. Did Garbo ever play Vanna?

But what fustian, after all, it is and how wonderfully funny the opening of the play with three quattrocentist Pisans in a kind of bastard chorus getting great chunks of undigested plot-material off their chests. Played as it stands, with these gentlemen exchanging items of information that all of them knew beforehand, it could set a contemporary audience rolling in the aisles. How, with Shakespeare's offhand, careless mastery before us, could we imagine that such stuff would serve? I see, by my English papers, that there is a revival in *Art Nouveau*. I trust it will languish before it includes this particular

form of romanticism: from here, it is but a short step to Wilde's
Salome which, by the way, the Wilkie Company played with great
success in India. As an unrepentant Shakespearean I sometimes
wonder if, with one or two exceptions there are no lasting criteria in
dramatic writing but only fashions. Already in the anger of the
young men we begin to hear whining overtones. M. Genet's black
plays may soon look merely grey. He may even achieve, before he is
forgotten, his full intention: he may end by disgusting us.

In the days I am writing about, the Angries, the Dirties, the
Blacks, the Existentialists, the Symbolists and the Frankly Dotties
were not yet in action. The talk was of Miss Horniman's authors, of
Granville-Barker, Schiller, Ibsen, Shaw, Galsworthy, Masefield,
Bjørnson, Strindberg (abhorred by Mr Wilkie) and interminably, of
course, Shakespeare. It is diverting to speculate on what our reaction would have been if the far-out plays of today had, by some
Einsteinian sleight-of-time suddenly flooded our stages: diverting
but idle, since there was no element in us to call them up, and plays,
like players, are indeed the abstracts and brief chronicles of their
times. We were still on the sunny side of chaos in those days. The
excruciating need for screams of protest was yet to come.

That was a winter of halcyon days for me. Nothing was lacking:
not even the addition of a blameless romance which for some reason woke a massive playfulness in Mr Wilkie.

'Has he popped the question?' he would hiss as I waited offstage
to make an entrance. Or: 'It's only a matter of persistence: you'll take
him in the end.' And once in a sort of schoolboy ecstasy: 'I've had
seven marriages in my company. All disastrous.'

I managed to draw and paint, lugging my heavy gear about the
country, and, without knowing it, I laid down a little cellar of experiences which would one day be served up as the table wines of
detective cookery.

I went on learning about the techniques of theatre: of the differences between one performance and another, of the astonishing
effects that may result from an infinitesimal change in timing, of how,
in comedy, audiences are played like fish by the resourceful actor. I
grew to recognize the personality of audiences: how no two are alike
and how they never behave as a collection of individuals but always
as a conglomerate.

'What are they like, dear?' the waiting actress asks as someone comes off.

'Slow.' Or 'Eating it.' Or 'Bone, dear, from the eyes up.' Or, with upcast eyes: 'Frightening, darling, but just frightening.'

Mr Wilkie used to say he knew what they would be like as he walked in at the Stage Door. There is no other sound in the actor's world like the sound on the far side of the curtain. If it swells and fills the auditorium with its multiple voice so that the theatre is alive with it, then his heart takes a leap and his diaphragm contracts. If it is quiet, he is apprehensive. If it is small he tries to think it is appreciative and warm. If it is big he rejoices and hopes to contain it.

I dressed with our elderly 'character' actress who was a dragon for superstitions. One must not whistle in the dressing-room, look through the curtain on an opening night, speak the tag at rehearsals or quote from *Macbeth*. Mrs Wilkie paid no attention to any of these shibboleths but I must confess that even now, if I catch one of my student-players whistling in the dressing-rooms, I send him out and make him knock to come in. This is a reflex action from the rockets I received forty-odd years ago.

At last, in the spring, the notices for the end of the tour went up. The present company would be disbanded and a new Shakespearean one formed in Australia. Some of my fellow players would rejoin but I would not be among them. I really could not pretend even to myself that there was a place for me in those plays.

On a wet night in Wellington I said goodbye and returned alone in the ferry to Christchurch. One of the first things I did was to wrap up Gramp's book and send it to Mr Wilkie. In return I received a ring of which, he wrote (and I could hear the Micawberish roll): 'It is a trifle of some reputed antiquity.' It was and is an enchanting ring.

There were to be other tours with other companies and many solitary train journeys in many parts of the world. In all of them, whenever I have found myself in a half-empty Pullman carriage, I have re-peopled it with those long-remembered companions. There is the flighty hat of Miss St John, and there, the toque of the character lady. A Pre-Raphaelite head is bent over a book, and beside it, a bullet poll with an impressive (if vaguely Humpty-Dumptyish) face. All the other hats and pates, bobbing in a constant rhythm with the motion of the train: The Allan Wilkie Company on tour in the year 1920.

CHAPTER 7

Enter the Lampreys

It wasn't easy to settle down again: to return to a pattern, that, however freely designed, turned about a small house, one's parents and a circle of quiet friends.

A new and lasting tie was formed in the person of an English cousin who, following the family tradition, had come out to seek his fortune in the colonies. He had gone straight from his Public School into the Great War, endured the shambles of the trenches and emerged, as I daresay some authorities would not scruple to put it, unscathed. He stayed with us for some time and from then until to-day has been 'a son of the house' whenever he enters it. His name is Hal. Later on his father and mother, who was my father's eldest sister, and their daughters and youngest son, Richard, settled in the North Island. They are still my closest family tie and the relationship, in many ways, is more like that of brothers and sisters than of cousins.

After my return to Christchurch I joined a group of fellow painters and worked away with only occasional, tantalizing meetings between intention and achievement. I went on writing and here I felt there was some kind of improvement. There came an offer from an English Comedy Company and I went off again for a three months' tour, this time with little encouragement from my mother.

'It will lead to nothing,' she said. 'Why do you want to do it? It's not the right kind of thing for you. *I know*.'

'I want to go.'

'You're making a mistake.'

I said I would find that out for myself and she withdrew from the argument.

Once more I was confronted by her attitude to the theatre. She knew about acting, she enjoyed meeting actors, she was ironically diverted by their shop-talk: she did not wish her daughter to adopt any part of their life or their behaviour. I believe her deep attachment to the Wilkies was first engendered by their avoidance of theatrical catchphrases or easy emotionalism.

The company I now joined was formed by Miss Rosemary Rees, a New Zealand actress who had spent her professional life in the English theatre. She is the author of a number of romances and had written a light comedy which we were to play throughout the 'smalls' in the North Island. Here was one of the earliest attempts to found a permanent theatre in this country.

We travelled in buses, trains and small coastal steamers and our audiences, never very big, were composed for the most part of provincial people, both Maori and Pakeha (European). It was a happy company: in it I made lasting friendships and learned a great deal about the tougher aspects of theatrical endeavour.

I began by playing a brazen adventuress of uncertain years and made, if possible, rather less of a success of it than of my somewhat similar part in *The Rotters*. Not, however, for long.

We had scarcely embarked upon our tour when the young actor who played the lively juvenile went down with scarlet fever and disaster stared us in the face. He had no understudy. For one hectic Saturday night our business manager was pressed into the service and the middle-aged character man grotesquely essayed the skittish boy. At the end of this extraordinary performance I heard Miss Rees lamenting that if only it had been one of the female roles, she could have engaged an English actress who happened to be at large in Wellington. I heard myself saying that I thought I could play the boy, 'Jimmy'. She leapt at it. All that night and all Sunday I memorized the lines. The newcomer arrived on Sunday afternoon and took over my old role. In the evening we rehearsed. The real Jimmy's suits were fumigated and found to fit.

Miss Rees suggested that I have my hair cut off but, willing though I was, I blenched at the thought of my mother's reaction. A wig was obtained from I don't know where.

On Monday we rehearsed all day and in the evening our character woman, a magnificent and much-loved old-timer called Katie Towers, screwed my abundant hair into a system of tightly strained worms and skewered them to my scalp. The wig was then adjusted over this hellish arrangement. I dressed and was called. I think I may say that I succeeded. The audience laughed, the company nobly backed me up and at the final curtain I was kissed by Miss Rees and the leading man.

Flushed with my unlikely triumph I wrote excitedly to my mother and received a snorter by return of post. I confided this reaction to Miss Rees who wrote, as she thought, tactfully and enthusiastically to my mother. With exquisite misjudgement, she held up as an exemplar, the late Miss Vesta Tilley whom she was careful to call by her title, 'Lady de Freece'.

I did not see the reply but to me my mother wrote that she was unable to discover why it should be imagined the antics of a music-hall soubrette could reconcile her to the thought of her daughter masquerading in male attire in a third-rate company. It was clear that she was miserable about the whole thing but I think the repressed but very real professionalism that lay at the back of her feeling for theatre, prevented her from precisely ordering me home. She realized that I had, however regrettably, staved off disaster. The show had gone on.

In the matter of short hair, although it was already fashionable, she was adamant.

I continued as Jimmy but I still suffered the agony of the wig.

I was also Assistant Stage Manager and since the Stage Manager was inclined to drink, the responsibility of 'packing in and packing out' on one-night stands was generally mine.

We played a remote town called Wairoa. After the show and with the help of the mechanist, I saw the set struck, packed on a lorry with wardrobe and props and taken down to the wharf. It was a warm, overcast night. My personal friend, the other girl in the company, was called Kiore (Tor) King and had been at RADA. With her I boarded a little coastal steamer at two o'clock in the morning. A single light showed the legend: 'Ladies' Cabin'. We groped our way into it, found empty bunks and crept into bed in the dark, thinking we were the only passengers.

I was just dropping off when a rich voice close beside me said profoundly: '*Wahine pakeha.*' (White women.)

A number of other voices answered. We had stumbled upon the only two empty bunks. The others were occupied by Maori ladies on their way to Napier.

They were companionable and handed round a bottle of port which Tor and I, not to be unfriendly, made as if to share.

The ship put out and when it grew light, the seas being heavy, we were all sick.

II

During this adventure the new Wilkie Shakespeare Company visited Christchurch. When my mother told Mr Wilkie of my inexplicable behaviour he said, 'I shouldn't trouble yourself. It won't last – I give the venture three months.' He was right, almost to the day. The Rosemary Rees English Comedy Company, like its successors, yielded to high costs and a small population and quietly folded.

I returned home but not to settle. Tor King came to stay with us. Tor was what my mother's generation (though not my mother, who did not relish such phrases) called 'a thoroughly nice girl', with beautiful manners and a 'thoroughly nice' background. She was also a great dear and as bright as a button. We talked endless theatre and presently I started to write sketches and we both began to think they might do and that it would be fun to try them out if we could find someone for the men's parts. Then we thought of the real 'Jimmy', now recovered from his fever and marking time at home in the North Island. We wrote to him and he replied saying he thought he could fix up a contract with one of the film managements for us to take half the programme on a North Island circuit.

My mother was perfectly complacent about all this talk and, without any thought for the extra trouble it must give her, readily agreed that Jimmy should be asked to stay. I think she was pleased that I was writing, particularly when I now essayed a one-act play.

This was, to me, a serious matter. I was still at the stage bypassed, one supposes, by modern youth, when the nebulous-romantic-picturesque-Borrowesque attracted me. Pierrot was not a dirty word and Granville-Barker's *Prunella* had wrought its blameless spell. So much so that my one-acter was a sort of *Prunella* in reverse.

I have not kept a copy of this play but I remember it pretty well. The plot is simple and derivative. There is, as the present idiom goes, this Boy and he is a Woodman and he is Kind of Restless and feels the call of the Great Forest and the World Outside and there is this Girl he is going to marry and she is frightened of the World Outside and so when she has prepared his supper she drops off to sleep in front of the fire and her boyfriend has a soliloquy while he listens to the wind going 'ohé' round the hut and he gets to thinking there is Somebody Out There, abroad in the forest. So he opens the window and calls out for whoever it is to come in and so Pierrot comes in, all wet with the Rain Outside and is very fey and talks about the Stroller's life and says it is Gay, in the original sense. Pierrette comes in and she is also very gay and fey, although damp, and speaks broken English but not the same kind as Anna the spy in *The Luck of the Navy*. And she fascinates the Boy and she and Pierrot tell him he is One of Them and she looks at the sleeping Girl and makes disparaging remarks about her. So the Boy feels the Call of the Outside which is somewhat heavily symbolized by Pierrot and Pierrette, and is tempted and works up to a climax and they forget to keep their voices down and the Girl wakes up and is frightened by their white faces. And they go silent and symbolic and stare at the Boy as they move backwards into the window and he says to the Girl not to be frightened, he will never leave her, no, no, no, staring at Pierrot and Pierrette. So they vanish through the window and the storm dies down. The Boy speaks the tag, 'They are singing. They will soon be up the shoulder of the hill.' Curtain. The piece was called *Little Housebound*.

When Jimmy arrived we read the play and he and Tor looked at each other and with one voice ejaculated: 'Havelock North.'

This was, and I suppose still is, a small and exclusive district in Hawkes Bay which was Tor and Jimmy's native province. By one of those curious runnings-together of affinities, Havelock North had become a cultural centre and thought of itself as such. There was an architect whose house was constructed of axe-hewn timber with enormous axe-hewn beams supporting nothing in particular and though the floor was not actually strewn with rushes their presence was implicit. There was a poetess in Havelock North and yoga regulated many of the families. Rudolf Steiner was a name to conjure with and handicrafts abounded. The esoteric found a fertile soil there. Eurhythmics flourished and psychic research was not ignored. In short, Havelock North would have provided the late E. F. Benson, whose 'Lucia' books are too little known today, with wonderful raw material.

There are girls' boarding schools in Havelock and Tor was an old girl of perhaps the most rarefied of these establishments. She and Jimmy both agreed that *Little Housebound* was the very stuff upon which Havelock North culture blossomed. We found that with this play and the sketches and Tor's repertoire of recitations which she performed with all the expertise of her RADA equipment, we had a full evening's programme within our grasp. We rehearsed like mad and I blench when I ponder on the outcome. It seems to me that now, as before, my mother must have exercised superb self-control during this period but still she did not discourage us: I was writing.

At last we all went north and I stayed with Tor and her parents, who were charming. It was arranged that we should do our show in Hastings, the nearest city; at two girls' schools and, of course, at Havelock North. I don't remember what the financial arrangements were but Jimmy managed them and we actually made some money. He then interviewed the cinema management and we were given a tour, taking half the programme and a share of the house.

Jimmy discovered that touring companies of five or more were allowed first-class railway accommodation at second-class fares. We therefore suggested to our respective mothers that they should accompany us, which, rather to our astonishment, they agreed to do. My mother arrived looking amused and away we went. Mrs King was the daughter of a general and gifted with the psychic powers that frequently manifest themselves, I have noticed, among ladies with martial backgrounds. She passed her hands downwards on either side of my mother without touching her and my mother agreed that from one hand there was wafted a cooling draught of air and from the other a hot gust. Upon this atmospheric basis they raised a friendship and my mother confided her own extramundane experiences, which, since I can vouch for them, may now be introduced.

My mother possessed a faculty which, if she had been a Highlander, would have been called the second sight. Can it, I ask myself, have stemmed from the great-uncle with Scottish estates who so disastrously expired in his family chaise? She was not at all proud of this attribute and generally preferred to ignore it but occasionally it manifested itself with such inconsequent emphasis that we were obliged to take notice of it. I shall give three instances of her powers, if powers they were.

It may be remembered that in my earliest childhood we were visited by my father's 'wild' brother, tubercular Uncle Reggie. He returned to England in due course. Some considerable time afterwards my mother, in the small hours of the night, roused up my father with the strange remark that: 'Reggie is about and I think he wants us.' My father assured her that she had been dreaming and himself returned to unconsciousness. My mother, however, re-enacting in some measure her role as Lady Macbeth, rose from her bed, lit her candle, took a pencil, consulted her clock and tore the current leaflet from the day-to-day calendar that stood on her dressing table. Having written the exact time upon this leaflet, she folded it, tucked it behind the bulk of the calendar, returned to bed and to sleep and, in due course, forgot the incident. She remembered it some weeks later when my grandmother wrote from England that at that very hour, sitting in a garden chair in the heat of the day, Uncle Reggie had incontinently expired.

The second example of her prescience occurred when I was teaching the small boy Colin, to whom I was very much attached. His parents had taken a cottage near us for the holidays and Colin was in the habit of paying a morning visit, often bringing me one of those warm knots of decapitated geraniums which children like to present. My mother was engaged, with my help, in the annual task of dusting and re-arranging the books which we accumulated in great numbers. She was gently, if reprehensibly, slapping two of them together on the verandah when she remarked that Colin was coming up the garden path and that he had his usual bunch of geraniums and wore a smart new Norfolk jacket. She asked me to meet him and keep him out-of-doors as she was busy. I went down one path and up another. I called. I explored the gully. He was nowhere to be seen. 'Funny little boy,' said my mother, slapping her books. 'He must have gone home again.'

The next morning he arrived saying that he had intended to come the previous day but had been a naughty boy and his nanny had forbidden him. 'And,' he said, 'I'd got my new coat on and I'd picked you a bunch of ginraneums.'

These two incidents can, I suppose, be explained on assumption of thought-transference. Both Uncle Reggie, in his extremity, and Colin, in his childish frustration, might be held to have set up some kind of telepathic communication. The third event is difficult to rationalize.

It also concerns a small boy – a cousin called Beynham Pyne. My mother, during her afternoon siesta, looked up from her book and saw a bed in a strong light with a little boy in it. He turned his head and smiled. She wondered which of her nephews this might be and, as was her habit with these occurrences, dismissed the matter from her mind. Some weeks later my aunt Madeline sent a message to say Beynham was to have his tonsils removed. She asked my mother to sustain her during the operation which was to be performed in the house. When my mother arrived they went into the sick room and she thought: this will be what I saw. But it was all wrong. The bed was in the wrong place, the light was coming from the wrong direction. Beynham did not turn his head. She thought: so much for *that*. She and my aunt went into another room and presently the nurse came to say the operation was successfully over and they could come and see the patient.

When they re-entered the room the bed had been moved into a bay window where there was a better light. Beynham turned his head and smiled at them.

Normally, as I have suggested, my mother did not discuss these odd experiences but Mrs King's hands blowing hot and cold had quite won her over. They beguiled our journeys with many an esoteric gossip.

This odd and companionable little tour concluded, we went our several ways: Jimmy to Australia where he joined the Marie Tempest Company and Tor, finally, to replace Vera St John with the Allan Wilkie Company. When I arrived home it was to a series of events that led at last to an enormous change.

Almost at once, I was asked to produce plays for several amateur societies. Our friend, Bill, who, like myself was equally concerned with painting and the theatre (that same Bill with whom we had travelled down the West Coast) left off being a schoolmaster and, having equipped himself in England, opened a studio of Drama and Dancing in Christchurch. To this end he was joined by his brother, the Fred Reade Wauchop who had played with Ellen Terry. They asked me to take over the drama department at their school and here I began to feel my feet as a director and coach. Everything that had been absorbed from my mother, from Allan Wilkie and from those subsequent and rather ludicrous ventures, now began to make sense.

At about this time an organization was set up in Christchurch with the intention of producing large spectacular shows annually for charitable purposes. My parents and I were asked to attend the first meeting. It was held in the showroom of a music shop among a shrouded company of grand pianos and here I met the little girl whom I had last seen almost twenty years ago in a carriage with a crown on the door. She had married, in England, the son of that house in Fendalton which I had visited with such delight. She had returned to New Zealand with her husband and three children to whom she was about to add the fourth and had been invited to sit on the organizing committee for this new venture which was called 'Charities Unlimited'.

In writing detective stories I have only once, with intention, based a complete family upon people I actually know. There can be no doubt, however much we may disclaim the circumstance, that fictional characters are pretty often derived, subconsciously or not, from persons of the writer's acquaintance. One may not be aware of this until after one has done with the book. In this instance, however, I wrote deliberately. Although the ages, sex, circumstances and behaviour of my imaginary family were not precisely those of its prototypes, its members were, in their, I hope, inoffensive way, portraits. I shall, therefore, make no bones about calling their dear originators 'The Lampreys'.

III

It so happened that a few days before the opening night of an elaborate pantomime launched by Charities Unlimited the producer became too ill to carry on. There being nobody else available, I took over. On the strength of this panic action I was asked to direct the next year's production. It was *Bluebell in Fairyland*.

I daresay it is a tedious commonplace to remark that most people find in their affairs a constant recurrence of themes that would have seemed to have died out. It is as if, after all, a kind of economy orders the ingredients of a life: an unsuspected design: as if, however much we are shaken up, we belong to some kaleidoscopic arrangement of which there are a limited number of fragments that are bound to make one of a series of patterns. One is tempted to think that coincidence is the rule rather than the exception.

I don't know who unearthed the script and score of this Edwardian piece fifteen years after Ned had taken me to see it as my first show but it was a happy augury that this was to be my first big production.

The senior Lampreys came to many rehearsals and became progressively involved with *Bluebell*. It is a children's 'musical', was written by Sir Seymour Hicks and has all the cosy sentimental ingredients, in the Victorian mode, for a Christmas entertainment. I had a splendid musical director and a ballet mistress, Madeline Vyner, who had trained with the Russians. The orchestra was excellent and the wardrobe mistress an expert. It was wonderful to have crowds to manipulate as well as individual players. The afterglow of Ned's and my delight seemed to reach over the years and shed an odd blessing on the venture. The two elder Lamprey children, who were about the same age as Ned and I had been, were also ravished by *Bluebell in Fairyland*.

After the final performance I went dancing with the Lampreys. In the early hours of the morning we drove to their house, twenty miles away in the country. Its doors opened into a life whose scale of values, casual grandeur, cockeyed gaiety and vague friendliness will bewilder and delight me for the rest of my days. If one can be said to fall in love with a family I fell in love with the Lampreys. It has been a lasting affair.

I must not try to ring the changes upon what I have written about them elsewhere and yet it is necessary, I suppose, to enlarge upon this first encounter since from then onwards, for some six years, I may be said to have occupied a seat on the Lamprey bandwagon. If

I were able to make an animated cartoon of this vehicle I would, I think, represent it as a sort of cross between a Rolls-Royce and a Dodgem car such as one sees at the fair. It would be driven jointly in all directions by a nanny, a very smart chauffeur belonging to another branch of the family and a Negro gentleman. It would travel at an uneven pace, cutting its corners, run in and out of ditches, and avoid head-on collisions by the narrowest of margins. Sometimes a vital part would fall off. Nobody would know where it was going and all the Lampreys would be very gay. Even when their hearts were in their mouths, they would laugh a great deal, saying: 'Isn't it *too* awful!' to each other. And they would be vaguely kind and stop for people who fancied a lift. These casual passengers would, if the Lampreys took a fancy to them, find themselves immensely flattered by information that the senior members of the family secretly confided in turn to each of them. Their eyes would open wider and wider as they learned of imminent financial and domestic disasters. They would feel self-important and would be scrupulous in maintaining the utmost discretion. If, by the accident of some unguarded remark, they found that they were all equally laden with identical Lamprey confidences their reaction would be one of bewilderment rather than resentment. They might observe that, with the Lampreys, seniority in years was in inverse ratio to conventional discretion. They would discover, if they stayed for any time on the bandwagon, that however frequently its parts disintegrated they would, after the fashion of all animated cartoons, be restored and the journey precariously maintained.

At the time of which I am writing, the Lampreys lived on a scale probably unmatched in any other New Zealand establishment except Government House. They were, however, tacking up towards one of their periodical financial crises when all the servants except the lady's maid and soldier-servant would be sent away, to be replaced by untrained Cantonese greengrocers wooed from their shops by wages slightly higher than those paid to their predecessors. This was an economy measure.

I spent most of my weekends with the Lampreys and joined in the desultory efforts to instruct the Chinese, who laughed a great deal. They were charming to the children and gave them many presents such as a sword made of coins to the son and heir and flagons of nauseating scent for the little girls who drenched themselves in it. They also invited us to interminable firework displays. Their names were Wong, Low and Percy Chew. They were baited by Mack, the soldier-servant, a difficult man whose wits had been a little turned by yellow fever. He was thought to be dangerous.

Percy Chew wrote a letter about Mack to their mistress.

Dear Madam,

Every morning he peep up his grim face of choler. Repeatedly ask what for breakfast. Reply egg. Constantly bang on saucepan loud hard noises. Continue to groan and grouch on daily. We wonder, madam, that you care to employ this churlish fellow.

Your Servant,
Percy Chew

Soon after this Mack hit Percy Chew and was dismissed. He became a hospital porter and bore, I believe, a grudge.

The ménage, apart from the peripatetic servants, consisted of Lamprey parents, occasional friends and relations from England, the Lamprey children (five after my godson was born), a nanny – Nanny Appleby who was the quintessence of everything that has ever been written on her species – a governess, French governess, and later a tutor. There were also two cadets who were said to be learning how to farm in the New Zealand manner.

Life with the Lampreys was enormously exciting and my week-ends grew longer. Sometimes they met. There was always some project toward, usually theatrical, and often on a most elaborate scale, as when the then Duke of York, following his father's earlier example, visited New Zealand. For this occasion we mounted a cabaret which he attended, having dined the previous evening with the Lampreys. They were involved in one of their recurrent financial crises and were down to a minimal staff. However, the English butler and cook came back for the dinner party. Little warning had been given and our preparations were hurried. Owing to the crisis the windows had not been cleaned for some time and the Lampreys argued a great deal about whether we should draw blinds and light lamps or allow the horizontal midsummer sun to reveal the imperfections. Finally, they settled for lamps but not blinds and so it came about that when the ducal entourage drove past the drawing-room windows it was afforded an uninterrupted view of myself falling in a series of serio-comic curtseys at the feet of one of the English cadets. Mr Moriaty, the village constable, had been alerted for the occasion. The appointment went a little to his head and prompted him to take an overdramatic view of duties which should have been confined to wearing his uniform, standing in the avenue and saluting at the appropriate moment. It was disconcerting to see, through the dirty unveiled windows, this large man, helmeted, sweating and doubled over his own bulk, dart from shrub to shrub in the garden. Keeping observation.

It is typical of a Lamprey occasion that while all of the Lampreys and I were grossly unmusical, we were successful in entertaining the illustrious guest with a nursery song at the piano. I can only suppose that he too was unmusical or that we were bad enough to be funny: I know we were bad. The royal cabaret on the following night was a triumph and made a great deal of money for deserving orphanages. Indeed, it was remarkable that while the Lampreys did not seem able to earn anything for themselves they were enormously successful in raising princely sums for good causes. What with these cabarets and an amateur vaudeville group called 'Touch and Go' which they sponsored and I produced, it was reckoned that while they were in New Zealand they raised directly and indirectly £12,000 for charities.

For two years the Lampreys held me as irrevocably in thrall as if they had been The Lordly Ones Who Live In The Hollow Hills. The children attached me to themselves as firmly as their elders. I have never been able to give very much emphasis to the age gap between myself and any children or adolescents with whom I become well acquainted. This lack of attitude has been accepted – indeed I think it has never been noticed – by the Lampreys. Although the eldest is almost twenty years my junior, we established a friendship that has gained in texture but is otherwise unchanged. Children are not nearly as 'childish' as people think: they are only inexperienced.

As for their elders, one grew accustomed to the off-beat rhythm of their fortunes. It became increasingly obvious that the financial crises were drawing closer together and the passages of rest growing more and more illusory. Gestures were made; table napkins, to the surprise of the butler, were abandoned. In an effort to cut down the laundry bills, enormously expensive washing and ironing machines were installed. The one, being insufficiently bedded, threatened to bolt and the other savaged many a handmade shirt and pair of Savile Row polo breeches before its intricacies were mastered. All the Lampreys made intermittent efforts to economize and then compensated for these bouts of abstinence by giving each other presents at the gold cigarette-case level. 'After all,' they would say to each other, 'he (or she) must have *some* fun.'

As we have seen, it is characteristic of the bandwagon that it never entirely collapses. It will show every sign of being about to do so and then suddenly set off in a new direction: downhill, and at a tidy clip. I suppose it wasn't really a great surprise when I heard that it was now to carry the Lampreys back to England.

We had discussed such a move often enough during those long, cosy, gossips that, however horrific their content, I so greatly enjoyed. Did Sullivan Powell cigarettes go out with the Second World War? If I were to find an unopened tin in some neglected corner and if I were to light one of them, should I not return to the enchanted house that smelt of them and of roses and a sweet-scented oil that was burnt in the drawing room?

It had always been understood that the children must be educated in England and the great obstacle was held to be the impossibility of raising funds for the move, let alone the schooling. It was perhaps a little confusing to learn that now, when financial disaster stared the Lampreys blankly in the face, their only possible means of salvation lay in the instant transference of the whole family, Nanny, a lady's maid and a tutor, by first-class liner via Panama to England.

So the house and farm were sold. The difference, a considerable one, between the price offered and the price required was settled by a billiards match played by the principals at a club in Christchurch and this, although they lost, greatly cheered the Lampreys. While the two men and their fellow club members were occupied with this contest, the wives and women-friends assembled elsewhere and made plans about how we would all meet in London.

At last the day came when our voices echoed through empty rooms. Sunshine poured in at the blank windows and dappled barefaced walls and naked floorboards. Everything was gone except, very faintly, the smell of a house that had been loved by a number of people.

IV

When the Lampreys had gone, their friends looked blankly at each other and felt rather as children do when the plug is pulled out of a swimming pool and summer goes down the drain. We told each other that it was no good being dismal and set about our lawful occasions. We even produced a cabaret in the grand manner.

I painted, and wrote verses, articles and short stories some of which found local publication. At that time, I had two ideas in my head: one for a full-scale novel with a New Zealand background and one for a detective story as an exercise, or so I thought, in technique. I wrote one or two short stories that I have never shown to anyone and have long forgotten. The manuscripts are lost and well lost, too. But there was one, influenced by E. M. Forster's earlier tales and perhaps by Walter de la Mare, which I have remembered. In it a benighted traveller found himself driving interminably down an unknown road into a valley too deep to be true. He came to a halt at last and was entertained in a submerged house by a hostess whom he took to be maimed in some way, since she lay on a very wide couch overspread with rainbow silks. She dismissed him and he was shown to his room. In the night he woke and heard the sound of wings. He looked out of his window and saw that she flew in great upward sweeps between him and the stars which appeared distantly above the walls of the abysmal ravine. Perhaps it is as well that this story is lost. I might find it foolish now and that, I suddenly realize, is a sensation I would not enjoy.

As for the novel, I wrote two chapters into which I tried to put mountains and a handful of people. In those days there was no talk, as there has been persistently in later years, of 'the New Zealand novel'. Or if there was, I was not by way of hearing it. The mountains and people chose me rather than I them and I found I wanted, quite passionately, to write about them. Perhaps if I had stayed in New Zealand I would have finished this book. I am almost sure that I would.

I did not stay. The Lampreys wrote gaily and affectionately from England saying that they were settled now and why couldn't I come? It was a lovely house, with lots of rooms, set in the woods and hills of Buckinghamshire. 'Do come, darling,' they said. 'Tell Betsy and Popsy' (for so they insisted on calling my parents) 'they *must* say yes.'

'Well,' my father said slowly, 'you've always wanted to go Home, haven't you?'

Not only had I always wanted to go but I had always felt quite sure that sooner or later it would happen. When I was about twelve years old, a silent film called *Living London* came to New Zealand and we went to it several times. It ravished me. It was extremely long, jerky and rather dim and it was not at all surprising. It did not contradict anything I had imagined about London but seemed rather to confirm my dreams. I mean real dreams as well as waking ones. I had dreamt often and vividly of The Strand and Piccadilly, of Ludgate Hill and Threadneedle Street. Always it was night time and I was alone in the crowded streets, exhilarated. Perhaps these dreams were engendered by my father and Gramp when they gossiped about Old Smoky and perhaps by *David Copperfield*, *Bleak House* and *Our Mutual Friend*, all of which I read when I was very young indeed. You may say it was a foredone, romantic and unreal London that I conjured up for myself.

I'm a compulsive spendthrift by nature but I had contrived to save some of my earnings, I had sold some paintings and I was commissioned to write a series of travel articles which, if they turned out well, would be syndicated through the New Zealand press. My father said he could manage the fare, if it was not more than £100, and also a modest allowance to supplement what I was able to earn. 'We have always lived quietly,' he said. 'We can do this. It would be a pity for you not to go.'

My mother agreed. I looked at her and saw a kind of anguish in her smile. I fell into an inward rage of compassion and love and resentment and, as so often before, hated myself for ever wanting to escape. It was terrible to know how good they were to me and how little I could do in return. This, I suppose, is the classic predicament of an only child. I have no doubt there are any number of surprising explanations and that Freud and the Greeks had a word for each of them and every one a *mot juste*. Is there such a thing as a daughter fixation? If so, I suppose it could be argued that my beloved mother was afflicted with it and I wasn't, under those terms, as beastly as I sometimes thought myself. A soothing exposition but not one which I find entirely persuasive.

There was no talk of when I should return and I was glad of that. I remember that we even speculated about a permanent family move to England but in a tentative, unreal sort of way. We seemed, almost, to be under some kind of spell.

Time went by and I started to pack about two months before there was any need to so much as think of doing so. I had taken a passage in a one-class ship called the *Balranald* of the P. & O. Branch Line, sailing to London from Sydney by way of South and Western Australia and South Africa. The voyage would take about ten weeks. Mine was a single berth cabin and cost £85. Its equivalent today would be thirty times as much, I imagine. I would cross to Sydney by trans-Tasman liner: first-class since it was widely held that any other accommodation was unsuited to a young female travelling alone on that line.

Encouraging cables and vague, pleased or funny letters came from the Lampreys. My ex-pupil, Bet, had already left by more conventional means of transport to stay with the Lampreys in England. Time seemed alternately to gallop and stand still.

The day of departure suddenly rushed upon us. I was to leave in the evening by the now familiar inter-island ferry steamer to await the trans-Tasman ship in Wellington.

'I really don't know why she's going,' said my father looking at my mother's and my own blubbered faces, 'if it makes you both so miserable.'

We had agreed that they should not come to the station. A friend was calling to drive me there. After dinner my father settled in his chair, opened his paper and lit his pipe. He caught my eye, nodded and made a hideous grimace which I ineffectually returned. My mother and I tried to behave unemotionally. When I saw headlamps coming up the lane, I hugged my parents and ran down the hill.

At once, as it seems to me now, with the closing of the house door and the slam of the garden gate, I moved into a new life.

CHAPTER 8

Northwards

In the antipodean autumn of 1928 the trans-Tasman steamer sailed down Wellington harbour between bush-dappled hills and through the Heads into Cook Strait. There are late afternoons in our part of the South Seas when the air is clear and the colour so lucid that it hurts. It was like that now. The South Island, although softened by the haze along the coast, was elsewhere brilliantly defined. The Seaward Kaikouras, those emphatic ranges, cobalt against a cerulean sky, floated above a Reckitt's Blue Pacific.

Our course was north-west. We sailed close in to the north coast of the South Island, passing D'Urville Island, Tasman Bay, Golden Bay and then Cape Farewell. As we stood out to sea and the land diminished, it collected itself into a country, something to be looked at from a distance, a discovery: New Zealand. Its colour intensified: it was now an astonishment. These were the last islands at the bottom of the world. One saw them that evening as the first canoe voyagers and Tasman and Cook saw them. They receded quickly, turned dark and presently were gone. I thought: 'How lovely they are. I wonder when I shall see them again.' I did not regret them.

Having never taken a sea voyage before but having suffered many a violent passage through Cook Strait, it did not astonish me when the next day proved stormy. The passengers, muffled and queasy, assembled in deck chairs and looked but greenly upon a mountainously heaving Tasman Sea and upon cups of beef tea. The elements seemed to get much rougher very quickly which I supposed to be normal and in the manner of Joseph Conrad, but it was nevertheless a surprise when quite suddenly all our deck chairs shot into the scuppers and discarded their occupants. An elderly gentleman's arm was broken. Beef tea was poured down bosoms. Several ladies screamed. A young man disengaged me from my chair and asked me if I would like to come and hear some of his records. We climbed, slid and ran down swinging passages and crawled up a companion-way to a smoking room where the young man played 'Hallelujah!', a very good jazz piece, on his gramophone. Several times the needle skidded across the surface and it was difficult to hear very well because of the thunder of the seas against our beam and the almost ceaseless crash of crockery as well as the incessant, ambiguous, basic hullabaloo. I hurried away once to be sick but I was enjoying myself and returned as soon as possible to my companion. We could only converse in shouts and all I can remember about him is that he screamed out that he was an old boy of the Merchant Taylors School.

When I went below to make some gesture towards dinner, I found a commotion of stewards in the corridor. The porthole in the cabin next to mine had been stove in. There was a general notice out that passengers were not to go on deck. One of the stewards said we were sailing in ballast and that it might have slipped a bit.

I attended dinner with perhaps a dozen other passengers but did not remain there long. The second officer and I were the only members of his table present. I rejoined my friend and we had quite a gay time of it in the deserted bar, drinking brandy and dry ginger which he said was a good thing and clinging to the tables when our anchored chairs threatened to decant us. I found that the brandy and dry ginger was not really a success and said goodnight. People always do tell one the Tasman Sea can be rough, I thought hardily, as I wedged myself down in my bunk. The noise was frightful but I think I slept quite a lot and I hoped that by the next day I would have found my sea legs. In the morning the stewardess said we had been hove-to in the night but I wasn't sure what that meant. 'Hove to *what*?' I asked myself as the Tasman thumped, crashed and hissed on the other side of the wall.

It continued violent all the next day but by the following morning was less so. Before dawn, on the fourth day, we came into Sydney Harbour. It never entered my head, until I heard other people saying so, that the passage had been in any way exceptional.

Sydney was my first big city and as unlike New Zealand, I thought, as it could possibly be. Remarkable, for instance, at dawn to see a lady on the wharf whose general aspect instantly recalled Sadie Thompson in Mr Somerset Maugham's *Rain*. She was encased in black satin and actually wore white boots with an overlap of calf and much jewellery. Her hair was the colour of new bricks and her face not so much painted as impastoed. She stood down there, all alone, and gazed through a black nose veil at the forward portholes below decks from which presently emerged the heads of stewards and able seamen. Words were exchanged. Presently she nodded, turned her back and with rhythmic jerks and alternating flash of highlights, hipped and thighed herself down the wharf. Life!

I had ten days in Sydney, staying with friends who were extremely kind to me. The Carl Rosa Opera Company was there and I was taken to the first night of *Turandot*, superbly presented and, or I thought so, gloriously sung. Sydney was *en fête* for the occasion – tails and white ties, orchids, jewels, dazzling décolletages: opera hats, even. But far, far better for me than all this splendour was the news that the Allan Wilkie Company was opening with *Henry VIII* at a big theatre in the academic quarter of Sydney. I felt a little as if I was in a picaresque novel where, however far I travelled, key figures would appear at rhythmic intervals.

Since we had last heard of them, Mr Wilkie had been the victim (if victim is the right word) of a disastrous (if disastrous is the right word) fire. It had consumed a block of buildings in one of which his entire wardrobe and property had been stored in readiness for a tour of New Zealand. At first this really did look like ruin: the insurance was far below the amount needed to set the company up again and, being a man of integrity, Mr Wilkie felt obliged to replace any personal belongings lost by his actors. They were asked to let him have a list of the contents of their cases and I am afraid that some very minor bit parts and spear carriers laid claim to astonishingly sumptuous raiment. Indeed, the elderly, rather raffish, gentleman who had not, in living memory, been known to appear offstage in anything but a seedy blue suit and a pair of wicked yellow boots, now turned out to have been possessed of a wardrobe calculated to set him up with credit in the Diplomatic Service.

While Mr Wilkie was still wondering what drastic action he would be forced to take, a splendid gesture had been made by his Australian audiences who raised a public subscription in grateful recognition, they said, of his making the plays of Shakespeare a living reality in their country. Be sure, he was off to London as fast as he could go and there, still in storage and for sale, was the superb wardrobe, and lavish scenery of the late Beerbohm Tree. So now, here he was, rustling in pure silk robes of Cardinal red to a full house and with a most superior company. 'Best thing that ever happened to me,' he would say, 'that fire.'

I had only a very sketchy notion of this play and had no idea what a rewarding actors' vehicle it is. I have seen it since, directed by Sir Tyrone Guthrie and cast up to the hilt, but there was a touch in Allan Wilkie's production that sticks in my memory as one of those moments of illumination that sometimes visit a performance and bless it. When Buckingham launched on his speech before execution and said to the hushed crowd: 'All good people: pray for me' they knelt, crossed themselves and began, just audibly, a prayer in Latin. It continued through to the end of the speech and I hear now a beautiful voice saying: 'when the long divorce of steel falls on me' and the slight upsurge of that background of prayer. The actor was an Englishman, Alexander Marsh, whose only fault was lack of inches. When my mother asked Mr Wilkie why he didn't put him on elevators, he ejaculated: 'My God, if I perched him any higher he'd fall off.'

Of course, I went behind after the show and it was lovely to see the Wilkies again. That was the last time I was ever to sit in front at one of their productions.

For ten days I wandered excitedly about Sydney. Flowers and fruit stalls blazed in the streets, the sun glittered on the famous and magnificent harbour which is a great deal bigger but less lovely, I swear, than more than one of ours in New Zealand. Sydney wears a brash, handsome, cocky look and has the air of knowing what it wants and going for it. Sydneysiders make New Zealanders look, I daresay, a bit dull, sheepish and provincial. This is the most positively antipodean city in the South Pacific. Neither geographically, ethnologically nor even historically do Australia and New Zealand resemble each other. We quite like each other: our common interests and our isolation from the rest of the world draw us together but there's nothing New

Zealanders enjoy less than being called Australians. Perhaps this is because we are insular and they are continentals.

The *Balranald* was to sail before dawn and I thought I would give less trouble to my hosts if I went aboard the night before. I was driven down in the evening by their chauffeur and I remember feeling, as he escorted me to the gangplank and handed my overnight bag to a brightly familiar steward, that this was not an appropriate mode of embarkation in the *Balranald*.

My cabin was forward on the port side and was exactly twice the size of its bunk. There was a washing-unit, three pegs, a porthole and no other means of ventilation apart from a small grille in the bulkhead. The only place for my cabin trunk was beneath the bed. To get it under, one opened the door, sat in the corridor and shoved with one's feet. When it was safely stowed I went up on deck. Why is it that on the beginning of a voyage, passengers look so objectionable to one another? Why is each dismayed at the sight of someone with whom, in a day or two, he or she will have struck up a pleasant acquaintance and later on, very likely fall in love? What, pray, has he or she subconsciously expected in the way of fellow voyagers? Argonauts and Nereids? The narrow decks of the *Balranald* were crowded with passengers all of them, no doubt, entertaining the strongest misgivings about each other. We herded into a dining saloon with strips of coconut matting on the floor and, sitting mum at long tables, consumed cold meat and beetroot. At about eleven o'clock I went to bed.

On that sweltering Sydney night the port was hermetically shut: a foretaste of many more nights in harbour. Watersiders were loading the forward hold about two feet away, as it seemed, from my head. Whine, judder, clunk, thump, rattle. I lay panting on top of the bedclothes and wondered when it would get light and I could go on deck. In the end, I fell asleep.

Strangely, I remember nothing of our departure but have an idea it was delayed. She was an old, coal-burning, freight-cum-passenger ship and we soon discovered that she was on her last voyage. Her liver-coloured sides would have done with a coat of paint. Her appointments were far from smart. I doubt if there are any one-class ships today at a comparable fare, offering such Spartan accommodation. Her master was an ex-naval commander who had been

stationed in Constantinople at the same time as a cousin of mine in
the Royal Scots. Eric wrote to him about me and after we had been
two days at sea I was commanded to the presence. Here was another
player of records, this time, appropriately, sea shanties, which were
less remorselessly canvassed in those days and sounded their best in
that setting. The master would give his guests liqueurs while robust
gramophone voices roared: 'Fa-a-r away you rolling river' and
'Spanish Ladies'. The night seas streamed past us and stars careened
across the portholes. It was all wonderfully consistent in tone and so
was the Owner himself. He was so like an RN officer in an Ian Hay
farce that he was scarcely credible. His face was red, his eyes blue
and, so it was rumoured, his temper exceedingly short. He was an
implacable disciplinarian and not greatly loved by his officers who
were forbidden to fraternize with passengers to any greater extent
than could be contained by a brisk walk round the deck at stated
times of the day. They must not sit or play games. He was obeyed but
his object, at least in one instance, was defeated since an ardent
romance developed between his fourth officer and a tough, bronzed
and cheerful young lady from Sydney. Everybody discussed this
affair including the lady, but nobody knew how such a degree of
complicated infatuation could be induced by the prescribed number
of circuits, eight to the mile, at a gruelling clip and under strict observation from the bridge.

There were any number of delightful passengers. Mrs Robertson,
a pianist, for example, the bones of whose left hand had been
broken by Dame Clara Butt. Dame Clara, it will be recalled, was a
famous contralto of Edwardian and early Georgian days whose
superb voice has been unfairly compared to a foghorn and who
was enormously tall and possessed a formidable physique. She had
been a student with Mrs Robertson and one afternoon, in merry
pin, had gaily rapped her over the knuckles with a ruler and at a
single blow transformed her from a concert pianist into her own
accompanist. Generously, Mrs Robertson seemed to bear no grudge
but undertook any number of tours with Dame Clara who did not
appear to be tortured with undue remorse. Her husband had the
wonderfully satisfying Lear-like name of Kennerly Rumford and
sang duets with his powerful wife: accompanied, of course, by Mrs
Robertson.

There were two amusing ex-public-school boys returning to England on what was left of their allowance, an English girl who was disembarking at Durban to marry a doctor and two young men whom she and I chummed up with. All I can remember of these pleasant fellows is the Christian name of one of them – Esmond. He was an enthusiastic British Israelite and lent me several books about the inscriptions in the Pyramids which I found profoundly unconvincing. There was an English actor of a lively disposition who organized ship's entertainments and invited me to help him and there were a retired naval officer who did sums all day and his wife who wasn't allowed to interrupt him.

Slowly and dirtily we steamed across the Indian Ocean and so infatuated with the voyage did I become that the increasingly dubious food and the stifling condition of the cabin did little to subdue my pleasure. With about a dozen others I used to haul my mattress along a corridor and up a companionway and heave it on the amidships hatch. There we lay, not perhaps very comfortably, listening at first to the sounds that a ship makes within herself; a complex of bells, the pulse of her engines, the hiss of her flanks through the night sea and the quiet movements of the watch. The stars were steady and luminous in the tropics and vague ideas about navigation made one feel they were important. I would fall asleep watching them and the night would go by in a little grey flash. Almost at once, it seemed, the quartermaster's voice was saying: '*Toyme* ter get up-er. *Toyme* ter get up' reminding me of Fred Scully and his '*Over*-ture and beginners'. Bare feet thudded along the decks. Already hoses spurted and fanned and sloshed into the scuppers. We would fumble up our unwieldy mattresses with fingers still nerveless from sleep and blunder off to our cabins which were already oven-hot.

We were nearly three weeks, I think, on the leg to Durban where the ship would spend two days coaling. Everybody was beginning to feel a bit jaded. When, on opening a folded slice of cold meat, I found it encrusted with small shells I made up my mind to cut loose in Durban. My friends were all collecting addresses of nice, clean, cheap little places to stay. I, who could afford it less than any of them, took what I hoped was enough money out of my hoard and resolved to spend the night ashore in a good hotel. I have never regretted doing this sort of thing.

This is not a travel book: I shall not try to write about Durban in any detail. Landfalls and arrivals on a sea voyage are, to me, a strange delight and this, the first in my experience, was immeasurably exciting. The impure land-smell reached out to sea and disturbed senses that had been scoured and simplified by salt air. A coastline, a pilot boat, shipping, buildings, docks, progressively encroached upon our exclusiveness. Details emerged: people on the wharves, a black man wearing, with perfect dignity, a bowler hat and a pair of corsets, who waited among his fellows, for us to berth. He was one of the gang of coalers. The gap between ship and dock narrowed. Bells rang in the engine room. Mooring lines were flung out and caught with bass-voiced ejaculations. The people on the wharf and the people in the ship stared dispassionately at each other. Friends exchanged greetings. Gangways were established. The *Balranald*, temporarily bereft of her somewhat vulgar personality, opened her bilges and indifferently relieved herself.

The pilot boat had brought a letter for my English friend from her fiancé saying he had been delayed by an urgent case in Johannesburg and giving her instructions about trains. Once ashore, she and I went by Zulu-drawn rickshaws from the port into Durban. I was not at all sure that I wanted to do this. I came from a country where it would be beyond the limit of anyone's imagination to envisage a member of one race running between shafts like a horse for the convenience of a member of the other. I didn't quite see that what was unthinkable for us should be OK in Natal. The Zulus, oiled, decked out in feathers and beads, superb men, stood by their rickshaws and shouted for custom.

I swallowed my scruples and we went that way from the port into Durban.

At the top of the hill my Zulu shouted and sat at an exact balancing point, on the shaft of his rickshaw. We coasted silently down the slope at what seemed to be a terrific speed, between glaring white houses and flamboyant splashes of colour.

The hotel was in a pleasant square and was cool and lovely. White turbans and white garments moved through shadowed rooms. Bare or slippered feet slapped discreetly down quiet corridors. I booked myself in and then, with some other of our shipmates saw my friend off in the Johannesburg express and set about exploring Durban.

I saw the Valley of a Thousand Hills from a height called the Berea and, returning, wandered about the streets until my heels blistered and the heat was too much to be endured. Back at the hotel I found my cool room and its own dark bathroom and for what was left of the day, I bathed and rested but was too excited to sleep. In the late evening I dined on a wide verandah of the hotel and watched the world go by.

Who was the fair young man who joined me during dinner and ordered, I think, a bottle of champagne? I fancy, he must have been one of a party at a nearby table and I suppose he must have been a fellow passenger: I didn't just pick him up. But I cannot recall his name or meeting with him on any other occasion. I remember that he asked me to join his party which was celebrating an engagement. I did so and supposed it was a South African custom to link arms and click glasses so ceremoniously. What a fuss! Having, out of excitement, slept not at all the previous night, and having walked, looked and stared myself to a standstill during the day and having taken, moreover, two glasses of champagne and some van der Hum with my dinner, everything now became hazy. I think I refused an invitation to go on somewhere and instead went straight to bed and to sleep for ten hours.

The next morning when, still footsore, I came out of the hotel, there, squatting by the kerb with his rickshaw, was yesterday's Zulu. He said, with a pleasing smile, that he was my boy and where were we going? My scruples about one human being trotting between shafts for another were honestly held and they now returned but were weakened by my blisters and confused by the attitude of the man himself. Obviously, he had waited there a long time when he might have been working elsewhere. He would therefore be a loser if I offered an explanation (which he would not understand or appreciate) and then, po-faced, tottered on my blisters in search of a taxi. Should I have given him a compensatory sum and a self-righteous commentary? An odious solution which he would no doubt have rightly interpreted as an insult to himself and his rickshaw. I took the rickshaw. He pointed out places of interest, nodded, smiled, trotted and uttered cries of greeting or warning to other rickshaws. Did he hate me in his heart, think me mad or not think about me at all? Without any shadow of doubt – the last.

He carried me to the native market, a place of enchantment. There were no white people about but a great strolling crowd of Indians, Negroes and 'coloureds' whose precise races I was unable to define. The shipboard diet of corned beef, suspect mutton, sardines, perpetual beetroot and plum duff had taken its toll. I longed for fresh fruit. Here, in a vast stone building, was a riot of pineapples, pawpaws, bananas and nartjies, that superb cross between a tangerine and an orange. Here were baskets with magenta motifs woven into them and wide beguiling hats. I bought a hat for fourpence and a basket for twopence which quickly became a cornucopea for elevenpence. I walked all through the market and came out in a colonnade occupied by Indian vendors of vivid cottons. Suddenly I wanted very badly indeed to paint. Without so much as a sketching block or a stick of charcoal to aid me in this desire and with the realization that it would in any case be impossible to set up an easel in the noontide heat and traffic of the market, I stared and stared, scribbled on the back of an envelope and hoped to remember. I *had* got a camera, bought in the ship, and I aimed it at the subject and thought that if the shot came out it would serve to jog my memory. Then I walked out into the glare on the opposite side of the market.

There he was, sitting on the kerb, nobly confident.

The last thing I did in Durban was to go to the theatre and whom did I see? Miss Sybil Thorndyke and Mr Lewis Casson (they hadn't yet been damed or knighted) and their small daughter, in a revival of an Edwardian drama.

It had been a lovely interlude. I decided to return to the *Balranald* that night as she was to follow her usual practice of sailing early in the morning. Surely, I thought, she will have finished coaling.

A row of taxis waited outside the theatre – I had half expected to find the Zulu – and I took one of them to the hotel to collect my things and then drive to the port. It was now close on midnight: very hot, still and heavily overcast.

The hotel bill was a little more than I had expected and I had treated myself to the play. As we jolted through the dark roads to the port – and it seemed much farther than I had remembered – I looked in my purse and found, as I remember, about ten shillings. Not enough, I thought; almost certainly, at this hour of the night, not enough. I would have to ask the man to wait while I got my hoard from the purser's office. A block of ice ran down my chest into my stomach and turned to a coal of fire. The office, of course, would be shut.

I hadn't noticed the driver and in any case it was very dark and he had a hat pulled over his eyes. I leant forward.

'Er. I say. One moment.'

'Yes, Madam? Forgotten something? Shall I go back?'

It was a very pleasant voice.

I explained. I said I was sorry and that I expected if I hadn't got enough money (I told him what I had) I could perhaps find the officer of the watch and borrow some from him or perhaps there would be time in the morning –

'Please,' said the voice, 'don't give it another thought. Of course it will be enough. Plenty. Really. I promise.'

Eton, Oxford and the Brigade of Guards thrown in. He did not turn his head. He drove on and made a little conversation. Had I enjoyed the play and was the hotel comfortable? And the ship?

I wondered if I had mistaken a private car for a taxi and he was amusing himself by taking me at my word. But no, it was a taxi and a very ramshackle one at that. Some young Englishman who had got himself into a scrape and was earning his return fare, perhaps?

When we reached the wharves and, finally, the *Balranald*, he said he would carry my things aboard. I said I could manage perfectly. He replied that he wouldn't dream of letting me go aboard at that hour of the night by myself.

I don't know what I expected to see when he moved into the light: something out of a glossy magazine I daresay, with a posh twinkle in his eye.

He was of middle height and carried himself like a soldier. When we arrived on deck and I emptied my purse into his hand, he took off his hat and I saw his face. It was grooved and pouched and empurpled. His nose was swollen and netted with veins. He had a three-days' growth of beard and his eyes were bloodshot. The hand he put out was grimed and tremulous and his clothes were filthy. He looked straight at me and said I'd really given him too much but would I like him to have the extra as a tip? I said yes, of course. 'That's awfully kind of you,' he said. 'Goodnight.'

'Goodnight. Thank you so much. Goodnight.'

II

They hadn't finished coaling. The decks were gritted with coal dust and as I reached my cabin – a disgruntled night steward unlocked it – the racket started. I suppose there had been a halt for some reason, perhaps a change of gangs. The porthole was sealed and the heat indescribable. The bathroom was locked.

I lay, for what was left of the night, bemused by heat and the crash of coals and by strange remembrances of the last two days.

A number of passengers, including the British Israelite, left the ship at Durban and we took on a great many Afrikaners, some travelling to Cape Town and some to England. The South African Dutch may, on the whole, be better to look at and listen to than this group that chance threw in my way for three weeks or so: better than the friends who came to see them off and stood, arrogant, small-eyed, muddily white, down there on the wharf. There is no value, of course, in a fleeting impression except, perhaps, for the light it may shed upon the observer. It never goes beyond the level of irresponsible journalism; snapshot judgement. If I had stayed for a year in Durban instead of forty-eight hours I would no doubt have learned of Afrikaners who contradicted every generalization I felt inclined to make about these people as we watched them that morning from the deck of the *Balranald*.

They had no bodily grace of feature, movement or behaviour and their voices were unlovely. What had they got that made them so sure of themselves? There were Africans down there visually putting them to shame. What had they got, these Dutch Natalese? Mastery, of course, as one saw. Among the Africans was a group of very small black urchins who laughed and danced on the wharf. Passengers threw coins to them and they shouted and grinned and showed off. One of them, a six-year-old, perhaps, executing a particularly lively prance, evidently overstepped some invisible barrier. An enormous Afrikaner turned on him as if he were vermin and hit at him and the child cringed and fell back. It was the ugliest of sights.

Perhaps this episode set those of us who saw it against the Afrikaners who came aboard. Perhaps it made us resent their arrogance and coarseness. They were the only fellow passengers in half a lifetime of long journeys, against whom I have taken in a big way.

There was a high sea running as we stood out from Durban: enormous blind rollers swelled and heaved themselves under a brilliant sun. The ship floundered up them, seemed to hover and then pitched and shuddered into the chasms between, taking it in green. A seasoned traveller now, I stood on the port side, held tight to the taffrail and exulted in the oncoming hugeness of the seas.

As I watched there rose up, astonishingly, quite close on our port bow, a great ship under full sail.

She towered above a crest and we wallowed in a trough: lordly beyond words she was, glittering, tall and a wonder to behold. She shone and strode the waters, making her own miracle, passed us like a dream and was gone. Nobody had seen her name. I would like to believe she was the barque *Pamir*, afterwards bought by New Zealand to carry food to Britain during the war. This was one of those moments that one aches to share with somebody: but with whom?

Heavy seas all the way to Cape Town where I was to be met by Uncle Freddie.

He was one of my father's six younger brothers. When, as I have related, my grandfather died leaving his widow and ten children less comfortably off than they had expected to be, there was a certain rallying round among the connections and this was matched by a determination on the part of the uncles to get out into the world as soon as they could and be at charge to nobody. There seems to have been no thought of university or profession for any of them. The Colonies, it was felt, were the thing. Uncles Arthur and Teddy plumped for Canada where they made and, in due course, lost, a fortune. Uncle Arthur, following in Great-Uncle Julius's footsteps (he who, it may be remembered, eloped with his niece's French governess), returned to England for a visit and persuaded the nurse of his own niece to join him in Canada where he married her without bothering to tell any of his relations. His reputation in the family was for headstrong behaviour. My father told me Uncle Arthur could never go to a prep or public school with any of his brothers because, so my father said, he was so jolly bloody-minded. Uncle Teddy also married in Canada and also forgot for some years to mention the fact. Uncle Teddy, it was, who on leaving school bought himself a suit which my grandmother considered loud and, in his absence, gave to the gardener's boy. When Uncle Teddy returned he encountered the gardener's boy who had foolishly togged himself up in his windfall. Uncle Teddy made him strip, there and then, and strode up the drive with a face of thunder and the suit over his arm.

During all these avuncular proceedings there were extraordinary involutions of snobbery and anti-snobbery at work. Willie, the boldest and gayest of the uncles, was offered a job by the husband of a cousin. This husband, my father said, was never mentioned without a certain change of voice since he manufactured biscuits. His wife was always called 'Poor Maude'. The fact that he was enormously rich and subsequently founded a peerage, made him, I gathered, less and not more congenial. However, Uncle Willie laughingly went into the biscuit offices and was in due course invited for the weekend to a large house in the country which he referred to as Cracknel Hall. He did not remain for long on such friendly terms as he discovered that his cousin-by-marriage grossly underpaid his employees. Uncle Willie went without appointment into the holy-of-holies, spoke his mind and was instantly sacked. The Boer War having conveniently broken out, Uncles Willie and Freddie volunteered, were commissioned and appointed to a good cavalry regiment. Dashing photographs were sent home to their family. They both went through the war, heavily engaged throughout and loving it. They did not suffer a day's sickness or the most superficial wound. When it was all over they decided to remain in South Africa. Uncle Willie, like his brother Reggie, became tubercular, was sent to a sanatorium and there married an English girl who was also a patient: both of them knowing that they had only a short time to live.

Uncle Freddie, nicknamed Criggy, also married and became permanent secretary to the Governor-General's fund, a job which he still held when I met him in Cape Town.

He was my father's favourite brother which was odd since he was deeply religious. ('Very sincere about it, though, old Crig. Funny thing.') When the *Balranald* berthed at Cape Town and I looked down at the people on the wharf, it was a shock suddenly to see my father. They were as like as two peas. Indeed, judging by old photographs of Granny Marsh as a still young and very pretty widow, sitting among her children on a croquet lawn, her sons all looked much alike. They are handsome, rather arrogant-seeming men with heavy moustaches that obliterate their obstinate mouths and an 'I'll see you damned first' expression in their eyes. Some stand in teapot attitudes: one hand on the back of a sister's chair, the other in a jacket pocket and the legs modishly crossed at the ankle. Others lounge back in their own chairs wearing knickerbockers and bow ties: elegant, huffy and grand. 'Conceited-looking lot,' my father used to say. 'Wonder if we were, what?'

With Uncle Freddie and his wife and two of their four boys, I visited an eighteenth-century house that had belonged to Koopmans de Wet: a very beautiful house that is kept exactly as it was when the de Wets lived in it. Each room feels as if one of the family must have only just walked out of it and is somewhere else in the house: sewing, casting-up accounts, counting linen or conning lessons. To visit there is like walking straight off the street into a Vermeer of Delft.

That was the only time I was to meet Uncle Freddie but from then until he died many years later, he wrote quite regularly and always remarked that he had greatly enjoyed getting in 'a nice lot of hugs and kisses', which was no more than the truth.

After Cape Town we steamed slowly up the west coast of Africa in enervating, overcast weather. A land breeze brought a sluggish, dank smell from the Gold Coast and a notice went up warning passengers to keep under the awnings as 'the sun was deceptive'. We stood close inshore and saw Accra and, later, Dakar and a fort that looked as if a film producer had decided to revive *Beau Geste*.

We had only one other port of call – a few hours, anchored in the roads off Las Palmas where we were supposed to take in fresh water. It proved to be bad and the doctor, who conformed only too accurately to every uncomplimentary and unfair legend one had ever heard about ship's doctors, roused himself sufficiently to issue an edict that it was unsafe to drink, either boiled or fresh. This resulted in a stampede on the bar which very soon ran out of everything except dreadful port and raspberryade.

Two nights before the end of the voyage a fancy-dress party was held. The weather was stifling. We had taken in a load of bananas which were stowed on deck in open wired bales between layers of their own tinder-dry leaves. I couldn't but think this a dangerous arrangement when I saw groups of passengers leaning against the bales, smoking. The smell, too, was very strong.

I had put on a scarlet paper carnival suit and feeling rather pleased with myself, had gone up on deck when I ran into a group of three South Africans. They were in a great taking-on. One of their party, a doctor, had become very ill and drifted between delirium and unconsciousness. The ship's doctor, run to earth in a cabin under circumstances where embarrassment was at a premium, had merely given orders that his brother medico was to be removed to the hospital and had then slammed the door and gone underground.

The friends were both furious and anxious and a little irked, I thought, at having their party upset. Who, they fretfully pointed out, could say what might not happen? He had warned them at the outset of his illness that he was in a bad way. He might die. They had decided to take watches between them. It was rather awkward, they said, because they had arranged . . . I said I would take a watch. I wasn't madly wedded to the fancy-dress party and anyway one of them would come and relieve me in an hour.

It was a strange experience. The unknown doctor, who looked dreadful, lay with his eyes not quite shut, turned his head from side to side and sometimes muttered unintelligibly. The stifling little hospital was dirty and unkempt. Surgical instruments flecked with rust lay haphazard in an enamel tray. Used towels had been thrown into a corner. The window was open and I listened to the giant whisper of the sea and distant sounds of revelry. Whoever had undertaken to relieve me evidently forgot to do so. I wished there was something to be done: fluids to be given or perhaps sponging, or ice packs to be administered. I wished the ship's doctor, in whatever condition, would look in.

I don't know how long I sat there in my scarlet paper dress. Presently there was no more music, the deck outside the window went dark and the ship settled down for what was left of the night. The patient had become so quiet that in a panic I felt for his pulse. His parched hand closed on mine. I leant forward and rested my forearm on the bed and so remained until at last the man who first spoke to me returned. He said he supposed I must like nursing. It was evident that however bereft the bar might be there were still supplies of alcohol in the *Balranald*. I said good night and walked *en fête* and alone down the coconut matting corridors to my cabin. Dawn was already established.

Four hours later I woke to the last day on board the *Balranald*.

Now the thing about names began. I wonder why these names should have had that particular effect? Was it just the easy magic of proper nouns, so indefatigably explored by poets? 'Harry the King, Bedford and Exeter, Warwick and Talbot, Salisbury and Gloucester' down to Kipling's list of fishing craft? Was it because one had so often heard these names and read them and was at last to see the places themselves? Or was it that, for someone with a great predominance of English blood in her veins, the sound of 'Land's End', 'The Lizard', 'Portland Bill', 'Beachy Head' and 'Sheerness' roused some atavistic emotion and abruptly established a heritage. Two men passed along the deck.

'We lie off Dungeness tonight.'

'I heard someone say we're to anchor off Gravesend until it gets light.'

My heart rose into my throat.

I went below and finished my packing.

Here, now, was England itself, close at hand, sliding composedly into the frame of my porthole. A lighthouse, the very tip and beginning of England, a breakwater, cliffs modulating into hills that looked as if they were mown like a lawn: a heraldic England in green and white. For a moment I remembered the West Coast of New Zealand as I'd seen it one evening nearly three months ago: remote, bereft of humankind, so old and so lately born out of primordial time. It astonished me to see now how the south coast of England bore an almost unbroken chain of habitation. I knew it must be so but it was surprising, nevertheless.

Already shipboard life was falling to pieces about one's ears. A radiogram from the Lampreys fluttered into the foreground and spread itself over my field of receptivity like the playbill in the film of *Henry V.* I had packed everything but my overnight necessities: for all the world, I might have been back on the inter-island ferry. My cupboard-cabin was blank and I don't remember, although the voyage had been a source of delight, that I felt at all sorry, as I would nowadays, that the *Balranald* had come to the end of her last ramshackle voyage. To all intents, I was ashore.

We did anchor off Gravesend and were to steam up the Thames at dawn to the docks at Tilbury.

Impossible to sleep. I knelt on my bunk and what I saw must have been much the same kind of thing that would be seen a few years later, during the bombing of London. A fire had broken out among the timber-yards at Gravesend. It made a red wavering hole in the night and I thought I could smell it.

Just before dawn the cabin steward made an isolated gesture. For the first time on the voyage he brought me a cup of tea. He said it would be all right to drink it: the water had been filtered. Since Las Palmas I had half-satisfied my thirst with the last of some Cape Town fruit. I thanked him warmly and had drunk half the tea when I found the rest of the cup was full of a thick, viscid, grey silt. There was no time to worry unduly about this. Light had entered the cabin, the ship was moving. Outside was the Pool of London.

It was still very early in the morning when we berthed at Tilbury. I expected that I would have to wait for at least two hours before anybody appeared but when I looked over the rail, there, among a handful of people on the wharf, was a Lamprey.

III

My childhood dream of London is in some ways clearer in my memory than the events of that first morning: they, indeed, have a dreamlike, wavering quality. Of the long drive through the East End into the City I remember little except, again, names. 'Limehouse' and 'Poplar', for instance, in those days evoked wonderfully sinister references to opium dens, gas-lamps wreathed in fog and wet stone stairs. The Commercial Road looked drab, broad and bald on that bright summer morning and held no romantic overtones.

I remember being told to look up out of the car window and there was the dome of St Paul's.

> Up the hill to Ludgate
> Down the hill of Fleet.

I thought, and the words jingled confusedly in my head. As if in answer there *were* bells, high in the air, clanging away above the roar of London.

'That's St Clement's Dane.'

There it stood like an island. 'Oranges and lemons' they were ringing as if there were no bombs in the future and they would sing it out for another three centuries or more.

'We'll have breakfast somewhere. There's a new place in Piccadilly we might try.'

The smell of the West End in the early morning. Hot bread. Coffee. Freshly watered pavements. Hairdressing parlours. Roses. Being a Lamprey place of entertainment it was, of course, an extremely grand restaurant. Why was it open at that hour, I wonder? I smell and see it and am surprised by the waist-to-ankle aprons of junior waiters. Eggs and bacon are ordered and then we are driving up a beautiful wide street.

'Do you know what that is?'

'Buckingham Palace?'

But it flashes up and is gone and so is the whole of the journey into Buckinghamshire.

I am not at all surprised to find myself being driven up a fine avenue to a Georgian manor house about three times as big and infinitely more impressive than the place that had seemed so grand in New Zealand and which, it may be remembered, had been given up as an economy measure. This is a lovely house. Behind and around it are gentle emerald-green hills, woods, and coppices, all beautifully groomed and tended and looking as if they came out of a medieval chronicle. Nor am I surprised, on alighting, to find everything shuttered and barred with large notices chalked up. 'Gone away.' 'Visiting Omsk and Tomsk.' 'Back in September.' 'For sale on Easy Terms.' This is one of the classic Lamprey jokes. They adore false telephone calls, dressing-up, diddling each other on railway stations and at garden parties, charitable bazaars and committee meetings. The head of the family once dressed up as an eccentric clergyman and with his wife – all scarves and beads – drove twenty miles into the country where he wrecked a charitable fête in his mother's garden. He made scenes about the prices, pocketed the clues in the treasure hunt and screamed out that the chocolate wheel (which I was running) was daylight robbery. Not until he shook his stick in my face did I recognize him. As most of the Lampreys are possessed of a considerable flair for acting and make-up, their on-goings are thought funny by people who normally detest and despise practical jokes.

We waited quietly on the portico and presently Bet and all the Lampreys inside took down the shutters and opened the doors. There was a fond reunion.

Again, it was no surprise to find (beside Nanny and the lady's maid) a butler, a footman and full domestic staff. The bandwagon evidently had had a coat of paint and a rebore.

It's no good trying to make a prim mouth about the older generation of Lampreys. Anybody who tried to do so, even the angriest young man of the fifties, would, if he knew them long enough, discover a sweetness of disposition, an absence of rancour and a generosity of spirit that, irritatingly enough, would seem to offset behaviour for which no logical excuse could be advanced. I, least of all, can shake a finger at their singular notions about money since I have never learned to take any interest in it apart from the pleasure or comfort it can give. Luckily this easy-come-easy-go attitude is offset by a pathological dread of debt, born, I am sure, of my father's strict integrity and nourished by a far from admirable and irreducible pride. The worst that I, who loved them, could ever find to think about my own generation of Lampreys was that they were, perhaps, not insensible of their cranky charm, nor as I think they say in the world of finance, of its potential. But that, after all, is an Irish characteristic and the Lampreys were nothing if not Irish. As for the younger generation; they, clever creatures, managed as they grew up to retain the charm and at the same time pluck out of thin air, a jokey sense of responsibility. They have in fact grown up, a process never quite achieved by some of their elders.

I have, of course, given a two-dimensional account of the Lampreys. I have disregarded shattering misfortunes beside which their financial crises are indeed no more than a joke. Nor have I tried to define their Christianity which is unshakable. There was a Lamprey whom in my story, where she appears as a child, I called Patch. Astonishingly, after Patch had grown up, she entered an Anglican nunnery which she always referred to as 'My Bin'. As a nun she was at once devout and unconventional, losing no chance of exploiting her cockeyed talent for practical jokes. She found she had mistaken her vocation and left before her novitiate had expired but continued, zealously, in her work for the Church. Essentially, she was a pioneer. She came out to New Zealand, lived on a pittance, founded an active and successful youth club, jollied up her parish, put heart into the aged, astonished the conventional and, as soon as all her pots were boiling satisfactorily, handed them over to her lieutenants and joined a medical mission in South Africa. She was a loving, generous, vulnerable and gallant child with the heart of a lion. I am sure that when she took this step she knew that it was to be her last adventure. They have built a chapel in her memory at the Mission.

But all these events were twenty years in the future when I first went to England in 1928. Patch was a very little girl then and a bit of a terror.

This was the age of *Decline and Fall* and *Vile Bodies*. Although my immediate Lampreys did not adopt the attitudes or conduct of a Lady Metroland or a Miss Runcible and indeed considered that such people went 'far too far', yet it must be confessed that those members of the clan who were, as we would now say, way out, might have served as models for Mr Waugh and, of course, they all talked the language. People and things were Heaven or shy-making, and, later on, too shying for words or too delicious, actually. All Lampreys are family-minded and love their young extremely. I remember hearing an aunt describe her favourite little niece in exactly these words: 'She's tiny, tiny, tiny tiny with blue blue blue blue eyes. *Too* much.'

For the next five years, this, apart from an occasional interlude with non-aligned friends, was to be the ambience in which I grew into the English scene.

CHAPTER 9

Turning Point

The feeling of unreality persisted. It was as if one lay down on a beach while wave after wave broke over one's head. This is not to suggest that it was anything but a wonderfully happy time for indeed I was with people in whose company I could never be anything but happy. The older children were home for the holidays, and my godson was now three years old, rather stout, and wholly beguiling. I wrote my syndicated articles, learned that they were becoming popular in New Zealand and began, I think, to develop some appreciation, at least, for cadence and the balance of words.

We were bewilderingly gay: a self-contained quartette driving up to London several times a week for dinner and a play and then going on sometimes to two or three places. 'Uncles' was the smart nightclub in those days and there one danced or inched at close quarters with poker-faced revellers of high estate or sat and listened to Hutch, a Negro entertainer whose popularity was supreme. 'It *couldn't* have been more fun. They had Hutch and everything.' Then there was the midnight floor show at the Savoy and a Tzigane band at the Hungaria. We went oftenest to the Hungaria and heard Colombo lead the band and saw him and all the fiddlers throw their bows into the air and shout while a little man like a troll went mad on the tzimbal. Richard Tauber was nearly always at the Hungaria and at some stage in the evening Colombo flourished up to his table and with an ineffable and excruciating leer, wafted a note or two in the tenor's ear. Sure enough, the plump little hands would extend, the shirt front inflate and out, mellifluously would come 'You are my Heart's Delight' while Herr Tauber's partner rested her cheek upon her palm and gazed pensively at her wine. Sometimes the Prince of Wales was there and sometimes Mr Michael Arlen and almost always, alone, at a table just inside the door, sat a strange figure: an old, old man with a flower in his coat who looked as if he had been dehydrated like a specimen leaf and then rouged a little. No one ever accompanied him or paused at his table. He looked straight before him and at intervals raised his glass in a frog's hand and touched his lips with it.

One night we asked the restaurateur who he was.

'A poet,' said Signor Vecchi, 'and once, long ago I understand, a celebrated personage. It is Lord Alfred Douglas.'

Those were the springtime years of the Cochran shows, of Cicely Courtneidge, Jack Buchanan, Evelyn Laye and Noël Coward. Drawing-room comedies had Nigel Playfair, Lilian Braithwaite, Yvonne Arnaud and Frank Cellier in the leads and nobody thought the worse of french windows. Charlot's Revue with Beatrice Lillie rioted at the Cambridge. The Lampreys had, for the most part, a gay taste in theatre and I think it was not until I began to explore for myself that I saw the experimental plays of those years.

This came about in August when the Lampreys shut up their house, gave their servants a holiday and went to stay with friends. I spent a short time with an aunt in Kent and a longer one with friends in London and with a most congenial Lamprey who was on the stage and had a house in Kensington. Now, I began to explore. I waited in pit-queues for matinées and came to recognize the street-buskers: spoon-players, a paper-tearer, an errand-boy who lowered the shafts of his cart, executed a brisk routine of hand-springs, took round his cap, and was off; the dismal woman who bellowed the story of her life beginning: 'I was a ninnercent girl,' and the terrible man with eyes like the Dead Drummer's who was led by his shifty-faced mate down the queue droning: 'Bl-i-nd, bl-i-nd' and collected, I daresay, more than any of them, so anxious was everybody to placate him and get rid of them both. Strangest of all was the man in the raincoat with unfurled umbrella, wild eyes and streaming hair and beard. He walked very fast with long strides, flourished his umbrella and glared about him. He solicited nobody but shot past the queue and down The Haymarket or Shaftesbury Avenue or The Aldwych or The Strand or Coventry Street. The last one would see of him was the ferrule of his umbrella gesticulating above the traffic.

After these superb preludes I saw a dramatization of Christopher Morley's *Thunder on the Left,* and, later, the first of the Priestley 'time' plays, Pirandello's *Henry IV* with Ernest Milton and a French tragi-comedy called *Beauty* with Charles Laughton. I daresay I have muddled the order of my theatre-going. As I look back there is still a haze over the first year in England so that although individual memories are sharp, sequences are blurred. The first Shakespeare that I saw in the West End was John Gielgud as a very young, petulant and smouldering Hamlet with, or so I thought, enormous promise rather than present achievement.

It was some time before I discovered the Old Vic which in those days was unknown to New Zealanders, but in due course I found my way to the Waterloo Road and became a galleryite at – could it have been? – tenpence a time. At the Vic, we were, I think, in the direct tradition of Elizabethan, Jacobean and Victorian audiences. The police constable on beat in the New Cut always looked in and watched from the back. Students, labourers, tough elderly women, nondescripts, deadbeats, and characters who might have made bombs in their spare time, chewed, drank, smoked and leant forward with their hands on their knees and the stagelight reflected in their faces. We stared down past a strange mechanism like the mock-up of a vast chandelier which hung from the roof outside the proscenium and helped to light the apron and main acting areas. If a player dried he would, as like as not, be prompted in strong cockney from the gallery and if he was inaudible he would be told to speak up in accents that were pellucidly clear to all the house. This sort of treatment, though distressing, is good for actors. The Vic, in those days, thrummed with a coarse, racy life that had no equivalent in the West End.

It was wonderful to be alone and at large in London. One early autumn morning I went by bus into the City and cashed a cautious cheque. I asked the teller what would be a good way to take for exploration and he came out with me to the street. 'If you go along there,' he said, 'and look up, you will see Gog and Magog. Take the next turn to the left, keep on uphill and see if you know where you are.' He smiled and nodded. 'Good hunting,' he said.

I have the poorest sense of direction and can get lost at the drop of a hat but it doesn't matter in London: a policeman or shopkeeper or any passer-by will always put you right and will take a lot of trouble about it. I found myself in steep cobbled lanes where draught horses with glossy flanks and rumps strained, plodded and skidded in the shafts of brewers' lorries. I looked in at a Wren church and peered into some Worshipful Company's hall. I smelt chemicals, spices, coffee and other exotics that I could not define. I climbed and climbed and had begun to think it was time to ask my way back to the West End when the buildings stood apart, the street flattened and widened and, as unexpectedly as on Arthur's Pass, seven years ago and thirteen thousand miles away, I looked into another world.

The Tower is a commonplace for Londoners: for me this first sight of it was like walking through one of those doors that in fairy tales always stand 'invitingly open'. It was like looking down into history. For one thing, although the sun shone, there was a light mist. It treated the keeps and walls as if they were mountains, separating them from their bases and veiling the river beyond so that everything floated a little. A company from the Brigade of Guards drilled in the moat, scarlet on emerald green, and the long, open-vowelled orders thinned by distance, rose above the sound of river traffic and the voice of the City and drifted up to the top of Tower Hill where a New Zealander began to feel London in her blood. I remembered the Esquire Marsh who was something in the Tower and kind to Fox the Quaker. I remembered the Tower was a place of infamy, courage and high stomachs, horror and martyrdom. An ignorant and passionate sense of historical continuity rose up in me. I had the first taste of the extraordinary buoyancy, the sudden quickening of all one's perceptions, the sense of belonging to, and being carried high, on the full tide of London: an experience that sooner or later comes, I think, to almost everyone who stays there.

I asked my way to the Mansion House and rode in glory on the top of a bus back to Piccadilly.

II

The Lampreys returned in the autumn and we all re-assembled. By all, I mean the family, my ex-pupil, Bet, the English cadet, Tops, who had been with the Lampreys in New Zealand, the two youngest children, who were not yet at boarding school, the household staff and me. Signs, elusive at first, like an unidentifiable squeak in the bodywork of the bandwagon, gave notice of an approaching crisis.

In the meantime, however, there was an adventure. The children's mother (to whom I shall refer in future as Charlot) was given a treat by *her* mother and I was included in it: a jaunt to Monte Carlo. All Lampreys adore Monte Carlo. Bet decided to come, too. It so happened that a week before we were to leave, a brother-officer of the Head of the House showed us a wonderful system which he had used with great success when last he had a fling on the green baize tables. This was just the kind of thing that inspires industry in a Lamprey. A domestic roulette was put into instant use. We were to take it in turns to spin the wheel and record the numbers and then come to a sensible and scientific conclusion about the system. Not a second should be lost, said Charlot.

'We mustn't be silly and go madly in for it without *really finding out*,' she urged. 'We must take it in watches at the wheel, not cheat over the results and keep our wits about us.' Dizzy, she said, would come to our aid. I should explain that there is a legend, based on a complete fallacy, that the first Lord Beaconsfield's blood is mingled with the Lampreys'. Dizzy is not infrequently invoked.

'Don't let's lose a precious moment,' Charlot said. 'To work, girls, to work.'

Can I remember the system? I believe I can. *En plein: – Zéro. Première. Quart. Onze. Dix-huit. Vingt. Et les deux derniers carrés.*

It was remarkable how often it turned up trumps on the domestic wheel. You might say there was no sense in it, we told each other and anybody who would listen, but here were the facts. And we would produce lists of figures. It was really very odd we would say, feverishly spinning. I know that in my heart I did not believe in the system and I doubt if either of the others did but – and this was a favourite Lamprey saying – we were having fun. Indeed it was highly characteristic that an inverted pyramid of close reasoning was owlishly erected upon a phantasmagorical premise.

When the time came for our departure, we counted up how much we could spare for the system and resolved to go no farther than it lasted. Away we went in the morning by the continental from Victoria. That night we slept in the Blue Train.

The wagon-lits and chocolate-uniformed porters, the dining coach, the swift journey out of Paris into the night and the shuttle-glimpses of French families in lamplit rooms: these were my first sensations of Abroad.

In the night I woke often and in ecstasy; the last time to hear outside, on an echoing platform, an incredibly melancholy voice chanting: 'Marse-i-i-illes' and to see the light of a lantern bob on the window blind. 'Marrr-sei-i-illes'.

When we woke up we were on the Côte d'Azur and the Blue Train had taken on a leisurely air. It seemed to dawdle a little by flowery platforms. Not far away was the full postcard blue of the Mediterranean. Villas glared blankly in the sun. Olive trees mounted like smoke up the flanks of the Maritime Alps. Everything shimmered and our coffee and brioches were delicious.

Well: there at last was Monte Carlo. I hadn't been much of a one for Phillips Oppenheim and William le Queux but I fancy they must have featured in those old *Strand* magazines in Dunedin and perhaps it was some memory of an illustration that made the whole thing conform so precisely to expectations: bland, meretricious and pleasing, like a studio representation of itself. 'Delicious!' said Charlot. '*Such* fun. *do* look.' And so it was.

We were given three enormous bedrooms opening out of each other. Our balconies overlooked a Franz Lehár backdrop with the marzipan cupolas of the Casino run out against it like a ground row. Edith Wharton deployed her posh Americans in such a setting: there is still an extraordinarily Edwardian flavour in the Monegasque scene.

In the afternoon we enjoyed the siesta, at five we sat under an awning taking tea and appallingly rich patisseries. At eight we dined and at nine walked down the hill through the gardens whose display of flowers in full bloom is said to be effected overnight in buried flowerpots. A blaze of salvia at midnight on Monday. A riot of petunias at 1.30 a.m. on Tuesday. I've never met anybody who has caught them at it but the legend persists and I hope it's true, it would be so precisely in character.

The French of hotels and places of entertainment seem to have a great liking for colour schemes ranging from chocolate up to ochre and relieved by baby blues and pinks that have gone off a little, the whole being garnished with touches of gilt. So it is, or was, in the casino. Heavy carpets, muted voices, muted smells, muted colours; chandeliers; the discreet click and rattle made by marbles skipping over metal and by croupiers' rakes dragging in the plaques: frescoes, in a subfusc scheme, of incredibly insipid *bergères*: had I expected something a trifle more rake-helly in the prevailing décor? I think I had. However, as one looked about one in the Salons Privés, there were, after all, footmen placing tables with champagne at the elbows of gamblers who had sizeable pockets under their lacklustre eyes. There were jewelled claws that hovered over the green baize, any number of cigars and heaps of plaques, worth Heaven knew how much, being spread over the playing fields in an idiotic and rather pretty design.

We chose a table and hit Monte Carlo with our system. I wish I could record some wonderful departure from what might have been expected but, no. All that night we were fortunate and the more we won the more we laughed. When we won we tipped and the murmur of 'Pour les employés. Merci, mesdames.' rose in a cosy murmur from the croupiers. At about two o'clock on a warm morning we walked back to the hotel and wondered if we would be hit over the heads and robbed of our bulging handbags.

It didn't disappear suddenly or even at a steady rate. Our fortunes wavered and the croupiers, as we overheard, referred to us as 'les dames qui rient'. When, after about a week, we were almost back where we started, we settled upon a method that is deeply despised by all true gamblers. We separated and we spent ages waiting for long runs on the even chances. After an even chance had turned up five times in succession we began to double on it, and, having won back a pittance grew bold again. I am not a natural gambler and would have sickened of this if it hadn't been for the Lamprey atmosphere that dottily prevailed and the strange habitués of the green baize. There was a lady dressed from crown to instep in the white cashmere of another decade with a heavy white crepe veil and white silk gloves. She appeared at a fixed time each afternoon, walking through the salons as if under the invisible escort of Wilkie Collins. A croupier told us she had an appalling disfigurement and nobody had ever seen her face. Edgar Allan Poe, perhaps, is nearer the mark. Or Hawthorne? One almost felt it had been necessary for the Casino to invent her. For an hour she gambled, not heavily, then rose and walked out, really very like a ghost.

Ladies, there were, of a kind that was entirely new to me. The croupiers referred to the most dominant of them as 'cette monsieur-dame'. She seemed to be having quite a pleasant time of it, running her finger round inside her collar and settling her tie. She wore a sort of habit and was perhaps by Isherwood out of Huxley. The disconcerting thing about many of the habituées was their tendency to seem as if they had been written by somebody not quite on the top of his form.

Several times I found myself next a bad-tempered, tweedy Englishman and his cagey daughter. They looked for all the world as if they had been taking the dogs for a walk right through the village and round. We thought them highly respectable and disagreeable and were rather ashamed of them for behaving in the way French comic papers expect the English to behave. It was astonishing to find that Miss Pittsin (as we had christened her) was quietly stealing my plaques. When I detected her at it and stared into her face in amazement, she made primming movements with her lips as if she'd caught me laughing in church. A famous French racing-cyclist there was, who introduced himself and was so astonished that we didn't fall into a rapture when he pronounced his name that he seemed to take a fancy to us and asked us to have drinks with him.

We made a number of acquaintances. Bet was greatly taken with a bald, elderly and wretchedly unhappy looking croupier whom she called Grumps. They spoke no word of each other's languages but she would sit beside him and give him her plaques to bet with. Sighing heavily he would push one after another on to some unlucky square and in due course it would lose and his colleague would rake it in. He would then raise his shoulders in a dismal shrug and he and Bet would shake their heads at each other. 'Poor Grumps,' Bet would say. 'He had no luck again.'

On our last day, having exhausted the pool, we had little individual flings and I suddenly found I'd won on 15 *en plein* and made enough to buy a coat and skirt. The others also recovered their losses and gained a little. We returned to England much exhilarated.

III

I have suggested, without any claim to originality, that in most lives there is a repetitive pattern; that incidents which on first occurrence seem to bear no relation to this pattern often turn out to be completely integrated and to have been merely waiting offstage for their entrance. I now come to a prolonged episode which might have been designed to make nonsense of this well-canvassed theory. It came about on an impulse, it lasted some three years, and it was ended, for me, by a tragic event quite unconnected with it. As far as I can tell it has had no influence on anything that has ever happened to me.

Charlot had an extremely illustrious grandmother who was once described by the Sydney *Bulletin*, a strongly antipodean journal, as being: 'the most highly decorated female in the British Empire *bar royalty*', a gloss of which her grandchildren constantly reminded her. Indeed, upon her eightieth birthday they enacted a charade (all Lampreys are superb charadists) in which the head of the family, heavily padded and bearded and speaking with a strong guttural accent, took decoration after cardboard decoration from a wheelbarrow manipulated by one granddaughter dressed as the Lord Chamberlain and pinned them all over another made up in character as the illustrious grandmother herself.

'Congrrratulations, Lady D. Would you turn r-r-round if you please, Lady D., there is no more room in front. Ach, so. Congratulations, once again, Lady D.'

Even at her advanced age, this lady occasionally caused to be organized functions for the raising of funds: usually for famine relief in India. On our return from Monte Carlo we found that a great bazaar was to be held and that we were expected to provide objects for an artsy-craftsy stall. Charlot and I established ourselves in the empty ballroom of the Buckinghamshire house with trestle tables, paint, wooden cigarette boxes, parchment, paper and a loathsome substance called Barbola from which one daintily fashioned rose-buds round the frames of looking glasses or the lids of glove boxes.

We created quantities of lampshades, blotters and funny rhymes for bathroom and lavatory doors. We decorated trays, bowls and trifles for what in an occasional access of hatred we called 'my ladye's toilette'. Charlot has neat and clever hands and when she sets her mind to a job she becomes a perfectionist. We made a great many objects and, in the event, a surprisingly large sum of money for famine relief.

By this time the current crisis had all but caught up with the bandwagon: it approached with the Christmas season and as usual long discussions, as enthralling as they were, of course, distressing, had set in. I don't remember which of us it was who abruptly exclaimed: 'Why shouldn't we make all these ghastly things to sell for US?'

The shop-girls idea was born.

We became immensely excited.

The plan was to make any number of gift-objects, take a lock-up shop somewhere in SW3 for the Christmas quarter, make what profit we could and stop. We called ourselves 'Touch and Go' after the vaudeville effort in New Zealand, and in doing so exhibited, at any rate in one respect, the most exquisite judgement. I don't suppose any two beings more ignorant of shopkeeping ever embarked upon it. We set to work anew and with the utmost enthusiasm. If it ever occurred to me that I would really be more sensibly employed in writing articles or even the novel that still nagged at me, I put the idea behind me for the time being. We were having fun.

We found a lock-up shop next door to Mr Green, the chemist, in the Brompton Road. One fine frosty morning we set up our wares in the window and retired to the basement to paint and glue and varnish as fast as we could in order to maintain replacements for what was sold. I remember a cold moment when one asked oneself: 'And if nothing is sold?' but it passed and presently the bell rang and we served our first customer: a Kensington lady with the inevitable dog on a lead. I must digress about dogs.

In respect of dogs I am a New Zealander. I like dogs. As a rule they have pleasant dispositions and either flatter one or make one uneasily compassionate by their excessive devotion. I very much like large, sensible dogs and sporting dogs. When dogs work they are splendid. A good huntaway, streaking down a mountainside and setting a great mob of sheep in motion is a noble sight. They are dirty, however, and can be obscene, and no amount of shampooing and twiddling will make anything but asses of them. In New Zealand they can give one hydatids and it would be idiotic to let them lick one's face even if one liked it. I never became reconciled to the South Kensington dogs. When they were not defecating on the doorstep they were shivering in their mistresses' embrace.

We toiled ourselves almost to a standstill over our shop. So busy were we in the last days before the festival that I stayed at the Rembrandt Hotel in order to open shop early. It was a white Christmas that year and London, to me, was wonderful. I was too busy working too hard to become disillusioned by the great commercial racket. Moreover I was living in a household of children and experienced a kind of realization of the winter fantasy I had, myself a child, made out of Christmas in the midsummers of New Zealand. I did not know what I believed, I formed no judgements about the way things were done. I simply felt that behind all the predictable performances there was something which, like Eliot's Wise Man, you might say was satisfactory.

Opposite the hotel was the Brompton Oratory. When the traffic was muffled by snow its tenor bell sounded very close. On my first night in the hotel, after I had gone weary to bed, a boy sang 'Adeste Fideles' outside in the cold. His voice was not so much sound as vapour or perhaps a tingling vibration on frozen air. Was he a chorister? It was very late for him to be out there singing all by himself. He finished and gave a little treble cough which was stifled before it ended. I imagined him wrapping a comforter across his steaming mouth and turning for home.

There was a great muster of Lampreys for Christmas: four generations of them and, except the youngest, they gave the impression of being prolific in the extreme. All Lampreys are devoted parents.

When our accounts were cast up it was found that we had made a surprising profit in our shop. This, of course, was fatal. The miasma of trade had infected us and we were unable to shake it off. Round the corner in Beauchamp Place there was a rather smarter shop to let on a yearly lease. We took it. After that I was a shop-girl in Beauchamp Place for two and a half years.

It was, and I think still is, one of those streets where established shops of considerable snob-value are occasionally interrupted by 'amusing' amateurish ventures that make their rather desperate little gestures, languish and are gone. We were less ephemeral and survived, I suppose, because we did most of the work ourselves. We became slightly less amateurish, never got on each other's nerves, made any number of ludicrous mistakes and encounters and added to the staff largely from our circle of friends. We crossed Beauchamp Place into larger premises and began to do interior decoration and specially made pieces of furniture.

It was upon this scene that the news broke of my mother's plans to come to England.

IV

It was astonishing and wonderful news. My father after retiring from his bank had taken up a number of secretaryships, I was beginning to be self-supporting, and the need for economy was growing less stringent. With his great generosity in all big decisions, my father said the visit could be managed and that he would do very well by himself as long as it was not for too long. So my mother sailed for England.

The ship berthed before we reached Tilbury and most of the passengers had already disembarked. I see my mother now, very clearly, sitting on deck waiting for me. She wears a sealskin coat and hat and her hands are clasped over her handbag. I seem to become airborne and shoot rather than run down the deck towards her.

'It's no good pointing things out,' said my mother on our way through the City. 'I can only nod and say things like "Fancy!" but I'm not really noticing. I'm floating.'

She continued to float for some time but when she came to earth, she did so to some purpose.

I don't remember how long it was after her arrival that the Lampreys' affairs swooped down to a particularly tricky crisis. It was not only the familiar state of near-insolvency but the distance that we found ourselves from our occupations. We were all working in

London, now: the Head of the House was in the City, Tops had become a new kind of cadet with a professional house-decorating firm and Charlot and I had our shop. Hours and hours were spent daily on the road. The lovely Georgian manor house was costing a fortune to run and on the firmly-held Lamprey principle that you must spend money in order to save it, a housekeeper had been engaged to encourage thrift among the servants. There had also been some odd sleight-of-hand changes in the staff. Chauffeurs had been converted into butlers. A pearl necklace worth some hundreds of pounds had been dropped in an empty chocolate box and burnt to blackcurrants. A private soldier from the Welsh Guards was pressed into service as footman. He was a talented mimic and one of our favourite diversions was to linger in the raspberry canes outside the servants' hall and hear ourselves being done to the life by Thomas. He was also, as it turned out, a prodigy of sexual prowess and wrought havoc in the morale of the female staff.

This was the general picture when the decision was taken to move up to London. From motives of economy.

It is not necessary to enlarge upon our search for houses and flats. Enough to say that there were outstanding arguments against unsmart districts like Dulwich, Notting Hill or Maida Vale where rents were low, and overwhelming reasons why it would be cheaper in the long run to be near Beauchamp Place and a good tube to the City. I must admit that I found myself in owlish agreement with the Lampreys on these issues. My mother offered no comment.

It was a lovely flat. Eleven rooms and charmingly panelled. SW3. Some of the servants were boarded out.

My mother and I also went flat-hunting and continued to stay with the Lampreys while we did so. Nothing could exceed the warmth of their hospitality but it was perfectly clear that when the children came home for the holidays there would be no room for anyone else. We found a basement flat, semi-furnished, in Bourne Street, off Cliveden Place on the borders of Pimlico: a living room with a divan for me, a bedroom for my mother, a miniature kitchen and a bath in a sort of cave under the footpath. It, too, was handy to Beauchamp Place, though not fashionably so. We were set up by the kind Lampreys with extra pieces of furniture from their store. So we kept house together and my mother became as deeply committed to London as I.

It was now that an old friendship was renewed. Dundas, nick-named Cis, and later, James, who had so gently enlivened my child-hood, was living in London. We all met again and it was as if there had been no interval of twenty years but that only yesterday he and I had been Mrs Finch-Brassy and Mrs Boolsum-Porter, sipping imaginary tea in the house in Fendalton. With James we saw another London: the London of the Caledonian Market and the Portobello Road, of junk stalls in Berwick Street and old print shops: the London of a youthful-elderly and quite successful professional actor with a private income who had been content to take what engagements came his way and when none came, settled into a state of sprightly reminiscence and the active enjoyment of many friend-ships. He was wonderfully kind in a hundred offbeat and unexpec-ted ways as, for instance, when his charlady of many years' standing confided to him that she had always wanted to see Paris.

'Very well, Mrs B., you shall.' And he took her there for a week-end to her amazement and delight.

The Jimmy of my own professional days (he of the scarlet fever) was in London, too, and playing with Sir Nigel Playfair in a piece called *Petticoat Influence*. He came often to the basement flat and so there was much talk of theatre. And after so long an interval my mother and I went to the early doors again. One of the most satisfy-ing of all our matinées was Pirandello's *Six Characters in Search of an Author* superbly directed by Tyrone Guthrie at the Westminster Theatre. I hadn't read it. I knew nothing whatever about it and that is the ideal way of seeing this play for the first time. It takes you by the throat and shakes the daylight out of you. If you long above everything to be a director, this is the play that nags and clamours to be done. I was broody with it, off and on, for some eighteen years before I finally got it out of my system in a burst of three separate productions in three separate countries. It may be a phoney play, its theme – that reality exists only in the mind of the individual – may be inconsiderable, but it remains, to my mind, more absolutely the pure material of theatre than any other piece of twentieth-century dramatic writing. One may discount its philosophy and dismiss its metaphysics (I do not altogether do so) but tackle it simply as something that happens in a working theatre and it crackles with immediacy. We were greatly excited by it.

Throughout these months, my mother didn't say much about the shop. She sat with us sometimes in our workroom while Charlot gummed maps on lampshades and I copied the patterns of glazed chintzes on to breakfast trays, firescreens and powder bowls. She enjoyed the jokes, was sceptical, I am sure, about the financial returns and indicated briefly that she thought I was on entirely the wrong tack. I think she worried about it and she certainly had cause to do so when the Great Depression came. We struggled on, appalled by the distress around us and horror-stricken by our inability to give work to the many, many people who appealed to us.

My mother watched and listened and said little. I am sure it was in some sort a comfort to her when, apart from the travel articles that kept going quite regularly, I began to write steadily in the evenings.

It started on a weekend when my mother was away on a motor trip with some friends. All day Sunday it rained and I read a detective novel from a little lending library in Bourne Street. I don't remember the author now, but think perhaps it was Agatha Christie. I was not a heavy reader in the genre but I had, off and on, turned an idea for a crime story over in my mind. It had seemed to me a highly original idea.

The murder game was fashionable in those days. 'Suppose,' I had thought in a blaze of inspiration, 'suppose instead of a pretence corpse, a real one was found.' I imagine some round dozen of established practitioners had already discarded this *trouveau* as being too obvious but I thought it was just fine. And now, on this wet Sunday, I went to the newspaper shop that was always open in Bourne Street and bought several penny exercise books and some sharpened pencils.

I don't think that before or since this weekend I have ever written with less trouble and certainly never with less distinction.

It was necessary, of course, to have a detective and having invented him to give him a name. The day before I began, we had visited Dulwich College Picture Gallery, interested in it, first of all, because my father was an Old Alleynian. I remembered how he had told me about the great Elizabethan tragedian who had founded the school and, of course, at Dulwich there were many references to him. 'Very well,' I thought, 'as a sort of compliment to Popsie I shall call him Alleyn.'

I wrote until late on Sunday night and, from then onwards, regularly in the evenings. The weeks went by and the penny exercise books grew into a pile. One afternoon when I got home from the shop I found my mother reading away at one of them. She took off her spectacles and stared at me with an air that I could not interpret.

'Is it any good?'

Like me she was not a great addict of detective fiction.

'It's *readable*,' she said and rubbed her nose. She gave a singular little half-laugh. 'I couldn't put it down,' she said and I don't know to this day whether I only imagined an overtone of regret in her voice.

I had never shown her or anyone else the beginnings of the New Zealand novel I had laid aside. It was now abandoned for good. I cannot remember what I did with the manuscript: got rid of it in one way or another. I had carelessly left it lying about and had had to listen to it being read aloud in a funny voice, not by a Lamprey. For some reason this had sickened me. It should not have done so to the point of abandonment. I think if the thing had been as insistent and compulsive and as promising as I had imagined I would have swallowed the incident with a certain fury and gone underground with my work. Later on I became quite accustomed to the odd Lamprey child reading what I was writing over my shoulder and shouting: 'Ha-ha-ha, listen to what silly old Ish' (for so they call me) 'has written now,' and even to a Lamprey grand-mama pinching my manuscripts and adding comic bits of her own. This is all good, healthy fun of an Irish inverted-public-school type. It is quite without malice and I daresay it prevents one from getting pompous about one's job. The Lampreys have kind hearts as well as coronets.

I have heard it said that in everyone's life there is a point of no return and if by this is meant any point beyond which one can never repeat certain patterns of behaviour then I think it is true. Perhaps a sudden confrontation with reality in a shape for which one is quite unprepared is not the least shocking way of passing this turning point. I am conscious that as it comes nearer I have tried to put mine off but here it is at last, no longer avoidable.

My mother and I knew, of course, that she would have to return to New Zealand but there was no settled date for this and we had been some months in our flat before my father wrote to say he felt that the time had come when a passage should be arranged.

She was wonderfully good about it. I knew she would like, above everything, for me to return with her but she didn't say so until a short time before she sailed. We looked at each other and I felt a desperate pang of guilt, an agony of compassion when I said I couldn't: that I would come before long but not yet: not now.

My mother stood by the rail with the other passengers and smiled brilliantly as the ship sailed. I returned to the flat and packed everything up for the carrier. I was to go to the Lampreys. When it had all been taken away and I looked at the dismantled room I was visited for the first and last time in my life by a complete emotional breakdown. It lasted, I think, for about three hours and then the Lamprey Nanny came. She always treated me as if I were a sort of extra charge. She rang and then rat-tatted. I had seen her grey cotton ankles and sensible shoes stump past the window and daren't not answer. She was unembarrassing and when I sobbed out that I felt as if I would never see my mother again replied: 'Stuff and nonsense' and made me drink hot milk and promise to come home within the hour.

V

The book was finished and typed. I had been given an introduction to my present agents and had been told that they thought they could place it.

I can never remember exactly how long a time went by but it could only have been about two months, before I had a letter from my mother saying that she was not well and that it might be rather a protracted business. And again I cannot remember how long it was or how many letters we had exchanged before my father cabled to say that she was very ill indeed.

On the third day after this I sailed for New Zealand. I had been in England for nearly five years.

Three months later, on a warm evening, my father and I faced each other across my old schoolroom table and divided between us the letters of sympathy that we must answer.

CHAPTER 10

New Ways

There are people: Chekhovian innocents, simpletons and dedicated bad men of the tyrannical sort, who never reach a condition that could be called maturity but merely arrive at a state of self-repetition. Most of us, however, could point to a time, often long after physical maturity has been reached, and say to ourselves: 'It was then that I, such as I am, grew up.'

My mother's illness, as cruelly and as excruciatingly protracted as if it had been designed by Torquemada, marked I think my own coming-of-age. In turning over the idea of this book I have found myself thinking of any event that might be worth recording as of something that happened before or after that agonized time.

My father and I settled down, I to keep house for him and write detective fiction and he to go on with his secretarial job, his gardening and his tennis. He was extraordinarily young in looks, in vigour and in disposition and was often mistaken, rather provokingly, for my brother. My first book came out. He read it in the old way with his hand shaking and the pipe jiggling between his teeth when he came to the exciting bits. I sometimes felt, that what with his wonderful absences-of-mind, his sudden tempers and his delight in simple achievements, he was more like my child than my papa. But it was not so. When I was least expecting it, he would bring me up with a round turn and make me feel more than a little foolish. We got along very well together.

My second book *Enter a Murderer* was finished. I enjoyed trying to get the smell and feel of backstage. This was a vicarious satisfaction:

I had not yet returned to any work in the theatre but painted a little and with a group of old student friends returned sometimes to
the mountains. My father generally came on these expeditions.
When, during the summer months we built a hut in the Temple
Basin above Arthur's Pass, he carried weatherboarding with the best
of us up steep flanks in a nor'west gale.

One great solace to us both was the return of dear James to New
Zealand and to the house on our hills where he and Cecil and their
devout spinster sister were attended by old family servants in a manner that was surely unique in New Zealand.

During our dark time, Mivvy had come up from Dunedin and
had been with us almost to the end. There was no one else who
could have given us the comfort that she did. When midsummer
came my father stayed with Mivvy and her husband at their fishing
cottage by the lake. They asked me to come, too, but I felt that it
was better for us to be away from each other for a little while before
we settled down. For the first time I was alone in our house on
the hill.

Presently, old associations began to re-assemble themselves.

There were Phyllis, my great student friend, and visits to the
house in South Canterbury and painting expeditions into the back
country. It seems now as if this was a curiously floating sort of time;
a time of recovery. The closest analogy I can think of is the experience of returning from a faint or an anaesthetic.

I was now to become familiar with both these sensations.

Nothing can be more boring than an obsession with one's ail-
ments. There are far too many Ancient Mariners of the operating
table. I shall merely recount that at this point a long-standing disability that hitherto I had contrived to live with, suddenly blew up in a
rather nightmarish fashion and I spent three months in hospital
undergoing a series of minor operations and a final snorter of a
major one. After which I enjoyed such astonishingly improved
health that I could scarcely recognize myself.

It was during my convalescence that I engaged in the only piece
of fiction that I have ever written in collaboration. This was *The
Nursing Home Murder* and my partner in crime was the extremely distinguished Dr Henry Jellett who was a member of the Lamprey
group in the halcyon days and now lived in New Zealand. He had

been one of the two doctors who saw me through my illness. The other was Sir Hugh Acland, a great figure in New Zealand surgery and, with his wife, a very dear friend.

When *The Nursing Home Murder* was finished we thought we would have a shot at dramatizing it and when the play was written, we saw no reason why I shouldn't produce it which I did with a group of experienced amateurs. This was great fun but an undertaking full of hazards. The last act is set in an operating theatre and involves the performance of an appendiectomy. Naturally, my collaborator – I was allowed to call him Papa Jellett – was a stickler for correct techniques. We rehearsed and rehearsed the actors who played the distinguished surgeon, his assistant, the anaesthetist (James) and the nurses, until they all said they would feel perfectly at home with any actual appendicectomy.

Papa Jellett himself made, out of felt, a startlingly realistic false abdomen with an incision and retractors to glut the horrified gaze of the circle. During the performance he sat in the stalls and secreted a small amount of ether. He stationed a genuine, fully-trained theatre sister in the wings to prepare the patient. Loud and frequent, during rehearsals, were our injunctions to the surgeons that if, by hideous chance, one of them should drop a glove he must NOT pick it up but say, 'Glove, Nurse,' in a bossy voice and Bet – the same Bet of Monte Carlo – would bustle up with a sterile replacement.

On the opening night there were many doctors in the audience which was a capacity one.

The performance, though warmly applauded, was not without its pretty disastrous moments. The assistant surgeon dropped a glove. He then picked it up. All the doctors laughed very heartily. Papa Jellett ground his teeth. The fully-trained theatre sister became so wrought up by what she could see of the action from the wings that she excitedly clipped her retractors, if these are the things I mean, into flesh instead of felt and the patient was wheeled on in the most exquisite agony which he had to support throughout the ensuing action while lying (like Miss Carter, the model) in simulated oblivion. Both 'surgeons' were too intent on passing the needle and tying off stitches to heed his muffled entreaties.

When in the earlier stages of this scene Papa Jellett released his ether, the abdomen was uncovered and the incision revealed, a professional actress from an English touring company screamed and fainted and was removed with difficulty from the auditorium.

Dear James ran a hypodermic needle into himself.

In all other respects it really went very well and played to full houses. We thought of sending it to my agent but our attention was drawn to *Men in White*, an American piece in a similar setting and we decided to allow our brainchild to sink into decent oblivion.

It was now that I learned to know the English cousins who had settled in the North Island with their parents. They came down one at a time and stayed with us; three sisters and two brothers. As I have already said, we grew very close to one another. My aunt was the eldest of my father's sisters. It was with her French governess (afterwards unseated in her wits) that her Uncle Julius, it may be remembered, eloped. When I first met my aunt she struck me as being extremely Tennysonian: one felt that she should trail in perpetual slow motion across rectory lawns, wearing a tea gown and a picture hat and carrying a parasol. I soon discovered that she shared, not only my father's 'Spanish' good looks but something of his absence of mind, his sense of fun and his stunning obstinacy. She was also an enthusiastic amateur actress. In the matter of religion, however, they were far from seeing eye to eye, my aunt being almost handwoven from the purest Anglican yarn and my father, as I hope I have suggested, a truculent rationalist.

When I stayed with my aunt we drove over a range of hills to visit Stella the married daughter and her husband and family; a girl and two boys. The elder of these boys was remote and dreamy; a vulnerable child, I thought, and was reminded of my own childhood. The younger was a tough, gay fellow, very alert, with a twinkle in his eye. I was much taken with my young cousins. In a few years the boys were to come down to boarding school in Christchurch and we were to know each other very well and establish a relationship that has been a delight to me. I had sometimes thought I would like to adopt a child. With the coming of the older of these boys I almost felt as if I had done so.

Perhaps, in the first instance, my older cousins and I agreed so well because they were still 'English' and I had been long enough in England to miss it when I returned to New Zealand.

We are often told by English people how very English New Zealand is, their intention being complimentary. I think that this pronouncement may be true but not altogether in the intended sense. We are, I venture, more like the English of our pioneers' time than those of our own. We are doubly insular. We come from a group of islands at the top of the world and we have settled on a group comparable in size but infinitely more isolated, at the bottom of it. We are overwhelmingly of English, Scottish, Welsh and Irish stock and it seemed to me, when I came back after five years, that we had turned in on our origins. You might say, I thought, that if you put a selection of people from the British Isles into antipodean cold storage for a century and a half and then opened the door: we are what would emerge. There have been internal changes but they have not followed those of our islands of origin. And I thought: it is the superficial changes, the things that matter least, which leap most readily to the notice of non-New Zealanders. Our voices and our manners have deteriorated to such an extent that many fourth-generation New Zealanders have a strong, muddled instinct that prompts them to regard any kind of a speech but the indigenous snarl as effeminate and even the most rudimentary forms of courtesy as gush. It is good honest kiwi to kick the English language into the gutter and it shows how independent you are if you sprawl in armchairs when old women come into their own drawing rooms. I refuse to say lounges.

And then, I thought, how complacent we are and yet how uncertain of ourselves! Why do the young ones say so often and so proudly that they suppose New Zealand seems crude and then, if you agree: 'Well, in some ways, perhaps,' why do they look so furious? I had forgotten what we are like, I thought. We really are rum. Or so it seemed to me when I returned.

I remembered that a young Etonian in England had said lightly to me: 'I hear we're not very popular in New Zealand.' I had been surprised by this and had said with perfect conviction that it was not so at all. Many of my friends in New Zealand had been English. My father and grandparents were English: it seemed a ridiculous remark. Now, on my return, I began to think about the bloody pommy thing and to speculate on the kind of within-the-family friction that has developed in my country. I tried to sort these attitudes out.

At once an over-familiar figure appeared: two-dimensionally, as if from the story-page of some early colonial newspaper. He was dressed in worn clothes of impeccable cut, his face showed signs of alcoholic indulgence, his voice was cultured and his manners charming. He was, in fact, the taxi-driver of Durban in the early stages of his decline. The Remittance Man. The chap whose people used the colonies as a wastepaper basket. Sometimes he was 'nobody's enemy but his own' and was treated with compassion. Sometimes he had pale eyes, slightly impudent, an amusing tongue and taking ways. He would stay too long: borrow too often. Sometimes he would not be the scion of nobility that he gave himself out to be and would go too far and land in gaol. Occasionally he would be all that he claimed and still go far too far and land in gaol. He appears from time to time, meets with hospitality and a certain degree of success, and inconsiderable figure though he is, carries far more weight than he should as a 'typical' Englishman. His legend has been, out of all proportion, a damaging one.

I began to wonder if the Remittance Man started our young men off on what they would call their 'independent' social habits. Perhaps. 'Polish is phoney, posh talk hides shifty ingratitude. Don't be polite – it's *plausible*.' Plausible is a deadly word in New Zealand.

And then, of course, there is the English immigrant. New Zealanders tend to take for granted the ninety-nine who settle in their jobs, are good mechanics, labourers, clerks, farmers or professional men. But they are too ready to cite as a prototype the one exception: the neighbour who borrows tools, leaves gates open and doesn't look after his fences. Bloody pommy.

I knew these generalizations were worth very little. I kept remembering how after a few mulish and disgruntled months in Britain my young fellow countrymen would begin to feel their history moving in their veins and would identify with the English scene. I remembered the warmth and intensity of their feeling for London. I contrasted this spontaneous absorption with the intractable way some of the untravelled ones behaved in New Zealand.

The New Zealand-Great Britain ambience is essentially a family affair. It has all the characteristics: the taking-as-read attitude to British ties and the spontaneous outbursts of irritation: the progression in the colonies from original involvement to casual acceptance and from there to adolescent rebellion with an awareness of the bond that exacerbates rather than reduces the conflict. I knew, too, that nothing could be more false than a pretence that the original attitudes have not changed. These are elements in a complex of which the family is a microcosm and the Commonwealth an enlargement.

I thought that, just as children who have been energetically bickering with their parents will close the family ranks with a bang against an outsider, so, if there should be another war, will the average New Zealander behave. But, of course, I thought, uneasily, there will never be another war. This was in 1933.

Like Bully Bottom, I could gleek upon occasion and to no better purpose.

The Arts in New Zealand, particularly the art of writing, have followed much the same pattern of development as the one I have tried to suggest. But whereas with the non-aesthetic New Zealander, the attitudes are instinctive and naïve, the writers have approached problems of their advance to national maturity with extreme self-consciousness, anxious analyses and an intensive and industrious taking-in of each other's washing. They are acutely sensitive to their position, greatly concerned, and rightly so, with the emergency of an indigenous genre but often disinclined to look beyond it for wider standards of comparison.

It is strange, I think, that with this fierce concentration on the New Zealand element, so few of our major writers have concerned themselves in depth with the greatest problem and surely the most interesting aspect of life in New Zealand today: the process of integration between two races and the emergence of many formidable difficulties that must be overcome before we can honestly claim to have realized the intention of our forefathers: that the Maori and Pakeha shall be as one people.

Four years ago, when I was in America and about to be interviewed for radio I realized from a remark inadvertently dropped by the questioner that she had expected me to be dark brown. When I said that I had no Maori blood but would be proud of it if I did, she looked politely incredulous. It did not at once occur to me that my first name had misled her: so many Europeans have Maori names in New Zealand. And then I wondered if ours is the only country where white parents give their children native names. If so, it is perhaps not too fanciful to see in this habit a reflection of the attitude which, however much we may blunder, has been ours from our first entry into these islands.

It is often said that we have no right when colour problems of Britain, Africa or America are discussed to argue from our own experience: it is on too small and insignificant a scale. I think we have every right. The very differences are significant. Our problems of integration, and they are real and cumulative, have developed out of a background of anxious determination to have the Maori people digest almost at one meal, our own slowly evolved habits of thought, behaviour and culture. We are what happens when certain attitudes are adopted towards a stone-age people who, officially, have never been regarded as an inferior race. The frictions and prejudices that undoubtedly exist spring from differences of behaviour and not from past injuries on the scale of the gigantic infamies in America and Africa. We are a picture in miniature of what happens when the dominant race adopts a civilized attitude and, inevitably, blunders from time to time in the efforts to realize its ideals. This seems to me to be wonderful material and it surprises me that it has not been searched in depth by one of our distinguished younger novelists.

On my return to New Zealand after five years, I found myself looking at my own country, however superficially, from the outside, in.

II

From that time until this evening, life has fallen for me into a constant though irregular rhythm. So many years in New Zealand, so many in England or abroad. Half the year in the theatre and half writing detective fiction.

In 1937 I returned for a year to England with Bet and another New Zealand friend. There was a joyful reunion with the Lampreys who were having a crisis, a meeting with Edmund Cork, my agent, and three months in Germany, Austria and Northern Italy. One German incident steps out very clearly from this adventure.

We were becalmed in Beilstein because Bet had pleurisy. It is a mediaeval town no bigger than an English village. It is flawless in its kind. The houses are joined together, there are windows in the roofs and even trees that grow like eyebrows over them. Little cars are drawn by oxen or cows and hay is hauled up and stored in attics. Hard by the little town flows the River Mosel which in those days was crossed by a ferry, propelled by the stream. All the people in Beilstein except the very old and very young worked from dawn to sunset on the vines and came down in the evening dyed a bright cerulean blue with copper sulphate. The oldest couple of all were Frau and Herr Koppel. They lived in two rooms, were very poor and sold stamps, faded postcards and wild strawberries which they gathered in the woods. They were too old for the vines. Koppel is a Jewish name.

We stayed in the house of the leading wine-growers, the widow Lippmann and her son. At one time it was a fortress and belonged to the Metternichs. Herr Lippmann spoke English very slowly and solemnly and was fat and in awe of his mama. I was writing and used to stay up late over my work, sitting out on the terrace among boxes of carnations and night-scented stocks. The river lapped and slapped at the landing and the air was very still, warm and heavy. When his mama had retired for the night, Herr Lippmann sometimes appeared rather timidly with a bottle of wine. One evening, the bottle was encrusted in mud because the Mosel had overflowed twice since that vintage. It was a glorious Bernkastler. Herr Lippmann, after ceremoniously doing a sort of 'Hoch!' thing and clinking glasses, entertained me with a conjuring trick involving a piece of string and a ring. As he had no patter it was all a little laborious. Gramp would have despised it.

By day, river craft carried hoards of *Kraftdurchfreude* up the Mosel. They flaccidly waved their handkerchiefs at nobody in particular, played concertinas and did *Heil Hitler* at the drop of a hat. Some rich people from Mannheim stopped for dinner on their way to a motor rally and the men, who had been prisoners of war in England during the Great War, introduced themselves to us and spent a long time telling us how wonderful was the régime and how you only had to say *Heil Hitler* to a stranger and he would embrace you like a brother. One of them cried a little out of pure fascist sentiment. It was wunderbar – like a miracle – what had happened, and all owing to the Führer. We were embarrassed and made noises. We had been told over and over again how punctual the trains were in Italy all because of the Duce and how clean and honest and joyous everyone was in Germany because of the Führer and how superb we would find the autobahns and autostrade: all because of totalitarianism.

One day, as I was writing on the terrace, I saw two brownshirts. They crossed by ferry and their jackboots made a clatter on the stone steps. Beilstein was noisy in the afternoons. The very small kinder yelled and fought and the old ladies screamed orders at them. German village children are very tough and noisy. Women shouted in neighbourly fashion from upper windows and in the schoolhouse the older children bellowed out a chanted table. 'Ein, zwei, drei – ' while their teacher screeched at them. Now, suddenly, all was quiet except for the sound of shutting doors and approaching jackboots. I went up to the girls' room which overlooked the little market square and we watched from the windows. The two brownshirts tramped in and out of the houses, and the whole of the little town seemed to echo with jackboots. They nailed something up on the notice board and tramped away. The doors opened quietly one by one and sound returned but in a subdued fashion.

That night the bell in the *Rathaus* was rung and all the Beilsteiners collected in the square. The Mayor read a notice and papers were handed out. I can see, now, cerulean fists crushing papers and thrusting them into pockets as the men turn away and go silently indoors.

Next morning I worked on one of the old battlements, approached only by a winding stair inside the wall. Herr Lippmann came out and was so white in the face that I asked him to sit down. We looked at each other across the small iron table and he said in his slow fashion that he believed he could trust me and that it would be a relief to speak. So I heard that yesterday's visitation was about the old Koppels. 'They are to be ostracized. No one is to enter their room or befriend them or speak to them.' They were not clean; they were

Jews. It would be better if there were no Jews contaminating the pure Nordic air of the Mosel. The thing that had been nailed up on the town notice board was a printed diatribe against Jews. '*Juden.*' '*Juden*' '*Juden.*' in black type with a hideous Svengali-like face glaring out of it. Something out of the most debased kind of sadistic comic strip; an obscene thing.

'So now,' said Herr Lippmann, 'they will starve or perhaps they will be taken away in the night. It has happened many times before,' and he told me of dreadful things, all the time looking nervously about him and listening in case there should be anyone on the stairs. He said that in the Metternichs' time they put a Jewish factor in charge of their property in Beilstein and his children married local peasants and thus introduced a dram of Hebrew blood into the community. I read in Herr Lippmann's face what we afterwards saw above his father's name on a gravestone in a hidden plot up in the hills—interlaced triangles.

After this I slept badly. A few nights later at about two o'clock on a stifling morning I heard the unmistakeable tinkle of the Koppels' shop bell and thought: 'Is that it? Have they come for them?' But there were no footsteps. I got up and looked down into the square towards the Koppels' door. A full moon had risen but I stared into an inky pool of shadow. After a time it cleared a little and there emerged the large, hopeless face of Frau Koppel, upturned to the night sky. She kept absolutely still and so did I. As the moon rose its light discovered her face and I suppose that warned her to hide because she went indoors and the bell rang again, very faintly. On several nights after this I heard it and once, a subdued murmur of voices. I think the Haus Lippmann was sending food into the Haus Koppel during the small hours.

Soon afterwards we left Beilstein. On our last day I went for a walk in the woods and by one of those long coincidences that one would never dare to use in a novel, I ran into a fellow New Zealander. He was a hiker – a student type and he was full of enthusiasm for the régime. 'I reckon,' he said, 'they tell you a lot of tripe about this outfit. I reckon it's great. Clean. Honest. Wonderful spirit. And look at the roads – wonderful!'

I returned to New Zealand in the following winter and a year later war was declared.

III

For seventeen years after my mother's death, apart from this journey in 1937, I enjoyed the vague, loving companionship of my
father and we were very happy together. On the whole ours was a
masculine household. For days on end the only other woman in it
was our much-loved housekeeper, Mrs Crawford, who looked after
my father when I was away. Sometimes, as in the old days, Mivvy
came up from Dunedin to stay and sometimes, of course, Phyllis and
other old student-friends, but by and large it was a male establishment with the emphasis on my father's generation rather than my
own.

On Sundays there were the Walker 'boys', James and Cecil (no
longer bearded), in the mornings and again to supper in the
evenings when they were often joined by Papa Jellett and Unk.
There was the same party, as a rule, for dinner on Tuesday nights.
After dinner we played Lexicon which James was dreadfully bad at.

Unk must now be reintroduced. He was my uncle by marriage, a
widower, a geologist of great distinction with wild hair, a startled
eye, a strange nervous manner and a mad disregard for the niceties
of wearing apparel. In these respects he was like a Professor in a
Whitehall farce and he was, I think, one of the most innocent beings
I have ever known. He used to camp out on our interesting volcanic
hills with a fellow savant for days on end adding to the rich sum of
geological research in New Zealand. When my aunt was alive, she
once invited me to look in Unk's rucksack. 'Would you like to see
what your uncle has packed for camping in the back country?'

A hammer, some rocks, a pair of knickerbockers and, tightly
screwed up and rammed into a crevice, his dinner jacket, wrapped
round a pair of hobnailed boots.

On one occasion, when he was to attend an international scientific dinner he fell into even greater sartorial extravagances. Because
some of the visiting scientists had not brought evening dress with
them, a compromise had been arranged. My aunt laid out all the
appropriate garments in Unk's dressing-room and sternly forbade
him to open any drawers or doors when he came in to change. He
was making a bonfire in the garden. She herself was dining out an
an earlier hour than he and she left full of misgivings.

When she returned and looked into his room she found chaos. Clothing littered every surface. All drawers and doors were open and their interiors in hideous confusion. She sorted things out and the conclusion she was obliged to draw from what seemed to be missing was so appalling that she was stricken into a kind of fateful immobility. She waited. At midnight Unk returned like Cinderella. He came through the house, having seen she was at home, shouting 'All right, all right. Very well. Very good. You need say no more.' (She had not uttered.) 'I am perfectly well aware. Very good.' The door opened and he stood shouting on the threshold dressed in the Donegal tweed trousers he kept for bonfires, a Paisley tie, an orphan waistcoat and his tails.

'You need say no more. My attention was otherwise engaged. Very good.'

One of his brother-scientists who knew him pretty well, afterwards told my aunt that about halfway through the party he was seen to be vaguely trying to pull his tailcoat over the lining of his waistcoat and presently, becoming aware of what ailed him, retired behind an armchair from where he upheld an animated conversation with a visiting savant.

His was an entirely different absence-of-mind from that of my father who used to laugh gently at Unk.

My father was particular in his dress and liked to wear a flower in his coat. He could never remember that he was getting at all elderly and remained extremely active, playing tennis until his eightieth birthday when I persuaded him to stop as it really was exhausting him. Soon after this his appendix perforated and Sir Hugh Acland removed it – his last operation before he retired. I could see, to my terror, that everybody except Sir Hugh expected my father to die and indeed he was awfully ill for several days. Thanks, as people say in agony columns, to skilful surgery, to the most devoted nursing and to a constitution that amazed everyone except himself, he recovered and took up bowls. When the war came he joined the Home Guard and ran about the hills hurling hand grenades and throwing himself flat on his face until his doctor forbade it. He then made camouflage nets but insisted upon using his own stitch which led to arguments. I became a Red Cross Transport Driver and did fortnightly duties on a hospital bus and also met returned wounded and drove them home. My male cousins enlisted: Richard, the day war was declared. He spent his last leave with us, wrote gaily from Egypt and died of wounds on Crete.

New Zealanders did not for a moment think there was any immediate threat to their own country. Again, the entire fit manhood of a small population was emptied out of these islands and it was not until after Singapore had fallen that it gradually became certain, as it seemed, that the Japanese would mount a full-scale invasion against us. We began to practise evacuating the hospitals and people built themselves retreats in the foothills. My father dug a funk-hole in the garden. Carried away by the creative urge, he roofed it with enormous pine logs which would have fallen on our heads at the smallest disturbance. We could hear and feel blasting under our hills where, it was rumoured, munitions were being secreted. Tank-stops went up along the Summit Road. A total blackout was imposed and by this time we were quite sure they would come.

A Lamprey cabled to me. 'Don't forget Japanese mothers nurse their children for seven years.'

My father put down four bottles of champagne against the peace but when it came and we opened them, their life had gone. They had been kept too long.

Now that the time has come when I must part with him, I wonder if I have managed to convey anything of my father. He was naïve and he seemed to many people, I daresay, to be a very straightforward, rather comical man, not madly successful in life. He was excitable and in minor crises was inclined to get himself into what my mother called fluffs but he was extraordinarily understanding and there was nothing I could not say to him. Even after his appendix he was able to do quite a lot of things he enjoyed. He played two small character parts in plays I directed. I used to walk round the set every night just before his entrance and there he would be, listening, with his ear at the door, for his cue. He would look at me and his eyes would snap and we would nod happily at each other and on he would go.

It was his heart that played up at last. He detested the disabilities of old age and was bewildered that they should be inflicted upon him. Not long before he died, being at my wits' end for something he could 'do' – old age is like childhood in this respect – I suggested that he might write down some of his considered opinions. He rather took to the idea. I fixed him up with one of my unused manuscript books and a pen and he sat out in the garden. I would look down and see his hand moving across the paper. For a time he wrote collectedly and with excellent precision. Granny Marsh. The Georgian House. Uncle William. South Africa. New Zealand. Marriage. Me. 'Our only child – our daughter: Edith Ngaio.' There was a wonderful broadside at the baleful consequences of organized religion.

And then the excellent clerkly hand began to waver. Sentences are a little confused. One day he looked up at me and said: 'I don't know, darling. This book seems so heavy.' I took it from him. 'Never mind,' I said. 'Never mind.'

It was a great sorrow when he died but there was no bitterness. I missed him dreadfully but wouldn't have had him to go on any longer than he desired. He died in the spring of 1949.

IV

It was strange to be the only one of our little family. To begin with I was desolate. For some years everything (and it was fortunate that writing is a housebound job) had been ordered to meet the condition of having someone increasingly dependent upon me. This was no hardship. With our improving resources I had found understudies, young friends as well as Mrs Crawford, who could take over for a day or two, or on rehearsal nights if I was engaged in the theatre. I had a secretary, Pam, who lived with us and was a great help and solace during my father's illness. She was a graduate of Canterbury University College and her arrival in our household was tied up with a series of ventures that have, I believe, brought greater satisfaction to me than anything else that has come my way. In order to write about them I must go back a little in time.

Immediately before and during the first years of the war, while my father was still extremely active, I had, between books, begun to do a good deal of direction for various *soi-disant* repertory societies in New Zealand. There were no resident professional companies in this country but the leading amateur bodies employed, as they still do, professional directors, staff, secretary, premises and theatres. The name repertory is an accepted misnomer since none of these highly developed societies ever presents a repertoire. They offer perhaps as many as seven separate major productions at intervals during the year and depend largely upon their membership to keep them solvent. Many of them play safe with box-office successes from England or America but most are prepared to risk one or two rather more venturesome pieces to appease the intelligentsia in their audiences and satisfy immortal longings in the odd administrative breast.

I was rewarded from time to time with pieces of this sort. Whenever I accepted such an engagement I would suggest a Shakespeare play and as often as I did so was met by little plaintive cries of refusal. I even offered to do them for nothing but the reaction, though wistful, was the same. People still talked about Allan Wilkie and about a tour of *Macbeth* with Dame Sybil Thorndike and Sir Lewis Casson, but they said things were different now: nobody wanted Shakespeare. A generation had grown up since then and another was on its way and none of them had ever seen Shakespeare. I could well believe that most of them had learned quietly to hate him since there are not many teachers of English literature like our Miss Hughes.

One day, in the third year of the war, two young men came to see me. They were undergraduates of the University of Canterbury, as it now is. Then, it was a college of the University of New Zealand. Their Drama Society, they said, had fallen into the doldrums. They had no money, no membership and no actors and they asked me to produce *Outward Bound* for the hell of it. I said I would.

With members of the cast liable to disappear overnight into the armed forces, we had a stiff time of it rehearsing this piece. Dear James came in to stop a particularly large gap and somehow or another the play was mounted. It was the first time I had worked with students and I found them extraordinarily congenial. They were arrogant, opinionated, sometimes mannerless and not always dependable: they were, in fact, New Zealand undergraduates – a turbulent lot. Of course, they were entirely uninformed about theatre techniques: no material could have been more raw or less perturbed by its own condition. Having no settled faults or mannerisms to correct, they started from zero and being extremely intelligent were soon passionately concerned with dramatic principles. Their gluttonous appetite for work and responsiveness under a hard drive were a constant amazement and their loyalty, once a relationship had been established, heartening above words. Their little theatre quivered with vitality.

It struck me, about halfway through rehearsals, that for all the appalling gaucheries, there were dynamic elements here that were not being exploded by the effective but slightly dated piece of whimsy they had chosen as their play. This production was followed by others very well directed by the professor of classics which I watched with great interest. When, the following year, the students again asked me to work with them I said I would if the play was *Hamlet*. They at once agreed.

I find it hard to write without extremism of the sense of release and fulfilment that suffused the time that followed. The only comparable experience, it occurs to me, is that moment with which I began this book, a moment of pure and recognized happiness when I embraced a honeyed tree.

That is not to say that all went smoothly with *Hamlet*. Not at all. There were nights, during the early rehearsals, when I thought: we must never, *never* ask an audience to sit through this mutilation.

Nowadays I wonder at my own temerity. How did I dare? With a totally inexperienced cast, ignorant not only of Shakespearean acting but of acting, full stop. Uninstructed in the simplest of stage techniques; enormous creatures some of them were, who would stand in front of each other, crowd into straight lines, teeter, speak out of the corners of their mouths and leave great gaps between speech and speech while they shifted weight from one foot to another.

As rehearsals went on, by the way, I discovered that rugby analogies could be very helpful and I used one of them, I am told, with merciless frequency. In trying to give these large, ardent creatures a sense of orchestration, to persuade them that Shakespearean dialogue is not a series of disconnected speeches but a matter of concerted passages, I used to tell them to imagine that they must build such passages up to their point of climax like halfbacks executing a passing rush towards the goal. There must be no meaningless pauses between speech and speech. If they occur the ball is dropped, the movement loses its impetus and the play comes to grief. No. The dialogue must pass cleanly from player to player with mounting tension until, at the moment of climax, it is clapped down between the goalposts.

By such images did the cast begin to think constructively of team-work, of the play as a whole, and, within this structure, to develop their individual roles with the aptitude I've already described.

Actually the footballers often got off to a better start than the 'intellectuals'. Some of these were enjoying a difficult adolescence, suffered from acne and Freudian elaborations and were gloomily inclined to sit about staring at one and to raise foolish observations in order to show how different they were. But after a time, and with any luck, they too would begin to accept the enormous challenge of a Shakespeare play and their own real importance, if only as spear-carriers, in doing so.

Apart from the basic fault of the unpregnant pause the students had no notion of the importance of phrasing, of concerted playing, of realizing the text in terms of movement or of thinking about it as a whole with a certain shape which must be broken down into movements within movements, minor points of climax among major ones, passages of mounting anticipation, of suspension and of rest. It was the old business of rhythm and form. I heard the Wilkie company twenty years ago, rehearsing on an autumn morning:

'Good morning, Mrs Hope.'

'Good morning, Mrs Jack.'

And now:

'Who's there?'

'Nay, answer me. Stand and unfold yourself.'

Is there anything to equal the moment when the thing happens: when suddenly there is ice in the air and the voices are lonely and apprehensive, when the superb pulse begins to thump and there we are on the battlements at Elsinore?

We played it in modern dress. I wanted, first of all, to get rid of Eng. Lit. and say to the players themselves and then to whatever audiences we might win: 'This is an immediate affair, it happens now and all the time. The predicament is ours.' There was a terrible shortage of all kinds of fabrics at that stage of the war and what material there was, was strictly rationed. We could not in any case have raised the wherewithal to dress this play in elderly Peter Pan or any other of the 'costume' conventions. As it was, I recollect, the King's dress tunic was made from baby's nappy cloth. His military aides-de-camp were dressed in such items of my father's and other volunteer officers' regimentals as had escaped the moth. The result was regrettably Ruritanian but the best that could be achieved.

Hamlet was played by an Englishman, nineteen years old when rehearsals began, who was completing his education in New Zealand. He was lame and of shortish stature with a resonant voice and a look in his face that theatre people recognize as that of an actor and call 'star quality'. His performance, by any standard, was remarkable. If it had not been for his physical disability he would, I am sure, have become an actor of great distinction. The Laertes, now a judge, was then a law student. He, too, had a voice of beauty and a sensitive and searching approach to his part. I was fortunate in these two young players.

We rehearsed for eight weeks and very intensively. At first I tried to mix hospital-bus-driving with *Hamlet* but was finally given leave of absence on cultural grounds.

Nothing binds human beings together more quickly than theatrical endeavour provided all is well in the company and the feeling of emergence and growth persists. These rehearsals were blessed with that feeling. The company, or so I like to believe, was visited by a sense of discovery and involvement and perhaps with something of the same exhilaration that rewards the successful learner on skis. They said, and they could have said nothing else that would have pleased me half so well, that the play was coming alive in their mouths, that it was 'real'. They willingly subjected themselves to an intensive cramming in basic techniques and to perpetual correction and an iron discipline. It seemed to me that, within the time allowed us, my best bet was to tell them as plainly as possible what I felt about the play, discuss this with them, listen, but not interminably, to any argument that seemed to be valid and then set the thing up in terms of concerted work, controlled and well-marked tempi and vivid movement. Upon that basis, I hoped, an honest and 'theatrely' realization of character could be built and the truth about the play in some measure discovered and conveyed.

From the toughest rugby player to the most owlish of the intellectuals, from the ferociously brooding adolescent to the mildest of the white mice, there was a superb response from the cast. For my part, I loved them heartily for taking fire as they did and was most grateful, as I still am, to those odd, responsive creatures for all the adventures upon which we have embarked together.

The Little Theatre at Canterbury College had been built as an assembly hall in the early days of the Province. It was in a style of architecture that we slightingly refer to as 'Dominion Gothic'. It had a little gallery, a raftered ceiling and the arms of the College above the proscenium. Sir James Shelley, an English professor of education who had been very active in university drama, had caused good lighting and an excellent cyclorama to be mounted. There was scarcely any room offstage and actors making a quick exit were prone to crack their skulls on a door lintel and then fall five feet sheer into a psychology cubicle. One could tumble backcloths but not fly them and the total depth, including the apron, must have been less than twenty-five feet. Crossing from prompt to OP was effected by squeezing through a filthy passage between the back of the cyclorama and the rear wall.

The seating accommodation was, lawfully, two hundred but we were known to cram in two hundred and fifty. As will be shown later this, potentially, was a dangerous practice.

With all its terrifying limitations, the Little Theatre had great character and an authentic atmosphere. As the rehearsal period went by I grew to curse and love it on equal impulses.

The Hamlet came to stay with us on the hills. He and James (who played the Ghost) and I would return exhausted after an intensive rehearsal, devour eggs and bacon in the kitchen at midnight and, talking in whispers so as not to disturb my father, would hammer out the problems of the moment. It was a glowing hazardous time.

Of all the plays in the Shakespearean canon, it seems to me, there is most conspicuously in *Hamlet*, an element that, not so much contradicts as it stands apart from, theory, research, comment and derogation. This is the singular flavour of Hamlet himself. It has been argued, and with much reason and any amount of textual support, that the Prince of Denmark is fat and flabby, amoral, a supreme egoist, cruel, rude, treacherous, subtle, and an idiotic bungler. He may be all of these things but it is difficult to imagine a performance by an actor who concentrated solely upon one or more of these aspects. If Charles Laughton who was fat, flabby, ugly and a superb actor, had elected to play Hamlet entirely in terms of the reverse side of the character, what would have happened? A fascinating speculation! Would his audiences not have come away exclaiming: 'But awful as he was you couldn't help liking him'? No actor as good as Laughton could have uttered certain lines without releasing the Hamlet magic. That the playwright himself saw Hamlet as an adorable prince is, to me at least, indisputable. Shakespeare knew, as so many of his commentators do not, that one is attracted to people, not by their virtues, but by that unfairest of all qualities – charm.

Our young Hamlet, in spite of the physical difficulty of his lameness, had the right ingredients: edge, rancour, intelligence, a quivering sensitivity and a certain wry sweetness. At first he was all over the place: unable to make his voice speak his thoughts, going full blast and arriving nowhere but presently the thing itself began to happen and here was an actor.

Two pieces of great good fortune befell us. The music for the production was written by Douglas Lilburn, then a young composer coming into full flower. Players were rehearsed. The violinist, Maurice Clare, at that time in New Zealand, heard Lilburn's music and with wonderful generosity offered to lead the group. So we had sounds that sent our hearts into our mouths, sounds that before the clock struck twelve and the curtain rose on Elsinore, spoke of the cold small hour and an unquiet spirit.

Suddenly, the dress rehearsals were upon us. Strangely enough, I remember little in detail about them except that the first one threw us all into despair. The pace, attack and vitality which had seemed to be established, faltered and wavered. There were longueurs. There were deflations. I blasted away like a furnace and then said all the things about 'bad dress, good opening'. We had two more and then, with the atmosphere almost giving off sparks like a cat's fur, we opened to a full house.

It must be remembered that for twenty years there had been no professional Shakespeare in this place.

Let me describe one performance. Three youths unable to get seats have climbed up into the rafters and straddled a beam. Someone is sitting on the top of the electrician's box in the auditorium.

The theatre is inside the university and upstairs. The Christchurch fire board has not yet concerned itself with our activities but we have had a complaint from the police about queues outside the booking office. The play has begun and I watch from the prompt corner. Opposite me, caught in reflected light from the acting area, a young man stands with his arms resting on the edge of the stage. When the players come close to him he draws back his hands but otherwise is immovable. I suppose he has effected an entrance by some unlawful means and has no seat. His face is extraordinarily intent and alive. Watching him, I think that the spirit of Bankside has come to life in New Zealand. So rapt, might have stood some young gentleman from the Inns of Court or a journeyman apprentice with arms akimbo on the apron stage of the Globe. It gives me great delight to watch this young man in the still, packed little house.

Theatre people are generally disposed to refrain from understatement when recounting a success and this is very natural in so hazardous an occupation. Surprise and relief as much as vainglory release our tongues when we succeed and surprise was our first reaction to the reception of *Hamlet*. I was much taken aback when, on the day after we opened, a tailor ran out of his shop and wrung my hand. 'The whole town's talking about it,' he said, and indeed, it soon appeared that he did not greatly exaggerate. Well then: 'let me speak proudly' of these student-players.

This was the beginning of an association that has lasted for twenty years. For me it has been a love affair.

Hamlet was twice revived and the following year we embarked on *Othello*. Somehow I contrived in the intervening months to write another book and take my turn at driving the hospital bus.

A strong nucleus from *Hamlet* was still at the university when we cast *Othello* and these players were now technically much better equipped. The ex-Laertes gave a sensitively realized performance as the Moor while Hamlet moved confidently into Iago. Under intensive and strictly disciplined rehearsal the company began to take up an attitude nearer to that of the professional than the amateur theatre. We had an extremely tough, capable, and rather arrogant stage-crew, most of them science or engineering students, who would try anything once and usually bring it off by a system of ferocious argument, terrifying rudeness and immense resource and expertise. I had the greatest confidence in them. We kept our respective tempers rather better than might have been expected and in the ripeness of time developed a mutual respect and affection.

Othello met with the same kind of reception as *Hamlet*. It became clear that, even if we extended our season for a longer period than the college authorities would stomach, we would still be unable to meet the box-office demands.

It was at this junction that a member of our executive who is now an administrator in the South Pacific, was seized with the notion of a tour in the long vacation. To this end he secured an interview in Auckland with Mr D. D. O'Connor, the *régisseur* who afterwards brought Stratford-upon-Avon and the Old Vic out to Australasia.

There followed a hectic period of suspense and then an offer from Mr O'Connor. He had been making enquiries and was prepared to tour *Hamlet* and *Othello* through the main cities during the long vacation. He would like, however, to see a rehearsal and would fly down if one could be arranged.

The Little Theatre was in use for examinations so we hired a room in town and set up our rostra in it.

It was a hot summer night when Mr O'Connor arrived. My great monsters sat on benches round the room in their shirt sleeves, looking as if butter wouldn't melt in their mouths. Elsinore rebuilt itself in a bare room under naked office lamps.

So it came about that after twenty years I was on the road again in New Zealand: this time with my own company.

New Zealand has a great many Edwardian and Victorian theatres, some in decent repair and others shedding dead paint like dandruff from old cloths that stealthily disintegrated in the flies. For this tour we played for the most part in the concert chambers of town halls. They could scarcely be less helpful to theatrical endeavour. In Auckland, in sub-tropic conditions, we had to keep the windows shut because of the noise of tramcars in the street. They were opened in the single interval and heavy, tepid air from outside dawdled into the steambath generated by a packed and sweating audience.

From the day the company began to work under full professional conditions, rehearsing in the mornings and with these rehearsals their sole concern, the temper and quality of the productions hardened and at the same time gained in flexibility, teamwork and control. In Auckland the actors had reached their full stature and were playing very freely and with great delight. One performance of *Hamlet* I remember vividly.

We did not take a formal curtain call. The actors, in single file, crossed the stage silhouetted against a blue cyclorama and that was all. On this night, as always, the house lights went up as soon as the curtain fell on this procession. The applause went on and on. The players, most of them, had gone to their dressing-rooms but the young Hamlet who had given that night the best performance of the tour, sat on the steps of the rostrum and cried like a schoolboy. This, no doubt, was a release, a kind of unwinding.

The applause continued.

'What's the matter with them?' said the stage director. 'Haven't they got homes?' At last it petered out. Hamlet sheepishly got up, grinned and said he couldn't think why he was such a bloody fool. Somebody gave him a grease towel and he began to remove his make-up.

'All right. Clear,' said the stage director. He looked through the curtain to make sure the house had emptied and drew back quickly. At the same time the applause started again, rose like a hailstorm and persisted. They were still sitting out there, almost the whole lot of them. In the end we had to reset the lights and parade as many of the company as were presentable. I have not known this happen on any other occasion in the theatre.

This tour was followed by a production of *A Midsummer Night's Dream* in midwinter when for part of the rehearsal period the fairies tripped winsomely in unheated premises with one of our extremely rare falls of down-country snow lying thick outside. Then *Henry V.* Then *Macbeth*, first in Christchurch in a larger theatre and later again on tour, under Mr O'Connor's banner. Precarious though its structure was and will always be, the student society had now established itself as a dramatic force in New Zealand.

In the last year of his life when my father grew more dependent upon me, I did not direct a play for the society but held a short production course of one-night-a-week exercises. From these and out of the accumulated experience of three years, a group of student directors emerged. They did some excellent work. One of them, John Pocock, now a distinguished historian, directed a most beautiful and moving production of *The Axe*, a play by the New Zealand poet, Allen Curnow. A student director who had not been concerned in my production, tackled *Venice Preserved* and made an excellent job of it. Later, he worked for the BBC. *Dr Faustus* was produced and *The Way of the World*. A group of three tackled an act apiece of Sartre's *The Flies*. There was a short season of one-acters. The standard throughout was lively and intelligent. The Little Theatre in those days was a quick forge and working house of thought.

These developments delighted me. I saw our group of young directors going forward under its own steam, with the Little Theatre becoming at once a training centre and a house for experimental plays. New approaches would be made by actors of integrity. Perhaps, I thought, it will be from here, who knows, that a professional theatre will at last emerge in New Zealand or, if not that, amateur actors who, being fully aware of the problems, stresses and technical demands of the stage, are prepared to play dangerously.

It was not long after my father's death that Mr O'Connor brought the Old Vic to New Zealand with Laurence Olivier and Vivien Leigh. I have recorded already the impact of *Richard III* and the honourable destination of Kean's coat. The student-players were, of course, much excited by this visit. They carried spears, they ushered, and as I and my fellow art students had done (long ago, now) they waited in queues, some of them all night, to get tickets. About three weeks before the company arrived we received a staggering request. Would we entertain them in the Little Theatre to a supper after the play and would we show them something of our work?

Putting, as far as one could, all thoughts of Bully Bottom and his tedious brief chronicle right out of mind, and refusing to cast Sir Laurence for the role of Theseus, I set feverishly to work. There was a certain new and most promising glitter in our minuscule firmament, a female one this time, Brigid Lenihan, who as an exercise in my production course, had worked with Bernard Kearns, one of our best men-players, on the first act of my obsession: *Six Characters in Search of an Author*. We plumped for this, built up as strong a cast as we could raise at short notice and rehearsed as if the devil was after us.

In the event, the performance was rough but not too bad and encouraging noises were made by our distinguished guests. This golden night in the Little Theatre was followed by a golden offer from Mr O'Connor. How would we like a tour of three Australian cities in January? Two plays would be called for. What about reviving *Othello* and completing *Characters*?

It is tedious to elaborate success stories. I shall take no more than a glance or two at our Australian venture. Here we all are on the trans-Tasman steamer, much excited, greatly possessed of that sense of partnership inseparable from all well-augured enterprise in the theatre. We have runs-through for lines on the boat deck, we re-learn about each other as travelling companions, we tingle with anticipation but maintain a cool and hardy demeanour.

With rehearsals called at 10.30 every morning over the past six weeks, the company has become fully integrated, has developed, I think I may say, a responsible, dedicated and mature attitude to the work in hand. We are all very conscious of this and try not to look astonished when movie cameras move in on us as we land at Sydney and there are press conferences.

The Australian press is, with several most honourable exceptions, opportunist, pseudo-American, curiously naïve and fairly impertinent. 'Now, the great big smile' they chant, aiming their cameras. Their picture pages champ with so many great big smiles, willingly or reluctantly induced, that one recalls with an involuntary shudder, the interior of some dental mechanic's cabinet.

Representatives of the press attended our rehearsals. They were amiable young men who said they would like to have some action pictures. Would I, they suggested, lie flat on my stomach on the stage with my elbows on the production script while members of the company, all with the great big smile, hung tenderly over me? Did I smoke? Yes, in those days I did, but was not, as it happened, smoking at that moment. Very well, would I light a cigarette? Just stick it in the mouth and let it dangle. I did murmur that it was not my practice to take rehearsals smoking from a prone position on a dirty stage but no attention was paid. Publicity is publicity, I reminded myself, and disregarding the covert grins and snide comments of my company, I lay down and lit a cigarette. The lights flashed. Next day the picture appeared with a bold caption. 'Ngaio (Nio) Marsh, eccentric

Maoriland novelist-producer. Lies on stage for rehearsals. Chain smoker.'

Mr O'Connor told us that for the first three performances the audiences would be thinnish and after that he expected a rapid build to full houses. He was right in this but one thing that neither of us anticipated was that part of the *Othello* wardrobe, together with the new dinner suit of Bob, our business manager, and travellers' cheques belonging to one of the actors should all be stolen from the theatre on the eve of our opening performance. It was never discovered who served us this scurvy trick although strange and fantastically improbable stories of professional resentment were brought to us.

We would have found ourselves in a pretty pass if Miss Doris Fitton's Independent Theatre had not come nobly to our rescue with handsome replacements.

The press notices made us blink. The players were compared, and favourably, with the Old Vic. Ecstatic praise was lavished upon teamwork, voices, attack and, particularly upon Biddy Lenihan. One couldn't believe one's eyes. It really was, we agreed, trying to keep the sickly grins from creeping over our faces, a bit too thick. 'You are not,' I said to the cast, 'anything like as good as all that,' and they replied: 'No, Mum' which was a form of address they had adopted and which had already been nauseatingly exploited by a gossip columnist.

Characters met with the same reception, or, indeed, rather more so. This had proved to be a good choice for student-players. Their intelligence, instinctive iconoclasm and command of pace were enormous assets. Sustained by buoyancy and lack of experience they actually welcomed rather than doubted the technical demands made by the play. It opens with a Commedia dell'arte gambit. Pirandello merely tells us that a company of actors is assembling for rehearsal and leaves the rest to the director. I wrote some five pages of dialogue as a framework upon which the players could improvise and between us we built a scene of preparation lasting about eight minutes up to the entry of the 'Manager' and the beginning of Act I as it is printed. It is a play that generates excitement. The theatre thrums and pulses with it – if this didn't happen at the outset the production would be a failure. It did happen, now. Every night I went out in front to get the feel of the house when those six black-clothed baleful persons were suddenly exposed and every night there was the same little miracle.

We played Sydney, Melbourne and Canberra. Before the end of the tour, Dan O'Connor made a new suggestion. He asked me if I would like to produce a company assembled in London from Commonwealth players and bring them out to Australia.

I accepted this offer.

CHAPTER 11

Exercise Heartbreak and Recovery

I returned to England in the summer of 1950. The Second War was over. Nearly thirteen years had gone by since I had seen the Lampreys. That is a long time. The children were all grown up and three of them had married. I did not at first recognize the tall blond young man who, with his elder brother, met us at Southampton. He was my godson.

Pam, my student-player-secretary, was with me. We had travelled in comparative grandeur and with her assistance I had written a largish chunk of a book. She was to go through the Production Course at the Old Vic Drama School. Another great New Zealand friend, Bob, who had been business manager on the student-players Australian tour, was also at that admirable, and ever to be regretted, school. He and Elizabeth, his wife, and I had settled to share a flat in London while preliminary investigations were made for the projected tour of which he was to be the business manager and stage director. After an interlude in apartments owned by an intimidating prima donna and furnished in a style that fluctuated balefully between that of a superior fortune-teller's parlour and an interior by Mauriac, we found an unfurnished flat in, of all streets, Beauchamp Place, and actually next door to the second premises rented by Charlot and me in our shopkeeping days. We furnished it mostly from junk picked up in or near the Fulham Road.

This flat was over an enchanting clock shop. During the night I could hear minuscule chimes, single tinkling bells, a gong, musical-box confections and the punctual wheelhorse observations of a dependable grandfather. There was even a French clock that tootled a little silver trumpet. 'There they go,' I would think, 'busy as bees all by themselves through the night.' It was like the setting for a Victorian fairy tale—by Mrs Molesworth of course.

I spent as much time as I could with Charlot. Our old quartette was now only a pair. Much of the past was to be unrolled, looked at and put gently away again. She was keeping house for the head of her family. I found the children were for me as they had always been, dearer than any others.

The head of the family had taken a house at Eze on the heights above Monte Carlo: a converted Saracen stronghold, we were told, carved into the cliff-face. Charlot and I joined his house party there for a fortnight and then, since the alpine atmosphere did not agree with her, came down to our old hotel, and, for a few days, revived old goings-on.

On the way back we stopped in Paris where I met my French agent, Marguerite Scieltiel. We breakfasted at her flat and then I signed a contract and was photographed in the act, and again in a raging gale, emerging incomprehensibly from police headquarters under the ironical scrutiny of the gendarme on guard.

It is always a surprise when I leave my own country to find myself 'known' elsewhere: I feel like a Willy Loman whose vapourings have turned out to be factual. If I have any indigenous publicity value it is, I think, for work in the theatre rather than for detective fiction. Of course, whenever I return to New Zealand I am always asked to write articles saying what I think about it *now* and even, on exceptional occasions, what I think about William Shakespeare, but seldom what I think about crime stories. This is just as well as there is a limit to what can be written under that heading. Intellectual New Zealand friends tactfully avoid all mention of my published work and if they like me, do so, I cannot but feel, in spite of it.

So it was astonishing, this time in England, to find myself broadcasting and being televised and interviewed and it was pleasant to find detective fiction being discussed as a tolerable form of reading by people whose opinion one valued. I suppose the one thing that can always be said in favour of the genre is that inside the convention the author may write with as good a style as he or she can command. As witness, for an instance, Michael Innes's wonderful *Lament for a Maker.* The mechanics in a detective novel may be shamelessly contrived but the writing need not be so nor, with one exception, need the characterization. About the guilty person, of course, end-less duplicity is practised.

In the seventeenth century the 'metaphysical' poets fitted their verse into diamonds, hearts and triangles. The convention was a silly one but within their self-imposed limits they occasionally contrived some pretty conceits. To do as much in his own medium is the aim of many a crime writer of the orthodox sort.

In London, my time was divided between prospecting for the new theatre company and finishing the current book: *Opening Night.* This was typed by another ex-student secretary who is assisting also in the preparation of this one.

The idea behind the British Commonwealth Theatre Company was, as its title suggests, a synthesis of players from Great Britain and the several arms of the Commonwealth, as it was then constituted. We were to try ourselves out in Australia and New Zealand and, upon the results of this tour, decide whether to continue and extend the venture.

In the meantime Bob and I poured over *Spotlight,* that vast *vade mecum* of the stage with its countless so-professional photographs: full-page and grandly taciturn for the stars, progressively smaller and more anxiously informative with the diminishing status of the entrants. We visited repertory theatres in many places, we inter-viewed actors and actresses from South Africa, Canada, Australia, New Zealand and India. We became accustomed though never, I think, reconciled to the heartbreaking sales talk that must not seem to be what it is: an airy cover for a chronic occupational anxiety. We tried to come to terms with the strange unbalance between talent and demand in what is perhaps the most over-populated profession in the world. I suppose that, every time a new play is cast in Great Britain or America, there are at least thirty adequate, unemployed players available for each part. Any one of these will give a sound enough performance and yet how difficult it is to cast a play to one's satisfaction. Harder still, as we gradually discovered, to form a company under the too exacting conditions we had set ourselves: a company in which each member should be a better than adequate representative of his country of origin, versatile, of satisfactory appearance, a good trouper, a reasonable being and prepared to leave Great Britain for at least six months.

While Bob and I were still engaged in this daunting pursuit the Embassy Theatre at Hampstead, under Molly May's management, decided to produce a comedy-thriller by Owen Howell based upon *Surfeit of Lampreys*. The Embassy was a club theatre running seasons of three weeks only. Mr Howell's play might well have succeeded but it did not do so, largely I think because the Lamprey flavour, present in his dialogue, was sadly missing in the production, which was much too heavy-going. The set was extremely lugubrious.

Not long after this disappointment Molly May, having heard something of our Australian tour with *Six Characters*, asked me to produce the play for her own management. I was given an excellent cast with Yvonne Mitchell and Karel Stepanac in the leads. We had only a fortnight's intensive rehearsal, at the beginning of which period I was struck down with a virulent attack of Asian influenza and a temperature of 102. A doctor, whose spouse was in the show, kept me on my feet with M and B's at night and benzedrine by day. I used to wonder, each morning, how on earth I was going to see the next eight hours' work through. I had changed much of the original production and I asked a great deal of my cast in the way of pace, attack and understanding. They responded nobly to what I cannot but think must have been strangely trance-like direction.

The Hampstead audiences were largely Jewish and continental: warm and big. The whole experience was heartening. Not that I saw much of it. I watched the opening night in a curiously unreal, floating condition, having eaten nothing but one raw egg a day for some considerable time. I then crawled to bed and later to Brighton and a wan recovery with Miss May for company. She, too, had been smitten by this beastly bug.

This illness left me with a chronic legacy which has been a great bore and which added in no small degree to the difficulties of the year that followed.

The Festival of Britain was in preparation. Miss May asked me to direct a season of English comedy at the Embassy throughout the summer. We were, however, to leave for Australia before the Festival opened so I had to say no.

At about this time another and, to me, most beguiling project was considered by Dan O'Connor. At Woolwich there was a theatre that had received bomb damage and not been repaired. The idea was that, if it could be made usable, a Shakespeare season should be held there during the Festival of Britain. Audiences would be able to 'take water to the play' going downstream by barge from Westminster Pier. One sparkling spring morning Tyrone Guthrie (he was not yet knighted), his wife, Bob and I, all went down the river to inspect this theatre. It was the gayest of jaunts. Tony Guthrie was in the middle of producing *The Barber of Seville* in a lovely liquorice-all-sort kind of setting and he and Judy sang bits of it all the way. We picked up the keys of the theatre at a pub and let ourselves in. The damage was extensive. 'No good, dear,' said Tony Guthrie after one glance at it. 'What a pity! Never mind.' So it was us for the antipodes, after all.

On an early March morning Bob, Mizzy, his wife, and I stood together on the deck of the steamer that carried us, with our company, to Australia. A light mist was already dissolving and the sun shone delicately over the Thames estuary. 'It's going to be a lovely spring day in London,' we said.

The six months that followed seem in retrospect to have had something of the character of one of those dreams that rocket to and fro between horror and reassurance. We opened in Sydney with *The Devil's Disciple*, a play that grew colder and colder in my hands the more I tried to blow some warmth into it. Dissonances of all sorts broke out in the company, the houses faded, gnawing anxiety and depression settled upon us. After eight weeks a decision was taken to tour New Zealand with *Twelfth Night*, a revival of *Six Characters* and *The Devil's Disciple*. As soon as we began to work on the new plays, the temper of the company changed and lightened. My health by this time was becoming increasingly groggy but I managed to keep this circumstance to myself and rehearsals prospered. *Twelfth Night* seemed to work its own miracle. We gave it a Watteau-like setting with delicate pavilions, striped silk awnings and a flowery swing in which the young Olivia dreamed her silly-billy fantasies. Biddy Lenihan in gallant blue made a darling of Viola. Feste, all frill and Watteau-esque stripes, was enchantingly realized by John Schlesinger. This admirable actor was already beginning to turn his attention towards film-making. Frederick Bennet, an excellent

Shakespearean, was a toby-jug Toby with a touch of elegance and breeding, and Peter Howell, later of *Emergency Ward 10* fame and later still in the cast of *The Affair* was a nicely batty Aguecheek. Peter Varley made a wonderful praying mantis of Malvolio.

Three years later the editor of *Shakespeare Survey No. 8*, the annual that is published in Stratford-upon-Avon, asked me to write an account of this production. I venture to re-introduce it here because it defines, as adequately as I could contrive, my feelings about the presentation of Shakespeare's comedies.

A Note on a Production
Of Twelfth Night

Each decade creates its own fashions in Shakespeare and only actors of distinction can survive them. The Shakespearean costumes of Macready's stage now 'date' almost as markedly as the crinoline itself. Is it not probable, moreover, that if we could look through the wrong end of our opera glasses at the Lyceum of the 1880s, the mannerisms of the lesser players would make us titter while Ellen Terry or even Irving would still command our applause? In the portrait of Garrick as Lear the authentic look of madness in his eyes effaces the oddness of his wig and costume. One is able to believe that his performance, if we could see and hear it, would transcend the mannerisms of his period.

Fashions in acting and presentation are as extreme as those that control the garments worn by the actors. The points of view held by producers, critics, actors and designers are forever changing: there is a feverish anxiety in our theatres to keep up with, or better still, anticipate the mode. It is in the presentation of Shakespeare's comedies that this kind of stylistic snobbism is seen at its extremity and it is about an attempt to escape from fashion that I propose to write, with specific reference to the comedy of *Twelfth Night*.

The modern producer of Shakespeare's comedies believes himself to be up against a number of difficulties. Much of the word-bandying is, he says, disastrously unfunny while many of the allusions are obscure and some so coarse that it is just as well that they are also incomprehensible. He must cut great swathes out of his script and for the rest depend on eccentric treatment, comic 'business' funny enough in its own right to amuse the audience while the words may look after themselves. If he is honest he dreads the obligatory laughter of the Bardolators as much as he fears the silence of unamused Philistia. These are reasonable fears, and, in my opinion, he does well to entertain them.

There are, however, contemporary producers who in their search for a new treatment of an old comedy forget to examine the play as a whole and fall into the stylistic error of seizing upon a single fashionable aspect of a subtle and delicate work and forcing it up to a point of emphasis that quite destroys the balance of production.

In 1951 it fell to my lot to produce *Twelfth Night* with a company of British actors on tour in the antipodes. As soon as I was made aware of my fate I began to look back at the many productions I had seen of this comedy. Some had been by distinguished producers with famous companies, others by repertory theatres and touring companies like my own. Of them all, the best, it seemed to me in retrospect, had been the simplest; the least pleasing, the most pretentious; and the most pretentious, those in which producers, actors and designers had apparently exchanged glances of dismay and asked each other what they could do to put a bit of 'go' into the old show. They had done much. There had been star Malvolios and star Violas. There had been remorseless emphasis on a single character or sometimes on a single scene. The words had been trapped in the net of a fantasticated style, lost in a welter of comic goings-on, coarsened by cleverness or stifled by being forced out of their native air. I had seen Andrew wither into a palsied eld, Malvolio as a red-nosed comic and Feste, God save the mark, as bitter as coloquintida or the Fool in *Lear*. I had seen productions with choreographic trimmings and with constructivist backgrounds. I had, however, missed the production on skates.

It seemed to me that my best, indeed my only chance, was to put aside everything that I had seen, forget if possible the current fashions in *Twelfth Night* and start humbly with the play itself. It is, after all, a very good play. If I venture now to retrace this production of *Twelfth Night*, it is with the hope that in doing so it may be possible to examine some of the problems of its presentation. Because it is also a very difficult play.

As I read it again I saw that in his story Shakespeare shows us the several aspects of love. He begins with Orsino's romantic absorption with the idea of loving the inaccessible Olivia and repeats this theme, burlesqued, in Malvolio's assumption that Olivia loves him. This in turn modulates into Olivia's completely unreal 'crush' on Viola. Through these three aspects of fancied passion he weaves three aspects of true devotion: Viola's for Orsino, Antonio's for Sebastian and, a delicate echo, the Fool's almost inarticulate adoration of Olivia. These variations on a dual theme are linked by the sun-dazzled flowering of Sebastian's love for Olivia, while skipping discreetly through the pattern is the buffo romance of Toby and Maria. Andrew's foolish acceptance of the role of suitor to Olivia is the final detail in an exquisitely balanced design. It is a pattern made by setting fancy against truth, dream against reality. Of course one did not hope, when one discussed the play with the actors, that an audience, in the ripeness of time, would go away muttering: 'We have seen a comedy of eight variations on two aspects of love.' One merely hoped that the production would be an honest one because the actors had referred their job back to their author.

As I prepared the script it seemed to me that if, following Stanislavsky's rule, one were to say in a single word what *Twelfth Night* was about, that single word would be Illyria. It chimes through the text nostalgically as if Shakespeare would make us desirous of a place we had visited only in dreams.

Viola.	*What country, friends, is this?*
Captain.	*This is Illyria, lady.*
Viola.	*And what should I do in Illyria?*
	My brother, he is in Elysium . . .

Andrew is 'as tall a man as any's in Illyria'. Maria is 'as witty a piece of Eve's flesh as any in Illyria'. And so it goes on. The rehearsal period was a journey in search of Illyria; the performance, we dared to hope, would be our arrival there.

And what happens in Illyria? By day the sun shines with a golden richness on boscage, on palaces and on well-tended gardens. At night a full moon presides over revels that for all their robust foolery are tempered with wistfulness. The inhabitants move with a certain precision. Toby, Andrew, Maria and Fabian step across their landscape to an antic measure, now lively, now reflective but always compact and articulate. Orsino, the Renaissance man in love with love, moons in the grand manner over the young countess

Olivia, whose principal attraction rests on her refusal to have anything to do with him. She, for her part, mopes with adolescent
excessiveness over the death of her brother. And moving between
these two strongholds of romantic nonsense are the Shakespearean
girl-boy, gallant and wise, and Feste, the errant Fool. The whole
most lovely play is set down in words that are so exact an expression of its aesthetic tone that one wonders how one dare meddle
with them.

However, meddle we must and one of our first concerns would be
the visual presentation of Illyria in terms of a touring company. How
must it look and what must its inhabitants wear? After consultation
with our young Australian designer, it was decided to use a Watteau-
esque décor. The dresses of Watteau belong to no precise historical
period: they are civilized, rich and fantastic, and they have an air of
freshness. We had three little pavilions of striped poles and airily
draped banners. There were flights of steps, dark green backgrounds,
platforms and a cyclorama. A traverse turned the half-stage into the
interior of Orsino's palace. A jointed screen in two sections mounted
on wheels and painted with a formalized seaport design was pulled
across for the front scenes. These changes, effected by two nimble
pages in view of the audience, took a matter of seconds to complete.
For the letter-reading scene, there was a formalized boxtree hedge
and a group of flamboyant statuary with which Toby, Andrew and
Fabian associated themselves to comic effect. A giant beribboned
birdcage, prominent throughout the garden scenes, afterwards
became Malvolio's mobile prison, being clapped over his head, leaving his legs free. The colour throughout in paint, fabrics and lighting
modulated from grey and blue-pink to full Watteau-esque gold and
turquoise.

As I read the play again, I caught – and who could miss them? –
its overtones of regret. It has a character that is, I believe, unique in
English comedy, a particular tinge of sadness that is the comple-
mentary colour of aesthetic pleasure. One listens to it with the half-
sigh that accompanies an experience of perfect beauty. This is an
element that has much to do with music and nothing at all to do
either with sentiment or with tragedy, and it is the quintessence of
Twelfth Night. The warp of regret is interlaced with a vigorous weft
of foolery. The producer's job is to retain them both in their just

proportion. It is because *Twelfth Night* is so gay that it is also so delicately sad.

I planned a swiftly running production with only one interval. This would come after the letter-reading scene and the coda of laughter that follows it. Toby would pick Maria up in a pother of giggles and petticoats and carry her off, Andrew and Fabian would follow arm in arm and the curtain come down. My aim at this stage of production was to catch the measure of the whole. That measure would be sustained by the occasional use of music. For this we chose Purcell's 'Golden Sonata', which seemed to me to be perfect Illyria.

It was now, when the script was plotted, the music chosen, the design in preparation and first rehearsal called, that I was most forcibly reminded of the influence of theatrical fashion upon actors. I had in my company a number of young actors and actresses who had worked under distinguished direction and one senior actor of great talent, experience and discernment. It was among the youngest players that the fashionable attitude to *Twelfth Night* was most tenderly embraced. At least two of them were consumed with the desire to play up the regretful overtones for all and more than they are worth. 'Infinite sadness' was a phrase much bandied about during the earlier rehearsals, minor overtones were remorselessly insisted upon, the horrid ghost of *I Pagliacci* seemed to lurk behind the boxtree hedge. I had seen all this sort of thing done and very cleverly done and had felt it to be an error in taste and discernment. The Fool in *Twelfth Night* is *not* the Fool in *Lear*, Malvolio's downfall was *not* conceived as a tragic downfall. He would not, therefore, be allowed to gloom himself into a sort of cross-gartered Richard II. No, he would be as acid as a lime and as lean as a praying mantis. He would have such an air of creaking dryness that when his transformation came about it would be as if he were galvanized into egregious gallantry. There must be no nonsense about making him sympathetic. Shakespeare disliked the fellow and so must the audience.

With Olivia I was able to air what had long been a fervent belief. There is another fashion in our theatres (stemming from who knows what forgotten managerial charms) that would make a mature woman of Olivia. For far too long, more than mature leading ladies have confronted us with the not very delicate prospect of solid worth extended in corseted melancholy upon some comfortless chaise longue, distressingly besotted with a girl-boy and finally marrying the latter's twin brother. Could anything be less Illyrian? I defy the fashionmongers to find in the text one single hint that the spoilt young countess is in fact anything but very, very young. There is not a ponderable note in Olivia, the bloom of adolescence adorns every word she speaks. Viola's impatience is with a girl of her own age who is making a little silly-billy of herself. Our Olivia was as pretty as a rosebud, her mourning was as nonsensical as Orsino's lovelorn dumps. Having shut herself up in a charming prison, she fancied herself head-over-heels in love with the first personable boy to walk into it and was exasperated beyond measure when he failed to respond. None of my cast had ever thought of Olivia being played in this key. The concept of the stricken dowager dies hard.

There are, however, no fashions in Violas. She has, as far as I know, withstood the most determined onslaughts of the modish 'fun' merchants and has neither hallooed Olivia's name through a megaphone to the reverberate hills nor yet disguised her fair and outward character in a track suit. Our Viola fulfilled the first require-ments of a heroine in a Shakespeare comedy by being an accom-plished actress, very young, intelligent and a darling. She moved through the play with charm, wit and good breeding. By the com-mand of a certain quality in her voice she was able to alight on her lyrical passages and in so doing bring about that sudden stillness in a theatre that tells an actress she is safely home.

And Feste? It was with Feste that fashion threatened most insis-tently to put up her unlovely visage, for it is through him more than any other of the Illyrians that Shakespeare shows us the reverse side of the coin of comedy. I had of late seen Festes who, by plugging at the minor theme in their part, had administered a series of excruci-ating nudges in the ribs of their audiences. 'Goodness!' they seemed to exclaim, in Morley's phrase, 'Goodness, how sad! Look!' But Feste is *not* Lear's fool. He must play against his own ruefulness and if he does this his ruefulness will speak for itself. It shows most markedly in the songs. 'Youth,' Feste sings, 'is a stuff will not endure' and 'What's to come is still unsure.' Beauty, he says, is a flower, and else-where the Duke reflects that

women are as roses, whose fair flower
Being once displayed, doth fall that very hour.

Viola agrees:

And so they are: alas, that they are so!
To die, even when they to perfection grow!

Olivia swears by the roses of the spring. The shroud of white in the Fool's song of death is strewn with yew and 'not a flower, not a flower sweet' on his coffin shall be strewn. This flower image is scattered through *Twelfth Night* like the daisies on a Botticelli lawn and it is Feste who most often expresses it. He wanders about the play mingling with its several themes. He is by turns listless and brilliant. He has an artist's resentment for Malvolio's criticism of his professional status and can be waspish. He is all things to all men and yet very much himself and very much alone. His devotion to Olivia drifts across the text with no more insistence than a breath on a looking glass. He can be ruined by an actor who sees in him a chance to make a big thing of a light part. He sets the tone of the play.

I felt that there should be some visual expression of his function and looked for it in the flower image. On Olivia's first entrance, Feste, who has played truant from her household, sets about fooling himself back into her good graces. Our Feste mutely asked her for the rose she carried. It was refused and given to Fabian, that oddly occurring character whose sudden appearance is thought to have some reference to the departure of Kemp from Shakespeare's company and the arrival of Armin to take his place. Fabian seems to have been brought in arbitrarily to replace the Fool in the letter-reading scene and perhaps to suggest a rival to him for Olivia's favour. It was to sustain this suggestion that Fabian escorted Olivia on his first entry. Later, on his line 'So beauty's a flower', Feste snatched the rose from Fabian and wore it on his motley for the rest of the play. At the end he was left alone to sing his wry song of the wind and the rain. At its close he laid down his lute on the stage and broke the rose between his fingers. The petals fell with a faint tinkle of sound across the strings. Feste tiptoed into the shadows and the final curtain came down on the lute and rose petals, vignetted in a pool of light. This use of a visual symbol in the rose was the only piece of extraneous production imposed on the play and even this could be referred back to the text. There was comic 'business' enough, certainly, in the buffo scenes, but it was kept in style and played strictly to the general tempo of the production. The result, surprising to actors and audience alike, was the discovery that the comic scenes in *Twelfth Night* are funny.

It remains to say that with the intelligent and patient cooperation of the actors this treatment of *Twelfth Night* became articulate. It was successful in performance. This, I am sure, was because we came freshly to the text and, seeking its true savour, bent all our thought and energy to serving it.

'If that this simple syllogism will serve, so: if it will not, what remedy?' None, I am sure, in any approach to the play that imposes an extrinsic fashion upon it. Whatever the style for *Twelfth Night*, it must be ingrain. Only so will it endure the wind and weather of production.

All went well with this play and with *Six Characters* for which the company turned out to be particularly well equipped. We achieved a pace and immediacy that I think bettered the London production. Basil Henson gave a compulsive edge to the Father.

We opened in Auckland with *Twelfth Night* to rave notices and packed houses whose enthusiasm seemed to mount as the season continued. I think if we had stayed in Auckland we might possibly have established a residential company making occasional tours. However, we were booked for the south and left while we were still 'turning them away'.

From then onwards our fortunes madly fluctuated. There were full houses in unlikely towns and half-empty ones where the auguries had seemed promising. People still tell me how excited they were by these plays. I know very well that Brigid Lenihan's performances were of a startling brilliance and the concerted work and general standard of acting at a pretty high level. What really defeated us were the conditions under which we had to tour. These were, as I now see, comically disastrous.

When, for instance, we arrived at a large theatre in a Southern city it was to find that the adjacent building was occupied by a Winter Fair and the theatre dock itself given over to a scenic railway, operated by machinery that might have been geared to the treadmills of Bedlam. It was patronized by revellers who screamed

industriously throughout the evening. In two of the West Coast theatres the antediluvian red, white and blue proscenium lights had
been broken, apparently by stoning, and there was not power
enough to supply our own equipment. In Nelson we had a full house
and twenty-five fuses during the performance. The switchboard
became so hot that the electrician could not touch it without whim-
pering cries of anguish.

We discovered, in secondary towns, once-pretty Victorian and
Edwardian playhouses that had fallen into neglect and were filthy.
In one of them there was no water for the enraged actors to wash in
and a major row at once blew up, as well it might. I learned more
about actors than had entered my wildest dreams when I was a player myself. One member of the company, who took umbrage rather
easily, toured an enormous album of photographs and press notices
eulogizing his past successes. I used to dread the appearence of this
tome which would be produced by sleight-of-hand, as it seemed,
when an insult had been suspected. The pages would be turned rapidly under my reluctant gaze and the more adulatory passages read
aloud while a dramatic forefinger stabbed home the points. We also
had our Job's comforter who liked to count the empty seats through
a hole in the curtain. 'Plenty of the Wood family in front tonight,'
this player would exclaim in a sort of gloomy triumph, like a near
relation of Cassandra.

We stayed our six months' course. The last performance was in
Blenheim, where rats darted in and out of the dressing-rooms, and
the rain, which was extremely heavy, found its way through the roof
and dribbled dirtily down to the stage.

I stood in the wings and watched and listened to Feste. There he
was, alone in his pool of light, singing: 'Heigh ho, the wind and the
rain.' He laid down his lute on the stage and broke over it the rose
that Olivia had given him. The petals made a little ghost sound on
the strings.

> But that's all one, our play is done
> And we'll strive to please you every day.

The next morning I said goodbye to Bob and Mizzy and to the
company. They were nearly all returning to England. I drove myself
down the east coast of the South Island, through the ranges, and
home.

II

During my long absence the English cousin and her husband with their two sons of whom I have already written, had taken care of my house so that I returned to my family. The boys had now left Christ's College and were making up their minds what they were going to do. They were immensely companionable and I think I may say that a bond, already established, was greatly strengthened during the three years that followed my homecoming. Finally they decided, the elder for the British Army and the younger for the RAF. We saw each of them off at the old railway station and I began to think what fun it would be if we could all be reunited in London.

I suppose the physical collapse that I had kicked offstage whenever it threatened to appear was bound to declare itself once my guard was down. It did so now and for some weeks I was more or less out of action. However, energy seeped back at last, and I began to write again.

My friendships, I find, on looking back down those parallel life-lines, have for the most part been long-standing affairs, many of them beginning in childhood. Now, I was blessed with one of the richest and most rewarding of them all: a new friendship-of-three, so naturally and quickly formed and so firmly held that it is hard to believe it is only twelve years old. Fortified by this and by cheerful reunions with student-players I took heart-of-grace and we began to plan a new production which would go into rehearsal when my book was finished. There stood the Little Theatre, warm and ready for us.

In the meantime, in 1953, the Royal Stratford-upon-Avon Company came to New Zealand starring Anthony Quayle, Leo McKern and Barbara Jefford. With the Sylvia of Glentui days for company, I took the car up to Wellington by ferry and drove some five hundred miles to Auckland for the opening night. I did this because I couldn't wait for them to come to Christchurch and because Tony and Dot Quayle are friends whom it was delightful to meet again and because Bob was assistant business manager and Mizzy, his wife, was with him. It was a great reunion. And then–the plays! *Othello*, *As You Like It* and *Henry IV, Part I.* A wonderful season.

While we were in the thick of it, I had a telegram saying that the Little Theatre had been completely destroyed by fire.

It had happened in the early hours of the morning. Some of the old hands were rung up and told of it. When they arrived the stage, curtain, auditorium and loft were all ablaze, and firemen concerned only with saving the rest of the building.

One of our players, dressed in pyjamas and mackintosh, ran up the stairs, plunged into the smoke and emerged with a smouldering bundle of papers – programmes and press notices for the most part. He would have gone back for more if he hadn't been held back.

It was a clean sweep; wardrobe, scenery, equipment, records, rafters that had been used during *Hamlet* as perches for an overflow of audience, odd little gallery, the apron, proscenium and loft – all gone. If it were true, as some people hold, that sound does not altogether die but leaves an echo of itself on walls and in the fabric of such places as our Little Theatre, what phrases, what jetting sounds went roaring up that night: Othello's opulent agony, the ghost's booming expostulations, wings in the rooky wood, Clytemnestra's death cries, Puck's laughter, the symmetrical bleating of Lady Wishfort and Faustus's cry of 'See, see where Christ's blood streams in the firmament.' What a bonfire!

New Zealand universities are under great pressure for space. More lecture rooms, more laboratories is the cry in our degree-factories, and it was quite clear that another little theatre was the last thing the authorities would think of building. We were in the wilderness.

It is in situations of this sort that the student is altogether admirable. No theatre? Very well, then, no theatre. Where shall we play? By some mingling of bluff with sob stuff and of effrontery with special pleading, we talked our way into the Great Hall – a Dominion Gothic interior in which a minstrel's gallery is not lacking. It is presided over by an enormous stained-glass window busy with New Zealand historical anecdotes and by portraits of distinguished alumni including Lord Rutherford of Nelson. Acoustically it is eccentric and unpredictable.

In this setting we persuaded the army to erect a three-sided arena and down in the circus thus formed we built a system of rostra and steps with a revolving unit in the middle, presenting as its several aspects, a stairway leading up to a pulpit, an interior and a tower. In this setting I directed *Julius Caesar* in modern dress. Three of the old hands came back for the production.

From that day until this, we have been a homeless society without a non-acting club membership and entirely dependent upon what we can earn. The students themselves produce plays, usually of the *avant garde*, in halls, common rooms and a theatre belonging to the local Repertory Society. Each year that I have been in New Zealand I have directed them in a Shakespeare play at the Christchurch Civic Theatre. This great barn is rather like a theatrical joke in bad taste. It was erected many years ago by a City Council profoundly convinced of its own expert's understanding of theatrical architecture. The Civic is the fine flowering of their confidence. The walls external to the proscenium are treated with a plaster trellis behind which organ pipes lurk and upon the surface of which medallioned nymphs and fauns musically caper. This motive is repeated as a frieze all round the auditorium. The circle is large and utterly remote from the stage. The general atmosphere is subfusc and far from intimate. There are, however, two portable aprons, the bigger of which extends over the front three rows of stalls and was designed to accommodate massed (and massive) choirs and augmented symphony orchestras. Christchurch is a musical city. This playhouse (how else to name it?) seats about 1100.

By using one or both aprons we have been able to throw the action out towards the audience and bridge the gap, psychological and physical, that yawns between stage and auditorium. In this theatre during the winter term, we have presented *King Lear*, *Henry IV, Part I*, *Henry V*, *Antony and Cleopatra*, *Hamlet*, *Macbeth* and *Julius Caesar*. Over a season of eight to ten performances we can expect audiences of between six and ten thousand. We have rehearsed in a condemned boat-shed with holes in the exterior walls, an earthen floor, occasionally pocked with puddles, and no form of heating. Also in a dog-show at a fairground: premises that were gloomy beyond all thought, icily cold and made filthy by the introduction of a furnace that periodically belched out massive clouds of soot. We have used a sort of giant attic where the players on the higher rostra crashed their heads against rafters, a parish schoolroom and a disused brewery – now a storage loft for old rags. Our rehearsals always take place in midwinter and under circumstances of extreme discomfort. You may say this is a kind of lunacy.

As for me, the time has come when, in the theatre as elsewhere it is appropriate, if one is so disposed, to look back, to ask oneself what one has chiefly desired to bring about, how far one has succeeded, and what conclusions, if any, may be drawn from the result.

I think the elements of stage direction with which I have most concerned myself are those of structure and orchestration. One's whole approach to a play can be governed by its architecture. The tone, style and impact of *Othello* reflect its form down to the last analysis of movement within movement, ascents to climaxes and their realization, pauses, passages of rest, phrase within phrase. It is of the first significance, I believe, that Iago's Satanic self-dedication: 'I am your own: for ever' falls exactly at the centre of this play. The structure curves up to this keystone and descends inevitably and in absolute balance to the reverse end of the arch. The character of the writing from the classic sweep of such speeches as the 'Pontic Sea' to an accurately observed need for compensation and relief in Iago's anti-heroic prose, the ease with which these transitions are achieved, and the whole anatomy of the play: these elements never obscure the pulse that beats so strongly throughout, but leave one, as director, to feel that a great wave is here and if you and your company can ride the crest you must come safely home.

It has become clear to me that far from restricting the individual actor, a keen observance of structure, of tempi and of concerted phrasing, releases his potential ability and leaves him free to move boldly within the design both as soloist, as interpreter and as a member of a team. As for the audience: without knowing precisely why, it feels itself to be involved and carried forward with the players.

The techniques of concerted acting are well understood by the professional actor: he is unhappy if he is not fed his cues in a way that gives him a good entry, if he is not responded to and sustained by his fellow players. He is sensitive to concerted phrasing, particularly in so far as it effects his performance. He will, however, sometimes resist these techniques and even destroy them if by doing so he can score a personal point. If he is a great actor with 'star quality' and the kind of dynamism that such players generate, we not only forgive him but, unless we are Brechtians, adore him for exciting us as he does. Let him break tempi and make nonsense of teamwork. He creates his own rules. The real struggle with the professional actor comes when he is not all that dynamic but technically pretty cunning and hell-bent on showing himself off.

By the student-players I have been given, not only a quick and lively understanding of the values of teamwork but a positive greed for the acquisition of stage techniques. Of necessity much of their work proceeds by short cuts, is rough, is over stressed but they are intelligent and responsive and they are never dull. This is particularly evident in their crowd work. Here each group in a mob, after diligent dragooning, is usually prepared to make an approach that even methodists might applaud. I have lately done a second production of *Julius Caesar* for the Canterbury University players. The continuity-rehearsals on midwinter Sunday afternoons in our comfortless buildings, generated their own heat.

Now, after ten years, the University is about to build another theatre. I have directed my last Shakespeare play in the Civic and perhaps my last for the Society. What I should like most of all would be to see a group of student and graduate producers carrying on the established tradition for vigorous, concerted acting, boldness, hard work, hard thinking and complete dedication.

I shall not lose touch with those of the players whom I know most intimately. They come often to see me and there is the very best kind of bond between us – the attachment born of working together at a hazardous task for which we share a great devotion. Together we have made those discoveries of Shakespeare that come, I believe, only to people of the theatre: only by way of acting the plays out before an audience, only by going a journey with each one on the terms under which it was written. Such journeys we have taken together. The iron discipline of rehearsal, fortified by the attitude of the students themselves, is as close to that of the professional theatre as I have been able to keep it. In directing I have myself received direction. Most students are above the average in intelligence: they are extremely quick to take a point and their approach to character can be as penetrating as any method actor's. Once they have learned the means of expression, how to make proper use of the player's tools: his body, his voice and his inward dynamo, they can be very good Shakespearean actors.

Some of the young men, having got their academic degrees, have elected to try their fortunes on the professional stage in England.

Several of them have won bursaries to London schools of drama, others have gone naked into the jungle. I am thankful to say they have all prospered. They write often and when I am in London we meet and take great pleasure in doing so. I think myself most fortunate in the friendship of these students.

III

During this last decade I have made two more visits to England. The first was taken in a Norwegian freighter, the *Temeraire*, with a New Zealand friend, Essie, who had found out about the line and suggested that as I was thinking of going anyway I should keep her company. The *Temeraire*, sailing from Outer Harbour near Adelaide in South Australia, took twelve passengers. She would carry wool, possibly to Odessa, making several points of call on the way though her Captain's orders, which were opened at sea, were quite likely to be changed. Ships of this line had been known to make an eight weeks' voyage without calling anywhere and deposit their desperate passengers finally at Oslo. Under circumstances such as these, arrangements would be made to tranship us to an English port.

It is a journey of nearly a week from New Zealand to Adelaide if you travel by surface. We arrived in sweltering heat twenty-four hours after the Queen had left and found the city still in a ferment with hotel accommodation at a premium. Here we awaited our embarkation notices and after about a week, received them.

On a very hot night we stood in an otherwise deserted customs shed at Outer Harbour while an official hunted through his files for our papers. It was some time before he found them and we were able to board a graceful ship that looked remarkably small in the moonlight.

As soon as we were shown our cabins I knew I would like the *Temeraire*. She was old-fashioned, odd and good. Her one bathroom was tanklike and primitive. The only passengers' common room was a small smoking parlour with a bit of deck outside. There was a little games deck above this and a narrow promenade amidships. Otherwise one sat or lay on the hatches. The dining saloon was just big enough to take three long, narrow tables. The stewardesses were two Norwegian college girls who were seeing the world and the steward was also a ladylike little thing. The wireless assistant doubled the parts of cabin boy and orchestra. Nothing could have been less like the organized fun of the luxury liners in which I had taken my last three voyages and no change could have been more refreshing.

Our cabins were unsmart, spotlessly clean, rather large and very comfortable. We stowed away our belongings, setting ourselves in order for a long voyage. The steward looked in and invited us to coffee and little newly baked breads. They were delicious.

On a very warm, still midnight we slipped away from Outer Harbour and when dawn came, stood well out in the Great Australian Bight.

I had not intended to embark such readers as have been kind enough to bear me company, on yet another sea voyage but I find my recollections of the *Temeraire* so pleasant that I cannot resist taking a longer look at them.

We were an oddly assorted company of passengers with little enough in common, one might have thought, but we got on extremely well together. Chief among us was a retired don, a Cambridge man, a classic: Professor S., late of Melbourne University. He was a delightful travelling companion and when we reached the Aegean Sea, spoke of each island as if its legend was an affair of yesterday. Mrs S., three other married couples, including Mr Thompson, the Dane, an excitable fellow, and his Australian wife, two unattached ladies, Essie and I, made up the full complement of passengers.

The Captain was a man of sentiment. He was fair and rubicund and inclined, out of social embarrassment, to giggle. His English was tolerably fluent and he was very polite. He was also a good commander and, one could see, respected by his officers.

When the midday luncheon bell was rung by the cabin-boy-wireless-assistantorchestra, everyone was expected to go at once to the dining room. Captain I. would be standing inside the door. As one entered he would bow and present one with a plate. Behind him on a side table were the smörgåsbord to which one helped oneself. They were always good. When everybody was seated the Captain took up his knife and fork and so did we. On a unique occasion one of the unattached ladies was late and we all sat, rigid with decorum, until she arrived. Captain I. received her apologies with an austere giggle. Even at breakfast the same protocol was expected of us.

The Captain had all our passports and therefore knew all our ages and birthdays. These he loved to celebrate. As if to oblige him, several of us had birthdays during the voyage. I was one. Dinner, on these occasions, was extra special. The ladylike and kind little steward whose name, Norwegian though he was, turned out to be Dan, also adored these parties, and caused the orchestra to play 'Happy Birthday to You' on his piano-accordion in the passage outside.

There was a cake with candles (tactfully unspecific as to numbers), wine and, as a grand climax, the Birthday toast, proposed by the Captain, in a long, involved speech that always made him cry. He would start off quite gaily with one or two careful little jokes but as soon as he got round to saying how nice it was to have whichever of us it was, in his ship and how well-behaved we were, his large blue eyes would fill with tears and his voice would tremble.

It so happened that our Queen's birthday followed all the others. Not her official birthday but her real one. I'm afraid none of her subjects among the passengers had noticed this circumstance. Not so, Captain I. He knew. He commanded the Birthday Dinner to end all Birthday Dinners. Dan decorated our nursery tables up to saturation point. The cook went away out on decorative icing and the orchestra played our National Anthem without the slightest hesitation. He also played 'Happy Birthday to You' which we were expected, always, to sing. And indeed all the Norwegian officers and Mr Thompson, the Dane, loudly gave tongue in their own languages. Naturally, we did, too, but it was a little difficult to know how to phrase the penultimate line.

'Happy Birthday, dear Queen Elizabeth,' would be redundant and 'Dear Queen' recalled President Roosevelt's letters to King George V. Too late one thought of 'Your Majesty'; the thing had already passed off in an ambiguous rumble.

Captain I. rose to propose the Royal Toast. He recalled Norway's close association during the War with Great Britain and the Commonwealth. He praised the House of Windsor. He reminded us that we and he and his officers and Mr Thompson, the Dane, were members of three great surviving monarchies. And gracious, as Hilaire Belloc would have said, *how* the Captain cried!

One episode of this enchanting voyage sticks most vividly in my memory. Essie had agreed to act as secretary for the duration and we used often to work in the evenings at my current book, *Scales of Justice*. On the night we sailed through the Dardanelles we resolved to stay up until we passed the beaches at Gallipoli, hoping to see them if the moon shone clear. It was overcast, however, and when we stood on deck at about one o'clock and peered into the dark we could only discern, very faintly, a glint of something that we knew was the beaches. The sea was dead calm and the air enervated and breathless. We had wished each other good night and were about to go below when we became aware of a cessation in sound and in movement. The *Temeraire*'s engines had stopped. We lay motionless somewhere, we thought, off the Hellespont. A rhythmic sound of paddling lapped into the silence. We crossed over to the starboard side and there, bobbing towards us in the blackness, was a lantern. As it drew nearer we saw that it hung from the prow of a caique.

The Turk in the caique, foreshortened and upward gazing in the lamplight, hailed us: 'Ohé, Captain!' and above us from the bridge, the Captain quietly answered him. Their common language was English which they spoke with a kind of biblical rotundity. It so happened that both their voices were deep and beautiful. Essie had her shorthand pad and pencil with her. 'Do take this down,' I said.

'Who are you, Captain?'

'The *Temeraire*.'

'From where, Captain?'

'Out of Adelaide with wool for Odessa.'

'How many souls aboard you, Captain?'

'Sixty-three.'

'Where are you bound, Captain?'

'For Istanbul.'

'Do you wish a pilot, Captain, for Istanbul?'

'I do so wish.'

'I have no pilot tonight, Captain. If you will, you may proceed without pilot to Istanbul.'

A pause.

'I will so proceed.'

'Good night, Captain. A safe passage.'

'Thank you. Good night.'

The Turk's teeth gleamed. He raised his hand. The lantern dipped, circled and bobbed away into the night. The engine-room bells rang and we began to throb again.

When I woke next morning and looked out of my porthole I thought: 'What quantities of very tall chimneys sticking up out of the mist and how romantic they look – they might be minarets.'

The mist dissolved and they were caught like the sultan's turret in a noose of light and declared themselves. They *were* minarets, of course. This was the Golden Horn and there was Istanbul and ahead lay the Bosphorus, the Black Sea and Odessa.

Of all the landfalls I have experienced: Hong Kong, for instance, or the Piraeus, Venice even, or Beppo or San Francisco at dawn, Odessa was the strangest, the most ambiguous, the most foreign. We arrived in the roads late on a spring afternoon and anchored there awaiting permission to berth. The sky was overcast and the sea dark and choppy. The city itself was simplified almost to a silhouette of onion domes, one of them flaming with the sunset, long roofs, dim flights of steps ('Ah, *The Battleship Potemkin*,' one thought), and the hint of a grandiose theatre down near the wharves. Professor S. talked of Genghis Khan, of barbaric splendours and terrors and the clash of ancient cultures.

The wind shifted. It now blew towards us from the land and carried with it the smell of occupied places and a most disturbing sound – the sound of a vast crowd of men, singing. Someone produced field glasses and through them we could just see that the steps and streets of Odessa and an open park or square were all swarming with people. The effect of this was extraordinarily dreamlike.

It may perhaps be remembered that as a child I had formed a romantic attachment for 'Russia', an attachment inspired in the first instance by what I suspect was a very slick piece of travel writing. My fantasy bore as little relation to Russia, I daresay, as the Pre-Raphaelite vision did to mediaeval Italy but the sight and sound of Odessa that evening revived it in an extraordinary degree.

The singing continued: vague, remote, gigantic. A flight of aircraft – Migs, someone said – roared overhead. A gunboat came out, encircled us and made off. A line of airships steamed out of port and into the open sea. It was all very odd and ominous we thought.

Apart from the gunboat nobody paid the smallest attention to us.

It was about now, I think, that one of the passengers pulled himself together and looked at a calendar. The First of May.

The Captain was annoyed and worried. He had not visited a Soviet port before and was, he said, uneasy about procedure. He had been sent a signal to the effect that it was forbidden to sound the ship's siren and that he was to remain where he was until he received further instructions from the port authorities. He told us that an official party would board us and that the passengers must remain in their cabins where they would be interviewed and might be searched. All passports, cameras and field glasses were to be handed over. Such were his instructions. 'I do not like,' he said, very red in the face. 'I very much do not like. I am obliged.'

We waited there, disregarded, until the next afternoon when a lighter came alongside, swarming with uniformed men and women: drab and businesslike. For the first time on the voyage a loudspeaker came into play. We were to go to our cabins and remain there until further notice.

My door was opposite that of the dining room which was ajar. The tables had been re-arranged by Dan to resemble an office. I left my own door open and sat on my little sofa from where I had an oblique view of the Captain, looking cross, seated at a table behind a mountain of papers and surrounded by Russian officers. A large-bosomed, frightening lady in a shiny navy-blue uniform and with the worst permanent wave I have ever seen, strode down the passage, observed me and shut my door very firmly indeed.

I was nervous. At that time, a particularly icy depression prevailed in the cold war. I had obtained what was held to be an adequate visa for the USSR and hoped to go ashore. The friends in New Zealand of whom I have already written were Estonians, exiled from their own country since it had been taken into the Soviet Republic. When one forms a close friendship one absorbs something of the life of the other partners and I had learned from them to amplify and, as it were, steady my childish dreams of their country. I had with me a parting gift: an old medal of St Innocent, patron saint of travellers. It is silver and has a hole cut in it like a window for the little brown, painted face of Innocent. There is also a legend in Russian characters. I had wondered, when we were warned of a search, possibly of our persons, what would be thought of Innocent, obviously a Czarist relic? When I asked the Captain's advice he said he thought it would be best if I posted the medallion to London from Port Said and added the possibility of its being stolen in Egypt was extremely high. So I kept Innocent and wore him under my blouse as I sat in the cabin and waited. There was also the book. It was now typed in triplicate. Would it be seized? Should I conceal a copy in a locked suitcase? But if they demanded the keys? In the end I distributed the typescripts in weighted heaps over my dressing table and little bureau and sofa. No deception practised.

After a long time, boots clumped down the passage. There was a rap on Essie's door and then a prolonged rumble of voices. Extremely silly, I thought, to be apprehensive but it would be rather nice when it was all over. What ages they were with poor Essie. Were they frisking her for weapons? Doors and drawers banged.

When, at last, they called on me they turned out to be an extremely pleasant and comely young officer who spoke good English and an offsider like something out of a hammy film of *Treasure Island*, with a scar running from his temple to the corner of his mouth and a villainous, hangdog manner.

I had to sign eight identical declarations that I had no firearms. While I was doing this, Scarface searched the wardrobe and drawers. There were other declarations, I have forgotten to what effect. The young officer said he understood I was an author and glanced at the typescripts. I said we had been interested in the gala sounds from the shore and he said yes, it was a great week in the year. There was a wonderful ballet at the Opera House. I said how lovely and I looked forward so much . . . He said unfortunately none of the passengers would be permitted to land. A fury of disappointment seized me. 'But my passport! I've got the special visa! They told me it was all in order.'

'I regret,' he said, nicely. 'No. Your passports will be sent up to Moscow but they are not sufficient.'

'Could you perhaps arrest me after we have berthed and march me off as far as the Opera House? I would be delighted if you would come as my guest. When the ballet was over you could march me back again.'

He was polite enough to treat this as a good joke and for the rest of the interview we got on very pleasantly, I thought, with lots of jolly laughter. Scarface stood inside the door and looked at nothing.

The young officer repeated his regrets, saluted, smiled in a friendly manner and took his leave.

Not long afterwards the loudspeaker said we could come out of our cabins.

The official party was assembled on deck and about to climb down a rope ladder to the lighter. My young officer emerged from a group and came face-to-face with me.

He cut me dead.

One by one they swung down the ladder and out of sight. He was the last to go. He hung back for a moment, turned and gave me a quick bow and a grin.

When we all met on our little games deck, the wireless officer told me how the formidable lady in uniform – she was, we supposed, some kind of commissaress – strode into his office and without a word wrenched out the salient fuses from his equipment, dropped them in a repellant reticule and strode out again. As far as the outside world was concerned we were now incommunicado.

For that night, all next day and the following night, we remained at anchor in the roads and no one paid the smallest attention to us. The Captain became apoplectic. It was rumoured that the delay was costing his company £300 a day. On the third morning, very early, and against orders, he caused a loud and long blast to be sounded on the ship's siren. It woke me for a moment but I fell asleep again and the next time I opened my eyes it was to see the flanks of a ship slide past the porthole. We were berthing.

It took ten days to discharge our wool out of Adelaide for Odessa. First of all the long probes, like skewers, had to be run through each bale. One remembered the old story and wondered, if a spy concealed in one of them would, on being transfixed, ejaculate 'Baa, baa'.

While this was being done a guard was mounted alongside us on the wharf. Three armed sentries. Not far away a diver was being lowered into the harbour. The winch was manned by a man and woman – a woman who according to one's inclinations was either splendidly symptomatic of muscular comradeship and sexual equality or absolutely terrifying.

Old ladies with headscarves and aprons, straight out of a fairy tale, swept the wharves with witches' brooms. When, at last, the unloading process was set in motion, one of the gigantic winches was worked by a young and good-looking girl. There she sat, high up in her cabin, like a goddess: Irma was her name, as we were to discover.

Furious as our Captain was with the port of Odessa he admitted, like the just man he was, that the unloading was the most efficient he had ever encountered. He added (and alas, I have yet to meet a merchant skipper who would not endorse his opinion) that New Zealand ports ('Excuse me. I regret.') were the slowest in the world. I understand that there is now an improvement.

By watching the watersiders all day and as long into the night as one was inclined, we discovered that the whole operation was ordered rather on the lines of those enchanting Russian dolls that fit inside each other. There was an overall superintendent of wharf operations and under him a cadre of the second rank who observed the main division of labour and, after these, a watcher male or female to each group of five or six workers. No doubt, at some nerve centre there was a superman observing the superintendent. This made for great speed and efficiency.

One of the watersiders was in love with Irma. He apostrophized her with all the frustrated ardour of a Romeo, day in and night out. *'E-E-E-Errrma!'*

Sometimes she would incline from her window and roar back at him.

Not one soul on the wharves or in the ship ever, ever glanced at the passengers. One evening I thought I would try if, by staring at the top of his cap, I could impel the amidships sentry to look up. I got a packet of cigarettes from Dan and leant over the taffrail and stared and stared. It didn't work. I took a deep breath and let out a gargantuan sneeze. He looked up. I motioned winningly with the cigarettes. He made: 'Certainly not. On no account' with his hands and resumed his correct posture.

Our officers were allowed on shore and had come back with accounts of the unbelievably high cost of almost everything and particularly tobacco. Dusk had fallen. The day shift was gone and the night shift not yet at work. The wharf was deserted. I leant over the taffrail, accidentally dropped the bright green packet of cigarettes on the wharf and walked away quickly. About ten minutes later, I returned and looked down. The packet had gone. The sentry glanced up for a moment.

I think it was on the following day that our wireless officer returned from a trip ashore to the seamen's institute or an equivalent establishment. He was anxious to show Essie and me a pamphlet that had been handed to him. It was in his own language, Norwegian, and was about countries in the British Commonwealth. In New Zealand, it said, the white capitalist reactionaries tortured the Maori slave population.

After a day or two I found a place on deck where I could sit with a writing block under cover of which I made rough little sketches of people on the wharves. There were sailors with red bobbles on their caps and two ribbons fluttering behind: incredibly hefty lady-watersiders with their broad Slavonic faces tied up like puddings: younger Amazons, still shapely and looking as if they ought to be parading in Red Square with swinging arms and bright ideological smiles. There were all the soldiers and the old sweepers and many beguiling and solemn little children. It would have been fun to come out into the open and frankly draw them all but this was considered inadvisable so I scribbled furtively and not at all well.

It was while I was doing this that I noticed my friend, the amidships sentry, stoop down and peer into one of a heap of conduit pipes that had been stacked on the wharf. He straightened up and made a signal to a soldier who was standing some distance away. This man came across, stooped, stared and walked rapidly away. Presently a car arrived with a senior-looking officer. There were no civilian cars on the wharves at Odessa. The sentry pointed to the pipe. The officer stooped and extracted from it a scrap of green and scarlet glossy paper. I looked down and saw that this was a corner of a book jacket or magazine cover. The officer drove away. That evening a top-looking brass and some satellites called on the Captain and told him he was to make it clear to everybody in his ship that no paper of any kind must be dropped overboard. All the following day two Russians in a dinghy paddled round the *Temeraire*'s seaward side, fishing with a net for the most unlovely *trouveaux*.

We moved to another berth at the farthest arm of the harbour and continued to discharge wool. There was a military establishment here. Soldiers drilled, ran, fell flat, crawled and ran on again. From a little hut, punctually at three every afternoon, there emerged a small boy wearing a shiny peaked cap, muffler, gloves,

belted blouse and baggy trousers. He had in either hand a little sister
in headscarf and long full-skirted dress and a staggering baby, also
gloved. They took a promenade, not too fast, not too slow and looking neither to right or left. Past the *Temeraire* and to a certain place
on the docks where they wheeled and returned. They were for all
the world like a woodcut from a Victorian nursery tale by Mrs
Juliana Horatia Ewing: such immensely solemn children and so
sedate.

At 11.30 a.m. on the fourteenth day the last bale went ashore and
the passengers were given final instructions. We were to assemble in
the tiny smoking room and remain there until further orders. One
heavily armed soldier stood inside the door and another on the deck
outside. Time dragged and we got hungrier and hungrier. Professor
S. and another passenger sang Gilbert and Sullivan very slowly and
lugubriously and we all joined in the chorus. The guard, not without reason, slightly smiled. After about an hour and a half, Professor
S. muttered under his breath and went out on deck. He was at once
ordered by gesture and ejaculation to return. Some time after two
o'clock, an officer and private soldier arrived. The officer put our
passports on one of the tables. We all confessed afterwards to a sensation of extravagant relief at the sight of the passports. This reaction
told us just how apprehensive we had been. But the passports were
not returned to us. Instead, the officer opened each one and made a
long staring comparison between the hideous photograph and the
original. He then handed them over to his subordinate together with
a flat black object which I felt sure was a camera and which was
quickly pocketed. They left us. We endured another long interval
during which Mr Thompson, the Dane, and Professor S. lost their
tempers and were damped down by their wives. We found out afterwards that during these interminable hours, the ship was subjected
to an exhaustive search. At three o'clock the guards went away and
the loudspeaker said we were free. When we got down to the main
deck the mooring ropes were being cast off and the engines were
throbbing.

And now, as a gap of dark water widened between the *Temeraire*
and the Odessa wharf, people down below, for the first time looked
up at us. They smiled and waved and we waved back; almost, it
seemed for a minute or two, as if there were two groups of human

beings wanting, before they lost sight of each other for ever, to come to some sort of understanding.

'Poor *devils*!' one of the passengers said.

But they didn't seem to me to be unhappy. They were shabby, hard-working and without any conspicuous vivacity. Beyond that I, for one, received no more positive impression unless it was of a sort of plodding acquiescence.

They waved for a little while and then turned back to their work.

Our next port of call, it was announced, would be Torreslavega on the east coast of Spain.

IV

The contrast could scarcely have been greater. From the bay, a few rows of little pinkish-pale houses stared at us. They had black window-holes in their faces and might have been painted on their bleached, salty background by Christopher Wood. We were halfway between Alicante and Cartagena in a little bay too shallow to allow an ocean-going vessel as modest, even, as the *Temeraire*, to come alongside the wharf. We anchored offshore.

Here was the other kind of totalitarianism: Catholic, picturesque, inconsistent, savage no doubt and, in the background, infamous, but on the face of it good-tempered and a bit ridiculous. The officials who boarded us in Torreslavega were armed to the teeth like bandits and rich in documents, but somehow it all boiled down to them joyously wolfing up any cigarettes that were offered them and suddenly waiving all formalities. All but one. They objected to Professor S.'s very conservative, waist-to-knee, old gentleman's shorts. 'I go ashore in no other apparel,' he said hotly. 'The thing is ridiculous.' The officials retired to the customs shed and after a longish interval, reappeared beaming, with a special permit that said El Professor S. would be permitted to enter Spain 'wearing his pantaloons'.

We were rowed to and from the ship by fisherboys of about twelve years old, who preferred cigarettes to pesetas. They sang, all the way: short songs of a kind that suited the warm weather and the dip of their oars – could they have been made up of the verses that are called *coplas*? The boys constituted themselves our escort and swaggered along beside us ordering off any lesser urchins who attempted to tag along and beg. They were tough, proud boys. We noticed that our particular one – was he José or Pedro or Carlos? – grew drowsy if we stayed ashore latish in the evening. Once, at about nine o'clock, while we had a drink in a sort of vague restaurant that was called a club he waited as usual, outside, but catching our attention through the window, laid his folded hands along his cheek, shut his eyes, inclined his head and by dint of mime, conveyed to us that he had been out all the previous night with his father's fishing boat. He had become, suddenly, a sleepy child and we were filled with remorse.

We were loading salt in Torreslavega. It was rowed out in dinghies, hauled up in buckets and tipped into the holds. This process allowed plenty of time for visits to Alicante and Cartagena. To this end some of us hired a car with a single-fanged driver who smelt more violently of garlic than one would have supposed humanly possible. He was incandescent with garlic. On the disgraceful road to Cartagena I sat in front and had the dubious good fortune to meet with his approval. Somehow or another, as we bounced and lurched over potholes we managed to conduct a basic kind of conversation, mostly by means of gesture for which he removed both hands from the wheel. Whenever I guessed his meaning he roared with laughter, dazing me with great hot gusts of garlic, pointing to himself and then to me and crossed his middle finger over the index one. Then, to indicate how well we understood one another, he hit me smartly on the suspender knob. It was a painful trip.

When we arrived in Cartagena he drove us into the slums and introduced us to his family, who were charming.

We lunched very late in a working-man's restaurant where the food was good and the patron obliging. In paying him we found an English sixpence among my pesetas. He turned it over, pointed to the sovereign's head, sighed like a furnace and shook his head. So vivid is Spanish gesture that it seems in retrospect that he must have spoken the phrases that he mimed: 'Ah, Señora, you are fortunate. Ourselves . . . alas!' As we left he laid his finger to his lips and drew aside an old coat that hung from a nail on the door. There were exposed two very faded photographs, one of the Queen and the other of the Pretender to the Spanish throne. It would have been nice if we could have brought him together with our Captain.

After a steady rumour that we would all be landed at Copenhagen, the *Temeraire* discharged her passengers at a small port in Wales. Bob (my old comrade of Commonwealth Theatre Company days) had found out about our arrival and telegraphed that he would drive nobly across England and into Wales to meet us.

All the other passengers had gone. Essie and I said goodbye to the Captain and the officers, sat on the hatch and told each other what a pleasant voyage it had been and how we would always remember the *Temeraire* with affection. It was quite late in the afternoon when the car arrived. We turned back to look at our little ship: elegantly graceful and unpretentious. As one does on such occasions, I promised myself another voyage in her some day.

V

There have been other voyages but not in the *Temeraire*: voyages to the Far East, to the USA and to Greece. Happy voyages in ships with a limited number of passengers and smart voyages in grand liners. There have been luxurious trains like the one from Kyoto to Tokyo and shabby comfortable trains like the old grande dame sweeping across the USA from San Francisco to Chicago, and innumerable joggings by branch lines in England. Flanders and Swan were here the other day and with their little dirge for fallen trains did awful things to addicts. Has Dr Beeching or his successor slaughtered that most amiable of branch lines: the one that potters to and fro between Leamington and Stratford-upon-Avon by way of Warwick? What are they going to buy with all the money they make from the killing-off of little trains?

The year 1955 was spent mostly in London where I took a minute and beguiling house in Hans Road. The two young New Zealand cousins were now commissioned in the Gunners and in the RAF respectively and, as we had so often planned, they spent their leaves with me. They were wonderfully gay company; everything entertained and delighted them. I used to see people in theatres and restaurants smile when they looked at them or overheard what they said: I suppose because they were so very un-blasé and so obviously enjoying themselves.

With The Gunner, I took what is perhaps the most spellbinding train of all, the Night Ferry to Paris: the train that is already French when you step into it at Victoria, that magnificently pours itself at speed through the night to the coast, stops and goes quiet. If you are still awake in your bunk you hear brief metallic sounds and then feel a lift and a suspended swaying. When you look out of your window the end of a jetty slides past and then – how strangely – a word with an arrow: 'To Dunkirk'. The Gunner was greatly excited. He stayed up until we were seaborne and called me repeatedly through the communicating door looking for all his six-foot-two, very much as he did when he first came down to school in Christchurch.

This was the year of Laurence Olivier's *Macbeth* at Stratford-upon-Avon. Bob and another friend and I drove back the hundred miles to London after the show and were so rapt, so involved by this extraordinary performance that the hours slipped by like a dream. The eldest of the Lamprey children, now a mama, and I stayed in Stratford for a week and I returned yet again by myself. I had become an habituée.

I don't really mind the 'Bard Industry' aspect of Stratford and what's more I don't think the Bard would have minded it either. It's better that there should be an olde radio shoppe, one or two souvenir absurdities and a display of handweavery that might well have been created for Miss Margaret Rutherford in character, than that the place should be put into a sort of sacred aspic and (like a perennial galantine in a passenger ship) taken in and out of the deep freeze and never marred by cutting. It is, I feel, not inappropriate that lorries and charabancs rumble over Clopton Bridge and along the London Road. One regrets, of course, that the theatre should have been built at exactly the wrong moment in the development of modern architecture. There may be something pretty silly about a modern hotel calling its guest rooms after Shakespeare's characters. (It would be fun to write for reservations stipulating: 'Either Doll Tearsheet or Pompey Bum, if you please.') But what may we not set beside these maggots? Captain Jaggard's bookshop. A walk at dawn or dusk across the fields to Charlecote. Groups of Warwickshire oaks that are also, and so clearly, 'a wood near Athens', a hilltop where poor Wat might have sat on his hinder legs listening, dew-bedabbled wretch, for the cry of the hounds. The Falcon Inn, which carries its age with grace and no gimmicks. A quiet church with a monstrous effigy to which you need pay no attention. And nightly, from early spring to late autumn, the sounding out before unfashionable cosmopolitan audiences of a music in words. This music so easily, so good-humouredly transcends all other spoken English in our history, that it raises a kind of laugh in the throat and heart whenever one hears it.

Of all the oddly divergent people, ideas and things that have attracted my devotion, I find most reason in my attachment to these plays. After writing this down it has just occurred to me for the first time, that if I had not directed ten of Shakespeare's plays I would have written ten more detective stories and been, I daresay, ten times better off.

How right I was!

VI

When I first applied myself to writing this book, it seemed to me that I would be obliged to make a sort of practical equivalent of that familiar experience which I have tried to describe in the first chapter. I thought that I must look on at myself: slide apart from my own image as if I were mis-focusing a camera upon it. And just as when the strange sensation of duality visits me, I always, by an involuntary act of defensiveness, return to my everyday self: so, I find, have I withdrawn from writing about experiences which have most closely concerned and disturbed me. What I have written turns out to be a straying recollection of places and people: I have been deflected by my own reticence.

It is with people that I would like to end this chapter: with some of the people who have formed its design. If, indeed, it may be said to have a design.

I look out of my windows, across the plains and there are the Alps. It is easy to find the shadowed valley where we camped and, further south, the entry into the Waimakariri Gorge leading to the high country, Arthur's Pass, the Main Range and Westland. The house is warm with recollections of Unk, Papa Jellett, Mivvie, Colin, Cecil and dear James: all of them very cheerful. But it is not just a house of recollections. There are at present, family visitors of three generations and many others going back as far as St Margaret's and even Tib's and there is a steady flow of past and present student-players. I am fortunate in my house and the people who come to it.

Three years ago, after two months of complicated and exciting voyages to Singapore, Hong Kong, Japan and the USA, ending with an unpleasant Atlantic crossing in a German liner, I landed at Southampton. With what seemed to me to be quite bewildering friendliness, I was given a telegram and shepherded into a train by two of the port officials. Green downs and spinneys fled past the windows and in a clearing in a wood there were English country-men, doing something leisurely with a cart and horse. I visited an unsmart bar in the train called, absurdly, a tavern. The pallid barman and tepid drink might have been Ganymede and Ambrosia. When the ugly backsides of Outer London's railroad houses began to close in, peculiar things happened in my throat, and when the Battersea Power Station, that unlovely inverted udder, loomed murkily forward, I actually cried with happiness and the sensation of Home. Is this sentimental? Very well, then, it is sentimental.

So, once more I was in London. In a little house in Montpelier Walk. Here it is, on the sunny side of the street, looking towards the dome of the Oratory and with the Prince of Wales, a decorous pub, in the foreground. I am visited once a week by a hoarse flower-seller (*'Anytime. All fresh.'*), by a whistling piano-accordionist who is rumoured to trade in filthy postcards on the side and by cheerful French onion-sellers. Jonathan Elsom, one of my student-players, on bursary at a drama school, is staying with me. My London secretary, who is also a friend of earlier days in New Zealand, is typing out a dramatization of *False Scent* which Jemima, the eldest Lamprey daughter, and I, have sweated out between us. (This play will, in the near future, be sold to a London management. Three years will go by. Jemima and I, by a kind of mental osmosis, will gradually absorb the truth about selling plays. We will discover that whatever may be said to suggest more precipitant action, the play may well be put into cold storage, occasionally taken out and blown upon and then put back again. At the moment, however, we are all wide-eyed enthusiasm.)

I await a visitor. Presently he arrives. Over six feet tall. Very erect. Very alert. The familiar Micawber-like voice and the stately periods roll round our little drawing room. He has been in retirement for many years but, as if the 'stroller's' drops of blood in his veins infect all the rest, he still travels a great deal. He visits his son and his old theatre associates in Australia, taking a devious course on the way.

'I had meningitis in Madrid,' he proclaims. 'A great bore, it was, but it has left no serious defects that I am aware of.'

'Four score and three,' he says. 'But not, I hope, greatly inconvenienced by the weight of years.'

Not greatly. Scarcely at all. Indeed, the years themselves disintegrate like mist and there he is asking me how I would like to be an actress or booming awfully with a coffin-plate crown upon his head, giving what-for to the witches.

The telephone rings. A falsetto voice tells me that the private secretary to Mr Chou En-Lai wishes to speak to me. I wait in a state of unsuspended disbelief until a second voice, speaking pidgin-English, says that Mr Chou will meet me in a certain little opium den under the American Embassy at thirteen hours GMT. I am to have a camellia clenched between my teeth and a copy of *The War Cry* in my left boot.

'And, darling,' says the voice, *'such* a crisis blowing up! You can't *think.'*

Jonathan is coming to dinner. We will speak for a little while of old times, but will soon turn to the present and Jon's future and what we are all going to do next.

CHAPTER 12

Second Wind

Perhaps I should have started with a heading *Twenty Years After*, which sounds like the title of a Victorian novel. Indeed I believe there was such a one and that it dealt with convicts in Australia.

It *is* in fact getting on for twenty years since I wrote the final paragraphs of the preceding chapter and almost as long ago since I last read them. The middle-aged woman is now very old. Her lines of perspective stretch out behind her and the beech tree is almost out of sight.

When we are young, old age is something that happens to other people. This attitude persisted in my father until he was well into his seventies. He once said to me that he always thought of himself as a young man and added in his surprised voice that he supposed that was absurd. I don't think he really believed it to be so or, if he did, gave a damn one way or the other. He preferred the company of my contemporaries. When his own – Unk or dear James, for instance – had reminisced at some length about the friends and events of their past my father would afterwards say fretfully that he found it all rather boring.

I resented the approach of middle age whenever I reflected that it had already overtaken me, but was almost too busy for this consideration to occur. Old age has caught me completely by surprise. It was the sudden onset of uncertain health that did the trick and the realization that the activity one most valued and passionately enjoyed was no longer possible. It must be packed up and put away with theatrical photographs and old programmes: a tidying-up process before a journey on which one will be obliged to travel very light indeed.

In this room there is a lovely old Hungarian chest, large, with five carved, smooth-running drawers and each drawer full to extremity with the detritus of theatrical endeavour accumulated through half a century. There are photographs in albums, the gifts of, I hope, affectionate casts, quantities of loose photographs in no sort of order and piles of old programmes. Every time I drag open an over-stuffed drawer I think I will reduce its contents to some kind of order and every time I then think of something more urgent or nicer to do and shamefacedly force back the drawer with all its contents jamming and slithering about inside. Unlike Kipling's Elephant's Child I am not 'a tidy pachyderm'. A popular song of the First World War was called 'The Trail of the Lonesome Pine'. My mother used to sing it substituting 'Untidy Daughter' for the last two words.

I have just finished a prolonged fossick in the Hungarian chest and have come up with programmes of the last three Shakespearean plays I directed. Two of them, *Twelfth Night* and *Henry V*, were special in that each was the opening production for a new playhouse: *Twelfth Night* for the Ngaio Marsh Theatre at the University of Canterbury and *Henry V* for the James Hay Theatre at the magnificent Town Hall complex in Christchurch.

The touching kindness of the Canterbury University Drama Society in calling their long-wished-for theatre after me made its opening a very moving occasion. I have written earlier in this book of a production of *Twelfth Night* for the British Commonwealth Theatre Company when John Schlesinger played Feste, and of my own feelings about the play. They do not change but I was now to learn how the expression of them would do so with a different cast. Student-players, like wine, blossom in maturity, yet retain a certain freshness of approach and a kind of knowledgeable delight in what they are doing. The cast of the new *Twelfth Night* were almost all of this sort: experienced but still young, disciplined but still exuberant. In the event this brought about a broader emphasis on the buffo element, particularly in the comic duel. I don't think I have ever before or since heard such laughter as this scene provoked.

While the overall orchestration retained its original shape, in detail there were many changes arising out of the actors' personalities.

But Illyria was still Illyria, a country halfway between a laugh and a sigh, and at the end Feste still laid his lute on the stage, broke his rose over the strings and tiptoed off into the shadows.

The *Henry V* production replaced one that was to have been directed by Sir Tyrone Guthrie who was then in Australia and came over to New Zealand for discussions. He was considering, I afterwards learned, somebody's re-arrangement of the mediaeval mystery *Everyman*. I have written elsewhere of Tony Guthrie and so have many of the theatre people who had worked with him. To me, he had been very kind indeed. It was delightful to meet him again but only too evident that he was no longer the provocative, brilliant, explosive Tony we had all known and so greatly admired. He was ill and soon to die.

And so, sadly, it came about that I was asked to direct whatever play I cared to choose for the opening of the James Hay Theatre. It was a formidable undertaking and at first I hesitated. But an irresistible bait was trailed before me. It was promised that we would have full use of the stage throughout the five weeks of rehearsal. After years of condemned premises, dirty, cold and balefully uninspiring, this was primrose news indeed. I fell for it.

In the event, such are the devils who beset theatrical endeavour that it turned out to have no more substance than a dream. Owing to strikes, over-optimism, unrealistic appraisements and the non-arrival of electrical equipment, we did not set foot in the theatre until twenty-four hours before curtain-up on the opening night. This meant working continuously through day and night, in a litter of electrical equipment, scenery, hammering and an atmosphere of near-despair. The first dress rehearsal, endlessly interrupted, was also a mechanical and lighting rehearsal. The second, uninterrupted, finished three hours before the curtain rose on the first performance. I had been given a committed and devoted assistant, Helen Holmes, and without her I don't think we would have made our deadline. On the night before we opened, she laboured right through. The workmen arrived in the morning to find her there and remarked that she was making an early start.

Apart from being obliged to endure this nightmare, I had been given a completely free hand.

Henry V was an appropriate choice for the occasion. Almost certainly it was Shakespeare's play for the opening of the newly-built

Globe Theatre. It had always seemed to me to be, in the first instance, a play about plays and playhouses. Like many another dramatist who was to follow him, Shakespeare was irked and frustrated by the theatre's limitations and excited by its potential. So he created 'Chorus' to explode upon the opening scene with his 'O, for a Muse of fire', to lament and apologize and exult and light a flame in the hearts of his unruly audiences. Again and again he came before them at that opening performance, four centuries ago in The Globe, to woo, to beckon, to reach out over the physical and emotional gulf that every actor must bridge. It is in the thoughts of the audience, he insists, that the reality of a play is born and he uses the word over and over again. The theatre, he says is a 'quick forge and working house' of thought. The audience must perform their part, they must 'work, work' their thoughts. '*Think*,' he urges, 'when we *talk* of horses that *you see* them . . .' 'You must', he says, 'piece out our imperfections with your thoughts.'

And of course it was Shakespeare who beckoned and roused up and implored. Behind the mask of 'Chorus' is the author himself making his age-old appeal: 'Like us, meet us halfway. Please. Please.'

To fulfil this role we brought out from London the young actor who, five years ago, had played Laertes for us in a production of *Hamlet*. Jonathan Elsom had won a bursary to a drama school in London and was now an experienced and successful actor.

He was to arrive a fortnight before we opened. We wrote, of course, repeatedly and at great length about the role which in the meantime he was to prepare. At last, and how vividly I recall this, it fell out that one day I was writing, not for the first time, that Jonathan must always be aware that it was Shakespeare himself who was speaking. I suddenly thought: 'But of course! Very well then! Let's go the whole hog and make it so.' I cabled him to get a Shakespeare wig made and finished the letter in the highest state of excitement.

We managed to preserve our secret from the rest of the cast. It was not until that first nightmarish dress rehearsal when they were all collected on stage that they found their author had joined the company.

The malign fates had one more kick in the pants reserved for us. On the opening night for fifteen agonizing minutes the curtain refused to budge. An electrical engineer arrived and at 8.15 it rose. And so, in that state of febrile, sick anticipation that crackles over backstages on first nights, we opened *Henry V.*

It worked.

The house lights dimmed. Eight trumpeters came out and sounded a fanfare. There was music. The curtain rose on an empty stage, clouds of mist, a luminous blue cyclorama and a solitary unmistakeable person who stood before it. As he came down to the forestage through the mist, the audience's recognition of him ripened into the sound that is the accolade of all players, and when at the end of the first chorus he asked them 'gently to hear, kindly to judge our play' it broke out again and in the shadows offstage we said to each other: 'We have a play.'

It ran for a season that could not be extended, to full houses.

'Thus far,' says Chorus at the end of the play, 'our bending author hath pursued the story.' And thus far I may, I hope, be forgiven for adding, did this bending director pursue her attempts to stage ten of his plays. When the curtain fell on the last night of *Henry V* it did so on my final Shakespeare production.

Theatrical endeavour is the most ephemeral of all the arts. When a season comes to an end it does so abruptly and completely and if, in whatever form and however explicitly or abstractly the cloud-capped towers and gorgeous palaces may have been suggested, they do indeed melt into air, into thin air. Canvas flats, stacked against a wall, a bare stage, a folded cyclorama and dust are all that is left of Illyria or the road to Dover, of Agincourt or Elsinore or the Blasted Heath. There will be some press notices. A few performances will survive for a time in actors' shop-talk, fewer still in books about theatre. Such a book, at least in part, is this.

What has been of lasting value in our student-players' Shakespearean ventures over the past forty years? Perhaps, first of all, that they *were* still student-players and attracted young audiences who otherwise would not have experienced the plays in performance and were fascinated by what they saw. One remembers the boy who stood with his hands on the edge of the apron stage for nearly three hours to watch *Hamlet*, the illicit sitters on rafters, and on the top of the lighting box because there was nowhere else to sit, the ones who came round after the show to ask questions, argue, propound. Above all, I think, there were those players, some in every production, who, after a few rehearsals would come to me and say they had not known that the plays were like this. Having, of course, had the pants bored off them by some pedagogue at school. Anthony Quayle once said to me that he was firmly of the opinion that teaching Shakespeare should be forbidden in schools. Remembering our exceptional Miss Hughes, perhaps the dictum should be given an additional gloss, 'except by a person of unusual ability'.

Of all the countless books that have been written about these plays over the last century I sometimes think that Granville Barker's *Prefaces* are the best. He was a playwright, a man of the professional theatre and also an academic. Knowing all about actors and the problems, limitations and liberties of playhouses, he wrote for the people who work in them. Because he was a scholar, and a man of sensitivity and perception, he wrote wisely of the texts. I returned again and again to his *Prefaces*.

When one is rehearsing Shakespeare there sometimes occurs a little miracle of a peculiar sort. One comes to a celebrated difficult passage upon which academic pundits have lavished pages of notes, a certain amount of guesswork, and pot-shots ending perhaps with the very persuasive conclusion that the text is indecipherably corrupt. An example is the speech about the 'dram of eale' in the second battlement scene of *Hamlet*. With many – not all – of such passages the baffled actor who is to speak one of them after, as it were, retiring to the study and mugging over all the commentaries, comes out no wiser than when he went in. He despairs. At this point he will, if he is an old hand, remember that his author, when he put words together, was a supreme master of sound and that the pulse of his blank verse is tremendous, the pauses imperative and that, with him, music and meaning are incorporate.

So the actor will experiment. He will repeat this devilish passage and for the time being pay no attention to sense but the sharpest and most devoted attention to sound. He will try and try again until shape, cadence, pauses and emphases *sound* right and while he sweats away at this exercise the door to interpretation has opened without him noticing and suddenly he knows without a doubt what he is talking about.

It is well to remember the conditions under which these plays were written: to think of some spring morning at the Globe Theatre when the Lord Chamberlain's Players were assembled under an open sky to re-rehearse a scene that went wrong at the last performance. Their manager, master and star-actor, Burbage, tells them the current show won't run longer than two weeks. Perhaps he says to his bit-part actor-playwright, 'See what you can do with this, Will,' and throws him a dilapidated old script. Or perhaps he asks him if he's got anything ready and if not, why not. And the bit-part actor goes away and writes *King Lear* in a fortnight.

It is no wonder, indeed, that many of the texts are corrupt: the wonder is that there are not more mistakes, more muddles, that the author himself did not slap in more careless or stock audience-informative minor scenes, or that insoluble confusions of time sequences, such as that which occurs in *Othello*, did not spill over into other plays. In that 'quick forge and working house' of theatre Shakespeare was not, could not be, a meticulous writer. He wrote at speed for a demanding boss and avid audiences. And, being a genius, more often than not he wrote like one.

In *Romeo and Juliet* he talks about 'the two hours' traffic of our stage'. Even allowing for poetic licence this is puzzling. *Hamlet*, played in its entirety, and without intervals, lasts about four and a half hours. Did the Elizabethan actor get up a terrific head of steam and execute his soliloquies at breathtaking speed? Did the dialogue rattle about the stage like bursts of rifle-fire? And were Shakespeare's audiences much, much quicker on the uptake than our telly-saturated viewers? I believe they must have been.

For a company embarking upon that journey with their playwright that all rehearsals call upon them to make, questions like these constantly arise. I believe that when their fellow traveller is William Shakespeare the actors themselves change a little on the journey. The more sensitive among them arrive enriched at their destination. If it is a happy company, a fine and lasting camaraderie is established. It delights me to record that this has been so with our student-players. We have explored together, striven together and, when fortune was on our side, succeeded together. I began by remarking upon the ephemeral nature of theatrical endeavour: this is the place to say that the bond that was established during our golden days endures.

Nowadays there are four major professional theatre companies in New Zealand and from time to time they all present one of Shakespeare's plays. Here in Christchurch, in the once-academic buildings that housed our original Little Theatre, is the Court Theatre with one of our earlier student-players, Elric Hooper, now a most experienced, widely travelled and gifted director, at the helm. From time to time English actors are imported for a season and are impressed by what they find. Our hope is that more of those student-players who made the hazardous decision, won a bursary to a London drama school and went professional, will return briefly, as Jonathan Elsom does, to give us a taste of their quality.

At the end of nearly every season when the cast still breathed the heady air of success and commitment, one or two players would come to me, hell-bent on becoming full-time actors. In almost every case they met with little encouragement.

The theatre is the most overcrowded profession in the world. In London when a new play is cast there are enough out-of-work, highly experienced and talented actors to fill each part over and over again. This may be one of the reasons why the standard of performance in the English theatre is so high; it is also a very good reason why any young enthusiast should ask him- (or her-) self how he would shape up in such a competitive field. And even if, after a long hard look at himself, he still believes he has a genuine potential, he must face this cruel reality: success often depends as much upon chance as upon ability. He must find himself an agent. He must be ready to endure exile in a wilderness where he waits, day after day in a bed-sitting room for the telephone to ring. And when, by some fluke, he is cast, it may well be in a small walk-on part that offers no artistic or financial potential but which, by this time, he is glad enough to accept.

Remembering these bleak prospects, one would be less than honest if one did not put them before any starry-eyed hopeful who does not want to consider them. Over the last thirty years and throughout fifteen productions there have been one girl and four young men who I thought would never be happy unless at least they tried, and who seemed to me to be possessed of that unfair and wayward gift known to actors as 'star quality'. Of the young men, one was unhappily lame. The other three have become well-known and well-established British professional actors and have prospered. The last, indeed, is now a star. And the girl? She was, I think, perhaps the most gifted of them all; largely an instinctive actress with a God-given sense of timing, a lovely voice and witchcraft in her ways. If all had gone well and she had lived, she must have shone very brightly indeed in that most precarious firmament.

Someone once said, and justly was it said, that madmen flock to Shakespeare as flies to a honey pot. The indisputable facts that are known about his life could be covered by three hundred words. Surmise and conjecture ranging from plausible speculation to stark, staring lunacy would, one is tempted to venture, fill as many tidy-sized volumes. Some years ago I used, at intervals, to receive from a gentleman in the Middle West of the United States of America, packets of diagrams purporting (I think) to illumine God-knew-what theory on the authorship of the plays and sonnets. They arrived together with pamphlets typed, cyclostyled, and in some instances printed on different-sized bits of paper. They were totally incomprehensible. In the margins exclamation marks, queries and arrows proliferated. Passages were scored under in scarlet ink and handwritten comments abounded: 'How true!!!' '*Bosh!*' 'See *Titus Andronicus* or *Pericles*??' And in one instance a possibly triumphant '*Ah-Ha!!*' The sender neglected to give an exact address so I was mercifully spared writing acknowledgements which may have been why these baffling documents stopped coming.

Arguments as to the authorship of Shakespeare's plays and the identity of Mr W. H., the subject of the publisher's dedication to the sonnets, range from the respectable to the thoroughly dotty.

There is one rebuttal to the anti-Stratford arguments that I have never seen advanced but which any actor would find irrefutable. Let us return for a moment to The Globe. The company is assembled. The new piece they are rehearsing is *Hamlet, Prince of Denmark*. In no time Shakespeare is being asked for explanations.

'Dear boy, what *do* you *mean* by "the dram of eale doth all the noble substance of a doubt to his own scandal"? Could you just give me a *line* on it, dear boy?'

Now. If somebody else wrote the play and if Shakespeare is in fact a Stratfordian semi-rustic clodhopper who has been told (by whom and why?) to pretend he wrote the play, how does he make out? He will be constantly badgered with such questions to which he hasn't a notion of an answer and to which his only response can be an oafish guffaw. He would not last a morning's rehearsal without being rumbled. And if anyone supposes that, Heaven knows why, the Lord Chamberlain's players were required to keep under their hats a piece of gossip of such an intriguing kind as this, they have no knowledge of what actors are like when they take a drink or two together.

I advance this hypothetical picture for the consideration of any anti-Stratfordian theorists who may chance to read these reminiscences.

I have already ventured to say that in a long association with student-players we contrived to establish as near a professional approach to our work as may be achieved by actors who have other commitments. This was made the more possible by long summer vacations and by the students' readiness to give up recreational activities and devote themselves absolutely to the production in hand. They came more and more to be wholly committed. I hope I am not arrogant in thinking – in daring to think – that in this process they became less insular, more civilized, more intellectually adventurous and perhaps more responsible beings than they would have been if they had submitted themselves exclusively to the degree-factory process that unhappily pervades our universities.

Directors' approaches to the plays vary, of course, enormously. Tyrone Guthrie manipulated his actors, I suppose it might be said, like a puppet-master. He experimented. He improvised. He would think of a treatment for a scene, orchestrate his actors' movements to bring out his reading, rehearse exhaustively and ruthlessly and scrap the whole thing if he decided it didn't work. 'No good. What a pity,' he would say. 'Never mind. Rise above.' And away they'd all go on a new tack.

Lewis Casson, on the contrary, prepared his elaborate production scripts beforehand. I have been told that he did this down to the last detail, marked the vocal inflections he was going to require of his actors as if in a music score and insisted on the strictest observance of them.

There are directors who go into huddles with an actor and have inaudible, interminable discussions while the rest of the cast hang about on the sidelines. There are directors who sit immovably in the stalls and others who are on stage, in front-of-house, all over the theatre. Some like to illustrate and to give inflections and require the actor to echo them precisely. Others never do this. They talk about the character in question, however small his role, and invite the actor to decide how, in any given situation, such a person would feel and react. From what I have already written of my productions with student-players it will be seen that this was the manner in which we went to work.

It was in crowd scenes of course, that the rank-and-file came into their own, most of all in *Julius Caesar*. For our modern dress production of this play in the Civic Theatre on a stage thrust out over the orchestra pit into the auditorium, we had a crowd of about sixty. They formed themselves into small groups of three, five and seven. Each group chose its own background – a working-class family of three generations, a cluster of students, members of a gang, down-and-outs, emotional women. I wrote sheets of cued dialogue for them, often using lines from other plays–*Coriolanus*, for instance, and the Histories. Some groups improvised their own dialogue. This was a hazardous undertaking and sometimes had to be checked. I remember a strongly New Zealand voice soaring above the crowd like a football fan's tribute: '*Look ut thet! Look ut thet! Hey! Watch it, mate.*' His zeal was admirable but, alas, it had to be modified.

Julius Caesar might have been subtitled 'The Mob'. In it Shakespeare demonstrates a sort of law of opposites – the bigger the crowd, the less responsible its individual members and their corporate reactions. When Mark Antony has finished with them the mob has the mass intelligence and amorality of a vicious six-year-old child. The director's job is to orchestrate. The volume of sound the crowd produces must be perfectly controlled and synchronized with the orator's speech. Overall there is one frightening crescendo that finally explodes into violence. Within this structure there are lesser climaxes for which Shakespeare gives occasional specific dialogue that must emerge above the groundswell. A woman gushes of Antony: 'Poor soul, his eyes are red as fire with weeping.' (Which they are not.) Her friends cluck with enjoyable concurrence. An aggressive male voice suddenly proclaims, 'There's not a nobler man in Rome than Antony,' and this when two minutes ago they had all been cat-calling and booing him. The mob under Antony's manipulation now becomes a single, idiot, menacing entity. To control, balance, order and shape this superb piece of dramatic writing is like conducting an orchestra and in the event I don't know which was the more exhilarated, the company or I.

And still, in all these productions, indeed throughout our association, I was obliged to take heroic short cuts. Techniques that a drama school covers in two years had to be injected in six weeks. The longer the casts the more arduous this process.

As time went on, a core of experienced actors emerged and were a stimulating influence on the newcomers. I have spoken of the ones who went further afield and prospered. Among them, and most emphatically, is James Laurenson. He came to us as a first-year teachers' college student and was cast for a small part in *Antony and Cleopatra*. (I telescoped a Messenger, Scarus and Dercetas for it.) It is difficult to find a place for an interval in this play. I took it after the Messenger's shattering news for Antony. 'The news is true, my lord . . . Caesar has taken Toryne.' Its effect depended entirely upon the way this line was given and Antony's reaction to it. As soon as I heard Jimmy's voice I knew we were home and dry. Later, when he came to deliver to Caesar the sword with which Antony had killed himself and announced: 'I am call'd Scarus-Dercetas,' it was the same. The next role he played for us was Macbeth.

In this same play, *Antony and Cleopatra*, there is a secondary part: Proculeius, a Roman soldier whom Antony told Cleopatra to trust. He was played by a newcomer from Westland who is still known as Proc to the old hands and is now the author of a number of impressive plays and a notable director of these and as many more: Proc, which is as much as to say Mervyn Thompson. In his autobiography, recently published, Proc indicates that I alarmed him beyond measure in this, our first encounter. I am glad I seem no longer to strike any chords of terror in his bosom.

A university drama society is by its very nature ephemeral. At the end of each academic year it burns out and one can only hope it will rise from its ashes when the new year begins. For this reason our auditions were always open to experienced players who had graduated and were no longer students. With us the play really was 'the thing' and must be served above everything else by the best of available talent. For me, when my active association with these players came, as it must, to an end, it did so in the happiest imaginable way. Jonathan Elsom crops up quite often in these pages. He is now well enough established on the London stage to take the dreaded risk of 'losing touch' by too long an absence from it. A year or two after his great success as Chorus in *Henry V* he returned and brought with him a script he had put together for a one-man show called *Sweet Mr Shakespeare*. He asked me to direct him. The first half dealt with what material we have relating to Shakespeare, legendary, apocryphal or positive, from the wildly unauthentic John Aubrey to soberly exact Ben Jonson. Jonathan, by a series of slight but entirely adequate quick-changes, was in turn an Elizabethan man-in-the-street, Aubrey, a sea captain, a pedagogue, Francis Meres, Robert Greene with his acid 'Shakescene' and 'upstart crow', Sir John Wooton and sundry gossips and commentators. The second half consisted only of sonnets and the little dirge from *Cymbeline*.

It was an elegant, accomplished and moving performance.

And now Jonathan and James are in London. Proc is a dramatist and director and lectures in his subject at Auckland University. Elric directs The Court. Canterbury University has its own handsome theatre and the Drama Society, as ever, has its ups and downs. Unhappily I am unable to follow them at first hand because the only approach to the auditorium is by flights of stairs which are not within my compass nowadays. John Pocock, one of the student-players of our early days and now a celebrated and august historian, was co-author with Bruce Mason, our most distinguished playwright, of a book called *Theatre in Danger*. In it they wrote of the times with the Canterbury University Drama Society that I have tried to describe. They called them 'the Golden Age'. For me, at any rate, they were all of that and that is how I shall always think of them.

II

Since the days when I wrote the preceding chapters until now I have concocted eleven more Alleyn stories, sandwiching them between five Shakespeare productions and have made trips to England and to Italy, Copenhagen, Yugoslavia and Vigo and those groups of West

Indian islands which I shall never cease to confuse – the three Bs: Bermudas, Bahamas and Barbados.

The five weeks in Rome may be described as pampered. I was lucky enough to stay with the Alister McIntoshes at the Residence of the New Zealand Embassy where Alister was established as our first New Zealand Ambassador in Italy. The Residence has since been moved to a no doubt posher but certainly less enchanting site than that house in 'old' Rome.

In a narrow side street off the exquisite Piazza Navona, it was reached by means of a lift and Primo, an eccentric porter who inspected all in-comers from some kind of invisible eyrie, where he could be heard indecipherably shouting. He admitted callers at once or, regardless of rank or distinction, caused them to wait, sometimes for an unconscionable time, in a rather dreary, dark little office. It was impossible to guess what line of reasoning prompted Primo to behave in this disconcerting manner. He roared a great deal and understood no English but he 'went with' the Residence and might not be discarded.

He was the cause of extreme mortification to Marcello who was a sort of unofficial master-of-ceremonies-cum-controller of the household. But before invoking Marcello, who is unique, I must pause for a moment in this impressive interior. It was an apartment occupying a whole floor and a half of a very large building and was leased to our government by a rich American lady. The rooms were enormous and nobly proportioned. There were some huge, dark, dimly classical and vaguely belligerent pictures. The drawing room opened on to a roof garden from which one looked out upon an operatic backdrop of windows, walls and Roman streets that might have been ordered by Franco Zeffirelli. I arrived in spring and the air was alive with swallows. They darted across the vision so fast that a single bird looked like a flight of little arrows.

When one left the Residence it was to walk into the noise of Rome, which is formidable: a conglomerate of excited voices, motor horns, church bells and millions of feet. Almost everywhere, it seemed, it was presided over by stone saints high up against a brilliant sky, making beneficent frozen gestures upon the teeming streets. I never tired of watching Romans in conversation. Two men, for instance, would greet each other soberly enough, sometimes gloomily: there would follow what might seem to be commiseration on the one hand and on the other tragic acceptance. Hands and eyes would be cast up. Shoulders would be clapped or stroked. Then, for no discernible reason, eyes would flash, teeth would be bared, voices would rise. Romantic profiles were advanced to within inches of each other. They were not yelling. A fight would seem to be imminent. 'Well, come *on*, then,' one would think, by this time oneself demoralized and, I'm afraid, longing for a scrap, 'get on with it.'

And then, without warning, these unpredictable gentlemen would burst into peals of laughter, shake hands extensively, clap each other on the back and part, refreshed, it was obvious, by their baffling encounter.

Marcello, then. Marcello is a handsome, exquisitely mannered Roman, a chartered accountant, I believe, by profession and a motion picture creator who with a partner won the prize for a documentary at a film festival. Unhappily this success persuaded him to venture further with disastrous results. At the time when the New Zealand Embassy offices, which were some distance away from the Residence itself, were being set up, he had secured an extremely humble job in them. From this embarrassment, after confirmation of his story, he was rescued and promoted to chief driver for the Ambassador and thence to the indefinable but immensely important role in which he is now cast. *Éminence grise* one might be tempted to call Marcello except that there is no suggestion of high-flown, off-stage manipulations or devious on-goings at any level, and not a hint of advancing himself above the role which he performs with such tact, adroitness and mastery.

It is the role itself which is elusive and impossible to define. He is still head driver and he drives beautifully, although you may not quite fancy certain tendencies. For instance when, in the hurly-burly of the terrifying Roman street traffic, another driver tries to put one across him, Marcello removes both hands from the wheel, puts them together and raises them in ostentatious and sarcastic prayer as if to say 'The Mother of God protect us from such as you.' He is of course too grand to lean out of his window and scream abuse.

When formal dinner parties were given Marcello was in the room throughout, presiding over the butler and footman who were engaged for these occasions and who did not seem to resent his presence. After a large reception when all the guests were gone, Marcello and Vera, his wife who assists offstage with the housework, would come in to say good night. Ceremonial, almost feudal, kisses were exchanged and compliments bestowed.

When sightseeing trips were taken Marcello achieved wonders. At Paestum, a magical place of temples and ancient marvels in the south, beyond Amalfi, he required a closed museum to be opened for us and at Pompeii again caused those notorious rooms with extremely explicit frescoes to be unlocked for our slightly embarrassed inspection. At the exquisite Villa Giulia where visitors' cameras are confiscated at the bureau, he excused himself for a moment and returned with the curator's compliments and our cameras which, to the scarcely concealed and understandable anger of tourist groups, we were allowed to use. Nobody knew how Marcello achieved these miracles, but if it was by graceful bribery it was at his own expense. Probably it was by an appeal to snobbery.

For, it must be confessed, Marcello is a great snob and was much gratified when visits were made to grand restaurants or smart shops. But he is also extremely thrifty and his gratification was tempered by considerations of expense. He admired the Ambassador and went completely but respectfully overboard for the Ambassador's lady. On one occasion when he was driving her to her dentist, she remarked that she was not looking forward to her appointment.

'If he hurt you I kill him,' Marcello alarmingly remarked.

Vitalia, the cook at the Embassy, was elderly, cunning and very, *very* devout. She did the marketing, but under the despotic supervision of Marcello to whom she had to account for every last centesimo that she spent. Every Friday evening if you passed the open door into the kitchen, there would be the wretched Vitalia seated with her account book at a table while Marcello with jabbing forefinger stood over her.

While I was staying at the Embassy, Vitalia came into her own. It seemed that in her native village there had lived a holy person now defunct and undergoing the long-drawn-out process of being made a saint. Vitalia as one, possibly the only one, still alive, who could bear first-hand witness to the alleged miracles, was constantly required by the Devil's advocate to do so. She gained enormous prestige by this circumstance and became unbearably smug: almost, one might have thought, as if she herself was in the running for beatitude. Marcello, maddened by her airs, teased her unmercifully, pretending he saw a halo coming and going over her head.

He has a sense of fun. A political election was in progress and one of the high-ranking candidates was a pompous, excitable but tiny minister who paced about the bedroom all night in a state of tension. His wife, Marcello said, had remarked that she would be glad when the election was over as she was getting no sleep with him walking to and fro under their bed.

Marcello speaks the sort of English that one had assumed to be made up by variety artistes impersonating Italians. When a pipe burst in the Embassy he really did say: 'I getta da plum.'

Perhaps I should have first tried to set down some of the wonders of Rome instead of remarking on the idiosyncracies of the staff at one of its smaller embassies. The truth is I have already tried to suggest them in a book that I wrote after leaving it. *When in Rome* is yet another detective novel but it is based on, and for the most part takes place at, a recognizable basilica – San Clemente in Via di S. Giovanni in Laterano. I called it San Tommaso but that was the only difference.

Doris McIntosh and I, driven and escorted as always by Marcello, first visited San Clemente one spring morning. To explore it is to walk downwards and again downwards through nineteen centuries into the age of Mithras. The present Basilica – one of the loveliest in Rome – is, as it were, the top layer of a superb historical cake. It was built over an early Christian church which was filled in with earth to support it but has now been excavated and restored by Irish Dominicans who have been in charge there since 1677 and began excavating in 1877. And still further down under this place of worship is a first-century *insula* or block of Roman flats. And there, in a grotto, at the far end of his sacrificial chamber and rising out of a bed of breast-like stones, stood the god who was born out of a stony matrix, a strange, smooth, plump figure, not child, not man, with a Phrygian cap on his long curls: Mithras. There he had stood, fixed and heavy, for nineteen hundred years and there we stood in his temple which was forbidden to all women.

I knew at once that I wanted to write about him and when we got home began to read about his cult and what is known of the rites that were practised in his honour. It was easy to fill the triculum with the bellowing of a garlanded bull and the reek of blood on hot stone.

We returned to San Clemente and on this second visit noticed how all the subterranean region where Mithras was fixed in his stones was filled with the sound of running water, because down there behind one of the walls runs an underground stream of pure water. It flows into the Cloaca Maxima about seven hundred yards away, close by the Colosseum.

Some six months later *When in Rome* was published.

But in the meantime Doris, knowing I was writing this book, thought she would like to visit San Clemente for the third time. Down she went through the now familiar corridors, nave and apse, past exquisite garlanded columns and frescoes whose colours are as bright as when they were painted, having been preserved by long burial in protective earth. And again down to the lowest level and the temple of Mithras. And to his grotto at the far end. It had been roped off.

Mithras was gone.

At first she could not, as one says, believe her eyes. After almost twenty centuries there was now only a litter of the breast-like stones into which he had been so firmly sunk and sealed! She returned up all the stairs to the bureau where the good brothers sell their cards and pamphlets and innocent little holy knick-knacks. By this time she was on friendly terms with them and was greeted, as usual, in the richest of Irish brogues. But the answers she was given were evasive and she came away none the wiser except that it seemed clear that the Dominican brothers had had nothing to do with the removal of the god Mithras, born of a rock, who was said to have banqueted with Apollo.

III

When I was in Rome there was a riot. At that time riots were of frequent occurrence. Beyond knowing that as usual it was political in character, and that students were heavily involved, I never really understood what this one was all about. It came to a head one evening. The belligerents assembled in thousands in the Piazza Navona, hard by the Embassy, and overflowed into our little side street. We watched from our windows.

It all seemed, in an odd sort of way, lackadaisical, more like a first 'take' for a film than the real thing. There were all the ingredients: a vast crowd of extras, students, shouting, a bit of singing here, operatically dressed police there, doing nothing in particular except lounge about and smoke.

As far as we could see, there was a great deal of noise but no fighting or making arrests. But there was naughty behaviour of an exasperating, idiotic sort. A group of young men who had been lounging near a motorcycle parked under our windows, half-heartedly turned it over on its side and, after several, unsuccessful attempts, set fire to it and walked away. This was followed by a group of about a hundred young men erupting out of Navona and running down the side street, followed, though not very fast, by some of the police. They were not the highly picturesque *carabinieri* but the work-a-day *corpo di polizia*. They did not attempt to arrest anybody and as soon as their non-quarry got to the far end of the street and stopped, the police, very sensibly I thought, also stopped and lit cigarettes. I don't remember any exchange of insults or threats or shaken fists, still less any baton charges. It was as if the director had shouted 'Cut' and everybody stopped acting. Meanwhile the background noise in Navona continued terrifically.

I am sure these rather limp demonstrations were by no means typical of Italian street demonstrations and riots as a whole but they did seem to me to be in paradoxical contrast to the ordinary street conversations that so often suggest belligerence and a violent approach to the most harmless of commonplace remarks.

While I was still in Rome I had a letter from Pammy, my former student-secretary, now a terrific passer of examinations and going great guns in Social Welfare. She suggested that I hire a car and that she come and drive it, being acquainted with Italy and the hazards of Italian motoring. When we had had our fill of this exercise we could return the car, no matter where we were, and take to the railroad. We planned to go to Perugia and thence to Florence for a week and on to Lucca to stay with friends who had a rural *palazzo* thereabouts. To Genoa then, by train. And so, by Paris and the English Channel, home.

Pammy, intrepid girl, arrived in the afternoon, collected the car and launched herself into the streets of Rome where she soon got lost. She asked her way of a driver with whom she found herself cheek-by-jowl in a traffic jam. He spoke English and offered to pilot her to her destination. So she followed him. The course he took was not direct. Presently she found herself high up in the world. He signalled for her to drive up beside him and stop.

She had arrived at the Tabularium on the Capitol and was looking down into the Forum on a fine evening – perhaps the most astonishing view in all Italy.

They leant on the wall and her guide, who was a dashing young man with a pleasing manner, pointed out the near-at-hand three columns of the Temple of Vespasian, and in the middle distance those of the Temple of Castor and Pollux and far away, darkly, the ominous bulk of the Colosseum. It was as if everything she had ever read or been told of Roman history had been unrolled, suddenly, in the evening light. Pammy was deeply impressed but a trifle uneasy. Her escort, perceiving this, removed his hat.

'I am a Roman gentleman,' he informed her.

'And I am very glad to hear it,' she warmly replied.

So he opened the door of her car for her, returned to his own and guided her back through chaotic traffic to the Piazza Navona and thence to the New Zealand Ambassadorial Residence where he took his leave, as a Roman gentleman should.

We left Rome the next morning and Marcello drove ahead and with careful signals set us upon the road to Perugia. And there I said goodbye to dear Marcello. For some years we exchanged Christmas cards. I expect he still does his splendid indefinable thing at the New Zealand Embassy and if ever he comes across this book I hope he will accept my greetings.

Before absolutely quitting Rome I would like to repeat a little legend which was much invoked at the time I was there.

The Pope was giving audience to a group of visitors and to each of them he put the same question: 'How long are you staying in Rome?'

The first visitor replied: 'Your Holiness, alas, no time at all. I am desolate but tomorrow I am obliged to leave. I shall have seen nothing.'

'Oh,' said the Pope, 'I wouldn't say that. It is possible, if you use your time wisely, to see quite a lot of Rome in twenty-four hours.'

And he moved on to the next tourist and asked him the same question.

'Your Holiness, unfortunately only three weeks. What can one see of Rome in three weeks!'

'Oh,' said the Pope, 'it is a very short time, certainly, but use it advisedly and you will be the richer for your visit.'

And he moved on to the third tourist and asked him the same question.

'Your Holiness, I am very fortunate. My company has transferred me to Rome. I shall be here for five years.'

'Five years!' exclaimed His Holiness. 'I'm afraid you won't see very much of Rome in five years.'

· IV

What a lovely drive we had that morning across the Umbrian plains. It was like seeing one quattrocento background after another, with little towns against rounded hills and surrounded by well-disciplined pastures and formal trees, all very fresh and cleanly defined. One middle-distance view I particularly admired was of Todi. There was nothing spectacular about Todi, no enormous church, no 'must' for the tourist. Simply a small mediaeval town that would have been none the worse for an angel or two flying decorously above the roof-tops and in the streets a bullock wagon and perhaps a man driving it wearing scarlet stockings, a smock and a rustic hat.

We stopped and photographed it and of all the photographs I took in Italy that is the one I like best.

That afternoon we reached Perugia and the Rossetta Hotel. It was like any university town in any other country that had been uplifted and translated into an Italian setting. We sat in an outdoor *caffè* on a high terrace and almost all the other customers were students and looked like students and behaved like well-conducted students. Quite a lot of them spoke either English-English or American-English, since the University of Perugia has summer courses for foreigners and is very popular. It had been a long day and we went early to bed.

The next morning, after breakfast, we drove to Assisi.

What do I remember of Assisi?

Great height. Up and up and then under a windy sky a long view from outside the church. The mist that had been drifting over Umbria cleared slowly and one by one, here and there, vignettes appeared of houses and farms and Noah's Ark animals. Foolishly I was reminded of the looking-glass view Alice had from the top of a hill above the chessboard country.

We stayed here for some time while a fresh breeze blew in the little village of Assisi.

At last we turned away and went into the church and of course it was the Basilica of St Francis and of course there was the Chapel of San Martino with frescoes by Martino Sierre of the Saint being nice to birds and an apotheosis with scarlet horses and a superb green and blue ceiling. As almost always in Italian churches, in spite of all these wonders, there was an air of everyday usage about the Basilica.

Instead of returning to Perugia we now drove deep into the mountains because Pammy knew of a remote grotto at Remo della Carcere where an order of monks lived in simplicity and hardly anybody else ever went there. So we went and were moved by it.

The next day we left for Florence.

Our entry into Florence was little short of hellish. To us it seemed as if the various approaches led into it like the radii of a spider's web but that, having passed through the perimeter, they broke up into a maze of lanes and passages into which we edged and out of which, with much ado, we gingerly backed. Our attempts to penetrate them closely resembled a certain slow-motion nightmare to which I am very prone: the one about not being able to get there. You move in a certain direction or seem to do so but The Others, persons who are always there in dreams and are always elusive and unhelpful, either misdirect you or don't seem to hear what you say but merely nod or smile or don't give you an answer because of something vague that you don't understand. They say they will tell you the answer (to what?) when they come back but they don't come back. On this occasion they seemed to be the sole inhabitants of the streets going into Florence. They came and went while Pammy left me in the car and ran after one of them showing him our address 'Pensione

Hermitage, Vicolo Marzio 1, Ponte Vecchio'. He pointed and gesticulated and seemed to make sense.

Pammy returned and started us off and suddenly we were there
at The Hermitage hard by the Ponte Vecchio. Only, when we stopped
and began to take our suitcases out of the car, there were policemen
saying we must move on. Somebody – a porter – came out of The
Hermitage and there followed one of the Italian street scenes with
which I had become so familiar. We were made to understand we
might park the car in some cloisters nearby, but only on sufferance
and not for long. We now decided the moment had arrived when
the car was more of a burden than a blessing and Pammy rang up
the local offices of the firm that had rented it to us and they collected
it; we paid their very moderate bill and settled into our rooms in The
Hermitage.

It was one of the nicest places I have ever stayed in, small but
wonderfully situated and beautifully ordered. There were two waiters, a porter and perhaps three chambermaids. The proprietors were
two middle-aged ladies who spoke fluent English. We did not have
a choice of dishes at meals but were served *en famille*, though at separate tables; the cooking was exquisite.

After dinner we walked about Florence in the cool of the evening
and were happy to be there.

We stayed for a week and every morning there was a new wonder. The year was 1968 and the wreckage left by the flooding of the
Arno was still evident: unbelievable high-water marks on the walls
of churches and the bases of monuments and everywhere, on both
gross and infinitely delicate surfaces, restorers were still at work.
Miracles of restoration were achieved – paintings were actually separated from damaged surfaces and laid on new ones.

Once again, this is not a guidebook which, in any case, I am not
capable of writing and all I can hope to do in the way of 'sights' is
give fugitive whiffs of my travels. To attempt this is rather like crushing a verbena leaf and finding oneself for a second or two in St Clair
and hearing the squawk of Gulliver the lame seagull and the sound
of the sea itself, when one was a child in Dunedin.

Other travellers are better remembrancers than I. My memory
has always been most eccentric, a thing of slipshod patchwork. Who
was a girl in my very remote childhood who looked out of a stand

of raupo in a riverbed and why did my mother say of her: 'Puck in the bulrushes'? Why 'Puck'? And how unbelievably young must I have been when I lay on my bed in a room with blue wallpaper and white flowers and, knowing my mother was resting on her own bed across the passage, wondered if I could stagger so far and did slide down and did stagger precariously across the passage and in at her door. I see her, really and truly I do, as if it were days and not two-thirds of a century ago, turn and smile her astonishment and hold out her hands. Why did my brain choose to retain this moment and no other of my remote infancy?

It is the same with travels and sights. Say 'Florence' and I see chubby rumps of Utrillo horses, comically improper. Then Donatello's little David, very smooth in hat and boots, then *the* David – Michelangelo's – and realize how huge are his head and hands and how lovely the line of his left thigh seen from the rear. Above all, Michelangelo's feeling for trembling flesh contrasting with firm flesh, expressed particularly in the veiled intensity of a mouth. For the hundredth time I see how little of the inner reality of art is conveyed by photographs and reproductions. Which makes me feel a bit smug, having experienced the reality. And after I've seen those things there is a kind of kaleidoscopic effect of quattrocento colour, clear pinks and blues and cardinal scarlet all as fresh as the day they were laid on, by Fra Angelico, of course: touching and truly devout but if I'm to be honest, no longer specific in my recollection. Not so the Botticelli. Aphrodite and her puffing zephyrs and dancing, well-conducted girls so often admired in coffee-table books, unlike the general surfeit of confused impressions, spring up in absolute clarity and perfection.

Well, for a week we walked and looked. There were other pleasures: a violent display of fireworks one night because there was some festival toward. We watched from the roof. And an evening up at Fiesole where high above Florence there is an open-air Roman theatre. Here a retrospective season of Antonioni's films opened with his early *Chronicle of a Love Affair*. We dined at Mario's and Signor Antonioni was at the next table. We went on to the theatre and there he was again, across the aisle, and signed Pammy's programme. It was a warm still night with the stars very emphatic overhead. *Chronicle of a Love Affair* is a remarkable and also an extremely long film. When midnight came and there seemed to be no end in sight we heard the bus for Florence start its engine and we bolted. We were only just in time.

When we arrived in Florence it was dark and silent and we were not at all sure where we had been put down. A lone taxi appeared. We took it and were back at The Hermitage by one o'clock in the morning and crept up to our bedrooms in the sleeping house.

V

The week (what would the Pope have said?) in Florence had been dazzling and one left it again saying, as one always does, that some day we would return. When it came to an end Vera, our friend at Lucca, collected us and we were driven across the top of Tuscany to San Concordio where she and her husband Ake lived in a sort of princely farmhouse with a gentle garden tucked into wooded hills. Vera is a distinguished painter. She and Ake had spent most of their lives in China where he was a top man in British espionage; in his own words, I'm afraid, 'A ball-bearing Mata Hari'. He was of Finnish descent but spoke English like an Englishman and Heaven knows how many Chinese dialects. He was also an authoritative sinologist. My great friends in New Zealand who had spent most of their lives in the Orient brought us together and in Lucca we had long gossips with, as Macbeth remarks in rather different circumstances, 'no more sights'.

And so after three good days with them, by train one Sunday to Genoa, where everything seemed to be called Christopher or Columbus or both, and then to Paris, where we spent a day with one of my student-players, Douglas MacDiamed, who lives there and is a painter of repute.

The English Channel was rough and for some reason that I've forgotten, a strike no doubt, the Dover train was extremely late. Instead of arriving at Victoria in the early evening we fetched up at London Bridge at midnight. There were not anything like enough taxis to go round. The porters were West Indians, some zealous and nimble in securing a cab, others lethargic and bored, ours the slowest of all. The last taxi had long gone, and so had he. There sat Pammy and I on our suitcases until two o'clock of a sweltering morning. Most of the lights were out when the last two black porters came off duty and said they had a car and would take us, if we liked, wherever we wanted to go as long as it was not too far. I wanted to go to the Basil Street Hotel in Knightsbridge and Pammy to a friend's flat nearby. So we thanked our rescuers and climbed in. They were kind and helped with the luggage and when we asked how much we owed them they said whatever we liked. I had five pounds and gave it to them and I wish it had been more because they brought a dismal night to a happy and gentle conclusion and we parted pleasantly.

I had been eight pampered weeks on my Italian travels and I now set about writing *When in Rome*.

CHAPTER 13

A Last Look Back

Until one has achieved publication the odds against appearing, however modestly, between hard covers seem astronomical. 'It couldn't happen to me' is the general feeling, or at least it was so in my case. I have related the circumstances under which it *did* happen and how by simply dumping my first Alleyn story with an agent and going out to New Zealand I escaped the awful humiliation of publishers' rejection slips, those definitive badges of being unwanted.

Nowadays, I suppose, like all professional authors, I am rung up or written to by people asking for short cuts to publication. It is not possible to reply in the way many of them obviously want you to. In my experience there are no short cuts. The only honest answer can be that all publishers are on the lookout for new authors but that few are prepared to risk the enormous cost of presenting a first book unless they are persuaded of its chances and those of a follow-up. It was this circumstance that prevented the publication of Allan Wilkie's autobiography, a remarkable account of his classic journeyings throughout the southern hemisphere with the plays of Shakespeare. Some old Wilkonians, including Hector Bolitho and myself, tried very hard but did not succeed. The publisher's reader's comments were favourable but regretful. One, the most august, from T. S. Eliot, had been left, by some oversight, in the typescript. It began 'This is a *nice* book', went on to praise it and ended, 'Unfortunately I am unable to recommend it for publication.'

The reason? It was what publishers call a 'oncer'. Needing copious illustrations, it would have been extremely costly to produce. By the nature of its subject matter the readership would have been limited to people who were of, or attracted to, the theatre. And there was no likelihood of a follow-up. But it *was* indeed a nice book. I recall one strange anecdote Mr Wilkie tells of a novice in his company. During a train journey, there came a sudden drop in the racket of their railroad progress in which this young actor's voice rang out.

'Ah, you may think I'm common,' he cried triumphantly, 'but you should just meet my people!'

I still lament the non-appearance of Allan Wilkie's autobiography. Many publishers seem to act in accordance with a yearly balanced programme or something closely resembling it: so many books by popular writers whose work is widely known and bound to appeal, so many with a limited appeal but of such literary, artistic, social or scientific interest that they will bring prestige to the firm that introduces them. Sometimes – very rarely – there comes their way a hitherto unknown author who has the mark of genius and for whom they are prepared to go overboard.

There is an anecdote told about my own publisher, Sir William Collins. He was an extremely tall, elegant man with something Puckish in his looks and great charm of manner. He had attended an International Congress of importance and when the luncheon break came and all the delegates were streaming down a corridor he was seen, head and shoulders above the rest, brandishing a bulky manuscript over his head and shouting, 'I've got the book of the century! I've got the book of the century!'

The book was *Doctor Zhivago.*

Many ringers-up or writers-in make their requests before they have set pen to paper or finger to keys. Often their friends have told them they ought to write a book and they intimate that they 'haven't got the patience' to do so unless they can be assured of seeing it in print. Many more suggest that I read their book and give them an opinion. Some send a piece without notice. One correspondent simply wrote on the back of a postal order for two shillings that he was prepared to collaborate and I was to insert the word 'Yes' in a morning newspaper of such and such a date. I lost the postal order and I suppose to this day he thinks I pinched it.

I wish very heartily that I could say some manuscript of outstanding merit has come my way over the last half-century but no such

luck. If it had I would have offered to send it with a letter of introduction to my agents. As it is I can only suggest to all enquirers that
they have mercy on me and provide themselves with a copy of the
current *Writers' and Artists' Yearbook*. It gives a list of reputable agents,
well-established publishers (with additional notes on how they like
to be approached) and offers sensible advice about finding out which
magazines or papers publish the kind of short story or article you
believe you can write.

It is foolish to send a piece on home-dressmaking to the *Poulterers'
Journal*.

Many years ago now, when I was beginning to get good notices
and increasing standing as a writer of detective fiction, my agents
and my American publishers asked me if I had ever thought of
'going straight'. They were kind enough to say they would be interested in such a departure and pointed out that many of the review-
ers emphasized the characterization and style of the books rather
than their sheer 'teckery and plot – contrivances which, I must confess, I never have been able to regard as anything but an exacting
chore. I have already suggested that in an age of much shapeless fiction the detective story presents a salutary exercise in the techniques of writing. It is shapely. It must have a beginning, a middle
and an end. The middle must be a logical development of the beginning and the end must be implicit in both. Economy as well as
expressiveness in words must be practised. One may not stray too
far from the matter-in-hand. I sometimes catch myself envying the
writers of fiction who can allow themselves long digressions into
whatever side issue takes their fancy and don't stop until they have
nothing more to say.

If my publishers' suggestion had come earlier I think perhaps I
might have entertained it. But I have never had much confidence in
myself as a writer and always think what I am doing at the moment
is awful and that I'm going to fall flat on my face and rise up with
egg all over it. This is odd because as a director of Shakespeare productions, beset by the terrors of first nights and all the rest of the
hazards of the game, I was persuaded, always, that what I wanted to
achieve was on the right lines and I think I always know, and
pretty exactly, too, just how far I have succeeded or failed in, as
actors say, 'getting a play to work'.

Because the books have done well I have been able to release my passion for these plays and my enduring love for the young actors with whom I have prepared them. It has been possible to forgo fees which a student society could not afford and so enable it to depart occasionally from the best known and therefore safest box-office attractions of Shakespeare's plays and tackle one that is not on the examination list and therefore will not draw block-bookings from the schools. So, in a way, the books have helped with the productions.

As time goes on, being interviewed about one's writing becomes more and more of an occupational hazard and demands more and more of a professional attitude. On being asked which of the books is one's favourite it is not easy to go dewy-eyed and behave as if one is stimulated by the question and is struck by its originality, particularly when, as in this case, the answer is that I haven't got one. Or else that the one I've just finished writing is my favourite because it's such a relief to have done with it. It would be much easier if the interviewer asked whether, apart from the Alleyns, I had any favourite characters. The Claires in *Colour Scheme*, The Boomer in *Black As He's Painted*, Inspector Fox and P.P. in *Hand in Glove* come to mind. I enjoyed writing about all of them. On consideration, I think perhaps I worried less about writing *Colour Scheme* and *Black as He's Painted* than I did with most of the others.

Inevitably, of course, I'm asked how many Alleyn stories I've written and inevitably, being me, I forget. I see, in the batch of reviews that has just come to hand, that they put it at thirty-two which surprises me.

Another evergreen enquiry is whether I've grown bored with Mr Alleyn. I haven't. Conan Doyle became so bored with Sherlock Holmes that he pushed him over the Reichenbach Falls and got for his pains an infuriated fan mail so huge that he was in the end forced to heave him up again. One of the letters, from a lady, merely said 'You beast.' So Holmes returned but it has been said that he was never the same man again. I incline to think that perhaps the trouble is that he was.

Since Sir Arthur's time, of course, a new kind of interviewer has arisen and what a job is his! The television probe! How grateful we must be to Mr Michael Parkinson who never shows off, never asks a silly question, never utters a bromide, always seems to be on-side with his subjects and neither flatters nor cajoles but crinkles into amusement and listens as a listener should, with quiet relish and enjoyment. Jolly nonagenarians, heart-transplanters, tenors, explorers, actors galore, authors, unrepentant homosexuals and ancient bewigged beauty specialists all walk into his parlour and succumb happily to his unostentatious charm. Has he worked very hard, one asks oneself, to attain such consummate ease?

The press interviewers of whom one becomes increasingly wary are young journalists attached to daily papers and, particularly, women journalists attached to women's journals, and, most especially, the young ladies who scorn to take notes. I have just read a quotation from an American *News of Books and Authors*. In it I am said to have 'reported' that I 'always smoke while writing'. I gave up smoking twenty years ago. The more inexperienced the reporter the less she enjoys being asked to let one see her story before publication and the more reckless her misstatements when it does appear in print. It doesn't happen on television, of course, because at least you're there and can contradict the soft impeachments.

The really terrifying televisual things, for me at least, are quiz shows. In character as an author of detective fiction, I was on a very tricky one for Independent Television in London. Outrageous and seemingly inexplicable events, said to have actually taken place, were put to the victims who were asked to give the true explanation. At the outset of this series I was smitten for the first and last time in my life with a devastating attack of lumbago. It struck me down when I was in the cellar of a London flat and it was so severe that I was forced to crawl on hands and knees across the kitchen and up two flights of stairs into a room where there was a telephone which I dragged down to floor level and rang a doctor.

He arrived in time to give me an injection in the lumbar region. This at least enabled me to become more mobile but wore off about halfway through the transmission, which was a live one. He repeated this treatment for the next appearances but was delayed on the final one. I waited till the last minute and then the friend who was staying with me got a taxi. She and the driver eased me into it. A press photograph was taken of the team that night. You can't see the beads of sweat that had gathered on my brow above the desperate smirk which I managed to flash at the cameras.

While I'm on about the author's complaints department I feel I must raise a piteous cry that publishers are probably very tired of hearing. It is a plea to the artist or photographer who does the book-jacket that he read the book or at least the passage the jacket is supposed to illustrate. The American jacket for the hardback of *Last Ditch* is a charming, rather old-fashioned pencil and wash affair that can only be made to conform with the text by assuming that the girl on the horse is galloping backwards at great speed into the ditch where her body will be found. I've had complaints about paperbacks. One from an English reader on the score of vulgarity so gross that she couldn't bring herself to buy the book as a present for a friend. It looked, said this reader, like a penny-dreadful in a sleazy book stall.

In *When in Rome* the clothes of a man who is murdered and thrown into a well are described in detail: Italian, black, alpaca-like suit, black tie and beret. On the paperback cover he is spread out, dry as a chip, on a marquetry floor wearing a natty blue business suit and felt hat.

The worst offence under this heading was the binder's transposition of two jackets and their titles. Infuriated purchasers, thinking they had found a new Alleyn story, discovered they had bought one with which they were already familiar.

I suppose, for non-authors, the best known pitfall in publishing is risk of prosecution for libel or defamation of character or plagiarism. There are famous cases: the one about a City personage who became so fed-up with the badinage of his friends and their quoting advertising jingles about a comical little man of the same very unusual name as himself, that he sued and obtained substantial damages from the firm that published them. There was a successful case against an author who created a disagreeable character and unfortunately gave him the same name as a person he had never met, of whose existence he had no knowledge but who sued and obtained enormous damages.

In one of my early books I introduced a rather unsavoury character called Luke Watchman. I received a charming letter from a real Luke Watchman but the coincidence was startling and might have turned out very differently.

There is, of course, a lighter side to occupational hazards. During the war when I was comparatively young and quite unused to any public appearances outside a theatre, I was asked to take part in a Brains Trust at a military camp. The other three performers were seasoned academics, politically pink and perfectly assured. Our audience consisted of active soldiers on leave from Guadalcanal, extremely tough and liable to cut up roughish if unamused by the proffered entertainment.

The hall where we were to perform was large and crammed to the doors with troops. We sat in a row on the stage. An officer had been detailed to act as chairman. He opened up by introducing us in turn by name and occupation and saying unconvincingly that he knew we would be given a fair hearing. He then declared the meeting open for questions from the audience. I noticed with terror that a soldier near the front was being nudged and muttered to by his neighbours and that they all looked at me.

After a deathly silence broken by the chairman saying, 'All right, men. Come on, now. Ask somebody something. Yes?' he added hopefully, having noted the reluctant warrior who now rose and turned scarlet in the face.

'Why,' he asked, staring at me, 'do people like reading about crime?'

The chairman turned to me and smilingly suggested this seemed to be in my department.

I should here explain that some provision had been made beforehand to guard against non-cooperation. Questions had been suggested to the troops. This, I have reason to believe, was one of them.

My mouth was dry and my stomach unruly. I remembered hearing a friend accustomed to public speaking say that the great thing was to start with a joke. The only military jokes I could recollect were about sergeants major.

I opened, in a voice that seemed to belong to someone else, by saying people might enjoy reading about crime as an alternative to committing it.

I then said, 'Suppose, for instance, one of you wanted to murder the sergeant major.'

I got no further. As one man the assembled strength broke into herculean laughter. They roared, they stamped, they hit each other on the back. They clapped and whistled.

This was extraordinary. Greatly taken aback but encouraged by my inexplicable success I held up my hands. There was immediate silence.

'Well,' I said, and hoped to sound breezily at ease, 'all right, suppose you *did* want – ' I got no further.

It broke out again, more boisterous and more puzzling than before. I noticed that the officers in the front row looked quite uneasy. At last, I again raised my hands and said, 'What is all this in aid of? Where *is* the sergeant major?'

At the back of the hall three enormous soldiers amid cheers from their comrades hoisted up into view a struggling figure on whose uniform the insignia of a sergeant major was clearly visible. He was pulled down again in a continued uproar.

I really don't remember how I got on after that except that they calmed down and the rest of the Brains Trust passed off without incident.

When it was over we were entertained in the Officers' Mess. One after another our hosts came up to me and asked me in the oddest manner, how 'I knew'. ('Wink, wink. Nudge nudge', almost.)

'Knew *what*?'

Then, furtively, they explained. We had drawn a full house because there was nowhere else for the men to go. And there was nowhere else for them to go because they were confined to barracks. And the reason they were confined to barracks was because that morning a stick of gelignite had been found underneath the sergeant major's bed.

I grew accustomed, after this dubious success, to speaking to very varied audiences. Seamen, for instance, of all sorts, from the New Zealand Royal Navy to the crews of large and small trading vessels at anchorage in Lyttelton, the port of Christchurch. They were always polite and seemed to be attentive. I remember one occasion when after I had sat down and the chairman had asked for questions and the usual silence had set in, a sailor rose and, in an expressionless voice, asked me what my name was and on being told gave a curt nod and sat down again. Disconcerting.

One does get asked very strange questions by strangers. During a long voyage I had found a quiet place on deck and had settled myself to write when an old lady, who looked and behaved like the late

Margaret Rutherford as Miss Marples, sat down nearby, edged her deck chair alongside mine and began to whisper.

'I have read all your tales,' she hissed and having waited for my emotion to subside, confided that there was a question she had always wanted to put to me.

She reached out a little paw and patted my manuscript. 'When you are writing your tales,' she breathed, 'do you know who committed the crime?'

A stock question is: how do you begin to write a book? I imagine that my way of beginning is unorthodox and silly. I try to behave sensibly and prepare myself by setting out the anatomy of the plot and the order of events and then inventing a cast of characters that this structure will accommodate. But that never lasts and the truth is that I most often start with characters alone and then have to find a milieu and circumstances and a plot that suits them. It becomes a matter of which of these people is capable of a crime of violence and under what turn of events would he or she actually commit one? I write very slowly, make a lot of alterations and lay myself open to the danger of repetition and self-contradictions which, when there has been a lot of rewriting, I fail to spot. If the publisher's readers also miss the boob it will ultimately be seized upon with glee by some babu in Pondicherry or a cock-a-hoop maths mistress in an establishment for middle-class maidens.

The stupidest brick I have ever dropped was to do with a play which I knew almost by heart. I mixed up two battles – Harfleur and Agincourt – in *Henry V.* In less than no time I did indeed get a letter of reproof from a babu in India.

A large number of the reading public for crime fiction are professional men and women; the very people, of course, who are best equipped to catch you out if you make a blunder – doctors, lawyers, soldiers, sailors, academics, all read these books and strangely enough, or so I am credibly informed, so do policemen – these latter perhaps because they enjoy a complete change from reality.

You might say the writer of a detective story is in much the same situation as a barrister whose practice is largely in crimes of violence. One gets up the case and in the process often has to do a lot of research in a number of fields: medical jurisprudence, police law, poisons, the drug racket, the arts, ballistics, the Judge's Rules or the laws of evidence. I have amassed a large collection of reference books and often am obliged to fag through one or another of them in search of some technical detail to which I will refer in a single sentence. No matter how plain sailing and simplistic you may consider the plot you've chosen, sooner or later you'll find yourself involved with technical concerns.

Suppose you decide that the crime is simply this: one man hits another man on the head with a half-brick in a dirty sock and leaves the body in a dark alley. Plain sailing you think? In no time your detective, and therefore you, are involved with the component parts of brick-dust, the various types of wool from which socks are woven or knitted and the places of origin of such microscopic traces of dirt as cling to the sock in question. Once the book is concluded you forget all this stuff and I'm told barristers who so confidently expound their expert knowledge to juries do exactly the same thing. The information has served its purpose: away with it.

Sometimes, however, things turn out oddly. One of the rare occasions when I began with a plot rather than with people was in writing *Scales of Justice*. A friend who was a member of the Royal Society and an authority on trout, told me that the scales of trout are unique in as much as those of one trout never have corresponded and never can correspond exactly with those of another. In this they resemble human fingerprints.

This, of course, immediately suggested a title and pleasing subject matter for a book. So I wrote *Scales of Justice* and in due course typescripts were sent off to my English and American publishers. To my astonishment the American script-reader wrote crisply in the margin 'Trout do not have scales.' I can only suppose she was thinking of eels.

It really is best to stick to backgrounds with which one is familiar. That is why Troy and I are concerned with painting and so many of my stories take place in theatres among those larger-than-life persons, actors.

Actors, indeed, make splendid copy. They tend to express every emotion up to the hilt. If they are pleased to see you they are enraptured to see you. If they are bored or depressed they turn the mask of comedy upside down and are desolate. If they are ironical or sarcastic they make jolly sure they let you know it with the well-timed sneer. It is not that they are insincere in their extravagances, it is their business and habit to give every reaction its due and then some. In that respect they can be said to be unusually truthful. This makes them good material for detective fiction.

I've said already that it never does to talk about a book while it is merely a fragile idea. I now break this rule by confessing that I have often dallied with the notion of writing a book about a company rehearsing *Macbeth*, which, as every actor knows, is thought to be an unlucky play. I have not found it so and do not subscribe to the superstition. It would be satisfactory to bring the two major interests of my life together for, as it were, a final fling and the actor's response to the situation as it develops could be an intriguing ingredient.

I hope I have one more book in me and I hope too I'll have the sense to call it a day if it turns out to be below standard. But my memory! As I have already confessed it has always been erratic, treacherous to a degree when the thing to be recalled is not particularly interesting but uncannily sharp when for some reason it was something that had attracted me. My father was a great singer-about-the-house and his choice in songs was Gilbertian. Patter songs, production numbers, romantic ballads, wandering minstrels, Lord High Executioners, jesters, judges, peers and policemen; he warbled away, taking his own time with them and it was often a very slow time. The other day I wondered how much of the interminable 'Nightmare Song' from *Iolanthe* might have lodged itself, unknown to me, in my wayward recollection. I had never attempted to memorize it. I started off and got, I think faultlessly, as far as words were concerned, to the end. But if you asked me to name all the characters in my latest book, *Photo-Finish*, as likely as not I'd be flummoxed. I suppose Freud would find something rather disgusting to dredge up about all this but I don't particularly want to hear it, though not for the reason advanced by my schoolboy cousin who, on being asked if he was interested in psychology, replied 'I'm a-Freud I'm too Jung.'

II

Time hath, my lord, a wallet at his back
Wherein he puts alms for oblivion

Ulysses in his elderly wisdom, is saying, and how marvellously he says it, that no one who has achieved recognition for his work can afford to rest on his laurels. It's no good, he says, for achievement to 'seek remuneration for the thing it was'. Keep it up. Go one better or sooner or later, out *you'll* go. Cold comfort for the lightweight novelist.

In contemplating the affairs of men, Shakespeare is a determined realist, perhaps the most unsentimental in our literature. In nothing does this attitude of mind declare itself more absolutely than in the passages about death. True, one must always recognize that in plays the situation and the characters stand like a veil between author and audience, but surely there are many instances when the veil is almost transparent, when the character does in fact speak for the creator. Can anyone read or listen to Claudio's speech about death in *Measure for Measure* and not believe Shakespeare's personal horror of it is there, before our eyes and in our own hearing?

Claudio is condemned to death. The price of his reprieve is that his sister buy it by yielding to the lust of the unspeakable Angelo. In the subsequent scene with her brother she takes it for granted that he will be prepared to sacrifice himself. He pleads with her.

Aye, but to die, and go we know not where;
To lie in cold obstruction, and to rot . . .

The speech is a horrifying and horrified confrontation with the physical ignominy that follows death and a terrifying speculation as to what may happen to the released spirit. One cannot escape the feeling that the poet himself had experienced these fears.

At the time when his small son Hamnet died, Shakespeare was writing *King John*. In this play another little boy dies. His mother says 'Grief fills the room up of my absent child.' Here, in these desolate words, the veil between the author's sorrow and his audience, it seems to me, is very thin indeed.

The Emperor Julius Caesar teeters between heroics and geriatric posturing. We are given one or two momentary back-flashes of the man in his heyday, particularly in his celebrated reply to the threat of assassination. He says of death,

It seems to me most strange that men should fear,
Seeing that death, a necessary end,
Will come when it will come.

The same acceptance of inevitability is echoed by Hamlet:

*If it be now, 'tis not to come; if 'it be not to come, it will be now; if it
be not now, yet it will come – the readiness is all. Since no man owes
of aught he leaves, what is't to leave betimes? Let be.*

In *King Lear*, the most pessimistic of all the plays, it is not only the
longing for extinction of the dying themselves that is expressed but
also that of the living, the onlookers, for release from the unendurable spectacle of death. Kent cries out,

O let him pass!
He hates him
That would upon the rack of this tough world
Stretch him out longer.

And as Kent speaks, the old King dies.

I cannot find that anywhere, except in the obligatory, conventional or ceremonial speeches of one or another of the characters, does
Shakespeare promise, through them, some happy continuation after
death, unless it be found in Cleopatra's proud boast that in the Elysian
fields she and Mark Antony, holding hands, will walk together.

In *Cymbeline* the little dirge for the supposed Fidele says consolation is to be found in oblivion. The dead boy has nothing to fear. He
knows nothing. To him 'the reed is as the oak'. 'Quiet consummation
have' is the poet's final wish for him and, one feels almost as an afterthought, a kind of politeness, he adds 'and renowned be thy grave.'

A very short time before his death the actor, Robert Donat,
recorded some of the poems that he liked very much and this was
the one he chose from Shakespeare. He introduces it by quoting an
old Lancashire woman who had once said to him that Shakespeare
was 'sootch a coomfort'. She was right. The solace this dirge offers is
not of the conventional kind but nevertheless there *is* comfort as
well as fear in the thought of oblivion.

In old age one begins to consider these matters. One hesitates to
speak of death to one's friends for fear of making them feel awkward. There is something a little *farouche* in being 'on' about one's
own demise. Luckily in this, as in so many other respects, there is
always Shakespeare. He says it all.

People sometimes remark on the gruesomeness of some of the
murders in my earlier books and are inclined to take the line of wondering how a nice old dear like me could dream up such beastliness,
let alone write about it. The idea being, I fancy, that perhaps the old

dear is not so nice after all. I really have no answer to this unless it be the one I gave to the soldier at the Brains Trust, 'Perhaps it's a substitute for committing crimes myself' but, with the deepest respect to the psychiatrists, I really don't think I'm sublimating any bloody inclinations lurking in my unconscious or id or libido or whatever it is and if that's the right way of putting it. I am, in fact, extremely squeamish and cannot read accounts of physical torture or cruelty to animals or humans without reacting most unhappily. True, in *Photo-Finish* a snapshot is skewered to a corpse but at least the victim was already dead when this indignity was inflicted.

And here, it occurs to me, is the place to confess that for some time now, I have seldom read crime fiction except when it was written by Wilkie Collins or, unresolvedly, Charles Dickens. Or, of course, when I have been asked to contribute a blurb for a book-jacket. I don't know why this abstinence has occurred; perhaps the pursuit of other writers' achievements became too much like a bus-man's holiday. Or perhaps I live too far away from my brothers and sisters in crime. In England it was a great adventure to get together with them at Crime Writers' festivities and to talk about the craft. Particularly was this so with Julian Symons and Harry Keating, joint victims with me on those Midlands tours when we paid for our lit-erary luncheons with our tongues. Julian is, of course, the doyen of the genre, and compulsive reading for all practitioners. *Bloody Murder* is the last word in critical appraisal. Harry's Inspector Ghote is always an enchanting read. Yet, if his creator and I had not met I don't expect I would have made the Inspector's acquaintance and thereby would have missed a great treat.

In my early days when I was still rather bemused by growing suc-cess as a writer and found it difficult to believe in it, I was invited, with my agent, Edmund Cork, to an initiation ceremony held by the Detection Club. Because of my isolation down-under I could not be considered as a possible member. There was a rule that a certain number of attendances at meetings every year must be observed. So it was very kind indeed of them to invite us to their party.

We dined, grandly, at the Dorchester and then retired to a private room where, or so it now seems to me, the only pieces of furniture were a lectern and two chairs against the wall. Edmund and I were placed in these, hard by the lectern.

This was before the Second World War and the Golden Age of the detective novel, as it is sometimes called, still flourished. The members present that I can remember were Dorothy Sayers, John Rhode, Freeman Wills Croft and Anthony Gilbert (who is a lady). Agatha Christie was a founder-member but was not there that night. E. C. Bentley, the extremely skilled writer of the classic *Trent's Last Case*, was to be initiated. To me, in the insolence of comparative youth, they all seemed to be elderly.

Everybody except Edmund and I left the room. I am sorry to say that in the deathly silence that attended our isolation we became very slightly hysterical but, so far, in control of ourselves. We spoke, I seem to remember, in whispers as if we were in church.

The door at the far end of the room opened and Miss Sayers entered, now kitted out in full academic regalia. She mounted the lectern and was near enough, if one had ventured, to be touched. I was dismayed to see that in the folds of her gown she secreted a side-arm – a pistol or revolver or six-shooter.

She was followed by the rest of the company. There were Wardens. The Warden of the Naked Blade (Freeman Wills Croft, I fancy) with a drawn sword. The Warden of the Hollow Skull, or perhaps I should say 'Death's Head', which was carried on a cushion by John Rhode and by a quaint device could be made to light up from within, and the Warden of the Lethal Phial (Anthony Gilbert) with a baleful little bottle. I am sorry if with the passage of so many years I have got objects and bearers mixed up. In their midst, looking shy, came E. C. Bentley. He was placed before Miss Sayers who now administered a long, complicated and very classy oath written by someone high up in the crime-writing hierarchy. (Could it have been Father Ronald Knox?) It was all about not concealing clues or making a policeman a murderer or (could it be?) having a Chinese character or arrow poison in one's book but I do not remember all the things one mustn't do. It was very impressive and beautifully phrased.

Mr Bentley took the oath, John Rhode switched on the Skull, Freeman Wills Croft, who looked like a highly respected family solicitor, rather gingerly flourished the Sword, Anthony Gilbert displayed the Phial and Miss Sayers, taking Edmund and me completely off our guard, loosed off her gun. The noise was deafening. I think I let out a yelp and I am sorry to record that dear Edmund, who has a loud laugh, laughed excessively.

The ceremony completed, we all went to the Detection Club's rooms in Soho and in great awe I heard them speak rudely about their publishers. A year or two later, on another visit, Miss Sayers asked me to dine with her and see them perform a skit on the Sherlock Holmes stories in which she was Mrs Hudson and I think Watson dunnit.

I am now a member of the Detection Club. Very kindly they waived their rule about regular attendances. They have, in some sort, been supplanted by the much bigger Crime Writers' Association which organizes trips abroad, presents awards and arranges for high-up policemen, pathologists, medical jurisprudents and all sorts of exciting authorities to address them. It would be lovely to go to these splendid parties.

It was some time after the adventure at the Dorchester that I first met Agatha Christie. She was kind and encouraging and struck one as being shy. I suppose it could be said that she was also an enigmatic person, since the mystery of her disappearance for some days during an unhappy episode in her past has been so often revived and, after her death, was actually used as subject matter for a book and film. We met several times and I like to remember those meetings. Nowadays, especially in America, a sort of 'thing' goes on about whether or not I have stepped into her shoes. I don't think I have and I wish it wouldn't. I don't think that, beyond the fact that we are both crime writers, we have technically very much in common. She is the absolute tops in plotting. Her books are at the apex of the classic style of detective fiction. A puzzle is set up and a contest between author and reader carried through to a surprise ending. She, almost always, is the winner. Her characters are two-dimensional, lively, extremely well-defined and highly entertaining. To call them silhouettes is not to dispraise them. (After all, what's wrong with the silhouette of a hawk-faced man in a deer-stalker hat and an Inverness cape?) You may say that in form and style Agatha Christie is a purist.

I, on the other hand, try to write about characters in the round and am in danger of letting them take charge. Continually I have to pull myself together and attend to the plotting and remind myself that this is a detective story and I'd better not start fancying myself in other directions.

Two years ago the Mystery Writers of America made me a Grand Master of their Society. (I expect they feel that Grand *Mistress* might be a bit equivocal – a little too suggestive of a *maîtresse-en-chef*.) John Ball who, as well as being a crime writer himself, has a successful film to his credit, was in New Zealand and invited me to attend the award-giving dinner in Los Angeles at which I would receive a china bust of Edgar Allan Poe. Unhappily I was not able to accept this very kind invitation even though Mr Ball wooed me with offers of a pavilion in his garden where I would be able to sit rather like an oversized plaster gnome and write. And so, to coin a phrase, Poe was posted. I look up at this moment and there, to my pride, he stands: *stylisé*, corpse-like, sheet-white, with closed eyes and black moustache, and there, fused into his pediment, is my name and the date, 1978. An uninformed person might make the silly mistake of supposing him thus labelled, to be me. I was very much touched by this handsome compliment.

III

I have been looking through the earlier chapters of this book and particularly at the concluding ones written some eighteen years ago. So many of the friends who appear in them can now only do so as memories. One has moved up into the front rank and the figures thin out. Jemima most sadly of all. Charlot. Bob.

And that Micawber-like voice no longer booms. In his last letter to me Mr Wilkie quoted the gravedigger's song: 'Age, with his stealing steps.'

There are now three Lampreys instead of five. I keep quite closely in touch with them. The most preposterous calamities, as well as very serious ones, continue to befall them. I wish we didn't live half the world away from each other but there, that's the way things have fallen out and with every letter I seem to hear those unmistakeable voices hailing me from the Kentish hills above West Malling or from somewhere on the fringes of the Devon moorlands or above the remotest Highland coastline or inland from Perth in Western Australia.

With the Lampreys is linked my cousin Johnnie Dacres-Mannings, the erstwhile gunner who, after a severe spell of tuberculosis which put an end to his term as a soldier, is now a most happily married papa and a successful figure in the world of finance in Australia and who, when I fly across the Tasman Sea to visit them, patiently tries to explain the, to me, totally inexplicable mysteries of high-powered banking. My understanding of money matters is on a par with Mr Micawber's but less disastrous as I have a compensatory horror of spending more than I can earn. For the rest I am content to leave it all to experts, which seems to keep them pretty busy.

Johnnie's eldest son, Nicholas, who is my godson, has just returned from England where he spent a year at Marlborough, rounding off his schooling. He was the same age as his father was when he first came down from the North Island to Christ's College. I am delighted to hear that Nicholas became warmly attached to the Lampreys with whom he spent his holidays and whose far from Establishment on-goings and punctual crises he seems to have taken happily in his stride. He and his papa are visiting me in the New Year which will be a treat of treats.

And now I look further back almost to where those lines of perspective meet and there are the tents in the bush at Glentui. When I was in England I visited Aileen, the eldest and last of the Burtons. Now a widow and living at Berkhamsted, she described herself as 'The Ancient of Days'. She got out an album of photographs with dry disintegrating fronds of New Zealand fern stuck between them. We turned the pages and, as old people will, became nostalgic, looked backwards over half a century and, for a moment or two saw ourselves as if it were yesterday. There we all were: the four Burton sisters, Sylvia, Mivvy, my parents, the two young parsons and the bearded boys. Back come the multiple voices of the river, of night-owls and of bellbirds at first light: the smells of woodsmoke, of sun-warmed canvas, frying bacon and cold, wet moss. 'Lovely holidays,' we said, 'they were lovely holidays.'

A pinch of friable leaf-dust had lodged between the pages.

It might have fallen from a black beech tree that on a warm morning in the foothills of the Southern Alps sweated little globules of honeydew.

Bibliography

A Man Lay Dead, London, Bles, 1934.

Enter a Murderer, London, Bles, 1935.

The Nursing Home Murder, with Henry Jellett, London, Bles, 1935.

Death in Ecstasy, London, Bles, 1936.

Vintage Murder, London, Bles, 1937.

Artists in Crime, London, Bles, 1938.

Death in a White Tie, London, Bles, 1938.

Overture to Death, London, Collins, 1939.

Death at the Bar, London, Collins, 1940.

Surfeit of Lampreys, London, Collins, 1940; US title: *Death of a Peer*.

Death and the Dancing Footman, London, Collins, 1942.

Colour Scheme, London, Collins, 1943.

Died in the Wool, London, Collins, 1945.

Final Curtain, London, Collins, 1947.

Swing, Brother, Swing, London, Collins, 1949; US title: *A Wreath for Riviera*.

Opening Night, London, Collins, 1951; US title: *Night of the Vulcan*.

Spinsters in Jeopardy, London, Collins, 1954; US title: *The Bride of Death*.

Scales of Justice, London, Collins, 1955.

Off With His Head, London, Collins, 1957; US title: *Death of a Fool*.

Singing in the Shrouds, London, Collins, 1959.

False Scent, London, Collins, 1960.

Hand in Glove, London, Collins, 1962.

Dead Water, London, Collins, 1964.

Black Beech and Honeydew: An Autobiography, London, Collins, 1966; revised edition, Auckland, Collins, 1981; London, Collins, 1982.

Death at the Dolphin, London, Collins, 1967; US title: *Killer Dolphin*.

Clutch of Constables, London, Collins, 1968.

When in Rome, London, Collins, 1970.

Tied up in Tinsel, London, Collins, 1972.

Black As He's Painted, London, Collins, 1974.

Last Ditch, London, Collins, 1977.

Grave Mistake, London, Collins, 1978.

Photo-Finish, London, Collins, 1980.

Light Thickens, London, Collins, 1982.

Death on the Air and Other Stories, London, HarperCollins, 1995; US title: *The Collected Short Fiction of Ngaio Marsh*.

Morepork

Morepork was first published in *Murderer's Ink* by Workman Publishing Company (USA) in 1979.

On the morning before he died, Caley Bridgeman woke to the smell of canvas and the promise of a warm day. Bellbirds had begun to drop their two dawn notes into the cool air and a native wood pigeon flopped on to the ridgepole of his tent. He got up and went outside. Beech bush, emerging from the night, was threaded with mist. The voices of the nearby creek and the more distant Wainui River, in endless colloquy with stones and boulders, filled the intervals between birdsong. Down beyond the river he glimpsed, through shadowy trees, the two Land Rovers and the other tents: his wife's; his stepson's; David Wingfield's, the taxidermist's. And Solomon Gosse's. Gosse, with whom he had fallen out.

If it came to that, he had fallen out, more or less, with all of them, but he attached little importance to the circumstance. His wife he had long ago written off as an unintelligent woman. They had nothing in common. She was not interested in birdsong.

'Tink. Ding,' chimed the bellbirds.

Tonight, if all went well, they would be joined on tape with the little night owl – *Ninox novaeseelandiae*, the ruru, the morepork.

He looked across the gully to where, on the lip of a cliff, a black beech rose high against paling stars. His gear was stowed away at its foot, well hidden, ready to be installed, and now, two hours at least before the campers stirred, was the time to do it.

He slipped down between fern, scrub and thorny undergrowth to where he had laid a rough bridge above a very deep and narrow channel. Through this channel flowed a creek which joined the Wainui below the tents. At that point the campers had dammed it up to make a swimming pool. He had not cared to join in their enterprise.

The bridge had little more than a four-foot span. It consisted of two beech logs resting on the verges and overlaid by split branches nailed across them. Twenty feet below, the creek glinted and prattled. The others had jumped the gap and goaded him into doing it himself. If they tried, he thought sourly, to do it with twenty-odd pounds of gear on their backs, they'd sing a different song.

He arrived at the tree. Everything was in order, packed in green waterproof bags and stowed in a hollow under the roots.

When he climbed the tree to place his parabolic microphone, he found bird droppings, fresh from the night visit of the morepork.

He set to work.

At half past eleven that morning, Bridgeman came down from an exploratory visit to a patch of beech forest at the edge of the Bald Hill. A tui sang the opening phrase of 'Home to Our Mountains', finishing with a consequential splutter and a sound like that made by someone climbing through a wire fence. Close at hand, there was a sudden flutter and a minuscule shriek. Bridgeman moved with the habitual quiet of the bird watcher into a patch of scrub and pulled up short.

He was on the lip of a bank. Below him was the blond poll of David Wingfield.

'What have you done?' Bridgeman said.

The head moved slowly and tilted. They stared at each other. 'What have you got in your hands?' Bridgeman said. 'Open your hands.'

The taxidermist's clever hands opened. A feathered morsel lay in his palm. Legs like twigs stuck up their clenched feet. The head dangled. It was a rifleman, tiniest and friendliest of all New Zealand birds.

'Plenty more where this came from,' said David Wingfield. 'I wanted it to complete a group. No call to look like that.'

'I'll report you.'

'Balls.'

'Think so? By God, you're wrong. I'll ruin you.'

'Ah, stuff it!' Wingfield got to his feet, a giant of a man.

For a moment it looked as if Bridgeman would leap down on him.

'Cut it out,' Wingfield said. 'I could do you with one hand.'

He took a small box from his pocket, put the strangled rifleman in it and closed the lid.

'Gidday,' he said. He picked up his shotgun and walked away – slowly.

At noon the campers had lunch, cooked by Susan Bridgeman over the campfire. They had completed the dam, building it up with enormous turfs backed by boulders. Already the creek overflowed above its juncture with the Wainui. They had built up to the top of the banks on either side, because if snow in the back country should melt or torrential rain come over from the west coast, all the creeks and rivers would become torrents and burst through the foothills.

'Isn't he coming in for tucker?' Clive Grey asked his mother. He never used his stepfather's name if he could avoid it.

'I imagine not,' she said. 'He took enough to last a week.'

'I saw him,' Wingfield offered.

'Where?' Solomon Gosse asked.

'In the bush below the Bald Hill.'

'Good patch for tuis. Was he putting out his honey pots?'

'I didn't ask,' Wingfield said, and laughed shortly.

Gosse looked curiously at him. 'Like that, was it?' he said softly.

'Very like that,' Wingfield agreed, glancing at Susan. 'I imagine he won't be visiting us today,' he said. 'Or tonight, of course.'

'Good,' said Bridgeman's stepson loudly.

'Don't talk like that, Clive,' said his mother automatically.

'Why not?' he asked, and glowered at her.

Solomon Gosse pulled a deprecating grimace. 'This is the hottest day we've had,' he said. 'Shan't we be pleased with our pool!'

'I wouldn't back the weather to last, though,' Wingfield said.

Solomon speared a sausage and quizzed it thoughtfully. 'I hope it lasts,' he said.

It lasted for the rest of that day and through the following night up to eleven o'clock, when Susan Bridgeman and her lover left their secret meeting place in the bush and returned to the sleeping camp.

Before they parted she said, 'He wouldn't divorce me. Not if we yelled it from the mountaintop, he wouldn't.'

'It doesn't matter now.'

The night owl, ruru, called persistently from his station in the tall beech tree.

'*More-pork! More-pork!*'

Towards midnight came a soughing rumour through the bush. The campers woke in their sleeping bags and felt cold on their faces. They heard the tap of rain on canvas grow to a downpour. David Wingfield pulled on his gumboots and waterproof. He took a torch and went round the tents, adjusting guy ropes and making sure the drains were clear. He was a conscientious camper. His torchlight bobbed over Susan's tent and she called out, 'Is that you? Is everything OK?'

'Good as gold,' he said. 'Go to sleep.'

Solomon Gosse stuck his head out from under his tent flap. 'What a bloody bore,' he shouted, and drew it in again.

Clive Grey was the last to wake. He had suffered a recurrent nightmare concerning his mother and his stepfather. It had been more explicit than usual. His body leapt, his mouth was dry and he had what he thought of as a 'fit of the jimjams'. Half a minute went by to the sound of water – streaming, he thought, out of his dream. Then he recognized it as the voice of the river, swollen so loud that it might be flowing past his tent.

Towards daybreak the rain stopped. Water dripped from the trees, clouds rolled away to the south and the dawn chorus began. Soon after nine there came tentative glimpses of the sun. David Wingfield was first up. He squelched about in gumboots and got a fire going. Soon the incense of woodsmoke rose through the trees with the smell of fresh fried bacon.

After breakfast they went to look at the dam. Their pool had swollen up to the top of both banks, but the construction held. A half-grown sapling, torn from its stand, swept downstream, turning and seeming to gesticulate. Beyond their confluence the Wainui, augmented by the creek, thundered down its gorge. The campers were obliged to shout.

'Good thing,' Clive mouthed, 'we don't want to get out. Couldn't. Marooned. Aren't we?' He appealed to Wingfield and pointed to the waters. Wingfield made a dismissive gesture. 'Not a hope,' he signalled.

'How long?' Susan asked, peering into Wingfield's face. He shrugged and held up three and then five fingers. 'My God!' she was seen to say.

Solomon Gosse patted her arm. 'Doesn't matter. Plenty of grub,' he shouted.

Susan looked at the dam where the sapling had jammed. Its limbs quivered. It rolled, heaved, thrust up a limb, dragged it under and thrust it up again.

It was a human arm with a splayed hand. Stiff as iron, it swung from side to side and pointed at nothing or everything.

Susan Bridgeman screamed. There she stood, with her eyes and mouth open. 'Caley!' she screamed. 'It's Caley!'

Wingfield put his arm round her. He and Solomon Gosse stared at each other over her head.

Clive could be heard to say: 'It *is* him, isn't it? That's his shirt, isn't it? He's drowned, isn't he?'

As if in affirmation, Caley Bridgeman's face, foaming and sight-less, rose and sank and rose again.

Susan turned to Solomon as if to ask him if it was true. Her knees gave way and she slid to the ground. He knelt and raised her head and shoulders.

Clive made some sort of attempt to replace Solomon, but David Wingfield came across and used the authority of the physically fit. 'Better out of this,' he could be heard to say. 'I'll take her.'

He lifted Susan and carried her up to her tent.

Young Clive made an uncertain attempt to follow. Solomon Gosse took him by the arm and walked him away from the river into a clearing in the bush where they could make themselves heard, but when they got there found nothing to say. Clive, looking deadly sick, trembled like a wet dog.

At last Solomon said, 'I can't b-believe this. It simply isn't true.'

'I ought to go to her. To Mum. It ought to be me with her.'

'David will cope.'

'It ought to be me,' Clive repeated, but made no move.

Presently he said, 'It can't be left there.'

'David will cope,' Solomon repeated. It sounded like a slogan.

'David can't walk on the troubled waters,' Clive returned on a note of hysteria. He began to laugh.

'Shut up, for God's sake.'

'Sorry. I can't help it. It's so grotesque.'

'*Listen.*'

Voices could be heard, the snap of twigs broken underfoot and the thud of boots on soft ground. Into the clearing walked four men in single file. They had packs on their backs and guns under their arms and an air of fitting into their landscape. One was bearded, two clean-shaven, and the last had a couple of days' growth. When they saw Solomon and Clive they all stopped.

'Hullo, there! Good morning to you,' said the leader. 'We saw your tents.' He had an English voice. His clothes, well-worn, had a distinctive look which they would have retained if they had been in rags.

Solomon and Clive made some sort of response. The man looked hard at them. 'Hope you don't mind if we walk through your camp,' he said. 'We've been deer stalking up at the head of Welshman's Creek but looked like getting drowned. So we've walked out.'

Solomon said, 'He's – we've both had a shock.'

Clive slid to the ground and sat doubled up, his face on his arms.

The second man went to him. The first said, 'If it's illness – I mean, this is Dr Mark, if we can do anything.'

Solomon said, 'I'll tell you.' And did.

They did not exclaim or overreact. The least talkative of them, the one with the incipient beard, seemed to be regarded by the others as some sort of authority and it turned out, subsequently, that he was their guide: Bob Johnson, a high-country man. When Solomon had finished, this Bob, with a slight jerk of his head, invited him to move away. The doctor had sat down beside Clive, but the others formed a sort of conclave round Solomon, out of Clive's hearing.

'What about it, Bob?' the Englishman said.

Solomon, too, appealed to the guide. 'What's so appalling,' he said, 'is that it's there. Caught up. Pinned against the dam. The arm jerking to and fro. We don't know if we can get to it.'

'Better take a look,' said Bob Johnson.

'It's down there, through the b-bush. If you don't mind,' said Solomon, 'I'd – I'd be glad not to go b-back just yet.'

'She'll be right,' said Bob Johnson. 'Stay where you are.'

He walked off unostentatiously, a person of authority, followed by the Englishman and their bearded mate. The Englishman's name, they were to learn, was Miles Curtis-Vane. The other was called McHaffey. He was the local schoolmaster in the nearest township downcountry and was of a superior and, it would emerge, cantankerous disposition.

Dr Mark came over to Solomon. 'Your young friend's pretty badly shocked,' he said. 'Were they related?'

'No. It's his stepfather. His mother's up at the camp. She fainted.'

'Alone?'

'Dave Wingfield's with her. He's the other member of our lot.'

'The boy wants to go to her.'

'So do I, if she'll see me. I wonder – would you mind taking charge? Professionally, I mean.'

'If there's anything I can do. I think perhaps I should join the others now. Will you take the boy up? If his mother would like to see me, I'll come.'

'Yes. All right. Yes, of course.'

'Were they very close?' Dr Mark asked. 'He and his stepfather?'

There was a longish pause. 'Not very,' Solomon said. 'It's more the shock. He's very devoted to his mother. We all are. If you don't mind, I'll – '

'No, of course.'

So Solomon went to Clive and they walked together to the camp.

'I reckon,' Bob Johnson said, after a hard stare at the dam, 'it can be done.'

Curtis-Vane said, '*They* seem to have taken it for granted it's impossible.'

'They may not have the rope for it.'

'We have.'

'That's right.'

'By Cripie,' said Bob Johnson, 'it'd give you the willies, wouldn't it? That arm. Like a bloody semaphore.'

'Well,' said Dr Mark, 'what's the drill, then, Bob? Do we make the offer?'

'Here's their other bloke,' said Bob Johnson.

David Wingfield came down the bank sideways. He acknowledged Curtis-Vane's introductions with guarded nods.

'If we can be of any use,' said Curtis-Vane, 'just say the word.'

Wingfield said, 'It's going to be tough.' He had not looked at the dam but he jerked his head in that direction.

'What's the depth?' Bob Johnson asked.

'Near enough five foot.'

'We carry rope.'

'That'll be good.'

Some kind of reciprocity had been established. The two men withdrew together.

'What would you reckon?' Wingfield asked. 'How many on the rope?'

'Five,' Bob Johnson said, 'if they're good. She's coming down solid.'

'Sol Gosse isn't all that fit. He's got a crook knee.'

'The bloke with the stammer?'

'That's right.'

'What about the young chap?'

'All right normally, but he's – you know – shaken up.'

'Yeah,' said Bob. 'Our mob's OK.'

'Including the pom?'

'He's all right. Very experienced.'

'With me, we'd be five,' Wingfield said.

'For you to say.'

'She'll be right, then.'

'One more thing,' said Bob. 'What's the action when we get him out? What do we do with him?'

They debated this. It was decided, subject to Solomon Gosse's and Clive's agreement, that the body should be carried to a clearing near the big beech and left there in a ground sheet from his tent. It would be a decent distance from the camp.

'We could build a bit of a windbreak round it,' Bob said.

'Sure.'

'That's his tent, is it? Other side of the creek?'

'Yeah. Beyond the bridge.'

'I didn't see any bridge.'

'You must have,' said Wingfield, 'if you came that way. It's where the creek runs through a twenty-foot-deep gutter. Couldn't miss it.'

'Got swept away, it might have.'

'Has the creek flooded its banks, then? Up there?'

'No. No, that's right. It couldn't have carried away. What sort of bridge is it?'

Wingfield described the bridge. 'Light but solid,' he said. 'He made a job of it.'

'Funny,' said Bob.

'Yeah. I'll go up and collect the ground sheet from his tent. And take a look.'

'We'd better get this job over, hadn't we? What about the wife?'

'Sol Gosse and the boy are with her. She's OK.'

'Not likely to come out?'

'Not a chance.'

'Fair enough,' said Bob.

So Wingfield walked up to Caley Bridgeman's tent to collect his ground sheet.

When he returned, the others had taken off their packs and laid out a coil of climbers' rope. They gathered round Bob, who gave the instructions. Presently the line of five men was ready to move out into the sliding flood above the dam.

Solomon Gosse appeared. Bob suggested that he take the end of the rope, turn it round a tree trunk and stand by to pay it out or take it up as needed.

And in this way and with great difficulty Caley Bridgeman's body was brought ashore, where Dr Mark examined it. It was much battered. They wrapped it in the ground sheet and tied it round with twine. Solomon Gosse stood guard over it while the others changed into dry clothes.

The morning was well advanced and sunny when they carried Bridgeman through the bush to the foot of the bank below that tree which was visited nightly by a morepork. Then they cut manuka scrub.

It was now that Bob Johnson, chopping through a stand of brushwood, came upon the wire, an insulated line, newly laid, running underneath the manuka and well hidden. They traced its course: up the bank under hanging creeper to the tree, up the tree to the tape recorder. They could see the parabolic microphone much farther up.

Wingfield said, 'So that's what he was up to.'

Solomon Gosse didn't answer at once, and when he did, spoke more to himself than to Wingfield. 'What a weird bloke he was,' he said.

'Recording birdsong, was he?' asked Dr Mark.

'That's right.'

'A hobby?' said Curtis-Vane.

'Passion, more like. He's got quite a reputation for it.'

Bob Johnson said, 'Will we dismantle it?'

'I think perhaps we should,' said Wingfield. 'It was up there through the storm. It's a very high-class job – cost the earth. We could dry it off.'

So they climbed the tree, in single file, dismantled the microphone and recorder and handed them down from one to another. Dr Mark, who seemed to know, said he did not think much damage had been done.

And then they laid a rough barrier of brushwood over the body and came away. When they returned to camp, Wingfield produced a bottle of whisky and enamel mugs. They moved down to the Land Rovers and sat on their heels, letting the whisky glow through them.

There had been no sign of Clive or his mother.

Curtis-Vane asked if there was any guessing how long it would take for the river to go down and the New Zealanders said, 'No way.' It could be up for days. A week, even.

'And there's no way out?' Curtis-Vane asked. 'Not if you followed down the Wainui on this side, till it empties into the Rangitata?'

'The going's too tough. Even for one of these jobs.' Bob indicated the Land Rovers. 'You'd never make it.'

There was a long pause.

'Unpleasant,' said Curtis-Vane. 'Especially for Mrs Bridgeman.'

Another pause. 'It is, indeed,' said Solomon Gosse.

'Well,' said McHaffey, seeming to relish the idea. 'If it does last hot, it won't be very nice.'

'Cut it out, Mac,' said Bob.

'Well, you know what I mean.'

Curtis-Vane said, 'I've no idea of the required procedure in New Zealand for accidents of this sort.'

'Same as in England, I believe,' said Solomon. 'Report to the police as soon as possible.'

'Inquest?'

'That's right.'

'Yes. You're one of us, aren't you? A barrister?' asked Curtis-Vane.

'And solicitor. We're both in this country.'

'Yes, I know.'

A shadow fell across the group. Young Clive had come down from the camp.

'How is she?' Wingfield and Gosse said together.

'OK,' said Clive. 'She wants to be left. She wants me to thank you,' he said awkwardly, and glanced at Curtis-Vane, 'for helping.'

'Not a bit. We were glad to do what we could.'

Another pause.

'There's a matter,' Bob Johnson said, 'that I reckon ought to be considered.'

He stood up.

Neither he nor Wingfield had spoken beyond the obligatory mutter over the first drink. Now there was in his manner something that caught them up in a stillness. He did not look at any of them but straight in front of him and at nothing.

'After we'd finished up there I went over,' he said, 'to the place where the bridge had been. The bridge that you' – he indicated Wingfield – 'talked about. It's down below, jammed between rocks, half out of the stream.'

He waited. Wingfield said, 'I saw it. When I collected the gear.' And he, too, got to his feet.

'Did you notice the banks? Where the ends of the bridge had rested?'

'Yes.'

Solomon Gosse scrambled up awkwardly. 'Look here,' he said. 'What is all this?'

'They'd overlaid the bank by a good two feet at either end. They've left deep ruts,' said Bob.

Dr Mark said, 'What about it, Bob? What are you trying to tell us?'

For the first time Bob looked directly at Wingfield.

'Yes,' Wingfield said. 'I noticed.'

'Noticed *what*, for God's sake!' Dr Mark demanded. He had been sitting by Solomon, but now moved over to Bob Johnson. 'Come on, Bob,' he said. 'What's on your mind?'

'It'd been shifted. Pushed or hauled,' said Bob. 'So that the end on this bank of the creek rested on the extreme edge. It's carried away taking some of the bank with it and scraping down the face of the gulch. You can't miss it.'

Clive broke the long silence. 'You mean – he stepped on the bridge and fell with it into the gorge? And was washed down by the flood? Is that what you mean?'

'That's what it looks like,' said Bob Johnson.

Not deliberately, but as if by some kind of instinctive compulsion, the men had moved into their original groups. The campers: Wingfield, Gosse and Clive; the deer stalkers: Bob, Curtis-Vane, Dr Mark and McHaffey.

Clive suddenly shouted at Wingfield, 'What are you getting at! You're suggesting there's something crook about this? What the hell do you mean?'

'Shut up, Clive,' said Solomon mildly.

'I won't bloody shut up. If there's something wrong I've a right to know what it is. She's my mother and he was – ' He caught himself. 'If there's something funny about this,' he said, 'we've a right to know. *Is* there something funny?' he demanded. 'Come on. Is there?'

Wingfield said, 'OK. You've heard what's been suggested. If the bridge *was* deliberately moved – manhandled – the police will want to know who did it and why. And I'd have thought,' added Wingfield, 'you'd want to know yourself.'

Clive glared at him. His face reddened and his mouth trembled. He broke out again: 'Want to know! Haven't I said I want to know! What the hell are you trying to get at!'

Dr Mark said, 'The truth, presumably.'

'Exactly,' said Wingfield.

'Ah, stuff it,' said Clive. 'Like your bloody birds,' he added, and gave a snort of miserable laughter.

'What can you mean?' Curtis-Vane wondered.

'I'm a taxidermist,' said Wingfield.

'It was a flash of wit,' said Dr Mark.

'I see.'

'You all think you're bloody clever,' Clive began at the top of his voice, and stopped short. His mother had come through the trees and into the clearing.

She was lovely enough, always, to make an impressive entrance and would have been in sackcloth and ashes if she had taken it into her head to wear them. Now, in her camper's gear with a scarf round her head, she might have been ready for some lucky press photographer.

'Clive darling,' she said, 'what's the matter? I heard you shouting.' Without waiting for his answer, she looked at the deer stalkers, seemed to settle for Curtis-Vane, and offered her hand. 'You've been very kind,' she said. 'All of you.'

'We're all very sorry,' he said.

'There's something more, isn't there? What is it?'

Her own men were tongue-tied. Clive, still fuming, merely glowered. Wingfield looked uncomfortable and Solomon Gosse seemed to hover on the edge of utterance and then draw back.

'Please tell me,' she said, and turned to Dr Mark. 'Are you the doctor?' she asked.

Somehow, among them, they did tell her. She turned very white but was perfectly composed.

'I see,' she said. 'You think one of us laid a trap for my husband. That's it, isn't it?'

Curtis-Vane said, 'Not exactly that.'

'No?'

'No. It's just that Bob Johnson here and Wingfield do think there's been some interference.'

'That sounds like another way of saying the same thing.'

Solomon Gosse said. 'Sue, if it has happened – '

'And it has,' said Wingfield.

' – it may well have b-been some gang of yobs. They do get out into the hills, you know. Shooting the b-birds. Wounding deer. Vandals.'

'That's right,' said Bob Johnson.

'Yes,' she said, grasping at it. 'Yes, of course. It may be that.'

'The point is,' said Bob, 'whether something ought to be done about it.'

'Like?'

'Reporting it, Mrs Bridgeman.'

'Who to?' Nobody answered. 'Report it where?'

'To the police,' said Bob Johnson flatly.

'Oh no! *No*!'

'It needn't worry you, Mrs Bridgeman. This is a national park. A reserve. We want to crack down on these characters.'

Dr Mark said, 'Did any of you see or hear anybody about the place?' Nobody answered.

'They'd keep clear of the tents,' said Clive at last. 'Those blokes would.'

'You know,' Curtis-Vane said, 'I don't think this is any of our business. I think we'd better take ourselves off.'

'No!' Susan Bridgeman said. 'I want to know if you believe this about vandals.' She looked at the deer stalkers. 'Or will you go away thinking one of us laid a trap for my husband? Might one of you go to the police and say so? Does it mean that?' She turned on Dr Mark. 'Does it?'

Solomon said, 'Susan, my dear, *no*,' and took her arm.

'I want an answer.'

Dr Mark looked at his hands. 'I can only speak for myself,' he said. 'I would need to have something much more positive before coming to any decision.'

'And if you go away, what will you all do? I can tell you. Talk and talk and talk.' She turned on her own men. 'And so, I suppose, will we. Or won't we? And if we're penned up here for days and days and he's up there, wherever you've put him, not buried, not – '

She clenched her hands and jerked to and fro, beating the ground with her foot like a performer in a rock group. Her face crumpled. She turned blindly to Clive.

'I *won't*,' she said. 'I *won't* break down. Why should I? I won't.'

He put his arms round her. 'Don't you, Mum,' he muttered. 'You'll be all right. It's going to be all right.'

Curtis-Vane said, 'How about it?' and the deer stalkers began to collect their gear.

'No!' said David Wingfield loudly. 'No! I reckon we've got to thrash it out and you lot had better hear it.'

'We'll only b-bitch it all up and it'll get out of hand,' Solomon objected.

'No, it won't,' Clive shouted. 'Dave's right. Get it sorted out like they would at an inquest. Yeah! That's right. Make it an inquest. We've got a couple of lawyers, haven't we? They can keep it in order, can't they? Well, can't they?'

Solomon and Curtis-Vane exchanged glances. 'I really don't think – ' Curtis-Vane began, when unexpectedly McHaffey cut in.

'I'm in favour,' he said importantly. 'We'll be called on to give an account of the recovery of the body and that could lead to quite a lot of questions. How I look at it.'

'Use your loaf, Mac,' said Bob. 'All you have to say is what you know. Facts. All the same,' he said, 'if it'll help to clear up the picture, I'm not against the suggestion. What about you, Doc?'

'At the inquest I'll be asked to speak as to' – Dr Mark glanced at Susan – 'as to the medical findings. I've no objection to giving them now, but I can't think that it can help in any way.'

'Well,' said Bob Johnson, 'it looks like there's no objections. There's going to be a hell of a lot of talk and it might as well be kept in order.' He looked round. '*Are* there any objections?' he asked. 'Mrs Bridgeman?'

She had got herself under control. She lifted her chin, squared her shoulders and said, 'None.'

'Fair enough,' said Bob. 'All right. I propose we appoint Mr Curtis-Vane as – I don't know whether chairman's the right thing, but – well – '

'How about coroner?' Solomon suggested, and it would have been hard to say whether he spoke ironically or not.

'Well, C-V,' said Dr Mark, 'what do you say about it?'

'I don't know what to say, and that's the truth. I – it's an extraordinary suggestion,' said Curtis-Vane, and rubbed his head. 'Your findings, if indeed you arrive at any, would, of course, have no relevance in any legal proceedings that might follow.'

'Precisely,' said Solomon.

'We appreciate that,' said Bob.

McHaffey had gone into a sulk and said nothing.

'I second the proposal,' said Wingfield.

'Any further objections?' asked Bob.

None, it appeared.

'Good. It's over to Mr Curtis-Vane.'

'My dear Bob,' said Curtis-Vane, 'what's over to me, for pity's sake?'

'Set up the programme. How we function, like.'

Curtis-Vane and Solomon Gosse stared at each other. 'Rather you than me,' said Solomon drily.

'I suppose,' Curtis-Vane said dubiously, 'if it meets with general approval, we could consult about procedure?'

'Fair go,' said Bob and Wingfield together, and Dr Mark said, 'By all means. Leave it to the legal minds.'

McHaffey raised his eyebrows and continued to huff.

It was agreed that they should break up: the deer stalkers would move downstream to a sheltered glade, where they would get their own food and spend the night in pup tents; Susan Bridgeman and her three would return to camp. They would all meet again, in the campers' large communal tent, after an early meal.

When they had withdrawn, Curtis-Vane said, 'That young man – the son – is behaving very oddly.'

Dr Mark said, 'Oedipus complex, if ever I saw it. Or Hamlet, which is much the same thing.'

There was a trestle table in the tent and on either side of it the campers had knocked together two green wood benches of great discomfort. These were made more tolerable by the introduction of bush mattresses – scrim ticking filled with brushwood and dry fern.

An acetylene lamp had been placed in readiness halfway down the table, but at the time the company assembled there was still enough daylight to serve.

At the head of the table was a folding camp stool for Curtis-Vane, and at the foot, a canvas chair for Susan Bridgeman. Without any discussion, the rest seated themselves in their groups: Wingfield, Clive and Solomon on one side; Bob Johnson, Dr Mark and McHaffey on the other.

There was no pretence at conversation. They waited for Curtis-Vane.

He said, 'Yes, well. Gosse and I have talked this over. It seemed to us that the first thing we must do is to define the purpose of the discussion. We have arrived at this conclusion: We hope to determine whether Mr Caley Bridgeman's death was brought about by accident or by malpractice. To this end we propose to examine the circumstances preceding his death. In order to keep the proceedings as orderly as possible, Gosse suggests that I lead the inquiry. He also feels that as a member of the camping party, he himself cannot, with propriety, act with me. We both think that statements should be given without interruption and that questions arising out of them should be put with the same decorum. Are there any objections?' He waited. 'No?' he said. 'Then I'll proceed.'

He took a pad of writing paper from his pocket, laid a pen beside it and put on his spectacles. It was remarkable how vividly he had established a courtroom atmosphere. One almost saw a wig on his neatly groomed head.

'I would suggest,' he said, 'that the members of my own party' – he turned to his left – 'may be said to enact, however informally, the function of a coroner's jury.'

Dr Mark pulled a deprecating grimace, Bob Johnson looked wooden and McHaffey self-important.

'And I, if you like, an ersatz coroner,' Curtis-Vane concluded. 'In which capacity I put my first question. When was Mr Bridgeman last seen by his fellow campers? Mrs Bridgeman? Would you tell us?'

'I'm not sure, exactly,' she said. 'The day he moved to his tent – that was three days ago – I saw him leave the camp. It was in the morning.'

'Thank you. Why did he make this move?'

'To record native birdsong. He said it was too noisy down here.'

'Ah, yes. And was it after he moved that he rigged the recording gear in the tree?'

She stared at him. 'Which tree?' she said at last.

Solomon Gosse said, 'Across the creek from his tent, Sue. The big beech tree.'

'Oh. I didn't know,' she said faintly.

Wingfield cut in. 'Can I say something? Bridgeman was very cagey about recording. Because of people getting curious and butting in. It'd got to be a bit of an obsession.'

'Ah, yes. Mrs Bridgeman, are you sure you're up to this? I'm afraid – '

'Perfectly sure,' she said loudly. She was ashen white.

Curtis-Vane glanced at Dr Mark. 'If you're quite sure. Shall we go on, then?' he said. 'Mr Gosse?'

Solomon said he, too, had watched Bridgeman take his final load away from the camp and had not seen him again. Clive, in turn, gave a similar account.

Curtis-Vane asked, 'Did he give any indication of his plans?'

'Not to me,' said Gosse. 'I wasn't in his good b-books, I'm afraid.'

'No?'

'No. He'd left some of his gear on the ground and I stumbled over it. I've got a dicky knee. I didn't do any harm, b-but he wasn't amused.'

David Wingfield said, 'He was like that. It didn't amount to anything.'

'What about you, Mr Wingfield? You saw him leave, did you?'

'Yes. Without comment.'

Curtis-Vane was writing. 'So you are all agreed that this was the last time any of you saw him?'

Clive said, 'Here! Hold on. You saw him again, Dave. You know. Yesterday.'

'That's right,' Solomon agreed. 'You told us at lunch, Dave.'

'So I did. I'd forgotten. I ran across him – or rather he ran across me – below the Bald Hill.'

'What were you doing up there?' Curtis-Vane asked pleasantly.

'My own brand of bird-watching. As I told you, I'm a taxidermist.'

'And did you have any talk with him?'

'Not to mention. It didn't amount to anything.'

His friends shifted slightly on their uneasy bench.

'Any questions?' asked Curtis-Vane.

None. They discussed the bridge. It had been built some three weeks before and was light but strong. It was agreed among the men that it had been shifted and that it would be just possible for one man to lever or push it into the lethal position that was indicated by the state of the ground. Bob Johnson added that he thought the bank might have been dug back underneath the bridge. At this point McHaffey was aroused. He said loftily, 'I am not prepared to give an opinion. I should require a closer inspection. But there's a point that has been overlooked, Mr Chairman,' he added with considerable relish. 'Has anything been done about footprints?'

They gazed at him.

'About footprints?' Curtis-Vane wondered. 'There's scarcely been time, has there?'

'I'm not conversant with the correct procedure,' McHaffey haughtily acknowledged. 'I should have to look it up. But I do know they come into it early on or they go off colour. It requires plaster of Paris.'

Dr Mark coughed. Curtis-Vane's hand trembled. He blew his nose. Gosse and Wingfield gazed resignedly at McHaffey. Bob Johnson turned upon him. 'Cut it out, Mac,' he said wearily, and cast up his eyes.

Curtis-Vane said insecurely, 'I'm afraid plaster of Paris is not at the moment available. Mr Wingfield, on your return to camp, did you cross by the bridge?'

'I didn't use the bridge. You can take it on a jump. He built it because of carrying his gear to and fro. It was in place.'

'Anybody else see it later in the day?'

'I did,' said Clive loudly. As usual, his manner was hostile and he seemed to be on the edge of some sort of demonstration. He looked miserable. He said that yesterday morning he had gone for a walk through the bush and up the creek without crossing it. The bridge had been in position. He had returned at midday, passing through a patch of bush close to the giant beech. He had not noticed the recording gear in the tree.

'I looked down at the ground,' he said, and stared at his mother, 'not up.'

This was said in such an odd manner that it seemed to invite comment. Curtis-Vane asked casually, as a barrister might at a tricky point of cross-examination: 'Was there something remarkable about the ground?'

Silence. Curtis-Vane looked up. Clive's hand was in his pocket. He withdrew it. The gesture was reminiscent of a conjurer's: a square of magenta and green silk had been produced.

'Only this,' Clive said, as if the words choked him. 'On the ground. In the bush behind the tree.'

His mother's hand had moved, but she checked it and an uneven blush flooded her face. 'Is *that* where it was!' she said. 'It must have caught in the bushes when I walked up there the other day. Thank you, Clive.'

He opened his hand and the scarf dropped on the table. 'It was on the ground,' he said, 'on a bed of cut fern.'

'It would be right, then,' Curtis-Vane asked, 'to say that yesterday morning when Mr Wingfield met Mr Bridgeman below the Bald Hill, you were taking your walk through the bush?'

'Yes,' said Clive.

'How d'you know that?' Wingfield demanded.

'I heard you. I was quite close.'

'Rot.'

'Well – not you so much as him. Shouting. He said he'd ruin you,' said Clive.

Solomon Gosse intervened. 'May I speak? Only to say that it's important for you all to know that B-B-Bridgeman habitually b-behaved in a most intemperate manner. He would fly into a rage over a chipped saucer.'

'Thank you,' said Wingfield.

Curtis-Vane said, 'Why was he cross with you, Mr Wingfield?'

'He took exception to my work.'

'Taxidermy?' asked Dr Mark.

'Yes. The bird aspect.'

'I may be wrong,' McHaffey said, and clearly considered it unlikely, 'but I thought we'd met to determine when the deceased was last seen alive.'

'And you are perfectly right,' Curtis-Vane assured him. 'I'll put the question: Did any of you see Mr Bridgeman after noon yesterday?' He waited and had no reply. 'Then I've a suggestion to make. If he was alive last evening there's a chance of proving it. You said when we found the apparatus in the tree that he was determined to record the call of the morepork. Is that right?'

'Yes,' said Solomon. 'It comes to that tree every night.'

'If, then, there is a recording of the morepork, he had switched the recorder on. If there is no recording, of course nothing is proved. It might simply mean that for some reason he didn't make one. Can any of you remember if the morepork called last night? And when?'

'I do. I heard it. Before the storm blew up,' said Clive. 'I was reading in bed by torchlight. It was about ten o'clock. It went on for some time and another one, further away, answered it.'

'In your opinion,' Curtis-Vane asked the deer stalkers, 'should we hear the recording – if there is one?'

Susan Bridgeman said, 'I would rather it wasn't played.'

'But why?'

'It – it would be – painful. He always announced his recordings. He gave the date and place and the scientific name. He did that before he set the thing up. To hear his voice – I – I couldn't bear it.'

'You needn't listen,' said her son brutally.

Solomon Gosse said, 'If Susan feels like that about it, I don't think we should play it.'

Wingfield said, 'But I don't see – ' and stopped short. 'All right, then,' he said. 'You needn't listen, Sue. You can go along to your tent, can't you?' And to Curtis-Vane: 'I'll get the recorder.'

McHaffey said, 'Point of order, Mr Chairman. The equipment should be handled by a neutral agent.'

'Oh, for God's sake!' Wingfield exclaimed.

'I reckon he's right, though,' said Bob Johnson.

Curtis-Vane asked Susan Bridgeman, very formally, if she would prefer to leave them.

'No. I don't know. If you must do it – ' she said, and made no move.

'I don't think we've any right to play it if you don't want us to,' Solomon said.

'That,' said McHaffey pleasurably, 'is a legal point. I should have to – '

'Mr McHaffey,' said Curtis-Vane, 'there's nothing "legal" about these proceedings. They are completely informal. If Mrs Bridgeman does not wish us to play the record, we shall, of course, not play it.'

'Excuse me, Mr Chairman,' said McHaffey, in high dudgeon. 'That is your ruling. We shall draw our own conclusions. Personally, I consider Mrs Bridgeman's attitude surprising. However – '

'Oh!' she burst out. 'Play it, play it, play it. Who cares! I don't. Play it.'

So Bob Johnson fetched the tape recorder. He put it on the table. 'It may have got damaged in the storm,' he said. 'But it looks OK. He'd rigged a bit of a waterproof shelter over it. Anyone familiar with the type?'

Dr Mark said, 'It's a superb model. With that parabolic mike, it'd pick up a whisper at ten yards. More than I could ever afford, but I think I understand it.'

'Over to you, then, Doc.'

It was remarkable how the tension following Susan Bridgeman's behaviour was relaxed by the male homage paid to a complicated mechanism. Even Clive, in his private fury, whatever it was, watched the opening up of the recorder. Wingfield leaned over the table to get a better view. Only Solomon remembered the woman and went to sit beside her. She paid no attention.

'The tape's run out,' said Dr Mark. 'That looks promising. One moment; I'll rewind it.'

There broke out the manic gibber of a reversed tape played at speed. This was followed by intervals punctuated with sharp dots of sound and another outburst of gibberish.

'Now,' said Dr Mark.

And Caley Bridgeman's voice, loud and pedantic, filled the tent.

'*Ninox novaeseelandiae*. Ruru. Commonly known as Morepork. Tenth January, 1977. Ten-twelve P.M. Beech bush. Parson's Nose Range. Southern Alps. Regarded by the Maori people as a harbinger of death.'

A pause. The tape slipped quietly from one spool to the other.

'*More-pork!*'

Startling and clear as if the owl called from the ridgepole, the second note a minor step up from the first. Then a distant answer. The call and answer were repeated at irregular intervals and then ceased. The listeners waited for perhaps half a minute and then stirred.

'Very successful,' said Dr Mark. 'Lovely sound.'

'*But are you sure? Darling, you swear you're sure?*'

It was Susan Bridgeman. They turned, startled, to look at her. She had got to her feet. Her teeth were closed over the knuckles of her right hand. 'No!' she whispered. 'No, *no.*'

Solomon Gosse lunged across the table, but the tape was out of his reach and his own voice mocked him.

'*Of course I'm sure, my darling. It's foolproof. He'll go down with the b-b-b-bridge.*'

Top: Edith Ngaio Marsh, aged about six months, with her parents

Left: The author with her spaniel, Tip

Above: Gramp

My father – "a purist in the management of field sports"

School – "I must have been hard to suffer"

"Aromatic smoke rose like a thanks-offering"

The Southern Alps of New Zealand from Cashmere Hills

Cobb and Co.'s Royal Mail coaches

Alan Wilkie and the author

Westland – "it looked and smelt the same"

My father – "playing tennis
until his eightieth birthday"

"A transport driver for
Red Cross" – the author
in World War II

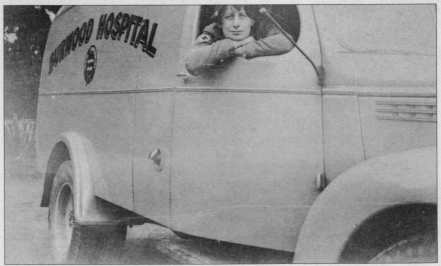

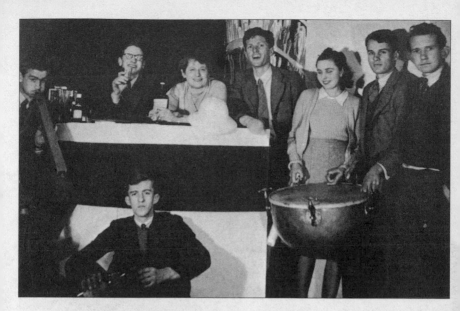

Above: Rehearsal, Outward Bound, 1941 – first production with student-players in Christchurch

Below: Australian tour, 1949. Brigid Lenihan (right) played Desdemona and Pamela Mann was Emilia in this Ngaio Marsh production of *Othello*

Emerging "incomprehensibly"
from police headquarters
"under the ironical scrutiny of
the gendarme on guard" –
Paris 1950

Director,
British Commonwealth
Theatre Company's
Australasian tour, 1951

Hamlet, 1958, with
Jonathan Elsom (left) as
Laertes and Elric Hooper
in the lead role. Both these
young Christchurch actors
subsequently established
themselves brilliantly in
overseas theatre. Hooper
now directs the Court
Theatre in New Zealand

Macbeth, 1962.
James Laurenson, who
later joined the Royal
Shakespeare Company,
Stratford-upon-Avon

Dame Ngaio Marsh, D.B.E.,
Buckingham Palace,
11 June 1966

Hon. Dr Litt.,
University of Canterbury, 1956

Julius Caesar, 1964, Mark Antony (Robin Alborne)
and crowd – "the rank and file come into their own"

Rehearsing *Hamlet*, 1968, with Jennifer Barrer and Mervyn Glue

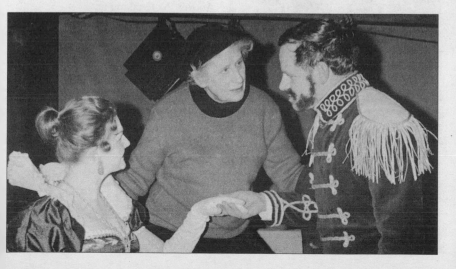

Twelfth Night was the play presented for the opening of the new Ngaio Marsh Theatre, University of Canterbury, Ilam, in July 1967.

Above: "Note-taking at rehearsal with my assistant, Mary Holmes."

Left: "Three merry men be we" – Frederick Betts, David Hindin and Vincent Orange, first night.

In 1972, the author produced *Henry V* for the October opening of the James Hay Theatre in Christchurch's new Town Hall complex.

Right: dress rehearsal – "The death of Falstaff".

Below: Jonathan Elsom rehearsing Chorus and (left) in makeup for this part

Guest of honour at the 1949 "Marsh Million" party given by Penguin and Wm Collins to celebrate the publishing of a million copies of Ngaio Marsh titles. From left: Ivor Brown, author and dramatic critic; the author; William Collins, publisher

First meeting with the late Agatha Christie – at a Crime Writers' Association "prizewinners party", the Savoy, London 1962

With Harry Keating (second from right) and literary luncheon guests during a Midlands tour, 1974

View on a misty day from the author's bedroom at
Marton Cottage, Christchurch – no alps showing

At the wheel of her Jaguar XK150 – the author, Christchurch 1980